ERRANT HOPE

ERRANT HOPE

SWORD SAGA BOOK ONE

Damien Jennison

Copyright © Damien Jennison, 2022

First hardcover edition, 2022

Editing by Luke Green and Alexander Kashev.
Book design by Alexander Kashev.
Cover by Sonja Juslin.

ISBN 979-8-4378-2521-1 (hardcover)
ISBN 979-8-4554-9928-9 (paperback)

Independently published.

https://kikoskia.com/

To my grandparents Flo and Frank,
who died before seeing me realise my dream.

Chapter One

"Hear ye, hear ye! Let you be warned that wolf pack sightings are on the rise! People are advised not to leave the village bounds after sundown, lest you wish to put your life in the hands of the Gods!"

—*Hayford village crier*

An uneventful day was always a bad one for Callum. His hands had barely been dirtied and his coin purse remained light. Standing by the well, he watched the daily life of the village go on, an outsider despite his years of residence. The looks he sometimes got from the others reinforced it; some gazed through him, others passed a grudging noise of acknowledgement. He'd at least made it through the winter, a cruel one by anyone's standards. The river had frozen over, the soil a nightmare to till. Idle farmhands when the snow piled up had meant even less work, dark nights spent sheltered but hungry and cold. Still, he'd eked on by, and the spring had brought with it new houses to build for families moving in from neighbouring villages. They'd been thankful for his help carrying building materials and running errands while they were settling in, but today was not those better times. Callum tried to tidy up the mess that was his brown hair, but the eternal battle was, as ever, futile. Brushing dirt off his rough green cotton shirt was just as pointless. With no sign of a caravan passing through, he reluctantly abandoned his spot by the well, hoping beyond hope that his luck would turn elsewhere. He gave a weak smile to someone who he recognised but got no response. It didn't take long for him to reach the marketplace where the bustling trade of the morning had started to die down. Those that remained haggled for final purchases or were collecting their gains. Callum didn't recognise anyone, and his heart sank as he realised he was too late for there as well. Then out of the corner of his eye, he noticed one of the few friends he had.

"Wandering without aim, I see?" Terrance was sat in front of his tiny shack as he often was, watching the world go by. A man in his sixties, he sported a well-trimmed white beard and not a hair on his head. His clothing was threadbare but had served him for more years than anyone cared to ask.

Callum walked up to him. The man nodded politely.

"Good afternoon." Callum afforded him the respect he felt was deserved. The old man just chuckled and shook his head softly, like he always did.

"Always so polite." His smile had a warmth no calamity seemed to shift. "How has the day been keeping you?"

"Not well, little work and not much prospect of it either. And what of you?"

"Things are going as they go." Terrance was watching the market himself. "There are a few traders there; you might still be lucky."

"I doubt it."

"An hour earlier, and things might have been different for you." Terrance indicated to empty stalls that normally bustled with life. "A wealthy man plans to host a banquet, bought up much of the trader's supplies. They say he might be hosting the duke." Callum sighed.

"A lavish feast when his people toil hard," Callum remarked, remembering tales of some of the more dubious taxes the ruler of the lands had instilled, all for peculiar reasons. He also knew of the people who spoke out against him that sometimes vanished, and the king raised not a finger to stop it. He couldn't blame Franci though, a child king ruling before his proper time. He may have been doing so with guidance from his regent, but that made the plight of the common folk little better. "Then again, who am I to judge the actions of the duke? I know little of what he actually does."

"To not do so would be folly." Terrance's remark drew a strange look from a passer-by.

"To speak so openly—"

"I'm an old man, who cares what I think?" Terrance grinned. "They would pillory me, execute me? They would think me not long for the world anyway."

"You, there!" came the call from down the street. Callum ignored it until the person spoke out louder, "Yes, you! Turn to me when I address you, commoner!" Callum did so and saw a man in regal attire, or so he believed. The colour of his shirt is what made him think of wealth, the purple of lavender flowers. What separated the figure even more from everyone around him was how clean he was. About Callum's height but twice his age, the forty or so year old man had long brown hair down to his neck and a stiff, lean face. The black hat he wore had a large white feather in it, complementing well the cloak of the same colour that just managed not to trail in the muddy street. Rings and a necklace of silver finished the picture of prosperity, but the two thugs that trailed a little behind him were a stark contrast, armed with clubs and wearing boiled leather jerkins.

"Are you talking to me?" Callum checked just in case. The man rolled his eyes overly dramatically.

"Yes, you simple-minded oaf," patronised the man. His accent wasn't a local one. "But now I see you and hear your mannerisms. Perhaps I have chosen poorly. Someone of sharper wit can better serve me—"

"If it's work you're offering, I will happily listen," Callum quickly interjected. "Unless it's illicit." Terrance frowned but kept his mouth shut.

"I am a man of noble blood, not a common criminal. Cuthbert of Geldran, I presume my reputation precedes me." Callum had heard of neither him nor the place. The man scowled at the lack of reply before his face returned to disdain. "Normally I would not lower myself to ask one of the common rabble for an errand, but it would seem I have no choice. The guard is, as of this time, unavailable for my task. Would you believe they said they were 'busy' with guarding the perimeters of the settlement? The nerve to refuse one such as I for such... trivial matters!" Callum's opinion of the man was dipping further by the moment as Terrance's frown deepened. He thought twice about his previous enthusiasm, but he needed this and the money it entailed.

"What is your task?" Callum asked. The ruffians that flanked their master were dubious of Callum. One pointed at something about him and shared a chuckle with his companion.

"There is a letter that I *need* to have delivered to my dear lady that resides in the next town over. I presume you know of it."

"Vaguely." Cuthbert huffed but continued.

"While my heart does long to see her, pressing matters keep me... in this place. The letter expresses things that you cannot possibly understand and should be delivered with utmost haste."

"Now?" Callum looked to the afternoon sun.

"Wolves roam in the dark," Terrance finally added. "Poachers as well, especially this time of year." The noble scoffed, the ruffians chuckled again.

"Am I to be scared by stories told to children? No, this is a task that I will ask you only once to fulfil. I am sure many others would wish to assist one such as I."

"Which is why you are asking a 'commoner', am I right?" Terrance smiled after his question, earning another scowl.

"You be silent. This conversation is between me and him."

"My friend has a point," Callum conceded. This provoked a stronger scowl. "And I presume there is payment?"

"My lady will reimburse you sufficiently for the task at hand, I am sure. She has money enough."

"I don't work on presumptions, I'm afraid." Cuthbert looked even more annoyed as well as surprised.

"I beg your pardon?"

"You promise nothing for delivering your letter and endangering my life. If your lady isn't interested in paying – or worse, has soured of your affections – it will be for nothing." He took a breath. "I'm afraid I cannot help you today. I wish you luck though." Anger turned to confusion, then flittered on bewilderment before settling on simmering annoyance.

"So, you wish bribery to perform a good deed." The noble's words were muttered quietly.

"A man cannot live on good deeds alone."

The ruffians on either side of the purple-clad noble began a step forward but were stopped by the jingling of a coin from a purse. Callum watched the noble reach for each piece of coin, noting to his surprise that it was silver, not copper that he drew out. With each coin the man assessed Callum's reaction, each one in turn until he reached five, placing them in a very small pouch. He tempered his excitement, trying to keep a neutral face.

"Here." Cuthbert tossed it to the ground flippantly. "This will no doubt suit your mercenary hunger." Callum quickly went for the money before another could snaffle it. "If this letter does not arrive to her post-haste, you do not wish to know the fury that I can unleash against you." Callum had already tied the pouch to his belt, his uncertainties having washed away; a walk to the next town over was worth far more than five copper, but this was silver.

"I shall set off immediately," he assured his newfound employer, "and not stop until the task is done." The man held out a very carefully sealed letter made of fine paper, which Callum took with equal care.

"See to it that you do..." The noble paused. "What *is* your name?"

"Callum, sir, Callum Igannes." The noble frowned once more.

"See to it that you do, Callum." He said the name with ominous emphasis. Turning away, the noble and his guards withdrew with purpose, quickly out of sight. Presented now with a mandate, he didn't give any words to his old friend and knew the man would forgive his wanting to leave while light still remained. With haste reserved only for more urgent things, Callum made his way to the perimeter wall.

The wooden palisade wall had existed for over a century, or so Callum had been told, erected to repel an invasion from the robber barons of the east that never came. Decades of neglect had taken their toll, but he didn't envy any bandits who tried their luck against it. Standing at the main gates were some of the guards that the noble had thought so little of. They were non-descript by their very profession, faces shrouded in dull metal and weathered leather, along with uniformly bulky armour. Of the few that weren't wearing helmets, Callum recognised one as the captain, a gruff and unappealing man of advanced years with a scraggly black beard matching the battle-scarred face. The other standing beside the captain lacked as many years behind him, although his brown hair was starting to recede and grey. Standing a few inches shorter than six feet just as Callum did, the guard had the frame to wear his suit of chain mail comfortably and a finely made halberd in hand. The younger guard's brown eyes met his own green ones, and he flashed a warm smile as Callum approached the open gate.

"You're travelling out into the wilderness?" another guard asked, a man watching him warily.

"I have a message that I must carry to the next town over as soon as possible," Callum answered honestly. Another guard looked over while stringing his crossbow.

"Too dangerous, wolves are out this time of year. Your journey can wait until morning."

"You can't stop me from going." Callum was determined, he had a job to do. The guard, about to respond, was interrupted by the halberd-holding one, who had moved away from the gate.

"When you've got a job to do, you do it." His voice was softer than the other man's but still had the coarse edge of a professional man of conflict. He turned to face Callum. "What's your name?"

"Callum," he replied promptly. "And yourself?" The captain was watching with a frown; he'd gotten a lot of them that day already.

"Saresan." The guard looked to the letter Callum held. "That message urgent, eh?"

"A very annoyed man of high birth asked me to deliver it." That prompted a smirk from Saresan.

"We had the pleasure of his royal up-tightness earlier today." The sarcasm put Callum at ease. He hadn't spoken to the guard much before in any settlement he'd lived in. Their stern demeanour had put him off; that, and he was usually busy himself. A handful bristled with more weapons than he thought reasonable, and a couple had bordered on appearing sinister. Saresan, however, seemed pleasant and approachable. "I hope it was a lot of coin he offered to you."

"Enough to make the journey through the night worth it."

"The woods *are* pretty dangerous at night. You got yourself a weapon?" Callum blinked.

"I've never needed for a weapon before. No one has gone at me with anything other than their fists."

"Punches won't fend off a wolf's claws, let alone their teeth." Callum felt a sinking feeling, picturing the feral beasts. Blood and gore flashed on his mind, mostly his own, along with fear. Saresan stroked his stubble in thought, right hand firmly holding his weapon. Then he stepped back and picked a heavy-looking mace that was propped against the palisade. "What you need is something to bash their brains in."

"I wouldn't know what to do with it," Callum told him. "I suppose I could get a staff or something from a trader." The captain narrowed his gaze as Saresan held out the metal mace, offering it.

"You'll be giving him *nothing*," the aged man barked to Saresan, arms folded. The other guards watched now, warily. Saresan ignored the stare he was getting. "That weapon is worth more than your week's wages."

"Would you rather the man was left to the fates? He's only borrowing it," Saresan objected to his superior.

"To him it's money in his pocket." The captain had turned his eyes to Callum, looking through him. It made Callum feel small and uncomfortable. "I know his type, they're all the same."

"I don't ask for charity. I'll manage just fine on my own." Callum's declaration did nothing to stop the captain from approaching. The captain glanced back at the guards watching the spectacle and they quickly returned to their duties with renewed purpose.

"Charity is wasted on people like you," the captain answered.

"And you're a poor judge of character," Saresan quipped quietly. His superior frowned once more, the wrinkles on his face comfortable in that expression.

"You're better?" Callum felt even more uncomfortable now, for causing a fuss more than anything.

"I don't mean to cause trouble." Callum doubted his words would make any difference. "I'll leave you in peace." Saresan shook his head and offered the mace once more. The captain's anger was ignored, leaving Callum to stare at it.

"And you'll leave with this weapon. You'll be returning here anyway." Saresan finally turned his head to the captain. "And if he doesn't return for whatever reason, you can take it out of my wages. Either way, the guard isn't out of pocket." The captain grumbled with dissatisfaction but said nothing.

"I do indeed intend to return, but I don't think I can accept your weapon," Callum insisted once more. A second later the mace had been given to him, the younger guard insistent in the action. Waiting a moment did nothing to get the offer to go away, so with reluctance he took hold of the mace. When Saresan let go, Callum discovered that it was not only heavy but unwieldy too, struggling to keep it upright; swinging it with one hand would be an impossibility. The captain of the guard remained sceptical and very unimpressed, but again he said nothing.

"Just bring it back in one piece with you much the same, and I'll be happy." Callum still didn't know quite what to do with the weapon, to hold it or try and attach it to his belt somehow. Either way, it was his for now. "And don't thank me, I'm just doing my job. Now get yourself gone. You've got a long journey ahead of you." Not needing to be told twice, Callum walked past the two and through the open gates. He glanced briefly behind him and then took a breath, setting his eyes on the path ahead as he began his journey proper, heading towards the forest in the distance.

"You're too trusting," the captain told Saresan gruffly, still clearly annoyed. "It's cost you before." The elder guard straightened out the sleeves of his jerkin. Saresan had never asked about the captain's battered breastplate, something that looked out of place as a singular piece. It had the hallmarks of being part of something far greater, perhaps a suit of plate mail. That kind of equipment was only held by knights and their ilk, and Saresan knew that his superior was not of noble blood.

"With all due respect, sir, bugger off." Saresan didn't have to take any crap from that man, and he wasn't going to. "It's my weapon to do with as I please. Besides, he seems a good man."

"It's a trip through the woods, not a battlefield." The captain folded his arms. "We've yet to have a single death this season from wolves or their ilk."

"He might've been the first."

"He could still be," came the retort.

"He's better prepared now." That provoked a tut and a sigh from his superior, one he ignored as he glanced towards the distance. Callum was slowly becoming a small and distant figure along the pathway that led towards a large patch of forest beyond.

"And what makes him so important anyway? Many more passed this day, more will tomorrow. You won't pay them any heed." When Saresan looked to his superior again and thought on it, he couldn't put a reason to why he had thought Callum was deserving of note; something just felt different for some reason. But no matter, Callum would surely be fine, he mused to himself. After all, it was only a forest.

Chapter Two

Callum found himself reaching the forest not long before the sun was due to set. Seeing the glowing orb in the sky dip ever closer to the horizon put him on edge; only now was the prospect of being in the countryside at night beginning to scare him. A deep breath helped to steel himself as he stepped beneath the canopy of leaves, beams of light breaching the blanket of green. The pathway was worn and well-trodden, but it gave him no comfort as even the vilest bandits used roads. Holding the mace that hadn't gotten any lighter firmly in his hands, he continued down the path deeper into the forest. He looked to the trees, cautious of them as if they were a threat rather than any figure who lurked amongst them.

"I'm just being stupid, there's no one else out here," he said to himself.

He couldn't see any other animals nearby; not even the sound of birds preparing for the night interrupted the quiet. The whole forest had an eerie sense of darkness despite the light, some of which he attributed to his newfound fear of the place. He noticed some torches up ahead on wooden poles, illuminating the old trees on either side of the path. One of them had burned out, but he grasped the other firmly and pulled it free from its stand after tucking away the letter in a spare pouch. The illumination and warmth brought with it a feeling of safety, one he hoped would last the night.

Callum felt the temperature drop as time wore on. He had only his thoughts for company, thoughts that started to doubt. Perhaps all the silver in the land was not payment enough for the danger he might face. He looked around again as he approached a river, stopping to drink a few cupped hands of water.

Crossing the small wooden bridge over it, he tried to distract himself by musing on what the silver he got would be used for. The noble had shown a lot of trust in him by paying some money upfront, that or desperation; a less scrupulous man could have taken the money and fled to another town, took on a new life, but he was no such man. The coin was not much to Cuthbert, but for Callum it was plenty. It would keep him going for many weeks, months if spent well. He considered the nature of his infrequent income, the long lapses in gainful employment. He hadn't had a steady job for over a year, where he'd helped a nearby village build a watchtower. He'd been offered a position in a rural guard there but turned it down; fighting wasn't for him. He had no stomach for it and was sure it would've shown.

The night had truly begun when Callum decided to take a moment to rest his weary legs. Finding a stump of a fallen tree, he sat down and tried his best to relax. The worries lingering in his head had so far been unfounded, his nerves no longer so frayed. He had little option now but to walk through the night and find a place to rest when he arrived at his destination.

Happening to look up, Callum glimpsed through the tree line a slow shooting star, an omen of events to come. If the omen was good or ill was a mystery for the sages, but from the as yet uneventful journey, he took it as the former. Reminded then of the time and his nagging hunger, he regrettably turned to the darkness of the road ahead before finding himself looking up again to the starry sky. He didn't know why he looked up a second time, but he noticed that the shooting star seemed... closer than before.

Standing up, he narrowed his eyes and raised the torch, hoping to see it clearer. The star grew wider, brighter and was moving very fast indeed. Before Callum had much time to react, there was a terrible sound akin to something tearing through the air, then searing heat and a white flash of light erupting from the ground right in front of him.

Dropping the torch in shock, Callum barely covered his eyes as he was knocked backwards and to the ground by the sheer force of whatever it was. Dazed and winded, it was a few seconds before he looked again, fearing that the bright light remained.

His vision was hazy, head light as he tried to survey the surroundings. What had once been part of the dirt path was now a blasted crater five metres across, its surroundings aflame and the ground densely scorched. The torch had been extinguished in the fall, lying next to him. The canopy smouldered with embers, a hole torn through it by whatever had caused the light. The whole area smelt of charcoal and glowed with burning embers that threatened to spread and envelop all like a hungry beast if they found fuel.

His head clearing a little, Callum tried to adjust to what had happened; had he survived a falling star, one of the gods which gazed down upon them from the night sky? He had never seen a god up close before, and so curiosity and wonder bested fear, bringing him to the crater's edge. Looking down, he didn't know what to expect, finding that at the centre of the scorch marks an object was embedded in the ground.

Looking harder, Callum recognised it as a sword, making him wonder a hundred questions; surely a sword couldn't fall from the sky: it had to have been buried in the dirt below the path. But who would hide a sword that way, an item of great value? It appeared to be about two and a half feet in length and looked plain; the metal was matted, tarnished and without shine. There was no remnant of the star, no body of a fallen god, and that made him nervous once again. Maybe it had vanished in the explosion, Callum mused, or perhaps returned to the heavens.

Afraid of the crater but still more interested about the prize in the middle of it despite himself, he stepped over the lip and moved closer to the weapon that was stuck – no, embedded – in the ground. Now next to it, Callum could see even more so how unremarkable the weapon was; he had seen depictions of knights in his younger years, and their weapons were pristine, elegant and wondrous. The edge of the discarded weapon looked sharp, not that he would have tested it.

He stared in silence and considered his options. Out of his mind a crazy idea emerged that he initially baulked at, picking up the blade. A falling star had hit it; the metal would scold his flesh, but then how had it survived the impact? Callum didn't know why his worries were being pushed aside by the curiosity that was often more dormant, and despite his mind warning him not to, he moved his fingers and ever so gently touched the handle of the sword.

Reflexively he pulled his hand back, but he felt no pain; there was only a slight tingling sensation in his fingertips that defied all explanation, entirely new but not unpleasant.

"There's no heat..." he muttered to himself as if saying it might make it more understandable. "How is that possible?"

Now seeking an answer, he carefully put the mace down then grabbed the handle of the sword with his entire hand. Again, only the soft, warm tingling was felt, this time slowly creeping up his hand. Then he found his grip had tightened around the handle without his knowing. He couldn't let go, the warmth travelling up to his wrist which sent him into a panic.

Now he deeply regretted his impulse, worried he'd angered whatever being had plummeted to the earth by taking the blade, punished for his folly and disrespect. In that frantic moment, Callum wrenched the weapon free from the dirt and was surprised at how little effort it took. It was as light as a knife, him squeezing the handle so tightly now that it hurt despite the wave of warmth that consumed his arm.

Suddenly, the strange sensation shot through his entire body and he felt drained of all energy, on the verge of collapse. Before he could, the void within him was filled with a pulsing strength that was agonising and then immediately not so. He did not fall, instead standing utterly refreshed and holding the weapon in his hand that had relaxed and was bereft of pain. He hadn't felt so good in his whole life, and even though fear lingered in his stomach, he stared down at the sword in disbelief; what had just happened?

The weapon now felt familiar, as if he had held it a thousand times before, but that wasn't so. Even as he tried to recollect the sensation that had utterly dominated him moments before, Callum found himself so used to the weapon that it was second nature to hold it. He knew he'd never held a sword before, let alone this one. He had to be dreaming, he concluded; he'd fallen asleep on the stump somehow, that had to be it. But he didn't wake, not even when he pinched himself.

The feeling of being watched snapped him back to his surroundings, eyes darting cautiously and frantically about. The smouldering flames around the crater were his sole source of illumination now, and around him he saw only trees and darkness. But he wasn't alone. Something in him told him that and he wasn't about to dismiss it.

Thinking the sword was perhaps a trap to lure people in, he was tempted to drop it and flee but decided otherwise; it was better to have a weapon in hand if trouble came than to relinquish his only source of defence. Stepping back from the crater, he grabbed the extinguished torch and relit it on one of the embers, trying to look around him.

It was then that a sharp stabbing pain in his head almost made him drop everything, only just managing to keep his footing. It was like something had been jammed through his skull, unlike any headache he'd ever had. Spinning in place, he caught sight of a pair of eyes in the woodland that was watching him, glowing unnaturally white. Perhaps it was a wolf, drawn to him by the flames and the falling star, but they were too high up for that. The pain in his head didn't subside, joined by a shiver that ran down his spine as fright once more gripped him. He held the sword tightly but clumsily; for all his newfound familiarity, he had no idea how best to wield it.

"Who goes there?" He tried to sound brave even as his voice quivered. "...I am armed and know how to use my blade!"

At his words more pairs of eyes appeared around him in the darkness, all staring straight at him. His fear threatened to surge into terror, now sure that the eyes didn't belong to wolves; no beast of the wilds had eyes which burned so bright. Turning to run, he saw his path back blocked by the eyes, the way forward also.

It was then that Callum felt an even more terrible pain shoot through his whole body. It took him by surprise, sending him staggering back into a tree which he leaned into for support as his muscles cried out for mercy. Clutching to his blade only through sheer force of will, he found the pain refused to subside. Thoughts of the river being tainted with a foul natural poison vanished when he heard the sound of claws digging into wood not far behind him. The beasts that surrounded him did not lunge, however, waiting for something; were they assessing him or mocking their prey? Even armed as he was, against so many, Callum knew he stood no chance as the pain endured. Then the eyes in the darkness ahead parted, a channel of blackness before him that he would've run to if his body had let him. The clang of armoured feet cut through the sound of crackling flames, his heart nearly leaping into his throat at who emerged into the light.

Taller than Callum by a few inches, the figure was fully encased in black plate mail, made to fit a man whose form was unnaturally lithe. The armour looked masterfully crafted, intricate runes and symbols running along where the plates joined, glowing with dark purple energies. It was far from complete, however; holes had been sliced through it at various points, most notably near the figure's right shoulder. The knight's helmet looked vaguely like a closed helm without a hinge to open the front, plumed with feathers of the darkest night.

Despite the shadows around them, Callum could see the eyes of the newcomer, entirely white save the pupil, unlike any man he'd ever seen before. They looked through him rather than at him, as if he were nothing and yet something. A flowing black cloak complemented the dark attire he wore, but it was riddled with tears and holes.

In his right gauntlet he held a sword longer than Callum's, handle enough for two hands if desired. Unlike his own, it was polished to a gold-tinted shine, excellently crafted, majestic and wickedly sharp. The tint was something Callum couldn't understand, but he had no time to question it, nor was he able to with the pain his body still felt.

The imposing and terrifying figure stood before him, not ten metres away. There was a chilling silence that not even the monsters out of view dared to break. Callum tried to back up, a reflex of fright, but the tree stopped him. The armoured figure did not speak but laughed instead, a deep tone Callum didn't expect from one so thin. It was quiet and tense, and Callum didn't know why it was happening, why any of this was happening. All he could do was hope that the man's intentions weren't malign, as slim a hope that was, as the laughter stopped abruptly.

"...*This* was all I had to do... to finally defeat you...?" His voice had a strange mixture of smooth confidence and desperate annoyance, conflicting emotions in a man seemingly assisted by so many strange things in the darkness. Callum had never seen them before, but the figure seemed to know him and indeed bore ill intent. Callum's arms shook with fear.

"W-what do you want with me?" He held his blade tight, pointing it at the figure as a futile threat, it wavering in the air. Despite how pathetic he must have looked, the armoured man did not advance, eyes fixed upon the sword.

"To kill you, once and for all."

Callum had known that before the angry words came out. He wanted to see if a way to flee was open, but he was transfixed on the figure, frozen in terror.

"You are alone now. They cannot shield you anymore, not here. Here, you are nothing!" He'd have been fine with being mugged blind and left unconscious at the side of the road, but this was his worst nightmare. Anything was better than death, but one question rang through his head over his panicked thoughts: why?

"...I haven't done anything to you..." Callum stammered weakly, knowing he had nowhere to go. Yet the final blow hadn't been dealt; what was holding back the knight? The figure glanced to his left suddenly, as if expecting something. After a second, he chuckled again, satisfied by the nothing which happened.

"For all you achieved, I see you for what you truly are now. You are not my foe, you never were. You are as the rest of you are, pathetic vermin." Callum was confused, horrified and afraid. "Your guardian will not come to your aid now. It looks at me but not me, and provided I end you in one blow, it won't turn my way."

"But I don't even know you! How can I do anything against you?" Words came only with great effort. Callum was even more desperate now, and he was considering begging for his life, a life he imagined would end very soon regardless.

"First I took from you your flower, now the roots shall be pulled from the soil." The armoured figure held his blade as if he was to charge forward and cut him down, then looked to the creatures in the shadows. "Kill him."

Callum's nerve broke and he attempted to flee at the command, past the tree he'd been up against and into the forest. Anything was better than waiting to die, as hopeless an effort it would be. Somehow his legs found strength, but as he turned, Callum almost collided with another figure who seemed to have appeared from nowhere.

As he looked upon the newcomer, the pain in his body ceased instantly, a tide of wellness that soothed his muscles but did not cleanse his terror. The same height as him, the newcomer was also clad in a full suit of plate mail. His, however, appeared to be made of the finest gold, ornate and intricate in craftsmanship. It lacked runes adorning it, starkly contrasting the dark and gloomy attire of Callum's newfound enemy. His helmet was a plain crusader design without adornment save a single green feather, the eyes hidden by shadow within. He had a shield made of the same golden metal, held in his left hand and adorned with heraldry he didn't recognise, a purple shield with a sword in the middle and two white feathers on either side. A flowing yellow cloak finished the image of a knight in shining armour, it moving with the wind gently. The man had his sword sheathed, though the handle was very similar to the blade that Callum himself held.

The black-armoured man was startled by the arrival of the golden knight. The eyes in the darkness had not moved, staring now at the newcomer rather than him. "...You!"

"You truly think I wouldn't know what you were planning?" The golden warrior had eyes only for his foe in black, ignoring Callum entirely. His voice was somehow familiar to Callum. He didn't know this man either, but his mind thought otherwise. "I see more than you give me credit for."

Still, the beings in the shadows did not move to attack, despite being ordered to; they were as wary as the one that led them, but why? How was gold an effective material for armour? Steel was a far better choice. Still, his own fear was near insurmountable, worried he'd be killed in the melee that was about to ensue. His legs had frozen up again, refusing to budge despite his mind screaming at him to run.

"I need only kill *him*," the other man rebuffed quickly, his previous confidence erased. "But if I must cut you down to do so, I shall."

"If you could kill me, you would have before, but you can't, can you?

You've only just realised this, and now you're afraid." There was tension in the air between the two warriors, as if both were waiting for the other to act.

"I am not afraid of you, you who are without your precious companions," the dark knight stated bluntly. "You cannot stop their deaths here." The golden warrior didn't flinch, so sure of himself.

"In times past you would have mocked with actions, not words. Your words are rich but empty, as is your intent." The dark knight clenched his sword. The air was almost charged with lightning.

"Kill him!" The order was repeated as a deep, booming shout that filled the air with hate. Callum was now in the middle of a battle that was no longer his, or was it?

Feelings of panic once again threatened to consume him. He then heard the voice of the golden knight softly speaking to him.

"Stay here."

The order seemed compelling, and it made him feel secure somehow despite the precarious situation. His body felt infused with a sensation for the briefest moment, but it faded into nothing just as fast. Something about the man was trustworthy even though they had only just met. From the edges of the illumination poured forth countless creatures, though Callum turned away before he could see more than the red of their being. He expected to be clawed asunder by them when a sudden pulse of white light emanated from the golden warrior beside him, a gentle glow of soothing energy. Callum could hardly believe what he was seeing; he had to be dreaming now.

"...Magic!"

The word was uttered in a whisper by him as if it wasn't so, yet his eyes didn't lie. Callum had never seen magic, only having heard rumours of it from drunk tavern patrons and those who spoke of it in hushed whispers. He'd dismissed it as old tales and warped legends, but he could not dismiss this, not now.

The warrior drew his sword then, and Callum saw that it was sheathed in the same white glow as its wielder. A single swipe in the air unleashed that energy in a lightning-fast wave of brightness, Callum shielding his eyes for the second time that night. In a moment it was gone, and so too were the red creatures Callum had not dared look at. Nothing remained; no blood or viscera lay before them, only emptiness and the black-clad knight who remained untouched. His attention was only on his foe who stood defiant and noble. Callum was in awe, forgetting that his way of escape was now open.

"You knew they had no chance," the golden warrior stated. His foe glanced briefly to Callum, and for the first time, the eyes looked *at* him. The stare was steely and focused in rage. Callum's supposed guardian stepped in front of him, asserting his vigil without words.

"You cannot defeat me."

The golden warrior raised his shield ready at that, his gaze levelled upon the man. He took a deep breath and readied his blade. An instant later the black knight shot a bolt of power of the darkest night, moving so quickly that Callum could barely react to its existence. But his shining ally did not waver, catching it with a quick movement of his shield, dissipating it. A chill quiet lingered after that for a few seconds too long.

"...Yes, I can."

There wasn't even the thinnest vein of doubt as the warrior spoke those words. In a moment his foe rushed forwards, a blur of darkness. The golden warrior vanished instantly, appearing a few metres ahead of where the two knights squared off. The blade of Callum's ally had similarities to his own, dull-looking and plain in comparison to the black knight's longer sword. That there was a parry at all surprised the black knight, and the two warriors' weapons again made contact, fighting at speeds that Callum couldn't even properly fathom; their movements were so quick as to be beyond human, and yet neither could land a blow on the other, the clashing of metal against metal a musical score of beautifully eerie composition.

After a couple of moments like this, the two darted away from each other and the dark knight took to the sky, floating up and defying all the powers Callum knew by remaining there. This startled him even more than he already was, watching the duel of these strange warrior wizards in petrified silence. The golden knight rose up as well a moment after, and the pair had a momentary stare-off before the dark one threw from his free hand balls of burning flame, large and travelling at incredible velocity.

As if expecting it, the man in gold enveloped himself in a translucent blue barrier that absorbed each of the fireballs in turn, it growing more red and fiery with each collision. After numerous such fireballs, the golden one focused the barrier into a narrow and intense beam of flame that was shot back at his foe, deflected by the black knight somehow parrying it with his sword. The beam scattered into a hundred streaking rays of fire that fell in all directions, catching much of the forest around Callum and setting it ablaze.

Within moments, his surroundings grew hot as the fire quickly spread and billowed smoke. He had to get out of there before he passed out from exposure, but there was no way to escape now, hemmed in by rapidly spreading inferno.

Looking up through the hole torn in the canopy by the falling star, Callum saw that the two warriors still battled above him, flashes of light and the sound of swordplay echoing into the night. The smoke was already intense and beginning to make Callum cough. He tried to move away, only to find that the golden warrior appeared suddenly from thin air next to him. Callum watched in silent amazement and horror as the man projected another blue barrier about him to negate pulses of green energy that had been aimed at him.

In that moment the glistening warrior looked to his charge once more. Callum could see from him a glimpse of concern and, even more oddly, pity. At that time, however, it was the least of his worries, for the dark knight lunged right towards them through the air, attacking his foe directly and right next to Callum. The dark warrior was trying to make an opening so he could strike at Callum with impunity, while the other did his best to stop that. Callum tried to step away, but his foot caught on a gnarled root, knocking him back to the ground.

"I will not fall! To your blade or any other!" The words of the black knight were seething, as hot as the burning fire around them. The golden knight countered without words, finally managing to strike at his enemy, his blade briefly stabbing into the man's chest plate. Callum was transfixed on the black knight, who looked at the hole in his armour as if it was an impossibility.

"You cannot stop that now," declared the golden knight, quietly and without pride. The response he got was filled with the anger of a thousand wounds but was unintelligible to Callum. Whatever was being said cut through his skin and seeped deep into his mind, an alien cry of anguish and fury. With a sudden movement, the wounded foe blasted at both the golden warrior and Callum an overpowering wave of fire. Callum felt the searing heat and then nothing, blacking out. His last vision was the golden warrior looking at him, staring deep into his eyes. Something about the look he knew, even as he plummeted into oblivion.

He had seen those eyes before.

Chapter Three

By Royal Decree of King Franci the Young, a duty is to be collected on the sale of products made of or containing silk. This is to be paid to your local tax collector at the week's end. Failure to do so will be considered an act of treason.

—*Notice nailed to a tree at the Sheep's Crossroad*

When Callum saw he was waking up in relative comfort, he knew something was wrong, though he was also relieved that he was waking up at all. He looked around and saw that the wooden walls weren't full of holes that let in the cold wind, so he wasn't at home.

His first instinct after that was to check himself over, searching for any sign of burns, injuries or otherwise. To his amazement and then relief, there was nothing save tiredness and an ache in his limbs. That quickly shifted to confusion, seeing now that he was in a proper bed with a straw mattress and a thin cover.

The mace Saresan had loaned him was propped up against the wall, a sight which made him question everything; perhaps it had just been a terrible nightmare after all. Maybe he'd made it to the town and merely forgotten about it, allowed shades of sleep to muddle with his head.

Yes, that had to be it; what he'd seen and experienced was just impossible. Magic didn't exist, nor did beings with burning white eyes or the knight who'd apparently recognised him. Seeing the sun through the window ahead of him, Callum guessed it was near midday, further supporting that none of those events had happened at all. Conversation from beyond the door to his left gave him pause.

"You think he will be awake now?" The first voice was eloquent and refined, a man of education. The second was one Callum recognized.

"Suppose so, can't hurt to check." What was Saresan doing there? Surely he was back in the village, didn't he have a job to do? Callum called out to those beyond the door.

"I'm awake." His voice was weaker than he thought it was going to be; had the journey taken that much out of him?

The wooden door opened, and the first one through was Saresan. He had a look of concern but was still smiling. The second to step through was half a foot taller, but the first thing that caught Callum's attention were the striking azure eyes of the man.

His hair was short, neatly groomed, and his face cleanly shaven, care and attention put into his appearance. He wore a jerkin and trousers befitting a man of high station, finely tailored and made of comfortable material. On his belt was a sword sheathed in a scabbard, the sign of knighthood. He was young like Callum, of a built body and tall, proud stature that spoke of arduous training and good eating. Callum tried to sit up as they both walked in, Saresan closing the door behind them. The guard walked up to the bed while the knight remained a few paces away, watching Callum carefully.

"You alright there?" His question was as puzzling as the man's presence.

"I think so." Callum looked over himself again, then back to the guard. "...Has something happened?"

"I was hoping you'd tell me. Folks in the village heard ungodly sounds from the forest, and when I went out to have a look with some guards, the whole place was ablaze." As Saresan scratched his head, Callum felt cold; surely it hadn't been true. "I wasn't going to rest until I knew what had happened to you. Found you by a crater right in the middle of it all, curled up and unconscious. It's a miracle you didn't burn to death."

The duelling warriors, the magical attacks that defied all explanation, the fire. It had to have been a dream, and yet apparently not.

Saresan furrowed his brow. "You okay? You look like you've seen a ghost."

"Was... there anyone else there?" Callum asked quickly. The knight continued to watch him as if appraising his words.

"Not a soul." He furrowed his brow. "Lightning or a torch knocked into dry grass, I say. The forest is gone, nothing but ash now."

"Some people say your survival is an omen," the knight finally interjected. "It is all the village folk will speak of."

"Village folk?" Callum turned to the window. "I'm back home?"

"Closest place I could bring you." Saresan shrugged. "Took you to the inn, had you put up for the night. Truth be told, the innkeeper's petrified of you. Says you're a curse and you'll burn the village down, like you did the forest."

"You don't think... *I* did that, do you?" Saresan smirked, patting him on the shoulder reassuringly.

"Of course not. I don't see you as the type."

The knight stepped up closer and spoke once again.

"I am Sir Azure Tellinton, knight of Felford and in service of our liege lord, the good King Franci. I arrived this morning, with the intent to pass through uneventfully. The turmoil of these events made me inclined to see you, to decide if what they say is indeed true."

"...And is it?" Callum asked, looking up at the tall knight.

"I am not sure, honestly." Azure rubbed his chin in thought. "You are very unassuming. I imagine a man with the power to destroy a forest like that would elevate himself to a position higher than a menial labourer."

"Exactly what I told you." Saresan glanced at the knight. "Didn't need to see him to conclude that."

"There *is* the matter of the possession we found you with, though." Callum looked to his mace. Azure shook his head. "Not that."

Saresan reached under the bed and pulled out something wrapped up in cloth, a cloth that had many large cuts through it. It was a shape that Callum recognized, and as the knight unwrapped it, the feeling of confusion was overtaken by one of silent fear.

It was the sword, no different from when he first saw it.

Any doubt of the night's events evaporated.

Azure was handed the blade, looking at it very carefully. Callum eyed the thing, and the knight noticed instantly. "So you know this blade."

"...I found it on my journey through the forest, before... Before I blacked out."

"What do you remember of your journey?" Azure asked then. Callum thought quickly; he couldn't say the truth, they wouldn't believe him.

"...I went to deliver the letter, but it got dark quickly. I stopped to rest for a moment, found the sword discarded by the road, and then..."

"Then?" Azure watched him intently.

"...I don't know. I'm sorry, I can't remember. Perhaps I fell asleep by accident." Callum doubted he sounded convincing, and the knight's look was a scrutinising one. It drifted to the sword soon enough, however.

"Try as I might, I cannot get a shine on this weapon. It must have been burned very badly to be in such condition. The edge, however, is sharper than anything else I have ever seen." He took the cloth the blade had been wrapped in, slicing through it with absolutely no effort. "And yet the blade lacks a makers mark."

"Whoever made that is a damn fine swordsmith, worthy of making any knight's blade," Saresan interjected.

"Are you going to take it away with you when you leave?" Callum hoped that he would; he didn't like being so close to it after what happened last time. Azure eyed the labourer, looked back to the blade.

"Until such a time as someone comes who can confidently verify that the sword is theirs..." He held it out to Callum. "...No. The blade is yours."

"But the laws—"

"Even with its sharpness, I doubt any knight would want it back in the condition it is in now." Callum exchanged a glance with the sword, feeling its presence and finding it unnerving despite his familiarity with it, a thing itself that should not have been. He took the handle of it with great care, hoping he'd wake again to find this a bad dream as well, the sword gone.

He did not, now holding the weapon again.

He darted his eyes around, looking for the darkly armoured figure, for the strange things with burning eyes that dwelt in darkness.

Nothing came through, and all the while Azure watched. "...Are you well?"

"Yes, I'm fine." He didn't sound confident, masking his fear poorly.

"Poor kid's shaken up. Not surprising," Saresan remarked. Then Callum remembered why he was on the road that night, guilt overtaking him. He looked around his person but couldn't find the pouch where he'd placed it.

"Did you find a letter by me? I must take that letter—"

"Yes, there was that," Saresan sighed. "Cuthbert wasn't at all happy to see you back here. I didn't find any note with you, in all the ash and embers it could have burned up anywhere. His objections can wait though; he can afford to lose a little time and coin, but a person can't be replaced. I'm just glad you're alright." There was a moment of silence, Azure pondering something.

"...There is still something I do not understand, that I cannot put my finger on." The knight looked to the sword again, then at Saresan. "If you would, will you show me the place where you found him?"

"It's not a far walk, can't see how it would hurt." The guard looked to Callum. "And I take it you'll want Callum to come along."

"Perhaps Callum returning to the scene of the event will trigger his memory, seeing how lacking it is at present." He said the last part with emphasis.

"You alright with that?" Callum nodded when Saresan asked, but deep down he was afraid of a repeat performance of the night before; would they even believe him if he told them? It would no doubt confirm he was the bad omen everyone was so afraid of. They'd lock him up as a precaution, or worse.

"...It can't hurt, can it?" Callum doubted the very foundation of his words.

"I shall meet you downstairs." Azure excused himself without waiting for a reply.

"A little stuck up, isn't he?" Saresan remarked with a grin once Azure was gone. That helped diffuse the situation, but only a little.

"Are they all like that?"

"Probably. First I've spoken with one, that's for sure." Concern flashed across Saresan's face. "You sure you're alright?"

"I guess I will be." Saresan patted him on the shoulder.

"Good man. Now come on, we might as well appease Azure so you can get back to working and I can get back to watching people come and go." Callum wondered how he'd be able to get his mind off what happened the previous night. Would the man who tried to kill him hunt him down again? Would the other knight again come to his aid? Trying to push those lingering thoughts back, he got out of the bed with a little difficulty, still feeling weak. Saresan watched him get up but said nothing.

"At least I kept your mace safe." Saresan couldn't help but chuckle.

"You did, yeah. You've got a much better weapon now anyway. Give it to one of the guards on the way out of the village, they'll know what to do with it."

"You mean the sword, right?" Callum asked hopefully.

"Don't think Azure would appreciate that right now," came the reply.

Picking it up, Callum could feel how much heavier the mace was in comparison to the blade he'd gained. With both weapons in hand, he walked with Saresan downstairs. Callum looked to the innkeeper, the man giving Callum a stare of barely suppressed fear as he quickly rushed into the back room. The various people sitting and trying to enjoy their morning food also watched with great suspicion. Callum was sure he could hear some mumblings about him, casting their watchful eyes over and especially to his sword.

Callum had often felt a little bit of an outsider in the village, but now it was palpable. Before they could step outside into the village at large, however, he was presented with the captain of the guard standing in the doorway. The old man – who he had yet to learn the name of, even after all this time – was very unimpressed about something. Saresan knew what.

"I make no excuses for what I did." Saresan again wasn't speaking in the most respectful tone, but it showed more reverence than before to the old warrior. "Only that it was right."

"And at the same time you abandoned the protection of the village to go off into a burning wood in search of one man anyone else would have left for dead." The captain was not in the least amused, and seemingly neither was Azure. "Do you have any idea of the danger you left everyone here in?"

"No more than they already are every time they sleep," Saresan replied. Callum was going to speak, but the stern look from the captain warned him to stay out of it. He did. "Three guards and myself weren't going to stop any brigands that chose to raid or wolves that wanted to feast on sheep."

"I've already talked to those three. They all pointed the finger at you as the instigator of your little rescue attempt." Azure then turned after the captain had spoken.

"You said nothing of your rescue attempt being against orders." Saresan met the disapproving tone of the knight with a slight shrug.

"Wasn't ordered to do anything one way or another. Used my own initiative, nothing wrong with that."

"When you are disregarding your duty, there is a lot wrong with it." Azure examined the man who was addressing Saresan. Callum continued to be silent, not finding a moment to interrupt. All the while his mind swam with the memories of magic and swordplay. Azure then addressed the captain.

"With armour such as your own, I wonder if you are a man of nobility. An odd place for someone of such station to reside, especially far from the trappings of civilisation." He spoke eloquently, more so than he had to Callum. The old man looked at the knight without the same level of reverence.

"I think you're mistaken." The captain was dismissive. "There's no 'sir' or lordly title in front of my name."

"Only one of noble birth may wear such armour," Azure insisted, referring to the breastplate, "even if it is just a small piece. It is crafted specifically for the wearer."

"Then the man who wore this must have been nobly poor. Found it in a smithy many years ago, and it would fit me and a dozen other of my men if they tried it." Azure looked even more aghast at that suggestion. Callum decided that now was the time to speak.

"If you're intending to punish him for his actions, I believe it would be what everyone would have done. It's their duty to defend and protect all the people of the village, and just because someone goes slightly out of the boundaries, it doesn't mean they are beyond the guard's duties."

"And by that logic you'd have the guard traipsing around the countryside every time a poacher goes missing overnight." The captain turned quickly from Callum, ignoring him and instead focusing on Saresan again. "Duties come before morals." Azure seemed unsure how to react to that comment.

"If you're going to kick me out, get on with it." Saresan was impatient. "I'm not sorry for what I did, and you know it. Stroke your beard all you like, I don't care for your pondering." He met the man's eyes. "If it happened tomorrow, I'd do it again."

"And that's why you don't have a place here anymore." The statement was a thud in the chest of Callum, who didn't believe what he was hearing. Heroics and endangering yourself were not what he thought losing your job would be provoked by. Saresan, however, shrugged.

"Fine. I'll get my things and be out of your way." He didn't seem bothered. "And being honest? Now I'm out from under your charge, I would tell you to get that stick out of your backside, but I fear it's wedged too deep." The guard stepped away from Azure and Callum. "I'll be with you in a moment." Callum was uncomfortable to wait, especially with the annoyed captain standing there. The old man was taken aback but quickly returned to a stern expression, which he aimed at Callum. The stare was piercing.

"I have no idea what happened in that woodland, and quite frankly, I don't care. But if you cause any trouble to the people I guard, you'll have to answer to me." Stern words from a stern man, Callum frowned, worried. It made him feel unsettled.

"How could I hurt anyone? I'm just a labourer." The captain frowned. Azure interjected then.

"He will cause no problems whilst he is in my charge, regardless of what is concluded." While that sounded more ominous than any half threat he could get from a veteran soldier, it seemed to placate the captain, albeit with a grumble and a scowl. As he left, Saresan returned with his halberd in hand and a small coin pouch that now hung from his side.

"Are you still intending to take us to the site of the event?" Azure enquired.

"No point not to." The guard shrugged. "The next town is along the way anyway. It's not like I'm going to find any more work here."

Stepping outside the inn, Callum saw that the streets were quieter than usual. Smoke rose into the sky from the direction of the forest, an undeniable reminder of what had occurred the previous night. Azure was standing by a magnificent black riding horse with chain barding that coped with the weight of the armour well. It was being tended to by one of the stablemen, who had just finished brushing the creature's mane. On the back of the horse was a large bundle wrapped in cloth, perhaps the knight's armour. Azure nodded to him and got onto the saddle of his mount, looking to Callum and Saresan almost expectantly.

"I guess he wants me to lead him," Callum commented to himself. Another glance at the surroundings found the atmosphere a little amiss. "Something going on today?"

"I think the taxman is coming, but apart from that, no," Saresan remarked.

"That'd definitely get people hiding." The former guard cracked a smile at that but said nothing more as they began to walk down the same route he'd had taken the day before, Callum hoping that history wouldn't repeat itself. He also hoped not to bump into Cuthbert, surprised the nobleman hadn't blustered his way towards them angrily at his emergence from the inn.

"Doesn't it bother you that you're out of a job?" Callum's question provoked another smile from Saresan.

"A guy like me can get work anywhere. They always need new hands, even at my advanced age."

"I wouldn't think of you as old." Saresan shrugged.

"It's old for my line of work." Azure followed behind on his horse, commanding respect from the populace by his mere presence. He carried the looks with pride, but mostly familiarity. The few people that they en-countered on the way out of the village gave Callum a wide berth, looking upon him fearfully. Terrance, sat in the same chair that he had been, made sure to look away as they passed. In all the years he had known that man, Callum hadn't put him down as the superstitious type. Maybe he was reading too much into it all; he wouldn't know until it all died down. He hoped it would be soon.

It didn't take long to get out of the village and once again down the road that would lead to the next town on. Even from that distance, Callum could see the smoking remnants of the forest that he'd been in the night before. A dark scar on the landscape, it spoke with a booming certainty of the destruction wrought there that night, visible to all but a mystery to everyone else.

"A shame, really," Saresan said to no one in particular. "It was nice woodland. Good game there to be had. You were in the middle of that, you know."

"I guess I was lucky." He knew better, but he still didn't think Saresan would believe him, not to mention Azure. Saresan chuckled.

"Must have used up all your luck in that fire. Don't go putting any bets on anything soon, that's my advice." The smouldering remains got closer as they walked, Callum able to smell the smoke even from there. Memories of the night were surfacing, but he kept trying to suppress them. The effort was futile, however. He gripped the handle of his sword tighter by instinct, expecting something to leap out at him from the nothingness. Azure stopped his horse and looked over at the scorched earth.

"You survived that," Azure half stated, half asked.

"I did."

"Unconscious."

"Yes...?"

"Without any burns or adverse effects from the fire." Callum didn't have a suitable reply for a moment.

"It seems rather unlikely."

"Exceedingly... for a normal man." Azure's eyes looked at Callum; he could feel them on the back of his head. That made him uneasy, but he turned to meet the questioning gaze of the knight.

"I *am* a normal man," Callum protested flatly.

"So you say." Azure looked beyond the former forest in the distance. "Perhaps you are protected by the gods, perhaps by darker forces. Either way, it warrants further investigation."

"What, you going to take him to a seer and have him 'divine' some portent about his future?" Saresan asked, getting a stern look in response.

"You doubt my judgement."

"Sure as heck I do." Saresan made a sweeping gesture with his free hand at the ruined forest. "Old men with beards who con people with illusions of great wisdom when they make it up on the spot and tell people 'the fates must have changed' if they're wrong?"

"He has not spoken an ill word to me yet," Azure retorted. "His wisdom has kept me on the true path."

"If you say so. So now we're here, you're just going to repeat the same questions as you did in the village?"

"As I said, it may trigger his memory of what happened that night."

Callum looked away from the knight, not wanting to give away what he knew. Azure didn't seem the safest person to tell it to anyway. "...*Do* you remember anything about what happened?" Callum took a deep breath, the pain and the terror in his mind replaying as he recalled the combat, the imposing figure, the rescue.

"...Nothing that I haven't told you, no. I'm sorry," he lied, hopefully convincingly.

The knight narrowed his eyes, as if watching his every muscle twitch. Callum was about ready to crack under the pressure, spill everything to the warrior who stared him down so.

"Give it a rest, the man said he knows nothing," Saresan's protest broke the gaze as Azure looked at the guard instead. "I'm sure if he remembers anything, he'll tell you, right?" Callum nodded quickly, flashing Saresan a thankful look that the older man either ignored or pretended to. Azure took one last look at the ruined forest and then again to Callum, exhaling a quiet sigh.

"...As you wish. You will still accompany me to the sage. He can tell more than I about this portent." The tone Azure used was no doubt just the way he spoke normally, at least Callum hoped so. The sword still felt too familiar in his hand. He wanted to drop it into the grass, forget about it and keep going on his way. What stopped him was the knowledge that he was just passing on the problem to someone else, to have another be burdened with it. "Well? We cannot get there if you do not walk, Callum." Looking up, he saw that Azure had tried to move ahead and had turned to see him not following.

"Sorry." His mumblings made Azure shake his head, almost in disappointment, before he resumed the slow trot of his horse. He caught up with Saresan who smiled at him.

"Could be worse. You could have died in that fire." Callum briefly wondered if it might have been better that he had.

"That's true." A pause as they walked in silence. "...This sage, is he a wise man?"

"Never met the guy, heard a few things about him though. Keeps to himself." He paused. "Most say he's a lunatic who claims to divine the future. A few others say he's an immortal wizard of limitless power. Azure seems to believe in him and that he's still alive, so at least that's something."

"You don't sound convinced."

"If there were people able to throw balls of fire around like pebbles, you'd hear about them a lot more than you do." Callum thought back to the fireballs of the previous night, how insignificant they seemed to be to both parties.

"But suppose this sage is what he says he is, that he can divine things."

"Then you'll find out exactly what happened that night, and Azure will get what he wants. Either way, you can travel under his protection until then, which isn't a bad thing."

"Then I'll have to get back home." Callum pondered home, feeling a little uneasy at the thought of being away from familiar surroundings for so long.

"Won't take you long, I'm sure. Then you'll be able to tell all the folks about the 'divining' over an ale. I'm sure it'll be a good story either way, eh?"

"I guess." Saresan once again had set his nerves at ease, something the man seemed to do well. Azure, on the other hand...

Chapter Four

The rest of that day's journey was in relative silence save a few passing remarks about their surroundings. Sticking to smaller out-of-the-way paths, Callum took in the rolling hills and peaceful countryside as he walked with Azure and Saresan. A few tiny hamlets dotted the landscape far from the worries he had, patches of golden wheat breaking the wall of greens. Azure had been casting glances at him from time to time, perhaps to glean a hidden motive or weakness, all of which made Callum feel like a prisoner despite the knight's manners and politeness. Saresan had noticed them as well but kept silent.

The knight's stare made Callum focus on his surroundings more than his companions, trying to distract his worries with the pleasant scenery. As the hours went on, he started to feel a niggling fear inside of him that wasn't caused by Azure's watchful gaze. From out of the dark corner of his mind, the eyes of the previous night's foes were creeping into his thoughts. The forests and the peaceful settlements were burned away, leaving only the curtain of glowing white eyes and the dark warrior. Furrowing his brow, he quickly cast off his concerned look so as not to draw suspicion, but something about those eyes bothered him. He didn't know why, but then he didn't know much about that night at all, a myriad of questions he both wanted and didn't want the answers to. His fear began to return as the sun made its steady descent to the horizon.

"Been a long day, huh?" Saresan's question had been unexpected, and for a moment he didn't even acknowledge it. Eventually, he turned, focusing again on the there and now.

"Rest would be good." A raised eyebrow from the older man set him ill at ease.

"You seem like you're somewhere else."

"I guess I am," he admitted, looking up to Azure. He seemed in a place of his own also, focusing on the road ahead. "Just thinking, on many things."

"At least you think. I've known people in my time who acted when they should've thought." He shook his head. "They were the messier deaths to clean up after."

"We will stop here, by this tree," Azure commanded, turning his steed to ride off the path towards a solid oak that had been there far longer than the road. Following, Callum watched the knight dismount and tie the reins to a strong branch, going through a routine he'd clearly done a thousand times. He retrieved from the saddlebags a grooming brush and began to tend to the horse's mane while Saresan settled down under the tree and stretched, relieved to have stopped. Callum didn't feel tired, but at the same time he hadn't been carrying a suit of chain mail on his shoulders either. The guard propped his halberd up against the tree and looked around the short grass.

"Nothing to hunt here," Saresan remarked.

"Only those with game permits are allowed to hunt in the wilderness," Azure then replied with a stern tone.

"Tell that to someone who needs to make a living," was the quick response. "Not everyone is born into wealth."

"The Tellinton family has upheld the honour of our people for seven generations and ruled with fairness and wisdom for that again. Our lands are a gift from our most humble and generous ruler for our continued service and our sword in times of war."

The words sounded rehearsed but were spoken with great pride, something that rang sour with Saresan.

"Right, sure."

"Not all are fit for the duty of upholding the great honours of knighthood, but I bear the burden with dignity and humility." Saresan barely contained a chuckle, which he hid as a cough. "I would not expect you to understand, nor do you need to." Saresan was about to say something else but decided against it, patting his stomach gently and shrugging.

"If you say so." Callum had begun to look at the sword again. The matted blade stared back, revealing nothing about itself. He held it in front of himself, assessing its weight as best as he could. Azure watched him as he tried to hold it in what he thought was a position ready to swing the blade. When he did so, it was clumsily, though the sound of it slicing through the air was distinct. It was as if the weapon cleaved the very winds in half, wounding the natural forces of the world.

"Balance your posture," Azure told him bluntly. He turned to see the knight watching him. "You do not want to swing so you put yourself off balance. Without a shield, you will wish to strike out while protecting yourself at the same time."

"And if that fails, kick some dirt in their eyes," Saresan added with a smirk. He ignored the knight's glare. "Sand works too. It gets them just as dead."

"I was just seeing how it handled, that's all," Callum told them. "I don't want to ever have to use it."

"Times we live in, you might not have much choice, what with brigands and cut-throats in dark alleys and the robber barons. I'd rather have a blade and never need it than be without it and get my neck slit."

He didn't have a reply for Saresan, putting his blade down after wrapping it up again in what remained of the cloth it had been bandaged in.

As the sunlight began to wane, hunger arose, Callum realizing he hadn't brought neither food nor his possessions with him. He hadn't much of either anyway so it wasn't a huge loss, but what he did have he'd worked hard to attain. He didn't bring it up either – he doubted Azure would understand. He probably had an entire castle to himself or something to that effect.

Ignoring his hunger as he had many times before, Callum settled down by the tree, wondering how quickly he'd be able to fall asleep in the open countryside. He hadn't been on the road like that for such a long time; he wasn't used to it.

"I don't know about you lot, but I am going to get some sleep," Saresan said, placing his chainmail off to the side. "Wake me up when it's sunrise." With that, the man shut his eyes. Callum watched Azure as he took the large bundle from his horse and unwrapped it on the ground, revealing pieces of a suit of armour. Callum immediately thought of the plate mail he'd seen the night before, and while Azure's set was similar to that of the golden warrior, it was far plainer and not forged from gold.

"You will assist me in cleaning this," Azure ordered without looking up.

"Can you not clean it yourself?" Callum asked.

"You will hold the armour still while I clean it." Standing up and heading towards the regalia, Callum held down the breastplate Azure indicated to. Azure began to polish the immaculate metal, an activity Callum saw as pointless; the armour looked fine enough and Azure's efforts seemed to be making no difference. "This is an activity my squire would normally do, but he is not here, and you are not him," Azure explained simply. Callum was silent for a while, but eventually mustered a question.

"So, you were trained by your father, I imagine?" Callum was curious.

"All knights are first assigned to other knights as squires, learning the ways of chivalry and the roles and responsibilities of knighthood first-hand from a paragon of said virtues," Azure stated, again almost trained to do so.

"So it would be possible for anyone to become a squire and be trained by a knight?" Azure indicated to one of the thigh plates, which Callum held down for him without a word.

"An absurd statement," the knight retorted quickly. "Only those of noble blood are able to comprehend and learn the difficult teachings of knighthood."

"You can't have always been nobility; people aren't *born* noble." Azure stopped then and stared at Callum sternly, angrily.

"Are you implying that my blood is not noble?"

"No, I'm merely—"

"You are merely *nothing*." Callum realised that Azure was gripping the handle of his sword. "Most other knights would not take your words so lightly." He gripped the handle a little tighter. "...Some would want blood for such an insult." Callum felt intimidated, on edge from the aggression of a man who until a moment ago had been so civil.

"...And you?" Azure looked at him for a moment longer. The knight then let go of the blade, exhaling a deep breath.

"As a man of such low birth, you clearly do not know what you are speaking of, so I shall give you the benefit of ignorance. I am willing to forgive those who know the error of their ways," Azure told him slowly.

"I'm sorry if I insulted you." Callum's response was quick. He had no desire to find out how sharp Azure's sword was.

"Indeed." Azure bundled the armour back up quickly, deciding against cleaning the rest. "Rest. We will travel much tomorrow."

The menace in his voice had all but vanished, as if the apology given had mollified him. His eyes, however, had something different to them, a hint of disappointment. Callum had hoped Azure would be willing to be questioned, but in hindsight, it was a foolish presumption; the knight's words during the day had been full of self-importance.

Azure settled down to rest, closing his eyes and drifting to sleep without difficulty. Only Callum remained awake now, looking at the horse. The steed stared back, but if the horse had any insight, it was keeping it to itself.

He found a relatively comfortable part of the grass and settled down on it, the night warm enough to not need a fire going. He didn't, however, close his eyes, afraid to. There was nowhere for an enemy to hide, but they had appeared out of nowhere before, as if part of the darkness itself. A repeat of the visit from the man in black was not what he wanted, but he couldn't fight fatigue forever. Despite his fear, Callum slowly found himself floating off into rest, hoping that his night was uneventful.

Saresan had been awake for a half hour. He'd watched the knight rise with the sun and begin his morning ritual to prepare for the day ahead. The former guard said nothing as he leaned against the tree, relaxing. Saresan knew that Azure would ask for his help at some point; the knight wouldn't be able to secure all the straps by himself, even if he had half the mind to let him try. He glanced over to Callum, who seemed fast asleep in an uncomfortable position. The knight had noticed his gaze, watching him silently. Saresan turned and folded his arms, expecting a high and mighty statement that never came.

"We going to have breakfast?" Saresan asked, half knowing the answer.

"We must head off soon if we are to make a good time."

"You're really keen to talk to this sage, aren't you? What do you actually think he can glean from tea leaves and stones?" The knight frowned as expected.

"The sage will tell me of any omens surrounding him." The last word had a particular emphasis, one of distaste. It made Saresan cautious, but the knight was in a talkative mood, and so he had to pry further.

"What omen can there be from a burning forest?" Saresan had an idea of what the man meant but wanted the knight to say it himself. "Forest fires happen."

"That man, unconscious and helpless, survived an all-consuming inferno without so much as a single burn. It is beyond luck." The guard stood up only when he saw that Azure now needed his help with the straps. Without needing to be asked, he began to secure and tighten those that the knight could not reach, one at a time.

"So why not go alone? It's not like Callum's going to run off anywhere, is it? If the sage brings up something odd, you can return and talk to him about it then." The knight's silence betrayed a lot more than words could. "...Unless you think he's dangerous."

"I think nothing of him yet." Azure's response didn't reassure him.

"On the contrary, sounds like you've half made up your mind already." He tightened one of the straps a little too much on purpose, watching as the knight grew uncomfortable. It was a small thing that he could do safely. "What's the worst the sage's going to say anyway? That he's some kind of warlock?"

"That is *not* a joking matter," Azure snapped suddenly. Saresan had struck a nerve. He'd seen such people with short tempers before, and this one was far better armed and trained than he. He secured the next strap properly.

"You believe in all that stuff? Magic and wizardry?" He went about loosening the strap that was too tight, listening as the knight began what sounded like a memorised speech, spoken verbatim.

"Those that practice in the dark arts of sorcery corrupt the very fabric of the lands with their foul taint. They twist nature to their whims and for their own selfish ends, to further their own station or to cause suffering to others. They must be dealt with, and their crimes answered for."

It was heavy stuff indeed, especially so early in the morning, but Saresan took it all in, then looked to Callum. His claim didn't add up.

"So, you blanket all of these people as... evil? That's presuming, of course, they even exist. You've seen one of these sorcerers before, I take it, to have such a strong opinion on them?"

"If I have seen them or not is irrelevant." Saresan almost chuckled but managed to suppress the urge, grinning in disbelief instead.

"It's entirely relevant. You think like that, and you'll likely send all kinds of people to bad ends, even if they're not a sorcerer."

"I have yet to see what good output burning down an entire forest yields."

"Again, you're presuming Callum did that." Saresan had finished with the straps on Azure's plate mail, taking a step back. Azure looked every bit the knight in shining armour, but he could see through the outward appearance to the pondering mind within and saw little virtue.

"I act only to protect the kingdom in the service of my liege," came the rehearsed reply.

"And what if the king was a sorcerer, hmm? What then?" Azure looked horrified at the very thought. "Well? Would the king have to be dealt with too?"

"The king is no sorcerer!" Azure's hand was close to his sword handle. Saresan had his halberd not a step away but knew it wouldn't be needed.

"How do you know?" There was a pause after that question, one that made Saresan smile. "You don't, do you? If the sage told you that Franci was a warlock—"

"He is *not*—"

"Do you really think Callum would take such a small payment from a noble, go out into the woods and set fire to everything with these so-called sorcerous powers, then leave himself to the mercy of the flames? Even if he had a way to protect himself from it, imagine what would've happened if someone had come across him and just stole everything he had, or worse, killed him?" Saresan took the step back to take his halberd in hand. "Why don't you just pass your judgement on Callum now if you're so sure he's guilty? Heck, why did you give him the sword so he could defend himself?"

"He would be no match for me in single combat," Azure scoffed.

"Like he'd use the sword if you're right, which you're not." Azure seethed silently for a few moments.

"I shall await the answer of the sage," Azure finally told him.

"And if the sage doesn't tell you what you want to hear?" Saresan could fill the gap that lack of response left behind. It didn't give him hope for Callum's situation, especially with the power that Azure seemed to hold in the area.

"We shall talk no more about this." And with that, the knight had killed the debate stone dead, leaving him to do the finishing checks of the straps. Saresan looked once more to Callum, knowing that he'd have to watch out more closely for the man he was beginning to think of as a friend.

Before he knew it, Callum's eyes opened. His back ached, but the relief at still being alive made that feel insignificant. Looking for the others, he found both his travelling companions were awake; Azure, now clad in his plate mail, was by his horse putting things into one of the saddlebags while Saresan was watching the spectacle, weapon resting in hand. Azure didn't acknowledge him, but Saresan gave a smile and walked up as he rose to his feet.

"Looks like you slept like a log," the man remarked. "Didn't want to wake you."

"A better night's sleep than I would have imagined for sleeping on the grass."

"We should get moving," Azure told them as he once again got on his horse, trotting gently back to the path.

"No breakfast then?" Saresan half-joked. His request fell on deaf ears. "Thought not. There'll be plenty of places to eat when we get to town."

"Few I would be able to afford," Callum remarked. Saresan's smile widened as they began to follow in the horse's wake.

"I'll show you my favourite taverns when we get there. They'll make sure you're well fed before you two go on ahead."

"And then you'll go and present yourself to the captain of the guard there." Callum didn't like the prospect of being alone with Azure. Perhaps telling the truth and getting it all over with was worth the risk, but still, he kept his silence.

"That's the plan." Callum noticed a hint of worry in Saresan's voice but couldn't pin down why it was there.

"I'll be sad to see you go," he told Saresan, who patted him on the shoulder.

"It's the way of things. I'll keep my eye on you while you're in town the best I can. They might think you're an easy mark."

"They?"

"The less savoury types." Callum thought on that.

"Even with a sword?"

"Point taken, but I'll watch over you all the same." Callum glanced at the sword once again.

"You don't have to."

"What are friends for?" He shrugged lightly. That made Callum return the smile given; he barely knew the man, but the word didn't seem out of place. "Should make it to the town today I think."

"I wonder what Azure will do when he's there," Callum muttered to no one in particular.

"Honestly? I don't really care what he does. He'll probably go and stay with a noble or something, that is if he doesn't force you to double-march right through and carry on your way. The guy doesn't realize that you're not on a horse."

Chapter Five

"It's like I said, there was a mad look in his eyes, and the muttering... It was no words I've ever heard before, that's for certain. I reported him to the guard right away, of course. They got to him before he could finish his hex, and a good thing too, or we'd all be under his spell by now. Said they'll pay me a silver after the hanging, but only if he confesses. Sure hope he does."

—*Tavern talk overheard in the Ox's Horn*

It took most of the day to get to their destination, and by then there weren't many people waiting to enter through the town gate. The large stone walls were imposing and weathered but had stood the test of time well enough. Walking along it were a couple of guards, whose job was to keep their eyes on the surrounding farms and the houses of those too poor to live within the walls.

A pair of rugged and thoroughly bored-looking men were standing in front of the iron portcullis, questioning those hoping to get in. Azure had a look of impatience as the guards spoke with a group of peasants about their cart of berries and forest produce. Callum was used to having to wait, taking it in his stride despite his stomach calling out in protest.

From the other side of the wall, Callum could hear the hustle and bustle of a place brimming with activity that refused to abate despite how far in the day it was. The weather being so pleasant surely helped, the air not too cold and no sign of rain in sight. The guards were now asking about a particular kind of red berry that the peasants had foraged, and for Azure that was the last straw. Riding up to the gate, he ignored the looks of agitation he got from people, who quickly realised who had barged past them and fell silent, a reverence Azure paid no heed. The guards looked up to the knight, not as impressed as the commoners were but still with some awe.

"Morning, sir," one said to him. "Nice weather, is it not?"

"The weather is of no concern to me. What is my concern is entering the walls of your settlement, an action you are delaying most disrespectfully."

"We're just doing our jobs, sir." Azure looked down on the pair as a man would glance at a scurrying rodent.

"You should learn a sense of importance, for my right to enter far exceeds that of these others. You would not leave your lord waiting." The guards looked at each other as Callum and Saresan moved up to stand with Azure. At the sight of Saresan, the guards smiled and promptly ignored the knight; Azure folded his arms, barely containing his annoyance.

"Hey, Saresan! Fancy seeing you here after all this time. Old grumpy-guts finally give you a day off?"

"Not quite." Saresan smiled. "He finally let me go, more like. Wondering if there was a place free with you lot."

"As long as it was nothing bad, I'll wager the captain will take you on." The other guard looked to Callum, a little confused. "Came with some interesting companions, I see." Saresan shrugged and indicated to Callum.

"Had to take care of this guy." Callum gave a weak smile, which was returned by the guards. "Forest burned down by his village when he was in it."

"I'm amazed he's alive."

"You're not the only one," Callum murmured, casting a glance Azure's way. Azure's patience had run out.

"Are you going to let us in or not?" the knight snapped.

"I need to know your business, knight or not."

Azure sighed and motioned vaguely to Callum with his free hand.

"I am escorting this man to the sage so that I can divine an omen from his survival. I feel that there is information to be gleaned from his... miraculous escape from harm."

The guards looked at each other again, as if they weren't sure what to think. Finally, the left one spoke.

"Well, if you believe in that stuff, I'm sure you'll get what you seek—"

"*If* you believe in it," interrupted the other guard. Callum noted wariness that had crept into his voice upon mention of the sage.

"Got to wonder where a man like that gets his 'wisdom' from."

Azure narrowed his eyes at that.

"His wisdom comes from many years of meditation, research and his faith in the gods," the knight stated firmly, ending the debate. "Now, will you let me and my two companions through?"

"Yes, sir," the left-hand guard said, indicating to a man atop the gatehouse to start raising the portcullis. "I hope your stay in our town is pleasant and—"

"Quite, you have wasted enough of my time. Come," he said to Callum as he began to trot calmly into the busy street ahead, seemingly ignoring all the people that occupied it.

"I'll be round the garrison in a bit, guys, just showing my friend here to a good inn."

"Sure thing, see you later," one of the guards answered before turning their attention to the next person in line.

Callum walked through the portcullis with the others and was immediately overwhelmed by the commotion beyond. Words and sounds surrounded him as everyone moved and acted as if part of a flowing river, moving along currents he couldn't see. He felt like an island of confusion and isolation until Saresan tapped his shoulder, drawing his eyes to a building not far down a side street and silhouetted by the setting sun.

"Right there," he said with a smile, "the Ox's Horn. You won't find a comfier bed or a better meal to rise to."

"You are going to stay *there*?" Azure's voice contained a palpable twinge of disgust. "A rowdy, raucous den of drunkards and vagabonds?"

"No better place in town on a cold winter night." The grin on Saresan's face was infectious.

"At least I will know where to find you," Azure mumbled, then looked at Callum with a half-glare. "I have business with the lord of the town that is for his ears only. I will be here at first light. We will travel to the sage then. Do not be late." He left a pause. "And do not leave town. I *will* find you."

"I've no intention of leaving," Callum replied, surprised to be cut loose, even if for only a night. "I'll be there."

"See to it that you are." The knight didn't acknowledge Saresan as he turned his horse towards the keep that towered over the other houses and started to make his way there, the people parting somewhat to give him room.

"He's quite a piece of work." Saresan shook his head and then turned to face Callum, extending his hand for him to shake. "If we don't ever meet again, it was a pleasure. You spend that money you got from Cuthbert wisely." Callum gladly shook the hand and nodded, smiling himself, a little sad to be saying goodbye.

"And if he comes after me?" Callum asked his friend. The guard chuckled.

"If he's coming after you for a handful of silver, he's got far bigger problems."

"I guess you're right." Callum smiled weakly. "Thanks for all you've done."

"It was nothing, least I could do. Take care of that sword." The last words reminded Callum of the reason he was there to begin with, glancing about for threats that weren't there. When he turned back, Saresan was gone. For a moment he felt adrift and without purpose, a feeling that never sat well with him. Deciding it was best to go somewhere rather than be an impediment to the flow of town life, Callum headed towards the inn. To his right, he spotted a few market stalls and scanned them briefly. Each one was selling different kinds of bric-a-brac, from small wooden crafts to salted meats. The sellers hawked their wares with years of experience, but even that was almost inaudible compared to the loud din all around him. As Callum passed the third store he stopped, noticing something that took his eye. The person immediately behind collided with him.

"Watch it!" the taller man hissed. He then noticed the sword and turned his gaze as quickly as he'd shouted. "...Sorry." A moment later he was gone. Was having a sword that pivotal to people's opinion of him? Did they think him a squire from the weapon alone? The storekeeper had noticed him lingering and began his sales pitch.

"I've got anything and everything you'd ever want, sir. Beef fresh from the spit, charms to keep evil spirits away. Anything you want I can provide!"

"What about that?" He was motioning to a battered and worn scabbard with an equally old belt. The man looked over his stall and noticed the blade that Callum was holding, giving him a most curious look that he'd have to get used to. The look then instantly dissolved into the smile of a salesman.

"If it fits, I'm sure it will work wonders! We don't want you carrying that thing around by the handle all day now, do we? You might chop some-one's feet off!" He motioned for Callum to pick up the scabbard. Callum carefully unwound the cloth from his blade, being careful not to ruin it in the process. When the stall owner noticed the dulled metal, his look shifted to curiosity. "An old heirloom, I presume?"

Callum compared the blade and the scabbard; the two matched one another well.

"Something like that," he said as he tried to carefully sheathe the blade. He found that it indeed was a good fit, sliding in firmly and snug despite the weapon's sharpness. He looked at the belt as well and guessed it would fit him also. It was worn and tired, much like himself.

"Like it? I am sure we can come up with a fine price for you!" Callum made an effort to conceal his coin pouch from the eyes of the man as the merchant tried to wager what kind of price he could ask. "Seven coppers and both are yours!"

"Five," Callum said quickly, looking him back in the eyes. Years of struggling to make do with copper had made him learn to haggle over everything. The merchant furrowed his brow at the counter-offer, but it softened quickly.

"They are yours."

He held out his hand expectantly and Callum paid from among his copper coins, though even with a discount, he was reluctant to part with it. He so rarely dealt with that amount of money in a single purchase, but it would make carrying the weapon much easier.

Callum slipped the belt through the rough loops in his trousers and fastened the buckle tightly, the sword now hanging at his left side. It felt odd having something there, even though other swords would surely be much heavier. "Tell your friends of my wonderful service!" Callum didn't think Azure wanted to know about the man, but he kept the words in mind.

Eventually, he found himself outside the tavern, a two-storey building of weathered wood. Boisterous singing and laughing could be heard from within, most of which was about drink and more drink.

Callum took a breath and pushed the door open, only for the stench of cheap ale to overpower his senses. People from almost all walks of life were drinking away their evening in revelry around tables in the large, dingy room and at the bar.

Callum quickly spotted the large open fire in the centre of the room and the whole pig being turned on a spit above it. Fat dripped into the roaring flames, sending the scent of meat through the air and to his nostrils. Barely anyone noticed him as he stepped inside, something he liked. He weaved through the patrons standing and trying to remain standing towards an unoccupied table close to the bar and sat down, relaxing properly for the first time since the whole ordeal had begun. He caught the eye of one of the servers that were dispensing drinks, a lady with a gentle, if forced, smile. She made it to him with ease.

"What'll it be, stranger?" she asked him.

"Stranger?" he repeated.

"I recognize all our regulars and even some who come here to forget." She looked him up and down. "You're neither of them. So, what'll it be?"

"Is there a room available for the night?" She thought for a moment and then nodded.

"Plenty, I think." He glanced into his coin pouch.

"...Will eight copper pay for it?" She looked bemused at the handful of coins he drew out.

"For the room, a meal and with a copper to spare," she told him. He began to wonder now if the street seller had indeed conned him. She took the coins eagerly, leaving the spare on the table and smiling warmly — in the way people who run a business do — before meandering through the crowd once more like it wasn't there.

Alone once more, Callum took in his surroundings and then noticed couple of people looking at him with some curiosity, but their attention drifted elsewhere after a short glance. One kept glancing back at him, however, a burly man that stared at him almost constantly. No, not at him, his sword. Callum met the man's gaze, and that finally prompted him to turn away properly. The man had many scars and a bandaged injury on his arm, which told Callum all he needed to know about the man's profession. The server returned at that point, ale in one hand and a plate in the other, upon which rested a generous slice of pork, potatoes and other vegetables. Callum hadn't eaten something so hearty for a long time, his eyes widening at the prospect. He was even offered a knife to cut the meat, something he hadn't been expecting.

"Everything good?" she asked, noticing his surprise.

"It's great, thank you. I just didn't expect so much."

"You get what you pay for. We pride ourselves on being the best in town." Callum moved the remaining copper coin across the table to her.

"Who is that man over there?" She followed his eyes to the burly figure that had watched him so intently. Her smile faded.

"He's trouble. Calls himself Grimsal the Slasher, doubt it's his real name. Been here a few weeks and loves to pick fights. I'd steer clear if I were you."

"Thanks," he said, slicing into the meat and taking a bite. It tasted as good as it looked.

"Let me know if you need anything else." She again vanished into the crowd, taking the coin with her.

Callum noticed Grimsal's eyes on him once more, lingering on his coin pouch. This time Callum returned a look faster, trying his best to seem brave. The two stared at one another for a couple of seconds before Grimsal finally backed down, turning to a man next to him and saying something lost to the din. Defeated.

Callum waited until he was sure the man wouldn't start watching him

again before settling into his meal. He tried his best to let the delicious fla-
vours of the food distract him from the worries of the next day, and though
it and the joyous atmosphere succeeded in doing just that, a quiet whisper
of concern refused to budge from his mind.

It was well into the evening by the time Callum went up to his room, though
the tavern itself was still as raucous as ever. His room was the first on the right.
Opening the door, he found it to be sparsely furnished with a wooden bed
and a straw mattress, as well as a large metal tub. The window had a shutter
that was securely fastened, and he was glad for that; he doubted the streets
beyond were going to quieten down even in the night hours.

Touching the mattress, Callum found that it was rather comfortable
despite what he paid, though not as much as the last bed he'd slept in. Fatigue had again caught up with him as he closed the door, not used to such
prolonged travel. He tugged an itchy yet serviceable blanket over himself,
and within seconds his eyes started to close, but as he turned over there was
a sharp pain in his side. Startled, Callum looked at himself quickly, only to
find that he hadn't removed the scabbard from his belt, the sword handle
poking him. Removing it with care, he looked at the blade once again as
he sat up, the hours of relaxation undone in an instant. He drew the blade
and sighed.

"...I wish I was rid of you," he said to the sword before chuckling at himself; it couldn't talk, he knew that. He then heard footsteps in the corridor
outside. He held the handle of his sword tightly, expecting something to go
wrong. The steps got louder until they stopped outside his room. Callum
stood nervously as the door opened with a loud creak. Standing in the doorway was a large figure who blocked the lantern light in the corridor beyond.

"Sleeping?" the gruff man asked him in a gravelly, mocking tone. Callum
noticed in the man's right hand a stout piece of wood. There was no way
out of the room, Callum knew.

"I was about to," Callum replied. "Grimsal, I presume?"

"Reputation precedes me," he responded, stepping out into the light
and revealing that it was indeed him. He had a malicious, black-toothed
grin. "So you know why I'm here."

"I can take a guess," Callum answered. Scared as he was, the man was
nothing like the figure in black; the stare wasn't as striking, his demeanour
not as menacing. That didn't make Grimsal any less threatening, however.

"I wouldn't advise it." The brute laughed at that.

"Or you'll do what? Just give me the coin pouch, and I might let you go with a bruising." Callum held his sword more firmly, trying to assume the stance that Azure had told him about the night before.

"I know how to use this," he bluffed with conviction. The ruffian eyed the dull, matted blade and snarled.

"I was thinking of taking your sword too, but now I've seen it, you can keep it. Don't think I could sell it even if I wanted to."

Grimsal took a step closer and Callum one back towards the bed as he held his blade tighter. The lantern behind Grimsal went out suddenly.

Unaware, the thug gave a sickening smile. "I'm going to enjoy this."

Grimsal was about to move but stopped suddenly, a look of shock on his face that quickly lost focus. The man tried to say something, but all that came from his mouth was blood. Then there was the horrifying sound of tearing flesh as, right before Callum, Grimsal was torn in two vertically from his chest outwards.

Guts and viscera spilled and gushed out of the growing gap as the man was rent asunder in the space of a second. Callum exclaimed in shock at the bloody sight but quickly looked beyond the pile of flesh to see a new figure in the doorway, larger than even the ruffian. Callum's breath stilled at the sight. He didn't have time to ask himself what kind of person was capable of doing that as the newcomer stepped into the light. The sight struck terror in his stomach.

"...No..."

Standing seven foot tall and splattered with blood was a creature covered in fine red scales save for its claws and eyes. The claws were sharp and bestial, body muscular and broad. It possessed an almost lizard-like head that looked directly at him. It lacked the spikes, horns or crests of its kind, however, possessing a humanoid shape that was at the same time alien. Its entirely white eyes glowed with unsettling energy and smoked with silent rage. Naked and lacking any gender-specific anatomy, it ignored the heap of meat before it that had once been Grimsal and watched Callum intently, muscles twitching as if it was holding back. Callum remembered all too well those eyes and what they meant; the man was still after him.

The creature lunged at him suddenly, teeth bared as it sought to catch him and claw him to pieces, just like it had Grimsal. Survival instincts kicked in, Callum diving to the side to avoid the creature's attack. It collided with the bed, wrecking it. In a blur, it turned its head and lunged out again at Callum, only just missing with its claws as he rolled aside. The thing was looming over him, wasting no time as it again tried to slash at his chest.

Callum swung with his sword in desperation, having nothing to lose. The blade sliced into its body with ease, the creature recoiling as it pierced its scaly hide. It bled no blood, instead oozing a black ichor-like substance from the injury. It looked at the sword, now stained with the thing's life fluids, and Callum too stared, amazed at what it could do, before swinging again clumsily.

This time the creature darted backwards, expecting the blow and easily evading it. Callum rose to his feet quickly and tried to strike again, but that was also dodged. The creature responded by backhanding Callum in the chest, knocking him across the room and into the wall with some force. He felt pain shoot through his system twice fold from the blow, struggling to remain standing. The hideous beast glared at his blade, Callum's heart beating like crazy even as agony pulsed in his head. He'd gotten lucky with his first strike. He wouldn't get such a chance again. Then there was a voice from the corridor beyond.

"What the...! Hey! Hey, you!"

When the creature turned sharply, it was struck by Saresan's halberd. Wounded a second time but not as deeply as by Callum's blade, it snarled with anger and bestial hate. The guard realised then what he'd attacked, his expression a mixture of horror and confusion that quickly faded when he noticed Callum's distress. A steely expression washed over him as he readied his polearm to fight. "Come on! Come get me, you... whatever you are!"

His goading paid off, the red-scaled monster surging towards Saresan instead. He swung for the thing's leg and drew ichor with a glancing blow which made it stumble. Callum was now steady, albeit with pain that pulsed through his head and back.

He watched breathlessly as the creature swung wildly, Saresan barely dodging back as he struggled to come to terms with its speed. The creature bull-rushed him suddenly, shoving him into the corridor and against the wall.

Callum felt dizzy but managed to stagger from the wall as Saresan only just managed to keep the creature's snapping jaws at bay with the shaft of his halberd against its neck. Callum moved with unsteady steps to strike at the red-scaled monster, but it noticed, swiping out at him aggressively. Callum retorted with an equally aggressive attack which took off its hand with practically no effort, something Saresan's halberd had been unable to do.

It growled loudly and angrily, ichor seeping from the stump as its fury only intensified. Callum barely noticed its remaining claw dragging through his shirt, digging into his skin as it retaliated instantly, instinctively. Agony consumed him, Callum stumbling back as he clutched his bleeding wound.

Desperation started to surge up inside his body, along with something... very odd. It was a quiet, tingling feeling that appeared to numb the pain but also confused him, not unlike what he'd felt when he first grabbed the sword. He ended up against the back wall, leaning on it for support as he found himself both exhausted and full of energy all at once. The creature turned from Saresan, reading to pounce upon him.

"Hey! Fight me!" the guard shouted as he tried for another swing.

It wheeled around on the spot and struck him firmly in the chest before his halberd connected. Saresan fell to the ground like a stone, groaning loudly. He gave a pained and apologetic look to Callum, as if he expected the end.

The tingling had crept up Callum's arms now, threatening to consume his entire body. It felt foreign and at the same time wholly natural to him, but it was overwhelmed by fright as he watched the creature step up slowly. Its sharp teeth were clenched, purpose clear.

When his fright was at its greatest, Callum felt an uncontrollable urge, unable to contain the strange feeling any longer. It overtook him as he looked up at the thing that was moments from killing him. He dropped his sword and his arm pointed to the beast, rigid with sharp needling pain. A sudden increase in temperature, brightness, agony. Then there was darkness.

Chapter Six

For the second time in as many days, Callum awoke in unfamiliar surroundings. The first thing he noticed was the cold, unyielding slab he was lying upon. The room about him was also of stone and dimly lit with torches, the scent of herbs catching his nostrils. He spied a robed figure in the corner who raised his head as he stirred and stood from his stool, moving over to him slowly.

"Please be still," the old man spoke softly as he checked a bandage that had been wrapped around Callum's chest. It was stained with blood, and only now did his body ache. The tingling sensation that had overwhelmed his body was a fleeting yet powerful memory. At least this time he knew it hadn't been a dream.

"Where am I?" Callum asked carefully, looking about for the sword. Sure enough, he found the blade in its scabbard propped up against the wall to his left.

"You are in the church. I have been tending to your wounds since your friend brought you in here." The monk shook his head as he pulled from his robes a small bottle. "I have never seen injuries like yours before."

"Saresan, is he alright?" was Callum's next question.

"He will be," the man said as he dripped a few drops of a green liquid onto the bandage. Its sting was nothing compared to the claws of the monster. "He had to carry you here, you were bleeding heavily and unconscious. He would not let us see to his wounds before he was sure you were being taken care of. He has taken a few blows, but nothing concerning." Callum took a moment before he asked the next thing, knowing it might get him into a lot of trouble.

"...What happened after I blacked out?" The older man looked at him, his wrinkled face momentarily unreadable before twinging with worry.

"...Your friend would not say exactly, only that you had been attacked by something and he had come to your aid. Apparently, the resulting fight knocked over an oil lantern and started a fire in your room." He left a pause. "Is that right?"

Was that a lie? He didn't know and wanted to ask, but now was not the time to question. For now, Callum tried to sit up, to get a better look around him.

"Please, you should be lying down."

He sat up anyway despite the pain.

"I don't remember much of what happened."

His response seemed to mollify the robed man.

"Of course. Sir Azure told me of your problematic memory." That made his heart sink; was Azure there? What time was it? Was he to be grilled a second time by the disapproving knight? "I shall tell him you are awake. You need rest."

"I'll tell him myself," Callum declared both with defiance and resignation.

"Please, you should—"

Callum ignored the man and slowly rose, placing his feet weakly on the floor. His footing wasn't as firm as he wanted it to be, but it didn't falter. He slowly walked over to the sword and retrieved it. He'd been tempted to leave it in the room but knew that Azure would likely demand he took it along anyway. Only then did he notice that he was wearing a different shirt; the monks had replaced it for him when he was unconscious. The old man made no effort to stop from him walking but did nothing to help either.

The door to the room beyond was ajar, and through the gap, Callum could see both Saresan and Azure standing in a small corridor with two exits. Callum guessed that the larger one opposite him led out of the building. The two were in the midst of a heated discussion.

"I told you, I was keeping my eye on him." Azure had his arms folded, not convinced by Saresan's words and watching him intently.

"And perchance you *happened* to see that someone had entered the tavern intending to attack him."

"That's right. So, I went up and helped him out. Turned out to be one of the local thugs, took a liking to his coin pouch, I'll wager."

"And the fire?" Saresan didn't appear fazed by Azure's stare.

"Caused by the scuffle. I think I knocked a lantern with one of my halberd swings, right before I got the killing blow."

"And tore him apart." Azure looked to the ajar door, spotting Callum and giving him a stern gaze. He quickly returned to interrogating. "There was little left to identify him as a man, let alone someone of ill repute."

"...I must have gotten carried away after I slew him, what with the fire happening and all, it was a bit of a blur." Then Saresan noticed Callum too and smiled. The man's eyes had an odd look about them, but it passed quickly. "Good to see you're awake."

"I'm trying not to make this a habit." Saresan smiled at that, but it didn't linger.

"I should hope so, it's bad for my health too." Azure then stepped up to Callum, his patience all but spent.

"I want an explanation for why the Ox's Horn tavern has burned to the ground and why there is a dead man in what was once your room." Azure's eyes narrowed. "Do *not* tell me you cannot remember."

"Hey, lay off," Saresan went on the defensive again. "He passed out from the flames and the smoke. Not to mention he'd almost been killed—"

"I am the one asking the questions. He will be the one giving the answers, not you." Callum wasn't sure if he preferred Azure's judging stare or the madness in the glowing white eyes of the creature he'd fought. Azure glared now, angry.

"...Like Saresan said, I passed out when the fire started. Grimsal came to my room to mug me and nearly succeeded, had Saresan not shown up." Callum couldn't completely hide his nervousness, hoping the lie would hold. The knight looked at him intently.

"The monk said it looked like *claw* marks on your chest." Callum had to think of something, fast. What came was a long shot, but that was all he had.

"...He had a dog," he mentioned then, pretending to just remember. "A huge beast that he set on me. It clawed at me before Saresan drove it off, with help from the fire." Saresan looked bewildered before clearing his throat and nodding.

"That damn dog! If it wasn't for its fear of the flames, I would have had my hands full. It bolted out the door and I haven't seen or heard from it since."

"You did not tell me of this... dog." Azure's pause was pronounced. Saresan shrugged again, settling back into his calm demeanour.

"I didn't think it was important."

"A giant dog was not important enough to be mentioned." Azure eyed the former guard.

"Well, you know, it was all kind of a blur. Callum's just brought it back to my mind. Combat's a hectic thing, eh? You'd know." There was a very awkward pause. Callum swallowed hard.

"...Quite." Azure's reply was measured and deliberate, the knight looking between the two of them. It lingered for far longer than Callum was comfortable with before the knight sighing deeply, "Your 'encounter' means I have to go to the lord of the town and do some explaining on your behalf.

You are after all in my care, and thus your actions are my responsibility. Even if it was all in self-defence, significant property damage has been caused and a man lies dead..." He gave Saresan a sideways glance. "...And a giant, near-feral dog is now loose upon the town."

"I'm sorry that I'm causing you such problems." Callum watched the knight sigh once more, agitated.

"I shall go and do that now. You will meet me at the town gate, where-upon we are going to make back the time we lost so we can reach the sage promptly. It seems I have more questions to ask of him now." The foreboding nature of the final statement wasn't lost on either of them as Azure excused himself from the church, stepping out into the street and mounting his horse.

The pair looked at each other silently. Only when Azure was out of earshot did Saresan speak.

"I don't think he bought it. A dog, seriously?" Saresan then looked concerned. "...What *was* that thing?"

"I don't know," he replied honestly, thinking back to the burning eyes from the night in the forest. He couldn't tell Saresan that, afraid of how he'd react. "It ripped Grimsal apart and then went after me."

"I've never seen anything like that before, and I've seen a lot of things. Looked like it came from the gates of the abyss." Saresan was watching him like Azure had, only without the sternness of the knight. Then he went to the door Callum had come through and closed it, speaking in a hushed tone, "...You don't remember what happened just before you passed out, do you?"

"From your expression, I think you do." He left a measured pause. "...What did I do?" Saresan thought about how best to word it.

"From your hand..." He shook his head. "This is going to sound really stupid, Callum."

"Please, tell me." Another pause.

"...Fire. Fire shot out from your hand." It took a moment for the words to sink in. When they did, Callum laughed; surely it was a joke. He was the only one that found it funny though, and that killed his mirth; he was being serious, but how could that be?

"You're sure?" Saresan nodded slowly.

"A blast of flame, unlike anything I've ever seen. It incinerated the... thing... as well as set the entire room alight. I think some of it came from your sword, but most of it was just from... Ah damn, that doesn't even make sense! But I know what I saw, it was fire!" He remembered back to the night of his woodland excursion, the two flying men as they battled with lightning and fire all over the place. Looking now to his hands he wondered what it all meant, even when he knew already. The revelation left him confused and very afraid.

"...You're saying that *I* shot out fire, from me?" Saresan nodded again and was about to pat his shoulder but hesitated.

"I didn't tell Azure. He doesn't trust..." Saresan paused, muddling through his thoughts. "All this time I thought it wasn't true, and here you are, Callum, proof that sorcerers *do* exist." Callum was alarmed at the word.

"I'm... what? I'm not a sorcerer!"

"If you're not a sorcerer, I'll be damned. I may have been distracted by the whole red monster thing, but I know what I saw! That was magic, and I don't believe in the stuff – well, didn't believe, anyway."

"But I don't have magic! I can't have magic, this doesn't make any sense!" He had to sit down, legs weak from the declaration and its implications, but there were no chairs. How could he have known? Maybe it was the sword, a vessel for occult energies, but it had come from him too, or so Saresan had said. The feeling moments before he blacked out returned to his mind, so odd and yet so much him. Had that been magic rushing through his body? How did that even work? "...It's just not possible." Saresan watched him, no smile on his face.

"Whatever you are, it doesn't change *who* you are. You're still you and you're a good man. I was just curious if you knew what you could do, that's all."

"You believe me, don't you? About the fire in the forest?" Callum couldn't hide his worry, but Saresan smiled, finally patting him on the shoulder at last.

"I believe you. You've had no reason to lie to me yet and I like to think I'm a good judge of character, but I'd keep this a secret if I were you. There are a lot more people like Azure than there are me." Callum smiled despite himself and the earth-shattering news.

"...Thank you." Callum looked at his hands again, puzzled once more. "It just makes no sense; how did it happen? Why did it happen?"

"Maybe seeing the sage will be useful after all if he can answer those questions for you. We'll find out soon enough, I think." As Saresan looked to the door that led outside, Callum was puzzled once more.

"...We?" Callum winced at his aching wound. "I thought you had a post to start working at."

"It can wait. Besides, I think Azure's beginning to suspect. I thought you'd be alright, but now I don't want to leave you alone with him just in case it goes sour."

"But your job—"

"They'll take me on no matter what. Besides, I'm on good terms with the captain here, I'm sure he'll be understanding." Saresan's grin did much to soothe his worries, if only for a moment.

"Really, you don't have to do this." Saresan chuckled.

"You're right, I don't, but I want to. What are friends for?" He smiled once again, then thought on something. "We need to get something to protect you." He was looking at where Callum had been clawed at.

"I can't afford armour, Saresan, you know this," Callum stated as Saresan opened the door to the streets, following his friend into the humdrum of market day.

"Good thing I know a few people, eh?"

Callum was sure that people were giving him odd looks, that they knew what had happened and who he was. Even as they weaved through the crowds eyeing the stalls, he dwelt on the revelation of his powers.

Why hadn't this ability shown up earlier in his life? Had his fear triggered it, even though he'd been scared before with no inferno bursting from his body? Why had he fallen unconscious? Thoughts on magic brought him back to the eyes of the golden knight. They were vivid in his mind and now more familiar than ever before. And his voice, it rang true to him, but why?

He stopped without even knowing it, standing before a long stone building that looked older than the others around it. Saresan opened the solid door in front of him and peered within. He seemed satisfied with what he saw.

"Wait here."

He slipped into the building, closing the door behind him. What was he doing, where was this? He noticed a couple of people that were definitely giving him looks and he tried to brush them off with a smile. They were looking at his sword, him gazing at it in turn; it had all started with that after all, a trigger to the cascading river of events he was swept up in.

He was so focused that he hadn't noticed Saresan come back out with something in his hands. "Put this on, it should fit over your shirt." He saw that he was holding a heavily tanned jerkin of thick material, stiff and worn.

"Did you just take that?" Callum asked quizzically, feeling bad already.

"They don't use this stuff anymore. Chain is better in almost every manner. Besides, you'll be bringing it back before you know it." Saresan's smile was ever-present.

"I don't feel right just taking it. Perhaps I could pay them for it?"

"They were in a heap in the storeroom gathering dust, I'd be surprised if they knew how many they had. Put it on, we need to go back and wait for Azure."

Saresan wasn't going to take no for an answer, and so he pulled the jerkin over his head. It was uncomfortable and irritated his injury, and yet he felt that much safer for knowing there was another layer between him and another wound like that. Saresan looked him up and down, satisfied. "You look the spitting image of a warrior."

"Really?"

"Well, you don't have the bulk for it yet, but I'm sure if you keep getting into fights that'll change."

"I don't *want* to get into fights," Callum replied as they returned to navigating the crowds. This time, people were giving them even more space, seeing that both of them were more visibly armed. "I just want to go back to how things were."

"The life of a labourer?"

"It pays my way." Saresan looked to his halberd appraisingly.

"And being a hired sword pays much better. A little more dangerous, sure, but what job isn't these days? Millers get caught in the grinding wheels; woodsmen get crushed by the trees they fell. At least as a hired blade, you get to pick your death, to some extent." He then glanced at Callum's sword. "Besides, I don't think you'll be seeing a normal life anytime soon, so you'd better get used to lugging that sword around."

"Once I see the sage, things will return to normal." Callum was beginning to doubt the words even as they came out. A child looked cautiously at his sword as they walked by a fruit stall.

"You've had more peculiar things happen to you in three days than I've had in my entire life, and I'm no spring chicken. Maybe Azure's right, perhaps the fates have picked you as someone special, who can say. Call it a hunch, but terribleness comes in threes."

Callum was left with that to ponder as they made their way to the town gate. Among the crowds he heard 'that one from the tavern' murmured, but he couldn't pinpoint who said it. As they approached their destination, he saw the as-ever disappointed Azure, waiting for them with a cold look. He was already mounted on his steed.

"And where have you—" Azure stopped his question as he noticed the jerkin that Callum now wore. "I see."

"Something wrong?" Saresan asked flatly.

"No."

"Not everyone can afford plate mail." The tension was so palpable that Callum could've grasped it.

"Not everyone knows how best to use it," was the retort as Azure looked to them. "I have secured horses from the lord for both of you, on the condition that they are returned as we took them from him." He then looked at Callum. There was a stern reprimand in the tone that was a warning aimed only at him.

"I'm surprised he let you borrow anything of his, how'd you manage that?" Saresan remarked, looking in the direction of the town gate.

"That is not of your concern." He then looked ahead, as if brushing off the question with a twinge of sadness.

"How did you know to get two?" Saresan then asked.

"I made an assumption. It seems I was correct." He didn't go into any more detail for a change. "They are waiting at the town gates; we shall ride from there." As if on cue, a guard made his way through the crowds towards them. In his hands were the reins of two horses that followed behind, one black and one brown, both with a finely made saddle secured to their backs.

"With our lord's kindest regards," the guard spoke flatly, handing the reins over to Saresan and Callum and leaving without another word.

Callum had never ridden a horse before, and so he stared at the creature with a vague sense of intrigue before guessing that he had to get onto it like Azure had many times before. Carefully he pulled himself into the saddle with some difficulty, keeping a firm grip on the reins; he expected the horse to try and bolt, rear up and throw him back to the ground. To his surprise, it did neither and waited there obediently.

"Well trained." Saresan had got onto his horse faster than Callum had.

"I would expect nothing less." Azure's tone was dismissive. The two warriors were bound only by their desire to accompany Callum and made no secret of it. He didn't want to think about when Azure's patience with Saresan would finally run out. The portcullis was already raised, Callum copying the motions Azure made as best he could to get his horse moving.

It was then that a familiar voice shouted angrily above the noise of the crowd.

"I *knew* it!" It was Cuthbert and his two annoyed henchmen. His cheeks were red with rage, the man forcing his way through the crowd even as it parted, with an accusing finger pointed at Callum. "You are as dishonest as you are foul!" How had he tracked them down?

"Ah," Saresan muttered, turning his horse to face the blustering typhoon. Azure looked at the upstart man sternly, clearly annoyed at being held up yet again. A ruckus developed around Cuthbert, who shouted louder still.

"My lady was most upset at the lack of notification of my events and activities! Now she spurns me! My heart aches from the pain *you* have wrought on me!" Callum had felt guilty already, now it returned two-fold.

"It wasn't my intention—" Callum began.

"I see through your lies! I should have followed my instinct not to trust you, but no, I was charitable, and look how you repay my kindness! Now you have a horse, armour and—" Upon seeing the scabbard, the man was even more aghast. "—A sword? Masquerading as a man of noble blood! I'll have you hanged!"

"But I—" Cuthbert then moved to stand in front of Azure's steed, one fist clenched as he pointed accusingly at Callum.

"Good sir, this... this petty criminal is sullying the name of your good tradition! By your honour, you should apprehend him!" Azure was not amused.

"Out of my way," the knight ordered. Saresan kept quiet, watching Cuthbert's goons carefully in case they tried something.

"But... but he is a thief! He has made himself fat off the silver I have worked hard—"

"If your silver is all you are concerned about, he will return it." Azure's statement didn't sound like a request. Callum removed the silver coins from his coin pouch, more than willing to return what he hadn't rightly earned.

"Silver alone cannot undo the dishonour he has brought me!" Cuthbert sneered, out for blood.

"He has business with me. Your grievance can wait until his return," Azure informed the noble bluntly. "Move aside."

Cuthbert blinked, lost for words. When they did surface, they were laced with anger.

"You would consort with—"

"Drop the pouch, Callum."

Callum hesitated, but he didn't argue with the knight's tone. The pouch of silver thudded onto the ground as he dropped it next to a puddle in the dirt. The noble stared at the pouch, speechless as the crowd talked amongst each other, along with a few laughs and gasps. Saresan chuckled, murmuring something lost in the commotion. "What was yours is yours again."

"A man of your station—" Cuthbert's goons finally stepped aside in deference to the knight, the noble now alone in his obstruction.

"Upon our return, you may talk to me of this in great detail." The knight spoke with measured eloquence, tempered with annoyance. "However, on this day, I have far more pressing places to be with him than here. The implications of our lateness there could have ramifications far deeper than your loss of petty coin."

"But this—"

"You have your coin and his apology. That will suffice for your honour."

"You would agree to travel with a man of ill repute—" Cuthbert was cut off sharply.

"Good day, sir." Azure's horse sidestepped and trotted past Cuthbert without another word, leaving Cuthbert in his state of shock. Saresan started to follow in, the noble catching his eye and sneering.

"How dare you—"

"Put a boot in it." The warrior smiled with mock politeness.

"I shall have words with your captain! You'll never work there again!"

"Way ahead of you!" Only Callum had yet to pass the now irate noble. He gave an apologetic look but said nothing, trying to catch up with the others by pulling on the reins, hoping the horse would move. It did so begrudgingly, starting a trot that Callum found uncomfortable. Still, he felt terrible; he'd fully intended to deliver the letter, had the events around the sword not interrupted. That Azure would talk to Cuthbert later didn't fill him with hope for the future, however, if he was still a free man by then. After all, they had yet to see the sage.

Chapter Seven

"Give unto others all that you can give, for they are of need.
Take unto yourself their grief and pain, for they are hurting.
Such is my bond and I shall keep it, for that is my duty in this life."

—*Oath of the Order of Pauper Monks*

Though clouds had slowly gathered above them as they travelled, the rain refused to come. Their progress unimpeded and the journey without incident left Callum with only his thoughts and fears for company. He couldn't help but look about him every once in a while for shadows that weren't there, drawing Azure's attention every time. Even when they briefly stopped to eat – something Azure held off on for as long as possible – Callum felt far from safe.

They travelled quickly to 'make up for lost time', as the knight put it, past the farmsteads until they reached a woodland that had signs of a lumber operation on its edges. The last place Callum wanted to be was in a forest, but the only alternative was to face Azure's ire, and so he ventured in in silence.

For hours they rode along a narrow but well-worn path, slowly descending into a small river valley. Beyond the river were two paths, one that ran alongside it and another which wound its way upwards. The ascending path was slowly being reclaimed by nature, and it was there that Azure's eyes were focused upon.

"The sage is up there?" Saresan asked, not getting an answer. "And we're expected to bring the horses along that path? Looks narrow."

"The horses will be fine," Azure replied confidently.

"It might be easier on foot," Callum suggested. "We could lead the horses by their reins behind us."

"Sounds sensible to me," Saresan agreed.

"If we go by foot, it will take too long." Azure's protest was ignored by the guard, who'd already begun dismounting.

"Doesn't look like the sage is busy right now." The joke wasn't taken well if Azure's stern stare was any indicator.

"The sage is often meditating at this hour but will surely make an exception in this case." Callum decided to dismount as well, and at that, Azure once again sighed, "Your fears of the path are unfounded, but if you insist in foolishness, then so be it." The knight got off his steed faster than both of them and led them all across the river and along the upward path, trying to maintain a brisk pace.

The path grew increasingly more exposed as they ascended, but Callum didn't have long to grow accustomed to the chilly wind before Azure stopped abruptly.

"People," Azure told them quietly. Callum was at the back of the group and couldn't see anything of the way ahead.

"If they're bandits, they sure picked the wrong group to waylay." Saresan checked the slopes about them just in case they'd walked into the ambush. Callum did the same but saw nothing out of the ordinary. He nearly reached for his blade but refrained when Azure called out into the distance.

"Hail! What brings you this way, strangers?" Nobody shouted back, but Azure turned to address the two of them quickly, "They're approaching. Two of them. Be ready."

Callum hoped it wouldn't end in bloodshed, be it from brigands or more of the red monsters. The lack of fright from Azure told him it wasn't the latter, and when the pair finally came into view, Callum wondered why he was so calm. The first figure was a man half a foot taller than him and broadly built, but it was the double-headed battleaxe in the hands that he'd noticed first. A dull shirt of chain mail with a plate of scale pieces strapped across it completed the image of a hardened warrior. The man's appearance was hidden by a full face-helmet, plain and without adornment. His brown trousers looked hard wearing and his boots were plated with metal, likely steel. Callum caught a glimpse of the warrior's powerful green eyes that watched them all with suspicion.

His travelling companion was a stark contrast to the foreboding figure that watched over her, a woman roughly his own age that stood a few inches shorter than he did. Her long blonde hair was tied back in a ponytail, clean and without tangles. Her bright blue eyes were striking compared to the grim warrior that stood beside her, catching his attention. She noticed his look and returned a smile of greeting, warm and welcoming. It felt genuine, melting away the fear of a bandit attack.

She wasn't as well built as the man next to her but was still quite trim. She wore a white linen shirt and trousers that were without blemish and brown boots that were speckled with mud. Over this, she wore a light blue cloak that was fastened around her neck by an engraved bronze emblem. That alone was more valuable than anything Callum had owned before finding the sword.

Something was hanging from either side of her belt, perhaps sheathed weapons. Neither group moved, waiting for the other to act first, but any tension in the air wasn't being felt by Callum. He and the lady watched one another a moment longer before he spotted her companion staring intently at him, almost a warning glance. He turned his stare away, not wanting to start things off on the wrong foot already. Saresan was the first to speak after another second, stepping forward with his halberd in only one hand.

"Didn't expect to see any other travellers out this way. The name's Saresan." The woman smiled once more in greeting and nodded her head.

"My name is Alexis." Her voice was soft and had the accent of someone from a higher station than Callum could ever hope to attain, possibly from the capital. Azure took notice when he heard her speak. She indicated to the man beside her. "And this is my brother Johnathan."

"Pleasure's all ours." It was Saresan's turn to smile, confident they were no longer in danger. He then motioned to Callum. "That's Callum, the other is Azure." Alexis looked at Callum once more.

"A pleasure to meet you all," she said to them. Azure then handed the reins of his horse to Callum and walked up to Alexis with purpose, Johnathan eyeing him now. The knight bowed, then removed his helmet to reveal his smile. Saresan rolled his eyes.

"I am Sir Azure Tellinton, knight of Felford in the service of our liege, the good King Franci." He offered his hand to take hers, perhaps to kiss the top of it. "Charmed to meet you, milady." She looked at the knight with an amused expression, not taking him up on the offer. Johnathan's posture showed disapproval, but Azure didn't notice.

"Nice to meet you," was her only response. Azure quickly realised he was being rebuffed and stepped back. Callum couldn't help but be amused by the spectacle.

"What brings you to this place?" Azure then asked, looking beyond them to the path ahead. "Are you too seeking the guidance of the sage?"

"I am," Johnathan replied, gruff and serious. Saresan seemed to be sizing up the tall warrior.

"Believer in all that stuff?" Saresan got no reply.

"We're heading there too," Callum then mentioned.

"You should address ones of such upbringing with the respect they are due," the knight chastised. She, however, just shook her head.

"There's no need for that," she explained, surprising Azure even though he tried to hide it. "If you're suggesting that we travel to the sage together, I agree. It's always better to be in greater numbers."

"We're already late. The caravan will not wait forever," Johnathan muttered, clearly not a fan of the idea.

"The caravan knows where to go if we take too long," she told him plainly. Johnathan looked once more to Callum as Azure put his helmet back on, taking the reins of his horse.

"Don't slow us down," Johnathan warned.

"We have had enough delays already this journey, so on that, you have my word," Azure remarked, it clearly aimed towards Callum.

"Words are cheap," Johnathan quipped, turning back to the road ahead and starting to walk without another word. Alexis followed a moment after, managing to keep up with Johnathan's fast pace. Saresan shrugged and joined the others down the path that would eventually lead to the sage's home.

The path continued to climb the valley with no abode in sight. Johnathan didn't look back once as they moved, his pace quick but not impossible to match. Callum once more brought up the rear of the horse procession, being much more careful than the others. Callum clutched his reins tightly, his eyes on the ground just in case a gnarled root or a jutting stone caused his horse to lose its footing.

Only when he noticed a shadow beside his own did he notice that Alexis had moved to walk beside him, watching him. Even though she'd said it was alright not to show deference, Callum was tempted to, trying to find the right words to greet her with. It was she that spoke first, however.

"You don't need to grip so tightly." She was unlike Azure. She didn't chastise him for his mistakes. He loosened his hands as instructed. "The horse will follow just fine."

"Thank you." That was the only reply which came to his head. He noticed Johnathan looking back for the first time, staring at him. It unsettled him, Callum looking to Alexis instead to distract from it. "I'm sorry about Azure, his greeting. I didn't know he'd do that." Only then did he check that the knight wasn't listening. He didn't seem to be for once, focused on the way ahead.

"You've no need to apologise," she replied. "I had an inkling he would try, such as knights are. What brings you all to see the sage?"

"Me." Alexis raised an eyebrow. "Azure wants to seek advice from him about me." That was all Callum was willing to give away; he didn't want her judging him for having strange powers or getting attacked by odd red monsters, never mind Azure being within earshot.

"I don't see why. You seem pretty ordinary to me." Callum found himself laughing at that, something he'd not done since his journey began. "What?"

"You're just the first person to have said that in a while, that's all."

"You seem normal for a squire, then."

"I'm no squire," came his reply.

"No?"

"I found this sword a couple of days ago. I'm holding onto it only because no one else has reclaimed it. Azure said no knight would want to use it."

"If it's sharp, that's all that matters," came her answer. "My brother often goes to the sage. I'm sure he'll have the answers for your knightly friend."

"Me too. I want to go back to what my life was before I started all this travelling."

"What were you before?" Why was she so curious about him? He was of a far lower station than her, beneath her notice.

"A labourer. A simple life, I know." Her look had moved to the winding path ahead as the forest began to clear, though her nod showed that she still listened. Then he decided to ask her a question or two. "What do you do, if you don't mind me asking?"

"My brother and I run a company of trading caravans. My parents worked from the capital and dealt mainly in unrefined ores. We've branched out into other items since we took charge. They made a healthy profit from their trade."

"And your parents?" Callum knew the answer already. Her smile dimmed in recollection.

"They succumbed to plague two years ago. They sent me away before I could get sick. My brother was lucky, he recovered." Callum wasn't surprised Johnathan had endured, strong as he looked.

"I'm sorry."

"It's okay, thank you though. In truth, we don't have much of a hand in the running of the business, we don't know the markets as our parents did. A friend of the family runs most of the day-to-day workings, giving us a small portion of the profits. He was close to my father, promised to take care of us if the worst happened." Her small portion was likely more money than he'd ever had, yet wealth hadn't gone to her head. He decided to change the topic to something not as downcast, mulling on how open she was to such a personal question.

"Why does Johnathan need to go to the sage?" She shrugged in answer.

"I don't know. He's been seeing the sage every now and again ever since my parents died. I don't normally go with him, but this time the visit coincided with a caravan group we were due to travel with."

The pair went silent, Callum unsure what to say. Her unreserved kindness didn't feel right; she should've been turning her nose up at him, ignoring his very existence, but no. He was happy for the company, but it didn't make sense, much like everything that had happened to him so far. Slowly, his mind began to drift to his magic, to the red creature, the night in the forest.

"Are you alright? You seem a world away."

"...Yes. Yes, I'm fine. I was just thinking." She nodded in reply and said nothing, walking alongside him for a bit longer before catching up with her brother, casting one more look his way before turning to the path. Left alone again, his thoughts returned to the sage and what they'd say about him. What if the truth came out? He was already in trouble with Azure and the local lord; if his magic was discovered, the web of lies he'd spun would ensnare him.

When it finally started to rain, Callum wondered if the gods had something against him. Perhaps they wanted him totally soaked and dishevelled when he was presented to the sage, or maybe they sought to delay him further to make the knotted nervousness in his stomach worse. Whatever the plan was, it was working. The exposed dirt path had become muddy, but the complaints among his travelling companions were few.

"Wonder if the sage saw this coming," Saresan joked. This time both Johnathan and Azure gave disapproving looks.

"The sage sees much," Azure responded. Callum saw the pathway widening ahead, giving the horses extra room to keep their footing. He felt then as if they were being watched. He stopped to look around, seeing nothing out of the ordinary.

"What's wrong?" Alexis asked, noticing his stillness.

"You need not worry yourself, my lady. His memory is... not all that it could be." It was a weak jab, but one nonetheless. The feeling wasn't going away, however.

"...Something's not right." Even as he spoke Callum couldn't see anyone, yet the feeling endured.

"If someone's out there, they'd think twice, I'm sure. We're too well armed to be easy pickings."

Saresan's assurances didn't make him feel any better. From the corner of his vision, Callum thought he could see a glint of white out in the open air. Turning, he saw nothing but rain. He tried to tell himself that it was just him worrying needlessly, but that didn't help. Quickly he caught up with the others, noticing that Johnathan was watching him once more, though Callum couldn't tell why. The path ended abruptly at the entrance to a natural cave, with a torch burning just inside.

"We have arrived," declared the knight.

"The sage lives in a cave?" Saresan was debating whether to take the torch.

"A quiet place of contemplation, far from the distraction of others. It is best to focus the mind, so he told me," Azure responded, looking back to the way they'd come.

Johnathan took the torch before Saresan could, walking ahead of the others and into the cave without a word. Azure was more concerned with finding somewhere to tie the horse's reins to, locating a pair of rusted metal loops hammered into a nearby stone. Saresan followed suit and took Callum's horse as well, tying both on the other remaining hoop before moving with the others into the cavern's mouth.

Now out of the rain, Callum glanced back at the downpour that they'd escaped from, then deeper into the darkness with a lingering feeling of anxiousness. It'd take a while for their clothes to dry, but did they have that long before they met the sage? The only route forward winded around a corner into the unknown.

"Let's just hope he's home," Saresan muttered. Callum secretly hoped he wasn't.

Johnathan moved deeper in without fear and the rest followed behind. Callum noticed Azure taking the rear, seemingly to block off his one avenue of escape. Moss and lichen clung to the walls and ceiling, but no animals took shelter from the cold and wet.

The cave had a chill of its own, unnatural and still. His imagination was running rampant with what the sage would look like and his powers; perhaps with but a thought the sage could divine his future, what little remained. The passageway narrowed as they headed further in, and when a fork in the tunnel presented itself, Johnathan made a left turn which led deeper still.

A minute later Callum spotted the light of another torch ahead, affixed to a worked stone wall and next to that a sturdy wooden door. A small trickle of water flowed from the rock into a natural basin, clean and fresh. Getting closer, Callum noticed that the torch shed no heat, but Azure ignored this, walking to the door and knocking.

He was surprised that the door opened at that. Johnathan didn't react.

"Maybe he's not home after all," Saresan muttered as Azure removed his helmet.

"Oh wise sage, we humbly seek your counsel on a matter of the utmost importance." Azure's words echoed through the caverns behind them, dying alone. Saresan shrugged.

"Shall we make ourselves comfortable?" came his suggestion.

"It is his sanctuary from others, we would be defiling it without his express invitation."

Johnathan ignored the knight's concerns and opened the door wide, stepping over the threshold. Azure frowned, but the warrior didn't care, moving out of sight. Callum, now curious at what was beyond despite his fear, stepped up to the entrance and peeked inside. He hadn't expected the ordered anarchy that sprawled before him, a pandemonium pinned in by the low roof and rough walls covered in painted runes and symbols. Items were all over the place, scattered into meaningless piles on the floor and across all available surfaces. Shelves were stocked to the brim with charms, strange concoctions and unusual sculptures of things that he'd never seen before. Contraptions of metal and glass stood motionless and inert in a corner, purpose unknown.

Through a small archway in the carved stone, there was a place that served as a bedroom and eating area, a cold fire pit within. Among all the knick-knacks, however, was no sage. Azure stepped within now, concerned.

"It was not like this when last I came here." His hand was resting warily on the pommel of his sword.

"We wait," Johnathan declared bluntly, standing by the entrance and setting his hefty battleaxe down.

Callum saw nowhere to sit and wanted nothing more than the fire pit burning so he could dry off. Alexis removed her cloak and hung it on an unoccupied peg by the door. She looked at the trinkets around them with curiosity while Saresan looked in the back area, likely for a way to light a fire. Callum followed him, watching as the guard found flint, charcoal and wood readily enough. It didn't take him long to get the fire pit going and Callum stuck close to it, thankful for its warmth. He could see the others through the archway, looking to them as Alexis spoke.

"I wonder how he finds anything in this mess."

"He will have placed them there for a reason." Johnathan was making sure not to move anything.

"Was he preparing for something big?" Saresan asked, his hands by the growing fire. "I don't think people daub things on walls just because they ran out of parchment."

"The sage is wise beyond all of us," Azure said to them. "His wisdom and insight into the workings of the lands let him see far more than the normal eye could. When last I spoke with him, he was in the middle of what he called 'a revelation moment'."

"Might explain a few things," Saresan mumbled quietly. Callum noticed then that the back room was tidy, a stark contrast to the main living area. It had plain walls, and the bed was made yet covered in dust. Saresan picked up a jar and looked at the contents, grimacing at the congealed mess within; perhaps the sage had not been there for some time.

"Callum said you were coming here to ask the sage about him," Alexis spoke to Azure now. Callum pretended to focus on getting warm as he listened. Azure looked to a skull that rested on a high shelf, dirty with age.

"It is not of your concern, milady." She was not impressed with his answer.

"I have made it my concern, sir knight, now please answer me." Azure stared at her, but she matched his gaze, waiting until finally he relented. Callum was more curious about that than the knight was.

"A number of strange events have occurred with Callum as the centre. Mayhap they are an omen of events to come."

"Strange events?" Johnathan suddenly took an interest in the conversation, turning to Callum. He pretended not to notice while Alexis listened on.

"Fires, two of them. Both he survived miraculously and with no memory of the incident. It would seem that he has more than a few connections to that most volatile of natural forces." Azure's disbelief was now only thinly concealed. Saresan was also listening less subtly.

"We told you what happened at the tavern," Saresan piped up. "Unless you don't believe—"

Chapter Eight

Just then, Callum felt something strange that drew his attention to the archway leading to the main room. He didn't know what that something was but had little time to ponder it. One moment there was nothing, and then someone was... there.

Standing in the archway was a figure clad in orange robes from head to foot, hands outstretched in a ritualistic manner. How had he got past all of them? Was there another entrance they didn't know about, or had it been magic?

It took a moment for the others to notice the new arrival. Saresan was startled, as was Alexis. Johnathan looked to the robes as the figure turned to the roaring fire pit, entirely unfazed by their presence. Callum could see the man's face now, young and with soft grey eyes that examined him, trying to glean something. Stroking his inches-long black beard in thought, the man considered a silent conundrum as he lowered his hood. Both his beard and long hair seemed untamed, yet all of it had a strange kind of order, a pattern. Callum had many questions but remained silent, aware that speaking out of turn might offend the sage. This had to be the sage; nothing else made sense.

"Where did you come from?" Saresan asked as Azure suddenly knelt in deference without looking to the new arrival.

"Oh, great sage, forgive our intrusion into your humble domain. We had expected you home and found you to be out on an errand of the utmost importance. We did not notice your arrival from one of your many hidden rooms of meditation," he proclaimed.

Alexis was warily watching the newcomer, his appearance still unexplained. The sage waved a dismissive hand, not even turning.

"Do not worry about it." The man's voice brimmed with self-confidence, almost sounding noble. Azure suddenly looked puzzled, as did Johnathan, who frowned.

"You sound... different." Azure was quiet.

"Younger, too," Johnathan added.

"I do not think so. I believe I have always sounded like this." The man walked into the main room, worry washing over Azure's face that quickly turned into shock. Johnathan reached for his weapon, the robed man shaking his head. "I would not do that if I were you. It will not end well." The sage smiled in greeting at Alexis. She didn't return it. What puzzled Callum most was how utterly unafraid the man was despite the brewing atmosphere of anger.

"You are not the sage!" Azure accused sternly.

"I never claimed to be, good sir. My name is Jinar Yelandan Fakkal Genai Lae, and the pleasure is all yours." That left Azure speechless, but Johnathan stepped forward quickly.

"Where is he?" came the demand.

"I am afraid the sage is a little busy right now."

"What did you do to him?" Johnathan was louder this time.

"Johnathan..." Alexis got her brother's attention, giving him a look that told him to calm down.

Callum didn't want the situation to explode out of control, but it was looking inevitable. He moved into the room and next to Alexis.

"This man is masquerading as the sage. I want to know why!" Johnathan stated. Azure finally found his words as Saresan watched the spectacle from by the fire pit, halberd close at hand.

"You will explain your presence here this instant!" demanded Azure. The robed man nodded in agreement.

"Very well, I am here because the sage is dead. Are you satisfied now?" Azure was once more robbed of a reply. Callum was even more stunned than both of them, not daring to speak in case he made things worse.

"What?! He cannot be dead!" The robed man was unmoved by the knight's eventual retort, stroking his beard once more.

"I am afraid he can. I daresay he has taken to his new profession most enthusiastically."

"Explain yourself this instant!"

"I arrived here a week ago to glean a few secrets I had yet to master, only to find him lifeless on the ground. His face was twisted in quite a horrifying visage of absolute terror," he spoke as if it was a matter of fact, smiling once more. "I buried the man and decided to try and discover the cause of his demise while waiting for someone to arrive, so I could break the bad news. Now you are here, you can let people know that he is, indeed, quite dead."

Johnathan scowled but did nothing, while Azure tried to gauge if he was being truthful. Callum doubted the knight would believe him.

"And who is to say you didn't kill him?" Johnathan accused, stepping closer. Jinar raised his eyebrow, though his smile did not fade.

"What good would killing him do me? I have no desire for his cave, and

I am in almost every respect better than he was. If there is any matter that *I* can assist you with—"

"No, there is not." Azure turned to the door, staring firmly at Callum. "We are done here, Callum. Come." What awaited Callum back at the town was far from answers, and now that the sage was gone, any hope of things ending well had vanished. Despite the fear welling in his stomach, he refused to follow. Azure noticed, waiting impatiently by the door.

"We came here for answers, Azure," Callum reminded him. Saresan was still, watching Azure intently; he too suspected things would get worse.

"And we cannot get those. I shall rely instead on my judgement and that of the local lord." That was what Callum had been afraid of. Alexis intervened at that point.

"The sage may be dead, but you have someone else who could help you. It can't hurt to ask Jinar your questions, can it? You lose nothing but time." Her words elicited little reaction.

"Time is a commodity we do not have in abundance. The night draws near." There wouldn't be any room for Callum to run if combat happened; Azure blocked the only way out. He didn't want to flee either, as it would only give Azure an excuse to plant guilt on him for crimes he hadn't committed. Saresan moved to stand beside him now, nodding subtly.

"To be a knight is to be fair and just, Azure. Right now, you're being neither." Azure glared at Saresan as the first word left his lips. "And I know what you're going to do when you take Callum back there."

"I refuse to listen to the falsehood that man will speak, nor will I tolerate *you* obstructing my duty to protect the people of this kingdom. I have tolerated you, Saresan, because I believed that you could be persuaded to see that which is before you. Clearly, I am mistaken." Azure held the handle of his sword, not drawing it just yet. That caused a shift in Johnathan's stance, unsure whom he was to levy his axe against. Jinar was indifferent to the looming threat, but Alexis was worried much like Callum was.

"And just what do you presume Callum is, Azure?" Alexis asked. "He's just a labourer—" She was cut off by the knight pointing an accusing finger directly at his charge.

"He is no labourer! He is in league with dark powers!"

The words persisted in the air, clinging defiantly to the very walls. Callum couldn't hide his guilt; his deception had been exposed, and sure enough,

Azure had known all along. Why had he strung him and Saresan along with this trek to the sage, knowing that deep down he'd act on his gut either way?

He turned away from the accusing stare Azure cast towards him, moving behind Saresan for protection. Alexis was dubious, but one look at Callum's face answered her doubt. It was not suspicion and fear that she showed, however, but sympathy, a glimmer of light in the gloom of despair. Johnathan was frowning, but not at Callum this time, while Azure looked vindicated.

"He cannot hide his crimes from the justice that seeks them. Callum cannot be allowed to continue his ways, to spread taint and destruction wherever he treads!" Saresan stood defiant, halberd now readied for combat. Johnathan was still considering his options, but he clearly didn't approve of something as Saresan spoke up.

"He's done nothing wrong. You know this. The fire in the tavern was an accident, and you can't pin the forest burning down on him." Jinar looked at Callum again, once more curious.

"I see you've been swayed by his silvered tongue," Azure remarked. "If you have any honour left, Saresan, you will stand aside and let me take him to face his punishment. Or shall I consider you complicit in harbouring a warlock?" Jinar's lips were moving silently, an island of calm as everything else crashed down around them. Callum hadn't come all this way to die, but what chance did he have? Azure would best Saresan, in the enclosed space a halberd was little good.

"This doesn't have to end in bloodshed!" Alexis had concealed an arm in her cloak, perhaps to reach for a weapon of her own just in case. Azure noticed.

"I see what is happening here, the subtle powers you weave, Callum! You model yourself the innocent victim while spiking their minds with pity! They may be weak, but *I* am strong!" Azure took a deep breath, trying to get his anger under control. Still, Johnathan didn't act either way. "If you had come with me, Callum, none of these people would have had to die as your pawns. You are truly without redemption."

Azure tried to draw his sword in a flourish, Saresan readying for a charge. Callum winced, expecting blood and pain, but neither happened; instead, there was that strange sensation again, this time far weaker and behind him. There was also Azure's confusion, as his blade refused to leave its scabbard, stuck firm. He tried again, once more failing and looking down at his weapon in puzzlement. Jinar chuckled to himself quietly as confusion rose rather than the surge of combat and peril.

"I believe that is quite enough, sir knight," the man declared. Callum spotted the subtle movements of Jinar's fingers and hands, an erratic pattern to them. Johnathan had spied the movements too and finally cracked a grin that didn't suit him. Azure turned his glare to Jinar now.

"...Of course, your lies are laid bare also," came his low sneer. With that, Callum quickly put the pieces together, astounded.

"...You're a sorcerer?" Denied his blade, Azure didn't rush forth and try to smash Callum's face in with his gauntleted fists. Instead, he watched with wary anger, waiting for his moment to strike.

"Are we not all sorcerers here?" Jinar smiled even as his gestures continued, passing a brief glance to Saresan. "Except you and the buffoon over there, of course."

Alexis shook her head, but Jinar simply nodded in reply. Her face went pale, in contrast to Azure suddenly erupting into even more fury.

"A cabal of taint!" decried the de-fanged beast.

A flash of metal betrayed the dagger that Azure had secretly drawn from a concealed location, rushing forward to strike at Jinar. The next few moments went by so fast that Callum barely reacted. Johnathan stepped forward to intercept the charging knight, raising his axe. Saresan readied his halberd against Azure, hoping to hit a weak point in his armour while Alexis stepped out of way, intently watching their foe's dagger.

Through what was a second that felt far longer, Callum's heart pounded wildly in fright, mind imagining the carnage that would follow. Jinar had neither weapon nor fear, reaching into his robes and throwing what looked like brown powder at Azure. As it hit ineffectually, he muttered syllables that Callum had never heard before and stepped forward. From the man's body, Callum felt... something. It was similar to the other sensations he'd noticed and it was building up intensely, sending his head spinning with dizziness.

He wasn't alone in his discomfort; Alexis seemed also to be affected as Jinar clasped the knight's arm tightly. Both looked to one another, one with hate and the other with disappointment as the something within Jinar seemed to shift through his arm, into Azure. Then there was empty air where Azure had been, and quiet once again descended upon the cave.

Callum blinked as his head instantly cleared, then blinked again. What had just happened? Where had Azure gone? He looked to Jinar for answers, but the man appeared drained, staggering as he tried to catch his breath.

Alexis too was stunned, but not as much as Saresan who was still ready for an attack that would never come.

"What the...?" Slowly the guard's halberd listed. Johnathan lowered his weapon quickly, silently watching them. Callum had no doubt that, had it turned ugly, the warrior would've shown just how skilled he was with that axe. Jinar caught his breath and then flashed a satisfied smile.

"Thanks to my quick thinking and skill, he has been dealt with." The sorcerer dusted off his robes as if nothing had happened.

"Dealt with?" The wording filled Callum with worry. "Is he dead?"

"Possibly," Jinar replied. Alexis frowned, letting go of whatever she'd been holding under her cloak. Callum was even more concerned.

"Possibly? What did your spell *do*?" he asked. Saresan had cautiously walked over to where Azure had been, moving his hand there as if expecting it to collide with something. It didn't.

"Normally I would have prepared the ritual more carefully and focused on a specific location to transport him to—"

"Transport?" Callum could barely believe it. Jinar's smile persisted.

"Do not sound so surprised, I am a sorcerer without equal." Johnathan exhaled at the self-praise but listened on. "The spell I cast is typically far more aggressive, propelling someone instantly from one location to another in such a way that would leave them little more than a bloodied pulp on the other side."

Callum tried not to think of the end result of such a spell on Azure but couldn't.

"A spell?" Alexis didn't seem to believe it either. "So what I saw was sorcery?"

"Cast by one of the greatest users of it in the kingdom, if not all the lands," Jinar added, "with mere moments to spare. I was only able to hastily cast it, which means that the force of his transportation would not be anywhere near as severe or precise."

"So he could be anywhere, in any state?"

Saresan was still looking at the air, still doubting what happened before his very eyes. Even though the situation had calmed, Callum was still on edge, worried that at any moment Azure would storm back in and cut them down or worse. This was compounded by so many new questions that would have to wait.

"I daresay if he appeared face-first in a muddy field to be ridiculed, it would be the least of what he deserves. His kind gives us a bad name through little more than hearsay and fear."

"Says the man who just admitted he reduces people to bloody smears," Saresan muttered.

"I try not to, but some people cannot be reasoned with, like your friend there."

"He was no friend of mine." Jinar smiled in response to the guard.

"Then there's no harm done."

"I'm not a sorcerer, how can I be?" Alexis again brought up the point Jinar had so casually mentioned, shaking her head.

"Through our father," Johnathan answered instead of Jinar, flatly.

"Our father?" Her words were barely a whisper, Callum watching as the same revelations he'd gone through dawned on her.

"He told me only on his deathbed. I kept it secret to protect you." Alexis was both grateful and annoyed all at once.

"While you went to the sage and learned more of your... of *our* power? And if it had unleashed itself without my control, what then?" The siblings stared at one another, neither speaking with words, Saresan wincing.

Jinar stepped between the two and smiled graciously at Alexis.

"Learning of one's magic potential can be quite eye-opening, especially if you were not told at a very young age like I was. If you seek to know anything else concerning your power, I will gladly teach you." The sorcerer was sincere enough, but Alexis shook her head.

"I'm afraid that won't be possible. I and my brother will need to catch up with our caravan in the morning. If I need a teacher—"

"I daresay you will find it difficult to locate one, wherever you go. There are a lot more people like your knightly colleague in the kingdom than I. Your brother will have come to the sage because he was one of the only people that would be willing to train another, at least that is what I presume." He got a vague nod from the warrior. "Perhaps his age made him unafraid of the consequences of being caught."

Callum wanted to believe that it was all over, that his life would drift back into normality, but now he couldn't shake the fear that the knight would track him down, provided he still lived. He wouldn't have a safe place in all the lands if that were the case, but what was his alternative save killing Azure, something he baulked at the thought of?

"I trusted the sage. I do not trust you." Johnathan was blunt and final.

Alexis seemed about to speak but decided not to.

"You can at least stay here for the night. There is room enough for all of you, and I would not trust the roads at this time." Callum was still wary, but he liked the thought of venturing into the dark even less. Johnathan wanted to leave, but Alexis spoke first.

"We will leave at first light, then," came her declaration, one Johnathan sighed at. Passing a look to Callum, the warrior stepped through the door to the cavern and out of sight. Alexis glanced to where her brother had gone and then to Callum, giving him a small smile. Something was clearly wrong, but he wasn't about to ask what, simply returning the gesture.

"There are blankets under the bed. You may debate amongst yourselves who gets the privilege of the bed itself." Jinar was already thinking about something else, examining one of the symbols on the wall with some interest. Saresan had moved to the doorway.

"If Johnathan isn't taking watch, I will. Who knows if Azure will come back," he told them. He exited before anyone could object, settling comfortably back into his profession. Callum didn't even have time to thank him.

"Then the matter of the bed is settled, Alexis," Callum concluded.

"You're welcome to it if you wish it," Alexis countered. "I've slept in wagons; the floor here won't be much worse." Awkwardness crept in without him realising it, expecting the debate to be over already. Still, she continued to surprise him with how down to earth she was despite her station.

"And I've barely slept in beds my whole life, the floor is familiar to me." Alexis and he looked into one another's eyes for a moment. "Please, take the bed. I'll be fine here."

"Only if you insist," she replied without annoyance, walking past him and to the archway. She considered something, then turned her head back. "If you aren't awake when we leave, I hope things get better for you, Callum."

"Thank you." And then she was out of sight. Jinar was eyeing him once again in that strange way he'd done before, staring at him but not *at* him.

"You have a lot of potential," the man began, stroking his beard. "And while you will likely never reach the lofty heights of my own mastery of the arcane, I see a bright future for you if you focus on the gift you have."

"It doesn't feel like a gift. It's all gone wrong since—" Callum stopped himself, even now afraid that saying too much would get him into even more trouble. "I appreciate the offer, but I cannot take you up on it, even if I have a thousand questions right now. I need to..."

The second time he stopped was because words fled him, leaving the fear of embracing the destructive powers he apparently had in their wake. It surely wouldn't end well.

"You need to think it over, yes. The first step is always the hardest, no matter how easily it comes. We will discuss it in the morning when the air has settled better." Jinar indicated to a soft-looking blanket bundled on the floor close to the entrance of the abode, Callum going over to grab it.

When he looked back, he found Jinar had vanished as mysteriously as he'd arrived, leaving Callum alone in a room cluttered with the possessions of a dead man. Had he used magic to vanish into nothingness? He was tempted to look around but didn't want to disturb Alexis, who was likely asleep in the next room.

His head was swimming with too many things to think about sleep, but his body would be objecting soon enough, demanding the rest it deserved. Even as he settled down and tried to come to terms with all he'd learned, Callum felt his fears clashing with one another; fear that his now undeniable affinity with magic would get him killed, fear that Azure would track him down. Worst of all, however, was the fear of change, all of it out of his control.

What say did he have, even if morning came and the knight hadn't run him through? He couldn't return home without the knight beside him, and even if he'd been vouched for, would that have quelled thoughts of dark magic, necromancy and corruption among the village folk?

He'd hoped that at the end of his journey there would be answers, but he'd only found more questions, more choices. He'd had so few choices that mattered in his life save earning enough to last another week, and now that was likely gone; what could he do now? So preoccupied was he with his thoughts that Callum didn't notice when sleep caught him. Even in sleep, however, he felt the sword hanging from his belt.

Chapter Nine

"And the stars shall fall to walk amongst us, wearing our skins and speaking our tongue. They will see our hubris and they will weep, for we have strayed from the path they set. They will turn their backs upon us, and we shall be forgotten."

—Prophecy of the Sage of the Hill

Callum rarely dreamed. When he did, it was often about strange things that could never be; impossible scenarios or half-recollected moments from years gone by, exaggerated into absurdity and beyond. Very rarely, they seemed so real that he could feel what he touched, smell the air and shiver from the biting cold. This one was different somehow, as if he'd truly woken up. What made him think otherwise was how still the air hung around him.

For some reason, his first instinct was to draw his sword, but he refrained, shifting the covers off himself and standing. There was no sign of anyone else around, and only then did he notice the absolute silence that pervaded, oppressive and unyielding. It all felt so wrong, and when he tried to wake himself up, nothing happened. Then he noticed that the door out into the cave was open to utter nothingness save a familiar sight that he wished wasn't so.

Two burning white eyes stared at him from oblivion, watching him. Panic leapt into his throat even though it was a dream, or was it? Had the others fallen to it already, him somehow sleeping through their deaths? He couldn't take a chance either way, too focused on fumbling for the blade at his side as he watched the creature in the darkness intently. The attack didn't come, Callum holding the sword ahead of him as what he knew of the scaled beasts was put to question.

"What are you waiting for?" he half-shouted, growing more afraid as the seconds passed.

Nobody rushed to the room, confirming once more that he was alone. The eyes of the creature shifted down a fraction to look at something else. Was it the sword it stared at? Did it desire the blade? Were they its owners, seeking to regain what they failed to get at the tavern when he defended himself?

More likely, it saw his only method of defence and was afraid, perhaps knowing what happened to its fellow before. Still, the creature didn't emerge, waiting for something he couldn't fathom. His breathing was light, body racked with nerves as finally he spoke again, voice weak, "What *are* you?" Knowing his dreams wouldn't answer, his breath stilled when they did.

"...I see." The voice was low, gravelly and unlike any he'd ever heard. Within the words was a restraint that was being tested, barely tempered disdain. It all sounded wrong, and he didn't want to know what it had seen but knew he'd find out soon enough. Now he was even less sure if it was a dream, Callum wanting to back away but his feet were heavy as lead.

"What do you want with me?" came Callum's second question, which quickly escaped and died in the quiet. The eyes once more shifted up, nearly making him shiver. It was a struggle enough to keep his arms from shaking. "If it's the sword you're after, it's caused me enough trouble as it is! You could've asked for it instead of your master trying to kill me—"

The creature emerged suddenly from the darkness but not to strike him, hunching down to carefully step over the threshold. Callum moved back in kind quickly, seeing that this creature was unlike the other he'd met, clad from head to foot in a black robe that concealed all features save for its towering height and burning eyes that stared from beneath the hood. The robe looked finely made, sleeves hiding the lethal claws of the creature that loomed. His sword seemed such a flimsy defence against the raw strength he was against, but still the thing did not strike. The eyes narrowed, however, now slits of light that pierced his soul.

"You have not met him," dismissed the creature quietly. Not wanting to find out the painful way if this was a dream or not, Callum answered quickly, hoping to keep the beast before him at bay.

"What do I gain by lying?"

"You cannot gain anything." At first it sneered, but that stopped when it stared longer. Without pupil or iris, Callum could only guess what was going on in that stare. "None who meet him live."

"I did. Someone saved me, a man in golden armour." Once again there was no flurry of action, just silent consideration, or so he presumed.

"No one can save you." The statement was chilling, spoken with quiet loathing. He gripped the sword tighter.

"I've killed one of your kind before." He tried to sound threatening, but his wavering voice betrayed fear. The creature didn't react to that news, watching him without a word. With the other of its kind, Callum had no time to consider his options, thrust into combat within moments.

"Your world will die. You cannot stop this." As if a matter of fact, the creature proclaimed doom, and Callum couldn't help but imagine it. So they intended to attack the kingdom, raze it to the ground. Why did this one give a warning, let them prepare? Surely it wasn't that confident of victory, but with how powerful just one of those things had been, what destructive might could an army wield?

"...Why? What have we done to deserve this?" He didn't expect a reply but was given one.

"Irrelevant," it replied, trying to step closer. Callum held out his sword, ready to strike the unwelcome guest, stopping it mid-movement. Was it afraid of him or the blade? "Your abilities *could* be useful—"

"I'd never work with someone like you."

He didn't know where those words came from, but he regretted them only as soon as he heard them. Where had the foolish bravery come from that had sealed his fate?

His head began to ache, followed by his entire body. The feeling grew stronger even as his foe revealed its clawed right hand, a growing ball of blazing inferno held within it. It was just a dream, but the heat felt more than real, his efforts to back away foiled by his every muscle crying out in pain.

"Death, then."

The orb of flame grew larger and hotter still as Callum's legs gave out in agony, making him collapse back on his blankets. He could barely keep hold of his sword as the scaled nightmare was a second from immolating him. Then, in his mind, he heard a loud shout, felt someone grabbing his shoulder. His mind was violently pulled from the realm of dreams to the waking world and dangers even more real.

Callum awoke suddenly, returning to the place he'd been moments before, only for real this time. Alexis was knelt beside him, shaking his shoulder firmly. Relieved and worried all at once, Callum noticed that she had a finely made dagger in her right hand, but the thought that she'd harm him didn't cross his mind. It had all only been a dream, fed by his worries and feasting on fear.

"He's awake!" she called to the open doorway urgently. That worried him, trying to stand. His muscles refused, however, Callum falling to his back again and groaning in pain. Even in a dream that pain had been real. Had the warning been real too? "What's wrong?"

"I can't get up," he told her. "My dreams, they—"

"Try to relax," she implored him, looking up when Saresan entered. The guard had a wound on his left arm which had been bandaged up. His halberd dripped with the black ichor of the scaled creatures, bringing everything from his dream into sharp focus. They shared a look that spoke volumes of what had happened while he rested.

"Is it morning?" Callum asked wearily.

"Still night. I've no idea how you slept through that, but be glad you did," she answered him. Saresan didn't let go of his weapon. Slowly the aches running through Callum's body lessened, allowing him to sit up weakly.

"Was it one of them?" Callum asked his friend, getting a grim nod. Alexis looked between them.

"You've met those... 'things' before?" She was both amazed and deeply concerned. Callum shivered from a final jolt of pain running down his back before the more normal aches of sleeping on the ground took over.

"In the tavern back at town. Were it not for Saresan, I wouldn't be alive now." Callum couldn't keep that secret anymore, not now that they'd seen one. Alexis nodded quietly, taking in what he'd said as the lies he'd spoken to her were being unwoven. The guard spoke quietly then.

"There were three of them out there, Callum, intent on clawing our faces off. No amount of shaking would wake you." Saresan looked at his wound. "If I hadn't been on watch..."

"You were, though," Alexis remarked. She paused, considering her next words. "All the scary stories in the world couldn't prepare me for seeing those things, their bodies just... vanished after you killed them. What *are* they?" Before she could get an answer, Johnathan and Jinar returned from the cavern. The warrior's chain mail was covered in ichor that refused to run off, a deep slice through it a testament to the strength the creatures possessed. Alexis got a look of relief from him, then it was Callum's turn to be stared down by the man.

"They were after *you*. Why?" Straight to the point, Johnathan clearly had no patience left.

"Why should he know?" Saresan answered. "What matters is that we're alive." Jinar was stroking his beard and watching Callum again. Almost all eyes were on him, once more the centre of events despite wanting nothing of the sort.

"Saresan says that you have met these creatures before, yes?" Jinar asked politely. Weakly Callum tried to stand, taking the hand offered by Alexis when she too got to her feet, an action Johnathan watched intently.

Callum didn't know where to begin, how they'd all react. Alexis was the only one showing her fear, but the others had to have felt the same. He looked beyond to the doorway, wondering why there'd only been three of the creatures sent by the black knight; a dozen would've overrun them, a hundred butchered them.

Taking a breath, he decided to start where it seemed most appropriate.

"I don't know what they are, or what they want. I thought they wanted the sword, but now I'm not so sure." Callum watched as Johnathan shook his head slowly. Saresan watched the door out, halberd ready for anything. Johnathan was dubious.

"No sword is that valuable," the warrior stated. Callum kept speaking, knowing that Jinar would ask him to either way.

"I had a dream that felt so real. The pain, it continued when I woke. That's why I couldn't move." Jinar raised an eyebrow at his words, attention ensnared.

"What happened in your dream, Callum?" Johnathan scoffed at the sorcerer's question but didn't interrupt.

"I was... visited by one of them, it was clad in robes. I thought it would attack, but it didn't. It just... watched me at first."

"And?" Saresan was occasionally glancing at the open doorway.

"It told me that it would kill me and that the world would die. It made a ball of fire in its hands and my body erupted in pain, then I woke up."

For a second, no one said anything. Then Johnathan chuckled in disbelief, unimpressed.

"And you believe this?"

Callum looked to the others, hoping that they wouldn't agree with Johnathan but knowing they had no reason not to. Saresan spoke first.

"I'm more surprised that it talked, the ones we fought didn't seem capable of it." Guard and warrior looked to one another.

"And based on my extensive magical knowledge, I believe I know what has happened," Jinar declared, walking over to Callum. He lifted his chin and examined it curiously, humming to himself as he did so. Callum waited patiently, hoping whatever he found wasn't bad. "You, sir, have experienced a magical sending."

"A sending?" Callum repeated.

"Someone communicated to Callum in his dreams?" Alexis guessed. Jinar nodded.

"Precisely."

"Is that even possible?"

"It is quite possible for one powerful enough and armed with the right information. As for why, I have a few theories," mused Jinar as he turned to Alexis, "most important of which is that the sender was trying to glean where Callum was through the dream, following the tether of their magical connection to our location."

"Which means this place isn't safe anymore." Alexis got a nod.

"My magic far exceeds the claws of those creatures, but they were few and lacking in strategy. The one Callum spoke of seemed to possess magic itself. A curious notion, for I was taught that only humans were capable of such feats. That aside, even though I would no doubt be victorious should they attack again, I suggest we relocate to somewhere safer before that happens." Johnathan had had enough, walking to the door.

"We've nothing to do with him or you. We're wasting time here, Alexis," he declared. She didn't move, however, looking concerned at all she'd heard and thinking it over. He noticed quickly. "Come on."

"And if those things follow us? They'd kill everyone on the caravan, not to mention us. You saw what they could do, do you think we'd stand a chance alone? The thought of them getting us..." Alexis trailed off, leaving Callum's imagination to fill in the horrific gaps. He wanted to say that she was better off away from him, but there was safety in numbers.

"You believe a stranger's word?" Johnathan was incredulous.

"I do." More than anything, those words surprised Callum. Johnathan wasn't sure if he was shocked or angry at the response, settling on neither emotion. "You should too. Father taught us to keep an open mind, and after what I saw last night and this morning, I have no choice but to believe him." Johnathan clenched his fist tightly.

"You barely know the man. Why trust him?" At that question, Alexis looked to Callum. He couldn't give her a reason to; he wanted to apologise, feeling guilty for dragging everyone into a mess not of their making, but couldn't find the words to begin.

"I just... do. If we leave, we'll be putting so many other people's lives at risk. I'm staying." She flashed a fragile smile to Callum, one he couldn't return. After a few seconds, Johnathan stepped away from the door and back to the others, doing so reluctantly. His gaze remained on Callum, silent.

"Then I believe haste is in order." Jinar left the room without another word, searching for something through the archway as Callum pondered on his sword. It had been the only thing that stopped the creature in his dream from striking, despite how unskilled he was with it. Saresan was already thinking.

"I'm all for sticking together, but where can we go? If they're willing to attack in a town and can find us here, where's safe?" The guard glanced to one of the symbols on the wall. "We've also no idea what they actually are."

"They die easily enough." Callum felt Johnathan's eyes on him as the man replied.

"They're stronger and faster than any man I've ever come across, scales harder than tanned leather. I don't want to know what you think a tough foe is."

"You managed to kill one," Johnathan replied.

"Without Callum's magic, I'd've ended up like Grimsal. Fair to say, we'd both be dead." Saresan glanced at the head of his halberd, perhaps considering how effective his weapon of choice was against them.

"The question is less what they are and more how nobody knows of their existence," Alexis thought out loud. "They are unlike anything I've ever seen before, monsters from nightmare. Who would be able to keep them a secret for so long?"

"Maybe they haven't been around for ages," the guard suggested.

Johnathan had gone back to watching Callum, waiting for something. It made him feel uncomfortable, but perhaps his stare was always like that; he didn't seem like the friendliest of people.

"Either way, I don't think asking one of them about it will work out. Makes me wonder about the one that talked to you, Callum. What was so different about it, apart from the obvious?"

Callum tried to recall back to his nightmare but couldn't remember as much about it as before, save the robes and fear unlike when he faced off the feral beast in the tavern. Callum thought on his words carefully.

"It's hard to put into words. I think it was trying to figure something out, what I can't tell you. I think it was... disappointed." Johnathan frowned, eyes looking away to his sister as Jinar returned. He held a leather pouch that bulged with red powder, not unlike the kind he'd thrown at Azure the night before. He had a confident smile on his lips.

"A short journey will allow me time to better research the nature of the creatures, to a place where I believe we will be safe for the time being. It will also allow me time to see just what your magic can do, Callum, if you wish it." Jinar smiled to Alexis afterwards. "The offer is open to all of you, naturally."

"And how far do you intend us to travel?" Alexis enquired, not returning the sorcerer's smile.

"Roughly three hundred miles, beyond the realms of the kingdom," Jinar told them.

Saresan was bemused.

"And how are we going to manage that this side of the season?" Jinar simply smiled more in reply. Alexis was eyeing the pouch, curious of the powder within. Callum had an idea of what was happening and didn't like the prospect of it.

"Magic, naturally. You are welcome to start walking if you would prefer."

"And you can take all of us?" Callum was curious.

"In theory, yes. I typically do not have others travel with me, but I do not see why not. It would require more magic, a smaller margin for error." Jinar opened the pouch and began pouring it around them, forming a rough circle. The tavern-talk of warlocks summoning dreadful monsters was coming into sharper focus after all Callum had experienced, wondering just how much truth was in them. Johnathan watched silently.

"Is magic truly that powerful?" Callum had to ask. "What couldn't it do?"

"You ask a question that people older and wiser than yourself have spent decades seeking the answer to. My knowledge of magic is, of course, extensive, but even I cannot see all that it encompasses." Johnathan shook his head as the sorcerer continued, finishing off the circle, "I think we can go ahead without ginseng. The seer must have used the last of his supply before dying." Callum looked at the others, wondering what they all thought of the peculiar situation they were in. Only Johnathan had an expression beyond neutrality, silently annoyed. If any of that was envy Callum couldn't say. Jinar reached to a small satchel on the ground, filled with bulky items.

"Why ginseng?" Saresan asked. "Does it have some kind of special properties?"

"Personally, I like it in my ale," Jinar remarked. "And I guess you could use it for some minor magic if you felt so inclined. Waste of it though if you ask me." Saresan was doubtful.

"Ginseng in ale?"

"You should try it sometime. Is everyone ready?" The sorcerer waited for an objection. Callum was worried, but his curiosity won out. He gave a weak nod.

"How does it work?" Alexis was looking down to the now complete circle of powder. "Is that rust powder?"

"It is essential to the success of the ritual, helping the arcane energies focus on the targets of the incantation. I will need you to make bodily contact with one another, a hand on a shoulder would suffice to make a chain, but the contact must remain constant. Try not to make any sudden movements or sneeze." Jinar looked seriously to them all in turn. "The gods help you if you sneeze."

A tiny part of Callum was still unsure about all of it; he was about to willingly subject himself to a spell, one that Jinar claimed would transport them all a vast distance but in truth was going to catapult him even further from his goal of an ordinary life. What if it went wrong and he was killed in the process or worse, wished he had been? Saresan placed his hand on Callum's left shoulder, starting the chain off. Alexis placed her hand on his right without hesitation. Johnathan waited a few seconds before gently holding his sister's upper arm. Jinar looked it all over and nodded approvingly, then assessing the circle of iron rust around them. Satisfied, he himself stepped within its boundaries and knelt down, touching it with his little finger and closing his eyes.

Quiet words were murmured, Callum and the others watching him. He noticed that Jinar's hand had started to glow a shade of red, initially muted but slowly growing brighter. Callum could feel the energy building up at that point, making his skin and hair tingle. Johnathan seemed to feel it also, but neither expected the circle to take on that glow, humming quietly. Jinar opened his eyes and smiled to himself, standing slowly and walking into the middle of the circle. He looked to Callum, having noticed his curiosity, and gave him a wicked grin.

"You will like this," he promised as he muttered an unknown word under his breath, pressing his hand to Callum's chest.

Chapter Ten

Callum felt a wrenching feeling in his gut, followed by weightlessness and nothingness. Barely able to look at himself before everything went white, it appeared like they were fading away into light. The next moment his mind felt without a body at all, free and unconfined, while also distorted and paralysed.

The sensation was in many layers indescribable and perhaps in some ways unable to be experienced, surpassing realms of human thought as easily as a bird flying overhead. He felt charged, full of energy and life despite his lack of self, and a moment after could see nothing but the sensation of brightness. He could feel, however, and it was as if he was hurtling at vast speeds, so quick as to be undetectable and yet noticed.

He remained in this state for what seemed like an eternity, wondering if something had gone horribly wrong. Perhaps he was now trapped in this un-bodied form forever, without being or substance. He could barely focus on fear, however, captured by the sensation and dragged along unwillingly to whatever conclusion lay beyond.

Suddenly, things came to a jarring halt. The world took on real form once again, and with it, a rush of sensory information entered his now reformed head, as solid as it had been before the spell. It pounded angrily in frustration, his whole body disorientated and confused. Without expecting a solid surface and lacking the strength to support himself, Callum crumpled to the ground while he tried to recover, to understand. His being felt like someone had taken an axe to it and exposed the interior to a furnace, though that quickly died away.

Managing to look around weakly at the others, he saw they had fared little better; Johnathan had barely managed to keep on one knee, gritting his teeth. Saresan's reaction was one of nausea rather than pain, having fared better than the others. Alexis would have fallen had Jinar not caught her gracefully with a suave look on his face, the sorcerer unaffected and his satchel on the ground by his feet. He looked down at her and flashed her a confident smile.

"A good thing I was here to catch you."

"Don't make a habit of it," she managed to reply despite obvious discomfort from the incantation's effects. Jinar shrugged and let go when she caught her footing, the others slowly getting to their feet with difficulty.

Callum was finding it hard to stand, struggling to find the energy. He took this chance to look at where they'd arrived, seeing a large open plain of wild grass illuminated in the moonlight, broken only by a dense forest in the distance. He couldn't see any signs of civilisation, a wild frontier as yet untamed by man.

Out of the corner of his eye, however, was a solitary bastion of familiarity, a barely concealed archway carved out of stone at the base of a large mountain. The thick rosebush would've fooled anyone at a distance, but being so close betrayed the corridor of darkness beyond.

"Hate to think what would happen if we'd sneezed," Saresan said to himself, finally standing. Jinar gave a joking smile.

"Oh, nothing would have happened. I just said that for a bit of fun." Saresan laughed, but he was the only one. "Well, here we are."

"And where is 'here' exactly?" Johnathan asked, staring at the tall mountain ahead of them. Callum was offered a hand by Saresan, finally getting onto his wobbly feet. He wasn't sure they'd hold, but he stayed standing, just. His head still felt light.

"This is where my master taught me, within that cave complex. He liked his privacy. I am sure by now you understand why. It is quite clement once you get further in."

"You want us to hide in another cave?" Johnathan frowned.

"Did you think there was going to be a sprawling estate, manned by servants, within a field of poppies?" Johnathan didn't reply; if he was satisfied was left unclear. "It will take you some time to fully recover from the teleportation. Do not worry, you will grow used to it the more it happens."

"It's not something I want to get used to," Saresan remarked, "but it wasn't so bad."

"Different people react to it in different ways, mainly depending on how much magical power they possess. It tends to kick the untrained sorcerer in the teeth a lot more than someone without magical aptitude, like yourself." He smiled proudly then to himself. "Of course, when I first teleported, I suffered no ill effects, no doubt due to my years of training in the mastery of the arcane."

"Will your teacher know of these creatures?" Alexis asked Jinar.

"If he did, it matters not, for he is dead. He did have a selection of tomes and research materials that were entrusted to my care. It is my hope that one of them will shed light on our predicament." The way Jinar spoke didn't make Callum feel any better about it all, wondering if there was going to be an answer. "That will occur while you rest, however. In the long term, I will try my best to train all of you in the arcane arts, the better to defend yourself if those creatures find us. The sooner we begin this, the better."

"When, not if," Johnathan corrected firmly.

"This place has remained secret for over a century, or so my teacher told me. I find it unlikely that any of those things will know of it."

"They found me before," Callum reminded them.

"With your knightly friend, anyone could find you." Jinar then turned to Saresan, smiling apologetically. "I am afraid that you will have to find something to keep yourself busy in the interim. I cannot teach you anything even if you wanted me to. You do not have the potential." Alexis raised her eyebrow at his wording.

"You speak of potential, yet Callum's power emerged without any training."

"The blood of sorcery is diluted or strengthened through the generations. It all depends on the amount of training the parents do to harness their power before they pass it on. Of course, new sorcerer blood in the family helps in that regard. I would guess, however, that your sorcerous parent or parents did not practice their art much. Perhaps you had an ancient ancestor who was a mighty caster in their day, I cannot say." Jinar turned to Alexis. "Your brother has a little more potential than you, but some of that might be down to previous training." She took a moment to think; even now, she wasn't sure of it all.

"...Me, a sorcerer," she said quietly to herself.

"Technically a sorceress, since you are a lady," Jinar spoke to her directly. "You do not see many of them these days. Most of them decide to call themselves witches. I wonder why they do; it does not change anything about them except make people trust them even less."

Johnathan was looking for a way to move the rosebush, finding that it was indeed planted.

"The truth of the matter, Alexis, is that magic is a part of you, whether you choose to accept it or not. I, for one, would not look a gift in the face and turn it away, especially if those things return. Training so many at a time will be a new challenge; at most I have only had two apprentices."

"What happened to them?" Callum asked. "Did they grow to become great magicians?" Jinar's face faded from its smile and he stroked his beard, pondering his next words.

"...Not quite. One of them was burned at the stake by an angry mob, and the other summoned... something. I am not quite sure what, save that it was not one of the things that attacked us. It consumed him alive."

Callum could imagine a thing emerging from a rip in the air, dragging a potential sorcerer into nothingness to be devoured.

"It cannot be helped. Since none of us will be sleeping anytime soon after that attack, who wants their first brief lesson?" No one jumped at the offer right away, but Jinar didn't take that as a sign of refusal.

Johnathan had uprooted the rosebush to open the way inward, but it was carefully replanted with a wave of Jinar's hand and a few muttered words. The feeling of energy was faint this time, but Callum noticed it; why was he noticing that more often now? Had he always had the ability to feel magic being used?

The cavern walls were worked surprisingly well, enough that Callum had to remind himself they were in a mountain and not a keep. Despite the lack of torches, there was illumination enough to navigate, but where it came from was a mystery. It was also warmer than he expected it to be even though the stone was cold to the touch, strangely comfortable in a way that Callum could only explain by presuming more magic was involved.

They turned off into the first room after ten seconds of walking, emerging into a large windowless area with a ceiling twice Callum's height. It was more illuminated than the corridor, again with no obvious source for the light. It was also entirely unfurnished save for some worrying scorch marks on the wall that looked old.

Saresan leaned in the entranceway, deciding to observe the spectacle rather than explore further in. Jinar observed his three students, each one anticipating what was to come differently; Johnathan was sceptical and Alexis curious, but Callum was simply worried that things would go wrong. Jinar reached into his satchel and pulled out a small cabbage. The reveal of the vegetable puzzled Saresan but also prompted a smile.

"The first lesson is quite simple and the most important one you will ever learn," Jinar explained, beginning to pace in front of the three students as he held the vegetable. "Controlling your power. This can take people days, weeks or even years. Some never truly learn, remaining wild and erratic casters who end up destroying themselves in one way or another. Of course, those people were not trained by myself."

He paced a little more before stopping and holding out the cabbage. "Imagine that you are cooking a pot of cabbage soup." Callum and Alexis looked to one other at the strange metaphor. "And you forgot the lid, left it at home. Now, you can control how much the fire beneath it burns by removing bits of wood, putting water on it or blowing into the fire, giving it more fuel and so forth. You want your cabbage soup to be delicious—"

"Is that possible?" Saresan butted in. Jinar eyed him.

"For the purpose of this metaphor, yes. You do not want it to boil over the pot and make a huge mess everywhere, however, not least because it is quite a nice pot and you just bought it yesterday especially for the occasion."

"Must be some cabbage soup," Saresan mumbled. Johnathan didn't look impressed.

"A poor cook will just keep the fire at the same temperature all the time, presuming that it will cook evenly at all times. This is foolish; while the cook may have time to do other things, he would be paying less attention. Before he knows it, the broth has boiled over the pot and scalded his foot. It was too hot to begin with, and he did not pay enough heed to see that. Now a good cook" — he smiled and looked at the cabbage — "a good cook will keep an attentive eye on his cabbage soup. He would notice that the fire was burning too hot, move his cabbage soup away so that it could cool while he tended to the flames. Eight hours later, he has a fine soup to share with his family, not to mention a perfectly fine foot."

"What does this have to do with magic?" Jonathan finally asked. "The seer focused on magical energies when he was teaching me, directing it into powerful spells that can defeat those monsters we fought, not strange stories about making awful food."

"But is it so strange?" Jinar asked.

"It is."

"Well, your old teacher is dead, so you are going to have to take your vegetable soup and like it. A solid foundation of knowledge is essential to mastering your arcane potential, and there is no better start to learning than this," Jinar pointed out as he eyed the tall warrior momentarily. "Now with what I told you in mind, I want you all to picture something in your imagination. Something simple, something basic..." Jinar thought to himself and clicked his fingers, still holding the cabbage. "Think of a stick. A short, wooden stick."

Callum closed his eyes, deciding to trust Jinar despite the niggling concerns in his head. It didn't take long to picture a stick, but he struggled to imagine the perfect stick. At first, it was too long, then too gnarled, and finally he thought of one with leaves before settling on a suitably stick-y stick. "I want you to map it in your thoughts, so that at a moment's notice, I could tell you to picture a stick and that is what you would think of."

There in his mind was the stick, short and thin, recently snapped from a tree. He couldn't see what any of the others were doing, but he imagined their sticks were similar to his.

"Now, this is where we get to the more taxing parts. I want you to picture the stick in your right hand, imagine that it is actually there. I want you to *feel* the tactile sensations of it. And when you do, I want you to make a waving motion using your left hand, with all but your little finger clenched into a fist, and murmur the words 'Gual Filliu Abaska', but only when you can feel the stick there."

"You're kidding." Again, it was Johnathan that voiced annoyance.

"Do not ruin your concentration. This is the best way to do it."

Callum tried his best to focus on the stick that was meant to be in his hand. Try as he might, the sensation just wasn't there: he couldn't trick his mind to make the stick come to be. He tried the hand gesture and murmured the words, but he felt nothing. No energy flowed through his body like before in the tavern, even as Callum felt emanations coming from others.

Opening his eyes, he saw Johnathan had just finished speaking the words, Callum watching in amazement as the warrior's hand flashed faintly purple. A moment later, Johnathan held a very weak and fragile stick, looking at it with a blank and unimpressed stare. Jinar smiled. "Not bad at all." Saresan was impressed, having glanced over while cleaning his halberd.

"Trivial," Johnathan said bluntly. Jinar then looked at the other two expectantly.

"And what of you two? Did you feel it there?"

"A little," Alexis admitted despite herself. "And I... do feel something building up in my arms, an energetic tingling. It's uncomfortable, like something is going to burst through my skin."

"That is good!" Jinar was enthusiastic. "You are receptive to the incantation.

Keep practising, it will become less uncomfortable as time goes on. And what of you?" He then turned to Callum, seeing his empty hand. "I presume, for you it was no problem at all?"

"...I felt nothing," he replied honestly. Jinar's face fell from its smile to concern.

"...Nothing," he repeated. "Nothing at all? Not even a little bit?"

"I felt Johnathan and Alexis's magic, but... nothing from me, no. I can't feel it. The incantation doesn't work." Jinar stroked his beard, then shook his head.

"Perhaps you are intoning it wrong."

Johnathan had by this point made another stick, putting it down with the first he had manifested from nothingness. Alexis had stopped with her efforts and was instead watching Callum as he thought and tried again. He muttered the words, pictured the object. Again, no tingling. He looked at his empty hand, confused.

"I don't think it's working," he told Jinar, glancing back at Alexis as she watched him.

"Hmm." The sorcerer was perplexed. "With all the potential you have, you should be knocking Johnathan's achievements out of the water." The tall warrior watched as he put down his third stick. "You are the first student I have had that cannot do this; the incantation does make it simple." Callum was disappointed with himself, considering how easily Johnathan was doing it and Jinar's surprise.

"Then what do I do next?" he asked his teacher, expecting an answer. Jinar, however, had begun pacing again, still holding the cabbage and mumbling to no one in particular. Johnathan by this point had made a small pile of little sticks and eventually stopped. Jinar then looked over to his one pupil that had failed.

"I will do some thinking, Callum. For now, I shall make sure the rooms you will be using are adequate. Even though you are all naturally eager to learn more, our rest was interrupted. A good night of sleep may help your magic flow better."

With that Jinar exited to the corridor and out of sight, cabbage in hand. Johnathan moved to lean on the wall in the far corner, waiting with a stern look about him. Callum felt even worse now, getting a sympathetic look from Alexis.

"He should have checked these things before he dragged us miles away from anywhere," Johnathan muttered. Callum felt the weight of his sword even more now, a burden that all of them hefted now. Alexis turned to the discarded satchel and walked to it curiously, all while Callum dwelt on everything that had begun his journey into isolation.

"I'm sure Jinar will find a way to make it work. He seems…" She paused. "…resourceful."

"It all looks absurd, if you ask me," Saresan remarked with a shrug. "Hand gestures, little phrases, reagents. Might as well just do a jig and sing a song while you're there. Don't know what any of that has to do with magic."

"Jinar seems to know what he's doing, he managed to teleport us after all."

"Can't say his methods don't work, but you didn't do that before, did you? Back in the tavern, you just unleashed flame and destruction. You didn't need to twiddle your thumbs and hum a hymn beforehand."

"Do you think there are bandits in the forest nearby?" Callum suddenly asked.

"What?" Saresan was taken aback by the change in topic.

"There's got to be some kind of settlement nearby, a forest is a great place for them to hide." Saresan shrugged again.

"You sure you're alright?"

"Yeah," Callum sighed as Johnathan checked the edge of his battleaxe. Alexis had pulled out a red book, which was locked, trying to discern its purpose. "It's just… my last experience with a forest wasn't great."

"Don't let it get to you."

"After all that's happened, how can I not?"

"We've alive, that's what matters." Saresan patted his friend on the shoulder. "The forest is far away, and even if someone is in there, they don't even know we're here. Those creatures are another matter, but we'll cross that bridge when we get to it." Jinar returned, bereft of his vegetable.

"The rooms needed a little dusting but are perfectly serviceable. The magical wards protecting this place are still strong, we should be quite safe here." Jinar's assurances didn't comfort Callum, but he doubted anything would.

"How did it know we weren't intruders?" Alexis asked.

"The wards would not go off with me here. Tonight, I will augment them to not perceive you three as threats. Unfortunately, there are only three bedrooms, and two are barely large enough for the beds within. I will be taking the quarters of my teacher so I can peruse his library of reference material, so I leave your sleeping arrangements to you." Johnathan moved from the corner, standing next to his sister.

"You and Saresan in one room. Simple." Johnathan indicated to Callum as the 'you'. Alexis thought for a moment before speaking softly to her brother.

"I would prefer if you shared a room with Saresan, personally," she told him. "I am sure you two could discuss many stories of combat together, after all." Her brother furrowed his brow in suspicion.

"So, you share with Callum." He spoke the name quietly. Callum wondered why she wanted that; surely it was better for her to share with someone she knew a lot better.

"Works for me," Saresan said.

"Is there a problem with that?" She stared down at her brother despite their height difference. They looked to one other until Johnathan grumbled under his breath and turned away.

"...Fine," was all he said as he headed past Jinar and to the corridor without another word. Callum and Saresan both looked curiously at that.

"What's up with him?" Saresan asked.

"I don't think he likes me," Callum said to them both.

"Jealous of your magic?" Saresan guessed as he went over to take his halberd. "Well, I think I'm going to turn in myself. Will we need to set a watch just in case the wards don't work?"

"I fail to see how those creatures can thwart the wards my teacher put in place," Jinar replied.

"Exactly." Saresan gave them all a smile. "Rest well, you two." And with that, he headed to get a few hours of rest before beginning his lonely vigil. Jinar noticed then that Alexis was holding one of his books, raising a curious eyebrow.

"I think you will need a few more years before you can comprehend the arcane secrets contained within." Jinar took the book gently from her, placing it back in the satchel that he picked up. He looked at Callum and smiled encouragingly. "With luck, I will glean some knowledge concerning these creatures while you rest."

"And if they find us?" Callum had to ask.

"Then they will have to contend with four sorcerers instead of one." Despite being further away from his home than he ever thought he'd be, he still didn't feel safe.

Chapter Eleven

CASPAR'S HOUSE OF DELIGHTS

YOUR WORRIES FORGOTTEN
YOUR WISHES FULFILLED
YOUR NIGHT SORTED

Find us on Penny Road. Ask for Cindra.

—Discrete pamphlet handed out by urchins

Only Callum and Alexis remained once Jinar went to study. Without a word between them, the pair left the training room, both stopping and waiting for the other to go through. He motioned for her to go first.

"Thank you." She smiled at his courteous gesture. Callum followed after her, looking towards the entrance where he spied Saresan leaning against the wall, weapon in hand. "I didn't want to be stuck in a room with my brother every night for however long we're here. At times he can be very overprotective." Callum found that he was glad to be speaking to just her again.

"Is there a particular reason?" Callum enquired as they passed a closed door on their right.

"He's always been like that in one way or another. I think it's the big brother in him, feeling like he has to watch out for his little sister. He can take it a bit too far though." She stopped at the next door and tried the handle, finding that it was unlocked.

Pushing it open, Callum saw that the room beyond was indeed small and furnished only with a bed and a pot beneath it. Unlike all the other places within the complex, the room was lit only by a small softly burning lantern that hung from the wall. It was also a little colder, perhaps to make the idea of rest all the more enticing. With how Jinar had spoken of the place's age, Callum was surprised at the clean blankets and fresh straw mattress on the solidly built bed frame. Only now, when he stared at a bed, was Callum beginning to feel tired; had he truly slept that well during his nightmare?

Alexis looked the bed over, nodding approvingly.

"This is nicer than I was expecting," he told her, putting his hand on the bed to check how comfortable it was. It would certainly be one of the nicer nights of sleep he'd ever had, provided he had no more strange dreams. Alexis stepped into the room and turned a metal dial on the lantern, the flame within growing.

"Looks like we'll be sharing the mattress," she said.

"I'll sleep on the floor; you can have the mattress." That prompted a smile from her.

"Not this time. Come in so I can shut the door." She didn't seem at all concerned like he thought she might be, Callum stepping into the room while she bolted the door shut.

He looked at the bed again, noting its size and trying to work out how best not to intrude on her privacy as they rested, concerned.

She looked at him and sat on the edge of the bed carefully. "I take it you aren't used to this."

He wasn't sure what to say, the words escaping him.

"Was it that obvious?" She nodded in reply.

"It's not something I'm used to either, but you shouldn't be nervous about it." He thought on that, looking to her as he considered just what to do. She, in turn, glanced back but said nothing. Then he realised he was staring and looked away, trying to think of something to say. Thoughts of the red monsters came to mind immediately, but that was the worst thing he could bring up, so he took hold of the next topic that flittered into his head.

"Tell me about yourself." It was the second-worst conversation topic he could come up with, confident he looked a total fool now. She'd told him so much already, more than he had a right to know.

She, however, just smiled, either not noticing his feeling of folly or ignoring it.

"You know more about me than I of you. Perhaps you should tell me a little about yourself." Somehow that seemed even more daunting than asking about her past; nobody had cared enough to ask before, why would they need to know anything about someone of such low station? And yet she'd asked, moving to sit on the far side of the bed. She waited expectantly, and so he got onto the bed himself, confirming that it was very comfortable.

"There's not much to tell that's interesting," he eventually began.

"Do you have a family of your own?" she asked, trying to pry out more.

"Not anymore," Callum answered. "I only remember my father, my mother died during childbirth. My father was a blacksmith, did the best he could for me. He died of plague, much like your parents did, when I was nine. One day he wasn't feeling well, the next I woke up to find him dead."

"I'm sorry." She looked apologetic.

"It's no worse than what happened to your parents."

"I was a lot older than you were." She was turned to him, watching his face as she spoke.

He wasn't used to someone paying so much attention to him, especially in such a small space. It wasn't much larger than the shack he'd called home for so long, but in that he lived alone with his thoughts and the cold draft.

"I accepted early on that life was hard, my father passing on was just another thing in it. I buried him, and then I had to fend for myself. I had no education, and no one was taking an apprentice, so I had to make my own way. If I have relatives somewhere, my father never spoke of them; I wouldn't know them even if I saw them." Alexis nodded sympathetically.

"I saw the suffering of those who struggled even if others in my situation wouldn't; my father would employ them with small tasks when he could. Still, I can't truly begin to understand what you must have gone through, to see your only relative dead."

"You've also lost people close to you," he replied back.

"But I still have people, a safety net, my brother. You had to grip to a sheer wall and keep climbing, or you too would fall into oblivion." He found her concern warming, smiling a little.

"It was just something I had to live with. It made me the person I am today." He looked down at his feet, for lack of anything else to glance at for the time. At that, she placed a hand on his shoulder. It was warm even through his armour. He grew used to it surprisingly quickly.

"I think your parents would be proud of the man you've become," she told him honestly.

He looked back at her, into her eyes once again and saw the sincerity in them. He somehow doubted that; would his father be proud of a man on the run, a warlock? Shifting, he felt his scabbard against his leg and ended up looking down at it.

She followed his eyes, then moved her hand towards the weapon. "May I?"

He felt suspicious of her despite himself, quickly wiping that from his mind; what did he have to worry about? If she ran away with it, all the better for him. He nodded, and as she began to reach for the handle, he unbuckled the scabbard from his belt and offered it to her. She hadn't expected that but gripped the handle, their hands touching briefly.

She drew his sword carefully, holding it in amazement. "It's so light."

"And it's deadly sharp. The edge would take your finger off at a touch."

"Are you speaking from experience?"

"Unfortunately." She looked back at him for a moment in silent expectation, waiting for some kind of explanation. "It was at the tavern, one of those creatures tried to kill me."

Her eyes scanned the dull sides of the weapon, examining the matted metal.

"I don't like those that strike out in anger, Callum. It always causes more problems than it solves."

"Are *you* speaking from experience?" he then asked, reading between the lines and instantly regretting it, looking away. "I'm sorry, I shouldn't have asked that."

"It's fine," she replied, careful with her wording. She handed the sword back, Callum carefully sheathing the blade as he turned to face her again, noticing now an expression of sadness. "My father, while a great merchant, was prone to fits of rage. It never led to people getting hurt, but they were still scary. I think my brother inherited it to some degree, but it's different with him. Perhaps he's been channelling it into his magic training with the seer, but I know it's there."

Callum didn't know how best to approach replying; being an only child, he had no experience of that. For a little while, he said nothing, trying in vain to come up with something to say.

Eventually, she sighed and removed from his shoulder the hand that he'd grown used to. "I'm sorry, it's not my business to lumber my worries onto you. You already have so much on your shoulders as it is."

"No, don't be sorry," he rushed out, catching her eyes as she started to turn away. "You're worried about him, he's your brother. It's understandable."

He then remembered something from earlier in the day, words she had spoken that popped into his head and danced a jig to present themselves to him. Somehow, she knew he was musing.

"What is it?" He thought on if it was worth mentioning it, deciding it couldn't hurt to ask.

"Earlier you said that you trusted me," Callum began, looking away from her again, hoping his words would form better when not facing her.

"Why? Johnathan is right, you barely know me." The pause before her reply made him nervous.

"Honestly? I don't really know." Alexis flicked a strand of hair from over her shoulder to her back. "You don't seem like a man who has any reason to be anyone but yourself. You have all this apparent power, and yet you aren't sure about it, you haven't let it go to your head."

"I can't promise it won't."

"And yet other people would, along with many other things." She spoke with certainty now, her thoughts more formed than his own. "You just seem like an honest man."

"I lied about what happened in the tavern to Azure. That's not the actions of an honest man."

"To avoid persecution," she rebutted. "I can't hold that against you. You shouldn't put yourself down so much."

"But I'm just a normal man. I'm not an all-power sorcerer like Jinar, not a great warrior like Saresan. And after what happened at the seer's home, I might get you all killed. You meeting me has already cost you so much."

"Not intentionally. I can't change the past, Callum, nor can you. In time, I and my brother will be able to return home, but for now, I might as well make the best of the situation," she concluded, smiling to him once more. "The morning shall bring new challenges and, no doubt, more strange training sessions from Jinar. I'm going to get some rest." Alexis sheathed his blade, then leaned over to place it on the floor by his side of the bed. She then took her blanket and pulled it over herself, Callum extinguishing the lantern. "Good night, Callum. Rest well."

Callum wasn't quite ready to go to sleep yet but didn't like the idea of venturing out into the corridor or the darkness of the wild countryside.

"You as well," he said back, staring into blackness as he got under his own warm blanket. Despite his best efforts to remain awake and avoid a repeat of the last nightmare, he soon fell asleep.

He awoke to the smell of cooked meat invading his nostrils, rousing him from his dreamless slumber. He was alone on the bed, the door left ajar. Callum was surprised that he was so well rested, stretching after getting out of bed. He then opened the door and followed the delicious scent. Turning into the training room, he found only Johnathan, sat on the floor by a small fire with a tender piece of beef on a spit. There wasn't any smoke rising from it, betraying that the flames were magical in origin. Where they'd managed to find a cow in the open countryside was a more curious question, but he was distracted from that by the look Johnathan gave him, entirely unreadable.

"Where are the others?" Callum asked, stepping over to the fire. Finding an unused knife and a plate, he cut himself a piece of the beef, trying it. It was crispier than he liked but still far better than his typical fare.

"How was your sleep?" Something about the way Johnathan made small talk made Callum uneasy.

"Fine, thank you. What about yourself?" Johnathan turned his eyes to Callum when he took a second bite.

"Alexis seemed happy this morning." Johnathan watched him take a second bite. That they were alone was concerning; a tiny voice in Callum's head reasoned that Johnathan had planned it this way, but that was absurd; there was likely a very reasonable explanation. Johnathan's axe was within arm's reach of the warrior.

"Maybe she slept well, the beds are quite comfortable." That answer made Johnathan frown.

"And?"

"And?" Callum knew the man was digging for something but not what. "We talked a little before sleeping, not about anything important."

"You *talked*." The words sliced through the air.

"About our families and other things." Callum took another slow bite. "Is that a problem?" Johnathan remained silent.

"No." That was a lie, but Callum didn't press the issue. It at least confirmed Alexis's statement about her brother being protective of her.

"You didn't answer my question. Where are the others?" Johnathan weakly motioned to the corridor.

"Jinar's looking for reagents. I volunteered to stay here just in case something happened while you slept." The better to keep his eye on him, Callum thought. With one final bite, his serving of food was gone. Callum thought of the others out there in the wilderness, hoping they were alright. Johnathan was still looking at him, eyes now judging.

"Yes?" Johnathan said nothing at first, which made Callum press the issue, "There's something you want to say, isn't there?" Johnathan then stood up, towering over him. It wasn't lost on Callum that he'd picked up his axe.

"Alexis may trust you," he finally said to Callum, "...but I don't." His answer brought forth even more questions.

"Why not?"

"Because of you, my sister and I are stuck in the middle of nowhere. Because of you, we're at risk of being attacked by those strange creatures." The axe's edge looked keen. "Those things are after *you*. Not me, not my sister, you."

"I didn't ask anyone to come with me, you were welcome to leave," Callum reminded him, provoking a sneer from the warrior. Tempted to put a hand on his sword, he thought better of it; why give Johnathan an excuse to think him a threat? "I'm sorry that you're involved in this, whatever it is." That only succeeded in making the warrior angry.

"Your words mean nothing. I don't see what Jinar sees in you, this so-called gift of power." Johnathan took a step closer, Callum moving back in response. The fear within him was making his fingers tingle, a glimmer of the sensation he'd felt in the tavern. He found himself focusing on the feeling, to better try and understand it. "It would be better for everyone if we just left you to your fate."

The implied threat made the feeling stronger, something that he clung to the memory of, trying to muster it. The tingling became a warmth in his hands that Johnathan noticed, eyes scanning down him curiously. He had no incantation to say or hand gestures to make, focusing instead on the raw emotion of his worry and the sensation in his body that remained even when his fear subsided.

He tried to think on the exact series of events in the tavern, the stinging pain and the desperation, but all that lingered was the image of all-consuming fire. Suddenly, Callum felt a rush of energy that threatened to boil over and he did nothing to stop it, startled as his hands erupted into flames. He felt the heat only momentarily before it vanished, Johnathan stepping back in an instant.

"What the…?" Johnathan was lost for words, and so was Callum when he looked at his accomplishment.

Two small flames danced in his palms, no kindling to fuel them nor burns on his hands. Startled, he clenched his fists to try and extinguish them but found that the fire persisted when he opened them. Was this magic, his magic? Any doubts he had about being a sorcerer had evaporated with that sight.

The warmth in his hands was weaker than before, fading slowly with each passing second. Johnathan was also staring at the flames, speechless. Callum took a deep breath, trying to control emotions that started to run rampant in his head at his success. Fear, excitement, fright, elation, intrigue, confusion; each fought for domination, each was beaten back by the others.

He looked to the flame in his right hand and found to his amazement that the glow from his left hand ceased in an instant. His left arm started to feel weak, then dizziness swam in his head. It had all been so simple, he thought, deceptively so. Perhaps he was making a mistake, thinking he was in control when truly these flames heeded no master. Curious, he decided to test it, no longer focusing on the fire. It faded into nothingness as his concentration ceased, his body slowly returning to normal.

"How did you do that?" the warrior asked quietly.

"I don't quite know," Callum replied honestly.

Taking another deep breath, he decided to try again, this time without the fear, hoping the memory of the tingling sensation would be enough. At first there was nothing, but after another attempt the feeling came again and he let it happen, this time letting it build for longer.

Instead of a small flame, his hand conjured a globe of fire, like the demon's spell he'd seen in his nightmare. He looked at it with a nervous smile, frightened and relieved all at once. It didn't make sense and yet it did so, but more important than that, he was in control. It was precarious, requiring nearly all his concentration, but it answered him rather than his feelings. Johnathan's face momentarily flashed with awe, then hardened.

"Beginner's luck." The compliment was grudging and quiet, the half-spoken threats of moments ago pushed back but not forgotten. About to ask about them, Callum heard the sound of someone quickly rushing down the corridor beyond, turning to see Jinar focusing completely on the globe in his hand, Alexis behind him with eyes wide in surprise. Before Callum could even start speaking, Jinar had moved forward.

"What did you do?" he enquired quickly, glancing at the fire and smiling widely. "*How* did you do it?"

"How did you know?" Callum felt a little weaker now, but it was manageable, even if talking made his concentrating on the spell difficult.

"I felt it, even though we were a hundred yards away. It was unlike anything I have ever felt before, so... raw." For a moment Callum wondered if the red-scaled creatures had noticed it as well, but no attack came. Alexis and Saresan entered the room, the latter not looking too surprised.

"Well, that's familiar." Saresan was a little out of breath from the run back. "At least you're not setting everything on fire this time."

"Does it hurt?" Alexis asked, trying to see any burns marks on him.

"I don't feel it at all. Why, is it hot?" Callum glanced back down to it.

"How did you do it?" Jinar asked again, excited. "What gestures did you make? The mantras, I must know!"

"I... didn't," Callum then told him. "I focused on a feeling, pictured the flames and... it happened."

"Nice one," Saresan complimented.

"Ah." Jinar's awe faded with that revelation, and he took a step back, examining Callum more carefully. "A surge of magical energy triggered by emotion, controlled with your willpower."

"Something wrong with that?" Saresan asked.

"Crude and prone to failure. It seems like you have it under firm control, however, despite your inexperience," Jinar's critique was exacting as he looked at the flaming fists appraisingly.

With that, Callum let the flames die, not wanting a repeat of the tavern incident to occur. It flickered and faded, all eyes on him as he watched his teacher consider what had transpired.

Jinar eventually smiled. "I would much prefer if you did things my way, but it is impressive nonetheless. If you can build upon it is more important."

"I'll try." Callum noticed Jinar had brought his satchel with him on their expedition out. "Did you find what you needed?"

"We did indeed. You would not wake, so I decided to show Alexis some of the more important herbs and reagents used in some of the more common rituals. Quite a nice day for it too." Jinar went to pick up the satchel once more, examining its contents briefly.

"No one in sight as far as the eye could see, none of those things either. We truly are alone out here," Alexis said, smiling at Callum.

That eased his concerns a little, but they still lingered, Callum remembering how easily the creatures had found them before. Johnathan was silent, watching the exchange without comment save his discerning stare. Jinar addressed Callum once more.

"My suggestion, Callum, is that you try that method of sparking your magic, so to speak, then try to control it with some command words and gestures. It seems fire comes naturally to you."

"And the rest?" Callum didn't know what encompassed that broad topic.

"I have an acolyte-level tome that may be helpful to you, all of you. It was written by my teacher and has some of the most basic spells that you might find useful, from conjuring elemental forces to fabricating simple items. Magic is a fine scalpel as well as a scalding hammer, after all."

"Did you find out anything about the creatures from your books?" Callum asked hopefully. The look he got back from his teacher wasn't encouraging.

"Alas not, but I have barely begun with my studies. All will become clear in time, I am sure of it. Let me go fetch that tome for you." Jinar excused himself with a nod and smile.

"It seems Jinar wasn't wrong about your potential," Alexis complimented. Johnathan turned back to the meat without another word, rotating the spit as he no doubt listened to them.

"I'm not really sure how it happened," Callum admitted.

"With enough practice that will change, I'm sure. When you figure it out, would you show me how to do it?" Saresan had joined Johnathan by the fire, taking a piece of meat for himself.

"Don't you want to learn the way Jinar is teaching? He's the expert after all."

"It's always good to keep your options open. If I'm tied up, I won't be making any hand gestures, will I?" He wondered about her reply.

"When are you going to get tied up?" he asked.

"Who knows what the future will bring." She shrugged while answering, smiling afterwards. He hoped it brought nothing bad.

Chapter Twelve

Azure had had to walk along the muddy pathways like everyone else and he hated it. He had found neither his horse nor bearings when he suddenly wasn't in that cave with Callum and the other warlocks. All he did find was himself on his back in a muddy field, rain pitter-pattering on his armour. The indignity of it all was something he hadn't spoken of to the farmhands who'd found him on their land; stubbornly and angrily he'd demanded that they provide him with their finest steed so he could make haste to the town, to warn the lord of the imminent peril he faced at the hands of evil. His anger had only grown when he was offered a mule.

The suggestion of a roof over his head and a meal to fill his stomach he'd rejected. He was not to demean himself further by associating with peasants. Instead, Azure had taken to the rough dirt road he found not far from the farm and walked through the rain and the night to find somewhere to orient himself. In the end, he resigned himself to sleeping under a tree and found that he recognised it as one he'd rested under before in the company of... him.

His sleep had been light, plagued with rage, waking him with a start. His only solace was that their taint hadn't rubbed off on him, his body un-corrupted by the dark energies their kind possessed. He had been travelling all that time with a warlock, deceived by him, with Saresan covering up his horrible deeds.

He'd suspected the labourer – if he ever had been one – of being one who used dark powers, but he had wanted to be sure, find a second opinion he could trust to confirm it. But the sage he knew was dead, or so the snake Jinar had told him. He couldn't trust anything that man said, he was just like Callum, just as deceitful. His mind went through the opportunities he'd had to finish the whole ordeal earlier, to go with his gut, imprison the man and be done with it. Sleeping in his armour had left Azure aching, but still he'd marched on, determined and stubborn. He made a direct route to the cave up in the hills, determined to finish what he had started; the man had gotten lucky the first time, his tricks he could anticipate, counter.

What had presented itself to him when he appeared at the cave after a day's walk was that the horses were still tied up at the entrance, thirsty but otherwise fine. Readying his weapon, Azure had stepped into the cave towards the seer's abode, preparing himself. As he got to the room, he charged forward, sword ready.

"Surrender—"

The place was empty, Azure alone. Where had they gone, why had they not taken the horses when they fled from his justice? Perhaps they'd used some devilry to hide, to conceal their nature and being from him. There was no trap sprung around him, no assailant skulking in the shadows, nothing. He stood in silence, his venture succeeding only in making him angrier. There were dangerous criminals on the loose; no one in the kingdom was safe.

Azure had to face the lord that he'd loaned the horses from, the man he assured would be handed all the evidence needed for Callum to be incarcerated, burned. He'd returned the horses, leaving them to the guards at the gate without a word. He couldn't return to the lord, though, for he hadn't finished his task; Callum wouldn't evade him again, without steeds they couldn't get far. There had to be a way to subdue them, to overcome their powers. He was a knight, the most skilled and noble of warriors, it had to be possible. He would have to consult some of the texts back at his estate, learn more about the best ways the knights of old killed them. One thing was certain; he'd find him and end him.

Callum wasn't sure where the week had gone when he looked back on it.

What had started as peculiar shifted into routine surprisingly quickly. The mornings were spent with Jinar teaching them, working to 'unlock the potential within them', or so he put it. According to Jinar, the best way to improve was always to practice casting spells, the better to weave the arcane energies they possessed to their whims and to fortify them. In the evenings, Jinar retired to his quarters and solitude, perusing texts that were off-limits to them. This left them time to practise magic on their own or explore the surrounding countryside from beyond the complex. Callum went outside only rarely, expecting the creatures to surge out of nowhere and rip him asunder. That thought persisted even when he remained indoors, but it began to lessen as the days rolled by without attack.

The weather had turned fouler as the week progressed, clouds darkening and rain falling with alarming regularity. The book they'd been given to study was entirely useless to Callum as he couldn't read, leaving Alexis to dictate what was written on the weathered pages. Most of the advice had little to do with magic, focusing on healthy living and the beneficial properties of herbs and minerals. What was about the arcane was interesting, but little of it meshed with his own efforts to cast.

After a few days, Callum had only succeeded in the most basic and primal of spells, and that was only with direct guidance from Jinar. Johnathan was naturally far ahead of both him and Alexis, ignoring the readings from the acolyte's tome and moving on to conjuring flames of his own with relative ease. The next time he created fire from nothing, the warrior gave Callum a steely gaze but no words.

Alexis had begun to grasp the basics of magic, progressing from conjuring sticks to the spells Callum had so much difficulty with. The tingling sensation within him resisted his attempts to summon it forth with words and gestures, but Jinar's curiosity about him had only grown as Callum grew more proficient at his own methods. Encouraged to branch out into other facets of elemental power despite his teacher's distaste for it, Callum found comfort in the flames he'd made before, now able to summon them to his hands easier.

As the days ticked by, he found that emotion was needed less to bring it to being, relying more on his will to make it exist. More nuanced applications of it also came under his control; offensive uses had quickly come to mind first, his first fireball small but potent enough to provoke surprise and another scorch on the wall. Even Jinar had been unable to critique when Callum snuffed out the magical flames of the fire pit and then relit them.

Johnathan hadn't been impressed, but he'd come to expect that. They'd spoken little, and when they did it was fleeting, with no mention of their near confrontation. Saresan had found a surprisingly large amount to do during the long hours of training and practice, exercising outside to keep in shape being one such thing.

All the time, however, Callum thought about why they were there, the threat to his life that still loomed over all of them. Jinar hadn't come forward with any discoveries on the creatures, the silence starting to annoy Johnathan.

Some evenings had been spent around the fire in the training room, talking about the lessons of the day and other things that came to mind. Alexis asked questions about Callum's magic, curious about how it worked. Sometimes, Saresan and Johnathan sparred, the latter stronger and faster but often losing in the long run to the guard's experience.

Saresan also told tales of 'his younger years', exploits in catching criminals and the strange things people see when their job is standing around and watching people go about their lives. Callum was often too tired after that to do much more than go sleep, Alexis also; they hadn't had a long conversation before sleeping since the first night.

The evening of the seventh day was no different to any other, with Saresan regaling the others with yet another tale.

"...Of course, everyone knows that an alleyway brute is confident only if there are others with him," Saresan's hands were animated as he described the scene, Alexis listening intensely. "So, from out of the shadows, his four friends emerged, grinning at me with dark intent. I took my halberd—"

"And fought them?" Callum guessed, expecting another amazing description of heart-pounding combat.

"I took my halberd and fell back to the safety of the street," the guard corrected.

"You didn't fight?"

"If I'd fought them alone, I wouldn't have lived. I returned to the garrison and told the captain. We assembled a team and went back, covering each other's backs as we rooted them out." Saresan looked to the fire and poked it with a previously conjured stick, memory in his eyes. "Heroics are all good in stories, but more often than not you're throwing your life away for an ideal most people don't care for. Pride's a dumb thing to die for when you're just doing your job."

"Azure would have argued bitterly with you about that," Callum said. Saresan stoked the fire and chuckled.

"He wouldn't have been fighting petty criminals in a dark alley," was his reply. "I couldn't see him besting that trap alone or running away with all that armour."

"Striking at the armour joints," Johnathan stated in a rare moment of engagement.

"One hit at the arm and you're spraying blood inside your gear. In three minutes, you're dead." Callum thought about Azure being struck down by the monstrous creatures, wondering how long he would last against them. Perhaps he'd panic, having overestimated his chances. Jinar had stopped listening, suddenly attentive to their surroundings. He stood up and moved from the others, catching Alexis's attention.

"Something wrong?" she asked.

"I do not know." Jinar's tone was distant, the sorcerer slowly heading to the main corridor.

Saresan had reached for his halberd already, standing at the same time

Johnathan did. Callum was on edge again, fearing the worst. About to reach for his sword, he felt a sudden jolt of pain in his head that he recognised and didn't all at once. Alexis felt it too, frowning in sharp discomfort at the same time.

It was the only warning they got before the sound of a bell echoing throughout the room startled him. "The alarm."

Callum's worry escalated into a fright. He drew his blade and got to his feet just as a figure entered the training room. Callum had expected one of the towering red monsters, but a man was their adversary.

Entirely clad in purple robes with the hood up and wielding a sturdy metal mace, he'd barely stepped over the threshold before Jinar unleashed a spell upon him with a momentary utterance. The sorcerer shot from his hands an arcing bolt of lightning so bright Callum shielded his eyes. A moment later the would-be foe had stepped no more, lifeless on the ground. Jinar had been the one to fell him, moving back into the room with his hands ready to unleash another spell. Questions about their enemy and amazement at their teacher's power would have to wait; they were in serious trouble.

"So much for being safe," Johnathan muttered, looking behind them just in case someone had stealthily appeared. Jinar had nothing to say about his astounding achievement, a stark contrast to his normal smugness.

"Now really isn't the time for that!" Saresan had rushed to the archway, daring to peek past it. He quickly darted his head back. "There's more of them."

"How many?" Alexis had drawn her daggers, waiting beside Callum with a serious expression. Callum could see the fear in her eyes despite the confident demeanour; he felt it too.

"Five, at least. They're waiting for something," Saresan answered back. Johnathan indicated to Callum accusingly.

"They're after him. We give him up, they'll let us go."

Alexis cast her brother a horrified look but had no time to voice her objection. Callum noticed movement from the edge of his vision, turning in time to see a second assailant that had managed to appear beyond the wards in the training room. This one was armed with no weapon save the magic weaved by his hands, energy made of glistening darkness.

Johnathan was closest to the new arrival and chose his axe over any spell, rushing the sorcerer. The assailant's spell fizzled when the axe hit, the figure crumbling with a scream of pain even as two more arrived, seemingly from nowhere.

Callum's fear made his magic easy to conjure forth, but he froze; slaying a monster was one thing, but killing another human? That they appeared to seek their death meant nothing; all Callum could think on was that beneath those robes was someone just like him, with hopes and fears all of their own. With a thought, he could blast them with flame, but he hesitated, afraid of killing even more than being killed.

Saresan had no such inhibition, locked in combat with an assailant in the corridor while Alexis and Jinar squared off against the two that had appeared. Alexis lashed out with her daggers while Jinar shot another bolt of lightning, aimed at the closest of the new arrivals. To his surprise, it dissipated, deflecting off a barrier that Callum only saw when it impacted, shimmering and momentary. What was even more surprising was that the magic appeared without any words or gestures.

"Do something!" Johnathan shouted to Callum, trying to rush the nearest of the two to him.

Even as Callum grappled with his conscience, however, the situation deteriorated rapidly; Saresan was assailed by a second, then a third warrior who held a sword point to his neck. Johnathan sprayed a gout of flame from his free hand while charging forward, but it was stopped by the same kind of barrier which had obstructed the lightning bolt. Then all at once, Johnathan stopped rigid, struggling in vain against a pulsing white glow that washed over his body, cast by the sorcerer not targeted by his spell. Alexis spotted Johnathan's predicament and stopped, a look of anger and pain in her eyes.

"Do not make it more difficult than it already is for him. His limbs bend to my whims," warned one of the robed figures, an older man. "Unless, of course, you wish me to break him."

Alexis's concern was plain for all to see, but still she didn't lower her weapons, not trusting the man. Callum wondered how many more were hiding out of sight in the corridor and, more importantly, how many of them were sorcerers. He'd got the impression that those with the gift were rare, yet here were these people that seemed to disprove that.

Jinar furrowed his brow, the atmosphere charged with tension as the stalemate lingered.

"How do you know of this place?" Jinar's question was measured.

"We watch all who leave us, your former master was no exception." Jinar looked to the robes, clearly not recognising them. "That he did not tell you was his error and matters not. You will come with us, all of you."

Callum and Alexis shared a look before he felt a sharp stabbing pain in his head, much like the one when the warrior in black had appeared. A moment later, Callum blacked out.

Chapter Thirteen

WANTED: Callum Igannes
For witchcraft and conspiracy to corrupt the kingdom

He is a man of average height, average features, brown
hair and green eyes. Be wary of direct confrontation,
for he is in illegal possession of a sword and has the
power to enthral others to his will with word alone.

Reward: Three silver for capture, one silver for his head

—Wanted poster circulated throughout the kingdom

Callum awoke with a splitting headache and an aching back, the latter informing him he'd rested on a hard floor once more. Quickly he noticed the grey stone walls all around him, the room illuminated by a faint orange glow but no torches. It was cold and slightly damp, lacking any amenities save space and silence. Callum had never seen the inside of a cell yet knew this was just that: he was a captive of the mysterious people in purple robes. Quickly looking himself over, Callum saw he was without his armour or blade.

"You are awake, that is good." Callum turned to the voice to see Jinar standing by a sturdy metal door without any visible handle. The man was stroking his beard in contemplation, staring into the distance. Whether the others were safe flitted into his mind, a worry that clung. "It would seem that Baldar hid a few unfortunate secrets from me."

"Baldar?" Callum slowly stood, relieved to discover no injuries on him save discomfort for a change. That he lacked his sword concerned him despite his want to be rid of it.

"My teacher. He was a highly skilled practitioner, and now I know why. I also understand his paranoia of being discovered... as well as how he came to die." Jinar looked at Callum then, smiling weakly. "But that is the past, the present requires our immediate focus. Are you unharmed?"

"I think so. What happened after I blacked out? Are the others alright?"

"I was under the impression that I was the first to be rendered unconscious, perhaps it was a spell with a blanketing area. Whoever these people are, they are no casters of parlour tricks. I only know of your location; the others are likely held in a different cell. I would almost be impressed with their efforts were it not for one oversight." Jinar turned his gaze to the imposing door that led out.

"And that is?" Callum couldn't see anything special about it save that it appeared sturdy.

"Firstly, they locked us up together, the two most capable sorcerers. Secondly and more importantly, the wards on this door are competent but flawed."

"There are wards on it?" Callum walked up to the metal and touched it, feeling cold iron and little else. "How can you tell?"

"Persistent magic has a lingering presence that you learn to recognise when you are as skilled as I am. It is simply a matter of discerning the correct incantation to unlock the ward, as it were." Jinar put his ear to the door, perhaps trying to listen to the magic residing in it, if that was possible.

"And what is the incantation?"

"One thing at a time, Callum. My mind has been pondering on the more pressing issues."

"Like how the sorcerers that captured us didn't use gestures or incantations?" Callum had remembered that peculiarity at the mention of magic. "Do they cast like I do?"

"That is unlikely, your method lacks refinement," Jinar dismissed him idly. "I was pondering these people's affinity with the red creatures."

"I don't see how they're connected," Callum said, watching Jinar mutter something under his breath, perhaps another incantation of his.

"Whoever they have guarding the room beyond this door enjoys talking to herself; I wager the hours are long and tedious. She mentioned a number of things, most of them inane and a number rarely uttered by the sane. Rest assured, Callum, at least a few of those creatures are here and I have a name for them now: demons."

"They don't look anything like the demons I've heard about. They have no wings, dripping venom or love for riddles." He remembered that tales of demons were often told to children so they didn't misbehave, whimsical stories of fancy that were innocent enough. Yet a few adults muttered darker rumours around the taverns, which Callum had dismissed as drunken boasting. Perhaps there'd been a grain of truth in them after all. "What else did she say?"

"She wonders why we were taken alive when they were under express orders to kill us. Who gave the order she did not say, but it is a curious twist, is it not?" Callum thought back to the short-lived struggle, guilt welling up.

"I'm sorry, I should have done something back when they came." Jinar nodded understandingly.

"I believe we would have been captured either way, Callum. The difference is, they do not know of your power and we did nothing to prompt more than incarceration. I did remarkably well back there, considering, and now we have them where we want them."

"...With us trapped in a cell?" Callum was dubious. "Are you sure they didn't hit you around the head?"

"We are trapped in a cell, yes, but within their complex, where we can learn about these monsters and perhaps even deal with them." Callum didn't like the sound of this plan at all but couldn't find anything appealing about remaining a prisoner either. Then Jinar grinned to himself, stepping away from the door. "So *that* is how it is done."

"What have they done?" Callum was urged to step back by a hand motion from his teacher. A few more motions later, Jinar let the magical energy build up in his body until he unleashed it with a delicate flick of his fingers. This ripped the door off its hinges and sent it flying forward, hitting someone with force and crushing them against the opposite wall. Callum flinched in surprise, then horror as blood splattered across the ground. Jinar smiled, satisfied.

"Shall we make haste?"

Callum was glad that he hadn't eaten any food that evening but found himself retching as a hand of the unfortunate victim twitched a few times before going still. He felt sick to his stomach, unable to look at the mess ahead of them.

"I cannot say that we will not be killing others that we come across, Callum; they will surely want to kill us. It will get easier in time."

"I don't think it ever will." Callum dared to look at the spectacle again, seeing no movement from behind the door.

"You would be surprised what you can get used to."

"I'm not sure I want to get used to it."

"One is rarely given the choice in such matters." Jinar carefully looked out into the wide corridor beyond and motioned for him to follow as he stepped out.

Callum emerged with his mentor into a wide corridor that had very few doors like the one they'd been behind. One to their right was open, revealing a room empty save for a single human leg bone, discarded and forgotten. The stonework was just like their cell, the ceiling higher but still a little short.

Torches that shed light but no smoke lined the walls, the corridor to the right ending abruptly, but to the left, it continued to a sharp right turn into the unknown. The place lay absolutely silent, unnerving him, a quiet they broke with each step. A muffled voice came from a door opposite and to their left, which Callum went to investigate as Jinar casually walked over to the crushed person, searching for something.

"Hello?" Callum raised his voice only a little, not wanting to alert a guard that they'd escaped. Then again, the crashing sound of the door would've caught anyone's attention if they were nearby. Callum got a response after a second, and though he couldn't hear exactly what was being said, he recognised the accent. "I think Alexis is in there."

"Then we shall free her." Callum waited by the door, keeping his eyes on the corridor leading further into the complex. The urge to see his sword returned grew within Callum. Jinar removed from the body a metal ring of keys covered in blood, moving over to the door and searching for a keyhole.

It took a couple of attempts to find the right one, the door unlocking with a loud clunk and swinging open when Jinar tugged at the handle. Sure enough, Alexis was inside, smiling in relief at the sight of Jinar and Callum. Johnathan was by her side, without axe or armour but still armed with his stern gaze. Saresan too was within, also lacking his equipment and leaning against the far wall. Alexis looked to the keys and furrowed her brow.

"You may thank me at a later date," Jinar simply stated.

"Are you all alright?" Callum asked, getting a nod from Saresan.

Johnathan stepped past him without a word, likely looking for a route out. Alexis stepped out more cautiously than her brother.

"I hadn't expected to be, and that worries me." She caught sight of the crushed person. "Did you cause that?"

Callum indicated to Jinar.

"Any weapons on him?" Johnathan enquired.

"Yes and no respectively," Jinar replied, then looking to everyone in turn. "It was the most expedient method of escape. My friends, we need a plan."

"Teleport out, simple," Johnathan shrugged.

"I am afraid not. This place has an inhibitive spell cast upon it, shielding it from the outside. I felt it upon waking, a subtle countermeasure that I am not surprised the rest of you did not notice. I would not like to try my hand at transporting us out of here beyond it, the results could be fatal. We will have to escape the old-fashioned way, if that is possible. The cell did not have windows, making me believe that we are underground." Jinar was stroking his beard yet again as they considered the ever-diminishing options.

"There's got to be a door somewhere," Saresan mentioned.

"Does there? Magic can do many wondrous things."

"Either way, fighting our way out isn't an option either." Saresan looked different without his chain mail but still seemed comfortable armed only with his fists. "The moment they find us, we'll be surrounded again, and I doubt they'll want to lock us back up."

"This is all because of you, Callum," Johnathan accused quietly, staring him down.

"Before you start and for the last time, nobody is abandoning anyone to these people, least of all me," Alexis quickly replied. "We are alive, it could have been much worse."

"It *is* much worse." Her brother folded his arms angrily.

"No matter what we do, we'll need our equipment," Saresan told them. "We don't stand a chance without it."

"But how would we know where that's kept? They're not going to tell us if we ask," Callum was looking at the other cell doors as he spoke. "We should check if there's anyone else locked up here."

"There's too many of us as it is," Johnathan bluntly replied.

"It can't hurt to check."

"Yes, it can. We should already be moving." Johnathan started down the corridor, not waiting for Callum to object. He certainly wanted to; the last thing any prisoner here deserved was to stay locked up when they had the keys to their freedom. What horrible fate lay in wait for them within the stone walls of this cabal?

"I hate to say it, but he is right, Callum. We should be moving," Jinar said to him. That didn't make it any easier to turn away, a feeling of guilt for betraying whoever was still incarcerated. Alexis looked sympathetic but had no words of comfort, following her brother and Jinar as they approached the corner. Saresan patted Callum on the back.

"We could do so much more," Callum said sadly, shaking his head.

"Not right now, we can't. Come on, let's go," Saresan remarked. Callum went reluctantly, passing a final look to the cells left unopened before he moved to catch up with the others. No matter the justifications given, he couldn't feel good about leaving them to their fates.

Their equipment was surprisingly easy to find, locked in a metal cage by the door leading from the prison, the jailer's keys opening both. The only item missing was Callum's sword, which surprised him; of all the weapons they had, his would've looked the worst. Did they know of its intense sharpness? He'd kept watch while the others got ready, putting on his armour afterwards, then looking carefully through the door beyond.

All Callum could see was a corridor exactly like the last. He'd expected people going about their activities or at least a guard on the other side, but the air was still. Saresan moved out first, followed by the others, the group moving slowly ahead. Callum expected an ambush every step they took, but as the seconds passed, his worries eased, if only a little.

Everyone was silent, but Johnathan kept glancing at him as they walked. The first door they came across was an oaken one on their right. Alexis walked up to it quietly and listened. She flinched when an agonised scream came from within. Everyone else stopped but she acted, opening the door wide and drawing one of her daggers.

"Stop—" She didn't listen to her brother, entering even as Saresan rushed to catch up.

There was a startled gasp from within, Callum moving up to see a sight that made his stomach turn. A woman was chained to a wooden table by manacles around her wrists and ankles, clothing worn but intact. Her face was frozen in an expression of unrestrained terror and pain, eyes blankly staring. From her burned lips dripped blood, telling him that nothing could be done for her anymore. Alexis had covered her mouth, observing the horrific spectacle in stunned silence, as disgusted as Callum was at the senseless waste of someone's life.

"Gods," Saresan muttered, shaking his head. Johnathan was looking to the path ahead, growing impatient. Jinar glanced inside, quickly turning his eyes away.

"There are those who would use unwilling persons as test subjects for experimental magical rituals," Jinar spoke softly. "I wager she was one of the unfortunate ones. Those that care little for the consequences of their actions are amongst the most horrifying and powerful sorcerers."

Alexis carefully walked over to the dead woman, closing the corpse's eyes after some hesitation. The door was closed on the scene when she emerged into the corridor, continuing onward even more cautiously than before. Callum couldn't get the lifeless gaze of the woman out of his head, the second corpse he'd seen that day. He couldn't help but imagine them captured once more, subjected to things worse than even what she had suffered. As they came across more doors, they listened carefully, expecting more terribleness but hearing nothing. Most of them were locked, and nobody desired to force them open.

"I wonder where they all are," Saresan asked no one in particular. "Some occult ceremony?" Only the quiet answered him, the group now presented with the choice of going left and right. The guard stepped to the corner and peered around, pulling his head back quickly. He held three fingers up, then moved his hand from right to left. While the others readied their weapons, Callum felt defenceless until he remembered his magic.

Again he questioned attacking people even when they were so abjectly horrible, nor did they know if the three coming were sorcerers or slaves conscripted to serve on pain of death. The others seemed more at ease with the prospect of combat save Alexis, who tried to give him a reassuring look. Then the three emerged from the right, a trio of purple-robed figures carrying parchments and books, a mace hanging from each of their belts. Their hoods were down, the closest man dropping his papers in surprise upon seeing them.

Johnathan launched a ball of flame without hesitation, setting the man's robes alight as Saresan stepped forward and swung with his halberd. Down fell the burning acolyte. Callum once more froze on the spot, unable to stop staring at the now-dead figure before him as the remaining two dropped their tomes also.

They reached not for their weapons but spells, the first conjuring a staff of purple flames from the air, the other preparing to hurl a ball of the same flames at them. A dagger suddenly punctured the staff-holding acolyte's chest, Alexis having thrown it to distract him enough that Johnathan could close the distance. Callum noticed, however, that in all the commotion, the final one was about to launch his spell at Jinar, and his friend wasn't ready for it, his attention focused on the one battling Johnathan.

Hesitation melted away at the thought of Jinar being harmed, easily drawing forth the magic within him. His only thought was protecting them from the flames, remembering the translucent barrier he'd seen before. Letting the energy rush through to his right hand, Callum tried to call forth the spell in front of him to shield as many as he could. A moment later the purple flame was shot in their direction, and Callum felt his magic being drawn upon as the shimmering blue came to be before his eyes.

Jinar and Alexis both were surprised by Callum's efforts, but not as much as he was, watching the flame impact and dissipate harmlessly. Callum couldn't maintain it after that, the collision straining and then breaking his tenuous hold on the magical energies. Startled by his efforts failing and his fellow being killed by Johnathan, the remaining acolyte tried to flee back the way he'd come. Jinar called forth a small globe of energy and it launched forward, seeking out its target with unerring accuracy. Callum heard the cry of pain as it connected, then a dull thud.

Stillness descended upon them once more, broken only by the crackling flames of the burning body. Callum tried not to look at the dead even as Jinar gave him a smile.

"I must admit, that was impressive," complimented his teacher.

"I couldn't let them hurt you," was the only answer Callum could give.

"I would have been quite fine, yet it seems I have underestimated your talent some." Jinar noticed Alexis had reached down for one of the parchments. "I would not recommend taking those, they may be laden with dark energies." She grabbed it regardless and carefully unfurled it. Then there was a sudden shout from down the corridor.

"There!" It was a woman, angry and loud. "They have escaped!" Callum saw that there were more purple-robed figures in the distance, one pointing to them as others readied weapons.

"Run." Saresan didn't wait for the others to follow his advice, taking to the corridor not travelled.

Callum didn't have time to grab one of the discarded maces, fearing a spell would hurtle their way at any moment. But where would they run to? The complex was like a maze to them; one wrong turn could trap them in a dead end. Still, they ran, darting around a corner, then another in the hopes of losing them.

An open door to their left presented an opportunity, all of them deciding in unison to rush inside and shut it without a second thought of who might've been within. Around them were wooden barrels filled with dried herbs, but Callum ignored that, listening for those chasing them. They rushed past and into the unknown quickly, his heart pounding the entire time. Alexis then noticed something he hadn't.

"Where's Johnathan?" she asked quietly. There was then a call from outside.

"Don't let him escape!" the woman acolyte declared loudly. Johnathan hadn't hidden in time.

Alexis's eyes widened in panic, her reaching for the handle of the door only to be stopped by Jinar grabbing her wrist.

"No," the sorcerer quietly implored.

"They'll kill him!" Angry and fearful, she tried again to grab it, but Jinar kept a firm hold.

"We cannot help him now." The sound of people running past them rushed in, then faded out within seconds, the four of them seemingly safe. Callum wanted to help, feeling powerless as the choice to remain hidden was taken from them. Jinar was right, however; revealing themselves wouldn't help him, only endanger everyone.

Only when it went silent did Jinar let go of Alexis's wrist. "He may yet elude them."

Saresan was doubtful, however, and Callum agreed but tried not to show it.

"We have to find him!" she quickly declared, opening the door to see if someone was waiting beyond it. "If we can catch up—"

"We do not know where they have gone nor how many of them there are, Alexis." Jinar was trying to be sympathetic; it was falling on deaf ears. "To give chase would be folly. We need to focus on ourselves."

"But..." She grew quiet, eyes cast down. Jinar couldn't give her any reassurance, looking back to the door. Callum placed a hand on her shoulder, Alexis glancing at it but saying nothing. He retracted it a moment later, sad that he could do nothing to make it all better.

"Initially I had hoped that we would be able to disrupt this group's operations, but they are perhaps too numerous for us to deal with alone," Jinar explained. Saresan shut the door carefully.

"You think the kingdom would listen to us if we told them?" The guard sighed, "We're way in over our head."

"Then I suggest more haste in our escape, so we may ponder this question in safer environs." Jinar opened the door slowly, checking as best he could before motioning for them to advance. Saresan nodded and followed but

Alexis and Callum didn't move. Callum wished he knew what words to say that would stop the tears she was blinking away.

"We'll find him, Alexis." He wasn't sure of that at all, but he'd try his best. She looked into his eyes, hurt but hopeful despite it.

"I can't leave him here, Callum." She was quiet, voice shaky.

Saresan looked back into the room. Alexis took a deep breath and walked out into the corridor without another word. Callum followed a moment later.

Chapter Fourteen

Alexis listened at every door they came across just in case Johnathan was hiding behind it, having evaded the acolytes and concealed himself safely. Those that weren't locked had nobody in them, small quarters with immaculately made beds and little else. Each time she didn't find her brother, Alexis grew more disheartened, nobody having anything they could say.

Callum tried not to imagine Johnathan being subjected to unspeakable pains at the hands of the sorcerers, but it flitted through his mind every once in a while. Even more than that though, Callum wondered why they weren't being hunted down by roving groups of guards and sorcerers. They couldn't have been considered unimportant: after all, they'd been captured.

After what seemed like an age but was likely only minutes, they came across the first open area of the complex, a square hall with a stone fountain at its centre that marked the coming together of four corridors. Water trickled from a large hand at its centre, palm closed. Each corner had a door that looked different from the others they'd seen, fashioned from older wood.

Again, nobody was to be seen, but a poster was attached to the wall nearby, one Jinar went to read. Saresan was watching their rear while Alexis eyed the doors beyond hopefully. The silence was starting to get to Callum, afraid the next loud noise he heard would be his last. His teacher frowned as his eyes scanned the elegant writing.

"That explains where everyone is." Jinar stroked his beard. "They are 'fulfilling the high seer's edict'. What that is, it does not say."

"Nothing good," Saresan quipped. Callum cautiously stepped forward into the open area, seeing a door immediately to his right that was a tiny bit ajar. He thought nothing of it, but then felt something familiar from that direction as he turned away. What that sensation was about he didn't know; none of the underground corridors were welcoming, and yet he found his curiosity sparked by that door.

He fought against this feeling at first, knowing it could very well be a trap to lure them in, yet only he had seemed to notice it. It didn't make any sense, but he found himself walking over to the door. If anything, he could see if someone was listening to their conversation, stepping carefully from the others as Alexis spoke, "Has that field you mentioned weakened?"

"I am afraid not; I imagine it encompasses all areas of the complex. Curiously, I have discerned that it only inhibits teleportation from within outwards."

Alexis spotted that Callum was moving ahead, deciding to check the one to the left at the same time. Now at the door where the strange sensation emanated, Callum saw it fling itself open, but before he could take in its interior, he was pulled within by a sudden, unstoppable force. It had to be magic, he thought, and a strong one at that, yet it didn't cause his head any pain. He realised then that he'd made a terrible mistake.

Turning as he stopped, Callum saw the door had shut behind him and pulled at the handle, only to find it stuck. What manner of lock kept it closed?

"Help!" he shouted, not caring if an acolyte heard as long as it got Jinar's attention.

"I'm afraid they cannot hear you now, magical dampening and all," came the reply from behind him. The voice was old, quiet and utterly without malice, but Callum still dared not turn. "Young man, you would already be dead if I wished it. I mean you no ill."

Callum was afraid yet had little choice but to trust the intentions of the person. He turned slowly, seeing that he now stood before a chaotic study. Books of different shapes and sizes were scattered about in large piles and stuffed ancient bookshelves along all the walls. In the centre was a table almost lost to literature, no doubt on subjects of magic or history. No glow illuminated the room, only a large candle on the table that burned brightly.

Sat in a comfortable-looking chair was a man of advanced years, nose in a thick dusty tome. Soft green eyes and wispy white hair reinforced his age, face lined with wrinkles and frame fragile beneath his purple robes. Callum spotted in the middle of the table what had drawn him to that place, his sword. It was unmistakable, resting on top of open books as if a paperweight. His first instinct was to rush forward and grab it, but that would anger the sorcerer in front of him – at least he guessed the man could use spells – forcing a fight he doubted would go his way.

"One of them knows I went this way. You should let me go." Callum spoke cautiously but firmly, watching the man who hadn't done so much as look up from his book. He didn't seem concerned by his statement.

"Quite impossible, I'm afraid. I need to keep you here, for your own good. In time you would run into people less considerate than I."

"Why should I believe you?" Callum was eyeing the sword despite trying not to. "You people do horrific things, I've seen it." Still, the old man didn't let up on his reading.

"Ah, to be young again and judge everything on first impressions." The man closed his book, reaching for a walking cane to help him stand. His posture was stooped. "There are those here who would enact terrible evils to learn secrets of the arcane. I am not one of those people, though there are few like me here now."

Something about how the man spoke lowered Callum's guard, even as he thought of his friends outside. They had to be trying to break in by now, to free him.

"And what is this place?" Callum decided to try and get some information out of the man if he could. The robed figure turned slowly to his books.

"All these I have read in my time. Studied, perused, learned almost by heart. I have been here since its founding, you know? We're likely the largest concentration of sorcerers in all the lands, originally united for one purpose: to enlighten people, find out how magic truly worked and teach others that it was something not to be feared." He muttered something too quiet to hear. Callum reflexively readied for a spell but nothing happened. "Our leader was…"

"Yes?" There was a pause.

"It was a name that started with 'G', I think. Gerald? No, Gregor? No, not that either," the man trailed off and weakly looked up to a book high up on a shelf, unreachable. "It doesn't matter, I guess, he's dead anyway."

"What killed him?" Callum tried the door again just in case. It didn't open.

"We asked questions all the time, especially ones we couldn't answer. What better way to learn more than to seek the unknown? We were the Astral Hand, the stars were in the heavens and we wanted to learn their secrets, a hand grasping for the truth.

"And then one day someone came to us and said that we were asking the wrong questions." The book high up moved on its own accord, slowly sliding out and hovering down into the man's hand, opening to a particular page. "Said that we should be asking what was *beyond* the Astral. Beyond the stars. Of course, we thought there was nothing – They were the gods and us their creations, the gifted species on our solitary world."

"Who said this?" Callum had never questioned what was beyond the gods, it seemed obvious; the night was full of darkness, the nothing that resided past the shining beings in the sky. No one could reach the gods to get past them, no mountain could possibly be tall enough.

"One day I rose to find out the High Seer had died and that this other man was taking over. Those that challenged him were never seen again. Whatever happened before that day…" the old man trailed off again, sounding sad. "We stopped seeking to enlighten people, turned to asking strange things I didn't understand then and try not to now. Been like that for ten years." He paused. "Or was it fifteen?" The book he was reading closed, hovering back up to its rightful place. "It doesn't matter either way. That is the past, only memories live there, and they cloud with time."

"Who is this person you keep talking about?"

"I think it's Alun, might not be though. Alex, Alfred? Doesn't matter, I guess, he doesn't care much for me. I'm an old, withered man who couldn't oppose him. They leave me alone to read my books and any others I wish, and I am fine with their occasional intrusions." Both now looked at the sword, then one another.

"It is your weapon, is it not? They took it from a young man, you look young." Callum was glancing back to the door, now concerned that Jinar hadn't got it open. Had something happened? Jinar would've left him behind if the need called for it, it made sense to do so. So friendly was the old man he kept forgetting that he was a prisoner again.

"It is," Callum finally answered, turning back slowly. "I found it."

"Magically fortified, unlike anything I have ever seen. I have seen many artefacts in my time, forged a few myself." The man took the blade in his hand, lifting it up carefully, finding it a little difficult even with its lightness. "This is made of no material I know of. They handed it to me to research for the High Seer while they dealt with you and your friends. I am to take it to him now, I might as well bring you with me. He will want to see you."

"And if I refuse?"

"You seem like a nice enough man, a shame you are wrapped up in all this mess. I suppose we all are, if they are to be believed…" Something about how the old man ignored his question made Callum wary to challenge him, quiet confidence that permeated his fragile body. His wording was also peculiar, but he put that down to age.

"What is the High Seer's edict?" Callum remembered then what Jinar had read. His words provoked a dark look. "Is it bad?"

"It is best you live without knowing, young one." The man walked slowly to his desk, reaching down with effort to retrieve the scabbard for the sword. He placed it on the desk, then grabbing a hefty tome at the top of a precarious stack. "Will you carry the sword for me? I need to take this book."

Callum blinked, surprised; surely the old man didn't trust him that much, to hand him a means of defending himself. Thoughts of escaping immediately came to mind, of bashing down the door and trying to find the others. The longer he thought about it, however, the more the old man's offer seemed reasonable. If anything, he could learn what was going on with the cabal and perhaps put a stop to it. That the man was likely a mighty sorcerer wasn't lost on Callum either, however, thinking on the great power his aged bones contained.

Taking the scabbard after a moment's pause, Callum quickly attached it to his belt, all while the man watched. He took the blade just as quickly, sheathing it. The familiar weight of the blade at his side was reassuring but he felt no safer, watching as the door opened all by itself, his benevolent captor walking past him slowly.

"Stay close, young one. The others will not bother you if they see you're in my custody." Callum looked through the door, hoping to see the others waiting for him. No friendly faces greeted him, once more exposed to the persistent silence of the grey corridors. There was no evidence of combat, which only made him more concerned. The old man slid past him through the doorway, ushering him on weakly with his free hand. Once more the temptation to flee took hold, but he thought better of it, instead keeping pace as they started to walk down the right-hand corridor.

"Why are you after me?" Callum doubted he'd get an answer. Sure enough, no reply was given. "If it's the sword, you could have asked for it." Again, he got no answer, left to ponder in the quiet broken only by their footsteps.

The pace was gruellingly slow, giving him time to think on the others and the growing worry that welled in his stomach as they drew closer to wherever the high seer resided. Once more he was going somewhere against his will, again with a polite captor guiding him along. When they eventually rounded a corner, he was startled to see a group of three acolytes talking to one another in whispers. In turn, they were surprised at his presence, their eyes drawn to the one that didn't belong.

"Go," the oldest of the three ordered, one rushing off into the distance. The remaining pair readied for combat but were dismissed by a weak hand wave, the scholar undeterred.

"He is my prisoner," said the old man. "I am taking him to his judgement."

"And you armed him?" came the accusing question.

"He has promised to come with me peacefully." The other acolyte was eyeing the sword at Callum's side incredulously. Callum stayed beside his guide through the endless halls as the two men moved in the way. The old man finally stopped, eyeing the young ones. "Do they not teach you to respect your betters?"

"We'll deal with him; you go back to your bedtime stories." The two stared down their elder but didn't attack despite their advantage. The one escorting him wasn't amused.

"You can try, but I won't let you. Now run along, I'm busy." Despite his frail physique, he stood imposing against the two younger casters. Perhaps age made him braver than he should be, old enough to have no fear of death, or maybe just stubbornness. The acolytes looked at each other, unsure how to react to the sight before them. Eventually one of them moved aside slowly, angering the other.

"The high seer will have your head for this disobedience!" Clearly, the cabal wasn't held together by friendship or camaraderie but fear, a powerful but corroding force.

"I will not ask you again to move, my time is valuable," warned the old man to the one who resisted.

"Make me."

"I'm sorry you have to see this, young one," he apologized to Callum in advance.

Callum flinched as he sensed the build-up of magic within their foe but was surprised that it was eclipsed by the power bursting forth from the old man, so great that his head swam with dizziness. Without a gesture or word, the young acolyte was shrouded in a purple haze and thrown violently into the wall next to him.

The unaffected one stared silently as Callum and his captor continued their slow walk past them, even as the now groaning sorcerer started to recover, even angrier than before. Recovering quickly, the sorcerer prepared another spell, allowing a lot of power to muster within his being. The old man didn't seem bothered, focusing on ahead rather than behind. Callum tried to summon his own energies but too late, watching as a bolt of dark energy shot their way.

It had the form of black skulls, jaws wide open as if screaming for retribution. The aged wizard stopped and sighed, clicking his fingers nonchalantly. A flash of magic from him later and Callum watched in amazement as the spell blasted at them lost form and fizzled. The one who'd thrown it was also shocked but only grew more enraged still. Screaming in anger, he prepared an even more powerful spell but didn't get the chance to do much more than prepare to cast it; without a second thought or a glance back, the venerable sorcerer conjured a streak of energy that guided itself towards its target.

The young caster had only a moment to realise his folly before it hit his head. When the energy had dissipated, the now headless sorcerer collapsed, stone dead. Callum and the remaining acolyte were horrified, but the old man simply grumbled to himself, "The young think they are so indestructible." The remaining man fled the way they'd come from, perhaps to warn others, but his captor didn't seem bothered; with the power at his disposal Callum wasn't surprised. What worried him was that this man wasn't in charge, that someone far stronger led this cabal of sorcerers willing to kill one another without a second thought. Escape had never been an option, not if the spells he'd witnessed were aimed at him in his attempt. Perhaps that would've been a mercy compared to what was to come, the unknown now all the more horrifying. He walked a little slower now, hoping the old man would match *his* pace and buy him a tiny bit more time. He didn't.

They encountered no more acolytes along their journey, though there were clearly some at work in the rooms on either side of the corridors they travelled down. Through one Callum could see a woman pouring strange liquids into a large bottle. She didn't look up from her work, focused entirely on the rancid-looking concoction she was creating. Another had people silently reading, perhaps studying arcane secrets.

Rounding a few more corners and traversing even longer corridors, eventually they came to a set of stairs that went down. The old man clutched Callum's shoulder firmly and teleported them, the sensation just like before but even more fleeting. Callum staggered woozily, getting his bearings only when he saw that they were now at the bottom of the long flight of steps. The old man was entirely unaffected and indifferent to the whole ordeal.

"I don't like stairs," he told Callum simply before continuing to move.

Callum's legs were weak for the first few paces but regained their footing soon enough. The floor they were now on was more decorated than the one above, tapestries of strange occult designs adorning the walls. Still, there were no windows, reinforcing Jinar's theory that they were underground. The doors in the corridor were closed, but through them Callum could hear sounds of unsettling things; screams of agony and gurgles of pain fought to be heard past the stone, making Callum long for the foreboding silence of before. He heard a quiet voice begging for mercy that quickly shifted into a cry of twisted suffering. The old man didn't so much as flinch, desensitized to it all.

Just what did the cabal hope to gain from torture like this? It did nothing but make him even more fearful of this Alun, the high seer. Ahead in the distance was a tall double door made of solid stone, guarded by two figures in full suits of chain mail tinted purple somehow. From coif to feet, they were covered in metal links, their faces concealed by helmets fashioned into the visage of monstrous beasts. They looked at the old wizard, readying their spears.

The old man stopped at last, clearing his throat.

"I have business with the High Seer. You will let me pass."

They both glanced at Callum, then his sword. A moment later they stood aside, watching them intently. The stone doors slid open, dragging across the floor with a grating sound. The room beyond was far gloomier than the corridor they were in, and Callum instantly felt the sensation that something was very wrong in there. It was familiar but he couldn't put his finger on it, a sense of darkness beyond the lack of light.

The old man glanced back to make sure Callum was following and walked into the darkness, unafraid. Callum was nervous, but the unflinching stares of the guards made him pick up the pace, following inside. The doors slowly shut behind him, leaving him in the barely illuminated gloom. Only then did he spot the burning white eyes of the demons on either side of him, four in all, instantly drawing his weapon ready to defend himself. They didn't move, however, which made him even more worried.

Another second passed and he heard the rattling of chains by every pair of eyes that glared at them, but no movement. Were they chained to the walls, captives of the high seer? He both hoped and dreaded it all at once, afraid of what the cabal hoped to learn from the monsters for their own twisted ends.

"Yes?" It was a powerful tone, coming from the back of the room. Callum couldn't see who the voice belonged to, but it was a man directly ahead of them. Was that Alun?

"I have brought him to you, high seer," the old man said into the darkness. He didn't speak with the reverence the high seer was apparently due, his tone unchanged. "I cannot glean any secrets from his blade, it is unlike any item we have seen."

"To be expected." The person appeared at ease in a room full of blood-thirsty monsters. It made Callum feel uneasy.

"Do be gentle with this one, he shows promise," asked the old man before turning away from the darkness. He gave Callum a nod. "I wish you luck, young one."

Chapter Fifteen

King Fredrin
King Alunya the Wise
Queen Jennifer
King Fredrin II
King Monroe
King Franci the Young

—From 'The Chronicle of the Yoven Dynasty', scribed by Anon

The door out opened again, light cutting through the shadows as the sorcerer left. Callum saw what looked like a throne forged of matted iron. A man was sitting on it, remaining shrouded somehow, perhaps through magic. When the doors shut once more, the darkness crept into his mind as well as the room, filling him with fear. The chains rattled once more, the creatures thirsty for blood, for death. Only once the commotion died down did the man ahead of him speak.

"So, this is the man they are so worried about," Alun stated. Already questions were being presented that Callum doubted would be answered. "The one they wished me to kill."

"Why haven't you?" Callum didn't know why he'd asked that question, regretting it immediately. No answer came for a few moments, leaving his fear to stew and spread. He held his sword tightly but doubted if he'd ever get close enough to use it.

"I am curious about what they see in you that I cannot." Callum could hear the man standing.

"A lot of people see things in me that I don't," Callum answered cautiously. "I've no idea why you're after me, what the Astral Hand would need of my sword—"

"We are the Silent Hand. The Astral Hand are no more, not that either will mean much to you. As for your sword, it is of interest to me but not my priority." Callum held the blade tighter, readying to fight to the last if he was given the chance and wondering how truthful Alun was being.

"Then why bring me here, torment me and my friends?" Callum then asked. "Are my friends still alive?" Alun laughed quietly, on the edge of the darkness that masked him. The robes he wore were black with a purple trim, much like the one demon in his dreams wore but with more finery.

"They are insignificant to me, and in many ways, so are you." He left another pause. "You live because you may still have use to me despite my orders. In a way, you remind me of myself, before."

"Before what?" Callum then asked, knowing better than to ask who ordered his death. Alun was too smart to fall for that. "The old man said you found something, something that changed you. What was it? What would twist you to commit such evil?"

Callum was buying time at this point, confident now that he wouldn't live to pass any of this information on. Perhaps he would be rescued at the last second by his friends, but that fleeting hope faded every moment it didn't happen. There was more silence.

"The truth." Another moment of silence. "It changed everything."

"Everything?" Callum was doubtful.

"If you knew what I did, you could neither deny it nor oppose what will happen here." Callum then looked again to the eyes of the demons, their murderous gaze.

"Are the demons part of your scheme? What of this final edict? What are you going to unleash upon the kingdom?" Callum's question provoked yet more quiet, interrupted only by chains to his left rattling more.

"My answer depends on whose side you stand on—"

Before Alun could continue, the stone doors were flung open, flooding the room with light which finally revealed Alun, standing as tall as Callum. Alun's face was pale from lack of sunlight, but it was handsome and charismatic, his brown eyes sparkling. His hair was short and black, neatly cut. Callum could see on his cheek a strange symbol that had been branded, unlike anything he'd seen before. He guessed it had some important meaning. The high seer's physique was hidden under his robes, and he was carrying no weapons save the doubtlessly large amounts of magic at his command. Alun looked past Callum to the people entering, making Callum turn also.

"We got one!" an acolyte shouted triumphantly.

Callum saw that three sorcerers were dragging Johnathan into the room, manacles around his wrists and fingers bound together with delicate chains. Bereft of his axe, the tall warrior was subdued, something Callum thought he'd never see. The two exchanged a glance, and not only did anger rise once more in the warrior, but Callum knew that Johnathan blamed him for all of this. Alun stepped back from the light, almost afraid of it. His expression shifted to anger, glaring with hostility at the ones who had disturbed his speech. With a wave of his hand, the three were flung out of the room with great force, crashing to the ground unceremoniously. The doors slammed shut behind them, plunging Callum and Johnathan again in the gloom.

"Did you find the others?" Callum asked Johnathan quickly.

"Of course, you got separated," Johnathan cursed. "If it wasn't for you—"

"Now is not the time to argue, Johnathan."

"When is?" The warrior raised his voice, "When we're all dead because of *you*?" Johnathan shoved past Callum, shouting into the darkness where Alun resided, "If you're going to kill me, get on with it!" Alun laughed gently at the ultimatum, unsettling Callum more than anything else he'd heard from the man.

"That does not need to happen." He then stepped a little further into view, making Johnathan's expression harden. "Not all of you have to die, not yet."

"If you want to kill him, go ahead." Johnathan spat. Callum had known they didn't get on, but to hear that shocked him, despite the truth of their meeting causing their plight. Still, Johnathan had brought up a good point, why were either of them still alive? Callum had only one guess and he didn't like it.

"You pick some unusual travelling companions if that is the case," Alun said to Johnathan calmly. "You are a man of strength, sure of your talents."

"So?" Johnathan was unimpressed, but it only confirmed what Callum feared was happening, hearing words laced with honey and venom.

"And yet here you are, powerless before me. You look at me and wonder 'what does he have that I don't?' If those manacles weren't on your wrists, you'd kill me and rescue your sister, wherever she is." As Alun mentioned Alexis, Johnathan glared harshly.

"Ignore him." Callum's warning fell on deaf ears.

"If you've hurt her—" Johnathan warned.

"I have done nothing to her. As we speak, she and her friends are running through this complex like rats, scampering from one hiding place to another. Right now, they have eluded death, but" — Alun paused — "it is only a matter of time, is it not? But enough of that."

"No!" Johnathan tried to move into the darkness but found himself unable to, stuck in place by a power that made Callum's head ache, "If anything happens—"

"It sounds like you have an issue with your friend here rather than myself. After all, is it not *his* fault that you are here, that she is here?" Callum shook his head, growing more afraid for Johnathan than himself now.

"Don't listen to him," he implored, but all he got was an angry look.

"I'm quite happy to stay here and exchange words while your sister courts death, but" — Alun smiled; outwardly it was warm, but Callum could feel the malice behind it — "it does not have to be that way." Johnathan watched him warily.

"You have me in chains," reminded the warrior. In an instant they unlocked, falling from his wrists and fingers with a clatter. Johnathan's eyes widened in surprise, looking to the high seer who observed the man.

"And now you are not," the high seer replied. Combat didn't start despite past words, Callum's companion glancing down to the forgone shackles.

"Johnathan, you can't trust him. He'll kill her no matter what you agree to. You're smarter than this."

"I think Johnathan is capable of making his own decisions, don't you?" Alun didn't take his eyes from Johnathan, watching his internal debate. "You have not even heard what I have to say." Callum kept a tight grip on his sword, hoping he didn't have to use it but knowing it was inevitable, one way or another.

Johnathan finally answered, annoyed.

"...Callum is right. I can't trust you." Alun didn't appear shocked.

"Why not?" asked the high seer.

"Your word means nothing, even if you unbound me. You're in league with those monsters."

"Am I?" Johnathan paused as the cabal leader shook his head, turning back to his throne of iron. "You know so little of me, of this place. You do not know what's to come, Johnathan, nor how things are."

"I know enough."

"You think you know, but you don't. These are things I have seen, the true truths of everything. I have passed the light of ignorance and entered into the twilight of enlightenment." Alun paused again. Callum had concluded that Alun liked pauses; perhaps he thought it made what he said more dramatic, stick in the mind better. "Not all can accept these truths. Perhaps *you* are capable of understanding it, maybe." Johnathan eyed him warily.

"I don't care about your truths, only my sister." The warrior took a half step back. Callum was even more doubtful that Johnathan would even listen to his pleas. He tried anyway.

"He doesn't care about anything, especially your sister."

"Shut it," came the rebuttal along with a harsh stare.

"As I said before, my issue is only with your friend," Alun reiterated. "You, I do not need to slay. It would be such a waste of talent."

"If that's so, I can kill you," Johnathan told him. Alun's chuckle was more pronounced than before.

"How quaint. I said you had talent, I did not say you have power, not yet. In time, you could..." He then left a much longer, lingering pause. It played on Callum's nerves. "...Perhaps even powerful enough to protect yourself from the coming omens, as well as your sister." There was an even longer pause as Johnathan listened. "I alone have the authority to save her, order my servants to take her alive rather than kill her. I see no reason to do that though. I have what I want right here, Callum and his blade. If you were *with* us, however, I would be more inclined to be merciful. The choice is yours, but do not linger, her life hangs in the balance." Johnathan and the high seer looked to one another, the former trying to assess the latter with seemingly no success. Callum didn't know what to say; he'd used all his arguments already and he doubted Johnathan wanted his opinion. Surely Alun was lying, he had to be, but then why do this if it was all a ruse? It was far easier to kill them and be done with it, but that hadn't happened.

"...Words are cheap," Johnathan finally replied, clenching his fists. Callum felt a surge of magic through Johnathan's body, ready to be unleashed. Alun simply smiled.

"Then I will show you." The high seer turned to Callum. "You must excuse us, Callum. I will deal with you afterwards, rest assured."

Callum was enveloped in a white aura, and with that, everything went silent. He tried to speak but his lips wouldn't move, cold and numb. He could barely breathe, frozen in place by the magic that bound him. He tried his own magic but found it wouldn't answer him, the energy around him muffling his own strength. All he could do was watch things unfold through the translucent haze. Johnathan looked to Callum, initially with surprise that shifted to fury aimed at Alun. Callum couldn't hear his shouts but they looked forceful, cast at the high seer who stood before him without any reaction. The warrior called forth flames that fizzled the moment they left his hands, disarming Johnathan of all but his fists.

Sure enough, the man charged at his captor, ready to punch, but was knocked to his feet with a blast of magic so strong a stabbing pain shot through Callum's body. Only when the warrior was on the ground did Alun speak calmly, eyes focused on the man before him. Johnathan responded with more angry words as he got to his feet, fists still clenched, ready to strike out again.

More than anything, Callum wanted to scream at Johnathan not to listen to Alun's lies, to fight even if it killed him, not that they'd get out of there alive either way. Desperation and dread flitted with the thought of watching Johnathan die before his eyes, with him powerless to stop it. The two went back and forth in an argument, Johnathan furious and Alun calm.

As time went on, however, something changed; Johnathan looked worried for a second before scowling and shouting once more, pointing to Callum for some reason. Whatever Alun said in response made him stare, trying to read something on the high seer's face. More words provoked a look of barely contained hatred, which worried him even more than he already was. Whatever deceit Alun was spinning to bend Johnathan's ear seemed to be working, drawing the eyes of his audience of one to give him the attention he no doubt sought.

Callum tried to break through the aura holding him, to warn of the forked tongue the seer hid, but his efforts were in vain, no power heeding his call to action. His eyes would've been hurting if the numbness hadn't taken hold, Callum unable to close them in a no doubt deliberate move to ensure he saw absolutely everything.

Within Alun's hand appeared an orb of dark blue light, swirling with mist, which Johnathan immediately turned away from, looking instead to the door. Something said drew his gaze back to the orb, made him step closer to it with words of his own as he stared within. At first, nothing happened, the globe's contents ever shifting but unchanging. Then the colour changed to a dark red, and Johnathan's eyes widened as he watched what wasn't revealed to Callum. Alun uttered a single word that he could lip-read.

"Truth."

Johnathan stepped back but the orb followed him, forced him to see what he couldn't wrench his eyes from as his face spoke where words had failed him. Terror, shock, disbelief, disgust, and through it all, rage. He went pale but could not avert his gaze, witnessing a pantomime of treachery the high seer was doubtless performing before him, until suddenly the orb went utterly black as if a shadow.

As the colour faded from the globe, so too did Johnathan's emotions, leaving only wordless despair in its wake. Alun took a step towards the warrior and spoke a few words, smiling and offering a hand for him to shake. Johnathan weakly looked to it, all fight gone. Then Alun looked behind him and up to something unseen, furrowing his brow.

A sense of urgency took him then, expression hardening as he moved the offered hand to Johnathan's shoulder, motioning for him to walk into the shadows. Without resistance, Johnathan stepped with their enemy, if he even perceived Alun as that now. The high seer passed Callum a look that chilled his being, suddenly content to leave him there.

As the pair vanished into the darkness, the aura around Callum weakened, feeling returning to his being, and more importantly, his voice.

"Johnathan!" He got no answer, moving after the pair into the gloom and finding nothing save the empty throne. Why had he been left alive when Alun had said time and again that his death was inevitable? The answer came with the horrifying sound of metal chains falling to the ground in a chorus of clangs, Callum knowing exactly what had happened. In a moment the demons rushed towards him, erupting into view with claws ready to rend him apart. All thoughts of Alun and Johnathan died as his heart thumped wildly, Callum swinging his sword at the first one that drew too close without thinking about it. The blade connected and sliced deep into its neck, decapitating it. The others had closed the distance in that time, one trying to claw at his sword arm. He wasn't going to let the demons rip him apart, the magic within him threatening to burst from his skin. He let it flow through him, a wide and wild spread of flames that immolated the demons. Unfortunately for Callum, the demons weren't distracted by their scales burning, continuing their attack. He swung at another of them that was practically upon him. Even as he took off one of the creature's arms, he knew there were too many of them for him. His luck had run out.

Then the room was flooded with light as the stone doors swung open, a lance of white energy flying past his head and through one of the uninjured creatures, slaying it.

"Callum!"

It was Saresan's voice calling to him, the guard rushing to his side and striking another one with a halberd swing. His chain mail was strained with fresh blood, but he was as ready to fight as ever, the two now striking together to fell the last of the red monsters. The ones already felled began to evaporate into nothingness, leaving no trace that they were ever there. Even though Callum had heard before of them doing this, it was still puzzling; what manner of things were they to vanish after death?

"I thought you were dead!"

"And I you!"

Callum was slowly calming down, turning to see that Jinar and Alexis were standing in the open doorway. His mentor had a scorch mark on his robes, the left arm of it stained with blood. He was observing the room with mild interest while Alexis was looking for something that wasn't there, concerned. None of her clothes were burnt but she hadn't escaped harm either, holding an injury on her right side.

"What happened to you? Are you hurt?" Alexis asked, scanning him with her eyes for any injuries.

"I'm fine, thank you. The door I went through was held magically by one of the sorcerers. What happened after I went in?" Callum asked back.

"They found us, and we had to flee, there were too many of them. Then we took a wrong turn."

"I concluded then that I was in fact far stronger than the ones in pursuit of us," added Jinar with a smile.

"You guessed and got lucky," Saresan chipped in with a chuckle, earning him a raised eyebrow.

"In matters of the arcane there is no 'guessing', especially for one as skilled as I. Once this was revealed to them, the acolytes were easily scared off by a show of my prowess. One that Saresan managed to capture spoke eagerly of this location in exchange for his life. That does not explain how you arrived here also, Callum."

Saresan had moved over to examine the iron throne, checking the arm-rests and the back.

"The man who kept me in that room brought me to Alun as his prisoner, along with the sword that he was studying," Callum replied, noticing how the ichor of the demons had run off it perfectly without any stains.

"We found more experiments like before, Callum," Alexis told him sadly. "Mercifully, they were dead when we found them."

"Most of them." Saresan shook his head.

Callum continued, "Alun said he'd been ordered to kill us instead of capturing us, he didn't say why. He was probably going to kill me, but then Johnathan was brought in—"

"Johnathan was here? Where is he?" Alexis asked quickly, hopeful.

"He... went with the high seer, I don't know where." Worry took hold at his words. Jinar stroked his beard in contemplation. "Alun was trying to persuade Johnathan to join them. There was an orb, Johnathan looked into it, and whatever he saw... it must have been horrible. Lies, but still horrible."

"They didn't say anything?" Saresan asked, having finished looking over the throne and finding nothing.

"I couldn't hear them: I was helpless inside that same white aura that trapped Johnathan before. He could've killed me easily, but he just... left with Johnathan into that corner, I don't know why."

Jinar walked over to the area of the room in question, placing his hand on the wall curiously. Alexis shook her head slowly, eyes cast downward.

"It doesn't make sense, why would he go with them?" she asked herself, looking to Callum in the hopes of an answer.

"He talked about power and the truth, offering to reveal it to him. He also mentioned you."

Her eyes widened, now even more concerned. Saresan began walking back to where Callum was.

"He used me as leverage?" She watched his face as he remembered the orb, the shouting. Saresan shrugged.

"Makes sense to me. He had no idea that you were alright, but how this seer knew you two were related is another thing," The guard said. "Your brother's got a short fuse, it wouldn't take much to set him off."

"We've got to talk him out of this. Whatever these people are doing, it can't be good if what we've seen here is a fraction of their intent."

Even as Alexis said that, however, Callum began to wonder if her brother would listen; between twisting Callum to be the cause of his problems to whatever the orb had shown Johnathan, it had sapped the fight from him, the will to argue. Callum hadn't eliminated the thought of magic clouding Johnathan's mind until it snapped to fit whatever scheme the high seer had, but surely he'd have felt something so powerful even through the trapping aura.

"We'll do our best." Callum could promise no more, trying to smile encouragingly. Alexis didn't return it.

Chapter Sixteen

The clicking of fingers made them both turn to the corner Jinar was in, smiling with satisfaction.

"I believe I have found where they have gone," Jinar said to himself, resting his left hand on the wall.

"Through the wall?" Saresan remained dubious even when the sorcerer nodded. "A corridor hidden behind it?"

"A magical portal weaved into the very stones. I am not surprised you did not notice it, cleverly hidden as it was. All teleportation leaves an imprint on the surrounding area, residual energy from the spell. Normally it fades over time, but I believe this wall has been imbued to act as a gateway, from one point to another."

Callum stepped up to the wall and looked himself, seeing nothing out of the ordinary. Touching it didn't cause his hand to fall through either, but there was a subtle warmth to the stones which he could barely feel, not unlike how the sun's light heated all it touched.

"Do you know where it goes?" Saresan asked.

"Not in the least," came the quick reply.

"What about activating it?" Alexis had walked up also.

"The possible ways to activate it are numerous. It can be through a magical incantation, a passphrase or an item acting as a key." Jinar stepped away from the wall, pondering what he'd uncovered.

"And you've no idea which one will do it," Alexis guessed, getting an idle shrug.

"Even if I were to correctly guess the type, the possibilities for each are theoretically limitless. Then you need to think of protective wards built into the spell itself, preventing those that try to activate it from doing so." Jinar tilted his head slightly as he stared at the wall. "My teacher told me of a few instances of his own wards activating, they were... Let us merely say there was not much left to dispose of afterwards."

"Is there anything magic can't do?" Saresan enquired idly.

"Bring the dead back to true life. My teacher sought a way to defeat death, but it claims us all one way or another."

"That's a relief," Saresan muttered, looking again at the wall. "So what do we do about the wall?"

"We wait."

"...For what, exactly? They went through it, why would they come back?" Saresan followed Jinar's gaze to Callum, who quickly understood what his teacher meant.

"They wanted me dead, unleashed the demons to do the job. He'll want to come back and recover the sword, and he'll use that portal," Callum realised.

"Very good, Callum. This is likely where he will come from, so we will wait for his arrival," Jinar answered.

"And then?" Alexis didn't like the sound of this plan. "He'll be far stronger than us, I imagine."

"We have the element of surprise, a most deadly weapon when used properly—"

In an instant, Callum felt another sharp pain hit him. This one was much worse, however, a blazing agony unlike anything he'd felt before in his life, excruciating to the point that he collapsed. Worryingly, Jinar and Alexis also struggled, his teacher barely remaining standing while Alexis crumpled, clutching her head and crying out. Saresan looked startled at this, wheeling around to find the assailant that had attacked them, but no one was there.

No sooner had it started, the sensation died suddenly. Callum could barely think for a few seconds as he tried to recover, but one thing flashed from his memory; he'd felt a feeling like this before, back when this all started, in the forest with the man in black armour. But it couldn't have been him: he wasn't anywhere to be seen. Jinar weakly offered Alexis a hand which she took, helping her up even though his footing was shaky.

"What the hell just happened?" Saresan asked quickly. "Was that a spell, one of those protective wards? Why didn't it affect me?" Callum struggled to stand, his legs arguing with him, but he persevered.

"I... I do not know what that was exactly," Jinar declared cautiously, still pained, "but whatever it was, it was powerful."

"...It was someone arriving," Callum announced with fear.

"That is quite impossible. No one could have that much power, it would rip their body apart," Jinar countered.

Callum wanted to tell them about his encounter in the woods, but even now, something held him back; they wouldn't believe him, and truthfully, he still didn't believe it entirely himself, wondering just how much of it had been his imagination and dreams.

"Suppose it is possible," Alexis began weakly, "that someone could have that much power. What would happen?" The sorcerer sighed, not quite ready to entertain the idea.

"Sorcerers like ourselves have magic within our being, and that can be detected by others of our ilk. When the levels of power are equal, it is almost unnoticeable, save through the use of magic that detects magic. I imagine you could learn to innately notice arcane energies as you would anything else, but I digress."

Jinar began to pace, Callum able to see the thought process on his face as he reasoned it out, "Now if someone or some spell is considerably stronger than you are and you have not taken precautions, you need no spell to notice it. The body of a sorcerer reacts to powerful magic as if it were an attack itself. At lower levels it is relatively minor, a headache or aches in the limbs..."

As he went on, Jinar started to grow more concerned as it slowly made sense. Saresan kept his eyes trained on the doorway out and the so-called portal, alternating his vigil. "At more drastic extremes, it would cause severe pain, disorientation..." Jinar trailed off.

"And what?" Alexis asked.

"Death, if the difference was so drastic." Jinar gazed to the ceiling. "If Callum is correct – and I do not yet believe that is the case – the dampening field around this complex would have shielded us from some of its impact. But it is quite impossible."

Callum thought about people like him who hadn't known of the power within them, dying where they stood without anyone knowing why. It made his feeling of guilt grow.

"Why? There are powerful sorcerers, Alun is one of them." Saresan was watching the portal now.

"Perhaps Alun was taking orders from someone," Callum guessed.

"Callum, if someone that powerful existed, they could..." Jinar went silent again, but this time he looked worried. "If you *are* right, we are all in some bother."

"So, what do we do?" Saresan shrugged. "What *can* we do? We don't know where this thing goes, where this person is or what they intend to do. We're just four people, we can't take on someone that powerful."

"We can safely assume that he has nefarious intentions, considering what we have witnessed here and this 'final edict' that we have seen mention of."

"Whatever we do, we need to decide quickly, before things get worse," Alexis told them with great worry. "People could be getting hurt." She went over to the wall Jinar had examined, trying to feel for something, anything to activate it. Jinar looked once more to the supposed portal while Callum was left to ponder their situation, thinking back on what his dream had warned him about, what Azure had said of him.

"This is all my fault," he declared. They'd all been right, now innocent people were suffering because of his power.

"I would hardly say you are the cause of all this," Jinar chipped in.

"But—"

"There's something different here, I can feel it." Alexis had her hand on a block of stone near the corner, feeling near the middle. Callum was about to approach when Jinar held a hand up quickly, eyeing what she'd found intently.

"Let me examine it," he requested, waiting until she'd stepped back before looking himself at the stone. "Curious."

Jinar pressed two fingers to the point in question carefully, smiling when it slid into the wall with a quiet click. An unnatural hum emanated from the corner, but there was no build-up of magical energy right away; only the noise's pitch rose, allowing Jinar the time to take a few paces back as Callum prepared for the worst.

A flash of energy made him dizzy, but it quickly passed. A disc of shimmering light winked into being before them as the hum died. It was definitely made of magic, and within it was the view of somewhere he found vaguely familiar, an empty street in the dead of night. There were no sounds from the disc, it was like a painting. But then they saw a young man run into view, terrified and clutching his stomach as it bled. Something lunged towards him and struck him down. Even in the shadow of night, Callum recognised the thing for what it was, a demon. Fright rose up in his stomach.

"Gods..." Saresan muttered, "they're loose."

Alexis was horrified, Callum more so. What could anyone do against those creatures, taken by surprise as they were? The gutters would run red with the blood of innocents, life torn from the community, and all of it because of him and the sword he'd found. The others denied it, but this had to be because of his discovery: they wanted him dead specifically. Something welled up in him that he didn't fight, couldn't.

"They'll kill everyone, we have to do something!" Callum told them.

He acted before he thought, stepping towards the disc in the hopes that it was more than just a viewing portal.

"We need a plan," Jinar said firmly, turning from the view. Callum couldn't look away, the demon's claws dripping with blood as it rushed away to find a new victim. He couldn't let it find someone, not when he had a weapon capable of killing them and the magic to protect himself and others.

Even if he could save one person, he had to try rather than wait for death to come for them. Throwing caution to the wind despite himself, Callum touched the disc before Jinar could stop him. He felt himself be pulled into it suddenly, then the same rushing sensation as teleportation.

Callum arrived with a stumble into the street he'd been watching, right next to the unfortunate man who'd been ripped to pieces by the demon. His heart lurched despite knowing what to expect, blaming himself for the death of a man he didn't even know. His ears tuned in to the pandemonium in the air, blood-curdling screams that echoed around him as others met their fates at the claws of the monsters.

Orange glows in the distance complemented by smoke were also worrying; an untended fire would ravage the town as terribly as the demons, perhaps more. What he didn't feel was the tremendous power that had knocked him down before, but something was nearby, a presence unfamiliar to him but strong. There was no shimmering portal behind him, and now that Callum was left in the dark side street alone, he thought too late on Jinar's urge for a strategy, fear rushing through him that he struggled to fend off.

What could he do alone even with his blade, his magic? It had been foolish to rush on ahead, but those thoughts faded when he was joined by the others, appearing out of nothing next to him. Alexis quickly recovered from the teleportation and drew her daggers, the wound she'd been holding no longer bleeding.

"May I say, Callum, that that was an ill-advised move," Jinar politely chided.

"And yet you followed me?" he asked back. Saresan wheeled around to examine their surroundings for enemies, halberd ever ready for a surprise attack. He spotted something that made him worry.

"This is where we were before, I recognise that tavern. If there's any resistance to what's going on, it'll be at the garrison," Saresan spoke quietly, as if he were wary that the walls themselves would betray their arrival to the demons. Jinar was giving Callum a stern look, speaking his annoyance without words, but quickly focused on the situation.

"You know this place better than us, lead the way." Alexis was about to move when Jinar indicated to her wound.

"You will need that tending to. I can use my magic to heal it if you wish," Jinar suggested.

"It can heal?" Callum asked.

"With a bright enough mind, one can achieve everything." Alexis took a moment to think about it before nodding in agreement.

Placing his hand on the bloody area, he muttered quietly and made a complicated motion with his free hand, drawing his magic forth into green energy that ebbed from his fingers to her skin. Callum watched as it bathed the injury and healed it rapidly before his eyes, surprised at the speed and effectiveness of it. Although the blood remained, the area was as if she'd never been hurt. The energy faded when he'd finished, smiling in satisfaction as he kept the hand there.

"My teacher spent years perfecting the ritual; in time I will teach you it also if you wish." Alexis looked at his hand, and then he removed it with a nod.

"Thank you." Callum wondered what emotion he'd need to think on to heal with his magic; perhaps Jinar would teach him too if they survived. That they'd endured their capture would be meaningless if the demons slew them now.

"Stay together, move quickly and don't stop for anything," Saresan told them. "The streets are already littered with the bodies of heroes." Callum wanted to disagree, but there was sense in the guard's words.

Together they moved out of the side street, presented with even more ruination and death. Bodies were strewn on the cobbles and doorways in various degrees of butchery; none had been armed, fleeing in the direction of a portcullis that led to the wilderness, which was shut. No demons lunged out of the shadows between buildings, the area hauntingly quiet despite the chaos all around.

As they moved, Callum looked at a doorway that had been battered down, a bloody handprint on the frame. There was no movement within, the sparse furnishings wrecked and flung about. He was frightened and on edge, unable to not look at each dead person they walked past. Saresan, in comparison, didn't pay them any heed, focused instead on the way ahead.

The screams had stopped; were they the only ones left? He couldn't hide his worries from Alexis, who gazed sadly at a woman's body that a raven was picking at.

They rounded one corner, then another through streets that once bustled with life, stopping when they came across what remained of the Ox's Horn. Burning out and abandoned, the husk now fitted in with its surroundings perfectly, the incident lost to the catastrophe about them. They didn't linger more than a few seconds, increasing the pace at the sound of combat in the distance.

Upon seeing the garrison, Callum's hopes sank; it wasn't the bastion he'd hoped it would be, surrounded by the corpses of those who'd given their lives to protect it. A few guards were still fighting along with a group of injured townsfolk, giving their all to survive against a trio of demons that had climbed over a flimsy barricade of wooden carts. One of the defenders spotted Saresan, and without a word, the desperation of their situation was conveyed with his expression.

Jinar muttered an incantation and brought forth lightning into his hands, blasting a hole through the closest demon's chest. When one of the surviving pair turned at their arrival, Saresan readied his halberd for the charge and Callum stood by his side, striking in unison as it scrambled over the carts to reach them. Callum barely thought about the attack, his instincts taking over as their combined efforts cut it down.

Alexis was surprised by a demon smashing through a door to their right, charging at her with deadly intent. Darting back from the rage-filled swing of the demon that narrowly missed, she stabbed at the creature's chest. The blades penetrated its scales but didn't kill it, forcing her to think on her feet as it snarled with hate.

She called upon her magic, a significant build-up of energy that shoved the demon back at speed, crashing into the very building it had come from. Jinar had turned to see the spectacle and created a fireball that he launched at the demon, the creature immolated along with the building. It had happened so fast the surviving guards and townsfolk had only just killed the demon they were facing, looking to their saviours when all went quiet.

"What *were* those things? By the gods, they've come to kill us all!" the younger guard asked everyone, looking at the bodies around them in horror. The townsfolk saw their chance and fled away from them all to a nearby alley.

"Stay here where it's safe!" They ignored the older guard, vanishing out of sight a moment later. Saresan moved past the barricade and exchanged a look with those that remained. "I don't know where you came from but I'm damn glad to see you!" Callum followed behind quickly, hoping that things within the garrison were better than they appeared.

"We need to speak to whoever's in charge," Saresan asked. "Is the captain around?"

"He was one of the first to go," came the damning reply. "No word from our lord either, I was starting to think everyone outside was already dead."

"What about the church?" The younger guard's voice was weak and fearful. "That's holy ground, they can't get in there, right?"

"Hell if I know, these things aren't like any beasts I've seen." The older one looked to Jinar. "You were the one that made the lightning appear, right?"

"We are on your side, do not fear," answered the sorcerer. Callum was watching everywhere around them, waiting for the next attack with his sword ready.

"Do you know what these things are?" the guard asked then.

"We have a few theories, but that is not important right now. We need to formulate a plan to get the survivors away, then rid the town of demons." Jinar got a fearful look from the already-spooked younger guard.

"D-demons?" he stammered, spear shaking in his hands.

"In name only, I believe." The assurance did nothing to calm the man's nerves.

"I knew it! We're damned, all of us—"

"That's enough!" the older one shouted, silencing the cries of doom. "We've had more than enough doom-saying for one lifetime."

"How many people are inside?" Alexis asked. The look she got wasn't encouraging.

"There were a lot more an hour ago, that's for sure. The things just keep coming, whittling us down. There are about a dozen innocents, all wounded. Three guards apart from us, plus Azure." Callum's eyes widened in fear.

"Azure?"

Chapter Seventeen

"The days of the Sage are upon us! His last prophecy was clear but not heeded, and now we pay the price for our folly! Look now upon your pride and despair, for only those of pure humility and kindness will pre—"

—*Final words of Mad Matt*

As if saying his name summoned the man, out from the garrison stepped the knight in armour speckled with ichor and blood. His cloak was tattered and his helmet dented, but he was otherwise unharmed, sword and shield in hand ready for a fight. The latter had a circular symbol daubed on it in blue that looked like the runes on the seer's walls. Immediately the knight saw who was before him and indicated to Callum with his sword point.

"You!" His voice brimmed with anger that surprised the guards, the noble tone almost drowned out. "The scourge of the kingdom returns to witness the suffering he has wrought!" Callum couldn't help feeling guilty but stood aside from his friends, shaking his head. Saresan had already readied his weapon again.

"You know these people, sire?" asked the older guard. "They saved us from the monsters—"

"A ruse to gain your trust, only so they can use you for their nefarious ends!"

"I didn't bring these things to the town, how could I?" Callum argued back. "We came to help!" Azure laughed in reply.

"No more lies, Callum, I see through your glamour now!" The knight motioned to his shield. "This sigil protects me and all in my charge from your taint, from the monsters at your command!"

"Perhaps if it were enchanted, you might have been correct," Jinar remarked while stroking his beard. "At present, it merely makes you look foolish." Azure stared at the sorcerer intently. Alexis stepped forward then, stopping only when the knight's sword was aimed at her instead.

"These things are here to kill everyone, Azure, us included! We're here to try to stop them, and we can't do that without your help," she argued. "You're meant to defend the innocent, Azure."

"I am, from your deception! I trusted you once when I should not have, I will *not* let my guard down again!" Azure was ready to charge forth but was beaten to it by a score of demons that emerged from the way the townsfolk had fled.

Callum didn't wait for them to close the distance this time, calling forth his magic and unleashing a cone of flame into the approaching rabble. It did little but burn some of their scales, Azure looking with surprise as the two guards moved forward to help drive back the demons.

Not wanting to be outdone, Jinar cast a far more potent spell, launching an intense ball of blazing inferno which immolated the first demon it touched, vaporising it. The younger guard clumsily attacked with his spear, the demon he was fighting leaping at his vulnerability and gutting him with a single strike of its claws, the screams of the man quickly dying with him.

Alexis paid the demon in kind by stabbing it in the head, allowing Saresan to decapitate it. Callum looked back to see the knight hadn't moved to aid them, watching him intently. Turning back to the fight before him, he swung at one of the scorched demons but missed, feeling its claws ripping through his armour and scratching his side. Crying in pain, Callum staggered back even as the demon didn't flinch, preparing to rip him to pieces.

Suddenly interposing himself between the demon and Callum was the previously reluctant knight, smashing his shield into its face so he could level his blade against it. Cleaving off its arm, Callum gripped his bleeding side as Azure skilfully dispatched the monster with another swing. The last one was disintegrated much like the first by Jinar, the area once more descending into quiet. Callum doubted it was for long, looking warily to the knight who'd been threatening their lives moments before, his sword still held ready. The older guard looked down at what was left of his comrade, shaking his head sadly.

"How far are you going to take your blind ignorance, Azure?" Saresan asked the knight sternly. "How many more people need to die like he did before you accept that we can help?"

"And how do I know you did not summon these creatures yourself to sway me into your service?" The sharpness of Azure's tone had dulled just a little. Callum sighed, frustrated.

"At this point, I don't care what you think of me," he declared wearily. "You hate me, fine, but a knight is meant to be noble and just. What's just about any of this? Right now, we need all the sword arms we can muster."

The two stared at one another, Callum not backing down this time; this was bigger than them. Saresan was ready for combat just in case, but Azure lowered his sword reluctantly, as if his very being was fighting it.

"...I do not trust you, Callum. If you try anything—"

"Thank you." Azure hadn't expected his reply, looking curiously at him. Saresan still eyed the knight warily but stood down from readiness. Callum looked at the older guard. "You need to get those left in the garrison out of here before the demons come back."

"And you should check on the church, they might still be holding out there." The guard nodded grimly. "If we make it through this day, the bards will sing of your bravery."

"It's Jinar Yelandan Fakkal Genai Lae, so you can pass it on to them," Jinar informed the guard, who nodded and went into the garrison alone. "My friends, we need to discover the source of these creatures and destroy it, as well as dismantle the cabal that is in league with them."

"A cabal?" Azure asked.

"It would take too long to explain. All you need to know is that they are quite evil, and you may kill as many of them as your heart desires." Jinar indicated to where the last group of demons had come from. "That way is as good a place to start searching as any."

"Perhaps the people at the church know something of this attack," Alexis suggested. "And hopefully they've seen my brother."

"If what Callum said is true, I hope for their sake they haven't," Saresan muttered.

They encountered nobody alive down the dark and winding back roads of the town; the corpses were numerous, however, hunched by closed doors as they'd desperately tried to find any sanctuary from their deaths. The group travelled in a silence broken by the occasional scream that caused them all to stop. The plumes of smoke were more numerous now, the fires consuming more with their insatiable appetite. Eventually Azure spoke.

"Do you have a plan for when you encounter this... cabal?" Azure spoke the final word with disdain. Jinar replied plainly and quietly.

"It is difficult to know what they are capable of or their numbers, if they are even here. The demons are and they are connected somehow, but beyond that I only have theories."

"The church is upon sanctified ground, blessed to repel creatures of evil, housing the purest souls of the kingdom. They will stand resolute against the darkness that sweeps this place."

"And how good are they at fighting?" Saresan asked as he stepped over a forgotten body.

"Those who tread that path forgo violence to better understand their connection with what lies beyond," Azure proclaimed with pride. Saresan didn't need to say anything to show how he rated their chances. Approaching the end of the side street, the guard looked around the corner and winced at what he saw.

"The church?" Alexis asked quietly.

Saresan shook his head slowly.

When Callum looked around the corner himself, his stomach churned uncomfortably once again at the horrific spectacle; nothing remained of the barricade in front of the main entrance save burning wood and charred corpses. Those that hadn't been lucky enough to be consumed by flames were being torn to pieces in their final, futile stand. The few who still fought had been overwhelmed. The ones who fled were caught with ease and killed, those that pleaded for mercy were given only death.

Callum couldn't look away, feeling cold as he watched barbaric cruelty unfold. Within seconds, the struggle was over, the demons pouring into the church's interior, where screams of panic and dread cried out before being twisted into sounds inhuman. No sooner had the creatures entered, they surged out, their terrible deed done, scattering in all directions in search of new victims. Then Callum noticed figures emerging from a building near the church whom the demons ignored, clad in the purple robes of the Silent Hand. One of them held a battleaxe that was familiar, but from that distance, he couldn't be sure if it was him.

"I think Johnathan is there," Callum whispered, concerned they'd hear with magic.

"Johnathan?" Alexis moved up to the corner, deeply concerned. "Is he alright?"

"Is he a captive of the warlocks?" Azure enquired, weapon ready for a valiant and likely pointless attack.

"We're not quite sure of that. I sure hope so." Saresan watched along with Callum as one of the robed figures stepped away from the others and observed the church, indicating to it with a sweeping motion of his hand. The guard looked to Jinar. "Please tell me you have a plan now."

"If your brother attempts to harm myself or innocents, I will not hesitate to kill him," Azure warned Alexis then. She glared angrily at him. "Though he is of your blood, I will not stand by while he commits evil."

"If you kill my brother, I'll kill you," she snapped back, the first time Callum had heard her anger.

"That's enough, both of you," Saresan butted in. "Geeze, you sound like my mother, rest her soul."

Alexis turned her back to the knight without a word, clenching her fist but unable to hide the worry for her brother.

Callum had no idea what they'd do, and it seemed the others also had no thoughts on it either. They couldn't just walk up to them and ask if they'd stop, but neither did they stand a chance against so many acolytes of the cabal. He looked again and noticed that one of the acolytes was looking right at him.

"You survived." In his mind, a voice echoed that wasn't his own. It was Alun, invading his thoughts through some twisted magic. "Do not be so surprised, Callum, you cannot hide from me. You *were* seeking me, were you not?"

Alun stared directly at him, motioning for the other acolytes to stay where they were as one started to approach them. Any element of surprise they thought they had was gone, replaced with the anxious fear that they had never been in control of the situation.

"You alright?" Saresan had noticed his discomfort.

"He knows we're here," Callum whispered, sure that Alun knew what they were saying too.

"Then we shall confront these fiends directly," Azure declared, stepping out into the open.

"I really think—" Jinar barely got a word in.

"Lay down your arms and surrender! I am warded against your evils and will bring you to justice, alive or dead!" proclaimed Azure as he strode towards the acolytes.

Saresan muttered under his breath but followed, knowing that they stood a better chance together. Alun didn't react to the knight's threat, nor did any of his companions, waiting for them to approach. Callum shared a look with Alexis and Jinar, putting on a brave face before they followed behind. When Alexis appeared, the man with the axe shifted, gaze focused on her. It had to be Johnathan, only he would do that.

Azure finally stopped less than ten paces from the group of acolytes, numbering seven including Alun. "Do you submit, foul warlock?"

Close as they were now, Johnathan was unmistakable; he was taller than the others around him and the only one armed. His gaze didn't shift from his sister, clearly concerned about something. The stand-off was tense, both sides ready to launch into action at the slightest provocation, but Callum knew how little chance they stood if that happened. Alun broke the quiet.

"Now that is a term I have not heard aimed at me for a long time. Wholly inaccurate too, but that is beside the point. That you survived and escaped our complex is impressive, Callum." The high seer didn't sound surprised. "Meaningless, but impressive."

"When the king hears of this, you will be rooted out from whatever hole you hide in. There is nowhere beyond the kingdom's reach you can seek refuge when it fights against evil!" Azure tried to stare down the high seer, but he didn't have Alun's attention.

"You talk far too much, sir knight. This kingdom verges on self-implosion, crumbling at the edges while it rots from within. The line of kings has grown weak, and your liege shall be the last, as much as I had planned otherwise. None of that matters, however. These lands are insignificant, as are all of you."

"I am Azure, most esteemed knight of the realm and—"

"That is quite enough of that," Jinar interrupted, stepping forward. Azure looked offended but remained silent, glaring at all the acolytes before them. "So, you are the ones bringing the demons to this place. Why would you do this? What do you seek to gain by killing all these people?"

Alexis clearly wanted to speak but refrained, perhaps unsure what words to use. Callum stood at the back of the group, knowing that despite everyone else talking, Alun was only focusing on him.

"What happens here is inconsequential, considering what is to come. You are wrong about the demons, however. It is not us who brought them here, nor do we control them. They do what they do, and we do what we do."

"Let my brother go." Alexis couldn't hold back anymore, imploring the high seer. Alun turned his eyes to her now, a piercing gaze.

"You think that we hold him against his will?" Alun smiled slowly. "Your brother joined us of his own volition. Ask him yourself." Callum was afraid they'd hear that, and Johnathan didn't deny it. She didn't move closer, afraid to.

"Johnathan, whatever they said to you about me, it wasn't true," she said to her brother. Alun surely wouldn't let him go: Callum knew this. Johnathan finally spoke, and his voice was different.

"Alexis..." The certainty and confidence in his words were gone. Instead, there was fear and a hint of sadness that pervaded them.

"Can't you see what these people are doing? All the people they've killed? They're evil, Johnathan. Innocents are dying even while we stand here! Look beyond what they've told you and see that, please..." she implored.

Slowly he stepped closer, Alexis not moving away. Azure readied his sword but Jinar shook his head; now was not the time for rash decisions. Johnathan had a haunted look about him that Callum only saw when he was within a few paces of his sister. He was also wearing a circlet around his head that had a spherical purple gem at the centre.

"...I can't. I know too much now not to act." Johnathan offered his hand to her, catching her shocked eyes with his own desperate ones. "You have to join me."

"What?" She stepped back, horrified at the thought.

"It's the only way you'll live, you have to trust me!" He was begging. "If you knew what I knew, you wouldn't hesitate. You have to trust me!"

"These people are mad, Johnathan!" Saresan was annoyed. "They want to kill everyone!" All the while Alun watched in silence, still smiling. The demons still rampaged while this was going on, distracting them from stopping further death, and he knew it.

"Everything I knew, everything I understood! It was all wrong!" Johnathan shouted, stepping closer to Alexis again. "You have to come with me, Alexis, it's the only way!"

"Johnathan..." Alexis was confused and hurt, barely recognising the man she'd grown up with.

"Please...!" Johnathan pleaded more desperately now. Callum had never heard him like that before, and from how Alexis reacted, neither had she. "...Please, trust me. You trust me, don't you...?" She blinked away tears, looking down. "...You're my sister. Don't you trust me?"

Alexis slowly looked up to Johnathan, pained. When she tried to step away, Johnathan grabbed her wrist, refusing to let her go.

"That's enough!" Azure could stand by no longer, placing his sword point at Johnathan's neck. The momentary distraction allowed Alexis to wrench herself free and step back, now next to Callum. She was shaking her head, unable to believe how dramatically her brother had changed.

"Are you alright?" Callum asked her quietly. She didn't reply. Her brother was confused until he locked eyes with Callum, bewilderment fading into silent anger.

"Oh, of course." No longer was he pleading. Instead, he spoke with wounded anger, "Of course you would trust him over me. It's been that way since you met."

"You know what they're doing is wrong," Callum told him. "Whatever differences we have don't matter; I don't want you to go down this path."

"You don't care what happens to me," Johnathan spat. "You've driven yourself as a wedge between her and I. She won't even trust me anymore! What lies did you speak to her?"

"Snap out of it, man!" Saresan shouted to him.

Johnathan was about to step forward when Azure stood in the way. Suddenly, Johnathan's battleaxe was wreathed in unnatural flame as he struck wildly. The knight managed to raise his shield just in time to deflect it but still staggered back from the sheer force of the blow, the sound of metal scraping across metal making Callum wince.

"Johnathan!" Alexis was even more worried, but now Johnathan ignored her.

"He is quite mad," Jinar said to himself quietly as Johnathan swung at Azure again, this time harder. Callum had to do something, even if Alexis didn't want her brother harmed. He couldn't read the mixture of emotions in her eyes as he stepped forward to help Azure, who was locked in combat with Johnathan. The warrior fought with a bitter zeal that was almost maniacal, swinging with all his might in the hopes of overwhelming Azure.

Callum struck out not at Johnathan but his weapon, remembering how deadly sharp his sword was. It cut through cleanly, sundering it into fragments that fell to the ground. Johnathan stopped for a moment, but his surprise quickly shifted to rage focused on Callum, the warrior turning to him.

Azure attempted to swing with his sword, but Johnathan lashed out with his magic, shoving him metres away and to the ground. Jonathan formed a new axe with a spell, made only of fire which burned wildly, much like his fury. Gripping the incorporeal weapon, he struck at Callum.

"Stop!" Alexis's plea fell on deaf ears.

Callum tried to block the axe, but it went right past his sword and hit him, the flames catching his clothing on fire. Callum fell down, rolling on the ground to try and douse the flames. Johnathan grinned darkly at the spectacle, readying his axe to strike again as Azure slowly got to his feet. Saresan rushed forward to defend Callum but was blasted back by the same force which toppled the knight.

"What do any of you know?" Johnathan shouted to them furiously. "You cannot see what I can! You do not know!" The burning of Callum's armour died in an instant, Alexis using her power to suffocate the fire. She offered her hand, which he took, helping him to his feet while Saresan recovered also. Azure looked at the rune on his shield.

"You cannot blame us for not acting on knowledge we do not have!" Jinar was the opposite of Johnathan, calm and collected. "You can tell us later—"

"Later?" Johnathan then laughed uncontrollably. It made Callum uncomfortable and scared Alexis. "There won't *be* a later! This whole world is doomed and everyone on it will die!" Saresan looked doubtful, but Callum remembered the dream with the robed demon, the warning that now echoed through him.

"What?" Alexis was almost speechless.

"This world will be cleansed!" Johnathan then told them, panicked and enraged all at once, "None who oppose him will survive! Fire will burst from the ground, the earth will crack and all will die!" He then turned once again to Alexis. "You *have* to come with me! Only then will you be spared!"

"What are you talking about?" she asked him, again with tears in her eyes. "Fire? Cleansing? Johnathan, this is madness!" It couldn't be possible, none of it. How could the whole world burn?

"I HAVE SEEN IT!" Johnathan screamed, pained, while his face paled as if reliving horrible memories. Then he looked to Callum, his eyes hardening into absolute loathing. "...And it is *your* fault! You brought this upon us!"

"Johnathan, I didn't—" Callum started.

"If you had given up the sword and yourself when you had the chance, we might all have lived! All of us!"

"Please, stop this!" Alexis begged.

Johnathan couldn't see beyond Callum, beyond what he intended to do. He moved up with furious determination, launching a ball of flame at Azure when he dared to try to stop him and knocking Saresan to the ground again when he charged forward.

Callum's fear grew into fright as he knew what Johnathan sought to do, unsure if he could stop the warrior with his sword and magic alone. Jinar was finally spurred into action but was interrupted mid-cast by a sudden detonation of his own orb of flame, triggered by Johnathan's barely controlled magic which knocked the sorcerer down. With tears in her eyes and no other choice, Alexis stepped in the way of Johnathan, daggers ready to strike at her brother.

"Don't do this!" she called to him, hoping that the true him heard.

He stared through her at Callum, shoving her out of the way as if she were an inconvenience. He ignored the bolt of flame Callum sent at him, setting his shirt alight and scorching his chain mail. Callum was surprised at how Johnathan was able to ignore the flames even as the warrior kicked him to the ground and raised his axe quickly to strike, to finish what he'd started.

"Die! For all the people you have damned!" Johnathan wailed, bringing his axe down on him. Callum couldn't block it, didn't have time to move. Azure wouldn't get there in time to stop it. He swallowed back his fear and closed his eyes, body tense as he waited for the end.

Chapter Eighteen

A moment passed, a crackling sound and a pair of screams piercing it, pain from Johnathan and shock from Alexis.

"No!" came her cry.

Callum finally dared to open his eyes and saw Johnathan standing over him, the flaming axe gone. Everyone had stopped still. Jinar's robes were smouldering; he was on one knee, his hand extended out with small arcs of lightning running over it. Johnathan slowly turned his paling face to his sister before his legs gave out, collapsing to the ground.

Alexis rushed to her brother's side and checked for a pulse, any sign of life. Callum was still trying to come to terms with being alive, saved by the one thing he hoped wouldn't happen.

"Johnathan?" Alexis asked weakly through tears. He didn't answer. She checked for breathing. "Johnathan?!"

Jinar slowly lowered his hand, closing his eyes for a moment in remembrance of one who had fallen. For just a few moments, Alun was forgotten about as the group looked at Alexis desperately trying to revive her brother. She tried to draw forth life by pressing down on his chest quickly, again and again. The body didn't stir. Saresan was about to say something but thought better of it. Callum staggered to his feet as Alexis started to cry at what she'd lost. He noticed the high seer's smile had grown wider, darker.

"I am so sorry," Jinar finally spoke with regret. She glared at him, tears running down her face. "I had no choice."

"You could have stunned him, knocked him out... Anything else..." she sobbed. She cried harder, having given up trying to rouse. Callum had no words of comfort; all of this was his fault.

"A pity, but his death was not without merit," Alun remarked off-hand.

The gem on the headband Johnathan wore started to glow with an inner light. It then pulled itself free, Alexis not fast enough to catch it as it shot towards Alun and settled in his hand. The high seer closed his fingers around it.

"What vile sorcery is that gem?" Azure asked in a shout, his patience with Alun long expended.

"Unfortunately for you, I have grown tired of watching this farce."

Alexis looked up from her grief, eyes red.

"...F-farce?" she stammered.

"It was more amusing than I thought it would be, but it is over now. I have what I want." Alexis closed Johnathan's eyes gently with her fingers, choking back a few more tears. Anger was taking over, however.

"You did this... for amusement?" She stood up slowly, eyeing the leader of the acolytes. Callum knew they stood no chance, even less now that Johnathan was gone, but he couldn't let Alun get away with what he'd done. They were outnumbered and outmatched, but perhaps they'd somehow manage. Alexis didn't seem to care for the odds, furious. "I will be the one to kill you, for Johnathan!" Alun chuckled quietly to himself.

"How touching," he remarked. Callum grabbed her arm when she tried to run at Alun, holding her back.

"He'd kill you before you made it." Callum didn't want to see her die as well, even less for such a futile gesture.

"If you are so powerful, warlock, why have you not struck us down?" Azure asked loudly, sword ready. He got no reply. "I think you are not as mighty as you claim to be, hiding behind words and lackeys."

"You are welcome to think that, and I assure you, you could not defeat me even if I were alone. The reason, however, is far simpler: I'm stalling until another arrives to kill you. Then the plan will be enacted." Callum and the others looked amongst themselves, save Alexis who stared with hatred and despair at Alun.

"The final edict..." Jinar muttered.

"In some ways, you are privileged to see what most do not, even if only for a short while."

A sharp stabbing pain flashed through Callum's body. He knew what this heralded, and it filled him with dread... or so he thought. Next to Alun appeared not the knight in black armour but the robed demon from his dream, the high seer not reacting in the least. Its arrival dispelled any illusion that the demon had been a figment of his imagination.

The desolation around them made his warning of the world dying ring truer than ever, fortified by Johnathan's frightened cries that lived only in his memory. The demon had arrived alone, eyes on Callum only; it was after him, none of the others mattered, and that made him even more afraid. Was all of this just to get him in the open, easier to kill?

Jinar was no longer calm, eyeing the new arrival with wariness while Alexis was clearly afraid. Saresan wasn't sure if his weapon was even useful against it, intensely focusing on its every move. Azure stepped forward with his sword ready to fight the newly arrived foe, emboldened with righteous zeal.

"So, you are the one who leads your monstrous kind against the good people of this kingdom! I am Azure Tellinton and by my liege, you shall perish on my blade!"

"That would be ill-advised—" Jinar's warning was ignored as the knight charged forth.

"For the king!" beckoned Azure, swinging his blade with all his strength at the demon's body. The blade not only failed to penetrate its scales but glanced off the black robes like they were steel. Neither Alun nor the demon turned to the knight; the acolytes watched and chuckled at his failure, which only angered Azure further. "What foul force shields you, monster?!"

"I see." The demon was still looking at Callum, disappointed. "He lives."

"Your dark magic cannot stand against my pure spirit!" beckoned Azure as he swung again just as ineffectively. Alun observed his attempts with some amusement now, smiling to himself.

"Azure, he's too strong for you!" Callum warned him, not daring to step closer.

"My will is stronger! Nothing can break it!" Azure proclaimed proudly, aiming to take off the demon's head with his next powerful strike.

The sword was caught mid-strike by the robed creature, stopping dead. Slowly the demon turned its gaze to the one who was trying to attack it, snarling silently. Callum watched as the metal crumbled as its grip tightened, leaving little more than the hilt intact. Azure hesitated before being struck in the chest by its claw, breastplate shattering and blood splattering on the creature's robes.

"Azure!" Callum cried out as the knight crumpled to the ground, motionless and bleeding. His heart sank; what chance did they stand against such might? Saresan moved back to stand by Callum, knowing that he'd achieve even less with his weapon. Jinar had begun moving as well, a small orb of flame ready in his hand to fling at a moment's notice. What good it would do remained to be seen. The demon ignored the fallen knight, instead looking to its bloodied claws with disdain.

"Thank you, Xiez, he was getting tiresome," Alun told his associate. So, it had a name and an odd one at that.

"You were to kill him," snapped the demon, looking up to Callum once more.

"And he will die. I simply—"

"Leave," ordered Xiez bluntly. The high seer didn't object, stepping back and nodding to his acolytes. Without a word they vanished into nothingness, Alun passing Callum one final smile before disappearing. Only the robed demon remained.

"You are the master that Alun works for," Jinar spoke carefully, keeping the orb alight in his hands. "The one who intends to raze the kingdom."

"Your kingdom is ash," Xiez declared bluntly, briefly glancing at the sorcerer. Alexis looked back to Johnathan's body: anger tempered with despair kept her from being rash.

"Perhaps here, but the people will rebuild."

"There will be no people." It spoke coldly but always with a subtle vein of anger, looking once more to Callum. "Your king is dead." Callum was speechless.

"His armies—" Saresan began.

"Dead." It left only one question that no one dared ask; why were they still alive?

"They cannot all be dead, demon. The kingdom is vast, and you are few," Jinar countered.

"It matters not to you."

Callum knew exactly what that meant and readied his magic to defend himself desperately. Before he could begin to muster his internal energies, a huge fireball was blasted at them, larger than any Callum had seen. Disorientated from the magic burst and terrified of his imminent death but barely able to react to either, he tried to erect a barrier to shield himself, but it was quickly overwhelmed by the sheer power of Xiez's spell. When it detonated in the middle of them, he felt a moment of searing agony as the flames consumed him, knocking him unconscious.

Callum was surprised to begin sensing things at all, more so without his whole body alight. Instead, there was a comfortable warmth that flowed through him, soothing his being. It certainly wasn't his own magic, but he had no time to consider who had saved him or how.

Quickly grabbing his sword without thinking, Callum opened his eyes to see the others being on the ground but starting to stir, apparently unharmed. Their skin was bathed in a soft green glow that blanketed a large area, similar to that which Jinar used to heal Alexis. There was also a white aura that was fading away, its purpose unknown.

His eyes shifted quickly to where Xiez had been; he saw that the robed demon hadn't moved from where it stood, their plight far from over. Its eyes weren't on him, which made him follow the gaze until it settled on another demon that was standing mere feet from them.

The other monsters he'd fought had been all but indistinguishable from one another, but this one had subtle differences that set it apart like Xiez; it was very slightly shorter and a lighter shade of red than the robed demon, and its regalia were a straight wooden staff and a plain brown cloak that flowed down to its waist.

The newcomer was staring back at Xiez, expression without snarls or anger. It had to be one of Xiez's associates, there to help make them even more doomed than they already were. They couldn't win as it was, another would merely seal their fate. The others were as surprised as he'd been at still being alive and unharmed, Saresan patting himself to check. Jinar was more curious at the green glow, quickly noticing the demon among them. Alexis had got to her knee, looking to the energy and turning to her brother, hoping a miracle had happened. Motionless he and Azure remained, drawing another tear that ran down her cheek. Xiez narrowed its eyes at the new demon.

"You would *help* them?" Xiez sneered.

Callum was even more surprised than he'd been minutes before. The demons were all on the same side, to destroy the kingdom, and yet an enemy of their enemy was before him. The staff-holding demon said nothing and didn't react when Saresan readied his halberd, the guard stopped only by Jinar holding his hand up.

A build-up of magic within Xiez was cut short by a faster one from the other demon that seemed far weaker. In an instant, Xiez was enveloped by a purple-blue mist that held the demon in place, as if the cloud was apart from time itself. The staff-holding demon turned to Callum finally, burning eyes looking at him rather than through.

"Approach." It had the same type of gravelly voice of Xiez but a little softer, missing some of the edges but no less friendly. Callum was wary, puzzled and worried all at once; he had no reason to trust this demon over any other. Alexis held her daggers tightly when she rose to her feet, eyeing the one that spoke with suspicion but knowing better than to strike at one more powerful. "The spell will not hold."

"Who are you? Why are you helping us?" Callum asked quickly.

"*Are* you helping us?" Saresan definitely didn't trust it. Jinar was deep in thought, considering their options perhaps.

"Irrelevant," it answered coldly. "I cannot teleport you away if you do not approach." Xiez shifted a tiny bit within the mist, already struggling against its confines with all its anger and strength. Callum was full of questions that he doubted would get answered.

"Where could you teleport us that would be safe from these things, from you?" Saresan was ignored by the demon who stared only at Callum. Why did these things like looking at him? It made him more uncomfortable than he already was, surrounded by death and destruction. Jinar looked up from his pondering.

"I believe we should go with it," Jinar declared. Callum was as surprised as the others.

"We can't trust that thing, look what they've done!" Saresan argued.

"I did not say we should trust it, merely that we take its offer. A high probability of death is more favourable than a guarantee." Xiez shifted more within its cloudy prison. "That, and we do not have the liberty of time to debate this further."

"But the kingdom! We can still save people!" Callum took a step closer to the demon. "If you say you're here to help us, you can stay and—"

"No," the demon snapped with finality, straining from the spell it maintained. That angered Callum more than he thought it would. The last thing he wanted to do was abandon this place to its grim fate, to ruin and emptiness. He remembered Johnathan's accusing glare, Xiez's prophecy. The people who'd died didn't know this, they'd had only moments of horror and pain before all ended without knowing why.

"I won't leave them!" he protested, readying his sword.

"You will."

"Or what? You'll drag me with you? I know how to use this!" The demon snarled quietly as the struggle against Xiez worsened, the robed demon nearly freeing itself before the mists could be fortified.

"Xiez will kill you. This cannot happen. Come." The words were forceful, falling just short of a direct order as it struggled to keep their foe at bay.

Callum was about to shout in anger when Saresan did so, but in surprise.

"Oh gods, it's Azure!"

The knight that Callum thought had died was struggling to his feet once more, gripping the remnant of his blade and wearing what remained of his armour and pride. The restorative magic the demon had used must've staved off death for him just in time, performing a miracle that Azure himself could not believe.

"Over here, quickly!"

But the knight did not move, remaining right in front of the entrapping mist as he looked around with a dazed expression that washed away into solemness. Jinar had moved to stand beside the demon cautiously, planning for betrayal but seizing the chance of hope it provided. Alexis stared at the body of her brother with tears in her eyes, wanting to go to him one last time.

"The body is but a vessel of the soul, Alexis. He is in a better place now." Jinar's words gave little comfort to Alexis, who hesitated once more before finally turning away and moving to the demon. Even Saresan had pushed aside his grievances with it, leaving only Callum and Azure not within arm's reach of the monster. Still Callum was wary, but Xiez was slowly besting the mist, beginning to shift within it.

"...All my training... for nothing," Azure muttered to himself. Each step Callum took to the demon was gut-wrenching, but the only other choice was folly. He didn't want to admit that, but he knew it.

"I must remove the mist to teleport us. At that moment Xiez will strike," the demon warned.

"Then we will be ready," Jinar answered.

"Irrelevant," came the chilling reply. Azure looked back to them after those words, to Callum. No longer was there hatred in his eyes, nor was there certainty. In their place was fear tempered with determination.

"...Then I shall hold the beast off for you," Azure declared, "until you escape." No one had expected his words, least of all Saresan.

"Don't be a fool, it'll kill you!" The guard shouted. But the knight shook his head slowly, stepping to within reach of the mist. He stared at Callum.

"A knight protects those who cannot defend themselves." He flashed a fragile smile of false courage as Xiez was almost free. Grief washed over Callum for the walking dead before him, hoping that he'd see sense and abandon the plan set in stone. "Know this, should we not meet again. I was... wrong about you all, but especially you, Callum. You... you would have made a fine knight, had I the wisdom to have seen it then."

With a nod, the knight turned and readied the stump of his sword, bending down slowly to recover his shield. The others meanwhile placed their hands upon each other's shoulders, ready for the demon's teleportation.

"Azure!" Callum implored desperately. "Don't do this!" He got a smile back, the warrior's eyes sparkling with inner strength.

"It is the only proper thing to do. It was an honour knowing you."

In an instant, the mist died and Xiez was free once more, the exact moment Azure struck with his broken blade. The demon was distracted by the ineffective strike for that one fraction of time, enough for Callum to feel the demon next to them grabbing his wrist tightly and the tugging magic of teleportation immediately afterwards. Before everything faded to white, Callum saw Azure's sword hilt succeed in piercing ever so shallowly through Xiez's scales. Then a foot wide hole was blasted through Azure's chest, the beam aimed at them. It was too late to reach them.

Then silence.

Chapter Nineteen

"When one chapter closes, another opens."

—*Proverb of the natives of Vedallan IV*

Callum wanted to cry. Only confusion and hurt kept tears at bay for that instant, clashing with one another in his head. He was alone in a room unlike anything he'd ever seen, with no apparent way out. All around him was metal save for where the light that somehow filled the entire room penetrated the ceiling.

Worse than the greyness all around was the quiet. It let his mind run rampant and remember everything he hadn't fully dwelt on when his life had been on the line just minutes before. He thought on the desolation, the hopelessness and the death, all the death. Lifeless eyes and dismembered corpses he'd gazed upon and been horrified by caught up to him, and he could no longer contain his sadness.

Callum slumped to his knees, tears once denied beginning to flow at last. They were for all of the people who had died because of him, for Johnathan and Azure who had died because of him. There was so much he didn't understand and would now never know; they were all gone. Terrance stuck in his mind, his old friend now just another body littering the village he'd called home. He wouldn't have even discovered why, what had caused the great calamity that had claimed his and everyone's lives.

And even with his apparent survival, where was he now? Where were the others? Was he now in a cell, trapped by the demon who'd supposedly rescued them? In those seconds that felt like an eternity of damnation, he cried, racked with grief. And it had all begun with the sword, the one thing he still had.

Everything had gone wrong when he found it, one disaster after another that ushered him to the dark and unforgiving place he found himself trapped in, and it has all been his fault. Even with his overwhelming sadness and lingering anger, throwing the weapon away seemed so pointless; it would still be there on the other side of the room, taunting him with its existence. It wasn't worth all those lives, but had it even been the cause of that? Had the demons wanted him dead before, had they even known of him before the blade? He wouldn't know either way.

He didn't notice the wall opening and sealing shut, but he did spot the shadows of the ones who'd entered. Despite his misery, he looked up, hand half-heartedly reaching for the weapon which ruined everything, to see that the two who'd entered were dressed so very oddly. The first looked about his age, with brown hair cut very short indeed, looking to him with dark brown eyes. His blue trousers and shirt were made of a smooth material that certainly looked like silk and yet... wasn't; it had none of the creases and looked far too fine to be anything a commoner could afford.

His shoes were polished and black, again made like no boot he knew. A thin armour plate adorned his chest, black and held by straps going around his waist and shoulders. On his back was an unusual metal object secured by some kind of scabbard, perhaps a club. Fresh-faced and roughly Callum's height, he had a confidence and commanding presence about him.

The other man was older and a little shorter than the first, wearing a face of weariness and fatigue. Black bags resided under his brown eyes, along with stubble that had been left to grow a little too much. His hair was unkempt and black, with twinges of grey poking through which betrayed his age, Callum putting him at about forty years old. His shirt was similar to the first man's but was white and riddled with creases and the odd black stain, the top button of three undone. His grey trousers were little better, with scuffed brown shoes finishing the image of a man who worked hard. Callum spied numerous worrying-looking items hanging from the person's belt, each of them strange and unknown to him. His mind immediately flitted to the Silent Hand and their love of inflicting pain, but one thing threw all that out of the window. In the man's hand was a plain white cup with a handle, its content letting off steam gently.

He wasn't sure what to make of the pair, but his instincts kicked in further, warning him not to trust strangers who were working in league with the demon that 'saved' them. He got to his feet shakily and finally drew the sword, not prepared to go down without a fight. The younger one noticed the weapon and flinched in shock, hands reflexively going for the device on his back. The older one held his hand up even quicker to stop him, turning his head to the man.

"Careful, we don't want to antagonise him." The man's accent was alien to Callum, and for a moment, he couldn't comprehend the words spoken to him. Then all at once they became clear as any other, though the man's tone lacked any local twist. It was sterile to his ears while also perfectly understandable, which brought up yet more questions he needed answering. Neither of them reached for a weapon, afraid of his.

"We don't mean you any harm," the younger one spoke carefully, his hand not moving away from what he'd been reaching for.

"Who are you?" Callum asked loudly through the tears he was failing to contain. "Servants of Xiez?" The pair looked at one another, the older one shrugging lightly.

"You need to calm down," the same man answered as he turned back, stepping closer. Callum stepped back in kind until his back was against the wall. "This is going to be difficult to explain—"

"You didn't answer my question. Who do you work for?" Callum's magic began to well up once more, fuelled by his emotions running wild and the fear which was building in his stomach.

"You are among friends." He had no reason to believe that, even if the younger man seemed sincere if a little on edge.

"I'll go get the sedatives just in case," said the older one, turning to the door, words Callum latched onto quickly.

"Who are these 'Sedatives'?" Callum quickly spoke. "Are they your masters?" The younger one glared at his counterpart.

"Simon!" he hissed quietly. "You're not helping."

"I'm never helping according to you lot, that's why you're all healthy and this thing hasn't fallen to bits yet." With that, the weary man left through the door that opened and closed as if by magic. He felt no such energies, however, making him question even more about his mysterious captors. Callum was considering his options frantically; perhaps he could overpower the club-wielding one now he was alone, find where the others were being held and escape. But where would they go, what would they do? If the kingdom was in ruins, who else could they turn to? The robber barons would be no safe haven, but perhaps they'd banded together against the monsters, put up some kind of resistance. The young man in front of him sighed before turning back to Callum.

"I think we got off to a bad start, let me try again," the man said to him. "My name is Daniel Cook. You are Callum Iangnes, correct?"

"Who told you that?" Callum watched him warily, waiting for the inevitable betrayal.

"Look, I don't know what happened down there, but you're safe here. They can't get you now, it'll make sure of it."

"It?" Callum took a deep breath, trying to calm down so he could focus better on what was happening while also being ready for anything.

"That... thing," Daniel gave his answer carefully. "It knew all of your names and where to find you, which I'm still amazed at, considering. It still gives me the shivers, even after all this time."

"Why would it want to save me and my friends?"

"It never told me its reasons and I didn't ask, about what the thing was or anything else. It paid in bars of solid gold, enough that you don't say no even if the job's being offered by a huge scaly alien from who-knows-where, even if it swears to kill you if you reveal its existence. What's important is that you're safe and in good health, remarkably good considering where you came from." The room had no windows, making Callum wonder if they were in another complex deep underground.

"Where are the others? And where are we?" Callum asked, still holding his sword firmly.

"They're safe, don't worry. As for where we are, I don't think you're quite ready for that one just yet."

They had to be underground, where else would be safe from the rampaging demons than deep within the bowels of the earth? Simon returned with a pair of clear cylinders with a plunger on one end and a tiny needle on the other. One of them contained two liquids that refused to mix together, purple and bright green. The other appeared to have only water in it. "Now, Callum, we need to give you some injections. They'll only hurt for a moment."

"A what?" Callum didn't like the sound of that at all. "If it's what's in those things, I'm not interested."

"It's for your own good."

"Do you expect me to believe that? I've only got your word on anything that's been said, you could be lying!" Callum couldn't move any further away, glaring at Daniel with suspicion. "Where am I, Daniel? Is this a prison where you keep the captives of Xiez?" Daniel shook his head.

"Just give him the injections, Simon," he muttered. Simon took one look at the blade, then stepped back to the door. "Where are you going?"

"He's not going to let me or anyone else near, and I don't blame him. If you can calm him down, then I'll administer them, until then I'm going to get another coffee." The door opened for him once more.

"Simon!" The man ignored Daniel and left. "He's insufferable."

"Are you going to tell me where I am or not?" Callum asked once again, losing his patience with the man. Daniel looked his way, clearly annoyed.

"We'll be back later, when you've calmed down." Daniel stepped through the door and Callum took his chance, rushing over to try and get out himself. It closed before he could see anything that was beyond, sealing him in the room once more. Angry and more confused than ever, he hammered his fist on the metal to no avail.

"Where am I?!"

He got no reply, silence returning. He didn't trust them: they were up to something terrible, and those 'injections' were a part of it. He had to get out of there, but he didn't know how to teleport or where to teleport to, he had no point of reference for where he was. Then he realised that in his hand was perhaps the best way to break free that any of them had, his sword. Perhaps it could cut through the metal walls with some effort, but cutting open the door was a bad idea; there'd be a guard detail waiting for him to try and escape, he'd have the element of surprise if he cut through a different wall. Turning to the opposite wall, Callum took a few angry steps and readied a swing.

"No."

The voice was of the demon that saved them, and it had come from the doorway. Startled, Callum stopped before the blade hit the wall and whirled around on the spot.

Sure enough, the staff-wielding demon was in the room, and he hadn't felt it arrive despite its apparent strength. Maybe there wasn't much difference in their power, the demon simply better versed in how to use its arcane energies. The confrontation he expected didn't happen, however, the demon simply staring at him. The look made him deeply uncomfortable, and he readied for a fight regardless, but still nothing happened. What was it waiting for? Finally, he spoke through his slowly abating tears.

"...Why not?"

"You would die," it answered flatly, the gravelly voice growing less alien the more he heard it.

"Are you threatening me, demon?" asked Callum. "I've killed your kind before."

"Beyond is death faster than any demon." This one was confusing, nothing like the other one that had spoken harsh words and condemned him and all he knew to destruction.

"You'll kill me anyway when Xiez tells you to." It didn't blink. Callum had only just noticed that their eyes stared unendingly, and it was strange.

"No," it repeated, tone unchanged.

"I don't trust Daniel and I don't trust you, even if you pretended to save us. Your kind kills everything they see, why should I think you won't?"

"Irrelevant." Callum took a moment to fully comprehend its answer.

"...What?"

"If you trust me is irrelevant. If I wanted you dead, you would be. I do not." Callum had been disarmed by its bluntness, finding nothing to object to.

"...Who *are* you?" he finally asked, hoping to glean some weakness from its answer.

"Tyrus," the demon responded simply. The name told him nothing, but at least the demon was answering his questions, more than Daniel and Simon ever did. If any of the answers were truthful was another matter.

"And you *claim* you're not in league with Xiez and the other demons." He was still doubtful, wary.

"Correct."

"Why did you save me and my friends?" It was the question burning brightest in his mind, Callum carefully watching the demon's being for the slightest hint of falsehood, even though its face was unreadable. "You could've saved anyone else. The king, his advisors, important people—"

"Irrelevant," it repeated.

"Why?"

"They were not important. You are." Its answer was direct, posture still neutral as it confirmed Callum's deepest fears; everyone in the kingdom was dead, all of them. Callum's anger welled up despite his grief and burst forth in his response.

"Why does everybody think that? I'm not important, I'm just... me! Is it not the sword you want? Alun certainly wanted it: he was ready to kill me for it!" He was half tempted to offer the blade up but thought better of disarming himself. "Enough people have died for me!"

"Many more will." The very thought horrified him. "Unless you stop him."

"Alun? Is he going to go after other kingdoms?" Callum was still used to the demons being aggressive and angry, which made working out Tyrus's motives much more difficult. He still didn't trust it, but Tyrus hadn't let so much as a twitch slip from its stoic face.

"To dwell on the past is futile," Tyrus stated. "You cannot undo what has been done."

"But it was my fault, all of it! If I hadn't found the sword, those people would still be alive!" Callum protested, frustrated at the sideways answer.

"No."

"Then what, Tyrus? What do you know about all this that I don't? Or are you going to keep hiding things like *they* did?"

He launched his harsh words at the demon who stood in the way of the closed door, as if it alone would fell the creature, but it did not. Tyrus stared at him for a few more seconds, then turned to the way out, the barrier splitting in two down the middle and sliding into the walls on either side.

Beyond was a long, grey corridor of metal on all surfaces, almost entirely featureless and unerringly straight. There was no sign of guards or the horrific implements of torture the Silent Hand would've had in a dungeon, just plain grey, interrupted only by more points in the ceiling where light illuminated the way. The demon stepped out of the room, but this time the door remained open.

"Follow," it ordered.

With his sword ready, Callum emerged out cautiously, still anticipating a trap that wasn't there. He trailed a few paces behind as he watched every door they passed, just in case it opened with an acolyte behind it ready to strike. The silence seemed to seep from the very walls, unnatural even compared to the previous place he'd been trapped within. At least no screams punctured the quiet, he mused grimly.

He wondered if any of the doors led to where his friends were being kept, if they too had only grey walls for comfort. Tyrus stopped by one of the right-hand doors, stepping through when it opened without comment. Callum took a moment to look within, seeing that the metal inside was not the same dull grey but a lighter hue.

A large table dominated a corner, and around it were six chairs, their design alien to him but they seemed sound to sit on. Against the left wall were metal devices that served no purpose he knew, along with equally metal cupboards built into the wall above the odd things. Again, there were the strange holes in the ceiling, only two needed to keep the room bright.

"Window," Tyrus announced to the emptiness.

Instantly, the wall opposite them faded into nothingness, revealing the night sky. It was cloudless and the stars were clearer than they'd ever been, but Callum couldn't recognise any of the shapes he normally could – the constellations were all wrong – and only then did he work out that he wasn't looking up.

"Are we walking on the walls?" He stepped into the room and approached where the wall had been, outstretching his hand. Callum was surprised when cold metal obstructed his reach, stepping back and marvelling at the powerful magic which made a wall invisible. "I have never seen this part of the sky before, are we on another continent? I heard tales of a land to the south very unlike our own."

"This is not the sky." Tyrus's reply made him look harder. Surely there was one constellation he'd find, hidden away where it wasn't meant to be.

"Of course it is, those are stars. You only see them by looking up at night."

"We are among the stars."

The statement was so absurd that it made Callum laugh. It just wasn't possible: no mountain was high enough to reach the stars. It had to be a lie, to distract from his imprisonment at the hands of the acolytes.

Yet Tyrus had opened the door for him when the others hadn't, answering his questions even if it held something back. He scoured the demon's face again for falsehood and saw nothing, it watching him without a word as he went back to frantically searching the canopy of stars before him for something, anything he knew. Then he saw something that didn't look like a star, a coloured dot that he pointed to.

"Magnify and focus." The demon's words made the view change instantly, the dot now large and clear. It was a sphere suspended in the heavens, of greens, purples and reds that swirled and shifted, as if in bitter conflict with one another. It was nothing like the moon he knew, grey and unchanging.

"What... is this?" Callum asked, amazed by its strange beauty.

"A world." Tyrus wasn't looking at the orb, only to Callum. "Not your own. You are no longer on your homeworld." The reply sank deep into Callum's skin as he tried to grapple with what this meant, how it fitted into everything he knew. He had always thought their world was unique, a place watched over by the gods, but there before him was another world, or so Tyrus wanted him to believe. He couldn't believe it, could he? It was all false, all of it and yet...

"...How many of these are there?" he barely asked the demon.

"Billions." Callum had no idea what that meant, and the demon noticed. "More than you can imagine."

He tried to, but the very idea was mind-boggling. If anyone lived on that world, they would look up and see different stars, breathe different air. Did the people down there even know of his world, his people? It made perfect sense and yet no sense all at once.

"But we cannot sail the stars," he was grasping desperately for a counterargument. "Even if there are other worlds, no people could live on them as we would never make it to them. How can you navigate a sea without current or landmarks?"

"Your world is not the origin of humanity. Your species germinated on a planet far from here, then spread to other worlds. They have been doing so for many thousands of years."

Callum slowly stepped from the view, finding a chair before his legs gave on him. It was surprisingly comfortable considering its strange design, but his mind wasn't on that. He shook his head, trying to fathom and deny what the demon told him. It couldn't have been true, it just couldn't.

"No, this is a trick," Callum replied quickly, "to catch me off guard, sway me to your cause—"

"You are one human out of many trillions. Your world is one of over a hundred billion planets—"

"No! That's not true!" His shout was ignored, Callum not understanding the size of the numbers but able to picture how vast they were and how tiny he was within them.

"A hundred billion planets orbiting hundreds of billions of stars in one galaxy. This galaxy is one of hundreds of billions of galaxies."

"You're lying—"

"You and your world lived in ignorance of the truth. In time, your people might have rediscovered what their ancestors lost, relearned the language of the wider galaxy that I had to impart to you via magic, but no more."

"You taught me their language with magic? If you can do that, why didn't you tell me *this* too?"

"Irrelevant. Your world is dead, Callum. Every human that lived on that world is dead. They killed them all." Tyrus looked to the window, to the world that mocked Callum. "*That* is what I knew that you did not. Now you know."

Callum wished he could remove the words that swam around his head forever, but they'd taken hold. He was thinking about the vast numbers of people Tyrus had talked of: crowds unfathomable and him deep in the middle, lost among the masses. He was nothing to them, nor was his world. All that he'd struggled and strived for was meaningless, all that had died did so for nothing. How many people were exactly like him, how many kingdoms had fallen in that day, only for twice as many to rise on faraway worlds so strange and magnificent that they defied explanation?

He slumped in the chair, shaking his head over and over as he tried and failed again and again to defeat what Tyrus had told him, the truths that it so bluntly decreed. A voice came from the room's entrance, startled.

"What are you doing?" Daniel wasn't pleased at all. "Do you want to drive him mad?!"

"You wanted him to understand. Now he does."

The demon didn't care for Daniel's reply, not turning to address the man. Callum didn't turn either, now looking at the stars blankly; how many people looked at them and thought their world was the only one? Had it been just those from his world, ignored by everyone else as they went about their lives?

Why hadn't the other worlds come to help when their kingdom was under attack? At least now he knew it was a metal ship that he was in, below deck as the boat sailed the black sea of the stars. It was the one thing he could work out, but it was a drop of fact in a still sea of unknowns that he'd been thrown into to drown.

"These things take time to do right, he needed to be ushered into it slowly. You're playing a dangerous game with his mind!" Daniel was clearly concerned, walking over to stand by Callum with his hand on the table.

"He will understand." Tyrus finally turned to Daniel and the man averted his eyes for a second.

"If there's anything left of him by then!"

"I will tell the others now. You will not need to confine them anymore," declared the demon. It got a glare from Daniel.

"Do you think they'll fare any better with it than he did? I won't let you smash their minds too!" Tyrus stared at him, then walked past without a word, not expecting him to actually do anything about it. Only once the demon had left did Daniel give chase, braver now that its burning eyes weren't fixed on him. He nearly crashed into Simon, who held the 'injections' in one hand and the same white cup in the other, the older man frowning at the spectacle, then shrugging as he entered the room.

Spotting Callum sat at the table, Simon pulled up a chair to sit beside him, placing the cup down. The liquid within was dark and had a strong smell, but Callum just stared at the view, trying to figure it all out and failing. For a second, no one said anything.

"It's called 'space'." Simon put the needled devices down by his cup, then took a hearty sip. Callum said nothing, he had no words that would mean anything to him anyway. "I've seen that look before, Callum. I can guess what that thing did."

"...I was told that the stars were gods, watching down and protecting us from harm," Callum spoke softly, full of emptiness. "They aren't gods, are they?"

"Sorry, but no. They're orbs that radiate heat and light, the reason most worlds can sustain life at all," Simon answered simply, putting down his cup carefully. "I can't say anything that will make it easier for you to understand, except that that thing wasn't lying. It doesn't make what you were doing on your world any less important, though." Callum's mind had drifted to Johnathan, and suddenly things clicked into place, making him feel even worse about everything.

"...He tried to warn us, but we didn't listen," Callum murmured to himself.

"Who?" asked Simon.

"Johnathan. He told us our world was going to end, that he'd seen the truth, but we refused to heed him. Did Alun show him what I saw, told him what Tyrus told me?" He didn't know, but the guilt only grew larger. Simon said nothing to begin with, considering his reply.

"He was Alexis's brother, yes?" Simon got a weak nod. "I don't know what circumstances led you to here, but we aren't in league with whoever is against you. If what the creature that hired us says about your world is true, and I hope it isn't, any enemy you had is dead now." The man paused, looking at the stars once more. "You seem to have experience with those creatures. Do you know what they are, aside from the first intelligent alien life forms encountered in the galaxy aside from humanity?"

"They're demons," Callum said quietly, head in his hands as he tried to make sense of everything once more. Simon didn't react to his answer, picking up his cup and needled devices, taking a sip as he stood.

"Do you want me to leave you alone?" Callum gave him no reply. "If there's anything you need to know, don't hesitate to ask for me. I'll help all of you in any way I can."

Simon left him to his sadness and solitude, dangerous things to be alone with. Callum looked up slowly. The view was different now, of stars even more strange than the ones before. Even if Simon had spent all day answering his questions, none of them would've filled the endless hole of knowledge ripped in his being by the fact that there was far more beyond Callum's world than he'd ever imagined.

He wanted to go back and tell people the truth, but they wouldn't have believed him; perhaps others had in the past, condemned as mad or worse by a society that wasn't ready for those facts. But there was no one left alive to tell, except those that already knew.

Chapter Twenty

By the time someone else entered the room, he'd been mulling over everything for what felt like an eternity. He'd thought on his friends, his world, everything from finding the sword to the death of Azure and all in between. Words he didn't understand swam within those memories: tiny ripples lost in waves of thought.

Only when the door opened and shut did Callum turn to see if it was someone he knew. A young woman with blue eyes stood in the doorway, a little shorter than him. Everything else about her was strange, starting at her short black hair, straight and neatly cut at chin length. Some of it was hidden under a brown hat that had a wide disc-shaped brim.

She wore a sleeveless white shirt of that same odd material he'd seen before, the top button undone. There were also folds around the neck which made a collar of sorts, its purpose unknown. Her brown gloves didn't cover her fingers, a huge oversight that made them pointless. The black boots she wore looked sturdy, however, the only sensible part of her attire as even her black trousers loosened the further they fell past her knee.

Hanging from a plain brown belt were two leather scabbards that held oddly shaped and unfamiliar devices. He guessed they were weapons, but what type he didn't know. Everyone he'd met so far was perhaps entirely unremarkable, but Callum had seen so little of the 'true world' he'd been dragged into that she caught his curiosity. She was looking to one of the metal units with a mischievous smile, then noticed Callum.

"Is that taken?" She was pointing to something on the metal device, a tin. Callum hadn't even noticed it. Chirpy and upbeat, her accent was as odd as everyone else's to him, but likely not to Daniel and Simon. Something about her voice pulled him from his gloom just a little, distracting him from bleak thoughts.

"...No?" he answered, the woman grinning in satisfaction as she walked over to claim her prize.

"Excellent." She pulled the lid off using a ring connected to it, sitting beside him without a moment's thought. She didn't think to offer him any of the green thing or the yellow crunchy bread within. It certainly didn't look appetising. "Name's Siobhan. Pleasure to meet you."

"I suppose I need to get used to hearing strange names," he replied. She smiled at him and shrugged.

"Probably. So, what do they call you?"

"Callum Igannes."

"Can't say I've heard of an Igannes before." Siobhan took a mouthful of the green and looked out to the view of the stars. She leaned back in the chair and put her feet on the table, crossed at the ankle. "Beautiful, ain't it?"

"I'm not sure that's the word I'd use right now," he replied, trying not to stare at that which had almost broken his mind before. Siobhan put the tin down, clasping her hands behind her head as she relaxed.

"Even now we don't quite totally know what's out there, in the last frontier. People get too used to it, the infinite black. I've flown it for a couple of years now, and it's never stopped being amazing. I'm a fighter pilot, you see." She noticed his blank expression at the term. "I have a ship like this, just smaller. It's my job to bail them out when they bite off more than they can chew, which I'm glad to say isn't often."

"You're... a guard then?" Callum asked.

"I prefer the term 'freelance fighter ace' personally, but I guess it fits." She glanced at his attire and then noticed the sword hanging from his belt. "Can I see it?"

"The sword?" His posture shifted to a guarded one. She noticed immediately.

"I've seen plenty of swords, but not an authentic one made by a real blacksmith." Siobhan shrugged once more, clearly at ease. "But hey, it's your sword."

Callum looked again at the weapon, reflecting on how protective he was of the very thing that had caused all his misery.

"...No, I'm sorry. People have tried to kill me for it, so when I get asked that, I get a little on edge."

"That's a good one," she remarked. Callum frowned. "...Get it? On edge? Sword? Never mind. I'm sorry, Simon told me you guys had had it rough. If you want me to go—"

"Honestly, I could do with the company right now. It's taking my mind off... everything." Callum drew the sword carefully and placed it on the table as Siobhan moved her feet off. Her eyes scanned it appraisingly as he warned, "The edge is wickedly sharp."

"It's... not what I thought it would look like. Not as shiny."

"It's how I found it: the sword won't take a shine. I don't know for sure, but I'm starting to think it may be magical."

Callum watched her as he spoke of magic, wanting to see what she thought of it. Perhaps it didn't exist beyond his world, but she wasn't startled by the mention of it.

"If you'd asked me a month ago, I'd've said I'd never seen magic either, but when a red scaly whatchamacallit vanishes right in front of you, you take notice."

"Is magic not common? I would have thought with all those worlds out there, there'd be large communities of sorcerers." Siobhan shook her head.

"If there are, they're damn good at keeping themselves hidden," she answered him, not touching the weapon and instead reaching for her tin of green and bread that she resumed eating. "Speaking of being hidden, you're going to want to get chipped so Z-Gen don't think *you're* hiding something. Simon's probably got that covered, though."

"Z-Gen?"

"I'm not even going to try and explain them to you yet, not while you're grappling with the basics. If I'd ever seen magic before, I didn't notice it, but technology's so invisible these days it might as well be magic sometimes. Once I met a guy who'd replaced the tip of one of his fingers with a laser pistol, barely noticed it before he tried to blast my face off. Good thing he was a lousy shot." Callum stared blankly at her, wondering what any of that meant. She noticed and chuckled, "Sorry, that's one of my better stories. It's also one of my only stories."

"So, magic... doesn't concern you?" Callum checked, surprised.

"I judge people when I see them, and you seem alright. A fish out of water, but you'll get the hang of it all eventually. Don't expect that reaction from everyone you meet, though."

Siobhan stood and walked over to the metal devices in the corner.

"You want something to eat?" she asked then. Callum's hunger hadn't been given a moment to voice itself, answering loudly when he thought about it.

"Did you prepare some food earlier today?" Callum asked, knowing there wasn't meat on a spit or a place to smoke fish. Siobhan opened a cupboard and considered her options, all of them tins like the one she'd picked clean and several metal bottles.

"You a vegetarian?" came her question.

"I don't mind vegetables if that's what you're asking."

Siobhan moved to her tiptoes and reached for a silvery bag that he hadn't seen before, then grabbed a plate and eating utensils that were as metal as everything else. She ripped open the bag, and Callum was surprised to see that the contents which poured onto the plate were hot.

Callum recognised the small potatoes and a kind of meat, but the rest of it was a mystery. Siobhan presented the meal to him, and Callum saw that there were some small beans mixed into the red sauce which had smothered the whole thing, making it look rather unappealing. He awkwardly took the eating utensils and cut himself some meat carefully, more used to eating with his fingers. It was warm enough, and the bland sauce murdered what flavour the meat had, but it was far beyond his normal fare in quality. She was watching him, curious about his reaction.

"Well?"

"It's... not bad at all. Did you cook this?" She laughed, opening a colourful cylindrical can at the top and drinking from it as she sat back down. There was writing on it, but Callum couldn't read it.

"I can't cook for crap, never took the time to learn. Not that you really need to, with almost any meal imaginable ready-made and packaged for your convenience."

"And you say you haven't seen magic," Callum remarked, taking another mouthful of the food now that his hunger had reawakened. The thoughts that had made him despair were muted now, distracted as he was, but they lingered in his head.

"It's just normal for me, but I see your point." Siobhan drank more from the can. "Simon told me about the others, what are they like? You're the first one I've talked to."

"The man in the robes is Jinar, he's my teacher of magic. Saresan's the older one, a guard by trade and handy with his halberd."

"And the woman with you?" she asked.

"I met Alexis by chance on the road to where Jinar was. She's stuck with me ever since."

"I see," Siobhan nodded, then a playful smile crept onto her lips. "So?"

"So?" Callum blinked.

"Are things okay between you two?"

"I don't know, we had to kill her brother." His tone was full of the regret and pain he'd barely stopped thinking on. Siobhan winced at his reply.

"Ooh, that sucks." She used such odd phrases, Callum relying on her reactions as well as the words to see what she meant. "That'd certainly put things on the rocks."

"I don't understand," he replied honestly.

"Turn of phrase, you'll get used to it all." Callum wasn't so sure that he would. "I was just asking—" Siobhan then stopped mid-sentence.

"Asking what?" he repeated.

"It doesn't matter, don't worry about it." She leaned back in her chair, taking another drink from the can. "Help yourself to some water from the tap or a can if you like, whatever you can find, really. I'll show you your room once you've finished up there. It's not much, the best we could get together on such short notice."

"Do you intend to have us stay for long?" Callum looked at the stars through the window that had once again changed, not able to see any worlds this time. "Then again, I don't know of anywhere to go anymore, so here is as good a home as I have."

"I don't know what's on the cards for you lot. The thing talked to Daniel about it when they were negotiating, but I don't think much negotiating happened. He saw a big payoff and didn't ask enough questions. To his credit, it's paid off so far, and as long as my wages keep coming, I'm happy." Siobhan put the now empty can on the table. "If it were up to me, we'd be landing on the first populated world so you could see everything first-hand."

"But it's not up to you, yes?" he asked, getting a nod.

"He owns the ship, so he gets the final say. Well, him and Monica, even though I've been here far longer than she has, but that's something else entirely." Siobhan didn't go into detail and Callum didn't ask; in time, he'd surely meet Monica and find out why. With so many things he was going to have to learn, Callum was brought back full circle to his musings on how large his world had suddenly gotten. At least now he was beginning to accept that he wasn't alone in it, no matter how many trillions of people there were out there or what a trillion was.

Chapter Twenty-One

"Hello, Universe! Welcome, ladies and gentlemen, one and all, to Ken in the Den at the Ten! I'm Ken, it's ten and we are in fact here in the Den, and my, do we have a show for you today! Not only do we have all the hot news from across the galaxy, but we're lucky enough tonight to have an exclusive preview of the latest entry in the Sword Slasher franchise! Make sure you stay tuned in throughout the whole show to learn all the fantastic details and keep your eye peeled for the seventeen flargls that'll appear on screen. Find them all, and you could win a year's supply of Proto-Paste, the only paste with 110 percent protein!"

—Opening of 'Ken in the Den at the Ten', Series 12 Episode 1,472

It hadn't taken long after finishing his meal for fatigue to catch up to Callum, held back before by terror, horror, grief and guilt. Siobhan led him through the grey corridors to his 'quarters', as she put it, but he didn't remember the route. The only familiar thing in the room he was left in was the bed, and it looked comfortable; even the chair he'd eaten at was softer than the straw he used to rest his head on.

Compared to the wooden shack he'd called home before, this place was a palace of decadence that made him wonder if this was the standard of living everyone enjoyed. A small window gave him a view of space, and he was told that saying 'lights off' and 'lights on' would do exactly that, controlling the illumination in the ceiling. He experimented with this for a minute, fascinated at how the light knew his voice.

He found that the small metal cube in the corner – two foot long, one wide and one high – was intended to store his possessions, of which he had practically none beyond his clothes, the sword and a handful of copper coins.

Attached to the wall and easily visible from the bed was a thin black rectangle, whose purpose was unknown and he didn't care to check. There was a second, smaller room which contained a strange kind of chair and an area behind a glass door which asked him how hot he wanted his 'shower'. Not wanting to experiment with things that might be dangerous and satisfied that the brightness in the ceiling was at his command, Callum let the room be plunged into darkness and tried the bed. The mattress was unlike anything he'd rested on in his whole life, springy and so soft. He wondered what kind of feathers it was stuffed with but decided not to check. The pillow was even softer, and before he knew it, he woke up; it had lulled him into an invigorating and peaceful sleep through luxury alone.

He didn't want to imagine what his dreams had been, thankful that he'd forgotten them upon rousing. What worried him instead was that he had no idea what time it was, outside still being stars and nothingness. Without the sun to dictate their day, how did they monitor the passing of those days? Perhaps for them, there was just awake and asleep, with everyone on their own personal timescale, a bewildering arrangement if there were as many people alive as Tyrus had said. He'd have to ask Simon what a trillion was when he next saw the man.

"Lights on." The room was slowly filled with brightness, and with it rushed back the memories of all that had happened to him, dragging him from his moment of comfort.

He noticed something secured to the wall which caught his eye, getting out of bed and moving to get a closer look. Drawn on a piece of very thin parchment was a selection of diagrams, with arrows dictating a path of events involving the small room with the strange seat. The pictures also pointed to his clothes and a handle on the wall he'd missed before, finding that pulling on it revealed a small hatch. He had little reason to follow the instructions but did so anyway, curious about what would happen. When all his clothes were in the hatch and he shut it, a soft whirring began from within and he went to the next step, entering the area behind the glass.

"How warm would you like your shower?" The voice was devoid of any emotion or accent, stilted as it came from the very ceiling.

"...Comfortable?" A moment after his answer, warm water sprinkled from the ceiling and it didn't stop.

At first, his reflex to find shelter kicked in, but he fought against it, now understanding what the diagrams meant; the room was all about cleanliness, and he was to wash his body with the water and the round block of soap on a tiny shelf. Callum had rarely owned soap but had tried to clean himself every day, yet this was far unlike anything he'd experienced before.

The soap was cleansing, helping him wash away the dirt and grime that he hadn't known was there. Callum examined a small bottle on the shelf, only managing to fathom what it was for when he saw little diagrams on the paper label that showed it being used on his hair. That felt even stranger than the shower itself, but he couldn't deny that the whole experience had left him cleaner than he'd ever felt.

He didn't need instructions to figure out the towel's purpose, having just finished drying himself off as the hatch in the wall opened. He caught his face in a reflective panel and took a moment to examine himself, seeing that he didn't need to shave just yet. He couldn't see the difference from his cleaning session, but he felt it, refreshed as he went to examine what had happened to his clothes.

"Unable to repair item of clothing due to insufficient matching materials. Replacements fashioned based on original items within hatch. We apologise for the inconvenience," the voice informed him. Callum picked up his clothes and immediately felt the different fabric they were made of, softer and stronger. His shoes and underwear had changed, however, replaced with brown boots and thin shorts.

The shorts were odd, but he could imagine himself getting used to them, putting on everything else afterwards. Even though it looked almost identical to his old attire, it was far more comfortable to wear. He was surprised that the boots provided were a great fit.

Listening to his stomach this time, he went to the door out of his room and watched it open without any input from him, stepping through into the grey corridor with the many doors that all looked alike. The corridor ended abruptly to the right, so he went left, checking every door in the hope that one of them would be the room with the food. One by one they refused to open, with no clear indicator as to why.

Eventually one did, and it revealed a room very much like his own save that it was occupied. Sat on the edge of a bed that hadn't been slept in was Alexis, head bowed in silence. Strands of hair had slipped over her face, and it was clear she'd been crying, not looking up to see him. Awkwardness set in quickly; he didn't know what to say, if she even wanted to hear anything he'd tell her. Still, she didn't look up.

"...I'm sorry. I didn't want any of this to happen," was all he could think of.

"But it did." Her voice was quiet and wavering. He turned slowly, feeling worse for apologising and reminding her of it all.

"...I shouldn't have disturbed you. I'll go," he told her. Alexis's eyes looked his way as she thought about something that fought with her.

"I'd rather not be alone right now," she conceded in a whisper.

"Then I'll stay," Callum stepped into the room, hearing the door shut firmly behind him as he walked to the bed and sat beside her, making sure to leave room between them. Still, he didn't know how to begin; nothing he could say would bring Johnathan back to them. Eventually, he swallowed his nerves. "I'm sorry, Alexis. You trusted me and I let you down, dragged you into this mess. It's my fault he's dead."

She lifted her again head and looked at him, tears welling that she blinked away.

"You didn't kill him, Callum. We tried to reason with him, but... he wouldn't listen." The pause was pained.

"And he was right, about everything."

"We didn't die," she corrected.

"Everyone else did," Callum sighed, shaking his head as he remembered the carnage and death. "The demon told me that everyone's gone, Alexis, everyone." He wanted to tell her things would be alright, but how could he when he didn't even know where they were? "I can't promise I can ever make amends—"

"Callum, please," she implored, a shaky breath following. "It's not your fault, none of this is. I know you blame yourself, but don't. I don't think we could've stopped it, nothing could." He didn't feel like his presence was helping, but he didn't leave, looking at her with sadness in his heart. She glanced at the window. "The demon showed me space, told me what it is, cast a spell so I could understand the others. I feel... I feel like a tiny speck of nothing, utterly insignificant."

"That makes two of us, but you're not insignificant."

"How?" Her eyes asked the question as much as her voice. Despite her loss, Alexis was trying to put on a brave face, perhaps for him.

"You're significant to me. You're my friend." Alexis blinked, unsure how to react to his words at first. For a moment, a weak smile crept onto her face, quickly washed away.

"...Thank you."

"It's only the truth," he responded, keeping her gaze. "If we ever meet Alun and his acolytes again, I'll do anything I can to avenge Johnathan and the people of our world." She shook her head in reply.

"You're not a man of vengeance, Callum, it's not in your heart." She was right, it wasn't. The seer couldn't just get away with the death of everyone, of Johnathan. She looked back to the ground once more. "Johnathan did it all to save me, but I would never have gone with him, and in the end, it was one of the monsters we fought that saved us instead."

"I don't know what it wants with us yet, but I'll find out," he promised, his words fuelled by guilt. "And if I can help it, no more worlds—"

"You can't promise that, Callum." At her words, he got the feeling that they weren't alone anymore and turned to the door, startled to see Tyrus standing there.

Only the staff and the cloak stopped him from jumping to his feet and drawing his sword, but he was still tempted, still unsure of its motives. Had it teleported in? How did it know he was there? Tyrus stared at him intently without a word, making him feel uncomfortable. Alexis ignored the demon entirely.

"Follow," it ordered, the door opening as it stepped through. Callum didn't want to leave Alexis alone in her sadness, but the demon didn't look like it was going to ask again.

"Will you be alright?" he asked her before thinking about how stupid the question was.

"No, I don't think I ever will be again. Thank you though, for being here." Callum reluctantly stood and, with one final look to Alexis, stepped out of the room, filled with pain but with a determination to try and make things right. If that was possible was another matter entirely.

"You will be trained," Tyrus abruptly announced once the door to Alexis's room closed.

"What for?" Callum asked. "Were you... listening to our conversation?"

"To defeat the one who leads the demons." Tyrus's declaration was without fanfare, but it hit him hard, mainly from how sudden it was. It was exactly what he'd just promised Alexis, but once again, Tyrus wasn't being clear.

"Xiez?" he asked.

"Keiran." That was a name he hadn't heard before.

"Is Keiran a demon like Xiez?"

"No." That sparked a memory in his mind, casting him back to that fateful night.

"Do you mean the man in the black armour?" Tyrus narrowed its eyes at him, answering his question without words. "I've met him before, when I first found the sword."

"You would be dead."

"Someone came and rescued me, a warrior in gold armour who matched the man blow for blow." Tyrus was watching his face intently, a stare he didn't like. "You don't believe me."

"It is a matter I will inform the Council of once I bring you to them," replied Tyrus.

"The Council? Is that who you work for? Are they a group of good demons?" Callum paused. "Are you even called 'demons'?"

Tyrus was the first demon that was actually willing to answer his questions, and so he seized the opportunity to ask them. He knew the conversation would steer back to Keiran eventually.

"Demon is sufficient," Tyrus remarked off-hand, staring now at his sword. Everyone was so interested in it, even their so-called saviour. "The Council are the oldest and wisest of our group, hiding from our kind to avoid death."

"Most demons I've met are savage monsters, why aren't you or Xiez?"

"They are consumed by their anger. I am not." The demon was answering with just enough information, Callum noted, not giving away any more than it felt necessary. "The servants of Keiran will hunt you down, kill you."

"Why, Tyrus? Why kill so many people just for me? I'm one man with a really sharp sword and a little bit of magic, why are they doing this?" Callum didn't get an answer, which frustrated him. "I seem to be so important to everyone, but no one's told me why; now you want to train me to defeat the leader of these demons, why?"

"Because you must." Tyrus turned its gaze from him, looking to the corridor ahead. Callum was waiting for the rest of the reason, but it didn't come.

"Or else what?"

"You will die."

"What do you know that I don't about myself that makes you think that I can take on the leader of these demons? With years of training, I might take on Alun, but if the man in black armour is Keiran, I saw what he can do. His power was... I cannot match that power."

"You will."

"How?" Callum raised his voice, which succeeded in grabbing Tyrus's stare once more.

"Without me, you will die. It is only my presence that shields you from detection by Keiran's servants." The demon snarled at him, Callum stepping back reflexively. "Your old life is gone. It will not return. If you are not willing, I will take the sword and find another. You would not live past the hour, nor will your associates."

"Are you threatening me?" Callum stepped back.

"Stating fact." They were damning words, but so frankly given that there was no misinterpretation possible; he and his friends were hostages of the demon, but the alternative was far worse if true. "You wish to avenge those who have fallen. I present an opportunity to do so."

His old life was gone, yes, but the one presented before him sounded little better. He had reason to doubt Tyrus's sincerity, of course, but then again, it had stated before that it had had many chances to kill them or to simply let them die. It had not, though, and for whatever reason, it needed him.

Glancing at the sword, Callum considered the 'offer' presented to him. Even though he'd tried to promise Alexis only minutes before to avenge the fallen, he wondered if he would ever be capable of that. Could he be that warrior, fighting and winning against the Silent Hand in this strange place? Could he best Xiez in combat? Or Keiran, for that matter? It would take so long to even begin to get close to their power, and by the sounds of it, they didn't have that long. He wondered where the warrior in gold was in all of this; perhaps he was already out there among the stars, fighting the demons, but surely that man's power was more than enough. Once again he had more questions than answers, but he'd settled on one thing at least.

"*If* you're going to train me, you'd need to talk to Jinar first. He's my current teacher," he finally said.

"Irrelevant."

"You could compare your knowledge at least." Tyrus had begun to walk down the corridor, setting a quick pace. Callum moved to catch up.

"His magic is inferior." They were moving with purpose, which made Callum think about the blank doors. How did the demon know which one led to where?

"How are you so sure?"

"He would have saved you himself."

The demon turned to a door that almost looked familiar and it opened. It was the room he'd eaten in the day before – or was it the night before? – and he saw Jinar looking at the view of the stars while stroking his beard in idle thought.

The sorcerer's robes were without burn marks, likely fixed in the strange hatch that had changed his own. Sat at the table was Simon, sipping more of his warm beverage and looking at something on a rectangular metal plate. Callum wondered if the drink in that cup ever depleted, considering how often he was drinking from it. Simon looked up briefly, not outwardly concerned to see the demon. Jinar, on the other hand, eyed Tyrus with healthy suspicion before smiling at Callum. It was a fragile smile. He'd surely been told all that the others had, of the true order of things. Had Jinar taken it any better than he'd done?

"It is good to see you well, Callum," his mentor greeted.

"You as well," Callum replied warily. Jinar noticed his tone, then eyed the demon once more.

"I will be training Callum, effective immediately," Tyrus declared bluntly to Jinar, not expecting the retort it got.

"Is that so?" Jinar raised an eyebrow as he spoke, smiling in amusement. "He has been showing great progress in the ways of the arcane, thanks to my tutelage. I do not think you can better my teachings." Simon put down the metal plate, attention snatched.

"You're both sorcerers?" Simon was clearly surprised, getting a smile from Jinar. "The demon only mentioned Callum's ability."

"The power of magic flows through my veins, as it does for my pupils, but that waylays from the matter at hand." Jinar met Tyrus's burning eyes, confidence brimming in his voice and posture. "Suffice to say, there are none better at teaching the arcane here than I. If you wish to prove me correct, by all means, explain your credentials."

"Unneeded," Tyrus retorted. Simon was frowning at the exchange, more when Jinar's expression hardened. Callum could feel the tension in the air and moved to dissipate it.

"I'm sure there's a way you could both train me, alternate lessons or something like that," Callum suggested.

"An inefficient use of time," countered Tyrus.

"Do you seek to provoke me, demon?" Jinar moved his hands into gesture-ready positions. "I will not be goaded into open combat so easily, but if you wish, we may engage in a duel of arcane wits."

"No one is engaging anyone in a duel of anything, least of all in the rec-room." Simon hadn't stood but was not impressed with either of them. "If you puncture the hull, we'll all get sucked into space. Save it until we're planetside." He paused. "On second thoughts, don't do that while we're planetside. At least move to the training room or the cargo bay, the walls are thicker there."

"Do you doubt my ability? I assure you: no harm will come to your ship while we duel." Simon didn't appear convinced by Jinar's assurance. "It will only be to first blood."

"Does that thing even bleed?" Simon enquired.

"A kind of black ichor," Callum answered before looking to his mentor.

He was worried, not for the ship but Jinar. The man had to know Tyrus's strength, and yet still he presented the challenge.

"So what say you, demon? First blood?" The demon said nothing, a moment of silence pervading the room. Then Tyrus raised its hand, and from it materialised several orbs of energy that launched themselves at Jinar with speed. Simon looked horrified at the spectacle, a sentiment mirrored by Callum as Jinar rushed to react to the quick volley of spells, hastily muttering and gesturing to conjure a defence.

He launched projectiles of his own that managed to hit three of the seven orbs, negating them into nothingness, but the others continued towards him. Dodging nimbly to the side, Jinar just managed to avoid the magic attacks, which dissipated before they hit the wall, but Tyrus surged forward, closing the distance between the duellists in moments.

Callum watched as Jinar reacted too late to the charge, Tyrus swinging at his chest with its staff. Callum heard the sound of bones snapping as the weapon connected, propelling Jinar back into the wall with some force. It was over before it had even begun.

"Good god!" Simon was up from his chair in an instant, rushing towards Jinar as he crumpled to the ground, face pale and in great pain. Tyrus stepped back to let Simon reach the wounded man and very carefully feel his chest, retracting the hand when Jinar groaned loudly. Callum felt guilty, knowing that Jinar's pain was indirectly because of him.

"You broke his ribs!"

The demon turned to Callum.

"Training will begin once I have convened with the Council," Tyrus informed him.

"He said only to first blood, and *don't* tell me his internal bleeding counts!" Callum was confused by the statement; surely, blood couldn't bleed within you as that was where it was anyway. Simon seemed to know what he was talking about, though, helping Jinar to his feet.

The sorcerer was uncharacteristically quiet, taking the support from Simon and walking with him out of the room, head hung low. Callum wanted to say he was sorry, but the words didn't come out. "I'll get you patched up: the medical room is just down the hall." That told Callum that Simon was a healer of some kind, but he wondered what could be done about broken ribs, barring some strange device that they had on the ship; at that point, Callum was prepared to believe almost anything about these people. Simon passed Tyrus an annoyed stare as he and Jinar left, the demon ignoring it. It didn't ignore Callum as he looked with anger.

"You didn't have to hit him that hard, Tyrus." Callum got a stern look back. "You could've killed him."

"The servants of Keiran will not pull their punches. You were fortunate that your adversaries did not kill you immediately. You will not have that liberty next time."

"You haven't told me what Keiran wants to achieve, Tyrus. He clearly didn't want to rule my world, because his servants have..." Callum paused, trying not to think on his world too much. "Does he want to rule all other worlds, carve a kingdom of his own from the stars?"

"Uncertain. When Keiran's servants strike, they cleanse the worlds they reach of all human life. Your world will not be the last," it responded.

"But surely these people have ways to resist the demons, right?" He got no answer. "That doesn't make any sense. These people have wondrous devices, they can sail the stars! How can you tell me that they can't fight the demons?" Tyrus turned from Callum and headed to the door. "Why won't you answer me?"

"You will train to defeat Keiran. The alternative is death at his hand."

Or the demon's claws, Callum thought grimly, watching as it left. He felt no better about the ultimatum set before him, still full of questions and silent dread. He'd got what he wanted, and yet not at all. Moments later the door opened again, Callum expecting more bad news to enter. Saresan was the bearer of no such thing, a broad smile on his face and bereft of his armour and halberd as he strode in, happy to see a familiar face.

"The black tiles on the walls, they come alive, Callum! They move with images and sound, some with people. I've no idea what they're talking about, but they're *there* and not there!" The guard's excitement ebbed when he looked at Callum's face. "You alright?"

"Not really," Callum answered honestly. "This is all a mess, I'm sorry for dragging you all into this."

"Sorry? I should be thanking you."

"For what?" Callum was puzzled.

"For saving my life, of course." His friend patted him on the shoulder heartily, but his cheer had faded. "If you hadn't gone to that forest, I wouldn't have gone with you and Azure afterwards to see that seer. If I hadn't done that, I'd've been none the wiser when the demons arrived, and I wouldn't have rated my chances. I know the rest of it is terrible, but if I'm still alive, I can work on making things better, no matter how strange things are beyond our world."

"They showed you space, I take it," Callum enquired. "What did you think?"

"It's a whole lot of nothing, but it's a damn pretty view. Daniel told me about all the other worlds and some of the things in them. He even showed me some of their weapons, but I don't like them."

"Are they those metal things I saw on Daniel's back and Siobhan's belt?" Callum got a nod.

"They fire no bolt or arrow I've ever seen. He called it a 'rifle', and when he loosed the shot, it was a… red beam." Saresan was thinking on his words even as he spoke them, attempting to make sense of it. "Thing is, the target he was aiming at was burned right through by it, heck knows how. He didn't need to load another shot, just pulled the trigger again and out shot another beam. I showed him my halberd and he was bemused by it, said that people abandoned hand-to-hand combat as their main attack method millennia ago, whatever one of those is. Can't say I blame them if they can make weapons that can kill someone so accurately from so far away. He encouraged me to learn to use one of those things myself."

Callum was reminded that he wanted to ask someone what a trillion was.

"And will you?" That provoked a chuckle from Saresan.

"Heck no. I was always a lousy shot with a crossbow, I doubt I'll be any better with their rifles. Besides, if I catch one of them off guard, I'll definitely get the element of surprise. I'm sure he'll want to persuade you to give them a try at some point, though." Saresan was looking to his blade. "But you lot have got your magic, so that'll even the odds if trouble comes to find us. We'll be fine as long as we stick together."

"Tyrus wants to train me to defeat the leader of the demons, someone called Keiran," Callum declared. "I don't think we have much choice in the matter either."

"It clearly had its own agenda from the start, but I'd rather be here than down there and dead like Azure." Saresan looked to the doorway. "Damn thing appeared in my room out of nowhere, you know? I don't think that thing knows what privacy is."

"Do you think we can stand up to this Keiran?" Callum asked his friend. "Eventually, once we've grown stronger."

"Once *you've* grown stronger. Unless you find some ritual that makes me like you, I'll be pretty much the same." Saresan walked over to one of the cupboards, reaching for one of the cans of drink. He turned it over, trying to find the way to open it. "When you said we don't have much choice, what did you mean?"

"Tyrus is shielding us from detection. If I refuse, it'll remove that protection."

"Blackmail, then." Saresan had found the ring that he pulled on, giving the contents a sniff before drinking. A grimace quickly swept his face, the guard looking again to the can with revulsion. "Gods, what died when they were brewing this? It's hideous."

"Is there ale in that?" Callum was offered the can immediately after asking, politely refusing with a gesture. Saresan left it on the side.

"There's something in it, but it sure isn't drinkable. Have you tried the food yet?"

"From the metal bags?" Callum asked. "Or did you eat something different?"

"Daniel was cooking dinner in his quarters, invited me to eat with them while he gave me the talk about everything. They cooked it together, he and his partner Monica, some kind of meat dish with spices I've never tasted before." Saresan started searching through the cupboards for a different drink. "She might be a warrior, you know, that or a blacksmith." He found a dark orange one, opening that. He frowned at the hiss which the can emitted, trying its contents warily. This time there wasn't a grimace, but Saresan clearly didn't like it.

"More bad ale?" Callum guessed.

"I've *no* idea what this is, it's got strange bubbles in it. Do these people drink anything that makes sense? I'd go for some water at this point." Saresan put that can next to the first one, giving up his search for a drink. "What do we know about this Keiran person, then?"

"Nothing, other than we'll be fighting him." Callum paused. "Now that I think on it, Tyrus only talked about *me* fighting, not all of us."

"Perhaps it only cares about you," Saresan told him. "I can't pretend to know how their minds work, but I do know that I'm not about to abandon you to face this alone."

"I can't ask you to do that—" Callum wasn't given a chance to explain his worries or fears, slapped on the back by Saresan as he walked by.

"You don't need to and I'm not going to take no for an answer, so don't try it." The guard smiled, but his confidence didn't ease all his concerns, thinking back to Azure's final moments. "I'm going to find Daniel. I need to ask him a few things, but I'll see if he knows anything about what the demon's planning. You never know, eh?"

Chapter Twenty-Two

Callum didn't linger in the room long, eating a small meal from what he could rustle up in the cupboards before exploring the corridors that made up the ship to distract his thoughts from everything else. Most of the doors still didn't open to him, and those that did were uninteresting; one small room contained a bucket and various brooms, along with shelving for bottles that he didn't spend long looking around, while another contained only metal boxes neatly stacked from floor to ceiling. Each one had words painted on them which he couldn't understand, but he guessed they were important for something.

Finding a flight of stairs that he descended, he ended up in a large open area with even more metal crates, larger and stacked higher than the ones in the small room. He guessed the room ran along nearly the entire length of the corridor above, making it at least a hundred metres in length. Strong-looking straps held the boxes in place, save a couple which were physically affixed to the floor with metal spikes that looked like they'd been hammered in. Those ones had a panel with buttons and a small black tile that changed in appearance every few seconds, words and numbers that again had no meaning to him.

He knew better than to touch the buttons, so he moved on, searching to satisfy his curiosity. He hadn't expected to find somebody there – the boxes were hardly going to grow legs and run away – and so nearly collided with the woman tapping one of the black tiles he'd seen before. She hadn't expected anyone either, stepping back quickly as her eyes scanned him, focusing on his hands and waist. When they settled on his sword, she relaxed, knowing who it was.

She stood about half a foot shorter than him, her hair catching his attention first as it was stark white and cut short. It was arranged into small upward spikes, perhaps held there with beeswax. Her amber eyes had moved from his weapon to look at his face appraisingly. She wore a dark green top that clung to her well-toned physique. Her black trousers were as clingy as her top, simple brown shoes rounding off her attire. Like Simon, she didn't appear to be armed with a weapon – Callum had now concluded that the apparatus on Simon's belt was likely for his occupation – but she could've knocked him unconscious with one swing.

"You must be Callum." She was the only person on the ship that had a definite accent, and it was one he vaguely knew. Urchins and people of the streets back on his world had a twang to their voice, and hers was a little similar. "Can't say you're anything like I imagined you'd be."

"What did you imagine?" Callum asked.

"Someone a lot more barbaric." She offered him a hand to shake, which he did. "I'm Monica."

"Saresan told me about you."

"Good things, I take it?"

"They were." He noticed she was still tapping at the black tile even when looking at him, snaring his curiosity. "What are you doing?"

"I'm checking the cargo manifest in preparation for the next planet we go to, making sure everything matches our records and the prices we'll expect to get per crate. It wouldn't have been much of a profit margin normally, but because of..." Monica trailed off, looking down at the thing she was tapping.

"Because of the demon?" Callum finished.

"I don't like that thing being on the ship. It could rip us to pieces if it wanted to, it's an alien!" Monica exclaimed before looking around quickly. Was she checking if Tyrus was there? "If it weren't paying us in gold upfront, Daniel wouldn't have thought twice about killing it. Do you know what people who pay that much upfront are like?" Callum didn't get a chance to answer. "It's paying for our silence, and I don't like it, I don't trust it."

"If it's any consolation, I don't trust it that much either."

"It's *you* we came here to rescue. You're apparently worth fifty tons of gold bullion. We could refit the whole ship with that."

Callum couldn't imagine how much gold that was, but it sounded like more wealth than any king. That spoke volumes about how expensive ships that sailed the stars were, making the fact that people had spread to so many worlds surprising. Monica paused and passed an apologetic look. "Sorry, I ramble when I'm worried."

"It's alright, but I really don't see how I'm worth a king's ransom to anyone. It's as surprising to me as it is to you." He smiled at her, wanting to reassure but not knowing if he could. "How long am I going to be here?"

"We're making one stop to sell our cargo and the gold, then we're taking you to the middle of nowhere, literally. The coordinates Tyrus gave us have nothing there. After that, we're free to do whatever we like, but I don't think

that's going to happen. That thing's scheming something and it's rotten."
Monica looked back to the crate next to her. "Do me a favour, Callum?"

"I can try."

"Talk to me about anything else before I start rambling again, would you?"

He had no idea what to talk about, even with all the questions in his
head; he certainly wasn't interesting enough to her that she wanted to inquire
about his life, he was just him. He settled on the first idea that came to his
head, speaking before he thought.

"Why is your hair white?" Callum quickly regretted asking that question.
"I mean, was it always white, or did it go white as you got older?" She stared
blankly at him for a moment then laughed, running her hand subconsciously
through the spikes.

"I bleached it when I was younger, then decided I liked it enough to
keep it. Had it genetically altered. Costly but worth it, if you ask me."
Monica watched him try to figure it out, grinning. "It grows like this now.
The spikes are gelled."

"It's very striking."

"That's why I like it. People turn their heads when they see me, and in
worlds with billions of people, that's an achievement." Monica moved the
tile to the side of the crate and placed it in a slot Callum hadn't noticed, so
fine was the seal. "Right now genetic alteration can only do stuff with hair,
everything else is either too risky or too difficult. Hair's only dead cells in
the end. They're looking at altering fingernail colours, but there isn't much
a market for that."

"Wait, hair is dead what?" Callum enquired, running his hands through
his own hair. "I take it you don't mean the kind of cell I'm thinking of."

"Probably not, no. You're going to have to do some serious reading
up on things." He gave her a blank look. "It'd be a lot of stuff, I know, but
you've got to start somewhere."

"You can read?" Callum got a look of confusion back, then incredulity.

"You can't?" she asked. He shook his head.

"Who was going to teach me? Only the rich can afford tutors, and besides,
what do you need to read that's important?" His explanation bewildered
her. "If something's really important, an official figure will tell the town
crier to declare it."

"So, what if you needed to sort out a shopping list?" She was grinning.
Callum guessed what a shopping list was by mashing the words together in

his head, shrugging in response.

"If I need to buy something I'll remember what it is, not that I could afford much."

"And when you had to work out taxes?"

"I just gave them what they asked for." She tried not to laugh.

"Wait, you can count, right?" He nodded. "Subtraction? Multiplication? Division? Quadratic theorem?" Callum had known the first one; the final thing sounded vaguely like the name of a distant lord that ruled beyond the robber barons. "Okay, the joke's over now."

"There was a joke?"

Her smile faded slowly as it dawned on her that he was being sincere.

"...Oh. I'm sorry, I thought you were pulling my leg." He looked at her leg and she quickly clarified, "It's an expression, another way to say 'in jest'?" His gaze returned to her face, Callum feeling a little belittled.

"I can assure you: I can't read. How many people that I'm going to meet can read?"

"All of them?" Callum was fast discovering that the gaping hole in his knowledge was even larger than he'd expected. "Education's free for everyone, it's expected. Educated people give back to the community far more than what they're taught." She let the words settle, then thought back on them and quickly corrected herself, "That's not to say you weren't useful, just likely less useful than—"

"I was an unskilled labourer who did odd jobs. It was a lot more common than you think where I came from." Monica was visibly relieved by his dismissal. "I'm used to being looked down on, but you're not intentionally doing so."

"I wasn't looking down on you," Monica told him. When she looked up, there was a grin once more on her lips. "You're taller than me, for a start."

Monica had suggested that she'd teach him the basics of writing, but Callum refused politely. Instead, he approached Alexis with the problem and asked very carefully about it. He hadn't expected her to say yes, the death of her brother still so fresh in all their minds, but she agreed to help him. It had been his plan to help her to cope with the loss of Johnathan, to keep her mind busy with something productive and to distract himself from everything that had happened.

Callum had never been one to waste time; he hadn't had the luxury of free time when on his world, always thinking of his next meal and the often-light coin purse at his belt. The letters didn't take him long to under-stand, a list of sounds to match shapes. Capital letters took longer, but their sounds were exactly the same. Only when the letters were strung together into words did Callum start struggling.

"If there are thousands of words, how am I going to learn what they all look like?" he'd asked. Sat in her room on the bed, she'd managed to find writing implements and some of that thin white parchment that had been used in his room for the picture instructions. "And how will I know what they mean?"

"That comes with time" — her voice was muted — "and repeated usage."

"How much time?"

"That depends on you. You never stop learning and it's never too late to start."

"It's a shame you can't teach me using magic like Tyrus did with the language the others use. It'd make the process so much simpler."

"You'd have to ask it about that. What I want to know is how it made this language as if it was our own. I barely find myself speaking how did we did back on our world anymore, it's... strange."

That made Callum realise that he too had switched seamlessly to the 'new tongue', as it were, a fact that surprised him only for a moment; with how strange everything else had been, that change had passed him by.

The only book that she'd been able to source had been from Simon, a thick manual that she worked out were schematics for the ship's engines. She'd had no idea what that meant and some of the words within the pages confused her, but he tried his best to understand. Eventually, they gave up on the book and she instead wrote words herself for him to learn.

It was clear to Callum that she was barely hiding her sadness as he learned far too slowly for his liking. She didn't smile through it all, and he didn't expect her to. The memories of the final hours on his world weren't fading as the days rolled by, and he doubted they ever would. It was after the third day that he found out that they'd be landing on a planet soon, a place populated by people who'd likely never heard of his world.

Daniel had suggested to Callum that he change his attire to something more fitting to the worlds they'd visit, but he didn't like the thought of that; he felt more comfortable in what he knew, and if there were lots of people, surely a few of them would be dressed like him.

Jinar was up and about again, but his pride was still wounded, the sorcerer keeping to his room as much as possible. Tyrus had no words of apology for Jinar or anyone else, not appearing to eat or talk with any of the crew or his friends. Callum was starting to wonder if demons needed to eat or drink at all, and more worryingly, he'd never seen one of them breathe or sleep.

What they did do, apparently, was meditate, a fact discovered by chance when he stumbled upon Tyrus's room. The room was completely bare save the demon's quarterstaff, which lay in front of it. Sat cross-legged on the floor, Tyrus rested its hands on its knees and stared blankly ahead, completely motionless. It hadn't acknowledged his presence, deep in whatever thoughts demons had. The gut instinct to defend himself when seeing a demon had faded for Tyrus, but he didn't trust it, not yet.

Simon wouldn't take no for an answer concerning the injections when they next met, but now that Callum knew of his profession, he'd been ready to hear what they were for.

"This one is a vaccination, usually given to babies in their first years. It'll make you immune to a multitude of illnesses that would've killed many on your world," Simon spoke of the dual-coloured injection first, then held up the other. "And this contains your IDC. It's short for Identification Chip, a tiny piece of metal that runs off the body's natural electric current. It proves who you are, holds information about your employment, residence and other minor things like a criminal record or standing health issues. It also acts as your way of paying for things, storing the data on your finances and bank balance. Practically everyone has one implanted in them at a young age, except for people like you."

"Is it safe to have a piece of metal in your body?" Callum had asked.

"It's usually implanted in the neck: you won't even feel it there. Once it's in, I'll get it to collect essential data, mainly your blood type. All you really need to know is that you'll raise a lot of eyebrows if you don't have one, and not the kind you'd like." He didn't stop Simon from administering both, the vaccination stinging a little. The insertion of the chip was more painful, albeit brief.

"That vaccination would've been thought of as a miracle by people I knew," Callum had informed him.

"You'd be surprised what people take for granted nowadays, Callum." When they got closer to the planet, Callum saw ships that sailed the stars like the one he was in, travelling on their own headings. They were nothing like the ships he was used to, metal constructs of odd symmetrical shapes. Little seemed to unify them apart from that, each one starkly different from the others. Some had markings on the hull that possibly served to identify them from a distance, but their meaning was lost on him. One curious design had sails around the ship, gliding through space on an invisible wind. Siobhan had tried her best to explain what each ship was for, pointing to each one as she saw them through the window of the common room.

"That's the make I have." She brought his attention to a trio of small, sleek looking vessels. The shape reminded him of an arrowhead, with tiny windows at the front and a small line of blue lights at the back, which he'd been told was the propulsion that allowed ships to move. On the underside were what looked like larger versions of the rifle that Daniel had, likely designed to fight other ships.

"The G-9 Bolt Light Interceptor. It's fast, nimble and packs a heavy punch. I call mine the *Silverbolt*."

"Flying straight and true to its target like a quarrel," he remarked, provoking a grin from her.

"Exactly." She was smiling widely. "Just made the last payment on it a few months ago, so it's all mine at last. They don't make them anymore, you know? The company was bought out by Z-Gen and they discontinued the line."

"I keep hearing that name." He watched the three ships turn away and fly off into the unknown. "Who are they?"

"They're the people that keep the galaxy safe, an army of sorts. I'll point them out if we ever see one, they stick out like a sore thumb. Just treat them like you would the guard back on your world, I guess." He considered the varying degrees of honesty that guards had, which did nothing to reassure him about Z-Gen.

Callum knew they'd landed when he was woken by the room juddering. Quickly showering and brushing his teeth – a new experience that Simon had had to explain to him, even though his teeth were apparently very good – he went to the common area so he could observe the world they'd landed on. He was surprised to see that the window was back to being a wall and wouldn't revert when he requested it. He went back to his room and saw that his window was also a wall. Confused, Callum sought out Daniel for an explanation but couldn't find him. He did succeed in locating Simon, looking as tired as ever and finishing off another cup of what he called 'coffee'.

"Where is everyone?" he asked.

"Daniel's outside with a client; the rest, I don't know. He'll be back in a couple of hours," answered Simon, looking at the bottom of his cup.

"Why aren't the windows working?"

"Again?" Simon sighed wearily. "They're always shorting out. I told him to get a replacement relay, before something more important breaks. I'll fix it before we set off."

"You fix the ship? I thought you were a healer." Callum watched as Simon shook his head and chuckled weakly.

"I trained as a doctor, but the last engineer we had left two years ago. Daniel didn't see a reason to hire another one, so I took it upon myself to learn how to keep the ship in one piece. One thing led to another, and now I'm probably the most overqualified ship's doctor you'll ever see. Of course, he doesn't pay me two wages." Simon again looked at his cup, his mind somewhere else. "Actually, I might as well fix that now."

"Don't let me stop you." Callum got a nod in return as the doctor left, muttering about 'a refill'. The conversation got Callum thinking about the fact that he hadn't found the exit to the ship yet, even though he'd explored nearly everywhere that wasn't locked to him. He decided to look again and didn't get far when he noticed one of the doors opening and Monica moving to stand in the doorway.

Spotting Callum, she smiled and gave him a 'come hither' motion with her finger. Immediately after making the gesture, Monica disappeared into the room, but the door remained open. She wanted him to follow, and his curiosity was caught; he approached the door and saw that she wasn't alone within. He'd expected something like his own room but saw instead a narrow corridor that could barely fit the multitude of people in it.

Siobhan was leaning against the wall a little inside, giving a small wave with one hand. Saresan was looking at the door on the other end of the small corridor, it both larger and heavier. He was bereft of weapons and armour, unlike Siobhan who had both her smaller rifles on her belt. Next to him was Jinar, who gave him a brief glance before looking back to the wall ahead of him in silent contemplation.

It felt strange to see him so subdued, but Callum had no words of re-assurance to give him. That Alexis was quiet wasn't surprising to him, but she managed a weak look of greeting that lingered only for a moment. Once he entered, the door shut behind him.

"Glad you could join us, Callum," Monica said to him. "Fancy going to see the sights?"

"Does Daniel know we're going?" was his first question.

"...Not quite." Monica's smile was sheepish now.

"Seems like he doesn't want us to see what's out there," Saresan piped in. "Thinks we might cause a scene."

"You're going behind his back?" Callum didn't like the sound of this, but Siobhan shrugged.

"He's just being paranoid. We'll only be out there a few hours anyway, long enough for you to get a taste of what the galaxy's *really* like. Maybe we can get you guys some proper weapons while we're down there too."

"A halberd is a proper weapon: it'll kill people just as dead as your rifles," the guard commented.

"When you can throw your halberd a hundred metres, maybe."

"You're welcome to stay if you want to, Callum, I won't stop you," Monica told him. Despite the risks, Callum was very curious about how people lived there, enough to throw caution to the wind but keep it within arm's reach.

"If you're sure it'll be alright." Callum got a grin from Monica.

"Daniel won't even notice. If he does, I'm sure I can talk him down." She winked at him, something he couldn't do himself. Monica pushed a button, and the large metal door opened to reveal an even smaller room and another large metal door. This one opened with a hiss moments after the first, revealing an extraordinary sight.

Chapter Twenty-Three

"In other news, the wanted criminal Felicia Jane Stoneson was appre-
hended today while attempting to leave spaceport. Z-Gen inspectors
were notified of her presence by a dutiful citizen, allowing them to
impound her stolen vessel and bring her to justice. If you wish to see a
complete list of her crimes, please consult the Z-Gen Public Database
at your convenience.

"Z-Gen would like to take this opportunity to again implore anyone who
has information on the fugitive Bastian Volso to please come forward."

—*News report from the Verin Verat Network*

Callum couldn't see the horizon, obscured by tall buildings made of metal and glass that reached up to the heavens. The overriding noise was an indecipherable din that was similar to and also nothing like the general commotion of town life. Emerging down a ramp onto the large metal platform with the others, Callum realised that it was night only by looking up, the vast quantity of unnatural light initially fooling him into thinking otherwise.

There was also no greenery to be seen anywhere, a jungle of man-made anarchy. Then he noticed how high up they were, a massive drop beyond the platform with only a metal bar at elbow height to stop people from falling to their deaths. Absorbed in taking in the surroundings, he cautiously stepped over to the rail and looked down at a myriad of walkways suspended between the tall buildings, themselves supporting streets and smaller buildings of their own.

Like layers of a cake, each segment seemed to be a town in its own right, blowing out of the water all that his imagination had pictured the world to be. Each walkway was crowded with people dressed in all manner of outlandish attire in a wide variety of colours, each one stranger than the last.

Alexis had pulled her cloak around herself, feeling the chill in the air that Callum had only noticed when his attention was brought to those around him. Saresan was speechless and Jinar looked on with a neutral gaze, assessing all he saw. Daniel's ship was truly massive – about a hundred and fifty metres long and thirty in height, at a guess – and very unlike the sailing ship he'd imagined it was. That the *Silverbolt* was nestled in it somewhere now made sense, though it was no less extraordinary. Everything on the world was so large compared to where he'd grown up, matching the colossal scale of the galaxy he was now an inhabitant of. It made him feel small once again, but Callum tried to shake that feeling off.

"Welcome to Gui-Lon," Monica told them, taking in the sight herself. "Not too different from my home."

"All the magic I have ever known could not match a single thing in front of me," Jinar spoke quietly, a rare concession of the limits of his power. "Was this all done without its aid?"

"It can't have been," Callum replied. "It would take an untold number of builders many hundreds of years to make something like this."

"The lift's over here." Monica indicated to a small area on the platform, red in colour. A waist-high plinth next to it had a single glowing blue button. "Stick together when we get down there. You get lost and we won't be able to find you."

"So how many people live here?" Saresan asked as they all gathered on the red square.

"Probably a hundred million, give or take," Siobhan guessed.

"That is quite impossible," Jinar remarked. "How would they sustain a population that large in one place?"

"Quite easily with enough forward planning. Some will live underground as well as in skyscrapers. A rich minority are on ground level, and the richest don't live in the city at all."

Siobhan pressed the button on the plinth, and slowly the square they stood on started to descend into the floor. The hole's walls were far from grey and featureless, however; on all sides were colourful and vibrant pictures on all manner of topics, most of them meaningless to Callum. The lift was a tight fit for the six of them, Callum stood in a corner with Alexis next to him. He wondered how strong the pulley system had to be to support all of them.

"Thank you for using Suprem-O Landing Pads Incorporated," a female voice told them from the floor of the lift. It sounded like she was speaking through a metal pipe. "This lift is here for your convenience and ease of use. Now heading to level twenty-three. While you are waiting, why not think about the dinner you'll get at the Suprem-O Eat-In restaurant? Now serving a thousand different meals at prices you'll find supreme! Third left after the lift's exit, second building. You won't be disappointed!"

"Who was that?" Callum asked.

"Can't go anywhere without being bombarded by advertisements," Siobhan remarked.

"So, this woman can project her voice wherever she chooses?" Siobhan chuckled and shook her head but said nothing.

"Estimated time until destination, forty-five seconds," the voice announced to them chirpily. Callum thought of bringing up something to talk about but could think of nothing, truly lost in a place where he knew nothing. Nobody else had words either, waiting the time out in silence until Callum felt they'd stopped moving. "Now on level twenty-three. We hope to see you again soon!"

The paved and cobbled streets he knew were nowhere to be seen. So too were the market stalls, horse and cart pulling produce fresh from the field. Instead, there was a sea of people all moving in different currents, some directly opposed to one another.

Siobhan watched the river, trying to guess the best way in. Monica didn't wait, motioning for the rest to follow as she walked into the flow without a second thought. Callum moved behind her quickly, not wanting to lose sight of her, and immediately became a motionless stumbling block for everyone else around him. One man nearly collided with him, passing a look of silent disdain as he walked around. The others followed his lead and they, in turn, followed Monica, the pace they walked dictated by how fast everyone around them moved.

"It would be easier to teleport to where we need to go," Jinar commented to them, looking around. "You need only tell me where we are headed."

"The last thing we want to do is draw attention to ourselves." Siobhan spotted someone in the crowd ahead of them by a building. "That's one of them, Callum."

The man was dressed in a white breastplate trimmed with red, with matching boots, red metal knee guards and white gloves. The breastplate had armoured plates hanging from the bottom which protected his upper legs, not unlike plate mail. Slung over his right shoulder he wore a gold cloak, it draped over his right arm and side, ending at the knees.

The helmet was also white, with a strange glowing red line running where the eyes would be. To either side of where the mouth would be – it covered by a grey metal grille – was a circular bulge in the helmet. The helmet's upper edges ended in two spikes on either side, with a third running from the middle upwards. The figure had a rifle in his hands, looking down at a young boy who was talking enthusiastically to him.

Was that a member of Z-Gen that Siobhan had told him about? Perhaps it was, maybe it was just a normal guard. He seemed heavily equipped for someone who was meant to keep the peace.

"He does not look like much," Jinar remarked.

"Looks can be deceiving." They passed the Z-Gen man, who didn't look away from the boy.

"Is this place always so busy?" Alexis asked.

"It's probably a bit quieter than usual right now." Monica's voice was almost lost to the din of the crowd even though she was only a few steps ahead of them. "It's evening, after all."

"Cities never sleep," Siobhan added as she looked at someone who nearly bumped into her, passing an angry look. She stuck her middle finger up at him with a smile in retort, turning back to the path ahead. "Everything open all the time, every day. People work all kinds of shifts: they need food and services just as much as everyone else. Their schedule isn't decided by the sun but by when their next shift is."

"Shifts? Is that a unit of time?"

"A variable one too." Siobhan looked around briefly after her answer. "So which place did you settle on in the end, Monica?"

"The one we looked at last night. Got some pretty decent reviews and the drinks are cheap," came the answer.

"Something bothers me about all this," Callum declared then.

"What's that?" Siobhan asked.

"If the city never sleeps, where can you find peace? If nothing is quiet, how can anyone be alone with their thoughts?" He looked to his left, the only direction which wasn't swallowed up by people. Below, above and all around were endless platforms of civilization, islands of life between mountainous pillars people called home. "How does anyone have time to be by themselves?"

"Many of the people here are more alone than you think they are, Callum."

Callum thought on Siobhan's words, how nobody looked to the others around them as they went single-mindedly about their tasks. The walkway they were on branched out ahead of them into even more paths, like a tree.

As he looked around, he noticed someone had stopped by the edge of a pathway opposite theirs, looking down with emptiness in his eyes.

He'd caught Callum's attention because of the fluorescent green of his clothing. The man was surprised that someone was looking at him, confused and unsure about something. Callum offered him a smile, which only made the man even more puzzled; was such a simple gesture so foreign? Slowly the man stepped back into the crowd, immediately consumed by it and gone.

"What was up with him?" Callum asked, realising then that only Siobhan was with him now. "Where are the others?"

"I saw you'd stopped, don't want you getting lost. The others are a little ahead," she told him. "If you ask me, I think he was going to jump."

"...Jump?" Callum looked down at the miles of air beneath, worried and confused. "Why?"

"Can't say what was going through his head. Whatever you did threw off his resolve." Siobhan looked back to the crowd of people weaving around them. "Let's catch up with the others." Callum decided that he'd be even more aware of his surroundings from then on.

After ten minutes of walking in relative silence, they took a route that was less travelled, though not significantly. It was approaching one of the tall buildings that stabbed the sky, dotted at all levels with illuminated signs that meant nothing to him; none had easily recognisable symbols to identify its purpose, but all were vibrant and eye-catching. Monica was directing them towards one place in particular, the source of an almighty racket that penetrated the commotion around them. Callum wondered if something was being built nearby; it was the only thing he knew that sounded similar.

"Well, there it is, Deff Pulse," Monica announced as they got close. The noise only grew louder, was it coming from inside? "Keep your eyes open for a table."

As soon as the door opened, Callum was hit by a wall of overpowering commotion and heat that made him hesitate about entering. Only Alexis hesitated also, casting him a look that clearly showed her opinion of the establishment. After a small delay the pair walked in, and as the door shut, Callum noticed how gloomy it was.

The walls and floor were black, and the tables and chairs equally dreary and uncomfortable looking. He looked around for the minstrels who were brutalising their instruments but saw no one playing. There were plenty of people dancing, or at least, they might've been dancing; he was worried some were unwell, convulsing and moving in peculiar ways. They were dressed in varying degrees of scantiness and were far too close to one another, in part because of how many there were in the small open area.

That people were managing to talk over the noise was surprising, but there was one familiar sight in the corner, a bar. Unfortunately, none of the drinks were anything he knew. One of the bottles glowed yellow in the dim light, which worried him. Only then did Callum see that the others had already walked off, able to find them only because Alexis's clothing stood out completely. They'd found a table in the corner from which Monica was clearing empty glass tankards.

He clumsily tried to navigate his way towards them, getting odd looks as he did. Callum was starting to hear words that repeated themselves in what these people called a song, mainly 'baby'. He wondered if the one singing had a fascination with them or really desired to have children of his own. When he finally reached the table, he noticed that Monica wasn't there and that two chairs remained. Callum sat next to Saresan, who chuckled.

"Thought we'd lost you there, or were you taking in the atmosphere?" the guard asked. "Drinks are on the way, apparently." Jinar was observing the crowds with mild interest, stroking his beard while Siobhan leaned back in her chair like it was the most comfortable thing in the world.

"Looks like we picked a quiet night," Siobhan remarked. "Shame we aren't staying, I was in the mood for dancing."

"It is a little dark for that," Jinar stated. "Also, there is not enough room to make the two lines." Siobhan gave him an odd look.

"I don't think you guys know what dancing is."

"I believe I am beholden to all the evidence I need to state the exact opposite." Jinar smiled to her, one of the first since his defeat. "Of course, if you wish to try and persuade me how wrong I am, I will bear witness to it."

"I don't think so." She looked to Monica when she arrived with a tray of beverages, all of them in those glass tankards. Callum and Saresan were handed what looked like ale, while Alexis was given something that was pink with a small parasol balanced precariously on the lip. She picked up the drink and eyed it before trying a little. It was clear that whatever it was, Alexis didn't like it.

"Thank you, but I would prefer an ale also." Monica took the drink back from her.

"Sorry, took an educated guess. Guess it wasn't that educated. I'll be back."

"Hey, what about mine?" Siobhan remarked after Jinar sipped his own ale.

"They don't serve things that cheap," Monica told her with a smile as she moved to leave. "But I can get you a glass of water if you like."

"Considering the smell of the place, if you left that on the bar side it'd be alcohol within the hour." Saresan's comment made Callum pause to consider the scent on the air, something he instantly regretted.

Within the general heat was a pervading presence of body odour and stale drink, far worse than any tavern he'd been in. For being so surrounded by people and among friends, Callum found himself feeling quite alone and isolated.

He looked out to the dancing crowd and noticed then that a Z-Gen soldier had entered the establishment. Nobody batted an eye to his arrival, even with the rifle in his hands. It made Callum look again at the dancers to see that quite a few of them were armed with weapons of their own, smaller and secured to their belts. Was the world that dangerous?

The soldier stepped through the gyrating mass without difficulty, people shifting to make room. Callum looked away, not wanting to attract the man's attention as Monica returned with ale for Alexis and a canned beverage for Siobhan. She didn't seem concerned about the Z-Gen soldier either.

"One of the staff found this down the back of the fridge. They're not sure if it's even made anymore." Monica passed it over to Siobhan, who caught it and looked at the design on it.

"It'll do," replied the pilot, opening it and taking a drink. She looked again at the design on the can. "I can see why they stopped making this. I hope he didn't charge you for it."

"Not much." Monica sat down.

"Too much, then," replied the pilot after she took another drink from the can. Siobhan then glanced at all assembled. "So what do you think?"

"Of the establishment?" Jinar asked.

"Of the world, of how things are. It's pretty neat, don't you think?"

"I don't like it," Saresan spoke first, shaking his head. "I'm used to busy places, but this is something else. Millions and millions of people crammed together, it just seems so lifeless."

"What do you mean?" Monica enquired, giving him her full attention.

"Back when I was a guard, I knew almost everyone where I worked. People could sit down and take a minute to think and talk, but here? You stop and you'll get trampled."

"Not every world's like this, you know?" Siobhan had finished the drink, the can discarded. "Some have barely anyone living on them. Others are almost entirely agricultural, or they store energy generated there to be shipped off to far-flung colonies that can't sustain their infrastructure without it. The galaxy is freaking huge, there are so many worlds that you can't judge them all on here. I just thought seeing a taste of what the galaxy might be like would help adjust you all."

"I think we'll need a lot more than a guided tour for that," Callum admitted, trying to picture the multitude of different worlds that might exist.

"We'll get round to that, or your demon friend might."

"He is no friend of mine," Jinar added coldly.

Callum noticed a shadow looming over the table and couldn't help but turn around. The Z-Gen soldier was right behind him, weapon in hand. He tried not to react, to suppress his nerves.

"Evening." The helmet distorted the man's voice a little, but Callum could tell he was young. There was no malice in his tone, nor was the rifle aimed at them, but Callum felt uncomfortable.

"And a good one to you as well, sir," Jinar replied before Monica could, smiling politely.

"Can't say I've ever heard that accent before," the soldier replied. He looked to be examining Jinar's robes. "Where are you from?"

"It is quite out of the way, you would not have heard of it, I fear."

"I've been stationed on four worlds in my time, try me." Callum had never asked what the world he'd lived on was called, if it even had a name. Jinar didn't know either but was doing a good job of hiding it.

"Vedallan IV," Alexis said quietly, surprising both sorcerers. "We're from Vedallan IV."

She'd clearly asked someone beforehand, a mistake that had almost got them in trouble, or had it? Perhaps Callum was just overreacting. The Z-Gen soldier looked at her for a moment.

"You're right, I haven't heard of there. Must be pretty out of the way for you to be dressed like that. Didn't think there were any backwater planets left in this area." Callum tried to work out if that was an insult, but it wasn't worded as such, nor was the tone demeaning. The Z-Gen soldier reached for a small device attached to his left thigh. "You don't mind if I scan you, do you?"

"For our chips?" Callum guessed.

"That's the one. You have been chipped, I presume?"

"Recently, we only left Vedallan IV a short time ago."

The Z-Gen soldier held the device close to Callum's neck. It beeped a second later, prompting the soldier to glance at the top of it. He then moved to Saresan, doing the same for each of them in turn until he finished with Siobhan. Everyone else was so at ease with it, but Callum couldn't stop his mind from imagining all the ways things could go wrong.

"Everything seems to be in order," the soldier declared. "Thank you for cooperating, you wouldn't believe the fuss some people kick up about it."

"You're just doing your job. Fancy a drink?" Siobhan said back.

"Not while on duty. Good night." And with that, the soldier started to leave, making Callum breathe a sigh of relief. Alexis smiled at him in reassurance, the atmosphere returning to the unnatural normal of the establishment.

"Seemed nice enough," Saresan remarked after drinking more. "I bet they aren't all like that though."

"Just as varied as all people are, I guess." Siobhan was eyeing Jinar's drink, waiting for a chance to take it from him.

The soldier had stopped amongst the dancing people, attention focused on the device he'd just used. Callum was watching him, and a chill rushed down his back when the man turned back to them. Slowly he approached them once more, holding his rifle in a subtly different way. Siobhan looked back to the soldier. "Something else you need?"

"Perhaps." His tone was different now, less conversational. "We've just received a report that a group matching your description were discussing 'teleportation'." Siobhan didn't react but Callum did, looking away quickly. "You wouldn't happen to know anything about that, would you?"

"Not in the least, my friend. Why, what is this teleportation you speak of?" Jinar smiled graciously, face unreadable, but the soldier wasn't looking at him; his gaze was on Callum, eyes hidden under his helmet. Now the red beam on it seemed dehumanising, but Callum was only remembering it, trying to focus on his mostly untouched drink. Monica hadn't moved, eyeing the soldier carefully as she tried to work out what was going on.

"That's what I'm trying to find out. Would you be willing to come with me to answer a few questions?" Callum was afraid now, that wasn't good at all.

"You can ask them here if you like," Saresan suggested. "Take a seat, we'll get you a drink."

"That wasn't a request." The words were stated firmly, eliminating any doubt of the soldier's intent. Siobhan's hands had drifted under the table out of sight and the soldier had noticed.

"I can assure you, whatever you think we have done—" Jinar was cut off sharply.

"Are you going to come with me, or will I need to call backup?" This was the same man who moments ago had been just like anyone else, now he was threatening them.

Callum couldn't stop his hand from reaching for the handle of his sword, just in case. He didn't want to find out if it was effective against the man's strange armour, but it was looking increasingly likely. Alexis was ready to draw her daggers, of the same mindset as Callum, which bolstered his conviction.

"Why do we need to come with you?" Callum finally asked. "Do you think we're sorcerers?" Monica swallowed nervously. The soldier paused.

"That's something we'll find out. If you're not, you will be released."

"And if we are?" Callum didn't get an answer to that. "Is there something wrong with that?" The Z-Gen soldier turned his head away.

"This is patrol thirty-seven, reporting in—" the man spoke quickly and quietly. Saresan stood.

"Oh god," Monica muttered, mortified.

"There's surely been a misunderstanding—" Monica began, trying to reason with the soldier. Saresan, however, grabbed the nearest object to him, a metal chair which he swung at the soldier suddenly. The loud clang caught the attention of everyone dancing nearby, watching in shock. Surprised, the soldier couldn't stop Saresan from pulling off his helmet and punching him squarely in the face. He fell to the ground with a thud, out cold. Saresan shook the life back into his hand as the group stared silently at the whole spectacle.

"Oh god!" Monica exclaimed in horror. The surrounding people, realising just what had happened, began to flee in panic.

"We need to go. Now!" Siobhan said as she got up from her chair, moving to head outside with the other patrons.

Monica followed quickly with a look of immense worry, while Jinar winced at the bruise on the soldier's face before departing. Callum remained, stunned at how quickly everything had gone so terribly wrong and hoping, despite everything, that the soldier was alright. Alexis grabbed his wrist as she passed, tugging him from his seat silently and prompting him to depart as the music finally died.

Chapter Twenty-Four

"What did you do *that* for?!" Siobhan exclaimed angrily to Saresan as they rushed out of the bar. Saresan was pleased with his accomplishment.

"I kept him quiet." The people around the bar had stopped, looking at the group with a mixture of confusion and fear. A few were pointing devices at them, purpose unknown. Monica was fumbling in her pocket for something as she looked to the walkways ahead.

"You knocked him out!" Siobhan was even angrier at his reply.

"Made things better though." Saresan got a glare.

"You made it worse, *much* worse!" She turned to Monica, who was fiddling with a small device. "Can you pick up Daniel?"

"Not here." She was worried, breathing lightly. "Maybe the message didn't go through."

"Fat chance of that." Siobhan looked to the others present, namely Saresan. "I'll have time to be pissed at you later, we need to get out of here. We make a break for the ship before his buddies show up."

"Jinar could teleport us there," Alexis suggested. "It would be—"

"No! No teleporting, no flashy crap! We're in enough trouble as is. We run!" Siobhan started down the walkway in a rush. She didn't break into a full sprint, however, and with the perilous walkways, Callum understood why. The others followed, Callum looking back to the spectacle and seeing some people helping the soldier to his feet. That was little comfort to him, however, fleeing once more, but this time from humans rather than demons. He hadn't yet drawn his sword but feared that he'd have to use it soon. It didn't take long for the more crowded sections of the walkway to become visible ahead, unaware and perhaps uncaring of the trouble Callum and the others were in. A voice came from the device in Monica's hand, and it wasn't pleased.

"Monica? Where the hell are you?" It was Daniel.

"We're outside," she admitted grimly, the device able to project her voice to him and his to her.

"We? You didn't take them out of the ship, did you? Oh god, what happened? Is it bad?"

"...Depends on if you class hitting a Z-Gen soldier with a chair as bad." There was a pause.

"Please tell me you're joking."

"I don't see what's so wrong with that! He was going to call for assistance!" Saresan remarked.

"Oh fuck." Callum didn't need to know what that word meant to know it was bad. "Are you alright?"

"How soon can you take off?" Monica asked. Daniel was talking to someone quickly, likely Simon. The sounds then ceased abruptly. "We're in trouble, big trouble."

"You think?" Siobhan was mad. "If we die, I'm blaming you."

"He was going to take us away," the guard protested. Callum was started to get tired from all the running. "Would you have preferred that?"

"I would've preferred if *you* hadn't mentioned teleporting!" Siobhan was glaring at Jinar now.

"While you all have valid points, I believe we should be focusing on the crowd of people ahead that we will not be able to run through. Perhaps if I used my magic—" The glare hardened when Jinar got to talking of magic. "Or we can ineffectually weave through. Either is fine."

"Stop!" came a call from ahead, a woman's voice. A Z-Gen soldier had levelled her rifle at them, the crowd dispersing quickly. Jinar ignored Siobhan's warnings and muttered a few syllables, gesturing with his hands before the soldier suddenly started to rise up in the air. Startled, she didn't fire on the group as they rushed underneath and past her through the rapidly depleting crowd.

"Sorry," Callum apologised even as Siobhan scowled at Jinar.

"Damnit, what did I just say?!" she shouted.

"Would you prefer she shot at us?" Jinar let the soldier fall to the ground after a few seconds, when they were far enough away for her not to give chase. All at once, two more soldiers blocked their way forward, one with an orange cloak ordering people away while the other shot at them with their rifle. The beam of red missed Jinar narrowly, the sorcerer stopping along with the others as the other soldier aimed his rifle at the group.

"Put your weapons on the ground! You're under arrest for assaulting a Z-Gen soldier!" beckoned the orange cloaked man. His gun was trained on Siobhan while the other was focused on Jinar, seeing them as the most dangerous threats. Callum's heart was pounding as he thought of their options; running would get them nowhere, but the last thing any of them wanted was to fight.

"This has all been a misunderstanding!" Monica implored, afraid.

"Weapons down!" The order was shouted once again, louder this time.

How many more times would they have to face soldiers, even if they avoided a fight there? About to reach for his sword in fear, Callum thought twice about it, sure they'd notice him drawing the blade, and instead decided to try his own magic. With no tells for his power, he focused the arcane might within him into a dazzling display of energy that he launched at the soldiers faster than he'd intended.

All present had barely a moment to react save Callum, who shielded his eyes just before the energy detonated into a blinding flash of light. He moved forward a moment later, the effect dying quickly as Siobhan muttered some less-then-savoury words from behind him.

His hope was that the soldiers were dazed, allowing him to use his sword to damage their weapons. He didn't want to kill them, even though the feeling wasn't mutual; they were just doing their job, and even though their dislike of sorcerers made no sense to him, if he could end it without death, he would. He barely drew his blade before he noticed that the soldiers hadn't been affected, weapons now aimed at him.

"He's a sorcerer too!" shouted the gold-cloaked one.

A spike of panic rushed through Callum that was overpowered just as quickly by confusion when he felt magical energy behind him. A moment later the man was knocked to the ground, hit in the chest by a searing bolt of flame thrown by someone else. The one left standing stared at his screaming comrade in utter disbelief. A hole had been seared through his breastplate, the skin beneath burned and blistered.

Callum was horrified at the sight, turning back to see that Alexis had cast the spell, the only one to recover in time. Her eyes shone with determination and regret, a feeling that he shared. The others regained their bearings from the flash at that point, Monica seeing the spectacle first.

"What happened?" she exclaimed, shocked.

The standing soldier took one look at the group and dropped his rifle, rushing instead to his fellow's side while reaching for something on his belt. Callum saw their chance to flee, but his heart bled for the man who suffered because of them. Siobhan took the opportunity, however, not looking back to the others as she rushed past. Monica was quick to catch up, but Callum lingered even as Saresan made his way ahead. The soldier was applying some kind of ointment to the burned man's chest, although it seemed to make the screaming louder rather than mollify it.

"Help's on the way, hold on!" the man implored his companion, ignoring the others completely. It was gut-wrenching to see, doubly so that he was the reason Alexis had had to do that. Jinar gave him a look that brought him back to his sense, reluctantly hustling away. The rifle that the soldier had discarded remained so.

Nobody else confronted them as they rushed to the landing pad, nor did anyone block their way; even when they moved out of sight of the previous confrontation, the walkways were far emptier than before. Those that there walking gave them a wider berth, making Callum think that they knew what they'd done. None of them had seen it, how was it possible?

Monica muttered all the way back and up in the lift, trying to get what she was going to say to Daniel straight in her head but failing each time. Alexis shared a look with Callum that spoke of far worse worries that lay ahead, echoed in Daniel's expression when they spotted him by the lift. He was frightened and furious all at once, rifle in his hands that didn't lower when they arrived. His eyes were only on Monica, who stopped dead in her tracks as she saw him.

"Daniel, I—" Monica was cut off.

"What the hell were you thinking?!" She was mortified and without a reply as Daniel looked to Siobhan. "Do you realise what you've done?"

"I didn't do shit, it was *them*!" Siobhan glared back.

"That is hardly fair—" Jinar got the glare aimed at him instead.

"You levitated someone!"

"He did WHAT?" Daniel exclaimed. That only made Callum feel even worse. "Oh god. We're criminals now, you know that?"

"Can't we reason with them?" The look Callum got from Daniel after asking that question made him regret it.

"Right now, my best bet is to kill you all and hand your bodies over to them in the hope that they don't think I'm complicit, that's how screwed we are!" Callum briefly expected Daniel to do just that, but he didn't, smashing his fist into the wall hard. "At least tell me you didn't kill anyone!"

"They will recover." Jinar was remarkably calm and measured. "We made the best of a bad situation, it could have been a lot worse."

"It IS a lot worse: you don't understand! Did they scan you?" Jinar nodded.

"I fail to see why that is important."

"They'll have your IDCs on record, which means they'll mark your files as being fugitives and me with you! We won't be able to go anywhere without being hunted down like... like dogs!" Alexis said nothing, far wiser than Callum had been.

"Daniel, I didn't mean—" Monica spoke shakily.

"Save it!" Daniel snapped, looking to Callum and his friends. "Give me one reason why I should let you on board!" Callum looked back to the huge drop around them but had no argument to give.

"You'd leave us here?" Alexis asked him. "Are you willing to have that on your conscience for the rest of your life?"

"When the alternative is death?"

Callum blinked and just like that, Tyrus was looming behind Daniel with narrowed eyes. Its appearance startled Callum, Jinar watching it with distrust.

It took a moment for Daniel to notice, turning in surprise which quickly melted into rage. "The deal's off, you... whatever the hell you are! All the gold in the universe isn't worth it if I'm too dead to spend it!"

"Irrelevant," retorted Tyrus.

"Don't give me that crap, you've ruined me!" Daniel moved to aim his weapon but stopped when the demon snarled threateningly. This was more like the creatures Callum knew, angry and hateful.

"Board," the demon ordered.

"Your stowaways are staying here! They're not my problem anymore, and neither are you!" Callum knew what was coming next and stepped forward, eager to avert it.

"The longer we spend arguing here, the more likely it is that those soldiers will catch up with us!" Callum told Daniel. "You can argue with us all you like, but if they do fight us, it'll be all of us, and we stand a better chance together." Tyrus didn't seem to care for his words. Daniel lowered his head and took a deep breath, clenching his fists.

"Daniel?" Monica was afraid, of what wasn't clear. Without a word Daniel boarded the ship, leaving the ramp down for them to do the same. Siobhan didn't think twice about following. Jinar and Saresan were close behind, the guard giving Callum a weary smile. Callum lingered along with Alexis, while Monica looked to where Daniel had gone, hurt and ashamed.

"Board," the demon repeated more sternly, aimed only at Callum. Did it care at all about the others? Daniel was mad and rightly so, but he had to understand that they'd had little choice, save going with the Z-Gen soldier to face whatever was in store for them. Was Tyrus's plan any better a fate, a foot soldier in a war he didn't yet understand? He didn't want to anger the demon further, however, taking one last look at the world which would never welcome them back again before boarding with the others.

"I'm sorry, Monica. The last thing we wanted was to cause you this pain," Alexis sincerely told her as the door closed. Callum didn't worry for Tyrus, the demon was likely inside already. No sooner had they moved back into the corridor of doors, Callum felt the ship lift off from the platform, something he'd never believed possible from seeing how huge it was from the outside. Siobhan was a little further down the corridor, walking past Simon who looked as tired as ever. He had none of the anger or worry on his face that Daniel did.

"I'm getting in the *Silverbolt* just in case things get even worse, and they will." Siobhan didn't wait for a response, pressing buttons next to a closed door and stepping through when it opened. Simon approached them then.

"I'm glad you're all in one piece." He glanced over them all to double-check. "I'd steer clear of the bridge if I were you, Daniel would flip his lid. Except for you, Monica, he needs you to copilot."

"I don't think he wants me there," Monica replied quietly.

"He still needs you."

She moved in the direction of the bridge, looking back to Callum with many emotions playing on her face. Reaching the end of the corridor, she opened the door that led to where Callum guessed the ship was controlled from. "Daniel told me everything, so I won't ask."

"If I had to make the choice again, I wouldn't hesitate," Saresan told him.

"You made the best of a bad situation," Simon agreed.

"Wait, you're agreeing with me?" The guard watched Simon shrug lightly, sipping from his cup.

"There's a saying my father has: things can always be worse, you could be dead." Jinar raised an eyebrow to that even as Saresan nodded in agreement.

"The way Daniel spoke, things are already bad," the sorcerer replied.

"Still better than the total cessation of experience and thought for all eternity. If you're alive, things can get better." Callum had heard that before.

"What do Z-Gen have against sorcerers?" Callum finally asked. "Siobhan didn't go into much detail about them before, only that we should avoid revealing our powers to them." Simon began to head to the common area, and Callum followed along with the others.

"Beats me. This is the first I've heard that they don't like you, but then you lot are the first sorcerers I've ever met. Perhaps they thought you were working with the Great Threat." The window in the common room had been repaired, once more showing the eternal blackness of space.

"The Great Threat?" Callum said as Saresan leaned against the wall just inside the room. "Another group like Z-Gen?"

"Or perhaps the demons," Jinar added.

"Details on the Great Threat are practically non-existent. There's been no eyewitness accounts from a survivor of their attacks. They don't happen often, but they're devastating," Simon had finished his drink, putting the cup on the table and turning his chair to them, "Z-Gen claims they send agents into our societies to weaken them from within in preparation for an attack. Whether that's true or not is another matter, but it would explain why they were suspicious of you."

"And why can't Z-Gen stop them?" Callum was thinking on their own world, its population reduced to corpses rotting peacefully in towns bereft of all but death. The thought sent a shiver down his spine, but the similarities weren't lost on him.

"The attacks would happen a lot more often if they didn't work to prevent them. When they do happen, only the local fleets can arrive in time to deal with it."

"Why wasn't everyone on that world talking about the Great Threat? A war on my world would be spoken of constantly." Callum got a vague shrug from the doctor as he reached for a device at his side, exactly like the one Monica had used on the walkways.

"When it's happened for as long as it has, it can all feel kind of distant, I guess." Simon turned his attention then to the device. "What's the situation, Daniel?"

"What do you think?" Daniel was clearly agitated. "We've got fighters in pursuit; they'll catch up in two minutes."

"Siobhan can take care of that." The doctor headed over to a small machine on the counter, sounding indifferent as he pressed a button.

"We're in enough trouble already! I'm not shooting down Z-Gen vessels!" There was a series of beeping noises from Daniel's end.

"And you think *not* shooting them will make them stop?" Siobhan's voice was coming out of the device now. Simon watched the machine dispense the liquid he drank so much of, though his attention was on the conversation. "I'm launching."

"I'm not opening the hangar."

"And you think I can't override it?" Callum could hear the pilot's grin through the device.

"Siobhan? Siobhan!" Daniel wasn't answered. "Damn it, she's going to get us all killed!" Callum didn't like hearing the group be torn apart by things they'd done. "Are they with you, Simon?"

"I'm not confining them to quarters." Simon took a sip from his cup, not raising his voice.

"That's not a request, Simon!"

"And if the ship gets damaged, I might need them to help me. You can be mad at them all you want when we're not being hunted by Z-Gen." Simon placed the device back on his belt.

"Will they ever stop hunting for us?" Callum asked, worried more about them than himself.

"They won't dedicate resources directly to it, if that's what you're asking, but neither will they let you be if they see you. Daniel may be blowing his top, but he has every right to be worried, there aren't many places you can go that don't answer to Z-Gen on matters of the law," Simon explained. Callum recognised the *Silverbolt* flying past the window, shooting beams of red far larger than he'd ever seen before. The ship shook lightly then, which made Simon look to the exit with a sigh. "If you need me, I'll be in the engine room monitoring the ship's status. Stay here or in your quarters... in case I need you." The doctor left with his drink in hand as the ship shook again, less than before.

"All this over magic, it is a shame," Jinar sighed as he stroked his beard. "I had hoped that persecution of those with arcane talent was something isolated to our world." Saresan had gone to the cupboards to search for a drink.

"So, what happens now, presuming Daniel kicks us off the ship later?" the guard asked.

"I have my doubts that will occur." Jinar watched Saresan open one of the cans, conjuring forth a drink of his own with a few mutterings and a finger click. It was in a rudimentary cup that obscured the contents.

"He's far past angry. Much as I don't want to admit it, if it hadn't been for Tyrus we'd be dead by now," Saresan remarked.

"*That* I doubt more so. Daniel is just one man: we could have easily taken him if the need arose." Jinar didn't sound like he relished that prospect, or was it that the conversation had shifted to the demon?

"And then Z-Gen too?" Saresan got no reply to that one.

"Saresan is right though, we owe a lot to the demon." Alexis's expression was neutral. "What puzzles me is why it's going to all this effort."

"It's because of me. Tyrus wants to train me to defeat the leader of the demons." It was far from the best time for Callum to tell the others, but waiting was worse; he didn't like keeping secrets, especially from friends, but it made him sound more important than he actually was. "I don't think I can do it, but we have little choice. It's the demon's magic that's protecting us from being noticed by the other demons."

"Presuming that Tyrus is not on their side," Jinar muttered.

"It would have no reason to save us back on our world if that were the case," Alexis pointed out. Jinar was still doubtful, sipping his drink as she continued, "There's something else that concerns me. The attacks of this 'Great Threat' sound similar to what happened to our world."

"I was thinking the same thing," Callum told her. The ship shook again, reminding them of the price they'd all paid to be having that conversation. Saresan looked back to the window as the *Silverbolt* flew past.

"Could be a coincidence. We don't know nearly enough about everything to make the connection." The guard sat down, watching the spectacle of combat that was just beyond the window. "You can ask Tyrus when you next see it, and if it's really going to train you, that'll be soon."

Chapter Twenty-Five

For a taste of perfection, there's no better than Otros Pale Blend. Ask your supplier to stock the ale your patrons won't be able to get enough of, now with a twist of lime to put an extra zing in your step!

You've only one life to live, so live it drinking Otros Ale.

—Advert from the Otros Ale Organisation

Siobhan claimed that she'd taken out half a dozen fighter craft upon her return, but Simon had a more accurate figure that was two shy of her boast. The damage to Daniel's ship had been described as 'mostly superficial' by the doctor, but the engine needed a check to ensure nothing had gone wrong. Callum presumed that was good news, but he hadn't seen Daniel since he'd entered the bridge. He'd heard him, however, arguing loudly with Monica about their situation, about their passengers and, worryingly, about themselves.

The mood on board was muted, with everyone keeping to themselves save Callum, who had no idea what to do with himself. He'd figured out how to turn on the strange viewing device on the wall and was immediately bombarded by vibrant colours and loud shouting of gibberish from people dressed in peculiar attire, addressing young children who looked a mixture of enthralled and confused.

He found out how to change what was on the screen before how to turn it off, seeing a brief snippet of a woman sat behind a table talking about them and what happened on Gui-Lon. It eliminated any possibility that they weren't criminals, branded as such by the woman and a Z-Gen official who proudly declared that they would be hunted down and dealt with.

Sleep was difficult, Callum unable to get the thoughts of the man Alexis had burned out of his head; the news that no soldiers had died in their escape was little comfort. Callum didn't know when he drifted off, but he was quickly awoken by the feeling of being watched. He knew who it was without looking as the door hadn't opened, Tyrus staring at him from beside the bed. That his hand was by his sword was surely a coincidence, he told himself.

"Why am I so important, Tyrus?" he asked again while sitting up, weary. Rest would not return soon. "Daniel had every right to try to throw us off his ship."

"Irrelevant," it declared. Tyrus always had its staff in hand. Was it to differentiate him from other demons?

"If you wanted someone to fight against the demons, Jinar would be a better choice. He's more skilled with magic than I'll ever be."

"Incorrect. You will surpass him in time," Tyrus replied. Callum couldn't picture that; his former mentor had such subtle mastery of his power, while his usage was brutish and blunt. Something came to mind that bothered him, unsure if he should ask the demon.

"But that doesn't make me more important than him."

"The others are expendable. You are not."

The demon was as uncaring as he'd imagined it would be, yet it was concerned for his life. No, that wasn't the right word. It was responsible for his safety and improvement, making him little more than a pawn in a game he still didn't understand.

"They're my friends. I won't sacrifice any of them, least of all for me," Callum declared defiantly.

"My duty is to train you to defeat Keiran. Your friends do not have the potential to defeat him. You do," it informed him.

"How do you know that?"

"Magic is second nature to my kind. We *are* magic."

Callum looked the demon over.

"You have spells cast on you?" He didn't feel any magic about the demon at that time, even though he knew its power.

"We are composed of self-sustaining magical energy, of physical form and intelligence. Humans are carbon-based, demons are magic-based."

"I thought humans were flesh and blood. Is that why you don't eat or sleep?" Callum tried to picture a creature made entirely of magic. Was their ichor like his blood?

"Demons lacks internal organs," it stated.

"Then how are you alive?" Tyrus paused at the question.

"How are *you* alive?" Callum hadn't expected his question to be answered with the same one, looking away to ponder it.

"My mother gave birth to me and since then, I've... been," was his answer.

"Three demons sacrificed a third of their being in a ritual to bring me to existence, weakening themselves in my creation," Tyrus explained. "I have no memory of a time before my existence, much like you. Unlike you, I came to be with the knowledge instilled in me by my creators."

"You have three parents?" Callum enquired, intrigued by that part of it.

"My creators lost control after the ritual and turned on one another. I alone survived."

"What?" Callum was alarmed. "I'm sorry, that must have been difficult for you."

"No." Tyrus's tone hadn't shifted in the least, as blunt as always. It left Callum feeling awkward but with more questions that he couldn't leave floating in his mind.

"Do demons treat their parents differently to us?"

"That they created me is irrelevant to me and them." They'd drifted far from the initial topic of discussion, but Callum was learning more about the demons with every question answered. What he was discovering didn't make them any more relatable, however.

"Surely they would've felt protective of you, you're their child." Callum was looking for the most subtle of reactions, anything. He got nothing.

"Demons are incapable of such bonds."

"You find it challenging to love?" Callum couldn't believe that they were incapable of it. They were intelligent beings, or so Tyrus had informed him; with that came empathy, surely.

"When I came to being, the first sensation I felt was near-maddening fury. The strong resist and become what I am, the rest turn feral like my creators when they lowered their guard to create me. We as a species are governed by that fury. There are certain emotions that we are incapable of feeling. Familial bonds are... one such feeling." Tyrus's hesitation at the end was telling, the first reaction he's got from the demon since the conversation began.

"You can't feel them at all?" Callum watched its face. "You can't laugh, smile, be happy?"

"No."

"That's... sad," Callum told it. "I don't know how I'd be able to live without those feelings."

"You do not miss what you have never experienced."

Tyrus had not a single hint of longing in its voice, watching him intently. Callum tried to think of never knowing joy or excitement, the hollowness that Tyrus had to feel that was only filled with anger.

"I'm sorry," Callum told it. The demon narrowed its eyes at him.

"You have more important things to focus on. Your magical training will start after your rest."

"Alexis and I think there might be a connection between the demons and the Great Threat." Callum looked away from the demon to the view of the stars that once more looked so different than before. "Do you know if there is one?"

When he didn't get an answer, Callum looked back, only to see that the demon was gone. He'd have to ask again when he knew it wasn't going to disappear. Alone once more, Callum tried to lay back and rest, but the will to sleep had been robbed from him by the burden of responsibility thrown onto his shoulders.

He was to train to fight the leader of the demons, or so Tyrus had said, a task he still thought wasn't possible. He knew so little about everything, and just him being had cost everyone so much. He recalled what Xiez had told him about his actions bringing pain to those he knew and couldn't disagree with it. What could he do against the leader of the demons? He had the sword, but anyone could use that, someone far more skilled with it and magic. But as he was finally soothed into slumber by the wonderfully comfortable bed, his thoughts drifted to the horde of demons that had ravaged his world, the death they dealt without discrimination to all they met. The world they'd fled from would be a slaughtering ground for them, the walkways turned into waterfalls of blood from those butchered by the clawed mass of red savagery.

Callum woke later with a clear head that quickly filled with the memories of the last week, as it had done every day since their rescue. For some reason, he hadn't expected Tyrus to be in his room again, watching him. It took him a moment to reassure himself that he wasn't in danger, or was he? The demon ignored his actions.

"I will train you now," it declared, turning to the door.

"I need to wash first, get ready for the day." Callum's heart had calmed down, now focusing on his hunger.

"Follow." Tyrus didn't leave room for compromise in its tone. The door opened and it stepped out and watched him, waiting.

Was it going to wait all day for him, or would its patience run out? Not wanting to find out the answer to that, he put on his boots and followed the demon out of his room. In silence it walked down the corridor, Callum struggling to keep pace with it as they passed door after door. He saw nobody else, nor was Tyrus getting Jinar or Alexis to come with them.

Tyrus led Callum to its room, standing in one end and watching him in silence. He waited for instruction but nothing came; what was it waiting for? Was he meant to show his magic to it, to see what he could do? The quiet continued until Callum broke it.

"Aren't the others coming?" he asked.

"Jinar refused. Alexis sleeps." Tyrus stared into his eyes. It had no books or learning aid in its hand, only the same wooden staff it always held; Callum was surprised it didn't shatter with its every strike. "What are you capable of?"

"My magic only appeared recently. I was attacked by a demon while in a tavern. I was cornered, sure I was going to die, and then... it just happened. I couldn't control it or stop it." Tyrus listened without reaction. "Apparently, I burned the whole building down, killed the demon. It knocked me out."

"A release of magical energy triggered by heightened emotions and a lack of control," Tyrus clarified. "That you did not suffer lasting repercussions is fortunate."

"What lasting repercussions?" Callum asked. He glanced at his hands, checking them for anything out of the ordinary.

"A human user of magic has a finite reserve available to them at any one time. It recovers gradually and, with training, can be improved. In your panic and with your inability to temper your magic, you expended your reserves and then fuelled it with your body." Callum thought back to waking in the church, how badly his being ached.

"I recovered quite quickly after that incident." Callum felt his magic surface, a subtle tingling at his fingertips.

"Exhaustion is the least of the consequences of over-exertion. Pain is next, then internal and external bleeding, weakening of the bone and muscle." Callum tried not to imagine that. "You falling unconscious was a self-defence mechanism of your body to protect yourself. Had you more control, you would have remained conscious and likely died."

"...Died?"

"Magic is powerful and dangerous. Inexperienced casters are some of the most dangerous." Tyrus looked at the wall behind him, it turning into a window so that they could see the stars. Its words echoed a warning he'd received once from Jinar.

"And the most dangerous?"

"Keiran." Callum was surprised he hadn't thought of that answer. "Some sorcerers willingly go beyond their limits to cast spells that exceed their power. A few will have paid with their lives. In time, you will know when you are at your limit, to best manage your ability."

Tyrus looked back at him then.

"Have you used magic since?" it asked. Callum tried to imagine the dire circumstances that led someone to cast a spell that would kill them, then shook off the ideas that came up before they dragged him down.

"A few times, in the enclave of the Silent Hand. I'm not very good at it, I can't cast as Jinar does," Callum admitted.

"Jinar's teachings are inferior. To will magic into the form you seek is the true manipulation of magical energy. Incantations and gestures allow easier casting at the cost of being intensely focused. Magic's only limitation is the mind of the caster." Tyrus brought a glowing orb of light into being with its free hand, it floating slowly in Callum's direction. He watched it, wary that it might be hot. "This knowledge is innate to my kind."

"If it's natural, why can't all demons cast magic? Most that I encountered charged at me with their claws and teeth." The orb was in front of his face now, Callum reaching out to touch it when he felt no heat. His hand went right through as if it wasn't there.

"A mind lost to rage cannot control magic. A mind distracted cannot focus on magic." The orb winked out of existence.

"Wouldn't this be easier if you imparted all you knew like you did before?"

"Impossible," Tyrus remarked. "Magic is too complicated for that to work."

"And language isn't?" The demon stared at him, leaving the question to die.

"Create an orb of light." Callum focused his thoughts inward on the energy in his fingers, feeling it move along his arms. He noticed the demon rushing towards him too late to stop it pushing him forcefully with its hand to the wall. The impact hurt and the surprise amplified the pain, Callum looking wide-eyed to his teacher.

"What was that for?" he shouted, rubbing his shoulder.

"Distraction in battle will kill you," warned the demon, hand gripping tightly onto his staff. He was grateful not to be on the receiving end of that. "You will learn to cast without thought."

"Magic doesn't come naturally to me, it resists my efforts." He was watching the demon cautiously, expecting another shove.

"You will bend it to your will until it breaks. You do not have time for failure. If Keiran and his minions find you, they will stop at nothing to kill you." Tyrus stepped away from him but looked no less threatening; it was intimidating by its very nature, tall and powerful.

"Does Keiran know that I'm working against him?"

"My rescuing you eliminates all other possibilities." Tyrus looked to the stars once more. Callum wondered what it was focusing on out there, every star looked the same from so far away. "You will need to improve before we reach the Council."

"Does he have a weakness, something we can seek out to slay him?" Callum got a glare back that silenced him.

"You already have it." Tyrus had to be referring to his sword, which he glanced at. As he did, Callum spotted a shift of red at the corner of his vision, his magic erupting within him even though he'd expected it to happen; the innate reaction to defend himself against a demon hadn't yet gone with Tyrus. His blade was easier to control than his magic, but he drew it too slowly, Tyrus reaching him and swinging with its staff. He flinched in fear that the demon would actually hit him, but its weapon stopped an inch from his face, motionless. His heart was leaping in his chest even as he stood unharmed.

"Fear focuses, hesitation kills."

"Why is the sword his weakness? And just who *is* Keiran? You must have some idea, even if it's just a guess." The weapon now drawn, he examined it attentively for the first time in a long while, trying to see what it saw. "It's very sharp and probably magical, but I don't see what else is special about it."

"The council will judge the full extent of its usefulness." Tyrus was watching the sword, he could tell that much. "As for Keiran, what is known is that he is a being apart from humanity and demons."

"He's something else?" Callum frowned. "An animal or beast?"

"Irrelevant. Defeating him is your only concern." Callum was reminded of what he'd just missed asking before, wondering now how receptive it would be to the question in the middle of their training.

"Are the Great Threat and the demons linked, Tyrus?" he asked.

"Presently irrelevant." Callum was getting annoyed with that word. "Your sole focus is training your magic. All other matters are secondary."

"Even if worlds fall while I do this?"

"Worlds will fall regardless. You are not strong enough to oppose Keiran, nor oppose a world-conquering force regardless of its composition."

Callum's annoyance evolved into anger that fuelled the urge to unleash his magic, one that he was suppressing. The demon observed him once more. "You will learn to focus magic without anger and fear."

"I still haven't agreed to help you defeat Keiran." Callum watched its body shift subtly, a change of stance which he wasn't comfortable with. "You speak as if I have."

"Yet you train with me. You understand the alternative."

He did, looking again at the demon's staff; did it know his mind, that he was going to try training despite his reservations? It was that moment when Tyrus tried to swing his staff again at Callum, but this time he was more prepared. His sword in hand, he swung at the demon's weapon wildly.

Despite his clumsiness, he cut the weapon in two, the top half clattering to the ground.

The demon looked at its weapon as it reformed to wholeness within moments. "Inadequate. You will improve."

The finality of its words told him that it knew his intentions. No matter what his misgivings were, Callum had to try for all those who'd died on his world, guided by the guilt everyone had told him not to hold onto.

The training had exhausted him, and though it had felt like all day, he and Tyrus had been going for only a few hours. Over and over again, the demon succeeded in catching him off guard, pointing out how slow he was to react, unprepared even when he knew it would happen at some point.

His efforts to make his magic come easier had been fruitless; without emotions to urge spells into being, it barely answered him. Eventually, Tyrus told him that the lesson was over until he could draw upon his magic without effort, leaving him to his own devices once more. It was obvious that Tyrus was annoyed by his lack of progress, though what did it expect after such little time?

Returning to his quarters and taking a much-needed shower, Callum was left with many things to ponder and all the time in the world to do so. He had no idea where the ship was going or if he'd get a warm welcome from any of the crew, so he decided to get something to eat.

Nobody was in the common area, Callum searching the cupboards and settling on one of the pouches that contained the meal he'd eaten before, looking up occasionally to the view of the stars as he ate. How many people at that moment were being pursued by Z-Gen because of the powers they had? Why did Z-Gen perceive them as a threat to begin with?

Once his hunger had been satisfied, he decided to find the one person on board who'd answer those questions for him that wasn't mad at them for the incident on Gui-Lon. He went down to the cargo area in search of them, knowing that was the only place he hadn't checked extensively. There were fewer containers down there than before, leaving an open area which would've made a decent place to train if Daniel would've allowed it, which was unlikely.

He thought he saw movement within the small maze of boxes, walking towards it and looking to his left to see an open doorway. The room was illuminated only by a soft blue light and there was a series of beeping noises coming from within, off-key and without rhythm. Walking to the door, Callum saw countless strange tools hanging off the walls and the source of the blue glow, multiple screens built into the walls and on top of counters around the edges of the room.

They showed pictures of odd devices and huge swathes of text he could barely read. In the middle was a metal table that had more devices on it, although they didn't look intact. A few of the screens started flashing red with a single word, and a moment later Simon emerged from a connecting room and rushed to tap various parts of the screens quickly. He hadn't noticed Callum, completely absorbed in whatever work he was doing. Callum thought against speaking at that moment, waiting for his rapid finger presses to turn the red screens into blue ones, the doctor breathing a sigh of relief.

"Is everything alright?" His question startled Simon, almost making him spill the drink he'd just picked up.

"Don't *do* that!" the doctor exclaimed, shaking his head. "Knock next time, alright?"

"The doorway was open, I'm sorry." At that, Simon turned his way and sighed, taking a careful sip of his drink.

"No, I'm sorry. You weren't to know what I was doing." Simon placed his cup down on the table and picked up two objects from it, attaching them together. "Nobody else really comes in here."

"Is this your workshop?" Callum guessed, watching him get a third object and attach it to the others.

"Might as well be, I rarely have to heal anyone. Your friend was the first time I fired up the medical room for more than a machine diagnostic in four months." Simon put the assembled item down, turning to the monitors.

"From here I can keep track of every system on board, find problems quickly and deal with them before they become major issues. Most of the time it's the same things going funny, of course, like the windows."

"At least it keeps you busy." Another of the screens went red, Simon glancing at it before picking up his coffee again. "Aren't you going to deal with that?"

"It usually sorts itself out, I wouldn't worry." Sure enough, the red screen reverted back to walls of text after a few seconds. "I'd rather be busy doing what I spent seven years of my life training for, but this pays just as good. Well, it did until now, anyway."

"I'm sorry." Callum got a shrug from the doctor.

"No point fretting about something that's already happened, it won't change anything. Not that I'm super pleased we're all wanted criminals, mind you, but it is what it is. Daniel wanted to drop you off on the first planet or space station we found, but we talked him out of it."

"How did you manage that?" Callum asked.

"Pragmatism," Simon answered, not waiting for Callum to say that the word meant nothing to him. "If we're wanted by Z-Gen, getting rid of you lot will only make it easier for them to capture us."

"Like you working as an engineer even though you're trained as a doctor."

"If I ever need to treat a cyborg, at least I'll have a better idea of what I'm doing." Once again, Simon answered the question Callum didn't get to ask, "A cyborg is a human with machine parts in them designed to replace biological functions. Almost any bit of the human body can be replaced with metal or synthetic alternatives that replicate or improve on natural specifications, as long as the price is right."

"Almost anything?" Callum was trying to process the image. "How does that work?"

"Medicine is a lot different to what you're probably used to, Callum. We have a deep understanding of how the body works and how it can stop working, be it disease or trauma. We can treat most illnesses routinely, allowing people to live as long and healthy a life as they choose to, without the risk of the black death killing you off." Callum's eyes widened at the mention of that deadly disease. "We had the misfortune of taking that one with us when we started colonising other worlds. Rats are a tenacious pest. We can't treat everything, of course, and complications occur, but all in all, it's a good time to be alive."

"It's a confusing time for me. Going down to that planet left me with far more questions than I thought it would. I felt like an onlooker viewing from afar, even though I was right in the middle of it," he told the doctor honestly, who smiled in reply.

"I can imagine. Your world was isolated from communication, so you're out of the loop. Even if people did know about all of this, they certainly wouldn't have told the masses." Simon finished his drink, leaning back on the table with his arms folded. "Not all worlds are like the one we went to, even if some will look similar. Every world has its own cultural traditions and quirks that they stubbornly cling onto while being able to communicate with almost any populated planet in the galaxy within moments. The human condition is stubborn like that."

"How many worlds are like mine?" Callum asked hopefully. "Perhaps when all this is all over, you can take me and my friends to one of them."

"I can't tell you how many of them there are, by their very nature they're not easy to find. There's all manner of other worlds though, each with a myriad of government types, from democracies to dictators and everything else you can think of. Do you think you could go back to a world like yours after all you've seen, however?"

More than anything Callum wanted exactly that, to wake up with all of the horrible events he'd witnessed since meeting Jinar being nothing more than a dream.

Wanting to distract himself from that thought, he decided to ask a different question.

"What is your home like?" he asked. Simon had started to fiddle with a tool from the table with a flashing light and a small screen for words on the top.

"My home? I was born and raised on a lifeless, dusty rock with an atmosphere thinner than a bald man's hairline, called Vetanus. The view from out your window was as boring as you can imagine."

"It had no life? How did you survive?" Callum had a chair in a corner pointed out to him, which he moved to a more central position before sitting down. Another screen flashed red for a few seconds before returning to normal.

"The same way we are now, in an artificial environment. I lived in a complex built into a mountainside, sealed off from the vacuum beyond. Machines generated gravity and heat, synthesized air and water. They even helped us grow our own food and mine ores from deep underground." Simon checked the screens for a moment. "If you didn't look outside, you'd've thought it was a fancy apartment complex."

"But you did." Callum watched Simon smile a little at his comment.

"That's one of the reasons why I decided to become a doctor, it's the kind of profession that can buy you a ticket off-world when a trading frigate shows up. I served on a few other vessels before Daniel picked me up."

"Do you miss home?" Callum's question provoked silence and a distant look from Simon that lasted a few seconds.

"I didn't at first. I was glad to be away from there, now I'm not so sure. Living on a ship or a space station isn't the same as having somewhere static that's your own. I wouldn't have picked Vetanus to be born on, but nowhere else is going to have the same feel as there." He looked to his empty cup. "Or maybe I'm just getting old, who knows?"

The room went silent save for another red flashing thing which stopped eventually. The talk of homes had only succeeded in making Callum homesick for the rolling green fields and fresh air of his own.

Simon was looking at his sword with curiosity. "Would you mind if I held onto that for a little bit?" Callum followed his eyes, a hand reaching for the handle of his blade.

"Why does it interest you?" he asked the doctor, trying not to sound wary.

"Scientific curiosity, I assure you. Your friends were talking about the weapon, and I wanted to see if any of their claims stood up to some tests." Simon smiled. "I wouldn't need it long and my equipment won't damage it. If what Jinar said is true, I doubt anything I have could." Callum thought on the request for a moment, then unsheathed the blade and offered it cautiously by the handle, deciding that he could trust Simon.

"Don't touch the edge, it might take your finger off." Simon nodded and took the blade, surprised at its weight.

"Not quite what I was expecting, the first of many mysteries, perhaps." Simon carefully placed it in the middle of the table. "I'll only need a few hours with it, three at most. Gives me something to work on rather than keeping the ship together. Anything else you need?"

"Actually, yes. I want to learn more about Z-Gen." Simon nodded and reached to one of the black tiles that were close to hand. "I can't read, so you know."

"You don't need to with this. If you tap anywhere on it and ask a question, the computer will search the ship's database and public-access information repositories to find the answer for you. You'll be able to find a lot about Z-Gen: for the most part, they like to be open about how most of the organisation works." Callum took the tile, finding it lighter than he anticipated it to be. It felt like glass in his hands, not what he'd expected at all.

"And Z-Gen won't be able to find us by me doing this?"

"No more than they can already by us flying around in space." That was less reassuring than it should've been, but he had what he'd come for, leaving the doctor to his work.

Chapter Twenty-Six

Callum had been staring at the glass object for a few minutes, unsure of how to phrase his question as he sat on Alexis's bed. He'd brought the device to her, curious if it would be helpful in her efforts to teach him how to read. She'd kept to herself since their return to the ship, worried just as he'd been about Daniel casting them out as soon as he could. He didn't know which angle to start his learning from; if the group were as large as it had been hinted at to them, where was best to begin? Alexis tapped the device carefully.

"Please explain the history of Z-Gen," she requested. To Callum's amazement, an image appeared to float in the air above the glass, as if brought into being by some magical force. The symbol was a golden 'Z' surrounded by stars, all encapsulated by a golden band.

"Z-Gen is a military organisation founded 2,802 years ago, full name Zettai Genforce." The voice that came from the device was genderless and artificial, yet fluent and easy to understand. Callum found it unnatural to listen to. "Originally based in the Zettai system, they were a mercenary force that protected the system from space piracy and interplanetary crime. They conducted operations with military efficiency and adherence to local laws, continuing to do so to this day. Due to continued success, their assistance was requested by neighbouring systems, allowing Z-Gen to expand its area of operations and scope. Over time, local governments found it more cost-efficient to outsource their military forces to Z-Gen. Such regions became more stable, as Z-Gen was the sole military power, rendering conflicts all-but-impossible without Z-Gen backing."

"I wonder why they gave up their military forces so willingly," Alexis pondered. "The lords of our world would never have bowed their knee to another."

"Perhaps that's why there were so many wars," Callum speculated.

"Among other things. They fought over territory, resources and beliefs. I wouldn't be surprised if kings waged conflict over the hands of princesses." Callum could believe that, thinking back to the child king that had ruled his home; what kind of man would he have become if given the chance?

"Do you wish me to continue?" the voice from the device asked.

"Please," Callum said after Alexis nodded.

"Z-Gen continued to expand its area of operations as more systems saw the stability that the organisation provided and wished to also be under their protection. As the organisation grew, it shifted from a mercenary operation to a full-fledged military force, with a chain of command to fit. Z-Gen reached its current size with the Great Terran Treaty, overseeing the protection of approximately ninety-nine percent of the colonised galaxy from threats without and within."

"The Terran Treaty?" Callum repeated, curious about that term.

"Would you like to hear about the Terran Treaty?" the voice asked.

"Are the Terrans part of Z-Gen?" Alexis enquired.

"The Terran Empire is a vestigial power in the galaxy that is independent of Z-Gen. I can go into more detail if you wish."

"No, thank you. Stick with Z-Gen." Callum then thought. "Actually, tell me about the Great Threat." The device didn't speak immediately, Alexis and Callum looking at one another.

"The Great Threat is a force that lies beyond current human colonised space. They are in a state of war with Z-Gen." There was another pause. "At present, three hundred and seven worlds have been attacked by the Great Threat." The number was soul-crushing to hear; how many billions of people had been on those planets?

"How many of those worlds survived an attack from the Great Threat?" Alexis spoke quietly, guessing what the answer would be, as did Callum.

"No worlds have survived an attack from the Great Threat."

"How many *people* have survived an attack from the Great Threat?" Callum asked next.

"There are no witness statements available concerning attacks by The Great Threat." Alexis shook her head as she heard it.

"That doesn't make sense, how could no one survive? They could hide or flee in a ship." Alexis was frowning as Callum imagined the piles of bodies, cities aflame. "How long have these attacks been going on?"

"The first documented attack by the Great Threat occurred one hundred years ago."

A hundred years. Callum had never heard of a war lasting more than a couple before both sides tired of conflict. A century of battles, and yet nobody on the world they'd been to had even mentioned it; was it that insignificant to them? Or had it gone on for so long that it was a part of their life, no more worrisome than stubbing your toe or the chance of rain?

Callum thought again on the possibility that the demons were the Great Threat; it made sense to him, but there was nothing on the records about it.

"What do you know about demons?" Callum asked the device. It paused.

"Demons have been an integral part of human mythology since ancient times—" it began.

"No, *the* demons. Scaled creatures, seven-foot-tall, users of magic."

Callum hadn't even noticed the door opening but Alexis did, glancing to whoever was there.

"They're nothing but trouble, that's what," Monica announced. That made Callum look up to see her stood in the doorway, arms folded. It looked like she'd been crying, but the only expression on her face was weariness. Her tone softened as she glanced between the two of them. "I'm not disturbing anything, am I?"

"Not at all. We were just looking up information on Z-Gen." Callum stood, her expression reminding him of their situation. "Look, I'm sorry about all this."

"I was the one that took you all down there, it's my fault." Monica looked to her feet. "I'd stay clear of Daniel for a while if I were you, he's still angry."

Alexis gave her a sympathetic smile.

"He has every right to be."

Callum wondered just how much Daniel and the crew knew about Tyrus's intent for him, the plan to train his magic to oppose the leader of the demons. He didn't want to bring attention to it and make their predicament even worse.

"Daniel..." Monica sighed, looking up to Callum, "Daniel overacted when we came back. I've been trying to talk him round, tell him that we can sort this out with Z-Gen if we can find someone to talk to about it."

"Do you think they'd listen to reason?" Callum was dubious.

"Not conventional reason, no," Monica answered. Alexis raised an eyebrow.

"Bribery?" She got a nod. "Would that work?"

"It'd require a serious amount of incentive for them to forget and the right person to make it happen. A commander, someone with the ear of one of the generals." That Z-Gen were susceptible to bribes didn't entirely surprise him; some less scrupulous guards would turn a blind eye for far less on his world. "It's better than doing nothing, that's what I keep telling Daniel."

"Perhaps you could ask Tyrus to help you with that," Callum suggested.

"It might be able to get you more things you could use."

"If it's all the same to you, Callum, if I never saw that thing again, I'd be that much happier for it."

For three nights, restful sleep eluded Callum. Sat on the edge of his bed, he rubbed his face and took a deep breath. He could've checked the time easily enough, but it didn't matter, the nightmares would arrive regardless.

It was usually the same one each time, more vivid and jaunting with each occurrence. He could see the fury in Johnathan's eyes this time as the man tried to strike him down. The swinging of the axe was normally when he woke up, severing his connection to the dream just as the flames touched his head.

This time had been different, however, Callum surrounded on all sides by searing flames which prevented his escape. Johnathan's clothes caught the flames as he readied for the killing blow, and Callum could only watch as the man burned. Skin and flesh melted off him, leaving nothing but a charred black skeleton. Not even with Callum's screams did it end; Johnathan still stood despite everything, as if his menace and anger alone kept him going.

The fire that had all but incinerated Johnathan then enveloped him, the skeleton's eyes burning white-hot with rage as he swung down with a chilling cry. The image had refused to shift from his mind even as he got up and paced, failing to silence it with other thoughts. He was likely the only one awake save for Tyrus, but he had no desire to get another lecture from his mentor at how he'd still failed to separate emotion from his spell casting.

Now wasn't even the best time to train, his thoughts scattered and yet focused all at once on terribleness. He tried to think of a happier memory, but this only brought his thoughts to the destruction of his world, and that made him feel even worse.

"Am I that much of a mess?" he asked himself.

He looked around just in case the demon had appeared, but much to his relief, he was alone. He stopped by the desk in his room, which only had his sword on it; Simon had told him that he hadn't been able to deduce much from his examination of the blade, but the data would give him 'a lot of bedtime reading'.

It was exactly the same as when he'd handed it over, the doctor true to his word. He pulled himself away from the spiral of disheartening thought he'd been caught in, trying to find anything else to focus on. He settled on the black thing on the wall which displayed moving images, turning it on with a press of his finger. A serious-looking man was sat at a desk while words scrolled around him, displaying information he couldn't yet grasp. The words the man spoke, however, were clear enough.

"...at this time. In other news, Z-Gen has released a brief statement on the interrogation of the wanted fugitive William Thompson Frederickson after his successful capture, following an ambush by Z-Gen forces on the rogue terrorist Bastian Volso." The man was stern and blunt, the voice coming from the corners of his room.

"Z-Gen are currently ascertaining his part in working with the Great Threat. This station has learned that a Z-Gen strike team were sent discreetly to raid what seemed to be a research facility on an otherwise unpopulated moon ten light-years away. Z-Gen declined to comment on the existence of said team, but the fact can only lead to the conclusion that they had uncovered the terrorist's hideout. What they found there is unknown, but it will no doubt cripple the future efforts of those he worked with, if not destroy them altogether. Z-Gen also refused to comment on the exact number of dead, but we have confirmed that two bodies were recovered from the scene of the ambush. They have assured us and the public that the threat Bastian Volso posed to all humanity has finally been lifted. Z-Gen has refused to confirm or deny rumours that Bastian Volso actually escaped from the ambush. We'll have more on this story as information emerges."

The man left a pause as information changed on the screen. "In other news, a freighter was damaged in a rare mid-flight collision when..."

Callum didn't know what 'terrorist' meant but gathered that it was a bad term. He pressed the screen again, hoping that it would turn off, only to find that the image changed to a woman enthusiastically talking about soap. He assumed it was soap as it wasn't in bar form, even as the lady extolled its many virtues to a somewhat disinterested man next to her that seemed to be considering his position in life.

He liked that even less, tapping again rapidly in the hopes that that would turn off the images, but it merely made what he was watching a lot louder. Quickly he tapped again, and the scene changed once more, to a confusing spectacle of multi-legged metal monsters locked in deadly combat with a fluorescent green horseman. He was attacking one of the creatures with what looked like an oar from a boat when the image suddenly cut to black. Callum breathed a sigh of relief.

"We'll return with *Sword Slasher 9: Fall of the Prism-Banes* after this commercial break," declared an overly dramatic voice. To Callum's horror, it returned to the woman talking about soap. This time the man was absent, and she was speaking a lot faster. He tried to turn off the screen again but was unable to, so he set out of his room to find someone who could, heading towards the common area. He was surprised to hear noise coming from there that sounded like the soap women again.

Opening the door, he saw that Siobhan was lounging back in one of the chairs with a drink in hand. More curiously she wasn't alone, Saresan sat beside her with a perplexed expression. That he was alive at all considering her rage when they were on Gui-Lon made him wonder just how they'd managed to patch things up, if they even had. Perhaps it was more pragmatism, as Simon had put it earlier, or maybe he'd missed the part where she'd shouted at him.

"...So, why is the glowing green centaur fighting the revenge-o-trons?" Saresan asked. "And what *are* revenge-o-trons? Do we need to worry about them?"

"What he doesn't know is that he's also a revenge-o-tron made entirely of demon-nanites that rewrite his memory every time he's just about to realise that." Siobhan took a drink after that.

"Demon... nanites?" Saresan slowly repeated, trying to work out if she was joking.

"They were created when the demon emperor was nearly caught in a black hole that he made to ensnare the warriors of truth in a never-ending battle with the creatures beyond the triangles that reside in non-space," she spoke as if it was all obvious. The guard noticed Callum and nodded in greeting.

"I didn't know you were up," he said to Callum. "You look like hell."

"I haven't been sleeping well," he replied, getting an understanding nod. Saresan seemed fine compared to him; what was his friend doing that he'd missed? Siobhan waved him over.

"Pull up a chair, it's about to get to the bit where the four rings of hope are used to dispel the shadows of the lords of despair!" She noticed his confusion. "I'll explain it all as it happens, don't worry."

"I can't make the images stop in my room," Callum informed them. "They only got louder when I tried."

"Just use the remote." Siobhan corrected herself quickly, "You won't know what a remote is, will you? That's okay, we'll sort it out later." The woman talking about soap was replaced by the green horseman, who conjured four multi-coloured rings out of nothingness that began to glow with an inner light.

"How many of these did you say there was?" Saresan was clearly struggling to make sense of what he was seeing. Considering the confusing mess on view, Callum wasn't surprised.

"Not enough. They're working on a new one, and the director promised that it'll answer the most important question of them all: if the demon emperor can truly be killed. I can't wait, it's going to be awesome!" Siobhan looked past Callum then, which made him turn around to see Daniel in the corridor. The man looked both exhausted and annoyed, arms folded and staring him down. Callum certainly felt small and guilty, looking away.

"I turned down your viewscreen." Daniel's voice cracked with anger he kept in check.

"I'm sorry," Callum sighed. "And not just about the noise. I know I can't change things—"

"You're right, you can't," Daniel snapped back. Siobhan winced. "The sooner you're off my ship, the better." Callum wanted to reassure him, but no words arose; what could he say?

"I'm sorry," he repeated, getting a glare. Daniel walked off, muttering to himself. Looking down the corridor, Callum noticed Monica in an open doorway, waiting for her partner. What was said between them was lost in the distance, but it seemed argumentative.

"He'll simmer down eventually. If he'll ever forgive you is another thing." Siobhan shrugged, eyes glued to the screen as four identical knights in bright orange armour charged towards a monster made entirely of lava. "Same goes for you, Saresan."

"Does this mean I need to watch my back when I walk about the ship?" Saresan half-joked. The momentary look he got made him go quiet again, the pilot quickly returning to her viewing as if nothing had happened. He wondered if rest would come even if he tried to sleep, but he lost nothing by trying. Saresan leaned back in his chair, pondering the scene before him on the viewscreen as Callum left the two to their late-night – or was it day? – viewing. When sleep finally came, it brought with it more nightmares.

Chapter Twenty-Seven

An Alpha-Level incident has occurred on Gui-Lon. Multiple GT agents involved. No fatalities reported on-world, though multiple Z-Gen personnel were injured. GT agents escaped world with assistance of collaborators. Four fighter craft destroyed in their escape with loss of all pilots.

Please find files on all persons involved in the incident attached below. Of note is the lack of information on the persons from Vedallan IV, a world recently discovered to be devoid of life. Investigations of Vedallan IV are ongoing.

Trajectory of escaped GT agents is unknown. Please inform your superior of any developments or sightings.

—Internal Z-Gen report

Callum woke with a start, sweating. His confusion was shunted aside immediately by the burning white eyes in front of him that belonged to Tyrus. He hoped it was Tyrus, anyway.

"Lights," he declared quickly, the room flooding with illumination that confirmed his suspicion. He didn't bother asking how long it had been there; Tyrus was unlikely to answer.

"Dress. We have arrived," it declared. He went for a shower, not caring if the demon objected to his cleanliness. It said nothing as he washed, the hot water splashing away the sleep that clung to him.

"Where are we?" Callum asked loudly, hoping it heard over the noises of the shower.

"Where we need to be." Tyrus was enigmatic as always. "Bring the sword." Oddly, Callum heard the door to his quarters opening and closing; had it actually left in a mundane manner, or had someone else entered? Washing quickly, he recovered his clothes from the machine and dressed, finding that his room was indeed bereft of the demon. Buckling his scabbard, Callum walked out into the corridor and looked for the others. Unfortunately, Daniel had encountered Tyrus, midway into a heated discussion.

"There's *nothing* here, Tyrus! It's the same as any other bit of empty space, just like I told you at the beginning!" Daniel folded his arms, passing a none-too-pleased look Callum's way.

"You will wait here for our return." Tyrus was focused on the man, looking down at him with a slight snarl.

"You said nothing about waiting, just to get you here! Don't try and change the deal on me; the second you're all off the ship, we're going!" Daniel shot Callum an angry look. Tyrus didn't turn to see who he was staring at.

"Come," the demon ordered, moving towards its room.

"We're not done talking!" Daniel shouted.

He was answered by silence as the demon entered its room, leaving Daniel to punch the wall in frustration and then immediately regret it, shaking his hand and wincing. Callum felt sorry for him but didn't want to become the new focus of his wrath, stepping past quickly. No words were spoken as he did so, quickly following after Tyrus to see that it wasn't alone; Alexis and Jinar were also present, the latter reluctantly if his body language was broadcasting correctly, sat in an armchair that hadn't been there before. Alexis gave Callum a weak smile that he returned before looking for the others and not finding them.

"The council will see us now," Tyrus declared without flourish.

"Are they going to meet us here?" Callum asked.

"No." The demon gave no further detail, waiting for something. Callum looked to his former mentor for clarity and only got a vague shrug.

"It has not spoken a word of how we will meet this council," Jinar explained. "And it is only us that are going. It would seem the council have no interest in non-sorcerers."

"Aren't you needed here to protect the ship from being found by Keiran?" Callum was worried about Daniel and the others, even if the feeling wasn't mutual with all of them.

"The council will shield them while they remain," Tyrus answered.

"Congratulations, Callum, you have succeeded in drawing blood from a stone by actually getting a question answered." Jinar slow clapped even as the demon ignored him.

"And what if Z-Gen finds the ship? Will the council protect them then?" Alexis was still concerned. The creature went silent once more. Callum felt something build up in the very air around them, similar in sensation to teleportation magic but also very unlike it. Alexis looked about with the same concern he had, and even Jinar grew curious at what was happening.

"How odd" — Jinar's declaration wasn't an impressed one — "that you would use a portal. The spell relies on close proximity to the connecting location, I imagine?"

"Less expenditure of magic to cast. Harder to trace," Tyrus replied.

"Trace?" Alexis asked as the build-up of energy around them grew to the point of discomfort for Callum.

"Casting leaves residual magic that dissipates over time. Stronger castings take longer."

"The portal magic must be powerful indeed." Alexis got a nod from Jinar. "Enough that we needed to be here for it not to be noticed immediately by the servants of Keiran."

"It will be open only for a short while. Be ready."

An instant later a tiny dot of darkness appeared on the far wall which unleashed a massive surge of power. It hit Callum's body as if a gust of wind, nearly knocking him off his feet. Alexis wasn't so fortunate, stumbling back into the wall as she recovered. Jinar seemed entirely unaffected and unimpressed by it all, but Callum was in awe enough for both of them.

The dot expanded rapidly into a rectangular opening which led into a swirling red and black tunnel of lightning. Where it led Callum couldn't see, but it felt wrong and powerful, as well as scary. Tyrus didn't hesitate in entering the doorway into the unknown. In an instant, it was gone. Callum had seen teleportation before, but he'd thought a portal would be different.

Jinar stood from his chair, it vanishing into blue sparkles as he approached the portal with an appraising eye. Did he not trust it, or was he seeking a flaw to ridicule Tyrus about later? He hummed neutrally before reaching out and touching it himself, vanishing as quickly as the demon had. Alexis and Callum looked to one another, neither wanting to go first.

"Together?" she offered.

"Is that a good idea? What if it does something terrible to us?"

Callum had stepped closer without realising it; was it dragging him towards the entrance, or was it more subtle, luring him with dormant curiosity? The portal almost seemed liquid and yet wasn't, confounding him enough that he reached out with one finger to test which it was. At the instant of contact, he was wrenched violently in, propelling him at speeds that bordered on painful through the tunnel of the crimson dark. The black lightning enveloped him, numbing any hint of pain instantly as if it was shielding him from what could've been. He had no time to be afraid.

After mere moments, he arrived at a place that defied all that he knew or had ever imagined. All around them were stars, but they didn't shine as bright, blurry and indistinct. The next thing he felt was his body tingling from the raw magic around him, the air oozing with it, but not to an extent that it hurt him. Then he panicked; how was he still alive beyond the ship?

He didn't trust that his feet had found ground, nearly falling when he saw that nothing was beneath him. Only when his mind realised that there were no stars at his feet did he work out that the floor was black as oblivion. A tiny red spark of energy crackled off it, further confirming that something was there, but he had so many questions that he hadn't noticed that the others were there with him. For once, Jinar was genuinely astounded, although he was trying his best to hide it.

"...Wow," was all Alexis said after a couple of seconds, captivated by the strangeness around them. Tyrus was unconcerned, but Callum had expected that.

"We are here," Tyrus declared flatly. Everywhere was so silent, yet the demon's words didn't echo. Perhaps the eternity beyond the ship was this quiet, but that didn't feel right to Callum.

"Where *is* here?" Alexis asked.

"A space between space."

"A pocket of being where there was none?" Jinar was stroking his beard, crouching down to examine the floor beneath them. It was no wider than two metres.

"Undetectable to the human eye and impossible to interact with. It is here and yet not, as is time." Jinar and Callum frowned, the former in curiosity and the latter bewilderment. "Here is apart from time."

"Apart from time? Then how are we moving?" Callum checked that his hands were, in fact, moving when he looked at them.

"We are apart from time," the demon repeated.

"That doesn't help."

"The time that passes here is apart from the time you experience—" Tyrus began again.

"Stop saying 'apart', please. It's not making any sense." Callum waited for the demon to continue, but it didn't. He shook his head. "Is time passing on the ship for Daniel now?"

"Yes."

"And it's passing for us too here?" Callum was trying to work it out in his head, two streams of time as if rivers that flowed and yet didn't. The analogy didn't help.

"Yes, but it does not affect you chronologically." Callum waited for a simpler explanation.

"What it is saying is that while we are here, we will not age," Jinar clarified. "Nor will we hunger or tire. Time passes for the convenience of existence, so that things can occur, but ignores us otherwise. I would presume that magic replenishment is unaffected by this, else your pocket of non-reality would not exist, correct?"

"That humans do not age here is an unintended side effect irrelevant to my kind."

"If you are apart from where we come from, why do you care about the demons or anything that's happening to us?" Alexis's question caught the demon's attention, earning her a stare. "Unless this place cannot exist sealed off permanently." It didn't speak or react further for a moment.

"The council may answer your question if you speak it," Tyrus informed her. Jinar grinned.

"So, there *is* something that you do not know." He was ignored by the demon, which had turned to the path ahead.

"Follow." Tyrus started to walk along the barely visible walkway, not waiting for them to keep pace. With how narrow their path was, the three walked in single file, with Callum in the middle. After only a few seconds of travel, their surroundings suddenly changed, as if by magic. Callum presumed that was how it occurred, though there'd been no portal and he hadn't felt the sensation of teleportation.

Perhaps the place they were in wasn't one unified location but multiple smaller ones bound by arcane trickery, like a series of islands with bridges built between them. Callum paused for a moment, considering that weeks ago, that line of thinking would've been alien to him, yet there he was, trying to make sense of it as best he could.

In front of him was a larger platform and other demons that all turned to face them. Tyrus stopped, as did the others. Afraid for a moment that they'd lunge for him, he was relieved that the group merely stared, but that was no less off-putting.

They nearly looked identical, but where he'd once seen uniformity, he now spied subtle differences. Some were a little taller, others had a darker shade of red for their scales and fewer still wore dark grey robes that hid all but their eyes. None of them had weapons, although if Tyrus was right about its kind, they didn't need them.

Tyrus narrowed its eyes at those who stared and they returned to their activities, quiet conversation that Callum couldn't catch the meaning of. It was in their language, however, which surprised him; he'd expected them to have a secretive tongue of their own. Were the demons humouring them? Tyrus started moving again, ignoring those around them as they passed. Callum stopped by a pair of demons who both turned to him, looking down as if he were nothing. He quietly cleared his throat.

"Hello." He was careful with his words but only got a sneer for his trouble, the demons returning to their conversation.

"As if we needed more evidence that demons lack charm," Jinar muttered.

Tyrus had continued to walk despite them stopping, stepping now on platforms that glowed with an inner red light. Callum felt powerful magic within the material; perhaps it was what provided the glow, but he couldn't be sure. Catching up, they walked in silence for another minute, Alexis still taking in their surroundings with great interest. Then they were somewhere else once more, Callum now sure that some kind of magic transportation was going on.

In front of them was a demon that was entirely unlike the others. It had a two-handed sword sheathed in a back scabbard that was secured by a leather strap across its chest, another weapon that would've fit in perfectly on his own world. Covering its eyes was a strip of black cloth that was tied around its head like a blindfold, but it failed to obscure the burning white of its eyes. Tyrus had already begun a conversation with the demon, making Callum wonder how instantaneous transport between the platforms actually was.

"What was once is no longer," Tyrus told the demon.

"The Council's vision is far beyond our own." The other demon's voice was different, but Callum couldn't pin down how. It also spoke a little more like he did, which was comforting and unsettling all at once. It looked beyond Tyrus to Callum. "Is that him?"

"Yes," replied Tyrus.

The other demon was trying to convey something with its face, but Callum couldn't figure out what; was it envy, anger or pity? Despite the cloth obscuring its vision, he felt its eyes assessing him. "Speak, Baylon. We lack time," Tyrus snapped.

The other looked to its fellow, not fazed by the sharpness of words.

"He must trust you," Baylon advised.

It was the first time Callum had heard a demon use that word and mean it, which puzzled him all the more about their ilk. They couldn't comprehend trust, surely.

"A liberty unaffordable by time," dismissed Tyrus. Baylon shifted.

"It is necessary, Tyrus."

"We will see the Council now."

Had Tyrus ignored Baylon, or were no words needed between them? Either way, the armed demon led them now and Tyrus followed, with Callum and his friends behind. Silence once more descended.

Baylon led them for many minutes, down red glowing platforms and past small groups of demons that all talked quietly and stared when they passed. Callum definitely didn't feel welcome, the glares they received barely falling short of provoking a sense of intrusion into the quiet solitude of their place beyond places. Baylon and Tyrus said nothing to one another, which did nothing to improve the atmosphere.

"What did you mean by that, Baylon?" Alexis finally asked after several minutes.

"I meant what I said," it replied, proving that it was equally as bad at giving answers as Tyrus.

"It is irrelevant," Tyrus clarified.

"I would say it is anything but." Jinar smiled politely, but there were no pleasantries attached to it. "What reason have we to trust you, Tyrus? You hold us hostage to the whims of your Council, whose aims may be no less nefarious than the ones of the leader of the demons that destroyed our world." Neither demon responded to him, which only made the sorcerer's smile widen. "Would we have been here as prisoners if Callum had not complied?"

"You would not be here at all," Tyrus finally answered.

"Jinar, I don't think now is the time." Alexis was ignored by the emboldened sorcerer.

"So, what *are* the motives of this Council? Do they really want to save humanity or just themselves? If they are so powerful, why are they not dealing with this problem?" Once more, neither demon replied at first.

"The Council will explain what they wish."

Tyrus wasn't getting angry, unlike Callum, who just wanted the point scoring to end; he didn't want it to end in bloodshed, least of all because Jinar wouldn't be the victor.

"So, you admit they are hiding things from us." Jinar stroked his beard.

"Jinar, please," Callum insisted, sighing. "Can you save this until afterwards?"

"Taking the side of your new mentor, are you?" Jinar commented with a raised eyebrow.

"I am taking the side of reason, as is Alexis." Callum shook his head, looking ahead just in time to see their surroundings change again.

Ahead of them now was something that almost looked like a structure, albeit nothing like Callum had seen before. A black rocky outcrop jutted from the edge of a large circular platform, as if wrenched from the ground that wasn't there. It had shapes vaguely like fortifications from a castle of nightmares. A sinister red glow emanated from what could've passed as windows, as well as a great power that pulsed within like a beating heart. In the centre of the platform ahead was a trio of demons standing in a triangular formation, motionless as they stared into the space between them. Jinar was examining the structure with a discerning eye.

"I cannot say I like your architecture," Jinar commented.

"It is optimised for the retention of magical power," Tyrus explained. "The walls absorb latent magical energies, which can be refocused for other purposes."

"I thought the material was jet," Alexis admitted, looking down at the platform beneath them. "It looks similar."

"Dark arcan. Created by the first demons that escaped our more feral kind. Originally it was used to hide our presence by masking the area with residual magic that overpowers detection spells. Later it was reasoned that this storage medium could be used for other purposes." Callum had an idea out of nowhere, connecting the conversation of the present with past teachings.

"You said before that your kind reproduces by using a third of their being apiece to create a new demon." Callum looked again at the three demons nearby, wondering if they were about to make a demon.

"Yes."

"Does that piece of you come back?"

"Humans grow stronger in magic with practice. Demons are the same."

"Why don't you use the magic that's captured by this dark arcan instead? Then all you'd need to do is impart knowledge through a spell, which wouldn't weaken the demons as much." Tyrus just stared at him, as did Baylon. "Right?"

Jinar was clearly impressed, nodding sagely.

"That... is a very sideways method of looking at a spell, Callum, but it does have merit," Jinar admitted, making Callum smile.

"Impossible." Callum's smile faded with Tyrus's reply. "Demons do not age as humans do. The imparting of knowledge must be instant, else the creature made would be no creature at all."

"Babies have no knowledge either when they're born, how is it different?" Alexis enquired as a presence of energy between the trio of demons started to grow.

"Humans have instinct. Demons do not," Baylon clarified. "Without the imparting of a third of our being, what was made would be mindless, no different than stone."

"A golem." Jinar clicked his fingers. "And a golem can be instructed, imparted commands by its creator."

"It has no will to think on its own, to be of its own. You cannot give it that, nor could we. Our race would not grow and, in time, would die."

Baylon was watching the ever-growing magical presence between the trio of demons. Callum wondered what was so important about it. Only after a moment did he notice that his hand was by his blade, worried without even knowing it.

"But what separates a demon from a golem? Are you not merely golems of magic instead of natural materials? And what of the feral demons we have encountered? If their actions were not out of instinct, then what compels them to kill?" Jinar stopped his questions when he noticed other demons arriving to witness the trio and their spell.

Callum knew now what was going on, that a demon was soon to be 'born' before them. Tyrus and Baylon approached the growing crowd, Callum eager to stay close to them in case it went wrong. The energy between the trio became visible, a red mist that grew denser with each passing second. The casting demons started to strain and tense, snarling from exertion and possible pain.

"What's happening?" Alexis asked Callum, stood next to him.

"It's a new demon." Callum held onto his sword now. "If it survives."

"If?"

The mist was forming a shape that looked vaguely humanoid, thrashing violently at the air and howling without a mouth to do so. Was this the rage that demons were made of, forced into physical being and given thought by a spell?

"What would kill it?"

"Itself." Tyrus spoke the words with finality, sharing a look with Baylon. "Be ready." Its fellow nodded, hand moving to the sword on its back.

The mist took form suddenly, solidifying into a demon that screamed in rage, its every muscle tense. It was clawing all over itself, drawing ichor with each scratch as it desperately tried to vent its emotions.

"Control yourself!" one of the demons implored, stepping closer. Suddenly, the newly born demon looked to its creator with a glare that Callum recognised all too well, menacing and feral.

"Get back!" Callum's warning was too late to stop it clawing at the one which made it.

The demon so swung at recoiled, clutching a wound as the other two backed up quickly. Baylon stepped forward without hesitation, drawing its sword in a fluid motion. The very act disturbed the crowd more than the feral demon did, them moving back further to give Baylon and Tyrus a path to approach.

The feral demon leapt upon the one it had already weakened, biting into its neck and rending at its chest. Baylon brought down his sword with startling precision, taking off the mad one's arm without so much as touching the one beneath, attracting its attention.

Tyrus unleashed its magic next, blasting it off and away, stepping over the wounded demon even as it began to struggle with its own pain. Baylon paid it no mind either, attention focused on the one-armed creature before them that rushed forward with a howl.

Callum wanted to go to the injured one but hesitated, afraid he'd be infringing on some cultural norm that would offend the demons.

Both Tyrus and Baylon raised their free hands, launching a spell apiece that seemed to mesh with one another, bolts of white energy spinning in unison as they hurtled towards their target. The feral demon made no effort to dodge and, when hit, disintegrated into nothingness before their eyes.

Neither caster had flinched, but Baylon now turned to the wounded one that was struggling to stand. It didn't sheathe its blade, approaching carefully as it dawned on Callum what was happening.

"They can heal it, right?" Callum asked Jinar, who shrugged.

"Perhaps it is too late," muttered his former mentor as Baylon had closed the distance.

"...I can control it...!" The words came from the wounded one through clenched teeth, ichor oozing from the open wounds.

Baylon narrowed its eyes, watching as it tensed and snarled, fighting against the anger within. It clenched its fists tighter and tighter, something Baylon noticed. Tyrus watched silently as Baylon attempted to place a hand on its shoulder, charged with the green glow of healing magic.

It was swatted away with anger and a glare. "*I* can control it!" The words were strained.

"No, you cannot." Baylon held its sword in both hands now.

Callum didn't want to witness it, turning away as he heard a bestial cry that was cut short. Baylon beheaded it without pause and with one swing, the body collapsing as the head fell with a thud. Both began to dissipate within moments, leaving a sickening feeling in Callum's stomach and doubts about how truly civilised these creatures were. The other demons around them dispersed without comment, returning casually to do what they'd been doing before as Baylon cleaned its sword with a cloth conjured by magic. Jinar hadn't looked away, frowning curiously as Tyrus returned to them.

"A demon lost to rage is lost to all." Tyrus looked to the structure they'd been heading to. "The Council is waiting."

"Don't you care that they died?" Callum asked. He looked for any sign, even the faintest flicker of regret.

"No." Callum and Alexis shared a look as his mentor approached where the Council resided. He was even less sure about meeting them now.

Chapter Twenty-Eight

Nobody guarded the way into the structure initially, but as they all entered, Baylon stood vigil at the entrance, giving Callum one last glance before it looked away. Something about it was different to how any other demon had looked at him, lingering longer than others had. That its eyes were covered made it even stranger; why did it wear the blindfold if it could see him? Could it see him? He eventually turned to the scene ahead of them, Callum looking upon a pool of red glowing liquid which emanated an eerie light. Even with all the dark arcan surrounding them, the intense magical energy in the air made him feel dizzy.

Jinar's eyes weren't on the pool, but rather on a series of seven columns. The rightmost one was the tallest, with every other two feet shorter than the previous. Sat on the top of each was a demon, but their scales were bronze rather than the red Callum was used to, almost mistaking them for statues. Each wore a red cloak that spilt down the pillar behind them. Callum spotted that the one lowest down was staring at him.

Not all of its scales were bronze, and its cloak touched the ground, so short was its pillar. Tyrus motioned for them to stay where they were as it approached the pool. There was no kneeling or reverence given by his mentor.

"You bring him before us," the one on the tallest pillar spoke first. Its voice was a little hoarser, but that would've been hard to pin down as different.

"I do, First," Tyrus replied.

"First? Is that its name?" Jinar asked himself. All eight demons present turned to Jinar then, staring him down. He raised an eyebrow in response. "Yes?"

"The First is its title, being the strongest. The Second is second, the Third third. The Fourth is middle, the Fifth next. The Sixth is inferior to all but the Last," Tyrus explained it quickly before turning back to the First.

"It was not your place to speak," sneered the First.

Callum hoped a commotion wouldn't occur, knowing they had no way out.

"Forgive my rudeness." Jinar wasn't very sincere.

"We forgive nothing, for it is not what we can feel," The First replied coldly. "It will, however, be overlooked this time."

Callum already felt like he didn't need to be there, but the Council's eyes were upon him, assessing and examining with all the subtlety of a poor pickpocket.

"He is not as strong as was perceived," the Second looked up to the First as it spoke.

"Potential is strength," the Fourth remarked, seemingly with no warning. Callum had a feeling this was going to get confusing very quickly. Alexis was keeping silent, watching the demons discuss their presence.

"Know your place, Fourth," the First snapped sharply, provoking the chastised one to look away. The First finally stared intently at Callum, which made him even more uncomfortable than normal. He couldn't read its expression. "I am the First, leader of this Council."

"My name—"

"Irrelevant." Callum didn't correct it, feeling immediately insignificant despite his supposed importance. "Your magic is weak."

"Humans are weak," The Fifth snarled, eyes narrowing on the trio. "Fragile, fleeting."

"Humans would not agree to a demon," the Third countered, earning a snarl back. "He will be trained to oppose Keiran as planned."

"Do they always debate like this?" Alexis asked Tyrus quietly, hoping they didn't hear. None of them reacted.

"Yes," Tyrus muttered back. Each demon seemed to know when their time was to speak, even though no signal was given in their debate. Alexis was looking at the Last now, the only one who hadn't spoken.

"If each one defers to the ones above them, what of the Last?"

"The Last speaks when no others wish to. It spoke thirty-two years ago." Alexis looked at the still silent council member with sympathy, something Callum thought he'd never see anyone do.

"What about when they're not among the Council? Are they free to talk then?" she asked.

"They are always one, the Seven," Tyrus replied with finality.

"You speak in pained knots at times," Jinar remarked with a sigh.

"Coming from you, that may be a compliment," Alexis muttered without malice. The look Jinar got from Tyrus silenced any reply he'd planned, then staring up at the Third who was replying to the Second.

"In times of war, humans follow their own that can lead them, regardless of their intent. Their history bathes in blood, but it is their own, not ours.

They will not accept us," the Third explained, glancing briefly at Callum after saying its mind.

"He will age, weaken, die. His foe will not." The Second stared down at the Third, matching its glare. Callum wanted to speak, ask what they intended for him or how they thought he'd ever be capable of defeating someone so powerful, but the words didn't surface; he was a mere spectator in an argument all about him. The feeling of being dragged along hadn't gone away since their rescue, but here it was intensified and entirely alien.

"You are aware of the threat your species faces," the First told Callum, giving him the first chance to disappoint them.

"Not entirely." The Council looked between themselves. "I only know that you want me to defeat the leader of the demons. I don't know his intent—"

"You will defeat him. That is all that is important," the First snapped. Callum looked away, uncomfortable.

"Weakness," the Second muttered.

"Why did you pick me?" Callum then asked, drawing his sword. The First watched the blade intently. "Is it because of this?"

"That is to be determined."

"What's so important about this weapon?" Alexis asked then. She got a glare from the First, but she stood her ground, unafraid. "We know nothing of your plans and you seem intent on keeping it that way, but how can we fight this foe if you reveal nothing?" Jinar nodded in agreement, watching as the First pondered her point. Tyrus was silent.

"It has similarities to the weapon that Keiran uses. It is assumed that the method of their creation is similar," the First spoke to no one in particular, no longer looking at Alexis.

"And I thought Tyrus was bad," murmured Jinar, stroking his beard. Callum spoke up once more.

"There are stronger sorcerers than me, why didn't you pick them? They would be better suited." A small voice in Callum's head hoped the demons wouldn't act on that.

"Less open-minded," Tyrus pointed out.

"And you *are*, are you?" Jinar frowned, ignored entirely by the demon.

"Less powerful." The Third got a deeper frown from the sorcerer, but he was again ignored. Callum shook his head, unwilling to believe it. "I can feel it."

"I have spent most of my life learning the ways of the arcane." Jinar patted Callum on the shoulder. "He has potential, yes, but I am superior. What makes you think you know Callum better than me?" Jinar folded his arms, defiant. Alexis didn't like that, wary of what was to come.

"The Last would break you like a twig," Tyrus answered for the Council, the sorcerer and the silent one among them staring at each other. Jinar chuckled for a second, but it died quickly as Callum felt the briefest glimmer of a colossal power that swam through his head and left it aching, Alexis reacting much the same. Jinar's arms slowly unfolded as the Last turned away from them all, staring at the walls of the structure they were within.

"You are an unknown element in our plan to oppose Keiran," the First revealed. "It is our intention to test your effectiveness against him."

"And what is your plan?" Jinar asked. "And what does Keiran actually seek to achieve? You have spoken little of this person's objectives."

"Our plan is our own. Tyrus is our agent in fulfilling it," the Third replied.

"Are we little more than tools to your council?" Alexis earned yet another look, this time from the Second.

"If it were not for us, you would be dead!" it barked, fists clenched. Its aggression startled her and Callum, Alexis taking a step back.

"But this is still an alliance of convenience for you."

"Sending Tyrus to save Callum put us at risk, a risk that we considered... favourable if the result was his safety." Callum had noticed that it didn't speak of her or Jinar as valuable, echoing Tyrus's sentiments perfectly. He also noticed the pause; was it difficult for the demon to admit that? "Protecting you also comes with risk. We hide from Keiran. If he were to find us, he would destroy us."

"So we are pawns," Jinar concluded. "Pawns in a fight for *your* existence."

"To save both us and your kind. You cannot do this alone. Callum will defeat Keiran. Tyrus will train him and hide his presence until he is ready." The First considered something then. "Measures will need to be taken."

"Such as?"

"Breaking the shackles of your mortality." Jinar chuckled again, something that the First found curious.

"You are speaking of life eternal," he was smiling, bemused at the thought. "It is impossible."

"You told me nothing was impossible with magic," Callum countered.

"True, but there are some are things beyond our grasp that no amount of training can achieve. Alchemists and scholars dedicated and wasted their lives on our world in search of immortality, my mentor included. Elixirs of life, divine blessings, meditation. Some would attempt combinations lethal enough to fell whole armies in the hopes of uncovering the missing ingredient to rejuvenation or better." Jinar paused then shrugged. "You or even I cannot achieve this state of eternal living."

Callum was trying to wrap his head around the very idea of it, living forever. He was excited about it, but there was a niggling worry that he couldn't shake, and then there was the fact that this was only to be a better servant to the demons.

The council left the silence to stagnate. "You know I am right."

"There are those of your kind who have achieved this already," the Second stated flatly.

"If people have achieved eternal existence, why have you not asked *them* to help you?" Alexis asked. "They would surely be stronger than us." She watched the Second as intently as Jinar was, him out of mistrust and her for entirely different reasons. None of the Council said anything, the Last turning suddenly, about to speak.

"We considered it," the Sixth spoke first, leaving its inferior in quiet. It looked dejected. Now Callum was starting to feel pity for it.

"He was disagreeable," the Fifth remarked.

"He would have been a better choice than this one," the Second answered back, then narrowing its eyes upon their charge. "But the vote said otherwise."

"A vote?" Callum didn't get an answer.

"I am surprised they agree on anything." Jinar looked to the First, guessing that it had ultimate authority to answer his queries. "So who are these people? Will we meet them?"

"Go," the First suddenly declared.

"It will be done." Tyrus nodded its head before turning to the others. As if they were no longer there, the Council started to talk amongst one another about things Callum didn't understand. From Tyrus's posture, it was clear that the meeting was over, as enigmatically as it had begun.

"I have a few more—" Jinar was touched on the arm by Alexis.

"I think we have taken more than enough of their time," she told him carefully, following Tyrus's lead past Baylon and out.

Jinar looked back to the Council, eventually nodding.

"Of course. After all, it is *highly* valuable." He lathered the sarcasm on thick as he walked out. Callum followed behind, with Tyrus exiting last as he glanced back at the seven, who were now utterly focused on themselves. Few questions had been answered, but a door to a thought inconceivable had opened, as well as a little more of the magnitude of what he was up against. Now that he was pondering it, the idea scared him that much more.

Tyrus remained at the entrance with Baylon, talking only when Callum and the others were far enough away that they wouldn't hear. They all got a look from the surrounding demons before they went back to their enigmatic duties. Callum finally sheathed his sword as Jinar looked back to Tyrus and Baylon, expression thoughtful.

"You don't trust them," Alexis guessed.

"They have given us little reason to, beyond our rescue. They make no secret of using us for their own ends." Jinar sighed, "Or should I say, using Callum for their own ends."

"I don't see why they think I'm going to be the strongest out of us three. You both outshine me." Callum was thinking more about the promise of immortality than trust, but he couldn't disagree with his friend on some of his points.

"I think you're stronger than me, Callum. Magic may come easier to me, but your spells are more powerful," Alexis told him, then looked to Tyrus. Callum still doubted that. "Them rescuing us was conditional, yes, but they're working to save humanity from the demons."

"Are they?" Jinar asked. "They are demons themselves, who is to say that their intentions are altruistic? From what I have seen, their kind is incapable of such gestures. Perhaps the Council wants to take the place of this leader of the demons." Tyrus turned its gaze to Jinar, staring silently for a few moments before continuing its conversation with Baylon.

"I think they heard you," she remarked with a smile.

"That we still live tells me they do not care. All that concerns them is us being their weapon in a place they are too afraid to inhabit themselves." Jinar shook his head slowly, pondering something that he kept to himself. "Expendable commodities that they can replace with relative ease."

"I think you're not giving them enough credit." Callum provoked a dubious look from his former mentor.

"And you give them too much. That their goals align with ours is only because they have decreed what our goals are, remember that. We still do not even know what Keiran seeks to achieve, yet I believe the Council does."

"You think they hide that from Tyrus?" Alexis asked, getting a nod.

"Among other things. It is one of the reasons I do not trust them."

"But we don't disagree to go along with their plan, do we?" Callum didn't get a reply right away.

"All we know about Keiran is that he and his servants want to kill us," Alexis said, looking back to the pair of armed demons herself, "Anything beyond that is speculation, but the Council's self-preservation is ensuring that we're protected as well."

"I'm still not sure if it should be me that they're relying on, but..." Now Callum found himself considering his imposed duty all over again. Alexis saw his pondering and posed a different question to Jinar.

"If this offer of eternal life is true, will you take it?" she asked.

"As I stated earlier, my mentor dabbled in the pursuit of immortality, more as time gained on him. The final theory he told me before his departure was of a concoction made of rare flowers which grew in the harshest regions of the lands. He said that the potion would extend life, a reward for the time and effort spent finding them." Jinar was focusing his attention on Tyrus as he spoke, "His plan was to transplant the flowers into a garden of his own, cultivate immortality at home. If he succeeded or not does not matter now, I guess."

"So, it was a fear of death that made him search it out," Alexis concluded.

"I believe that was a secondary concern. He was a powerful sorcerer in his prime, though I will overtake his achievements shortly. He was also a man driven most by wanting to excel, become the best that he can be. Eternal life would have let him see just how far his power would go. In many ways, I am much like him."

"If we were meant to live forever, why don't we already?" Alexis's question provoked a smile from Jinar.

"If we were not meant to be masters of the magical arts, none of us would have the gift by your logic, yet some of us do. It is my belief that one day all of us will be sorcerers, that magical bloodlines will spread amongst humans enough that those without the power will cease to be."

"Yet Gui-Lon didn't need magic," Alexis replied, following Jinar's gaze. "The people there have devices that serve all the purposes you can conjure."

"Except immortality."

"For now."

Tyrus approached them once more, looking to Callum exclusively.

"I will inform Daniel of the location of the one who will assist us in rectifying this oversight," Tyrus told them bluntly.

"Oversight?" Callum frowned at the wording of their mortality. A moment later, another of the portals that brought them there appeared and Tyrus stood by it, staring at Alexis and Jinar. With a shrug, Jinar touched it and vanished to the other side, likely Tyrus's room. Alexis gave Callum a look before following.

"Keiran will use the connection with them against you," the demon warned suddenly when Callum and it were alone. Surprised, he turned to see its eyes narrowed on his face, watching him. Was it really asking him to distance himself from the few people he still knew? Anger flared up inside of him that he quelled, not wanting to get on the wrong side of the demon.

"They're my friends, I won't do this without them." Tyrus said nothing, watching him with its unreadable expression. "We work better together." Callum noticed that Baylon was also observing him, turning its head away slowly after a moment.

"They are a weakness he will exploit," Tyrus clarified. "They will not be as strong as you."

"And I'm weaker by myself than I'll ever be in a group."

"Incorrect," the demon told him, flaring up his annoyance once more.

"This isn't up for debate, Tyrus. If you want us, then it has to be *us*, not just me." Callum stood defiantly before his mentor, somewhat surprised that it was in him. Tyrus narrowed its eyes a little more before its expression returned to its normal bestial nature.

"So you say." Callum didn't know if the demon was angry at him or not; the lack of a snarl or aggressive stance didn't help. Baylon was looking at him curiously, as if it was about to speak. Callum met its eyes, but no words came from the armed guardian of the council. Seeing its weapon again prompted a question in Callum's mind, but he decided not to ask about it; he'd hopefully get another chance later. Looking back to the portal, he had little alternative but to use it, giving the alien landscape around him one final look before letting himself be dragged through the maelstrom of magic, back to the barely more familiar surroundings of the ship.

Chapter Twenty-Nine

"Now, I know you're all bored to death of hearing about it from everywhere else, but we here at Ken in the Den at Ten do not shirk our responsibilities to the public. With that in mind, let's go over this as quickly and as directly as possible, so we can go back to providing you with the entertainment you so desperately crave.

"If you suspect that someone is an agent of the Great Threat, do not hesitate to inform Z-Gen. It is your duty as citizens of the galaxy to ensure that our worlds remain safe from the threat they pose to us all. Any information you can provide, no matter how insignificant it may seem, could make the difference between life and death for billions of people.

"If you, yourself, suspect that you are an agent of the Great Threat, you are encouraged to hand yourself in to the authorities for questioning. As you won't be able to take advantage of the reward for your own apprehension, however, I somehow doubt you'll be doing that. And that concludes the obligatory message from Z-Gen; now we go to the section I like to call 'Whoops, How Did That Happen?'"

—Extract from 'Ken in the Den at the Ten', Series 12 Episode 1,499

Tyrus's room was empty when Callum arrived save for himself and the demon. He questioned why Jinar and Alexis weren't there until he remembered the shift in time when they'd travelled through the demon's domain.

Perhaps it had been longer than a minute since the others had arrived. Tyrus didn't seem bothered, the portal having already vanished as the demon left in the direction of the bridge. Simon was close by and could guess where Tyrus was going.

"Daniel won't be happy to see you," the doctor warned.

"Irrelevant," it responded flatly. Callum didn't need to stop by Simon, the doctor following them with his beverage in hand.

"Were we long?" Callum enquired.

"Not really, an hour or so. Why?"

"I was curious, that's all."

The door at the end of the corridor opened and Callum saw the bridge for the first time. In front of him was another window showing space, but the walls were nothing like his quarters; strange devices were built into it, each with buttons and dials, as well as the interactive screens that displayed information alien to him. At various points were not-so-comfortable chairs, Monica sat on one of them with her eyes focused on the image of a world, red and brown in colour with a ring around it. Daniel's chair was in the centre, larger and more comfortable looking. He was looking at a screen that was connected to the chair's right arm by a rod. As they entered, Daniel's chair turned to face them, the man none too pleased that they'd returned.

"We are done here," Tyrus declared bluntly, approaching him.

Daniel warily watched the demon as it got closer. Monica had turned to watch it also, muttering something to herself.

"Am I finally rid of you?" Daniel asked it, not getting a reply as the demon pressed on the screen by him. This brought up a translucent image with countless white dots arrayed in a seemingly random order, along with blobs of different colours. One dot was marked in red, making Callum conclude that it was a map of sorts, charting their position among the infinite sea of stars. Tyrus pointed to one of the dots some distance from the red one.

"Second planet." The image zoomed in on the dot, a bright, orange star with five orbs circling it. The second one from the star was various shades of sickly green, and as Daniel read the information that appeared alongside it, it was clear that wasn't a good thing.

"Are you kidding? The planet's atmosphere is so acidic the ship would never be able to take off again if we landed." Daniel shook his head as Simon watched on, sipping his drink. "Why do you even want to go there?"

"We're going to find somebody," Callum answered, omitting the reason why. Daniel frowned.

"Nobody could survive there, not even one of you." Daniel aimed his words at Tyrus, who didn't react to them. Monica stood up, pressing a button by her chair as she did.

"We did what you wanted us to do, brought you here. Can't you find somebody else to help you now?" She was hoping for an answer Callum knew wouldn't come, the demon not even turning to acknowledge her question.

"They're going to have to, because we're not taking them there." Daniel was hardly imposing in front of the demon, but his expression was stern.

"I don't care how much money or cargo you offer us, you staying here any longer will just make things even worse! It's going to be damn difficult to pay off Z-Gen as it is, without you and the others stirring things up again!"

"If we leave, you'll all be in danger," Callum warned. "Tyrus being here means that my presence is hidden from those that want to harm me. If you left, you'd no longer be protected by that." The last thing he wanted was another argument, but it seemed unavoidable. Simon listened with interest, but Monica was shocked and Daniel angry.

"You said there was nothing to worry about," Daniel muttered, words aimed at the demon.

"I said it was irrelevant," Tyrus replied.

"Who wants him, why?" Monica's voice was quiet, a worry over her face that made Callum feel all the more guilty for the pain he'd inflicted on them already.

"And why should we believe you? What proof do you have about any of this?" Daniel was watching Callum's face, waiting for his answer so he could try to ferret out falsehood.

"You don't have to believe me, but that won't make it any less true. I wish it wasn't, but it is." Daniel smiled to himself then, but it wasn't a good smile.

"...What happened to your world is your fault, isn't it?"

Callum blinked, taken aback by the sudden question as it brought back painful memories of home.

"I did a little research while you were away. Vedallan IV is little more than a burned-out husk now, it's got a lot of scientists baffled. This 'enemy' came after you, and Tyrus paid us to bail you out, didn't it?" Again, Callum said nothing. "So who are they, Tyrus? Escaped criminals that hid out on that world to avoid notice?"

"There's not a weapon around that can reduce a world to ash like you claim," Simon remarked, coming to Callum's defence.

"There's always the nukes that people hid away when they were being banned centuries ago." Simon finished his drink as Daniel spoke, the pilot levelling a stare against him which he shrugged off. Monica had looked more concerned when the word 'nuke' was mentioned.

"Even if there were caches, you'd have a hell of a time smuggling enough of them to incinerate a world," the doctor remarked.

"What's a nuke?" Callum asked then. "It sounds dangerous."

"It *is* dangerous. They're weapons of destruction so terrible and indiscriminate that nobody dared use them for fear that everyone else would in retaliation."

"So where did they go? Why did people stop making them?" The doctor gave Callum a grave look.

"When eleven billion people were vaporised in two minutes, the galaxy woke up." Callum couldn't imagine how huge a fireball had to engulf an entire world, hoping he'd never see it in person. "The Great Terran Treaty was the result."

"And the rise of Z-Gen as the great power in colonised space," Monica added.

"If what Tyrus says is true – and I have no reason to doubt its sincerity – then it doesn't matter what these people want Callum for. We're already criminals as it is, anyway," Simon remarked.

"But we can solve that," Monica reminded them.

"A commander won't just sit down and wipe the slate clean after we spaced a score of their fighter pilots, Monica. Bribes work for petty crimes, but what we did was big. Better to spend that money on stocking up the ship and some repairs."

"For what? It won't get us out of trouble." Daniel was still unconvinced.

"By the sounds of it, we're in far more bother than just Z-Gen." Simon placed his cup down on the devices, folding his arms.

"If you'd told us—" Daniel began to speak to Tyrus, but the doctor cut him off.

"And if you'd talked to us about it before accepting on our behalf, things might've been different. As it stands, we'll make the best of a bad situation."

The room was quiet, Monica giving Daniel a look.

"Get out."

Callum knew that Daniel was referring to him and didn't wait to be told again, exiting along with Simon. Before the door closed behind them, he could see Monica walk over to Daniel. The feeling of guilt remained, and nothing he thought of made it go away. Tyrus was also gone, as it often did.

"You didn't have to stand up for me there," Callum said to Simon.

"No one else was going to," he replied as he walked off in the direction of his workshop. Whether they would head to where Tyrus wanted them to go was almost a non-issue; the demon had a way of persuading people, he was fast discovering.

While Callum didn't find out what Daniel and Monica discussed, their course was set to the location Tyrus had indicated, a world that Simon described as 'a death trap'. Callum's days fell into a routine of training his magic and avoiding Daniel, something which wasn't difficult as the man rarely ventured away from the bridge or his quarters. Callum spent the rest of the afternoon after training with Alexis, though his efforts to learn how to read were made more difficult by exhaustion; Tyrus had told him to push his body to the limit, the better to see what that limit was and fight against it, and that left him aching and weak.

Then Alexis arrived, intending to be trained also. She didn't wait for approval, and while Tyrus didn't give it, nor did the demon expel her. Alexis couldn't hide her own fatigue during the training sessions, even more tired than he was. Jinar remained absent, preferring his own methods and teachings to the ones Tyrus imparted.

As for Callum's reading lessons, progress was slow, but more words were starting to make sense to him. The topic of her brother hadn't come up since the last time, but Callum noticed each time he emerged in her mind. She'd become distant, lost in thoughts he was loath to drag her from for fear of disrupting the process of mourning.

Turning on the viewscreen in his room afterwards was often a moot effort, it showing him little of interest barring the occasional news statement. He'd at least mastered how to change the 'channel', as they were apparently called, and adjusting how loud it was, including a handy tip to instantly quiet it at a single press. On one such evening, there'd been mention of an upcoming event concerning a man called Ken who lived in a den of some kind.

"Coming up after this coverage, of course, is the man of the show, the host who knows the most and the coolest cat that's all that, Ken in the Den at Ten!" the man presenting the very dull show said enthusiastically. "Bringing you up to date on the hottest events and news all across space and time, it's the one-stop show for those who want to be in the know!"

Callum quickly turned the screen off; he questioned how much one person could know about the galaxy. On the topic of immortality, Callum had been guarded with who to tell of it, speaking of it only to Saresan. The guard wasn't excited, however, the thought of eternal life provoking a dismissive shrug. The news spread quickly after that, becoming a conversation topic despite the lack of detail as to how it worked. Monica was thrilled at the thought of being forever young.

"Is it even possible?" Monica had asked while eating dinner. All the worry and annoyance of the previous days had been washed away with the revelation. "I suppose anything must be possible with magic, but living forever?"

Simon had been preparing his coffee at the time. "Levitating people is one thing, living forever is quite another," he muttered, taking a sip. He'd prepared no food of his own, nor had Callum ever seen him eat. What was in the drink that made it so tasty and sustaining, he wondered.

"So? Would you take it?" she asked Simon eagerly.

"No." Simon sipped his drink as Monica blinked in surprise.

"Why not?"

"Because I'd have no idea how it works, that's why not. If there's one thing I'm quickly learning about magic, it's that nobody knows in the slightest what makes it go, and if I'm going to have any persistent effect infused into my being, I'd like to be doubly sure nobody can corrupt it or turn it off without me knowing about it, or worse." Simon leaned back in his chair. "Unfortunately, it's not a subject I can look information up on without it being highly illegal."

"If we're already criminals, what's the harm in it?" Callum asked.

"It's generally not a good idea to stack more offences on top of the ones you already have, but I suppose there's not much worse than what they want us for."

"I've been meaning to ask, Simon: what *is* in that that makes you drink it so much?" That question made Simon chuckle quietly.

"A little magic of our own, Callum, called 'caffeine'." Simon moved back to the machine that made his drink of choice and placed a small cup underneath it, pressing a button which poured the black liquid from a nozzle. "Milk? Sugar?"

"I don't know. I'll try it as it is." Monica smiled to herself as Simon carried the cup over to Callum, placing it before him. He could feel the heat rising from the liquid, something he wasn't at all used to in his drinks. Nevertheless, he put it to his lips and drunk cautiously. Immediately his tongue protested at the sharply bitter taste, Callum swallowing it with difficulty much to Monica's amusement.

"You get used to it," she told him.

"I'd rather not." Callum pushed the cup away, only thinking that he might've offended Simon after the fact. The doctor didn't seem to mind, drinking his own without so much as a shrug. Callum reflected on the drink before him, one of the few things he could avoid growing accustomed to in a galaxy that would likely always be strange to him, no matter what the others told him. If the promise of eternal youth turned out to be true, it was about to become even stranger.

The days rolled by without incident, which Callum found surprising, considering how much trouble they were in. Monica had explained that they had to be ready for an attack at any time; all it took was a single scan of their ship for their crimes to be laid bare before a Z-Gen crew. Siobhan's eagerness to pilot the *Silverbolt* in combat again had been clear; she'd been tending to her fighter craft during the day in the hopes of using it once more, but the call to arms never came.

His sleep had been light the first few days, each night pulling him gently into an uneasy pattern stilted by nightmares and the background thought of the Council's demands of him. He hadn't told Daniel and his crew of their goal to defeat Keiran and stop the demons, unsure how he'd even go about starting that conversation.

With Daniel still angry with them, his fear had been that he'd snap and dispatch Callum himself with his rifle. Jinar and Alexis had remained quiet about it as well, perhaps also debating when the right time to mention it was. And so, the routine of training his magic and learning to read remained largely unbroken save for the late hours.

He'd been happy to learn that playing music with an instrument hadn't died out, even if the device Siobhan played looked only vaguely like a lute. Thinner and longer, it was made of neither metal nor wood and had a cord that ran from its base to a black box which amplified its reverberating tone. It didn't sound right to him, possessing a metallic twinge that was unnatural yet seemed entirely familiar to her. Callum couldn't deny that she was skilled with it, able to play without looking where her fingers went.

Eventually, he woke up one day to hear that they'd arrived at their destination, showering quickly to get to the bridge with the others. He wasn't surprised to hear Daniel arguing with Tyrus upon his entrance, the image of the green world projected between them. Monica was stood by him, warily eyeing the demon.

"Your friend can't be there, and I'm not landing my ship in that atmosphere," Daniel told it frankly. "You're welcome to do your vanishing trick if you like, but don't think I'll be putting myself at risk to bail you out." Callum wondered if he'd try if it were possible. Siobhan was sat in a chair with her feet propped up on the device next to it, mindful not to accidentally press any buttons. Simon was next to her, drink in hand as he listened to the debate. Jinar, Alexis and Saresan were to the right of the entrance, all of them keeping a healthy distance away from Daniel.

"Teleportation is naturally the wisest course of action, but it would be wiser to leave some persons behind, just in case of unforeseen complications," Jinar mused.

"Well, I'm not staying behind," Monica replied.

"Nor am I. If we have to stay here, I'm damn well keeping an eye on you this time," Daniel spoke to Callum in particular.

"We could always cut for it," Siobhan suggested with a smile. Callum spotted that Siobhan was wearing an armoured plate vest on her chest much like Daniel's, only beige and smaller. She reached for a pack of cards in the back pocket of her trousers. "You can even pick first." Callum was surprised to see that they were the same size as the playing cards from his world, though naturally hers were made of better material.

"Don't you have a marked deck?" Monica frowned even as Siobhan began shuffling.

"I don't think there was a tavern I went to that didn't," Saresan quipped with a chuckle.

"It's not this one, though." Neither Monica nor Daniel seemed to believe her. "They have red backs, this deck's green." The pilot stood up and approached the pair, finishing her shuffling. "You two pick first."

"Why do you want us to pick first?" Monica enquired, suspicious.

"Then I'll draw first." Siobhan shrugged. Saresan chuckled again as she shuffled them again.

"I was never any good at cards," Callum muttered, remembering the one and only time he tried it. His coin purse had been that much lighter by the end of the night, a day's work gone in a few hands.

"You can't hide what you're thinking," Alexis answered. He didn't know if that was a compliment or not until she smiled at him. He returned it, looking back to Daniel, who'd taken the deck from Siobhan and was now shuffling it himself.

"*I'll* draw first, then you." He looked to Siobhan, then Monica. "Then you." He took a thin selection from the top.

"I'm sure if it's that important, we can make two trips," Callum suggested. "But it might not be needed, especially if we can be taught how to do it."

"And then I can improve upon it," Jinar added. Siobhan didn't even look at the deck, taking her split without hesitation. Monica eyed her with suspicion but quickly focused on what remained of the cards, carefully splitting them into two equal segments. Daniel revealed his card first.

"Jack." He was confident that was enough. Siobhan didn't react but Monica smiled, showing her card now.

"I guess we know who's staying behind, eh?" Her card had nine diamonds on it, Monica even more confident of victory. One corner of Siobhan's lips curled upwards as she slowly revealed her card.

"Yeah, I think we do." The pilot had ten diamonds on her card. Monica immediately protested.

"You cheated," came the accusation. "You knew you were going to pick higher!"

"It's all luck in the end," Saresan commiserated. "They won't be long anyway."

"They?" Alexis asked. "You're not coming?"

"I'm not really fussed about it all. I'd stay by myself, but I'd be more likely to make this crash if something went wrong and I had to press buttons to solve it."

"You know we don't have enough suits for everyone, Daniel," Simon reminded. "Unless you've got a magical solution for that too."

"Suits?" Callum asked.

"Zero G-E suits. Self-enclosed, with oxygen and environmental control. Not sure how well they'll hold up against an acidic atmosphere in the long run, but I doubt the man of mystery we're there to see won't have his own enclosed environment."

"Like a suit of plate mail then, shielding the wearer from all harm." Callum got a nod.

"Something like that."

"Wait, you're coming with us?" Siobhan was surprised. "I thought this wasn't your kind of thing either."

"Scientific curiosity. Personally, if I were immortal, I'd pick a nicer world to live on," explained the doctor.

"A world like this is the ideal cover for one who can out-live their foes with ease, but I do agree in part," Jinar theorised, stroking his beard.

"All of this still doesn't solve the problem of there not being enough suits," Alexis reminded them.

"They are unneeded," Tyrus stated, moving between them without another word. Callum knew what was coming, moving beside the demon in preparation for teleportation. Daniel looked on at the spectacle.

"Physical connection is required for the teleportation spell to function," Jinar informed him, "to allow the magical energies to affect everyone." Simon set his cup down and joined them, standing next to Saresan.

"That's weird," Daniel muttered.

"*Any* physical connection is sufficient if you are wary of hand-holding," joked Jinar as he took his place by Saresan.

Callum ended up between Tyrus and Alexis, with Daniel being as far away from the demon as the circle allowed. Callum placed his hand on the demon's scales, finding them to be far smoother than he'd thought they'd be. He was about to reach for Alexis's shoulder, but she beat him to it and took his hand in hers. They looked to one another for a moment; it had been a little surprising, but it wasn't uncomfortable, her grip gentle. The circle now complete, Callum began to feel the familiar sensation of teleportation magic.

"So, anyone got any good songs?" Siobhan joked. Callum forgot the warning Jinar had given them about teleportation until it was too late, the spell whisking them away to places unknown in an instant.

Chapter Thirty

For the first time Callum felt no different after teleporting, but the three unfamiliar with it weren't so fortunate. Siobhan managed to stay standing but was clearly dizzy, while Daniel fell to one knee, clutching his stomach with a groan. Simon was prevented from falling by Jinar quickly catching him, the doctor having the worst reaction of the three.

Callum quickly took in their surroundings and a lungful of air, finding that it was perfectly breathable. Expecting demons but finding none, his momentary fear faded as he looked upon the inside of a cave, illuminated only by an orb of light Alexis had conjured, which she held in her free hand. The stone around them was grey, the air muggy, still and silent. Daniel retched, trying to recover from their instantaneous transportation.

Only then did Alexis let go of Callum's hand.

"What the hell was that?" Daniel groaned as he retched a second time.

"Teleportation."

Tyrus gave no further explanation, looking at the dark grey stone that arched above them. Simon had regained his footing and was looking also at the ceiling.

"An enclosed cave system," Simon remarked. "The atmosphere would have made finding this place impossible with scans."

"Not with magic," Jinar countered.

"Then perhaps your 'magic' can find where this person that we're meant to find is." Daniel had finally got to his feet, face still pale. Callum couldn't feel the presence of a powerful sorcerer, but he was fast learning that that wasn't a sign there wasn't one nearby. Daniel reached for his rifle, holding it in his hands, just as Siobhan now had her pistols drawn.

"Are those necessary? We're not here to hurt anyone," Callum asked.

"Better to be safe than sorry," Daniel replied.

"Self-defence." Siobhan's answer made more sense to him.

"Futile gestures," Tyrus remarked as it headed towards an opening in the cave wall ahead of them. Neither of them put away their weapons, taking the rear as the group followed the demon into the narrow passageway. Something felt off about the passage to Callum; the walls were too rough, the direction of their travel too straight.

"This place doesn't seem natural," he voiced his concerns just as a drop of water splashed onto Siobhan's hat.

"Are you implying this person *created* a cave system to live in deep underground?" Daniel glanced behind them. "That's absurd. Why would they want to hide in a cave anyway?"

"I cannot speak for the person's motives," Tyrus responded, much to Daniel's happiness.

"Finally, something you don't know," he muttered.

"The collective knowledge of all humanity is nothing to the limitless eternity of the universe." Daniel didn't reply to that, continually checking behind them as they progressed further in. Ahead, Callum could now see light, then a metal wall as the passage opened out further. Again, Callum could feel no magic nearby, telling him that the wall with only a single flickering light was exactly what it appeared to be. There were no visible ways forward, but Jinar smiled to himself, walking past the others and standing by the wall with a discerning gaze.

"A clever ruse, but it is not enough to fool one such as I," Jinar announced, flexing his fingers before he muttered a select few words. After a pause, he began muttering again with more deliberate gestures. The wall began to shimmer.

"Jinar—"

Callum barely got a word in before something lashed out at Jinar violently. A bolt of white energy jumped from the wall and hit the sorcerer in the chest, knocking him back and to the ground.

"Whoa!" Siobhan pointed her guns at the wall instinctively, expecting an attack that didn't appear.

Callum took a second to react to the whole thing, by which time Jinar was already standing up slowly, dusting off his robes that were now singed where the bolt impacted. Simon rushed to his side but was shooed away with a dismissive hand wave.

"It was far from fatal, thanks to my preparations beforehand," the sorcerer declared.

"But it could've been." Alexis wasn't impressed.

"For a sorcerer of my calibre, this spell is little more than a parlour trick, but your concern is heart-warming." Jinar smiled back.

"If it was magic." Simon was alternating between examining the wall warily and looking Jinar over with a healer's eye.

"It is, and a crude application, if I may say so."

"I'm starting to get the feeling we're not expected," Siobhan said to no one in particular. "It'd go a hell of a way to explaining why Jinar got zapped."

"Not entirely accurate terminology. The magical barrier I conjured protected my body in the moment of impact," corrected the sorcerer.

"Of course, how obvious." She rolled her eyes even as he smiled back. "*Are* we expected, Tyrus?"

"No," the demon answered.

Callum wasn't surprised by that answer, having seen how they thought and debated amongst one another. Daniel sighed in frustration, once again looking behind them.

"Of course we're not expected, why would anything go right?" he sighed, frustrated.

Callum was looking to the metal wall with curiosity, thinking about what Jinar had done to be attacked by the bolt of energy. He had an idea.

"Wouldn't the spell in the wall need to expend some magical energy to fire off that attack, Jinar?" he asked. Jinar glanced his way and nodded. "Do you think it needs a living target it hits?"

"There is only one way to find out, Callum: experimentation."

Jinar muttered more words, conjuring a stone into existence with a flourish of sparkling light. Alexis bent down and picked a handful of smaller ones from off the ground while he was doing that, throwing one at the wall. Callum and Daniel both flinched as it made contact, seeing a second magical bolt turn the stone to dust. After that discharge part of the wall changed, a door revealing itself. Jinar looked to his own rock, subtly dropping it to the ground when no one was looking. "As I said. A crude warding spell, easily thwarted." Callum noticed a panel beside the door, similar to the ones on the ship.

"Fortunate for you lot, I have a master key that'll get us past any lock," Siobhan declared. She walked forward and looked at the panel for a moment before shooting it with her right pistol. It sparkled and crackled as the door opened slowly.

"That could've very easily put it on lockdown," Daniel chastised.

"But it didn't. We could've teleported past it either way, right?" She shrugged. Tyrus didn't wait for the others, entering into the darkness beyond without so much as the announcement of their intentions. Callum quickly followed behind, afraid the door might close on them at any moment. The gloom was banished by a flood of light seconds after his entrance.

Callum had expected more metal walls within, an interior similar to the ship. He was pleasantly surprised to see the natural materials that he associated with proper houses. The walls were panelled with fine wood, and the furnishings were of oak and comfortable looking. The floor was polished marble, with an immaculate rug in the middle with intricate designs woven into it. A stone fireplace to the left finished the decorum, logs burning slowly, with an armchair facing it.

Callum had drawn his sword; the pleasant surroundings made him no less wary. His eyes drifted to what almost looked like a window on the wall opposite the fireplace, only to see that that was exactly what it was. Beyond, he could see a beautiful view of untouched countryside on a cloudless day, an impossibility considering how deep underground they were. There were no doors he could see, but that didn't mean they weren't there. He stepped forward and the others followed him in. Siobhan whistled at the sight before them, while Daniel stood by the entrance, with his gaze firmly on the cave they'd left.

"Talk about swanky," Siobhan said to herself. Before anyone else could speak, a voice spoke out to them, source unclear.

"I told your kind never to come here." It was a man's voice, deeper than Callum's and sterner also. Simon looked to the armchair to check if it had suddenly become occupied. It hadn't.

"You've been here before?" Alexis asked Tyrus, not getting an answer.

"If you could beat us, you would have," the demon retorted.

"Are you *trying* to pick a fight? I thought you were here to get immortality from him," Daniel asked, more worried than ever as he stepped further in.

The door they came through closed with a thud. Callum's heart started to race, feeling a fight was imminent now that they were trapped by the stranger.

"A non thinks he can master death, grovelling to his better as a puppy does before its master. Pathetic." There was calm malice in the voice of the non-present person that made Callum very uncomfortable, questioning if any of them were strong enough to go against him.

"A non?" Callum hadn't heard that phrase before but guessed it wasn't complimentary.

"The Council has an offer, Kole." Tyrus was looking directly ahead, not focusing on anything as it spoke.

There was a pause, the momentary wait a nervous one for Callum. Finally, the figure revealed himself, appearing out of nothingness directly in front of Tyrus. Six feet tall and middle-aged, the stranger had short grey hair and a goatee beard of the same tone. All of it was immaculately maintained, his face without blemish. He wore a white shirt with a collar and an armoured vest similar to Daniel's atop it. Over both of them was a brown sleeveless coat that stopped only at his ankles. Black trousers and polished black shoes finished the look, the well-built man looking at Tyrus with apathetic grey eyes, arms folded.

"Doubtful," Kole muttered, not taking his eyes off the demon.

Callum couldn't see any weapons on the man, but magic was as deadly as it was concealable. Daniel and Siobhan both had their weapons trained on the man, who hadn't so much as blinked at the threat they posed.

"Invisibility, how very novel," Jinar remarked with a smile.

"Enough to be hidden from you," Kole countered, still not turning from the demon. Jinar raised an eyebrow in response, smile unwavering.

"I'm Callum Igannes, and this—" Callum was cut off sharply as he offered a hand to shake. Kole's tone was dismissive.

"The pleasure's all yours. I don't care who you are." Callum slowly retracted his hand but noticed that Kole had glanced briefly at his sword. If he was intrigued, he couldn't tell, the man's expression was unmoving.

"He has potential," Tyrus told him.

"Your Council knows I exceed all of them."

"He's modest, too," Simon muttered.

"I am here to negotiate. Nothing more," Tyrus stated then, as if wanting to silence the chatter around it. The effort succeeded.

"Uh-huh," Kole half responded, turning his back to them and taking a few steps away. A book appeared as mysteriously as he had before, open and levitating at a page that he began to read.

"Why live in a cave?" Siobhan asked him. "Hiding from someone?"

"Yes, as it happens, nosey demons and their entourage of tag-alongs." Without fanfare, Kole's feet left the ground, and he was lifted up into the air to a bookshelf Callum hadn't seen until then, the book following him. Above Kole the ceiling was much higher, a tunnel of books and tomes all around him in sturdy wooden shelves. "I don't need to justify myself to you."

"Are you immortal?" Alexis asked. Kole didn't levitate down as she moved to see him better, Callum stepping closer as well. The sorcerer didn't look down either. "How old are you?"

"I stopped counting after three hundred," he replied dismissively. "You would too."

"And your family?"

"Dead, not that I care." Callum hadn't liked this man much to begin with, but his opinion was dropping even lower with each thing he said.

"Why wouldn't you care? They're your family," he asked Kole, doubting he'd get a straight answer. Surprisingly, the man looked down at him, expression stern.

"They deserved what they got."

"How can you say that?"

The look he got from Kole shifted to a glare, a warning he heeded quickly. Returning back to the ground, Kole looked at the wall near him, and the very wood shifted to create a portal through, turning molten like lead. Callum hadn't seen such magic before, but he felt the power behind the spell, unlike the others Kole had cast in their presence. It made his head ache for a moment as Kole stepped through to the room beyond, leaving the way open for them. Had he intended that effect to show his power? Tyrus went through without a word, leaving the others to decide if they too wanted to follow.

"No way but forward." Daniel wasn't at all happy with the fact, his gun lowered.

"What *did* he mean by calling you a 'non'?" Callum asked.

"How should I know?" came the response as Siobhan followed in the demon's wake.

"I believe it is a less-than-polite word for someone without the gift of magic, a 'non-sorcerer', as it were," Jinar guessed, looking up to the elevated bookshelves with intrigue. "I can understand how someone could enter that mindset, not that I agree with it."

Callum was curious at what lay beyond the open 'door', and so, with sword still in hand, he stepped through, hoping that it didn't shut behind him as the way out had for Daniel.

Callum felt a strangeness in the next room, unlike anything he'd experienced before. Magic seemed to be everywhere and nowhere all at once, pervading the very air, giving it charge, but it wasn't like it had been in the home of the Council. It made him question if anything he saw around him was real at all or if it was just another illusion, carefully weaved by Kole's magical talents.

A much larger space than the last, it was far from neat and well organised, with books and parchments scattered across a large desk in the middle of the room. The open tomes had been left that way for some time: a thin layer of dust had settled on the exposed pages. More bookshelves lined the walls from floor to ceiling, five metres of knowledge broken only by another large window that showed a scene that wasn't there. This time it was a woodland in the late afternoon, the sun's rays piercing the tree line as a gentle wind blew through the branches.

There was no sound coming from the window, Callum noted, not even the birds that surely would've been singing at that hour. The lights hanging from the ceiling were metal chandeliers, with candles that illuminated far more than they should have. It struck Callum then that there were none of the strange devices of metal or the technology that Daniel's ship was full of. It would have made the place quite inviting, were it not for the unfriendly man who populated it.

"Well?" Kole asked the demon expectantly, arms folded once more.

As the others filtered in, Tyrus produced an orb from nothing as Siobhan found a chair to sit on, leaning back. The orb had a reddish gas within it, but the feeling of intense magic drew Callum and his two sorcerer friends to look at it. The magic within the orb felt familiar to Callum somehow. Daniel once again stuck by the hole in the wall, which sealed itself when he so much as looked at it, while Simon found himself watching the orb with his own curiosity.

Kole glanced at the orb dismissively. "So you've contained magic within glass. Am I meant to be impressed?"

"A specifically treated receptacle that captures a demon's essence on death, preventing its loss through dissipation," Tyrus explained. It reminded Callum of Johnathan's death and the small gem that Alun had been so intent on keeping. Had that trapped his magical power for some nefarious purpose, or did it work differently?

"So?" Kole wasn't looking at the orb anymore.

"You lack the power to make your immortality permanent, fuelling it with your magic. This will rectify that." Kole was checking the demon's eyes for falsehood, though Callum doubted he'd notice from that.

"Where did you get the essence to fill that globe?" Daniel dared to ask. Not surprisingly, Tyrus didn't answer.

"Likely an encounter with feral demons," Jinar guessed, getting a look of shock from him. "We have had our fair share of meetings with them." Daniel's eyes narrowed on Callum.

"How many more secrets do you all have?"

"You were welcome to ask at any time," Jinar replied with a small smile.

"And what are you wanting in return?" Kole seemed a little interested in the prize offered, though he was doing a good job of hiding it.

"The spell for immortality," Tyrus was blunt in its answer. Kole finally looked properly to Callum and Alexis, clearly unimpressed. It made Callum feel side-lined, trying to shove that feeling aside with little success.

"A decade of research, wasted on *them*?" Alexis looked just as unimpressed with him.

"Do you accept?" Tyrus didn't try to justify its bargain, watching with absolute patience.

Jinar was now reading one of the open books, focused entirely on the words written within. Callum was expecting Kole to refuse and expel them from his home at best. He didn't rate their chances if he decided to remove them more violently, it all over within a few bloody seconds.

"I will entertain the notion that it may work, but not in front of your pawns." Looking to one another for a moment, the pair vanished into nothingness.

Callum didn't feel the magic used by either caster. Daniel looked back to the way they'd entered to see that it hadn't opened up again.

"And now we wait," Simon stated, finding a chair to sit in.

"As prisoners," Daniel added.

"Did you think he'd be serving tea and biscuits? We did just break into his home."

"Something else the demon didn't tell us we were going to do." Daniel didn't let go of his gun, looking at the decorum with suspicion. "So who is this enemy of yours, Callum? Is it one of those creatures?"

Alexis had picked up a book nearby and was flicking through the pages, reading with interest.

"I'm not sure," Callum admitted.

"Not surprised that it's keeping you in the dark too." Alexis was reading more intently and then stopped.

"Dragons," she said out loud.

"What?" Daniel frowned.

"This is a record of their existence, information gathered by scholars and sorcerers over the ages."

"Dragons don't exist, they never have."

"People thought magic didn't exist at one point, but I've seen more than enough to sway me," Siobhan chipped in, moving her feet to the table as she leaned back further in the chair. Jinar looked up from his own reading, listening in as the debate continued, Daniel still dubious.

"Magic is one thing, but dragons? Might as well say pixies and fairies are real while we're at it. People can write whatever they want, it doesn't make it true."

"I don't see this man as the kind to keep records that are inaccurate, especially with how long he has lived." Alexis turned a page. "These dragons were apparently massive and could survive in space..."

"Nothing lives permanently in a vacuum," Daniel countered, turning his head to the doctor among them. "Back me up on this one."

"There are some species of invertebrates that can survive in space for an extended period, so I wouldn't say it's impossible. Nothing is, just astronomically unlikely." Simon appeared a little odd without a cup of coffee in hand, standing by a bookshelf lined with black tomes without words on the spines. "But something as large and mythical as a dragon would've likely been recorded in more mainstream records. What else does it say about them?"

"They had no towns or cities as we do," Alexis continued. "They're far more intelligent than humans also."

"He has books on alchemy, divination, even necromancy, and that is just what I see scattered on this table," Jinar told them. "This man is indeed erudite in matters of the arcane. His collection would have put the accumulated lore of my mentor to shame, but all the knowledge in the world is for nothing if the one who owns it does not heed it."

"He doesn't use incantations either." Callum got a raised eyebrow from former his teacher. "I know you don't like or trust Tyrus, but you might learn something if you listened to what it has to say, even if you only use its knowledge to better your own methods."

"My methods are tried and tested through many generations and have served me well all the years I have used them," Jinar countered proudly, no longer smiling.

"It *did* defeat you easily, though," Simon reminded the sorcerer. "Opening your mind to its teachings can't hurt. It's how technology became what it is today, through iterative experimentation."

"So, is this something that anyone can do, casting magic?" Daniel interrupted, annoyed but also mildly interested and trying to hide it.

"Magic runs through bloodlines, and I am sorry to say that you possess no such talent," Jinar informed him.

"Just by looking at me?"

"My teacher trained me in noticing those with the spark of aptitude, and for you there is none." Jinar glanced back down to one of the open books before him as Daniel shook his head, saying nothing. In the quiet that ensued, Callum once more felt that strange magical presence in the room, faint but persistent.

"So, when that magic in the orb is used up, is the demon in it dead?" Siobhan enquired to no one in particular. "Or is it already dead?"

"The more interesting question is if it was ever alive by our definition, but I imagine whatever consciousness it had is gone," Simon answered.

"What about its soul?" Callum asked. He only had a faint presence of magic behind him as warning of the demon's arrival, turning to see it there. Daniel was the only one to look surprised, though the others looked in its direction save Simon, who had picked up a small book that he was skimming the contents of idly.

"We do not possess souls. On death, we cease to be," the demon replied bluntly. Siobhan chuckled at the answer.

"Like all of us do," she muttered, shaking her head.

"The soul is what makes us who we are," Callum refuted, getting a nod in agreement from Alexis. Siobhan looked between them and then to Jinar, who also nodded after a moment.

"The soul has long been catalogued in magical texts as a tangible element of a person, the one eternal aspect. Even death cannot shatter the soul, Siobhan," Jinar explained.

"Absurd," Daniel murmured.

"I won't tell you not to believe it, but I don't. We're flesh and blood, and when we go, we go." Siobhan looked to one of her pistols as she spoke, eyes running along the barrel, "Speaking of which, how did it go?"

"He is casting. It will take time," Tyrus told her. Callum wondered about the risks of a spell like that, one which froze the body in eternal youth; how many had lost their lives in such magical experiments, destroying themselves as the process backfired? He decided not to ponder that thought long.

"Answer me this though, Tyrus," Siobhan suddenly began. "If you had a soul – if they exist – would you become more human? More..." She paused. "Can't think of a good word, just... more." Simon looked up from his reading, his interest piqued by the philosophical direction the conversation had taken.

"Irrelevant," the demon stated. "To desire to be human is a human trait."

"Some robots want to be more human, AI too."

"Created by humans, for humans. Some of my kind debate that their path to self-control is one of self-improvement, to better what we are made of. Fewer still believe that demons can 'earn' a soul." Tyrus was going into a lot more depth than Callum was used to. He wasn't sure if he liked it. "I do not miss what is impossible for me to have."

To Callum, the thought of a creature without a soul was a sad thing, a being without a part of itself, yet the demons never had that crucial piece to begin with. But as Tyrus said, he couldn't judge the demons fairly as he wasn't one; what seemed incomplete to him was whole to it, even if some of its kind wondered if they were, in fact, all they could be.

Kole's return to the room wasn't instantaneous like Tyrus's had been, slowly floating down from above them with a spell powerful enough that Callum couldn't help but notice. His expression was neutral, but the orb of magic was now perfectly clear and empty. Something was different about him, intangible and indescribable but there. All eyes were on Kole, likely how he wanted it as the sorcerer finally reached ground level. Tyrus held its hand out expectantly, and with a quiet sigh, Kole returned the orb to the demon, it vanishing with a shimmer not a moment later.

"Well? Don't keep us in suspense, did it work?" Siobhan's feet had left the table, her sitting straight now.

"Yes." Kole folded his arms, perhaps impatient already with the questions.

"Awesome, so when are you casting it on us?" she quickly inquired. Kole ignored her, instead looking to Callum and the other sorcerers present.

"The Council really think these three can take on Keiran?" He was doubtful, focusing his attention on Callum most of all.

"You're welcome to join us," Callum suggested, getting a look of disbelief from Daniel. "You're obviously skilled with magic, we could use someone with your experience." At that Kole laughed, managing a smile for the first time. Eventually, he stopped, expression returning to normal.

"I have more important things to do. I wouldn't be joining you: you'd be joining me."

Kole conjured a burning rune, whose shape was so complicated that it made Callum dizzy just looking at it. It morphed and shifted at random, but there was a pattern buried deep beneath the visible chaos. Something tried to latch onto his memory as he stared at it, thoughts he hadn't pondered that clung until he looked away from the symbol in discomfort. They faded moments before the symbol vanished, Jinar's eyes lighting up in barely contained wonderment.

"Fascinating," he declared in a whisper, stroking his beard.

"What is?" Alexis enquired.

"That rune. It was a magical receptacle of knowledge. I imagine it is tailored only to imprint in the mind of the one whom the knowledge is destined for."

"You have what you came for, now leave," Kole ordered, ignoring the sorcerer's question. The wall by Daniel once again opened up, along with the metal door beyond it.

"Perhaps we can exchange theorems another time." Jinar got a look from Kole. "Very well, we shall teleport to our ship and leave you in peace."

"You think your quaint magic can get through the dampening around this place?" That question provoked a sudden burst of activity from Tyrus, turning its head to the way they'd entered, fists clenched. Alexis's eyes widened in worry a second later, Callum connecting the dots as well.

"That means the spell hiding us..." At her words, Daniel was immediately concerned.

"But how would they know where to—" Then it clicked in his head, and fright washed over his face. "Oh god, Monica!" he exclaimed, rushing to escape Kole's home in a frantic panic. Callum shared his deep concern but had no time to voice it.

"Cancel your spell, we need to get to Daniel's ship now!" Callum implored Kole even as Siobhan and Simon followed Daniel out just as quickly.

"That's your problem, not mine. Out." Kole turned his back on them, looking to a discarded tome. Tyrus headed out then, leaving only Jinar and Alexis on either side of Callum.

"Please, you can help us—"

"I will not ask again." Kole's warning sent a chill down his body. Only annoyance broke through his apathy.

Callum was about to plead again, but Alexis grabbed his shoulder firmly.

"We need to go, now."

He didn't remember following her out into the caves, nor them teleporting; his mind was awash with fear and anger, swirling in a pool of confusion and worry. The demons had found him before in a galaxy of billions of worlds, a ship among the stars was no different. He didn't know what was waiting for them, but the one thought which did ring loud in his mind was that someone – or something – would be waiting.

Chapter Thirty-One

For some, space travel is a necessity of business, but why spend those long weeks slumming it through the stars?

Wouldn't you rather have:
  - Penthouse-level comfort with amenities tailored to your specific needs?
  - Hand-crafted wood-panelled interior walls and premium carpeting throughout?
  - Two CryMax Alpha Cryogenic Pods?
  - On-board emergency medical systems for dealing with the aches and pains of a busy work life?
  - Fully automated ship systems so you can focus on what's important?
  - Your very own butler droid, customized to your wishes?
  - State-of-the-art laser defence systems for asteroid destruction?
  - Lifetime parts and service guarantee?

Sound good? Ask your dealer for the EX-7 Gold Personal Transport: Make the Journey the Destination of Luxury

—Advert

Their arrival had been more jarring to Callum than usual, but he barely had time to take in his surroundings as before him was a figure clad in familiar purple robes who had turned at their appearance.

It was a Silent Hand sorcerer, already preparing a spell, but it was neither magic nor his blade that felled her; a beam of red hit their assailant, first in the chest, then the head. She fell back against the far wall, very dead, scorched flesh around the points where the beams had burned through.

Callum turned away from the horrifying sight to see that Siobhan had aimed one of her pistols faster than the sorcerer could cast, still accurate despite her shaky footing from the teleportation. They were far from safe, however; if there was one, there'd be more.

"They truly were spared," Jinar muttered to himself. Daniel moved to the door quickly.

"Stop." At Simon's order, Daniel did. "You know that's going to get you killed." The doctor spoke quietly but firmly.

"I have to find her!" Daniel was barely containing his panic, gun gripped tightly.

"And Saresan too." Callum wasn't surprised that his friend wasn't on Daniel's mind, even if they were both on his. "Is there a way to see where the Silent Hand and Monica are?"

"The bridge has the camera feed, but if they have any sense they'll be there." Siobhan was thinking, pistols aimed at the door. "We could split up and search the ship."

"Impractical," Tyrus declared. "They know the location of the ship, opening up conventional options of attack. We must leave this area." Daniel was frustrated but couldn't find words to voice it. Callum didn't want to speak his mind, doubting it would help, as the last thing he wanted was Daniel even angrier at him.

"Just who are we dealing with here?" Daniel finally asked. "Are these some of the enemies you've made?"

"In part," Jinar conceded. "They are members of a cabal of sorcerers in league with the ones that seek our deaths. They are from our world."

"A cabal of sorcerers?!" Daniel was aghast at the news.

"Will they not have heard the shot?" Jinar enquired to Siobhan then, ignoring Daniel's reaction.

"Possibly," Siobhan replied quickly.

"You're being hunted by sorcerers? That's just what we need, sorcerers AND Z-Gen after our hides!" Daniel clenched his teeth, taking a deep breath. "When this is over, you're going to tell me everything that's going on, or I'll shove you lot out the airlock!"

"Now is not the time for this," Alexis implored calmly. "We need to work together if we're going to survive. Tyrus is correct, we need to move the ship."

"If the demon wasn't here—"

"The demon *is* here, and right now it's our best chance of getting out of this alive," Simon interrupted sharply. He waited a second for an objection but didn't get one. All the while Callum thought on the peril Monica was in, the demons that would be lurking around every corner ready to lunge at them. "If we move together, we can reach the bridge and then relocate the ship. Once we have eyes on the other rooms, we can make plans from there. Does anyone have any objections?"

"It seems sound to me," Jinar agreed.

"Good. You take point, Daniel, you're the soldier after all."

"You might need this then," Siobhan told the doctor, offering him one of her pistols. Simon shook his head.

"I swore an oath not to take life, I'm not about to break it now."

"I think Hippocrates would forgive you." But Simon stuck to his convictions as the others readied their weapons. Siobhan went back to holding both pistols ready. "Your loss."

Callum tried to steady his nerves while Daniel approached the door with his rifle ready. He briefly wondered if the Silent Hand were having the same problems that he and his friends had in adapting to life beyond their world. Nothing Alun told them would've prepared them for the truth, that much was certain.

Daniel opened the door and checked both directions in the long hallway before giving a nod to Siobhan, who stood beside him. The man was clearly distracted, despite his eyes attentively focusing on the way to the bridge. There were many doors between there and where they were, each one possibly hiding an enemy. Callum could feel no magic being used around them either.

Before they'd gotten more than a few paces away from Tyrus's room, Callum heard the sound of a commotion from one of the rooms to the right. Daniel motioned for the others to follow him quickly as he hustled to the door for the common area.

The sound was clearer now as Callum stood with him, sword ready. It seemed like a struggle was happening within, but the sound of a heavy thud made him wonder whether it was already over.

Daniel opened the door and took a quick look before moving back into cover.

"Two of them," he told them as Callum quickly rushed in, eager to help whoever was under attack. "Wait!"

There were indeed a pair of sorcerers in front of the table, each one armed with a weapon much like Daniel's, who quickly turned from their original target when they saw him enter. Callum's gut instinct to protect himself took hold, but momentary panic made concentrating on a spell all but impossible. The magic that rushed through his arm was sudden and he could barely control it, but its effect worked, a momentary shimmering shield absorbing the beams of red before it fizzled into nothing. The sorcerers' surprise was cut short as Siobhan and Daniel fired, felling the two of them with a few shots. Callum's heart continued to pound, so close he'd been to death and yet managing to evade it.

"Are you alright?" Siobhan asked him.

He just nodded weakly before he noticed that on the table was another sorcerer. He was unconscious but breathing, his face bruised and nose bloodied. Callum then spotted a figure which slowly stood from behind the table, one that he recognised without thinking about it even as Daniel readied his gun to fire again.

"Hold it, it's Saresan!" Callum urged, rushing over to his friend.

The guard had his left hand pressed against his right side, where his shirt was bloody. In his right was one of the beam weapons the sorcerers had been using, held like a club and splattered with blood. It was slightly bent and buckled.

"You're wounded!"

"What kept you?" Saresan chuckled as he saw Simon move over to him quickly, "It's just a graze, it looks worse than it is."

"I'll be the judge of that, sit down." Saresan did as he was told, the doctor lifting his shirt to examine the wound that indeed looked bad.

"Where's Monica? Was she with you?" Daniel quickly asked the guard.

"No idea, sorry. We weren't in the same place when everything went to hell," Saresan apologised. The others moved in quickly, Siobhan watching the corridor they'd left. Jinar noticed the unconscious man on the table.

"Dare I ask what happened to him?" Jinar enquired with distaste.

"Not long after you guys left, they started showing up," Saresan replied, watching as Simon reached for one of the dead sorcerer's robes to rip off some makeshift bandages. "I darted into here, but one of them spotted me. I grabbed his weapon and then beat the crap out of him with it."

"I'm glad you're alive, I feared the worst," Callum told him.

"More than I can say for the gun," Siobhan remarked. "Corridor's still clear."

"So, what's the plan?" Saresan winced when his wound was bandaged.

"Whatever the plan is, *you're* staying here," Simon told the guard firmly. "You put too much strain on yourself, and that wound will get worse. I won't take no for an answer."

"I can help, you know that. All I need is a weapon."

"You had one until you smashed it up," Siobhan reminded.

"A *proper* weapon," came the correction. Saresan looked to Tyrus. "Just use your hocus pocus on me and I'll be good as new."

"An inefficient use of reserves that may be needed for a true threat," Tyrus retorted bluntly. Its claws clenched a moment before relaxing.

"You're staying here and that's final." Simon wasn't in the mood for debate. Callum was surprised that more hadn't come to check on their fellows in the common area. Daniel was growing impatient, glancing back to the door periodically.

"And if someone finds you? What are you going to do, heal them to death?" Siobhan asked with just a hint of mockery.

"I shall remain with them while the rest of you tend to the bridge. Their power is nothing compared to mine." Jinar smiled confidently as he stood beside the doctor and his patient. "Do what you must, we shall be fine." Callum nodded but was concerned all the same as Daniel looked back to the corridor.

"Still clear. Let's move." Daniel stepped out, quickly followed by Siobhan. Callum and Alexis weren't too far behind. Last out was Tyrus.

The corridor remained empty as they hustled towards the bridge. Callum had expected more resistance, but the loud conversation audible through the door gave them all the warning they needed. Daniel and Siobhan stood on either side of the doorway again with their weapons ready. Wanting to avoid a repeat of their entrance to the common room, Callum stood against the wall by Siobhan, Alexis mirroring him next to Daniel. Tyrus didn't budge, watching the doorway intently.

"What's the plan?" Siobhan whispered to the others. "Open the door and blast them?"

Tyrus vanished and the conversation beyond stopped suddenly. A noise of surprise was cut violently short with the sickening sound of flesh being rent from bone. Neither Daniel nor Siobhan moved, exchanging looks, as the screams of bloody agony and flames gave way to quiet. Daniel was hesitant to open the door but did so, immediately regretting looking in as he quickly retched.

"Good god, what did you *do*?" he exclaimed.

Callum dared to look within himself and saw a horrible mess. The floors and walls were splattered with blood as well as errant body parts that once belonged to what remained of the sorcerers within. Two had been burned beyond recognition, sprawled near the doorway that was scorched black. One unlucky victim yet lived, groaning in unimaginable pain as he attempted to drag himself across the floor away from Tyrus, who slowly approached. Only the demon's claws were bloodied, dripping gently as it loomed over its target.

Despite everything, Callum felt great pity for the man.

"P-please..."

The sorcerer's pleas were answered with the staff Tyrus conjured into being, hitting him with it again and again with such force that it splintered after the third strike to his head. Callum hadn't been able to look away, disgusted at the brutality he'd witnessed from his mentor.

Tyrus stared at the now-dead sorcerer as its staff reformed itself, whole once more. The moment of rage seemed to pass, and it once more returned to relative normality. Was that how it wanted him to deal with his enemies, like they were little more than cattle for the slaughter?

The demon looked at him silently, not justifying its behaviour or caring what he thought. Callum walked further in, mindful of his back being exposed to anyone who saw them from down the corridor. Siobhan tried not to look at the remains scattered around the bridge as she headed to one of the devices in the wall, holstering her pistols and quickly pressing buttons.

"Looks like they haven't tampered with the navigation systems at least," she told them as Daniel stepped in. "Where to?"

"Anywhere as long as it's not here." Daniel then indicated to one of the discarded rifles as he headed to a different device. "Take that and watch the corridor, Callum, I need to check the cameras." Callum looked at the weapon curiously.

"I wouldn't know what to do with it," he honestly replied.

Alexis was trying not to look at the dead as she picked up one of the weapons, holding it roughly like Daniel had been his own.

"Point and pull the trigger. There, now you know."

Callum sheathed his sword and grabbed one of the firers of red beams delicately, finding that it was lighter than he thought it'd be. He quickly found the trigger, but it didn't feel right in his hands. Callum stood by the door, Alexis taking a position opposite. Half expecting a sorcerer to emerge from one of the many doors before him, he tried to keep an eye on all of them at once.

Struggling to keep the gun still, Callum doubted he'd even hit someone with one of the beams if they did emerge. Alexis's aim was far steadier, making him wonder what he was doing wrong. Tyrus was still silent, watching the view of space change as the ship started to move.

"I've found her," Daniel declared then. "She's near the escape pods, beyond the cargo area. Doesn't look like she's being chased by anyone, thank god. I've deactivated them, just in case."

"Are there other sorcerers on board?" Alexis asked. Daniel pressed a few more buttons.

"...None."

"Maybe we got them all," Siobhan sounded hopeful. "Wishful thinking, I know."

"We should bring her here either way. Callum and I can go to her," Alexis suggested. "That way you can stay here, in case they did something to the ship that you haven't yet noticed."

"I'll go with them, just in case," Siobhan stated, drawing her pistols again. Daniel immediately objected.

"No way, I'm going," he told her.

"If something goes wrong, I don't know how to get it working again. You never taught me beyond the basics, and right now your copilot is trying to bail." The two stared at one another, Siobhan not yielding to her captain. "Your head's not in the right place, Daniel, you know it." Daniel finally averted his gaze with a worried sigh, shaking his head.

"If anything happens to her—" he began.

"Like we'd let that happen. Come on, I'll lead." Siobhan headed through the door after quickly checking the corridor.

Callum and Alexis followed behind, him still holding the beam weapon awkwardly as he looked back to Daniel. The man was staring at him with a look of blame that Callum couldn't shake off even when the door closed. Tyrus was following a few steps behind them, guarding its ward as they descended into the cargo area. No ambush was waiting for them.

"So who are these sorcerers, Callum?"

"They are a cabal of magicians from our world, in league with an army of feral demons," Alexis answered as they moved between the large crates.

"And they want you dead why?"

Callum saw their likely destination, a secure-looking door similar to the ones on the way out of the ship.

Siobhan glanced around before she headed to it, tapping a complicated sequence of button presses into the panel beside it that almost sounded musical. "All but one of the pods have been launched."

Callum suddenly felt uneasy, sensing a magical presence that was both strong and oddly familiar. He didn't know anyone that powerful that was a friend, yet the sensation made him lower his guard before becoming even more worried. Alexis frowned.

"Someone is there." She'd felt it too.

"Maybe Alun." Callum didn't relish the thought of that.

"Not strong enough," Tyrus informed them. The scream of fright from beyond the door sent a shiver of fear down Callum's spine.

"She's in trouble! Open the door!" he shouted, ready with his weapon to fire at a moment's notice. Siobhan obliged and, with Alexis and himself, opened fire on the purple-clad figure whose back was turned to them. He hoped that they weren't too late.

Callum was as surprised as the others that the figure hadn't fallen in the hail of red beams. The purple robes were untouched, but he'd neither seen nor felt any magic that could've resisted the withering attack. Siobhan was amazed, weapons still trained on the person and so very tempted to shoot again.

"He didn't even flinch…" she muttered, shooting again to no effect.

Callum dropped the rifle and reached for his sword as he started to see features of the person that was eerily familiar to him. Standing in a wide corridor basking in gloomy illumination, the man was tall and broad-shouldered. It reminded him of someone, but it couldn't have been him, it simply wasn't possible.

On the left wall were four doors, the closest of which was open and led to a tiny room with a chair and some panels and buttons. Beyond the man he could see Monica at the very end of the short corridor, armed with a pistol of her own, which she'd likely used to fell the dead sorcerers in front of her before the newcomer's arrival. She was terrified, constantly glancing at Callum with pleading eyes.

"You're outnumbered, give yourself up!" Callum declared loudly, hoping that it'd work.

Slowly the man turned to face them, and it was then that recognition struck Callum like a lightning bolt, freezing him in place. Those powerful eyes were ones he could never forget, burned into his memory. Alexis gasped, scanning every feature of his face in utter disbelief and puzzled joy.

"…It can't be…" Her voice was a wavering whisper, the rifle clattering to the ground as the sight of the man. "…It can't."

All the while Tyrus watched from behind them silently, staff gripped tightly. Callum knew it was ready to fight at a moment's notice and so was he, and yet every part of his being was fighting that urge despite himself; it just wasn't possible, but his eyes didn't lie, neither had that feeling before, which he now recognised as the man's magical presence that he'd grown used to in the short time they'd known each other.

"You *know* this guy?" Siobhan was incredulous, watching the figure with distrust as he finally spoke.

"Hello, sister." Johnathan's voice was as it had always been, the warrior's stoic expression softening into relief at the sight of Alexis. It was all him; not a single thing was out of place, save that his magic was far stronger than before, but then he'd always been more skilled. He held his axe firmly in hand, and under his robes were little more than black garments, the man having cast off his chain mail for the protection of magic. Callum spied a headband which had in its centre the purple gem he'd seen before, glowing with a soft inner light. Siobhan was puzzled but quickly narrowed her gaze in suspicion.

"Wait, isn't he meant to be dead?" she asked warily, expecting a spell flung her way.

Johnathan did no such thing, looking only to Alexis, who was trying to blink back tears.

"...He is," Callum answered softly.

Something was wrong, very wrong. This had to be a trick, a scheme of Alun's to catch them off guard, but no sudden strike came from the cabal leader, nor were they engulfed in flames. But Jinar had killed him, he'd been sure of it. Even if somehow he'd lived, the demons would have made sure to finish him off once they'd escaped.

Johnathan hadn't moved since turning to them, perhaps also hesitant to fight. Callum's gut said not to trust anything. Monica tried to move to them while Johnathan was distracted but was stopped by a translucent wall of magic that blocked her in. She pushed at it, hammered it with her fists, but it did not yield, nor could they hear her shouting to them.

"How...?" Alexis no longer quelled her tears, stepping a little closer. Johnathan reached his hand to touch her face.

"Alexis." Callum's voice stopped her, something that made Johnathan turn to him with disdain. The warrior's hand slowly moved back to his side. "It can't be him."

"I am glad you survived, Alexis. I had feared…" Johnathan trailed off, his eyes returning to her.

Now that Callum had heard him more than once, he noticed that the man's voice was distant somehow. Callum glanced back to Tyrus, checking that it was still there, which the demon was; was its inaction a sign that it wasn't sure of victory, or was there something else going on?

"But how? I don't understand…" Her happiness was mixed with confusion and sadness, a mess of emotions that fought for control.

"It doesn't matter, what matters is that you're alive." Alexis's eyes drifted to the purple robes that her brother was clad in.

"You still serve Alun, don't you?" Alexis dared to ask, afraid of the answer. Johnathan paused to consider his answer. On the man's face seemed to flash a moment of pain that was quickly hidden. "You've seen all that's beyond our world just like we have, yet still you side with the Silent Hand?"

"If you're Alexis's brother, then let our friend go. Heck, join us!" Siobhan hadn't lowered her pistols, still expecting a fight. "Tyrus can hide you from them just like it's hiding us."

Monica had stopped trying to break through the barrier, watching in fear at the exchange she couldn't hear.

"Whatever hold Alun has on you, we can break it. We'll find a way," Alexis assured her brother, hoping for the answer Callum knew would never come.

"Only with me will you be spared, Alexis; you know this. You cannot defeat Keiran." Johnathan's voice didn't have the desperate zeal it had possessed on their world; instead, there was a quiet sureness which his deep voice radiated.

"I know you did all this to protect her, but you don't know that we can't defeat Keiran." Callum's words once more earned him Johnathan's attention, a glare that he now felt was emptier than before. Its strength had changed, a hollowness that sent chills down his back.

"I have seen his power. There are none who can." Johnathan's words were laced with anger and hate, all aimed at him. In immediate contrast, he held out a hand to his sister and spoke gently to her, "Please, Alexis, come with me. Please!" She looked at the hand and, for a second, seemed to be considering his offer. Then she stepped back to stand beside Callum, something that made Johnathan scowl.

"…I can't," Alexis said quietly to her brother, her heart breaking all over again. "You have to see that what you're doing is wrong. Whatever Alun told you is wrong; can't you see that?"

Johnathan wasn't looking at her anymore, instead staring at Callum as he gripped his battleaxe in both hands.

"Still you are swayed by his lies?" came words full of anger. "Everyone that meets him suffers, Alexis. Our world burned because of him, and you *still* follow, still believe?"

Siobhan had been silent throughout the exchange, but Johnathan's words were making her trigger fingers itchy. Alexis was pained by his words, Callum more so as they were all true. Alexis finally answered her brother.

"Because he's doing what's right. You knew what that was once, but now..." She choked on her words, reaching for her daggers with shaky hands.

"Now..." Johnathan shifted his stance, readying for battle as Callum prepared his sword reluctantly. A solitary tear ran down Johnathan's face.

"I don't want to fight you, Johnathan, but I won't let you hurt Monica or anyone here."

Callum felt magic tingling through his skin even as he spoke, ready to be unleashed with a thought. "I'm sorry."

Johnathan's eyes flared with rage; the head of his axe suddenly wreathed in blue flames of fury.

"How *dare* you apologise to me!" screamed the warrior as he rushed forward, swinging with such arcane might that it made Callum dizzy.

Chapter Thirty-Two

The strike was stopped by Tyrus teleporting to interpose itself between Johnathan and the others, his staff shattering upon contact with the axe's head. Callum stepped forward to assist his mentor but got a warning glare from the demon.

"He is too strong for you," Tyrus declared loudly, conjuring another barrier between them and Johnathan, blocking an impressively devastating amount of flame that their foe unleashed.

Callum couldn't understand how Johnathan had managed to grow so powerful so quickly compared to him. Beyond both barriers, Monica looked on at the combat, face pale in horror at the prospect of immolation.

"You need my help!" came Callum's objection as he moved to stand beside Tyrus, his sword ready.

Siobhan took one look at Johnathan striking the barrier blocking him with his axe and decided to step back slowly, knowing when she was outmatched.

Alexis hadn't acted, fighting against the fact that it was her brother. There wasn't time for the demon to object as Johnathan smashed through the barrier that separated them with a blast of magic potent enough to set Callum off balance.

Johnathan swung for him, his arms now engulfed in the blue fire that seemed not to harm him. Callum was too caught up in the fray of combat to be terrified now, managing to parry the axe before launching a spell of his own, a pushing force to make some distance between them. Johnathan smiled darkly as he was shoved but a few metres.

"You were always weak, cowardly, choosing your own life over everyone else!" Johnathan spat at him, readying another powerful spell. Still, the barrier entrapping Monica held strong.

"Do you really think they'd've spared our world if I gave myself up, Johnathan?"

Callum's objection earned him a bolt of flame which he only just cancelled with a barrier, one that almost entirely consumed his magic reserves. They had to distract Johnathan enough that Monica was freed, but how? Johnathan's magic seemed to be without limit.

"Go!" Tyrus ordered more angrily to all of them, staff back in hand and whole.

"He'll still die." Johnathan's eyes were only on him now as he unleashed his magic.

Callum's strength failed him instantly, struggling to stay conscious as he slumped to his hands and knees, barely gripping his blade. Something was leeching his very energy, dragging it forcefully from him in a way that quickly sent pain running through his entire being. Tyrus's efforts to stop Johnathan were interrupted by a near-constant blast of flame from the man's free hand.

"Stop!" Alexis ordered her brother, rushing forward to stop him despite the pain it caused her.

At the moment when Johnathan saw her draw daggers intended for him, he hesitated, the magic gripping Callum faltering as he saw what his actions had driven her to. Indecision gripped him, the barrier trapping Monica shimmering briefly before Alexis closed the distance.

Channelling her magic into the blades she wielded, they glowed with a soft white light moments before she struck him. Johnathan's survival instincts kicked in despite himself, shielding his chest from the blows and instead allowing the daggers to sink deep into his right arm.

Callum felt his strength return to him slowly, reinvigorated by magic instilled into him by Tyrus, who had gripped his arm, but there was also the tugging pull of teleportation; the demon sought to spell him away from danger and Callum fought the urge, unwilling to leave any of them to fight alone. The spell failed to wrench him from the room, his mentor snarling in anger at his stubbornness.

Only when Alexis stepped back from her brother with surprise and horror did Callum look at the man's wounds to see that it did not bleed.

"...What...?" Her words were gasped.

Johnathan looked at the two punctures in his flesh that refused to leak, staring at his sister with an expression of surprise and pain.

"What the hell?" Siobhan had backed up to the doorway out, staring in disbelief as Callum finally got to his feet, trying to comprehend what they were witnessing; what powerful enchantment allowed Johnathan to defy the body's natural order like it was?

"I'm trying to save you, why can't you see that?!" Johnathan shouted, voice pained.

"What did they do to you?" Alexis couldn't look away from the injury, daggers gripped tightly. Tyrus stared at the sorcerer, standing between him and Callum, ready to defend its charge.

"...What needed to be done."

Johnathan's voice was straining, likely from the agony of his wounds, but within his body was a tremendous magical strength that Callum couldn't deny; somehow, he was even stronger than Alun had been on their world, defying all that he knew of the progression of arcane power.

"It's not Monica you want, it's me," Callum told Johnathan then, moving away from behind Tyrus.

"No," Tyrus warned harshly, glaring at their foe.

"Well, I'm here. Let her go!" Johnathan's anger melted away into a smile that didn't sit well with Callum. The warrior dropped his axe, nodding slowly in agreement, which gave Alexis a glimmer of hope to cling to.

"I will."

The build-up of energy was intense and instant, one palm pointed to Alexis. From it, a surging force shoved her violently into Siobhan and through the door, the pair colliding hard into a cargo container. Callum saw Johnathan's other hand press against the wall where the pods had been, just as the barrier containing Monica vanished. Taking her chance, she began to rush towards him, but he'd figured out what was going to happen, terror gripping him. Tyrus struck out with a bolt of energy, too late to stop Johnathan.

"Monica, don't—"

The hole in the wall Johnathan created was large, opening the corridor to the beyond which the stars swam in. The door out thudded shut in an instant, sealing their fate. Johnathan was still smiling to them as he was pulled out into space by an unstoppable force, the very air being wrenched from the corridor and dragging the sword from Callum's grip as he and Monica were pulled towards the gaping wound in the ship.

Fright and panic overtook Callum in that second, unable to grab or keep hold of anything as the ragged doorway to oblivion waited to envelop him. It was stopped only by Tyrus grabbing his wrist, the demon having warped the very floor to swallow its feet, providing a desperate anchor. But Monica wasn't so secured, his friend petrified as the blackness pulled her closer. In that heartbeat, Callum couldn't grab her but Tyrus could, reaching forward with its clawed hand.

Her hand managed to reach the demon's and gripped it, but it didn't grab her in kind. Tyrus's eyes were not on the woman they'd tried so hard to save but the sword that was just out of its reach because of her. Without hesitation, the demon shook its arm to wrench her grip from it, reaching forward to rescue the blade instead.

Many emotions flashed across Monica's face: shock, betrayal and finally the realisation that she was going to die. Words were lost immediately as she was sucked out of the room, but her face spoke volumes of terror. Callum tried to shout, but there was no air to carry his despair.

She was gone.

Teleported back into the cargo hold by Tyrus, Callum immediately collapsed to his knees as a wave of despair hit him, trying to come to terms with what he'd witnessed. A sickness rose in his stomach, followed by tears that he shed for the woman who'd died, and for what? His mentor held the sword it had saved by the handle, the price paid. Alexis and Siobhan had only just got to their feet, and while the former looked to Callum with immediate concern, the truth of what had happened dawned on Siobhan, looking to the still shut door in loss.

"What happened? Where's Monica? Is Johnathan...?" Alexis asked him before following Callum's gaze and finding out the answer herself.

Tyrus stepped up to Callum, towering over him as it offered the sword back. It was that which triggered anger which burst forth without his control.

"You could have saved her!" he shouted, glaring up at the demon.

"No," Tyrus declared flatly, still offering the blade. Its answer repulsed him, Callum standing to his feet.

"What happened?" Siobhan repeated Alexis's question, watching the demon carefully as Callum pointed an accusing finger at his mentor.

"No?! That weapon wasn't worth her life, nothing was! There had to be another choice, another way!" His words didn't so much as make Tyrus shift.

"There was not the time to save both," it replied. Siobhan listened on, shocked at all she was hearing and her pistols back in hand.

"But you could have *tried*!" Callum exclaimed, shaking his head as the tears kept coming, breaths shaky. "You could have—"

"You saved his sword instead of her?" Alexis was aghast at that thought. "You're supposed to be protecting us!"

"Incorrect. My duty is to protect and train Callum to defeat Keiran." Tyrus tried to hand Callum the sword, but he refused it; it had been bought with Monica's blood, her look of dread that he'd never forget. "More will die. Her death was necessary—"

"No!" Callum was aghast.

"YOU!"

A cry of grief-stricken fury echoed through the cavernous room.

Daniel had arrived, firing upon Tyrus as soon as he had a line of sight. Callum was startled at the beam of red which almost hit the demon, dissipating instead on a momentary barrier it brought into existence effortlessly. The sword clattered to the ground as Alexis turned to Daniel with sadness and shock.

Siobhan quickly moved away from the demon so as not to be hit by mistake. Tyrus stepped in front of Callum, wishing to shield him from the man's wrath as he kept firing, each shot failing to connect thanks to its magic. Tyrus didn't react to the shots otherwise.

"You fucking let her die!"

"Daniel—" Callum tried in vain to reason with him.

"And YOU!" Daniel didn't stop firing as he shouted beyond his target. "It's your fault they came here, your fault she's dead! I should've killed you when I had the chance!"

A build-up of magic within Tyrus told Callum exactly what was going to happen, fright leaping into his throat. In a single second, the demon teleported in front of Daniel and swung its staff at him, shattering his rifle and knocking him to the ground in one swift action.

Alexis gasped, while Siobhan raised her pistols to fire upon Tyrus as it readied to unleash a spell upon him at point-blank range. Callum shouted in desperation, not thinking on the words as that would've taken too long.

"Stop!" he beckoned in futility.

Amazingly, the demon did stop, standing above the wounded man with its hand clutching a fireball that burned brightly. Siobhan didn't fire but only just, the atmosphere of panic gripping all of them.

"Let him go!"

"He seeks your death," Tyrus responded, ready to finish what it had started.

"No one else dies, not for me!" He didn't remember picking up the sword, but it was in his hands as he stepped closer.

He saw the pain Daniel was in, physically and emotionally, and knew the man was right: it was all his fault. Callum saw Simon rush into the room, quickly assessing the situation and focusing on the demon.

"Step away from him," Simon demanded, unafraid to order the massive creature.

"No." Tyrus let the flames in his grasp grow stronger as Daniel tried to reach for a pistol.

He screamed in pain when the demon stepped hard on his wrist, an unnatural crunch making Callum shiver and Siobhan flinch.

"You hurt him again and I'll hurt you a thousand-fold," Siobhan warned loudly even through her fear.

"You're a fucking monster!" Daniel was in tears as he shouted, letting his hate flow into the words even while he whimpered in pain.

"That only one died in the attack was improbable," the demon commented coldly.

"How can you say that? Monica was—" Siobhan began to object.

"One human," Tyrus interrupted sharply, drawing all eyes to it. "Keiran's servants eradicated a world to kill Callum."

"And that makes him more important than her?" the pilot shouted, making the situation even tenser.

"Yes." Siobhan didn't quite know what to say, but Callum did, outraged.

"I'm not! That's what I'm trying to tell you! I'm not going to throw people away just to try and achieve the Council's goals! You can't expect me to be so... so heartless! She was my friend!"

"Irrelevant."

"How do you expect me to trust you if you're going to sacrifice anyone on a whim?" Tyrus finally stepped off Daniel, Simon rushing to examine his wounds as the demon stared at Callum. The fireball still burned in its grip.

"Trust is a human weakness. I am to train you as instructed by the Council. You may partake in the alternative if you wish it."

Callum remembered the alternative, and as much as his heart bled for Monica, to throw away her death by letting it all be pointless was worse. It did nothing to endear him to his mentor, it who had acted more monstrous than the near-mindless ones of his kind they'd killed before. Siobhan was watching Callum and the demon, unsure of where this would lead but on edge nonetheless.

Callum sighed sadly and shakily, the concession Tyrus had been waiting for. It turned then to Daniel, who was being helped to his feet by the doctor.

"If you insist on his survival, Callum, then he shall live. I will not hesitate to defend you from *all* threats. Remember this."

Tyrus vanished, leaving behind bleak silence, broken only by Daniel's pain and sobbing.

Callum felt drained and utterly responsible. He wanted to apologise to them, but what could he say?

"I'm sorry." The words came out anyway, expecting nothing but scorn for them. The look he got from Daniel was one of utter loathing, stabbing deep as he was helped out of sight.

"You've no need to apologise to me," Alexis told him quietly.

She was clearly torn up about Johnathan, old pains exhumed and thrown upward into the air along with a hundred more questions, but none of them seemed to matter at that moment.

"…I don't think anyone can blame you for what that guy did back there," Siobhan said quietly. She had holstered her pistols. A sad calm had taken hold of her. "We all tried to save her; look how much I helped."

"I still feel responsible."

Callum looked down to the sword, the thing which had started everything off. Was it truly worth the lives of others, of Monica? That he was even considering the question made him angry.

"That's the sign you're still a human being, not like… that thing. It *is* a monster." Siobhan glanced back to the closed door she'd been flung away from. "If your brother's meant to be dead, Alexis, what was he doing there? Was it magic that made someone look like him or something?"

"I… don't know," Alexis conceded, looking back herself to the door with sadness. "But I know it was him, even if it makes no sense."

"I'm the least qualified to tell you you're wrong, but damn it I wish things made sense right now." Siobhan was silent for a moment. "You sure that thing isn't going to turn on us, Callum?"

Callum considered her question grimly, remembering how quick it had killed one of its own without remorse.

"I hope not."

Chapter Thirty-Three

Protect The Public
Shield the Innocent
Uphold the Law

Enlist in Z-Gen today!

—Z-Gen recruitment poster

Days passed in an eerie quiet. Monica's death weighed on the minds of everyone on board, though few talked about it; Daniel remained in his quarters after Simon had finished treating him for his injuries, not emerging even to eat. There'd been no demand that they be thrown out the airlock or left on a planet to fend for themselves, only silence.

Jinar shared what little they knew of their foes and the Council in the first days after the incident. None of that made Monica's passing any easier or soothed the tensions between them and Tyrus, who'd remained in its quarters in silent meditation since its angry outburst. Jinar had smiled to himself when hearing of that, the first time the supposedly superior teacher had shown weakness.

Saresan had been treated shortly after Daniel, his wound healing fast. The guard regaled everyone in time with what happened on board and then switched his time between exercising and weapons training, using a metal staff until Jinar created a replacement halberd for him using his magic.

"It'll do for now," Saresan had remarked at it, giving it a swing to check its balance.

Alexis was also more detached than before, trying to come to terms with the apparent resurrection of her brother. Callum didn't ask for any reading lessons, sure that she wanted time alone once more.

He knew that there was no way Johnathan would've ripped a hole in the ship if he wasn't going to survive it, likely teleporting to safety before the deadly effects of space took hold. He also knew that there was no way that the man could've even been there if Jinar was right about returning from the dead, yet there he'd been.

His nights were plagued with even worse nightmares than before, each one of Monica suffering a terrible fate and him barely unable to save her no matter what he tried.

He resigned himself to watching the viewscreen in his room when rest was robbed from him. Rarely was there something interesting to watch, but he'd learned a few things about how it all worked; every news outlet had differing ways of presenting information, some inserting their own opinions into the narrative while others remained impartial. Often to get the whole picture on an incident or item of interest, Callum had to switch between a few different people to piece it together, something he found annoying. On the fourth night of restlessness, one news item caught his attention, spoken by a tired-looking woman with a very neutral accent.

"...And we'll have to return to that story later. We've just received word that Geladan has been placed under quarantine. We have been unable to ascertain the reason, but we believe that it is another bold attack by the Great Threat. Z-Gen have refused to comment on the situation, save to say that everything is under control and that the problem will not spread to outlying systems or other planets within the system. We got this statement from the general of that region, Cadmus."

The picture changed to a tall and imposing man who stood with a bulky rifle in his hands. He was a man of war, the scars on his face telling of his experiences. Callum's eyes were caught by the metal in places where flesh should've been, his entire left arm forged of what he guessed wasn't steel and his left eye gone. In its place was a grey orb that glowed a deep red in its centre, a feature of the middle-aged man Callum found disturbing.

Callum didn't know what to make of seeing a cyborg for the first time – he guessed the man was such from Simon's description of one – but he didn't have too long to ponder before Cadmus spoke.

"As yet we don't understand the nature of the threat Geladan faces, so the quarantine is a precaution." His voice was gruff but powerful, stare not deviating. "But know this: if it is the Great Threat, then I will not hesitate to protect the people of this galaxy by crushing them with the full might of Z-Gen. We will make them fight for every inch of land they try to hold, and I promise you, they will not win!"

The picture returned to the woman at her desk.

"General Cadmus of Z-Gen and we hope that the situation on Geladan will be dealt with soon. If you have any concerns about friends or loved ones, do not hesitate to approach a Z-Gen official or soldier, they're there to serve."

He switched to something else, hoping to find something that would distract him from his mind's torments. A part of him found watching the screen strangely lethargic, an urge that he ultimately fought against by turning it off. Maybe some spent their whole lives sat like he was, seeing much but experiencing nothing.

He thought on the people of Geladan, hoping that they were going to be alright, but worry wouldn't leave his mind. Images of people fleeing in terror from demons persisted, the bloody result of the masses trapping themselves in their panic making him seek another place of quiet. Leaving his quarters, he noticed Siobhan and Jinar were standing outside Tyrus's room in mid-discussion. Jinar spotted him and smiled, the invitation for Callum to approach, which he did.

"But why won't it work for me?" Whatever the conversation concerned, Siobhan was disappointed.

"The spell is tailored to only work on one who possesses arcane talent. For why, you would have to ask its architect, but considering his opinion on those without magic, I do not believe there is much to deduce," Jinar answered.

"Does having powerful magic make people assholes by default?" she enquired, prompting a raised eyebrow from the sorcerer.

"Am I not a perfectly pleasant person to speak to?" The question was said with a smile.

"And humble, you forgot that part." Jinar ignored her eye roll, then addressed Callum.

"I am surprised that Tyrus did not seek you out. It is waiting for you, to bestow immortality at your convenience." The sorcerer paused. "That is a rather odd phrase to say, is it not?"

"I'm surprised you said yes, considering how sulky you are around it," Siobhan piped in.

"Even that thing understands that my arcane supremacy is an invaluable asset, despite its mutterings to the contrary."

"Did I mention how humble you are?" Siobhan remarked.

"On several occasions."

"What does it involve?" Callum didn't notice anything different about Jinar, nor was his magic any different.

"I am afraid it is rather unimpressive to experience, unlike the ramifications of its casting if, of course, it actually works," Jinar remarked. "But I will not delay you any longer, lest the demon grows impatient. I have some arcane experiments to perform. You are welcome to join me if you wish, Siobhan."

"Sounds positively thrilling." She did nothing to hide her sarcasm.

"I assure you: it most certainly is. Nothing is more awe-inspiring than the arcane."

"Thanks, but I think I'll pass. I've got to give the *Silverbolt* some tune-ups just in case Z-Gen shows up."

Callum entered the demon's quarters to see it stood in the centre of the open space, staring right at him. There was nothing that Callum associated with the idea of a powerful spell; no magical circles, reagents or chants, nor was there a strong presence, just the demon waiting in silence. Its staff was absent, leaving only the cloak to separate Tyrus from the savage killers he knew most demons to be, though at that moment the distinction was blurred.

There was still a great discomfort and anger with being near it, but still, he had come when asked. Callum waited for instructions but got nothing more than a continued stare, slowly stepping closer until the demon conjured an orb of demonic essence into its hand.

"Closer."

Tyrus wasn't making a request and he didn't question it, walking up so that it was within reach, ever knowing that his sword was at hand. The demon put its claws to his chest, and slowly the light within the orb faded as a build-up of magic ebbed from the demon into him.

The energy was stinging but not painful, and to begin with, his body tried to resist it. The sensation grew in strength and overwhelmed him before a brief flash of intense agony struck. Then it was gone, leaving Callum feeling no different than he had been before aside from a dull ache that was already passing. In many ways, the sensation was very much like when he first picked up the sword, and yet not.

"...Is that it?" he asked warily. "Did it work?" Tyrus stepped away from him, the orb it held now empty and vanishing back into nothingness.

"Yes," Tyrus replied.

"How do you know?"

"It is our nature to know the workings of magic," came its reply.

He looked at his hands, trying to detect the faintest of glimmers that he was not as he'd been before, only to find nothing different. Jinar had been right; it did feel anticlimactic, but in the back of his mind was the knowledge that, if Tyrus was being truthful, the spectre of death no longer followed in his shadow to reap him when his time came. He wasn't quite sure what to think of it.

"I will offer this to Alexis, then you will continue your training."

"For how long?" Callum asked.

"Until you are ready. The ship is being piloted to a nebula, where you can train more safely."

"If we're going to get stronger, wouldn't it make more sense to directly help people rather than hide?" Tyrus stared at him. "We don't know what Keiran is doing, but there's still the Great Threat. That's a danger to everyone, and we could—"

"Needless risk." Its refusal was to the point and expected, but he wasn't going to give up so easily.

"We can't just hide away and pretend their attacks aren't happening." He remembered again Monica's expression moments before her death. It sent a chill down his spine. "By the time I'm ready to face Keiran – if I ever am – then there might not be anyone left to save."

"That you accept it as your responsibility is progress, but *my* responsibilities are clear." Tyrus wasn't yielding, and it only made him more frustrated.

"But how you want to do things won't work, facing Johnathan showed us all that." Tyrus clenched its fist at the mention of Alexis's brother; was the incident a sore point for it too? "All the training in the world won't help us if we don't get to apply it to something real."

"You are not ready."

"I wasn't ready way back at the start of all this, but I managed, somehow. If more are going to perish—"

"Many more will die," Tyrus stated coldly.

"*If* they are, then it has to be doing something worthwhile." He then remembered Azure's sacrifice, the bravery he had in the face of certain death. What would he have thought of their hiding, cowardice in the face of the enemy?

"Training is essential to your goal."

"You're not seeing the point I'm trying to make, Tyrus." He wondered now if it ever could think about it like he was.

"Your point is irrelevant." That sparked Callum's anger further.

"Monica wasn't irrelevant! She was one of the many people your Council is trying to save, why can't you see that?" Tyrus didn't respond immediately, simply watching him with its lifeless eyes.

"Her death was..." — Tyrus again paused, as it was trying to find a suitable word — "circumstantial."

"Circumstantial?!"

"You believe there was a choice. That is incorrect. The retention of your weapon is an extension of the protection of you and is essential for you to defeat Keiran." Tyrus didn't snap at him, explaining simply as if he should've already known the answer, "Were it possible to save Monica, I would have, but in the fight against Keiran, her life is not worth your blade. No life is."

Callum drew the sword slowly, staring upon Monica's weregild. The Council wanted him to be a warrior, a leader, but who would follow him into death by choice? Did his friends follow him willingly or out of fear that Tyrus's protection would be rescinded? In the back of his mind, the question of if he was as expendable as Monica had surfaced; would it sacrifice him to save the sword? He tried to push that thought aside, think about something else before his thoughts drew the conversation down an even darker path.

"Why is Johnathan alive, Tyrus? Jinar killed him," was the question that surfaced instead.

"I am not sure he is, not entirely." Alexis's voice made him turn, his friend standing in the doorway. She stepped in, looking thoughtful as the demon watched her. "I didn't mean to interrupt; I was told by Jinar you had the spell ready."

"I do," Tyrus replied.

"How long have you been there?" Callum asked. She gave him a very weak smile.

"Not long."

"What do you mean, not entirely alive?" Callum frowned. "Your wording is very specific."

"I've been thinking about it since the incident, trying to make sense of how he could be here when he had... died." The word still caused her pain, less than the first time, however. "Jinar has been musing on it too, but I think I've come up with a theory if you'll listen."

"Of course," Callum agreed. Tyrus said nothing, which was as good as they were going to get.

"The gem on his headband. It was something he gained only after he joined the Silent Hand, and Alun was keen to retain it after Johnathan was killed. It had an inner light to it then, a glow, unlike anything I'd seen before." Callum nodded.

"That is, until recently. The orbs that contain demon essence, they glow with an inner light also."

One such orb appeared in front of Tyrus at her mention of it, levitated in place as the red energy within it swirled. Callum wondered just where the demon was storing those and how many it had. "Could it be a similar thing? That Johnathan is somehow... trapped inside it?"

"A possibility," Tyrus answered, much to Callum's surprise. "If Alun had prepared a contingent spell to ensnare a soul upon death into a suitable object. His soul would be tethered to the object and would need to remain in close proximity."

"But what would that make Johnathan? Is he alive or not? And how can we save him?" Callum was thinking back to old tavern tales of those who defied death, none of which were even close to the truth they were discussing.

"Irrelevant," dismissed the demon. "He is in league with Keiran."

"Only because he thought it would save me." Alexis was a lot calmer than Callum thought she would be at that statement, her voice full of hope.

"Your efforts to sway him were ineffective."

"With research, we might be able to reverse the spell, return him to his own body." Callum's suggestion was met with a stare from his mentor.

"Unlikely. His original body was likely destroyed, and any new body he possesses was created by magic."

Tyrus looked at the red essence within the orb with indifference. In a way, Johnathan had attained what he had just now, Callum thought: eternal life at a terrible cost.

"If we could break the gem, would his soul be free?" Callum was trying to imagine what his soul being apart from his body would feel like but couldn't begin to picture it, only that it would be horrible.

"He will not hesitate to kill you, Callum," the demon stated. "You must not hesitate either."

Alexis took a deep breath.

"Would breaking the gem free him?" Callum wanted a straight answer.

"Possibly," the demon conceded.

"If we can save him, we should. Even though he doesn't like me, I can't leave him in such a state. I don't expect you to understand, but I won't turn my back on him, even if..." Callum's words petered out; Johnathan's dislike of him had been obvious and was the last thing he wanted to remind Alexis of. Tyrus paused.

"The man you knew died on your world. Your sole focus is training to defeat Keiran. All other objectives are insignificant." Still the demon didn't budge, not that Callum expected it to, no matter how much he argued.

Still, he felt that the singular focus on his training was wrong, a fact that made him reflect; at the start he'd been so reluctant to be a tool in the Council's battle, but already that was shifting and he hadn't even noticed until then. It unsettled him, but not as much as things he'd noticed about Johnathan that he was seeing in a new light with Alexis's theory; the hollow look in his eyes, the shift in his voice, all of it spoke of a painful emptiness that made him pity the man, even though his actions had led to Monica's death.

But was Tyrus right about his redemption? He refused to believe it: seeing the affection the man had for his sister proved that there was some small part of him left in there somewhere. Tyrus held the orb of demon essence and looked to Alexis, ready to use the spell that would bestow immortality on her. After a breath, she nodded in readiness and the process began.

"Her theory does have merit, as well as fitting into my own thoughts on why Johnathan is as he is," Jinar said as his eyes scanned a series of glowing glyphs suspended in the air.

Three days had passed since they'd been bestowed eternal life, something Callum still hadn't gotten used to yet. He'd gone to see his friend, only to find that the sorcerer's room was far different to his own, the walls covered in arcane diagrams and more runes. While there were no shelves of reagents or dusty tomes, it felt every bit like an occult study, the very air charged with energy. Numerous metal pads displaying walls of text were discarded around the small room.

"What is your theory?" Callum was stood in the doorway, watching Jinar consult one of the metal pads and muttering some words. The glyphs in front of him shifted to a new, more complex pattern at Jinar's whim. What meaning they had was still a mystery to Callum.

"We did not find any of those headbands on the other members of the Silent Hand that tried to board this vessel, nor did we see them back on our world before Johnathan. It is my belief that Johnathan was forced into his current state without his knowledge or consent, to test if the process was possible." Jinar touched one of the glyphs and it dazzled a brilliant white before vanishing. "My teacher spoke of less scrupulous magicians who used their apprentices as the subjects for arcane experiments, not wanting to endanger themselves."

"That's horrible! Who'd agree to that?" Callum got a shrug from his former mentor.

"Remember when you burned down that tavern?"

Callum nodded.

"If I had approached you and offered my services, would you have said no?"

"I wouldn't have let you experiment on me."

"There were many competing methods of magical research on our world, each with their own advantages. Study of the theoretical can only get you so far, but I would never do what Alun has likely done. If he deems the results a success is something I cannot say." Jinar glanced back to the metal pad in his hand.

"What are you reading?" Callum asked then, walking over to glance at the words. He couldn't understand many of them.

"This text details the studies on the power in ritual words, compiled by a Sella Larsen. Her writings are not well structured, but the reasoning is sound. She was apprehended by Z-Gen before the end of her research." Jinar placed the pad gently on the bed.

"I thought Z-Gen would try and prevent anyone from reading things like that since they dislike sorcerers so much. Where did you get it?"

"It was not too dissimilar to how some would repress tomes, burn them as heretical. The basements and hidden libraries are no longer physical, or so Simon told me, buried among so much worthless information. He showed me some of it, and it was less orderly than the study of a scribe after a gust of wind." Jinar changed the glyphs again, this time into a single large one with a multitude of shifting triangles. "Most of what is there are but legends and lore, folk tales waved away as piffle. It takes a learned student of the arcane to see the fractured wisdom within the mass of text."

"How did you know where to start?" Callum was looking at the metal pad, seeing another word he understood.

"I did not know where to begin, but I knew who would. While Simon complained about assisting me, I am starting to believe that he quite likes being overworked as he assisted me regardless. Once he showed me how to search for information, it was merely a matter of following the breadcrumbs scattered about until they led to a veritable archive of forbidden lore, a thousand thousand intangible scriptures." Jinar transformed the single large glyph into numerous smaller versions that began to shift and change at random. "They confirmed another thing I have suspected since leaving our world, that sorcerers did not originate there."

"For Z-Gen to dislike them so much, there have to be others like us out there: Kole is proof of that. But why did our world end up as it did instead of full of tall buildings of glass and metal?" Callum imagined what he'd have been doing on such a world; was there even a place for people like him in a world where structures scraped the heavens?

"That I cannot say. What sorcerers exist out there are likely in hiding, afraid of apprehension by Z-Gen under their draconian laws prohibiting the practice. One possible theory is that the people who first landed on our world were attempting to hide from their retribution, but we have no way of confirming that now. It would certainly explain why there were so many proficient in magic amongst the populace." Jinar stroked his beard in thought as the glyphs winked out of existence, one after another. "Upon examination of the numerous apprehensions throughout the galaxy, I have seen little evidence to support that there was a threat posed by sorcerers. They have committed very few crimes, save that of being what they are."

"It's good to see you like this again." Callum smiled.

"One does not improve through inaction, my friend; it is as you all said. Only through work and practice can I surpass Tyrus once more." Callum wondered if Jinar would ever be able to surpass the demon, the gulf between their power already so wide. Jinar then glanced at Callum's sword. "If I asked to borrow your blade, would you let me?"

"You wouldn't be the first. Simon looked at the physical properties but couldn't find out much."

"Magic is much more than the vessel it is contained in, else my own would be both unstoppable and exceptionally charismatic." Callum found himself chuckling, reminded of more innocent times that now felt so distant. "Perhaps Alexis would be willing to assist me in my research."

"It can't hurt to ask her."

"I think she would take the idea better if you suggested it."

Callum wondered why he thought that, only to be interrupted by the room being plunged into darkness save the final glyph, which winked out of existence a second later. Jinar conjured an orb of light, Callum drawing his sword out of fear that the Silent Hand had found them again.

"We should get to the bridge." Callum got a nod, and together they exited into the pitch-black corridor. While he hoped that nothing major was wrong, his gut said otherwise.

Chapter Thirty-Four

The bridge still had light, Jinar dismissing the glowing orb as Callum quickly spotted Siobhan looking at the projected image of a ship that was very unlike their own. She glanced from it at their arrival, looking disappointed.

"You seen Daniel?" she asked. Callum shook his head and she grumbled in annoyance, "Shit."

"What's wrong?" Callum looked back to the dark corridor just in case the captain was behind them. He wasn't.

"A Z-Gen cruiser, that's what. They're giving chase." Siobhan went to Daniel's chair and started pressing buttons. "No idea how they found us, but well, they found us."

"Can we outpace them? Fight them?" Callum asked. Her look said it all about their prospects, and worry rose in his stomach. "What can I do to help?"

"Not a damn thing unless you can get Daniel in here or use your magic to make it disappear." Siobhan then pressed a red flashing button on the chair, which beeped.

"I can certainly try. How large is it?" Jinar asked. He walked up to the image, examining it with curiosity and not outwardly showing concern at their predicament.

"At least twice as big as this ship." Siobhan's answer was quick.

"I would need time to think on it."

"You've got five minutes, tops." She then pressed a button on the left armrest. "Simon? We've got a problem, a big problem."

"I know." The doctor's voice came from the corners of the room, like the music had in the bar they'd visited. He sounded weary and agitated, no doubt due to their situation. Callum went over to one of the screens that were flashing red, trying to make sense of what it was warning about. There was a selection of numbers that seemed to be counting down ominously. "Daniel?"

"Didn't answer. What are our options?"

"Our turret out-ranges the typical armament of a Z-Gen cruiser, but it'll only scratch the paintwork. It wasn't designed to take out military vessels. They launch fighters and we can take a few of them out, but short of a miracle, we're at a huge disadvantage." There was a pause. "We're in firing range in one minute, they'll be in three."

"The nebula?" Siobhan was hopeful.

"Seventeen hours." Jinar frowned as Siobhan muttered something incomprehensible under her breath. "I've overridden Daniel's viewscreen and sent a feed of our scanners, I don't have authorisation for anything else." The door behind them opened, Alexis entering with her own orb of light.

"Z-Gen have found us," Jinar informed her simply.

"I doubt they can be reasoned with," Alexis said to them as Tyrus appeared by Siobhan. The pilot was too focused on moving to another device to notice, tapping screens and buttons quickly. The demon said nothing, watching as the chaos grew more intense. "If you tell us how to pilot the ship, Siobhan, you could go in the *Silverbolt*—"

"It'd take too long, and I don't feel like being ripped apart by that thing's point defence." The lights flickered suddenly and one of the devices sparked and crackled, smoke rising from beneath the buttons. "What the hell was that, Simon?"

"Best guess, a long-range laser battery."

"Not THAT! What's the damage?" she shouted. All the while Callum stood there, unsure of how to help. Jinar began muttering as he focused on the smoking device, only to get a glare from Siobhan. "You douse that in water, and you'll fry it."

"Suffocating the flames, however, will not." And with a pulse of magic and a smile from the man, the smoke ceased. "You are welcome."

"The damage?" Siobhan repeated the question to Simon, ignoring Jinar's smugness.

"Good news or bad news?" Simon asked.

"Cut to the chase."

"The main energy conduits are fried. No damage to the engines or the secondary conduits."

"Are we still accelerating?" she asked.

"Best I can give you now is minimal propulsion plus life support and gravity. Can't turn off the distress signal now we've taken damage, as you know. Anything else is pushing it."

"And the turret?" Jinar enquired.

"If we turn off heating and oxygen, but if we lose any more conduits, I won't be able to turn them back *on*."

"Do it." Siobhan's eyes were drawn to the door, glaring. "What the hell kept you?"

Daniel and Saresan had arrived, and the captain looked in a bad way. Stubble had settled on his face, along with black bags under his eyes. Clothing and hair dishevelled, Daniel didn't even acknowledge Callum or Alexis, walking past them to his chair and slumping down in it, while Saresan gave Callum a look which said that he knew what was happening.

"Man the turret." Daniel was in no mood for an argument, and neither was Siobhan, going to another device and bringing up a display of space as she stood ready.

"Is it as bad as I've heard?" Saresan asked.

"Much worse, I'm afraid," Alexis answered.

"Just can't catch a break, can we?" Callum wanted to help but had no idea how; he didn't know how to fix conduits or how to damage a massive ship of metal without being able to see it.

"Get me more engine power, Simon," the captain said to the doctor.

"Can't be done." The doctor's statement was followed by the familiar sound of him sipping coffee.

"I'm ordering you to do it!" Daniel shouted.

"Well, let me know when you find me the forty man-hours to repair the conduits, and I'll get right on that for you. I'll be here, precariously balancing our remaining power output so the rest of our systems don't fail in the meantime."

"Don't be a smart ass, Simon!" Daniel didn't get a reply. "Simon? Damnit!"

"Can you protect the ship, Tyrus?" Callum asked his mentor just as the lights went out in the bridge again. This time, only a dim glow returned and half of the screens around them remained black and lifeless. The dark brought with it equally bleak thoughts for Callum, who still felt powerless to stop things from getting worse. Siobhan thumped the console in front of her in frustration.

"Shit, we've lost the turret!" she declared.

"And so, the crows descend upon the carcass," Jinar muttered reflectively.

"You're not helping!" she snapped back quickly.

"If you gave me something to do, I would gladly assist."

"Quiet!" Daniel shouted angrily, silencing them both. "Simon?" Silence. "Simon!"

"We've got a hole in the cargo bay, collateral damage to the secondary energy conduits. Engines have shut down to avoid overloading, we're running on auxiliary power. We've also got damage to the ship's main system controller, meaning we can only have one non-essential system up at any time till I can fix that."

"That all sounds bad," Saresan commented.

"How did they hit us so precisely?" Daniel let anger run rampant in his voice.

"Z-Gen have access to almost every ship schematic that's ever been made. With the right one, it'd be no more difficult than surgery," the doctor replied. Daniel slouched in his chair further.

"Can you get it fixed or not?" came the captain's question.

"A week, minimum, and that's not taking the hole into account." Alexis noticed one screen that had lit up with a green image that caught her eye, walking over to it and reading. Tyrus approached Callum, gripping his shoulder as it tried to teleport him. He wrenched himself from the demon's grasp quickly.

"I'm not leaving them to die," he objected loudly. The demon's actions had drawn the attention of Jinar and Siobhan, the latter staring warily at Tyrus once more.

"My duty is to—" This time Callum interrupted the demon.

"If your duty is to protect me, then help me protect them, because the only way you're going to get me to leave them behind is to kill me!" First, he wondered where those words had come from. Then he wondered if Tyrus would do just that, but instead it just stared at him with a snarl.

"And you'll have to kill me too." Saresan stood beside his friend, halberd ready to strike at a moment's notice. Surprising Callum, Tyrus stepped away without a word, the first time it had conceded anything to him. "I thought not." The thought of teleportation stuck in his mind, lodging there for a reason he couldn't fathom.

"This says that there is a communication waiting for us," Alexis announced. "I imagine it's Z-Gen."

"Why would they wish to communicate with us now? They have a clear advantage." Jinar walked over to Daniel's chair, getting a warning stare from him that was ignored. "Answering it may gain us more time." The screen ahead of them changed to a view of a Z-Gen soldier standing in a room not too dissimilar from their own bridge. There were other soldiers sat with controls around them and a pair of armed guards at the door leading further into the vessel. The one staring at them wore a red cloak and was bereft of a helmet, a middle-aged woman with short black hair and a stern look on her face. Everyone turned to look at her, Callum noticing that she was currently staring at him exclusively and with disdain, an expression he was familiar with.

"The hell do you want?" Daniel was annoyed and downcast.

"I am captain Colette of the Z-Gen cruiser *Gorgon*," she answered firmly and with authority, eyes shifting to look at Daniel. "Your vessel has been identified as the *Winter's Mourning*."

"So?"

"Your crew are wanted for crimes against Z-Gen and the people of this galaxy. Surrender and you will be brought into our custody, else your ship will be destroyed with you on it. Our scans indicate you have no functioning escape pods, I would take this into account when you are making your decision." One of the soldiers on her bridge noticed Tyrus and stopped in his tracks.

"What is *that*?" The soldier was clearly shaken.

"Something that will not be a problem soon, private. Report to the medical room for an examination," Colette replied, still looking at Daniel.

"Captain—"

"That was not a request, soldier." The private did as requested, giving them a few seconds of reprieve before the Z-Gen cruiser inevitably opened fire on them. Daniel wouldn't surrender and Callum didn't want to find out what they did to sorcerers in their captivity, but the alternative was worse. Tyrus again tried to teleport him away and he moved away once more, but this time something clicked in his head. It was absolutely stupid, but it was perhaps their only hope.

"I have an idea," he whispered to Alexis, mindful that Colette was watching their every move. Tyrus watched with a snarl as he quickly went to Daniel's chair, pressing the button which communicated with Simon, speaking before the captain could object, "Simon, how far away is the Z-Gen ship?" The annoyance on Tyrus's face instantly vanished. Alexis too understood his plan, motioning for Jinar and Siobhan to come to her, which they did. Siobhan looked puzzled, but Jinar answered with a knowing smile.

"What are you doing?" Daniel asked angrily.

"A kilometre right behind us, why?" the doctor answered. Colette was watching Callum now with impatient curiosity as he too rushed to the assembled huddle at the back of the bridge.

"I have given you ample time to come to a decision, so I shall request one last time that you surrender to us," Colette told them.

"Blow us up for all I fucking care!" Daniel told her with enough vitriol to surprise Colette for just a moment.

Callum reflected on his plan and wondered how wise it would be, but what other option did they have, save the absurd? The momentary pull of teleportation as Tyrus transported them was when Callum drew his sword, knowing that they'd be flung from one desperate situation to another.

A flurry of actions around him muffled the fear within Callum's heart. Their arrival on the bridge of the Z-Gen ship had surprised every soldier present, but they needed no order to reach for their weapons.

Jinar was faster, letting loose a beam of intense heat which scorched right through one foe before he could rise from his seat, body quickly engulfed in flames. The others hesitated at the display of arcane power, looking to one another, though some had their rifles in hand. Many looked to Tyrus, those without helmets doing so with fear and confusion. Colette turned from the screen which showed the bridge of their ship, as surprised as Daniel was shown to be. She already had a pistol in hand.

"Greetings and well met," Jinar said to the captain with a flourish. Siobhan was unimpressed.

"What kind of snappy one-liner is that?" she remarked.

"I would suggest surrendering, Captain, unless you wish to see the full extent of my arcane power," the proud sorcerer continued.

Callum doubted they would get that concession, surrounded as they were. Colette pressed a button beside her and the bridge was plunged into red light, along with the wailing drone of an alarm. At that moment, the soldiers that had been sat quickly rose from their seats and drew their weapons. They fired without hesitation, but their shots hit the barriers he and the other sorcerers conjured in front of them, a haphazard shield wall that blocked the volleys nonetheless.

Quickly, the soldiers stopped. Some checked their guns in puzzlement, and that was the opportunity Jinar used to cease his barrier so Siobhan could return fire, puncturing their armour with ease. Saresan broke from the group then too, a battle in full flow that Callum joined alongside his friend. Saresan swung with his weapon, but the halberd's edge didn't break through the soldier's chest plate, which he sorted by punching the helmetless man in the face. Callum's sword had no such difficulty, slicing through his foe entirely.

Only then did he realise that it was the first person he'd ever killed directly by his own hand. The brutality of his strike made him unwell, but he had no time to ponder it, caught in the maelstrom of combat. Tyrus had no such qualms with killing, having set a score of soldiers alight and leaving them to burn as it dealt with the two guarding the door.

Alexis was focused on Colette, advancing on her with a dagger drawn. When the captain fired, Alexis created a shimmering barricade that reflected the beam back on the pistol, as if a mirror bouncing sunlight, destroying it.

Disarmed, Colette drew a large serrated knife and lunged towards her. Alexis had reached for her second blade, parrying the soldier's strike with her right dagger and slashing with the left at Colette's face. The captain tried to move back but not fast enough, the edge cutting through her cheek. She recoiled back in pain, clutching the wound, which Alexis used to advance and press a blade to her throat.

"Drop your weapons!" she demanded of the remaining soldiers, who did just that.

As quickly as the combat had begun, it was over. Saresan kicked the soldiers' weapons away from them, Siobhan training her guns on each one as he did so.

The dead were numerous and grisly, Callum noticing that he'd killed a second person in the melee without thinking about it. The man's face was twisted into an expression of pain that clung to his thoughts. Callum looked away as quiet returned to room save for the beeps of devices all about them. Daniel had been silent during the explosion of violence, clearly annoyed that they'd survived despite the implications if they hadn't.

"I did warn you of my arcane power," Jinar reminded Colette smugly. Colette had moved her hand from the gaping hole in her cheek but didn't struggle, ever mindful of the cold metal at her neck.

"Now, we would still be more than willing to accept your surrender, if you wish."

Callum hoped that she'd agree.

"The word of one with the taint is meaningless, as is your goal," Colette told him firmly. "The Great Threat will not triumph, this day or any day."

"Taint?" Alexis repeated the word. "You are referring to our magic, I presume."

Colette said nothing in reply.

"You're mistaken, we're not with the Great Threat." Callum got a weak chuckle from the captain at his words.

"Then what's that?" She was looking to Tyrus, who in turn was watching her.

Something clicked in the back of Callum's mind, but it didn't get a chance to surface, smothered by him dwelling on those he'd killed. Still, he didn't like where this was going.

"Irrelevant," Tyrus stated bluntly, walking up to the commander.

"...You can talk." Colette was surprised and worried at the revelation.

"Yes," it answered, now within arm's reach of her. The wailing noise ceased, then was replaced by a stilted voice.

"The boarding alarm has not been cancelled. To preserve Z-Gen intel and property, this ship will self-destruct in ten minutes. All access to ship archives and controls have been disabled. All Z-Gen personnel are encouraged to board the nearest escape pod, which will open to their registered code phrase and Bio-Identification. If this alarm has been activated in error, you are encouraged to board the nearest escape pod." The voice ended as abruptly as it began, leaving them all in silence.

"...That doesn't sound good," Saresan muttered.

"Protocol is clear; the destruction of the Great Threat is second to none. Cadmus would have it no other way." Colette was now resolute, staring down Tyrus. "You lose."

Tyrus teleported away immediately, leaving the news to sink in with the rest of them.

"You'll die too!" Siobhan protested.

"And?"

A whole new fear arose in Callum as he tried not to count every second they had left. Ten minutes seemed like a lot, but he knew all too well how quickly a day could flash by.

Jinar looked at the remaining soldiers, who hadn't reacted much to the news of their imminent death.

"Do any of you happen to know if this... 'self-destruct' can be stopped?" He was met with silence. "Am I to presume that you do not know or are playing ignorant?"

"Guess they don't want to get to the escape pods that desperately, do they?" Saresan chipped in.

"There's no way to turn it off," one of the soldiers declared.

"You expect me to believe that?"

"It's the truth." The guard watched Colette for a moment, her expression unwavering.

"Let them go," Callum told his friend. "There's no reason to keep them here."

"There's plenty reason if they're lying." Siobhan had holstered her pistols, looking to one of the screens near her. Her attempts to bring things up were met with a low toned beep. "Damn it, this thing's locked up tight."

"They're not lying, why would they? Just let them go," Callum repeated.

Saresan shrugged and stepped back, but it took longer for Jinar to heed his request. They didn't move, however, watching the sorcerer intently. He sighed and spoke calmly to them.

"You have my word that I will not harm you if you head immediately for the door. Now go and remember the mercy you have been given. Perhaps one day you will deign to give it to another."

None of the soldiers made a move for their weapons as they quickly left the bridge. Now only Colette remained as their prisoner.

"You really think they're going to take that to heart?" Saresan asked Jinar.

"Not one bit."

"Likewise."

Tyrus returned as the guard spoke, but not alone; still shaky from the teleportation, Simon looked more fed up than usual, armed not with a weapon but an array of tools and a small metal pad.

"Will *someone* tell me what's so important that I need to leave our ship precariously close to losing all essential systems?" asked the doctor loudly.

"This ship is going to self-destruct in less than ten minutes," Alexis answered quickly.

"And you expect me to do *what* about that? I don't know the first thing about the architecture of Z-Gen's computer systems!" Simon approached a screen next to Siobhan and pressed it, summoning the low toned beep. "That said, I know what a system lock-down looks like."

"Can you get rid of it?" Callum asked hopefully.

"That depends on a lot of things, but I don't think you'll like the answer." He glanced at Colette. "You got a coffee machine here? I left mine back on the ship." The captain looked more quizzically at him than she had at Tyrus speaking.

"I think that may be one, it has a lot of drink receptacles by it." Jinar indicated to a device in the corner of the room.

"Make yourself useful then. Black, strong." Simon removed a metal panel and started to fiddle with wires and boxes that Callum didn't recognise.

"Why don't you just teleport us back to our ship?" Saresan suggested.

"Collateral damage from a Z-Gen cruiser blowing up a kilometre away would be my first guess," Simon answered simply as he pulled a red wire out.

Alexis hadn't let the dagger shift from Colette's throat, watching her to make sure she didn't so much as shift toward a screen. Jinar went to get Simon a drink.

"Your efforts are amusing, like a colony of ants being flooded," the captive captain mused.

Callum didn't know what to say to that, but he could imagine the desperation of the insects, their futile hunt for safety.

"Tell me about the Great Threat," Tyrus then demanded of the captain.

"Why say what you already know, monster?" One of the boxes by Simon sparked, and the voice that had previously announced doom returned.

"Attempt to bypass ship systems lockdown detected. Reactivating and engaging automated countermeasures. Please remain where you are," it declared.

"Damn," Simon muttered, replacing the panel quickly. "This ship has combat robots."

"Damn's right!" Siobhan crouched behind a metal chair and trained her pistols on the door as Colette smiled darkly.

"What's an automated countermeasure?" Callum asked. The answer came in the sound of a heavy thudding noise from beyond the door, rhythmic and louder with each passing moment. Callum had no idea what to expect but held his sword tightly, magic ready to defend him and Simon if needed. All the while he was ever mindful of the silent countdown, whose progress he'd manage to lose track of.

"Be ready," Tyrus warned as the door opened for the unwelcome guest.

Half a foot taller than Tyrus and made entirely of metal painted white, the vaguely humanoid figure was large, bulky and entirely unnatural. It lacked a head and had giant weapons where its forearms were meant to be, comprised of multiple spinning barrels. Siobhan fired immediately, but her shot didn't even hit the robot, impacting on an almost invisible and crackling barrier much like their own magical ones but different.

"Oh shit." She quickly dragged another chair to her.

The metal beast replied to her aggression with a withering hail of beams aimed at no one in particular. Scattered and unfocused, the attack hit consoles and devices, sparking and exploding as it sought to deal chaos as well as death.

Alexis let go of Colette to defend herself with a brief barrier, the captain breaking for the door immediately while Callum and the others were distracted. She moved forward without fear of the robot, and to Callum's surprise, none of the beams hit her. Siobhan attempted to take a shot at the retreating soldier, but the suppressing fire forced her to duck back into cover, the chairs faring poorly against the attack.

Tyrus protected both itself and Callum with its magic, freeing him up to protect Simon. The doctor's concentration had been shattered by the laser fire, him abandoning his work to duck by the panel. Saresan had found a small space beneath one of the consoles which he'd hidden in, but Callum knew they couldn't do this forever; his magic was fast running out, and the others would be faring no better.

The robot had stepped forward enough that Colette could move past it into the corridor beyond, giving them one last look of hatred before she left.

Callum knew they had to do something, but what? Siobhan had shown that beams of their own would be ineffective, and if the thing had protection like their own barriers, how could they bypass it with magic? Even if he could've used his magic safely, to do so would leave Simon vulnerable to the metal monster, as he couldn't use two spells at once.

"I'm open to suggestions!" Siobhan shouted, rolling away from what remained of the chairs she'd been behind to another one.

"How is that thing attacking with its protection up?" Saresan asked the others. Callum's magic was almost depleted, and there was only one option left; his sword hadn't failed him yet, but was it sharp enough to slice through the thing firing at them?

"Teleport me next to it," he ordered the demon.

A look of worry flashed over Alexis's face, and he expected the demon would object, but it did not, grabbing his shoulder. The tugging sensation was shorter than usual, giving Callum no time to reconsider his plan before he was directly in front of the beast. There was a hum in the air around it, and now that he was closer, the protective barrier was obvious, everything past it a darker shade and a little blurry.

The thing reacted to his presence, aiming its weapons at him, which he instinctively struck out at.

His blade cut through the barrier and the first weapon, but it didn't react to the injury. He then swung the weapon horizontally across its chest, but not before it fired.

That was when his magic failed and he felt horrendous pain rush through his chest, a burning agony. His swing faltered, but still it bit into the beast before he fell to the ground. Something detonated within their foe, the beams and the barrier dying.

Tyrus had already sprung into action, blasting the metal monster with a bolt of energy which finished what Callum had started, a large hole torn through it and flames erupting from what remained of the metal beast.

Chapter Thirty-Five

What lies beyond life? After many millennia, the question remains unanswered. There are, of course, people who have claimed to see what's beyond during near-death experiences and the like, but none of those can be... measured. You can run tests, but they're not going to give you anything beyond biological and psychological readouts, and that tells us nothing.

There have been enough books, arguments and papers on the subject to run a ring around all of colonised space, but I shall still throw my thoughts into the ether: there's only one way to truly find out what's on the other side, and once you do, you're hardly able to come back and tell everyone. So, in my opinion, it's best not to worry about it. What's most important is living the life you want to live while you're alive to do it.

—*Extract from the Foreword of 'The Secrets to a Truly Happy Life, Vol III' by Professor Harvin Vundro*

Callum struggled against unconsciousness. His efforts to internalise the pain failed and he cried out. Simon had been about to go to him when Alexis and Jinar rushed to his side first, leaving the doctor to again focus on the system lock-down. Both sorcerers knelt down on either side of him, Alexis wincing at the injury he hadn't seen, using what magic she had left to soothe the pain.

"You are a brave man, Callum," Jinar informed him as he too used his own magic to heal. "Foolish, too, but both tend to travel hand in hand."

"Is it...?" Callum got a nod from Alexis.

"Stay still," she implored him as the healing energies concentrated in his chest.

A few seconds later the energy faded, but to his relief, the pain did not return. He touched where he'd been hit and couldn't feel a wound there, standing up slowly with Alexis helping him. She was still concerned: it was written all over her face as she too checked where the injury had been.

He wondered now why Tyrus so willingly let him throw himself into danger when it was the demon's duty to protect him at all costs. Had it been a test of his abilities?

"Next time you have a plan like that, please try to let us know."

"I'm sorry, I didn't have time to think it through," he told her.

Saresan and Siobhan had emerged from their places of cover, the guard walking over to the remnants of the robot and tapping it with his halberd cautiously. It didn't whirr into action, blocking the corridor which led deeper into the ship with what was left of its being. Siobhan, meanwhile, had moved to be beside Simon, watching the screen he had begun working again with concern. "At least the thing isn't a threat anymore."

"I think I've got into the lowest priority systems, nothing that'll stop the self-destruct though," the doctor declared, pressing at the screen. He then frowned, looking at another screen to his left. "...Scanners show another ship rapidly approaching."

"Z-Gen?" Alexis checked.

"Does it matter?" Saresan turned from the metal monster. "We're wanted criminals. Anyone with sense will finish us off and claim whatever bounty is due."

"They're opening up communications, I don't have the authority to deny it," the doctor warned. "Audio only."

Callum expected to hear the firm words of another Z-Gen captain ready to open fire on the ship, but instead, the screen showing Daniel cut to black as a very different voice started speaking.

"Who is receiving this communication?" It was an old man, throwing Callum's theory up in the air; did soldiers in Z-Gen serve that long? Everyone looked at each other, unsure of who'd answer. The doctor shrugged.

"I'm a little busy to talk to him right now. They can hear you anywhere on the bridge," Simon reminded them, once again removing the panel he'd been working behind. Jinar nodded and began to speak, much to Siobhan's concern.

"Greetings. My name is Jinar Yelandan Fakkal Genai Lae. What is it we can do for you?" There was a moment of pause, Callum waiting for things to get worse.

"...I have heard of you." The man's reply prompted a raised eyebrow from the sorcerer and a smile.

"Clearly my reputation precedes me."

"You're wanted by Z-Gen for many crimes, dead or alive," the old man responded.

"Nice one," Siobhan muttered.

It wasn't clear if he was friendly or not, but there was a warmth to the man's voice that endeared Callum to him, a kindness that pervaded even that statement.

"It was all a misunderstanding," Callum spoke up then. "We never intended to hurt anyone and were only defending ourselves. This ship crippled our vessel, forcing us to board it to prevent further damage." He was afraid, but that had to take a back seat to the truth. Again, there was a pause.

"And who am I speaking to now?" the voice asked.

"My name is Callum Igannes. This ship is going to self-destruct, and we can't stop it, would you be able to help?" Another pause. "I know you only have my word for it, but we mean you no harm."

"I'll see what I can do," came the surprising answer that no one had expected. "We have a few ways of stopping things like that."

"Isn't that highly illegal?" Siobhan asked. She didn't get a reply. "Just who *are* you guys?"

"I think that's a conversation best had in person. All that's important now is that we currently share a common interest. We will board the *Gorgon* and do a full sweep once we've stopped the self-destruct."

"And how can we trust you?" Saresan was understandably sceptical.

"I don't think you're in a position to deny my help, but be assured that I'd much prefer I get to know you than your corpses."

The screen returned to showing Daniel, who was now in a silent conversation of his own, likely with the same person. It left many questions without time to provide the answers, but that they weren't dead was a small beam of hope in the darkness that surrounded the ship infinitely.

"That they wish to help us despite our criminal status is indeed curious," Jinar declared. Simon continued to work frantically, coffee hardly touched as he alternated between fiddling with wires and pressing on the screen. "Perhaps they seek to place us in their debt."

"Strangers don't go out on a limb without there being something in it for them," Saresan agreed. "Question is what they want."

"From wanted criminals? Probably something dangerous and as illegal as shutting off the self-destruct." Siobhan was keeping a wary eye on the door out just in case another metal monster appeared. "That, or they're criminals themselves who caught a distress signal and came to plunder. At least we know now that news of the chair incident reached the galaxy at large."

"I saved us a lot of trouble: you know that," Saresan objected.

"Whatever their reasons are, they have the power here." Alexis watched the door too. The dagger she'd wounded Colette with was still stained with her blood. "No matter how it ends, Z-Gen will not forget what has happened here."

"As if our reputation with them could be any worse." Siobhan looked at a screen by her, which had information scrolling down it quickly. "Think you should look at this, Simon." The doctor glanced over then turned his attention to the words exclusively, sipping his coffee.

"If I'm not wrong, and I might be, this is a military-level brute force attack program." Simon watched it intently.

"From our mysterious helpers?" Simon nodded to the pilot. "You think it can break the lock-down?"

"These things are designed to take down planetary defences in minutes, a single ship would be no match for it. How they have it, I can't begin to wonder."

The screens that hadn't been hit by the metal monster's onslaught suddenly activated, displaying information similar to the kind Callum saw on their own bridge.

"System lockdown rescinded. Self-destruct sequence halted," the neutral voice declared in a very broken manner. Simon breathed a sigh of relief, shaking his head.

"We've got a ship docking with the airlock. I imagine that's our new friends. It won't take them long to sweep the ship and get here, a minute at most." Simon finished his drink. "If you don't mind, I'd like to be taken back to our ship now." Tyrus walked over to the doctor, vanishing with him the moment it gripped his shoulder. Siobhan went back to eyeing the entrance to the bridge with guns now drawn.

"There's no need for that, surely." Callum still had his sword in hand, but he couldn't kill anyone on the other side of the room with that. "They've saved our lives; we owe them a chance to explain themselves."

Tyrus returned without the doctor, standing off to the side out of view of the door, waiting for the saviours. Callum worried about what the demon would do when they arrived.

"They're just as likely to be looters. Better to be safe than sorry," Siobhan answered him.

After half an hour, the door on the far end of the corridor opened and a soldier stepped through that was dressed quite differently from the Z-Gen crew. His armoured uniform was dark purple and rather plain, save for the elbow pad, kneepads and shin guards which were lighter in colour. The shoulder pads were flatter than Z-Gen's and extended outward, ending at an acute angle. The full-face helmet was also plain, with black goggles where the eyes were and a fine mesh over the mouth. In his hands was a rifle, similar to the Z-Gen ones but sleeker, made of dark grey metal. He didn't aim the gun at them.

"They're here!" he called back. Only then did the man look to Callum. "We don't mean any harm."

"Neither do we you," Callum replied, even though Siobhan hadn't lowered her pistols yet. The soldier advanced past the remnants of the robot, pushing it aside with some exertion. Immediately upon entering, the newcomer noticed Tyrus, raising his weapon to the demon quickly.

"What the...!" the soldier exclaimed loudly. That he hadn't fired immediately was a good sign, but still, Callum spoke quickly.

"It's with us," he tried to explain. The newcomer looked back to the corridor.

"Sir, don't come in—" Too late the soldier's warning came as a figure entered the bridge who was definitely not a man of war. He also wasn't the dirty and savage trickster that Siobhan feared but a very old man indeed, well into his seventies. The same height as Callum, he had long, thick white hair which rolled down his shoulders. Matching it was a regal and tidy beard. His eyes were something Callum was drawn to, brown and warm, bolstered by a soft smile. His face was lined with the wrinkles of age, but his body had seemingly not weakened, standing without a stoop and of average build.

He wore a fine grey cloak that went all the way to the floor, sealed with a plain metal clasp at the top. Underneath the garment, the man wore a simple yet finely made green shirt and darker trousers, capped off with smart black shoes that had a shine. He was armed with no weapons, that fact catching Callum's attention almost as much as his eyes. He was every bit not what Callum had expected to see with the voice they'd heard, and there was something familiar about how he presented himself.

The man almost immediately noticed Tyrus, and his calm expression warped into shock, deep fear and recognition. Another soldier emerged from the corridor, levelling his gun at Tyrus as it looked to them coldly. Tension once again flooded the bridge, moments away from another bout of horrific violence Callum wanted so much to avoid.

"Please, we're not going to hurt you," Callum protested in vain. Jinar was muttering under his breath.

"Drop your weapons, all of you!" the second soldier demanded.

"No," the old man ordered weakly. "It's... it's alright." His breaths were deep, trying not to stare at the demon.

"But sir—"

"That's an order." The words pained him, but the soldiers did lower their weapons.

"Sir."

"You will mention this... thing to no one." The old man's voice hardened.

"Yes, sir." They weren't happy about the situation, but Callum was. The old man stepped up to Callum and offered his hand to shake, the first person he'd met among the stars who'd extended that greeting, one he gladly accepted.

"I take it you're Callum. It's nice to meet you, all of you." Though he looked to everyone, his gaze never deviated to the demon. Tyrus, in turn, was watching him with suspicion, at least that was Callum's best guess. "My name is Telanthir. We have taken control of the vessel. There is no one else aboard."

"Your arrival is well timed. Did you come in answer to the distress signal?" Alexis asked politely.

"We were returning home after visiting another system and came in the range of your signal, yes. Z-Gen law decrees that we are obligated to investigate and assist in any way that's required, provided there are no aggressors in the vicinity."

"And so, you assisted by boarding a Z-Gen vessel?" Jinar was watching the man's face intently.

"Deactivating the self-destruct prevents potential harm to other vessels attending the situation, and there was every chance that you were not what you claimed to be. The protection of Z-Gen property and intelligence is of paramount importance to them."

Telanthir's answer was very carefully worded, Callum noted. The two soldiers with the man were keeping their attention focused on them all, even though their guns weren't raised.

"Where are you from?" Siobhan then enquired conversationally.

"Not far." Telanthir glanced to Callum's weapon of choice. "Though I'll wager for you it will seem many leagues away."

A third soldier entered the room, taller than all but Tyrus there.

"There's one room we can't access, sir. The bulkhead won't open short of explosives." The man had an authoritarian tone, of a broad build and holding a rifle larger and bulkier than the others'. "We'll detonate them on your command."

"That was not your decision to make. What's your name, private?" another soldier chided, as a sergeant would a militiaman.

"Davis, sir. Private Davis Thomson Jones," replied the private immediately.

"We are here on a mission of mercy, not sabotage," another soldier firmly explained. The soldier had raised his voice, which caught Telanthir's attention.

"It's quite alright, sergeant. It pays to be thorough in such unique circumstances." Telanthir then addressed Davis, "We'll have a look beyond that door once I've finished speaking with our new friends."

"Sir." Davis nodded.

"Oh, and make sure all record of our being here is wiped from the ship's logs before we leave." Callum frowned at that.

"Sir."

Telanthir looked back to Callum, addressing them all.

"Your ship was quite badly damaged during your encounter. We would be glad to bring it back with us to our world. You can stay at my estate while it is being repaired."

"Estate? You must be a man of considerable wealth," Jinar remarked.

"What's the catch?" Saresan was dubious.

"There is no catch, nor obligation. You are quite welcome to stay on this ship or your own, but yours won't be space-worthy before another Z-Gen vessel comes to see why the *Gorgon* didn't report in after encountering you, and I doubt commandeering a Z-Gen cruiser will benefit you in the short or long term."

Again, Telanthir spoke with carefully chosen words, all the while being civil and pleasant. It didn't stop Callum from trusting him though; his skill with language spoke much of his position of leadership, a talent he lacked. Siobhan was also sceptical, sat on one of the consoles with her arms folded.

"Gotta agree with Saresan on this one, you're giving a lot for nothing in return. What's your long game here?" she asked.

"Only that you allow me to be your host for the duration of your stay on my homeworld." Telanthir smiled back to her. "If money is your concern, all that I offer is without charge." That only made Siobhan more suspicious.

"Surely there is some way to repay your generosity," Alexis enquired.

All of the soldiers present were now watching Tyrus warily, especially Davis. Callum understood their distrust perfectly, for who would look upon something so alien with anything other than aversion? That made him reflect on how used to having the demon around he'd become, while also finding it so out of place.

"Generosity is its own reward, my lady. What do I call you?" Telanthir enquired in turn.

"My name is Alexis, and these are my friends Jinar" — she indicated to him, then to each other person in turn — "Saresan and Siobhan. The demon is called Tyrus."

"...What *is* that thing?" one of the soldiers asked carefully.

"It would be difficult to explain beyond that it is not human," Alexis answered.

"Not human...?" The soldiers watched Tyrus even more carefully, apart from Davis, who was keeping his eyes on the others now.

"A pleasure to meet you all." Telanthir gave a subtle nod to them all barring Tyrus.

"Generosity is the puppet of desire," the demon spoke for the first time in the man's presence, prompting looks between the soldiers.

Telanthir focused his gaze even more on the others.

"Not all offers of friendship are given with condition," Callum countered his mentor. "And I think we should go with him."

"No," came the swift and inevitable response. "It further increases the risk of discovery by our enemies."

"If Z-Gen can find us out here in space, then the Silent Hand can find us in a nebula, and if we're caught out there, who will come to our aid?" He didn't get a response. Telanthir didn't react at the mentioning of the Silent Hand. "Who will repair our ship?"

"Our discovery was chance," Tyrus snapped.

"And we are being presented another chance here." Alexis gave a nod to Callum as she spoke, Telanthir watching the exchange with interest, though he continued not to look to Tyrus. "We would be foolish to turn down such generosity based only on your desire to keep Callum safe. There's nothing to say that these people are a threat to us. If they'd wanted us dead, they would have destroyed our ship and this one with their own, not come to meet us face to face."

"Not all threats are overt and obvious," Saresan mentioned then.

"And not all kindness is laced with venom. I agree with Callum, we should go with them." Her agreement with Callum bolstered his resolve. Tyrus glared at Alexis, an action she didn't react to.

"And if I'm going, you have to come with me," Callum told his mentor. Tyrus remained silent. Siobhan shrugged.

"Guess we're going with you, old man." She stood from the console.

"Looks like the group's spoken." Saresan was still wary, but Telanthir was delighted at the decision. Jinar hadn't expressed a view either way, stroking his beard in contemplation, but he hadn't objected.

"Then I shall get your vessel on board our ship as soon as possible so we can be on our way. You may come aboard on our boarding craft if you wish."

Tyrus was silent, but Callum was sure he saw its eyes flaring a brighter white than before. Angering his mentor was becoming a regular occurrence, but again it didn't act on the threat to abandon them; or had he simply not reached the point where its patience would run out?

Chapter Thirty-Six

Callum saw little of Telanthir's ship from the small windows of the boarding craft, but it was huge, easily capable of taking Daniel's ship into the 'hangar', as it was referred to. The hangar was accessed by a massive airlock, the better to avoid unfortunate accidents, or so he was told by the shuttle pilot.

Daniel hadn't been at all happy with the idea of going with Telanthir, but with the lengthy list of battle damage to the ship he had little room to argue, nor did he press the point, returning to his quarters with a sullen glare.

Tyrus elected to remain on the boarding vessel, more likely, Callum mused, out of a desire to be left alone than consideration for the commotion it would cause with its presence. He didn't doubt it would be keeping an eye on him in one way or another.

Siobhan was the exact opposite, excited upon their exiting the small boarding craft at the sight of twelve fighter craft sharing the positively cavernous room that accommodated Daniel's vessel easily. Portions of it were full of metal crates much like the ones Callum had seen before, only even larger. Another corner had what he guessed were workstations, sealed off from the rest of the room by a transparent wall, with people attending to things he couldn't make out at that distance.

There was a powerful quiet in the room, but what sounds did break it echoed in the emptiness around them over and over. The vessels that had caught Siobhan's eye looked sleeker than hers, the metal without tarnish or scorch marks from beams. Each one was perfectly uniform save a symbol that he guessed was used for identification. How they differed otherwise from the *Silverbolt* he didn't know. Listening to Siobhan talk with the one pilot present didn't help him understand any better.

"Is that a TX-V Avant?" she asked with a grin.

"Yep," came the answer.

"Quad barrel laser cannons?"

"Yep." The pilot had a panel at the bottom of the frontmost fighter open, tinkering with various tools.

"Triple-layer reinforced armour?" She was positively giddy.

"Yep."

"Mark VI Predictive Dodging Parameters?"

"Mark VII, upgraded last week." Her grin widened.

"Not bad." She touched the hull of the vessel carefully, looking it all over. "Shame the G-9's better." The other pilot chuckled.

"You're kidding, that old thing? Not a chance." Her smile shifted to one of a challenge.

"Oh really? AI assistance is one thing, but there's no beating intuition and the knack." She patted the man's ship and stepped back. "We get in a fight, I'll gladly show you just how an 'old thing' can teach you some new tricks."

"You keep thinking that." The pilot moved under the fighter to work on its belly.

"Did you understand any of that?" Saresan checked. Callum shook his head. "Glad it wasn't just me."

Telanthir led them out of the hangar as people approached Daniel's vessel, likely to begin fixing it. Looking at it from the outside, the damage was obvious, two large holes blasted through the hull as well as a third from the incident with Johnathan, gaping scars that would heal only with work.

Everything about Telanthir's ship seemed newer and lighter, the corridors a whiter grey and wider than on Daniel's vessel. There were crew and soldiers, both keeping themselves busy at consoles or travelling from one place to another. Some were in conversation about things Callum didn't understand that well. They all watched the procession pass with some interest, and each gave Telanthir a respectful nod or, in the case of the soldiers, a salute.

In a short space of time, they'd already ascended two flights of stairs and descended as many more. How many floors did the vessel have, how many people? Telanthir left them at the entrance of a small dead-end which shot off the main passageway, four doors down it. Business on the bridge demanded his attention, he told them, explaining that if they required anything, all they needed to do was press the panel by the door and ask.

Stepping up to one of the doors, Callum looked in to find that it was a double bedroom, half again the size of their individual quarters on Daniel's ship. A lot more was crammed into them, but efficiently so; a compact cooking area was built into the wall by the door, and a viewscreen folded out from the ceiling in front of it. A small door off the side led to a space no larger than a shower, containing that, a toilet and a sink.

The beds were a little small, but the design of their bases implied that they could fit together if needed. Despite its size for two people, the accommodation felt cosy rather than cramped, the walls a light cream and the floors a

subtle shade of red. The conundrum of who'd share with whom was solved far quicker than Callum thought it would've been.

"I shall share with Callum," Alexis suggested, then looking to him, "if you wish it."

"I see no problem with that," he told her. That made Siobhan grin.

"Then this one's mine, unless someone else wants in on my movie marathon. They got *Journey to the Demon Dimension* and *Fall of the Prism-Banes* back-to-back in an hour." The pilot only got a raised eyebrow from Jinar in reply. "Oh, go on. It'll be fun!"

"I am afraid my time will be spent musing on the secrets of the arcane, otherwise I would gladly partake." The sorcerer did little to hide his sarcasm.

"Oh, come on, you'll love McZappo the Warlock!" The eyebrow rose a little higher.

"I doubt his credentials."

"I can give you a brief rundown of the character if you like." Siobhan was very eager to explain.

"No, that is quite—" The pilot didn't wait for him to finish his reply.

"Well, originally he was called Fedinard Arcran IV, and he was the wielder of the Lance of Truth, a legendary weapon forged through the sacrifice of the pure-hearted soul of Calastrin." Simon went into one of the rooms with a shake of his head. A quiet beep followed. "She died when the resurrected demon emperor traded her soul with his own and shattered it into five fragments during *Sword Slasher 5: The Time of Truth*. The other fragments were collected by the Phantom Avenge-o-trons when they pierced the Ghost Shroud, and with them—" Jinar vanished at that moment, disrupting Siobhan's tidal wave of words. Saresan smiled.

"I think I preferred it when the tall tales were told by drunkards in taverns. They made more sense too, by the sounds of it," replied the guard.

"You'll be hooked once you start watching, mark my words." Alexis and Callum looked to one another. He wondered if she too was making a mental note not to watch the first movie in the apparently long series. "Your loss. Well, I can't stand around here all evening, a tub of popcorn and a night of awesomeness await." With that, Siobhan went into the room next to Simon's.

"Every time you think you're a bit closer to understanding it all, something like that pops up." Saresan tried to enter into Simon's room, but the door wouldn't open. "Guess that means I'm with he-who-never-sleeps."

"He who never sleeps?" Callum was curious.

"When Jinar has a magical theory on his mind, he's up all night pacing and muttering to himself. I'm used to a bit of background commotion, but the sounds of his spells, or incantations, or whatever he's doing aren't what you'd call soothing." Saresan sighed, "But it is what it is. I'll leave you two to sleep. Take it easy."

"And you as well," Alexis said back as Saresan entered the room Jinar was in, blue glyphs shining brilliantly within that the sorcerer was pondering.

When the door shut behind them, Alexis went to the right-hand bed and laid upon it. Her weariness was something that was only just starting to creep up on him too, having silently stalked his every move since the hectic combat and only now choosing to strike.

"No matter how comfortable a bed is, my sleep has been troubled." She'd closed her eyes, hands clasped on her stomach. Callum sat on the edge of his bed, not quite ready to turn in yet.

"Because of Monica?" He was feeling hungry now too, making him wonder when he last ate or drank anything.

"Among other things."

"Johnathan's return has weighed heavily on my mind as well." He finally settled back on his bed.

He hadn't even taken off his shoes, but he didn't care. The soft mattress was soothing away aches he'd only started paying attention to, save all the worries on his mind which no amount of comfort could take away. Even his hunger was slowly being shoved aside.

"I heard most of your debate with Tyrus about wanting to help others directly," Alexis told him then, confirming what he'd suspected. "You're not the only one who thinks that way. He does well at hiding it, but Saresan is at his wit's end of boredom."

Callum took a deep breath before speaking.

"So much has happened in a few weeks, and yet it feels like nothing has. The days have begun to blur into one another with our training being the focus." He turned his head to see her eyes were open, staring at the ceiling.

"Even as we train, I think on the destruction the Silent Hand might be achieving while we stand idle." Her voice simmered with anger. "But even if they were doing that, we have no idea where they are. I know we can't teleport too far, but we cannot presume that they are also as limited. They might have portal magic like the Council do. I don't know, I just..." She fell silent, but Alexis didn't need words.

"I know." At his answer, she turned her head to look at him. He wanted to voice all his concerns and worries, but what good would burdening another with them be, especially her? She had a world of woes all her own, to stack his on top would be cruel. Her eyes watched his own. "I'm sorry."

"For what?"

"I've caused so much pain already. For you, for Daniel, for... everyone." It was his turn to gaze at the ceiling, a futile attempt to distract from the thoughts that clung to him.

"You also saved my life."

Somehow, he could tell Alexis was smiling, but it gave him no comfort.

"Your life wouldn't have needed saving if this hadn't happened."

"Callum." That made him look back to see that she wasn't smiling but looked worried instead. "You cannot look back at what you cannot change and lament, it will destroy you. I spent many nights thinking about how I could've got through to Johnathan, caught what was happening before it and..." She trailed off once more.

"I'm sorry," he said again.

"I'm starting to think you'd apologise for the sun rising if you were given the opportunity." He was about to reply when she shook her head. "But now is not the time to think about all of this, as hard as it will be. We're guests of Telanthir, and by the sounds of it, honoured ones. We can consider our future course when we leave wherever Telanthir is taking us, and we can only do that after we sleep." She pressed a button by her bed and the room went dark. "Rest well, Callum, alright?"

"I'll try, thank you. Goodnight." He wished he could just tune it all out, but the thoughts kept on going, a danse macabre of future horrors that would not abate. Closing his eyes, Callum wanted desperately just to rest and forget, but the silence did little to help.

The only way Callum knew that he'd managed to get to sleep was that upon waking, he wasn't in the same room. He was in an even more comfortable bed, under white linen sheets and above a feather mattress.

The sun shone through an open window, its warmth washing away all the weariness of the past. He stretched contently, refreshed and relieved; for a moment, he wondered if it had all been a terrible nightmare as he no longer had the sword on his belt. But this wasn't his wooden shack, and it was far too extravagant to be a room in the inn. The stone walls were painted white, and the furniture around him was too well built to be affordable for any poorer than a baron. Suspicion started to set in, as did worry when he sat up, seeing that his clothes were all white and soft on the skin.

Something was wrong, but everything around him said otherwise, arguing a strong case. Quickly getting out of bed, he moved to the window and felt the breeze upon his face, looking out to a pleasant landscape of forests and fields, soft greens and a clear blue sky. From the corner of his eye, Callum noticed a door of a slightly darker white leading out. He heard a voice from beyond it, someone calling for him. It was a woman's voice that was vaguely familiar but also unlike any he knew.

"Who is it?" he asked, stepping up to the door.

"Come outside, Callum, it's beautiful!" A name was pulling at the edge of his thoughts, did he know this person? "You have to see it."

More convinced than ever that he was dreaming, Callum wasn't sure if he wanted to wake up. He turned suddenly, expecting Xiez to be there, but there was no one, just himself and his paranoia.

"Who are you?" was his next question. The voice was now different, or was that he recognised it?

"Who do you think?" It was Alexis. She sounded happy. "Come on, it's wonderful out here."

The door didn't have a handle. His mind doubted.

"Why don't you come in here?" Again, he looked to the window, spotting birds flying in the distance.

"How can we go on a walk if you spend all day indoors?"

That sounded... nice.

He put his hand to the door and felt the warmth beyond it. Quickly, it got hotter until he had to pull his hand back as stinging pain rushed through his palms. The brightness faded from the window and he could smell smoke. Looking up, he saw the roof ablaze with black flames.

Too late he tried to avoid the collapsing beams that burned with something horrifying. As one knocked him to the ground, his clothes themselves burned but with no heat, smouldering black with dying embers.

The walls of the room had crumbled to dust, and beyond was not countryside but wasteland, empty of all but hopelessness. Grey surrounded him as far as the eye could see, burning with the dark fire that pulled brightness to it, suffocating it. Nothing lived, nothing grew save grief and empty promises.

The skies were black, and a mist of black-grey began to advance upon him from all sides. He reached for his blade instinctively but there was no weapon there, he'd known that from the start. Alexis was nowhere to be seen, no one seemed to be anywhere, but there was something in the mist. Within it, he spied vague figures, monstrous and alien to him.

He called on his magic but it didn't answer, fear gripping every part of him as he knew there was nowhere to run. A faint cackle could be heard, not coming from the mist or anywhere. Looking again for Xiez, he saw no one, but as he stopped focusing on the fog, it advanced faster on a non-existent wind until it was all around him. Only then did he hear the whisperings of the beasts of the fog.

They spoke words unknown, gibberish and nonsense that meant nothing and explained everything. Quickly he grabbed a piece of charred wood to defend himself and swung at the still vague figures around him, but they remained just out of his reach each time. On the third swing, one lashed out at him with a wispy claw that caused no injury but hurt immensely.

Despite his suffering, he fought harder, but each effort was punished with more pain until despair took him and he fell to the ground, curling up as the fog consumed him. He couldn't fight it, nothing could. The beasts laughed and murmured a thousand truths and ten times falsehoods, Callum forgetting them instantly but knowing they were told.

In that moment of confused revelation, agony and terror he awoke silently and suddenly, breaths erratic and body light. He frantically reached for his sword and felt it there, stilling his thundering heart but a small bit; it had been a nightmare, a terrible nightmare that was already fading into haziness, but it took with it all desire to return to sleep.

Did it mean something, a warning of horrors to come? He had no talent for interpreting dreams, but that one had left him feeling hollow, staring weakly into blackness as he tried to hear even the faintest whisper of a beast out of view. Was there anyone that could defeat Keiran? Perhaps none could.

Corporal Mateo moved down the corridors of the *Viridian Eclipse* with haste, knowing that the general expected direct communications to be delivered promptly and by hand. Other Z-Gen soldiers saluted as he ignored them, navigating the labyrinth of passages by memory alone. Space had been his home for the past five years now, the feeling of solid earth under his feet a distant memory, replaced by the thud of boot upon metal.

The news he bore was a mystery, the general the only one authorised to read it, which made him curious of its contents; only news of the Great Threat and direct communication from other generals bore such secrecy. He stopped at the door to the general's quarters and pressed his right hand to the panel beside it, the identification chip within the glove granting him access. As the door opened, Mateo caught part of the conversation his superior was having with one of his black-cloaked commanders.

"It doesn't matter who they dredge up to replace Kalton, they'll be just like the others," Cadmus spat.

He was looking out to space through the large window behind his entirely metal desk. The commander next to him was wearing her helmet, an unusual sight considering her rank. What was less of a surprise was the infantry laser cannon slung over her back, as all officers under Cadmus were expected to fight alongside their soldiers at a moment's notice.

"There's only me and Felix left of the old guard now, and they'll be pushing for him to retire within the decade."

"Others see as we do, sir, those who bear the scars of the enemy. We keep Z-Gen strong." The commander's voice wasn't one Mateo recognised, but her tone was powerful, carrying an unwavering presence.

"And how many of them will survive as you did?" Cadmus didn't get a reply, his robotic hand clenching. "No, they get ground up and spat out like I nearly was, but I refused to die, and when they wanted to discharge me, I fought them with more hatred than I have for the Great Threat!"

Mateo stood in the doorway without saying a word, looking at the sparse room. There were no luxuries or decorations beyond the essential, a metal chair behind the table and a few screens that displayed vital information for the region of space Cadmus oversaw. The only thing out of place was an uncomfortable-looking bed that hadn't been slept in, small and forged from a single piece of steel, topped with a very thin mattress and no bedsheets. The commander noticed his presence but said nothing, which only made Mateo feel more out of place. She returned to watching Cadmus. "The High Marshal listened to Kalton, and he listened to us, but now they're both gone."

"Kalton died in a freak accident and a heart attack took Gernan, that's what the reports say." Cadmus was disgruntled and quiet, robotic hand still tightly closed.

"I served as leader of the *Gladius* fleet for three years and I still had to fight tooth and claw to get to where I am, but not her. I warned the other generals that if we couldn't decide amongst ourselves who'd take the position of High Marshal, the Board of Commanders would have to elect a replacement, but did they listen to me? Of course they didn't! Now Terri Anderson is in charge, 'a new leader for a new Z-Gen', some are saying." Cadmus let a laboured chuckle escape his lips. "An upstart commander with no legitimacy! If I didn't know better, I'd say Gernan and Kalton's deaths were too close together to be a coincidence."

"But you know better. Do you have reason to doubt them, sir?" the commander asked without hesitation.

There was a pause.

"Well?" Cadmus said loudly. He wasn't speaking to the commander anymore. "Are you going to stand there all day, or do you have something for me, corporal?"

Mateo stood to attention quickly and approached, hoping a reprimand wouldn't follow. He presented the information pad without a word and the commander took it, looking over the first layer of encryption the data had.

"The encryption is intact, sir." The pad was taken by Cadmus, holding it in his hand of flesh as it began decrypting before his eyes.

"You heard nothing of our conversation, corporal," Cadmus ordered sternly. Even without seeing the general's eyes, Mateo knew their intensity and nodded.

"What conversation, sir?" he answered back.

There was no reply, and so he started to step back, only to have the commander shake her head very subtly. Mateo remained, waiting patiently as the general read the report. Staring at the stars helped keep him calm, still expecting stern words for his intrusion. Then Cadmus groaned in anger and threw the pad down violently, startling Mateo as it shattered upon impact. The commander didn't flinch or look at the destroyed device, her eyes still on space while the general slowly gazed upon his robot arm, which was clenched so tight it was a wonder nothing had broken. Deep breaths followed, and slowly the metal digits loosened.

"The *Gorgon* has been crippled." Cadmus was seething.

Mateo hadn't seen him this angry before, not even in battle. It unnerved him, but still he remained, not wanting to provoke that rage on himself.

"The tainted?" the commander asked flatly, unconcerned by her superior's fury.

"...Unaccounted for." He raised his metal arm up to look at it, the limb lost while earning his final promotion.

"They will be detained. No one can hide from Z-Gen forever."

"They will be *killed*." Cadmus turned to Mateo, face twisted in hate. "Send a code ZX-4 to all ships in that area, priority Night-7. Now!"

Mateo didn't wait, rushing out of the room with none of the formalities that should've happened. He had no idea what ZX-4 or Night-7 meant, and that told him one thing: they were protocols only the highest-ranked officers knew, and if they were aimed at the tainted who evaded capture on Gui-Lon, then they were about to learn how terrifying the power of Z-Gen was.

He began to pity them for that, but no, there was nothing pitiable about the tainted. They were agents of the Great Threat and a danger to all around them, with their hideous powers that corrupted all. They would be brought to justice, alive or dead, and if he was lucky, it would be him who'd be there to pull the trigger that ended the threat they posed to the galaxy.

Chapter Thirty-Seven

1) All vessels must obey instructions given to them by Z-Gen personnel.
2) All vessels have a duty to investigate an active distress signal and render assistance if possible. This will then be reported to Z-Gen at the earliest opportunity.
3) You are prohibited from firing upon life pods and other emergency evacuation vehicles, regardless of the situation.
4) Criminals categorised as Space Pirates by Z-Gen are an exception to rule 3, though their deaths will invalidate any bounty for their capture.
5) The ship's captain is to maintain a record of the vessel activities while out of spaceport, as well as retain all flight data. This is to be surrendered over to Z-Gen personnel upon their request for examination.
6) No littering.

—Universal Laws of Space Travel

The week that followed was bereft of sleep for Callum, fearful that each night would bring more horrifying dreams. If they did, he had no memory of them; still, he was afraid, waiting for exhaustion to take him to his slumber. Alexis said nothing of his restlessness, but she couldn't hide her concern.

He didn't have words to reassure her, she'd have seen right through them anyway. So he said nothing as he sought to try and enjoy his respite from training; Tyrus hadn't approached him demanding it, and creating balls of fire from nothing would likely upset the crew, so he kept what spells he cast subtle and brief, trying to ensure his skill didn't dull and nothing more.

There were many places for him to explore even with the restrictions placed upon them by their 'clearance', whatever that was. A nearby communal area was where he typically met his friends, spacious and full of tables and chairs which were often occupied. The crew of the vessel didn't mingle with them, and compared to their apparel, his friends stuck out like a sore thumb. Saresan asked for an ale on the second day and was given something that neither he nor Callum recognised.

"It's blue." Saresan watched it as it fizzed.

Siobhan had no such reservations and had already downed her first glass.

"And it tastes horrible. Lime and peach do not go together," Siobhan told him. She was eyeing Saresan's glass. "Fancy another?"

"What kind of ale has fruit in it?" Saresan moved the glass away from him with a disappointed sigh. Siobhan snatched it up quickly.

"Probably to mask the terrible alcohol," she answered between big gulps.

Callum was wary to ask for a drink himself and so decided to try and make a glass of water. He pictured the receptacle and the liquid in his mind as he weaved his magic, but the result was haphazard, the glass uneven and wobbly. What was inside it Callum wasn't sure, but it was too viscous to be water. A man sat at the same table had noticed his spell and decided to move to another one further away. Callum moved the glass to the side carefully, feeling no more welcome from the man's reaction.

"Why would you want to mask it? If I wanted fruit, I'd squeeze some oranges," Saresan told them. "Ale is meant to be bitter, without that it's not real ale. And why *are* you drinking that if you hate it?"

"Because it's free? I don't say no to free booze, and neither should you. Want me to get you another one?" The pilot stood up with both her empty glasses.

"No, thank you." She shrugged at Saresan's answer and went to the machine in the corner where the drink had been dispensed. "Blue drinks..."

A passer-by had noticed Callum's concoction and gave it a curious look. Lifting it up to smell the liquid quickly warned him away, placing it back with revulsion.

The other areas they had access to aside from the corridors were recreational in purpose. Some were large open areas where people met and sat on benches around plants that managed to live on a ship, often having big windows for viewing the stars. There were also places to eat and drink, but none of them resembled the taverns he was used to. Even if they had an atmosphere he liked, the looks he got from people when he was by the entrance of them told him that he wasn't entirely welcome. That feeling pervaded everywhere, he'd noticed: that they were there only because Telanthir wished it, or perhaps that was him imagining things.

Saresan split his time between taking full advantage of a training room that the soldiers on board frequented and watching the viewscreen in his and Jinar's room. He'd found a channel where people fought in a large metal arena for a crowd. That they battled against robots most of the time 'took all the fun out of it', as Saresan put it, and when there weren't robots, the sparring was always non-lethal.

The lethality of the robot contests was debatable to some of the people commentating, as they believed that robots weren't truly alive in the first place. Callum wasn't sure if he agreed; the robots received injuries and sought to protect themselves, and their 'deaths' were just as brutal as any person's if not more so, as apparently most were repaired and sent right back out to battle once more. It made him think of the metal monster they'd fought on the *Gorgon*, wondering if it had been afraid when his blade was moments from ripping it apart. The crowds seemed to have no such thoughts, cheering the fights on and betting heavily on the results.

Callum found a place called 'the observation room', which he spent some time in. Although it was in the middle of the ship, there were views of space in all directions, and with a simple command, those views would shift to the desired size. Callum was amazed at the maximum setting, where nothing but a mass of stars was visible everywhere he looked. That quickly shifted to lingering horror as he remembered Monica, floating lifelessly out there somewhere, and so he left.

One soldier had questioned his sword being there, but his superior informed him of the exception to the rules the blade was. The same soldier mentioned 'his liege', which was a phrase he knew well but was surprised to hear; Callum had thought that kings and monarchs were not a thing of the wider everything he was now a part of. How stubbornly had traditions held for there to still be princes and royal demesne?

He also caught the name of where they were going, Otros, but when he asked about it, Callum was only told that the planet was 'just like any other, only smaller'. That conjured images of overcrowding and artificialness as far as the eye could see. He remembered his home fondly but tried to think of other things before memories of the dead returned.

The day of their arrival at Otros was a remarkably unceremonious one, and it began with Callum being asked by a soldier to head to the hangar at their earliest convenience. He needed only to shower and allow his clothes to be cleaned, and somehow was still one of the last to arrive, along with Alexis.

Tyrus wasn't present but Daniel was, and he looked exhausted as well as annoyed to be out of his room. Callum guessed the demon would make its own way down to the world; it certainly wasn't going to let him out of its sight with Telanthir.

The craft they boarded had comfortable chairs against the walls in two parallel lines, cushioned and red. With Simon on his left and Siobhan to the right, Callum watched the others secure the fabric straps that kept them in place so he could figure out how they worked, then fastening himself in also. Daniel sat closest to the door, staring blankly ahead. The doctor was twiddling his thumbs until he caught sight of the pilot boarding.

"Any chance of a coffee?" Simon's face sank when the young man shook his head.

"No food or drink on the shuttle, I'm afraid. No exceptions," the pilot replied.

"Is Telanthir not coming with us?" Alexis enquired.

"He went planetside earlier, to make ready for your arrival. He said you would understand."

"Of course." She nodded back, the man entering the cramped cockpit then.

The door to it was left open as he prepared for taking off, manipulating panels and buttons with such ease that it appeared natural.

"I'm sure we can get you one when we land," Siobhan told him.

"Like you did on Bedral?" The doctor passed her a glare.

"Are you *still* holding that against me? I said I was sorry!"

"Sorry for what?" Saresan asked. Jinar was watching the exchange with amusement as the door out closed and they lifted off, heading for the airlock.

"Last year she blew the power conduit for the cannon during a routine inspection, after insisting that she didn't need reminding about how to do it." The doctor folded his arms slowly. "We spent a week down there waiting for parts, and you said the exact same thing to me then. And what did we find when we got down there?" He waited for her to answer.

"Surely it can't be that bad." Callum was curious.

"Bedral is the only damn planet I've come across that's banned non-medicinal stimulants grown or produced planetside. Can you imagine how much a simple thing like that being missing changes a world's population?" Simon asked them all.

"Devastating, I'm sure." Siobhan let her sarcasm run rampant. "We found some imported stuff for you, didn't we?"

"It tasted like dirt."

"And the stuff you chug is high-grade?" came her counter. Simon gave her an unimpressed look back and Saresan chuckled. "What?"

"I believe there was a saying on our world that suits this situation," Jinar explained. "Do not cry murder when you yourself have killed."

"The only thing she murdered was a cup of coffee." Simon got a laugh from Saresan.

"Asshole." She caught Jinar smiling more. "You too."

Callum could see that they were in space now, small windows appearing behind them all once they've cleared Telanthir's vessel. No planet was visible yet, just endless stars.

"And what did I do to deserve your wrath?" Jinar asked innocently.

"Don't play dumb with me."

"I assure you, I am incapable of that level of stupefaction."

Her scowl was answered with a polite smile as the planet came into view for Callum. To his surprise, they were already rather close, and it was blue-green in colour, giving him a faint hope that this world was in some way better than the others.

"Initiating atmospheric entry," the pilot informed them as the windows shut once more.

A few odd noises came from the cockpit and Callum could see flames outside, but with each second the planet grew closer. The pilot didn't seem worried, but Callum had a lingering fear regardless, one that proved to be unfounded when space slowly faded away into nothing. A sky of blue drowned it, and he'd expected metal and glass as far as he could see, sprawling settlements that had consumed everything in their path. What he saw instead was so eerily similar to his strange nightmare, but only when the expansive plains of green broken by scattered forests and rivers didn't vanish into grey oblivion did he believe his eyes.

"Well, that's a sight for sore eyes," Saresan muttered at the beautiful scene, nature untouched in all its splendour.

Callum now knew what it was like to be a bird soaring high, and he envied the view they had. Flying over a large hill, he caught sight of the high rising structures, but they were far different to the last ones he'd seen; they didn't pierce the heavens, nor were there platforms between them crammed with people. The settlement was large but not without limits, and curiously, it was perfectly circular, making him wonder how they managed such a feat of planning. Their vessel wasn't the only one flying to the city now, other small craft heading to landing areas on top of buildings or a central location dedicated to it. Each ship was wildly different to the others. The streets below were busy but not cramped, and he spied trees planted along the pathways on either side of larger causeways used by metal vehicles. The sight of small spots of greenery among the metal monoliths warmed his heart, but none of them compared to everything around the settlement, as if nature was laying siege to it. They landed with a muted thud.

"We have arrived. If you'll follow me once we disembark," the pilot informed them as he stood, opening the door for them and exiting. Callum undid the securing belt and left the craft.

Stopping once he'd scaled the stairs, he felt the warmth of the sun on his face and couldn't help smiling at the old friend he hadn't know he'd missed. It was a little smaller in the sky than on his world, but it was the same yellow disc that watched over them.

The temperature was comfortable, and the cloud cover minimal, with birdsong in the trees around them. Within the walls of the estate was a simple yet wonderful garden, grass cut neat and short, as well as trees and winding paved pathways. Despite the hustle and bustle around them, the place was so quiet and calm, a tranquil puddle of peace that he could see himself getting used to.

Ahead of them was a large three-storey building made entirely of fine stone. The roof was tiled with slate and the windows filled with stained glass, every bit the home of a grand duke but with the tell-tale signs that he was far from home; soldiers armed with rifles patrolled the outside in pairs, and four guarded the large open archway leading to the main door, itself wood riveted with metal and painted green. Siobhan whistled.

"Swanky." She was impressed.

"And expensive," Simon muttered, getting a nod from the pilot.

"If you'll follow me." The pilot began walking, and Callum followed with the others down the main path to the entrance.

Daniel trailed behind, looking at his surroundings with contempt. Callum caught his eye and got a look which quickly made him turn away, thinking instead on Tyrus not being there; if its presence was required to shield them from detection, just how close was the demon and where was it?

"I've been in a place like this once," Saresan told them. "Merchant had a break-in. I was surprised he even knew what'd been taken, with all the rooms full of stuff. He called himself an art collector, you know, but I'll be damned if half the things in there were art."

"Lots of questionable sculptures?" Siobhan joked.

"Paintings of cows, would you believe."

"...Cows?" Siobhan paused. "Did he breed them or something?"

"They are a versatile beast and a valuable trade commodity," Alexis explained simply as they approached the door. The guards took one look at them and blocked the entrance.

"I'm going to have to ask you to surrender your weapons here," the pilot insisted with a trained smile. "It's standard procedure for everyone who enters. You will have them returned when you leave."

Callum was wary of handing the sword over, remembering the concerns Tyrus had voiced. Siobhan shrugged and drew her pistols, handing them over to one of the guards, who took them. Alexis's daggers forced him to cup his hands, and when he spotted Saresan's halberd, the man had another guard open the door for him a crack.

"I'll be back," came the assurance before he slipped inside.

"Telanthir rarely receives visitors, I'm sure you understand," the pilot told them. "Unfortunately, he has outlived many of his friends and former colleagues."

"Getting to such a venerable age was an uncommon feat on our world, though I had imagined it not so impossible here." Jinar was looking at gardens as he spoke, stroking his beard in contemplation, likely on some deep arcane mystery. "How many years past his seventieth is he, if it is not rude to pry?"

"Seventy? Telanthir celebrated his one hundred and seventeenth birthday last month."

Callum had to take a moment to make sure he'd heard that correctly; how could someone live that long? It made Terrance's feat of survival trifling in comparison. There was little difference in appearance between his old friend and their host, did people stop changing after a certain point?

"Surely you jest." Jinar was rightly dubious.

"You can ask him yourself at dinner tonight, you are to be his guests at a banquet in your honour."

"Double swanky," Siobhan quipped as the guard returned empty-handed, taking Saresan's halberd and looking over Jinar and Daniel. Daniel hadn't brought his rifle with him but did surrender his knife reluctantly. Callum drew his sword exceptionally carefully and looked at it, wariness still clinging to him. He had to give it up, yet something in his head fought against the idea. He'd get it back, surely, he had to believe that.

"Be careful with the blade, it has a sharpness unlike any other," Callum warned as he passed it over handle first. The guard nodded and disappeared back through the door. Now relinquished of the weapon, Callum felt a little better, but the worry lingered.

"The staff will show you to your rooms. If you desire anything, you need only ask one of them."

With doors opening at last for them, a spectacular room of polished marble floors and magnificent luxury was laid out before them, a grand staircase leading to the upper levels with a deep red carpet running down – or was it up? – the stairs. Wood panelling and white walls were broken by fantastically painted pictures of great value. Never in Callum's wildest dreams had he expected to see such a sight, let alone be welcome within it. A smartly dressed man and woman approached them with a polite smile, indicating to the staircase.

"Welcome, we've been expecting you. Please follow us."

Decadence.

It was the only word Callum could come up with to describe the room he'd been assigned, and now that he was alone, it made him uncomfortable. The walls were of intricately carved panelled wood, and the light above him a wonderful chandelier that must have cost a fortune in labour alone. The four-poster bed was so grand that he dared not touch it, though he could smell a subtle and pleasant fragrance coming from the pillows and bedsheets.

He saw not a hint of grey metal or a viewscreen, his only source of entertainment being a bookshelf chock-full of tomes that he doubted were on his reading level. Two doors with glass windows led to a small balcony, allowing him to overlook the gardens around the estate and consider just what was going to happen. He'd even been assigned a set of clothes to wear to the banquet later, handed to him by one of the soldiers.

"If the suit doesn't fit, let us know," she'd told him before leaving.

Callum tried it on to find that the clothes fitted him exceptionally well, wondering how they'd got his measurements so exact. He didn't think much of the style, but he wasn't going to refuse a simple request from his host. Not seeing the sword reflected back in the full-length mirror in the corner was odd, as was how he looked in general, at least to himself. He wore a white shirt with buttons all along the middle, and over it a black jacket with long sleeves. Complementing it were smart-looking and smooth black trousers, along with polished shoes. There was also a long length of fabric which he couldn't figure out the purpose of; it was too flimsy to be a belt and one of them had been provided, so he stuck it in a free pocket to work out later.

Even with how comfortable it all was, the outfit felt like a façade, dressing him up to look 'normal' rather than who he really was. A knock on the door interrupted his thoughts and he went to open it. Standing in the doorway was Jinar, dressed much the same as he was. The only difference was that his shoes were a little pointier at the end, the one piece of individuality that made him miss his friend's orange robes.

"Greetings." Jinar smiled. "Are you ready? Telanthir will be expecting us shortly, or so I have been told."

"I guess." Callum stepped out of his room and closed the door. He caught sight of a striking picture of a beautiful sunset and remembered it so he could find that place later. "Have you seen any of the others?"

"No, but I am certainly looking forward to it." Jinar's smile told him everything Callum needed to know, though he wasn't sure which person he was referring to. "Surely you are also, if only a little."

"It didn't cross my mind," Callum admitted.

Jinar patted his shoulder.

"Give it time, it may yet do so."

They began walking down the corridor in the direction of the stairs. The art on the walls were portraits of various men and women in regal poses that signified their importance. Approaching the huge staircase, Callum stopped upon looking at the last picture, seeing that it was Telanthir that had been painted. His hair had streaks of black and he looked markedly younger, standing in front of a wooden desk with an almost burned-out candle. His clothes were mostly the same, but the gold on his head made Callum's eyes widen in disbelief. It was a crown Telanthir wore, unadorned with gems but still a sign of great power. Jinar had spied it too and raised an eyebrow.

"Well, that is interesting," his friend remarked.

"Telanthir is a king?"

He thought back to their encounter, how the man acted, and was dumbfounded; rulers were never so approachable or... like him. They had great responsibilities and power, with wealth and station that put them so far above ordinary people, and yet Telanthir had spoken with him as if they were equals. It didn't make sense, how could it? Jinar read a plaque beneath the painting as Callum tried to come to terms with what he's learned.

"It can't be," he uttered.

"King Telanthir Callahan D'Otros, age eighty-two," Jinar confirmed.

"He barely looks fifty."

"Unless the man has illusions of grandeur, I would say it can be and is. You are welcome to ask him at the banquet."

"It would be rude of me to." Callum looked away from the painting and they continued to walk, slowly descending the stairs.

At the bottom they spied Siobhan, her attire unchanged save for the absence of the armour chest plate and her hat, the latter making her look almost completely different. She waved to them as they made their way down.

"Glad you finally decided to show up." She motioned with her thumb to the large doors to the left of the stairway. "You're late."

"Rather, everyone else is early, as no celebration truly starts without my presence," Jinar told her. Siobhan rolled her eyes. "Besides, my arrival will turn more heads this way."

"We're still waiting on Alexis, but I'm starved enough as it is. What say we get in and tuck in?"

Chapter Thirty-Eight

Callum approached the large doors, and a quiet knock made two attendants within open the way for them. The room beyond was massive, and dominating the middle was an oak table twenty metres long and three wide. A feast was laid out upon it: all manner of foods piled on large silver trays, along with a selection of wines and beverages that made Callum's mouth water. He'd never seen so much food before, least of all food he was allowed to eat.

Windows that almost rose to the ceiling lined the back of the room, glass spotless as it let the late afternoon sun bathe the table in light. There were enough red cushioned chairs around the table for all of them, including one for Tyrus that was unoccupied.

The demon was stood at the end closest to them, turning to see Callum arrive with its unreadable expression. At the head of the table sat Telanthir, who smiled at them, careful to not look upon Tyrus.

Behind the king was a grand fireplace that burned heartily with fresh logs, and above it, a large picture that was entirely covered in white cloth. Daniel, Simon and Saresan sat to Telanthir's left, the doctor already armed with a coffee. He'd changed only his shirt, while Saresan was dressed like Callum, though he didn't appear to be comfortable in it. Daniel hadn't changed and was slumped in his chair, a mostly empty glass of wine in his hands. He was staring at nothing, sad and distant. A space between Daniel and Saresan was quickly occupied by Siobhan, who was eyeing the food hungrily.

"Thank you all for coming," Telanthir said warmly, his voice easily reaching all of them. Callum and Jinar took their seats on the other side of the table, their host glancing then to the empty one to Callum's left. "I presume lady Alexis will be joining us?"

"Shall I go and check on her, sir?" one of the attendants asked.

"No, let her take her time. I'm sure no one is in a hurry to get started." Siobhan's stare at the roast chicken ahead of her said otherwise. "Feel free to have some of the red in the meantime. It is a fine vintage."

Callum reached for a jug of water, seeing no ale on the table. Saresan had reluctantly poured some wine into his glass.

"You got anything harder?" Siobhan asked idly.

"Spirits more to your taste?"

"Not fussed, just harder."

"I will have someone find something for you," Telanthir told her.

The other door attendant left in search of that. He held the door open, and when Jinar turned his head, Callum did also to see that Alexis had arrived. She wore a full-length white dress that fitted her well. Plain and without adornment, it went down to her feet and was held up by straps that went over her shoulder. She didn't announce her arrival with any fanfare, but it hadn't been needed; being the last one to arrive, it caught everyone's attention easily. Telanthir smiled politely at her.

"I'm sorry that I'm late," Alexis said to him, moving to sit beside Callum. "It took some time to find something for me to wear."

"Do not worry, we were happy to wait," Telanthir told her. Alexis reached for a glass and started to pour herself some wine carefully.

"You look nice," Callum told her honestly. It made her glance at him in turn.

"Thank you, as do you."

A man entered with a trolley with a huge silver bowl on top, from which he began to serve soup. It was reddish in colour, Callum smelling tomato and a hint of beef: a fine meal all by itself, but there was so much assembled before them that there was no way he could make a dent in it. Siobhan was going to try, ignoring the soup given to her and taking a leg of chicken, which she started eating without using the large amount of cutlery provided.

"Please, enjoy any and all of the food." Telanthir tried the soup and nodded to the attendant. "Excellent, as always. Please give my compliments to Frederick."

"Of course, sir." The man left, but not before eyeing Tyrus warily. The demon glared back.

"Why are we here?" Daniel made no effort to hide his annoyance, not touching his soup. "Surely not because you're short of dinner guests."

"Daniel." Simon's quiet warning fell on deaf ears.

"He's hiding something, just like *they* were," Daniel spoke hatefully, staring at Callum. The old man eyed him curiously but not with anger.

"No matter what we speak of here, you are my guests above all else. You are under no obligation to stay. Once your ship is fully repaired, I will arrange transport to your vessel if you wish it. Unlike Z-Gen, I bear you no ill will," Telanthir spoke plainly, giving Callum no reason to doubt his words. "No one here will talk of your visit, of that I swear."

"Do you think I'm stupid?" Daniel spat. "No one gives all this and expects nothing in return. What do you want?" Telanthir blinked.

"Geeze, cut it out already!" Siobhan told him with a mouthful of food, already reaching for more. "You made your point." Daniel slumped further back in his chair, brooding.

"So why are we here?" Saresan repeated the question, though without the malice. "There something we can do for you? A 'you scratch my back, I scratch yours' kind of deal?"

"All I ask is that you listen to what I have to say." That sounded simple enough, Callum thought; Telanthir had been pleasant so far. "Let me start by saying that I know all about your exploits on Gui-Lon, including your criminal records. I do not intend to use that as blackmail to strong-arm you into any action. Z-Gen has no power here."

"Did you get to the bit about Saresan and the chair?" Siobhan asked with a grin and a frown from the guard. Telanthir nodded. "I bet you weren't expecting that, eh?"

"The news broadcasts about the incident used security footage from the bar. I am quite aware of the circumstances of the unfortunate incident, and I commend you for there being no casualties while planetside. Be assured that there will not be a repeat incident when you leave Otros, they have no military garrison present."

"I thought Z-Gen were almost everywhere." Callum thought back to their arrival on the planet, realising now that he hadn't seen a single Z-Gen soldier on the streets.

"Almost everywhere, yes. There are pockets of space where their authority is limited or, in my case, non-existent. The Great Terran Treaty is the document that everyone remembers, but there have been smaller agreements made throughout history, and the Otros Accord was one such thing. Signed 703 years ago, it grants this system autonomy from Z-Gen in all respects. It was a very savvy piece of negotiation, struck when Z-Gen were weak in this area and needed to allocate vessels used to defend this system for other purposes."

"And in return, what do they get?" Jinar sipped his wine, holding the glass like a goblet.

"The restrictions placed upon Otros are minor, along with standard protocols like free passage of Z-Gen ships through our space and free trade. Mostly, we ensure that no space pirates use this system as a spot for an outpost where they can launch their operations. The Otros Accord was aimed primarily at military matters, freeing us from their rule with minimal strings attached." Telanthir dipped some bread in his soup. "It's not something that could be signed today, of course. Z-Gen are... not what they once were."

"You took a great risk rescuing wanted criminals, Telanthir." Alexis was eating the soup without bread, her wine barely drunk. "Am I to understand you don't hold Z-Gen in high regard?" Telanthir briefly turned his eyes to his bowl.

"Under Z-Gen, the people of the galaxy are united by one banner, seeing themselves as one people." Telanthir didn't look up as he spoke. "Without Z-Gen, the galaxy would descend into anarchy, a thousand upstart empires trying to carve out their fiefdoms in blood."

"But do you dislike them?" she asked again.

Telanthir brought his gaze up from his food but looked to no one at the table, instead staring at Tyrus. The demon looked back, and it was clear to Callum that the man was having difficulty maintaining eye contact.

"...I have seen your kind before," he stated.

His quiet declaration surprised not just Callum but his mentor also.

"When?" it asked quickly.

"A long time ago, when I was much younger." There was a pain in his voice, memory in his eyes.

"How long ago?"

"...I have not thought about it for so long." Telanthir could look to the demon no longer, pushing his bowl away. He waved his hand dismissively. "Leave us." With a nod, the attendant that was serving them exited without a word.

"I thought the demons were only after us, what do they want with you?" Saresan enquired after swallowing some beef. Telanthir stood and looked to the fire, hands clasped behind his back. He sighed quietly.

"My primary duty to this world is as a diplomatic envoy. I am as much an ambassador for peace and cooperation as I am a figurehead, travelling to far-off systems to seek unity in the galaxy. Occasionally there would be problems, but with Z-Gen overseeing everything, what did I have to fear?"

"Kings do not normally go to meet people themselves, has that much changed?" Callum got a quizzical look from Saresan. "Telanthir is a king."

"You're kidding." The guard looked him over more carefully and with disbelief. "He doesn't look much like one." Daniel just scowled at the news.

"Callum is quite correct, I am a king," Telanthir replied. Siobhan looked up from her full plate in interest. "As old as the lineage of my family is, the title is mostly ceremonial in this day and age. Aside from my duties as a diplomat, it entails little more than some traditional functions and minor political activities. It's been many centuries since laws were decreed from this house."

"Sweet, I've never met a king before." Siobhan chewed on another leg of chicken. "So that vessel we came here on is yours?"

"I do believe we are deviating from the original matter at hand." Jinar had finished his glass of wine, sitting up in his chair. "You mentioned that you have seen a demon before, please explain." Telanthir had a sombre expression as he stared ahead at something that wasn't there. Tyrus watched the king intently, impatiently.

"Sixty-three years ago, my ship was attacked by unknown assailants, far from any planet in deep space. We were on our way to attend a conference of the local systems when it happened." Telanthir took a light, shaky breath. "There was no ship, no airlock breached. Before the security teams could be mobilised, we'd lost half of the vessel to... to..."

"The demons." Callum whispered the words, but Telanthir still heard them, nodding ever so faintly. "You don't need to say anything else: we've fought them before."

All eyes were on the king, which made him look up to the shrouded picture. Callum knew what was going through Telanthir's head, the horrible and pointless death that would've left the corridors of his ship sprayed with blood. Telanthir took another breath, closing his eyes.

"Why would they target your vessel?" Jinar asked.

"I don't know, but they did," the king answered weakly. "I was in the security room when it happened, looking over some camera footage of an event the Chief wanted my thoughts on. He was out of the room when the lockdown happened. All I could do was..." He swallowed slowly. "...watch as they worked their trade." Callum had lost his appetite, and he wasn't the only one, Alexis setting aside the bread in her hand. Siobhan kept eating.

"If you survived that, then why doesn't everyone know about the demons? The news networks would gobble that right up." Simon was listening intently. "Unless you didn't tell anyone, but why would you do that?"

"A Z-Gen cruiser picked up our distress signal, en route to the same world we were. They could've had no idea what they were up against, but they boarded and purged the monsters with brutal efficiency. In a matter of minutes it was over, or so I thought." Telanthir went quiet, opening his eyes and looking into the fireplace at the dancing flames. "They gathered up the survivors on the bridge and asked them something, I couldn't tell what because I didn't have an audio feed. Their commander entered and said a few words, and then... and then..."

The king's voice wavered, cracked with sadness and tears he managed to hold back. Siobhan finally stopped eating, as lost for words as everyone else. Callum imagined the next horrifying moments in the story, and he felt a mere fraction of the pain Telanthir was going through.

"You can't be serious," Simon muttered, startled.

"...They shot them. Gunned them down like... cattle."

Telanthir closed his eyes again, hand holding onto the mantelpiece as if for support. Now the tears flowed, all the while Tyrus watched with narrowed eyes. Not a shred of empathy flashed on its face, but how could it? The king barely continued.

"...Among them was my wife and daughter. They burned the bodies, left no trace of them." The pain in Callum's chest magnified into grief for a man he barely knew. Now he knew what that picture was, why it was covered.

"How did you survive?" Alexis asked the question carefully.

"I lied," came the simply put reply. "I deactivated the camera feeds, deleted the viewing logs. When they finally found me, I asked them what had happened, feigned ignorance in front of one of the very soldiers that killed them all."

"And he believed you?"

"Yes. He told me space pirates had attacked the ship and that there were no other survivors. They'd holed up in the bridge but were killed by grenades, incinerated. The man lied to me, and in turn I lied to him, and that is the only reason I'm still alive today. The incident was reported galaxy-wide, investigated by Z-Gen, but the truth never got out. No one knew it but me and Z-Gen." The king breathed deeply, his hand on the mantelpiece clenching. "If they'd known what I saw, heard what I'm telling you now, I wouldn't be here. They'd've killed me long ago."

"But why would they hide it?" Callum had to ask. "And why tell us this now?"

"I wouldn't have, but when I saw..." Telanthir turned his head to Tyrus. "...when I saw that, I knew you knew, and I couldn't hold it in any longer. You now know the truth as I do."

"That the demons are the Great Threat," Tyrus finished without fanfare.

"Yes. And I want you to prove it."

There was silence at first.

"Bollocks," Daniel shattered it. "You're telling me we've been at war for a hundred years with those things, and *no one* knows about it? No one survived an attack, no communication left planetside? That's impossible!"

"Incorrect," Tyrus replied.

"Why would they be attacking worlds? What do they seek to gain?" Simon asked himself.

"You don't seriously believe him, do you?" Daniel was incredulous and angry. "There's no huge conspiracy, there can't be! How could Z-Gen keep it all secret?"

"By making sure no one who discovers it survives," the doctor countered. All the while Telanthir watched them without a word, exposed and vulnerable.

"But we've got our evidence right here." Siobhan indicated to Tyrus. "We parade it around the news channels, and they'll have to believe us."

"Evidence of my existence is not evidence of a link between the Great Threat and the demons," Tyrus answered.

"No way." Daniel shook his head again and again. "No fucking way. I don't buy it, I can't! Listen to what you're saying: that every time these demons attack, Z-Gen swoops in and keeps it all hush-hush?"

"They monitor almost all interplanetary communication within their space, control how it flows through the galaxy," Simon told him. "All it would take is a press of a button, and nothing goes far beyond the planet's atmosphere. The same thing blocks the news channel from broadcasting." The doctor didn't stop there. "People will have tried this before. Even if something *had* got through, their PR department likely mopped up what's left."

"Bloody PR," Siobhan murmured.

"You can't seriously believe him!" Daniel was getting angry at being ignored.

"I believe him," Callum said back.

"You would, you're an idiot."

"Daniel!" Siobhan's shock was cast aside.

"This is the sob story of an old man who wants to twist our arm to do something illicit. You'd believe anything that tugged at your heartstrings." The king stared at Daniel, who looked back angrily. "All we have is your word for all this, you were the only survivor, or so you say. What proof do you have?"

"Telling you this has put my life in jeopardy, is that not enough?" the king answered calmly despite the accusations flung at him. Daniel had no such restraint.

"Only if you're telling the truth, which you're not!"

"I've seen a lot of things that I couldn't have imagined were real in just a few weeks," Callum began, unable to keep quiet anymore. "I've seen ships that fly through space, cities with more people than my entire kingdom. I've looked on as an outsider with no knowledge of how it all fits together, but we've seen Z-Gen. We saw how the captain of the *Gorgon* reacted to Tyrus; we've seen how they treat sorcerers. It makes sense."

"Does it? Does it really?" Daniel argued back. "The way I see it, this is all slipping into place a little too neatly. He's feeding you exactly what you want to hear to make you sympathetic to him!"

"If Z-Gen were as good as—"

"What do *you* know about Z-Gen anyway? You're from a backwater nowhere!"

"Just listen!" Callum stood up, angry at Daniel and unable to hide it. The man was quiet. "If my king had known, back on my world, that there was an army of monsters that they were losing to, he wouldn't tell the people this. Why would he? It'd rip the kingdom apart!"

"Z-Gen are unlikely to lose against feral demons," Jinar chimed in.

"If they were winning, they'd have no reason to hide it, would they?" Alexis countered.

"News of sentient alien life would turn our galaxy upside-down anyway," Simon interjected. "Your kind would hardly fit the generally accepted image of what's out there, Tyrus."

"But how are they victorious against Z-Gen?" Jinar asked again. "They have powerful long-range weapons and spaceships; they could attack the demons from the air and be impervious to their claws."

"Unless there are more demons like Xiez." Alexis got a weak shrug from Jinar. "You, yourself, always say that nothing can withstand arcane power; Z-Gen would be no exception. And if they saw magic used against them, they would be fearful of any sorcerer working with the demons as the Silent Hand do. That would be all the evidence Z-Gen need to conclude that any sorcerer could be in league with the Great Threat."

"If there's an army of those things out there, the galaxy has to be told, and that's something we can do," Siobhan said between her mouthfuls of food, eating a little slower now. "They can't fight what they don't know about."

Callum was expecting an objection from Tyrus, but it didn't come; where was the stubborn insistence that they had to hide away and train, ready themselves to face Keiran? This was exactly what it didn't want them to do, and yet there was no word against it. Had this news changed the situation that much?

"Why would you agree to all this? You want humanity in a panic?" It was Daniel's turn to stand up, furious and upset all at once as he shouted at the pilot, "They ruined our lives, they killed Monica! We owe them *nothing*!"

"Doesn't mean I'm going to sit back and let the demons do what they're doing, if Telanthir's right!" Siobhan downed a glass of wine. "You don't think I cared about Monica? She was my friend, damn it! Yes, she's gone, but that doesn't mean we should refuse to help out of spite." Callum kept quiet as the argument escalated.

"Simon?" Daniel looked at the doctor darkly. He said nothing. "Why do you both trust them all so blindly? Why am I the only one who sees what's so wrong with this? Do you want the galaxy to live in constant fear of the demons, gripped in terror? What good will that do?"

Daniel stopped shouting suddenly, a calm washing over him that didn't seem right. "You know what? If you want to go off and get yourselves killed, fine! But you'll be doing it without me *or* my ship!" Only Tyrus wasn't surprised by his declaration.

"Daniel—" Simon barely got a word in.

"No! I've fucking had it with all this and with *you*, Callum!" An accusing finger was aimed at him, which made Callum feel even worse than he already did.

"What about our things?" Siobhan got a glare back.

"Fuck your things!" Daniel snapped. The pointing finger was shifted to Tyrus. "And you! I hate you even more than him! Not once did you even think to say sorry for her, not once!" Daniel had nothing but unbridled loathing for the demon, but it just stared through him coldly.

"An apology would be as insincere as it is irrelevant. You are unnecessary."

Callum felt the chilling bite of Tyrus's words seep into his skin, a quiet descending upon them all. For a moment, Daniel seemed overwhelmed by utter insignificance, only for that to be smothered by his anger rekindled.

"Rot in hell."

Without another word, he walked towards the large doors leading out and swung them open so hard that the attendants waiting beyond were startled. He ignored them and left, but not before casting Callum and Tyrus one last look of hatred.

Chapter Thirty-Nine

"But Jazz-O-Tron, not even the smooth sound of your quantum saxophone can drown out the ritual of the seven clones of the Demon Emperor!"

"Maybe so, Grondo of the Twelve Souls, but how will the Fairy Force penetrate the Time Barrier and destroy the time loop the universe has been in if I don't distract them from summoning the REAL Demon Emperor from the virtual dimension?"

"But you'll die!"

"I can't die, I'm a robot."

"You know damn well what I mean, Jazz-O-Tron! I won't let you throw away your life like this!"

"But I must—"

"Damn it, I love you!"

"I know."

"...You know? I've been trying to tell you for seventeen million years, and you've known all this time?!"

"Of course."

"Why didn't you tell me you felt the same way?"

"I don't. Jazz is my one true love."

"...Oh, Jazz-O-Tron, I can't stay mad at you. Just promise me you'll come back alive."

"The only thing I can promise is that there's about to be one heck of a smooth saxophone solo! Jazz powers, ACTIVATE!"

—Clip from 'Sword Slasher 12: Battle for the Past of the Future-Past's Future'

The silence lingered for a few more seconds before Simon sighed wearily, rubbing his brow.

"Well, that was a mess," he muttered.

Daniel was gone, and with him their ship, but that was insignificant to Callum. More than any other feeling, worry surfaced, knowing that Daniel was abandoning the magical concealment that Tyrus afforded the rest of them, vulnerable and visible to the servants of Keiran. Tyrus had let him go knowing that, though any thought that it hoped he would be captured and killed was dismissed, remembering that Tyrus didn't feel hope.

"I'm sorry," Telanthir apologised unexpectedly. Hurt still played at the edges of his tone. "I feel responsible for this."

"It was a long time coming, I'm afraid. If it hadn't happened now, it would've later. Still, I don't like it," Simon conceded. Saresan stood up.

"I'm going after him," the guard declared. "If he's not in that magic of yours, Tyrus—"

"There are other ships." Tyrus was dismissive of the situation. "And matters to discuss."

"Don't you care that he's gone? He isn't in a good place, Tyrus, who knows what he might do!"

"We have matters to discuss." Tyrus turned its attention to Telanthir.

Saresan was torn between giving chase and staring down the demon but ultimately sat once more. Callum understood Tyrus's thinking, but he didn't like it. He was just as worried as Saresan, but nothing he could say would make Daniel come back.

"I will have our security forces keep an eye on him while he is on Otros, of that you have my word," Telanthir assured Saresan, looking to the way out himself. "I understand his pain though. There was a time when I felt the same: angry and hateful. Time did much to erode those feelings."

"I fear time may not be on his side." Alexis got a nod from the king.

"You may be right, but I promised you all that I would not keep you here against your wishes. His is a wound that I cannot force closed." The king moved back to his chair, sitting carefully and looking to the barely eaten banquet. "Your... demon is right. We have matters to discuss if you are willing to assist me in finding proof."

"I will." Callum still expected blunt refusal from Tyrus, but again it didn't emerge. He was also a little surprised that he was agreeing to help but, upon reflection, found that that surprise was in itself surprising...

"I as well." Alexis nodded in agreement.

There were no objections from around the table, which made Telanthir smile weakly.

"You don't know how happy I am to hear that from you, my friends." The king leaned back in his chair. "My coffers are not bottomless, but I have plenty of resources at my disposal. Money, supplies, weaponry and a safe haven from Z-Gen are what I offer you, among other things."

"We'll need a ship now too," Saresan added.

"That may be a little more challenging, but not beyond my means."

"You put your world at risk without its consent," Tyrus warned the king, bringing the brief mood of enthusiasm to a shuddering halt.

"The parliament don't know you're here, I'm sure I can keep it that way," Telanthir replied.

"Collusion with us brings your world to the attention of Keiran." Tyrus didn't go into any more detail, but that it had at all was far from the demon Callum had first met on his world; it didn't care about anyone, why warn the king at all? He decided to fill in the blanks himself.

"The demons that we have encountered have a leader called Keiran," Callum explained. "We don't know much about him, but he appears to have a long and powerful reach. He also has human allies that collude with the demons; to what end, I don't know." Callum hoped the explanation wouldn't ward off Telanthir from helping them, but he couldn't leave him in ignorance. "I do want to help, but the last thing we want is to put your world at risk because of it."

"Is it not already at risk? Now that I have a chance to protect the people of this world and, by extension, all other worlds, I can't refuse it. Parliament may not understand now, but if I approach them with irrefutable proof of the demons' intentions, they will have no choice but to act."

"And if we cannot find this proof?" Jinar was watching their host carefully.

"You'll find it. When you do, the galaxy will finally know the truth. Z-Gen would be able to quash the rumours of a single crew, but not the parliament of Otros." The king's confidence was beginning to return. "We, as a species, can then create a united front against our common enemy and perhaps turn the tide where Z-Gen has failed to."

"Z-Gen already has a united front," Simon interjected.

"And look how well *that's* going." Siobhan reached past the doctor to grab some roast potatoes. "When was the last time Z-Gen actually stopped the invasion of a world by the Great Threat? Oh, that's right, never."

"If it were the demons, that would be understandable with their use of magic to reach worlds." Jinar was stroking his beard, watching the king, who had a glimmer of hope in his eyes. "Do not think us ungrateful for your offer, we are not. The threat we face, however, is very real and very dangerous. If Z-Gen cannot withstand it, your world will not either."

Telanthir thought for a few moments, but his conviction didn't fade.

"My only other choice is to send you away and watch as other worlds fall to the Great Threat. Maybe I won't live to see Otros fall, or it might happen next year, next week. Perhaps tomorrow the monsters will surge through the streets like a river of death, consuming everything in their path." The king stood once more. "No. I cannot, I *must* not let that happen. If you agree to uncover the Great Threat for what it is, then you'll have all the support that I can give you. It is better to try and fail than to sit back and let it continue."

"Why trust us?" Callum asked then, catching the king's attention. It still felt odd to be talking to one so powerful like that, as if he was like them. "You know little about us."

Telanthir smiled faintly at the question.

"My life has been all about understanding people, seeing who they are and what they care for," Telanthir began. "I have seen wolves that linger in shadows and strike in packs, vultures that wait for weakness and pick at carcasses, snakes which poison and corrupt. You are none of those things. Someone out to trick me wouldn't be trying to dissuade me right now, warn me of risk."

"Or we'd be doing exactly that to make you *think* that we're good people." Saresan was leaning back in his chair. "We're criminals, remember?"

"Only in the eyes of Z-Gen. Perhaps if you can find the proof we need, you wouldn't be criminals any longer." Callum was flattered, but still he worried, and not just because of the risk the king was taking; Tyrus hadn't spoken for quite a while, and it was one with the ultimate leverage. The demon was silent for a few seconds more.

"The Council will be informed of your offer and the information you have provided," Tyrus told him.

Callum had expected much more than that; another argument, objections and counterpoints, but instead there was just... that. He had to concede that demons remained confusing and strange to him.

"There is a council of your kind?" Telanthir was curious.

"Another shall take my place until my return." Without another word, Tyrus vanished into nothingness. Telanthir blinked once, then again, unaccustomed to the demon's ways.

"That went better than I expected," Alexis admitted.

A moment later a black-red portal appeared where Tyrus had once been, startling Telanthir and the others who hadn't seen one before.

"You were saying?" Saresan grabbed one of the knives on the table, a poor weapon but better than nothing.

Callum was on edge despite seeing a portal like that before, half-expecting feral demons to emerge from it and attack them. It was Baylon that emerged, however, the portal closing behind the armed demon no sooner had it arrived. Siobhan quickly caught on that Callum recognised it, but she continued to eye the creature warily. Telanthir managed to contain his shock better than last time, but Tyrus hadn't appeared as dramatically. Baylon looked at those assembled as it declared its intentions quickly.

"Do not be alarmed, I mean you no harm." The demon held its sword firmly by the handle.

"Got a funny way of showing it," Saresan answered back.

"One cannot be sure how humans will act when presented with a demon." Baylon's reply was not as bluntly delivered as Tyrus would have done.

"Are all your kind so capable of bypassing our defences?" Telanthir asked carefully, unsure how to address the newcomer.

"Yes," came the reply. Baylon let go of its sword, looking to Callum as the king pondered the implications of that answer. "I will oversee your concealment while Tyrus is debating your deviation."

"Deviation?" Callum was confused.

"Your actions are a direct deviation from the goals set by the Council. They will not be pleased with this development."

"Why?" Callum didn't get an answer. "Are all demons as cryptic as Tyrus?"

"Most are worse," Baylon answered. "The Council even more so. You would do well to stay on the good side of the Council, Callum."

"They have a good side?" Jinar joked.

"Okay, who *are* the Council?" Siobhan finally asked. "They some hoity-toity bunch who shout till they get what they want?" There was a moment's pause.

"Mostly, save they spend too much time arguing to get what they want." Jinar thought on that. "What *do* they want, Baylon? They were very secretive about it when we first met them, I am sure they are hiding something from us."

Telanthir continued to watch the spectacle with both great wonder and some small degree of horror.

"Their purpose is to oversee and protect the demons within the enclave and ensure their survival. Beyond that, I cannot say." The demon spoke factually, but Jinar wasn't entirely convinced, watching its face closely for any tells. As far as Callum knew, they had no such things.

"You cannot say because you do not know, or because you cannot tell us what you know?" the sorcerer dug deeper.

"It is not my place to answer that question," it announced to them. That didn't reassure Callum, but that they had not been abandoned already filled him with some hope that this agreement would go ahead.

"You got any more of this?" Siobhan was pointing to the turkey slices which had been devoured by her alone, her attention torn away from the demon and back to what was important: food.

Telanthir had quickly excused himself to discuss something with his head of staff, but not before giving them free rein to explore the grounds. The only exception was the king's own quarters and those of the staff, but Callum didn't feel that needed to be said. Baylon declared moments after the king's departure that it would relocate to a place where it would not be noticed, vanishing much like Tyrus usually did.

Left by themselves, the group slowly drifted away from the still plentiful banquet save Siobhan and Simon, the former continuing to eat her fill while the latter poured himself a glass of wine and enjoyed the quiet that had fallen on the room. Jinar had found a library and was immediately lost to it, enquiring with a bemused assistant as to the number of magical tomes they had on the shelves. Callum returned to his room and stepped out onto the balcony, looking all around at the bustling city beyond the walls of the estate, the high-rise buildings somehow managing not to cast a shadow on the palace grounds despite their prominence.

The palace's quiet no longer felt right when he could see everything surrounding it, the peace encircled by a world it refused to accept. It reminded him somewhat of himself. Thoughts of the risks Telanthir was prepared to take to expose the Great Threat flitted across his mind, each of them worse than the other.

He didn't doubt what the king said, but Tyrus's warning was a wise one; if the servants of Keiran discovered the help he'd offered them, would they seek to kill him too? With his daughter dead, his own passing would leave the crown in dispute, bringing a premature end to the royal bloodline. Would the palace be torn down so another monolith of metal and glass could be erected, wiping all trace of the king's legacy away?

Thoughts of death brought him to Daniel, regretting now that he hadn't given chase himself and tried in vain to persuade him to stay. Had the Silent Hand already caught him, or was he still being masked by the concealment which the demons had granted them? The ruination of his life had come at their hand, and that truth hurt Callum, but it was impossible for that pain to equal what Daniel suffered through.

A smaller part of him wondered if the man was correct; what if there truly was nothing to Telanthir's theory, that the attack on his ship all those years ago had been an isolated event of horror? It was possible, but so many things were possible that he gave up thinking on them, instead musing on the countryside beyond the city.

He couldn't see it, but he knew it was there, untouched and wild. It reminded him of home, and perhaps, if he closed his eyes long enough out there, he could pretend this was all in his imagination. But it wasn't, it couldn't be. What he'd witnessed was no fabrication of his mind, nor was the task that had been placed upon their shoulders.

Still, with Tyrus gone there was a moment of pause, a break in the feeling that he was always being observed. Just thinking on that made him wonder if he was in fact alone, turning quickly. No one was there, however. Nobody observed him from the gardens below either.

He reached out with his arms immediately around him, just in case an assailant was hidden with magic, and then stopped himself; he must've looked like a fool, fumbling around at nothing on paranoia alone. If Terrance had been there, he'd have shook his head and reminded him that at times, his head was aloft in the clouds. He missed home.

"Hey," Saresan's voice came from behind him. He hadn't even noticed the door being opened, so caught up in his search. "You alright?"

"Yes, sorry. I didn't hear you come in: I was miles away." His friend walked onto the balcony with him, looking out at the view. He seemed far less amazed than he was.

"I know that feeling." Saresan leaned back on the door frame, arms folded. "I've been thinking."

"What on?"

"There are probably more worlds like ours out there, forgotten about by everywhere around them. Do you think they're just like home? With swords, spells and kingdoms?"

"I don't know. Each place we've seen is so different. Perhaps those forgotten worlds went on a different path to ours." Callum was trying to imagine those paths. "Why do you ask?"

"Just for when this is all over... if it is." Saresan trailed off. "It doesn't matter. If Telanthir and Tyrus can see eye-to-eye, we'll be off solid ground and back into space in no time. I can't say I'm super thrilled at the thought of hunting down the demons, but without Daniel's ship we're in a bind."

"Do you think he's alright?" Callum looked back out to the city.

"I don't think he'll be alright ever again. I just hope he doesn't do something stupid, but we can't stop him now." Saresan stepped from the door frame to stand next to Callum, leaning on the balcony. "Telanthir reminds me of my uncle, you know."

"How so?" Callum didn't keep his eyes from the view.

"Determined to do right, no matter the cost. Ended up with a knife in his back, face down in a ditch." Saresan shook his head, but after a few moments he chuckled to himself. "Jinar has some of Telanthir's staff out there, looking for things for him. He wrote them a pretty long list."

"Magical reagents?" Callum guessed.

"Clothes, actually." Callum was puzzled and Saresan chuckled at that. "He's been mentioning it on and off since we went to Gui-Lon, saw all those people. He wants to 'liven up his image', or so he said. Can't say I'll be doing the same. What about you?"

"Hmm?"

"Getting new clothes. Getting... 'with it'."

"...With it?" That didn't sound natural coming from Saresan. He did cringe at it being repeated.

"Siobhan's words, not mine; didn't know they'd rubbed off on me already. Jinar had passed the topic by her, and I don't think she discouraged him at all. Maybe he thinks she'll be impressed, I dunno. I think he's barking up the wrong tree, personally."

Callum heard the door to his room opening the second time. He and Saresan turned to see Telanthir waiting in the corridor. The king smiled politely, though something was clearly on his mind.

"May I come in?" the old man asked. Callum nodded, and so Telanthir entered.

"Still not used to you being a king," Saresan admitted. "And definitely not one who's over a hundred but looks so much younger. How does that work?"

"Very expensive medication, gene treatments and good, healthy living, my friend, though I've been doing a little less of the latter than I'd like the past week."

"Surprised you aren't demanding we use your proper titles."

"I am no king of yours, there is no need for such reverence."

"How did your talk go?" Callum asked then.

"I have a plan and the resources to make it happen. I'll need to locate a pilot willing to come with us that won't talk of our mission, but there are always people like that." Telanthir paused, frowning to himself. "Provided your demon associate has agreement from its council, whoever they are."

"I hope so. Thank you, by the way, for your kindness. I didn't expect it to be given so freely by anyone I met."

"Kindness is a gift so easy to give, yet rare to be given in this day and age. Every act of compassion makes the galaxy that little bit better," the king proclaimed verbatim. "My father taught me that, and his mother before him."

"People were hardly kind on our world, but Gui-Lon was a very impersonal place," Callum recalled.

"I've been to Gui-Lon a few times, and I'd like to say it's the only world like that, but it's not." Telanthir walked out onto the balcony himself then, glancing about the grounds before he spoke again, "Have you heard of Geladan, by any chance?"

"It was attacked by the Great Threat not long ago, Z-Gen went there to deal with it. I imagine it suffered a fate similar to our own world. Why do you ask?" Callum had an idea where this was going.

"The attacks from the Great Threat are infrequent and unpredictable, and I wager Z-Gen are good at eradicating what evidence remains of the demons." The king watched as a ship took off from a tall building, heading to the stars and beyond. "I know that the creatures don't leave bodies, but they aren't invisible to security cameras. Somewhere on that planet there must be evidence of the demons that we can recover."

"Won't Z-Gen be watching that world like a hawk?" Saresan asked. "We wouldn't get anywhere near it before we're noticed."

"But I can," the king told them. It was what Callum had been thinking he'd state.

"With your ship? Won't Z-Gen know you attacked the *Gorgon*?" To Callum's question, Telanthir simply smiled.

"We were very thorough in blocking Z-Gen's communications and hiding our identity, it's very unlikely they discerned who we were," the king told them with a knowing smile. "I will admit that this is not the first time I have searched for evidence. I made sure then that my efforts would not get Otros in trouble, and I can do so again. What's different this time is you and your friends. I didn't have access to those with magic in the past."

"Not many sorcerers on Otros, huh?" Saresan enquired.

"There might be one, perhaps two in the city. Whether they know of their gift is another thing, and even if they do, they'd be terrified of coming forward for fear of persecution. You are the first of your kind I have knowingly met, and there's three of you." The ship that had taken off had vanished from sight, the king looking back to the high-rise buildings around them. "I can arrange to meet with Fernisan, the president of Gerasal. It's in the same system as Geladan, and I have a few things I can discuss with him, to make it seem legitimate. While I'm there, your ship could travel to Geladan in secret and see what you can find, along with a few of the soldiers from my ship to assist you."

"I'm surprised people meet up in person. With all the wonders you have, surely it isn't needed." Callum was thinking on the way the *Gorgon* had communicated with their vessel, sending pictures and sound through the vast nothing of space instantly.

"Long-range communication is fine, but I think it takes away of the personal touches of diplomacy. Besides, Z-Gen cannot so easily monitor a conversation when you're in the same room as the one you speak with. Some even send robots to talk for them, a halfway house, as it were."

"We fought a metal monster Z-Gen were using, why aren't there more of them? It would save lives, surely."

"People have been suggesting it for centuries, but the arguments against it are always the same; they don't want to make an army of emotionless robots, which are stronger, faster and smarter than humans, that might go awry and start killing people. An irrational fear, mostly, but if AI didn't occasionally go haywire, they wouldn't have to put inhibitors in." Telanthir looked to see if they understood what he'd said, which Callum sort of did. The king continued, "Now imagine an army of them running with one hive mind, and then *that* goes wrong. Or worse, they are programmed to be the tools of a conqueror. You can see why they're not popular, even if human soldiers are far less efficient and cost-effective."

That Callum could do, the demons immediately coming to mind.

"You said you'd have some of your soldiers come with us, what will you tell them about the dangers we'll face?" The last thing Callum wanted was people blindly stumbling into the demons, subjected to horror without their consent.

"There are a few that I can trust with this information, mainly the ones that saw Tyrus already on the *Gorgon*." Telanthir paused in thought. "You still might get noticed on your way to Geladan, of course, but it's that much less likely with you already in the system."

"That's not much of a plan," Saresan said frankly. "A lot could go wrong."

"It's the best I can do, I'm afraid, and the longer we delay, the less likely there'll be anything for you to find."

"We've had worse, but last time it went belly up Tyrus bailed us out." At Saresan's mention of the demon saving them Telanthir looked troubled. "It was a surprise to us too."

"I wasn't aware that their kind was capable of restraint... or intelligence." Telanthir was choosing his words carefully, dancing around raw memories. "Seeing that demon has made me ask a lot of questions, none of which I have answers to."

"I'm not sure we can provide them either. Tyrus is..."

Callum trailed off, trying to think of nice things to say and coming up short. He resigned himself to saying what came to mind instead.

"Tyrus is Tyrus," Callum stated. "Focused to a painful degree on the goals it's been given above *all* else. I don't hesitate to think that it would lay down its life for me if it had to."

"I'm sorry, but I can't believe that to be true even if you do," Telanthir said then.

"I've seen first-hand the horrors that its kind can commit, but there are those among them that are more... human isn't the right word at all." Callum thought some more.

"Less monstrous?" Saresan suggested. "Say what you like about it or my lack of trust for it, it did save our lives. It wanted something from us, of course, but there you go. There are others like it, we mentioned one of them back at the table. That one is more of the 'kill everyone' kind of demon, just with magic."

Tyrus appeared out of nowhere, but this time Callum sensed it arrive. He didn't presume that was out of politeness, however, looking over with the expectation that it would be stood there exactly as it always was. Sure enough, Tyrus's garb and expression were unchanged from before, looking to Callum only. The king took longer to face it, trying not to meet its eyes right away.

"What did they say?" Callum waited apprehensively for the answer.

"There was much debate on us working with others," Tyrus stated, still ignoring Telanthir.

"Business as usual, then?" Saresan quipped.

"Did they make a decision?" Callum watched as Tyrus approached the king. Telanthir instinctively tried to step back but was already at the balcony's edge, staring up at the towering beast with bravery.

"There was disagreement, but ultimately they decided to take advantage of the resources you offer." That didn't sound right coming from Tyrus. "You will provide us with a ship, sufficient crew and anything thing else Callum requires."

"They were so against the idea of anything else but training until now. What's changed?" Callum needed to know, wanted to better understand his mentor.

"The wishes of the Council," it replied without explanation, speaking again to the king it loomed over. "You will provide what we need."

"That was always the intention, I assure you." Telanthir didn't smile, even though it was what he wanted. "I would offer to shake your hand to seal the deal, but I don't know if it's customary for your... kind."

"It is irrelevant, as are your words. Secure what we need."

"There's no need to be rude," Saresan objected.

"Time was wasted with frivolous festivities, time better spent training and seeking out evidence of the demons being the Great Threat."

Callum didn't try to reason with Tyrus; it was as wasted an effort as the feast, in its eyes at least. He took solace in the small concession Tyrus had forced upon the Council, something he doubted it took well but had to obey. It was an alliance of convenience for the demon and the Council both. The question Callum asked himself with worry was how long they would tolerate Telanthir before his usefulness ceased in their eyes, just as Daniel's had for Tyrus. He hoped it wouldn't come to that.

Chapter Forty

It was another day before Telanthir had everything sorted for their departure. Callum spent most of it trying to relax, but his mind kept returning to the task ahead of them and the enemies he was likely to face. Only at night was he able to clear his mind of the many worries that plagued it, staring at the stars in the sky. None of them were in the right place, but it was as soothing as always, allowing him to sort his thoughts.

He wasn't sure how ready they were, despite their training. He hadn't seen Telanthir during that time, his staff always informing him that he was busy on an important errand undisclosed to him, even though he knew its purpose.

Siobhan and Simon had managed to recover what possessions they had from Daniel's ship, who'd relocated them with just enough care that nothing was damaged into haphazard piles outside the airlock. They would be taken up to the ship ahead of them, all the better for a speedy departure in the morning.

The *Silverbolt* had been relocated by one of Telanthir's fighter pilots, carefully flown to a landing pad below ground level behind his palace. The grass apparently slid away to reveal a vertical shaft that led to the underground facility, allowing guests of the king to arrive at his home directly and keep their ship protected. Jinar told him that Siobhan had insisted on checking the ship over herself to make sure Daniel hadn't done anything, even though it'd been looked over by someone already.

Of Daniel there'd been little word; even though his ship was on a landing pad not far from the palace, the man himself was nowhere to be seen. Callum had been tempted to go find him but thought better of it; the last person Daniel wanted to see was him, no matter how much he worried.

Jinar had indeed changed his attire, though most of what he wore was still orange. His robe was shorter, ending just below his knees, and was not only tailored to fit his figure but also lacked a hood. The sleeves ended above his elbow, but he now wore a long-sleeved orange shirt underneath that ended at his wrists.

The front of his robes and the end of the sleeves had a star motif worked into the fabric and dark purple gems that lined the tail and cuffs. His trousers were black and smart, his shoes now laced and pointed at the ends, with the same dark purple gems running back from the tips upward. He'd made effort to have his hair and beard cut and styled while still sort of keeping them as they were. It was a stark contrast, positively formal compared to the humble robes he was previously clad in – the only thing humble about him, Callum reminded himself.

Once again Telanthir didn't join them on their journey back into space and to his ship, but Callum was certainly glad to have his blade returned to him at that point. Attaching the scabbard to his belt, he felt more complete than he should have. Callum took one last look around before he embarked the vessel in front of them, leaving the fresh air and warmth of sunlight for never-ending darkness.

"We'll be back," Alexis tried to reassure him, but it was little comfort, his mind whirring on all that could and likely would go wrong.

Nobody said anything on the journey up, Simon watching a small crate at his feet diligently. At first Callum thought it was coffee, but that smell came from a large flask he drank from. Upon their arrival in the hangar of Telanthir's ship, a young and keen green-eyed soldier was waiting for them. He was the only man in the cavernous room, making Callum wonder if Telanthir had arranged that so Tyrus's inevitable arrival didn't panic people. Standing the same height as Callum and clad in the purple armour of Telanthir's soldiers, his black hair was thick yet managed, and a rifle was holstered on his back.

"Welcome back to the *Janice*," the man said to them. "I'm sergeant Wilkinson Peters, the commander of the soldiers on board. Since you're going to be here for a while, I thought it was best we had an introduction."

"It's nice to meet you, Wilkinson." Callum smiled as he spoke, trying to start their friendship on a good footing.

"Everyone calls me Will." Saresan was helping Simon carry the crate off the vessel, the last two to disembark. The pilot started his preparations to return back to Otros. "Your demon has already arrived, damn near scared my security team half to death. We've assigned it quarters far from the heavily populated areas of the vessel. I hope it'll keep out of sight for the most part, but from what I've been told, we might not be so lucky."

"It does what it wants, to hell with anyone else," Saresan muttered as he carefully lowered the crate to the ground. "What's even *in* here, Simon?"

"My tools and workbench," Simon answered with a shrug.

"Not medicines?"

"This ship will have plenty of them."

Will looked to the doctor at that.

"I've had time to look over your credentials. You're by far the most qualified medical practitioner we have on board, not to mention a competent engineer."

"I don't feel it," Simon grumbled. "Where am I putting all this?"

"Leave it there, we'll have someone bring it up later. Let me bring up the floor plan so you can pick your rooms." Will walked to a large metal box and picked up a metal pad that had been discarded.

A few presses later and he stood before them with the layout of the ship's rooms displayed in a projection that highlighted the location that Callum guessed they were in. A few other locations flashed up then in yellow. "I've taken the liberty of assigning you quarters by the bridge, Callum, just in case we need your presence." One room at the top briefly flashed.

"I don't mind where I am, but I don't see why you'd need me there. I don't know how ships function." Callum was already second-guessing that it was Telanthir's idea.

"Telanthir is the captain of the ship, of course, any major decision will be made by him. He suggested that you be available at short notice just in case a topic that you specialise in comes up."

"You are talking about the demons, yes?" Alexis asked. Will nodded. "What has Telanthir told you?"

"Telanthir entrusts me with everything, that was no exception."

"And you believe him, I take it." Alexis got another nod.

"Telanthir is my liege, but he's also my friend. He's not lied to me before, so I had no reason to doubt him then. Now that I have seen your demon with my own eyes, I have even less."

"That thing is no friend of ours," Saresan muttered.

"You don't know how much hope you've given my liege: a confidence I hope you don't break." Will watched each of them in turn for signs of falsehood.

"Would that we could tell you that all we have experienced is a façade." Jinar was examining the projection. "With so many choices, I do wonder—"

"I'll have that one." Siobhan pointed to a room seemingly at random. Will glanced at her choice.

"If you wish," Will answered. With a tap, the room greyed out.

"There." Simon indicated to a place far away from the middle of the ship, close to the rear and to where Tyrus was apparently housed. "And get a coffee machine in there, would you?" Will cast a curious look at the doctor.

"It's not worth seeing him fed up, trust me," Siobhan warned.

"I don't care where you put me, a room's a room." Saresan shrugged. Alexis was pondering the choices before her, but Jinar needed no such time.

"There will be optimal," Jinar announced, answering the question that didn't come. "That way I will be equally accessible to almost everyone, should they require my vast knowledge, tutelage or someone to speak to on a quiet evening." The sorcerer gave Siobhan a look, prompting a frown in retort.

"Sod that, I want a drink. There any good bars, Will?" She got a quiet chuckle from the sergeant.

"There's the one most of the soldiers go to, you'd be welcome there, and far as I know, your drinks are on Telanthir." Siobhan lit up with excitement.

"You should've *started* with that! Who's with me?" Siobhan headed towards the exit without another word. Saresan shrugged and followed.

"Maybe we'll catch you there later," he said to Callum as he left. Jinar looked again at the map.

"Where is this place they are headed?" Jinar enquired of Will. As the Sergeant pointed, the sorcerer muttered a few words and, with some hand gestures, teleported away. This came as a surprise only to Will, who looked around for Jinar quickly.

"Magic. You'll get used to it." Simon was looking over the crate again while taking another drink from his flask.

"Telanthir said some of you were capable, but I've never seen it before," the sergeant told them honestly.

"You'll be seeing a lot more of it with Jinar around, trust me." Simon stepped away from the box. "I'll find my room later; I've got to deal with something."

Callum knew exactly what that meant as the doctor left them. Only Alexis remained alongside him now. She hadn't yet decided, or had that already been sorted before their arrival?

"I'll show you to your room, Callum," Will told him, indicating for him to follow.

Winding through corridors and pathways that Will seemed to know like the back of his hand, they stopped in front of a large lift that opened upon their arrival in front of it. They weren't alone in it, a couple of crewmembers already inside, focused on their own work. Like the other lifts on the ship Callum had been on, it was spacious and clean, pleasant music playing as they went up. There was even a machine that filled cups with beverages built into the wall.

"This is the main elevator. It can access most floors, and there are signs all over for it. If you get lost, someone will happily point you to where you want to go," Will told them. "You and your friends have been given clearance for the officer elevators as well. They're positioned so you can reach critical locations on board in the fastest possible time. Well, when you're not using magic to get everywhere."

"Jinar and Tyrus are the only ones who do that regularly," Alexis told him.

"How many people does this ship have? A hundred?" Callum asked.

"The normal crew complement is roughly eight hundred active crew and a security detail of eighty soldiers." That amount baffled Callum; that was a small town floating through space, how did it function? "Right now, we're running a little thin on the ground, so there's only four hundred crew."

"Are there always that many soldiers?" The lift stopped as Alexis asked that question, it clearing of everyone barring them.

"They pilot the squadron of fighters, as well as some land combat vehicles. They also act as the security team on board. With the Great Threat around, you can't be too careful." A downward arrow appeared on a screen next to Will. He waved his gloved hand over a panel beside it, and the arrow changed to one pointing up. When it opened up again, Callum was presented with a corridor with two doors on each side and a large set of double doors at the end. "You'll be using the smaller lift to the right of this one most of the time, the crew elevator is slower."

"Is the bridge ahead?" Alexis got a nod.

"Telanthir's quarters are the first door on the right, mine is the second." Will pointed to the door closest to the bridge and on the left. "That one's yours, Callum, and that one next to it is yours, Alexis." Had she picked that out of all the choices, or was that where Will had chosen?

"Thank you." She smiled. "Where will you be if we need you?"

"If I'm not on the bridge or training in the firing range, I'll be in my quarters. If you ever need anything, there's a panel by the door where you can summon someone who'll try to help you. If it's more serious, don't hesitate to find me."

"We will, thank you," Alexis replied. Will excused himself with a nod, heading back down the lift after she and Callum had stepped out.

"I didn't know your room would be next to mine." Callum tried to make it not sound like an enquiry but failed.

"Is that a problem?" In her voice was a hint of concern.

"Why would it be?" he asked back, approaching the room that was his.

It didn't open when he got close, nor was there a handle he needed to turn. He quickly found a panel with words above it on a plaque that he couldn't read. Pressing it caused the door to open. Weeks ago, he wouldn't have thought to even try that.

"Identification confirmed. Welcome, Callum Igannes," a stilted male voice declared.

"After you," he said to Alexis.

"Thank you." She stepped inside and stopped right past the door. "... Wow."

Following her in after she stepped aside, he too was surprised. It was twice the size of the room in Telanthir's palace, with walls half of panelled wood, half painted white. The floor was covered in a dark blue carpet that looked expensive and soft. The bed was a four-poster similar to the one in the palace but even more expensive looking. The wall opposite had a large viewscreen, and facing it was a long red chair, cushioned and comfortable looking. By the door was a series of counters and appliances that he recognised as being used in cooking, as well as cupboards above them. Another open door by them led to the shower room.

Crossing the room to check out the final door on the other side, he found that it was a large wardrobe of sorts, with the suit he'd worn to Telanthir's banquet hanging from a metal bar, suspended in the air by a wire contraption it was draped over. He would never have enough clothes to fill that up, and he wondered if anyone that wasn't a king would either. Alexis had moved to the bed to touch the mattress, feeling it spring back up quickly as she pressed down.

"This room is far too big for just me." Callum looked to the wall opposite the entrance to see a panel beside it. Callum pressed it, almost all the wall fading away to become a massive window, revealing the stars in all their beauty. "I've got nothing to fill it with, and even if I did, we won't be on it too long."

"That may change in time. A lot of things already have." She was sat on the edge of the bed, looking around to the surroundings he'd have to get used to. It was opulence that he didn't deserve. "You're still worrying though."

"I am." He sighed, staring out into space with his arms folded.

"You're poor at hiding it. The Council picked you for a reason, Callum."

"I still don't know what they saw in me though, if I can do this." He didn't know what she saw in him either; she had such faith in his ability, trusted him despite the many times that trust had caused her hurt.

"And yet the Council chose you." Alexis stood up and walked to stand beside him, gaze at what he was. "You doubt yourself too much, Callum. We can only do what we can, no more."

"Tyrus expects far more than that, everyone does." He checked behind him just in case the demon had been summoned by his thinking of it, but they were still alone.

"Considering where we began on this road, I'd say that we've done remarkably well. You should too." She patted his shoulder, it soothing his concerns a tiny bit. She turned back to the room and focused on beneath the bed, stepping over and looking underframe.

"Is something wrong?" Callum asked.

He spotted it then, the glint of metal from something wrapped in black fabric that she was pulling out carefully. Stepping up, he saw a note pinned to it, which he removed and looked at. Focusing on each individual word, he tried to read what was there.

"I... hope... this..." He narrowed his eyes, Alexis watching as he put her teaching into practice. "...Halps...?"

"Helps," she corrected with a smile.

"Helps." He nodded, continuing slowly, "...In your... your..." The next word was long and complicated, defeating him more soundly than any demon could. He offered the note to her, which she accepted. "I'm sorry."

"Why? You did well to reach that far," she told him as she skimmed the text. "I hope this helps in your efforts to uncover the truth. It should complement your weapon of choice nicely. Telanthir."

Callum removed the fabric and was stunned at what was underneath. It was a hauberk of scale, glistening and without blemish. Its sleeves were long, and the metal plates were secured to a fabric inlay to prevent chafing. Underneath it was a yellow cloak, long enough to flow down to his ankles. He marvelled at how something so simple as a piece of armour could be so beautiful, so masterfully crafted. What surprised him more was that the only thing which made it look unlike armour from his home was how shiny it was.

"Telanthir had this made for me?" Callum couldn't believe it. Alexis picked up the hauberk, expecting it to be heavy but lifting it with ease.

"It's exceptionally light and, I'll wager, stronger than any steel from our world." She looked over the armour, then him. "You should try it on."

He took the hauberk when it was offered. It was no heavier than his shirt, but the metal was real; he couldn't quite figure out how that worked. It made slipping it on over his clothing a simple matter, amazing him more when he found that it was a perfect fit.

Alexis took the cloak and stood behind him to fasten the simple metal clasp around his neck. It sat on his shoulders comfortably, as did the armour, and it was by far the most expensive thing he'd ever owned. He marvelled at it as Alexis looked him over once more.

"It suits you, Callum."

Spying a mirror by the wardrobe, he walked to it and examined himself fully. Dressed like he was, he almost looked like a different person. Was this the Callum Igannes that only a few months ago was struggling to save money for the winter months? He almost didn't recognise his own face for a second, the look in his eyes. The Callum he'd known was gone and was never coming back. He should've felt pride, but instead sadness welled up. Alexis stood behind and a little to his right, looking over his shoulder at the reflection.

"If Azure could see you now, he'd've been quite angry." Alexis gently laughed to herself. "He'd say something about you 'desecrating the traditions of knightly regalia with your common shoulders'." He didn't miss the knight's indignant fury, but remembering the man still made him melancholy. "I wonder what he would have thought of all this."

"It's probably best he never saw it, what society has become," Callum replied.

"He certainly wouldn't have liked the weapons of war, I agree." She looked from the mirror back to space. "To kill a proud knight with a single beam of red light would have been unthinkable to him. He would've been dead before he could draw his sword..."

He pushed the thought aside, stepping away from the mirror and considering what they were setting off to do. Perhaps all they'd achieve was their death. He found that Alexis was looking at him then with a warm expression, their eyes meeting. She was just as they had been when they first met, but he knew she'd experienced as much as him, if not more. She eventually broke the connection, but as she looked back to the stars there was a moment of nervousness.

"Let's hope I can act the part," he remarked quietly.

"I think you'll do fine just being yourself."

The stars began to move, their journey beginning just as Callum felt a presence behind him he wished wasn't familiar. Sure enough, Tyrus was but a few paces away, watching in silence. This time he was glad the demon was there, however; he had questions that needed answers but doubted Tyrus would provide them.

"How much disagreement was there among the Council about working with Telanthir?" Callum asked, turning to face it. Alexis did the same.

"Much, initially. In time, only the Second objected," it answered simply.

"Such consensus sounds like a rare thing." Alexis got no answer. "But is the Council's vision so inward that they hadn't seen evidence of this before?"

The silence continued.

"Will they be assisting us with more resources of their own? Perhaps Baylon could join us on Geladan," Callum asked.

"To offer more would imperil our own safeguards and theirs." Tyrus ignored the view of space, looking only to its pupil. "If the Great Threat is the demons, if they remained on Geladan, you will be noticed."

"We might face Xiez," Alexis mused.

"Or Keiran," Callum added.

"You are not strong enough to defeat them. If they are there, you will retreat, no matter the cost." Callum knew exactly what the demon meant by that. "The Council were unhappy with the progress of your training."

"Why? I've been working hard. What do they expect from me?" Callum wondered how they knew that, unless Tyrus had told them and deemed it insufficient itself. "I'm stronger than I was before."

"The Council expects training at the expense of all other pursuits," Tyrus told them.

"I don't think they quite understand how different we are from your kind," Alexis remarked, finally getting the demon's attention.

"In almost all ways you are inferior." She folded her arms.

"I don't think so. Most of the demons we've met are near-mindless beasts."

"They are not our kind," Tyrus snapped.

"But they are, just lost to the same anger that exists in you, Baylon and the Council. The only thing that separates you from them is control, and that's something we don't suffer from." Tyrus snarled silently, but Alexis continued without fear, "You claim the demons are superior, yet if they were, they wouldn't be cocooned from the galaxy, hiding away."

"Keiran seeks our destruction over yours. Without the enclave, you would also be found and killed," Tyrus answered. "Eliminating Callum remains one of their high priorities, but we are an even higher one."

"They can't be afraid of me. The sword, maybe, but not me." Callum looked once more at the blade.

"You have potential yet untapped, which Keiran wishes to destroy."

"We all do," Callum corrected his mentor.

"You are my primary focus."

"I used to be your only focus," Callum reminded it. Tyrus narrowed its eyes at him. "The sooner you accept that we're a team, the stronger we'll be together."

"You are stronger alone." Tyrus refused to yield, as he expected.

"That doesn't make any sense," he objected.

"The connections you forge with your companions will be used against you. Daniel was weakened by his, you will be by yours." Alexis stepped towards the demon then, staring up to its eyes, which it cast down upon her dismissively.

"What you call weakness is one of our greatest strengths," she said with certainty.

"Implausible," it sneered.

"Your kind can't feel what we do, how can you say what makes us strong? If we hadn't been together on our world, we'd've died before you could've saved us. It's the people we know and care for that are the reason we fight, to protect them from harm." Alexis glanced back to Callum. "I'd give my life to save Callum, and I know he'd do the same for me." He nodded without hesitation.

"His life is more important than yours," Tyrus told her.

"No, it isn't," Callum spoke up then, wanting so desperately for Tyrus to understand. "It doesn't matter if I'm stronger than her or have the sword. You let Monica die to save me, but that didn't make her any less important to Daniel or anyone on board. If you told me to let a hundred people die to kill a thousand thousand demons, I wouldn't do it."

"Why?"

"Why?" Callum could hardly believe the question. "Because it's wrong!"

"It is an acceptable exchange," it corrected bluntly.

"No, it isn't!" He was nearly shouting. That didn't surprise Tyrus. "What good is any victory if the path to it is littered with corpses?"

"Your world died. Many more worlds will die. You cannot stop this," Tyrus warned him.

"Watch me try," he swore.

Tyrus observed him and stared at his right hand, Callum following its eyes to see that he'd instinctively reached for his sword handle. Had he expected an attack, or was his conviction so strong that he was willing to fight for it there and then? How had he come to this, debating the very task he'd struggled with accepting only weeks before? When had he changed?

"If this isn't what the Council wanted, why pick me?"

"I cannot speak for the Council's decision. Initially, I believed they had chosen in error."

"And now?" Alexis stepped back to stand beside him.

The demon looked at her, then him and then back to her.

"You are weak and flawed, unprepared for the conflict that is to come."

"At least we can change. You can't," she said back to it. Tyrus paused.

"I... do not *need* to change." The hesitation was something Alexis latched on to.

"Why not?" The pause persisted. Callum watched Tyrus as it considered, a rare moment for the demon. "We know nothing of your kind, but you know even less about us. A little more empathy would go a long way to making you a better teacher."

"Impossible."

"Then whatever's closest. Just..." She sighed. "Just try and put yourself in our shoes for just a moment. Just one moment." Callum thought the demon was going to snap at them, but instead it just stared. After a few awkward moments it vanished, leaving Callum to wonder if any of what they'd said had sunk in.

"Tyrus was right about one thing," Callum eventually conceded, "we do need to do some training. Perhaps Telanthir has a place in mind for us to use." For the first time in a while, Callum didn't feel like Tyrus was watching him. Whether that was true he didn't want to check.

Chapter Forty-One

"I can assure you, Z-Gen have conducted a thorough search of the area where the incident occurred, and they have confirmed with near-absolute certainty that the criminals were working alone. Furthermore, there's no evidence that they have remained in the system.

"I have been in conversation with General Cadmus himself about the matter. He has promised me that the ones responsible for the disturbance will be captured and brought to justice. Furthermore, he has promised more soldiers patrolling our streets to ensure that such an unfortunate incident never occurs again. The safety of our citizens is my and Z-Gen's utmost priority, and we'll be working even more closely in the future."

—Statement from the Interim Chief Speaker of Gui-Lon

Daniel had rerouted most of the controls of the *Winter's Mourning* to the panels on his bridge chair and set up a few makeshift displays to its sides that showed the engine and general ship diagnostics. He hadn't yet figured out how to control the turret from there, nor was he sure if any of the functions he'd set up would work for long, but he wasn't thinking on the long-term; he wanted to get as far from Otros as his ship would allow, away from Callum.

Thinking of the man alone would've provoked anger if his head hadn't been pounding from a terrible hangover and lack of sleep. Every night had been the same, restlessly tossing and turning in bed as memories of Monica rushed through his mind, all stained with loss. His military training had taught him about the brutalities of war, but nothing had prepared him for the shattering pain of her death.

Everyone had lamented the tragedy, but it had been no accident; the demon had murdered her, snuffed her life in exchange for the weapon of its charge. A blade had been worth more than her, and it sickened him more the longer he thought about it. Her death was on endless repeat at the back of his head, try as he might to shut it out. He reached for the bottle by his chair as the automated take-off procedure began, only to find that he'd drunk the last of the cheapest gin he could find on Otros. He was sure the bottle had been bigger than that, but it was empty.

The security forces of Otros had been watching him, tried to pry on his destination, but he hadn't one to give them; he'd sold all his cargo for a tidy profit and sought things to buy, but the world had no impressive goods for him to trade, not that he'd be able to sell any of it anyway. Evading the security forces had simply been a matter of waiting for the right opportunity, and once he was up in the air, it hadn't taken long to exit the tiny bubble of Otros space. Out there was a galaxy of opportunity, even for someone wanted for a list of crimes so long that he'd be locked up forever were he captured.

He knew a man who knew someone that could make people effectively disappear for enough money, build him a new identity that would defeat Z-Gen's intense scrutiny. All he had to do was get there, and with enough care he could manage it. He slouched deeply into his chair as the autopilot continued to guide his vessel through space to the colleague whose friend's services he never thought he'd require.

Sleep took him forcefully, but it was plagued with horrors and grief that he couldn't forget even when a communication roused him. Too drowsy to stop it, he found himself looking at a Z-Gen corporal in full military attire and a green cloak through the bridge's viewscreen and only somewhat caring; if they were going to blow his ship up, at least they'd do it quickly.

"Hello, Daniel." The soldier spoke almost conversationally, expression hidden under his helmet. "You don't know me, but I know a lot about you."

"So what?" Daniel was far past politeness, but the corporal didn't appear offended. His bridge crew continued working diligently on their tasks, as if their conversation didn't matter. Perhaps it didn't.

"My name is Corporal Mateo, but I doubt that's important to you," the soldier told him. There was a pause. "I'm sorry for your loss."

"Fuck you," Daniel spat, trying to terminate the communication on his end. It failed. This man didn't care about Monica, nobody did apart from him. How did he even know about all that? He expected a barrage of laser fire tearing through the bridge, but nothing happened. Anger quickly bled into frustration. "Well, what are you waiting for?"

"I'm sorry, I don't quite follow." Daniel didn't buy that for a second. "You're here to kill me, so do it."

"It's perfectly within my power to kill you, yes, but my orders are to apprehend you for my commander so you can be questioned," Mateo answered him calmly.

"So do it, I don't care." More than anything, Daniel just wanted to go back to sleep, even with the nightmares that would come with it.

"Again, I could. Your ship is no match for mine, but I like to think of myself as a pragmatic man. Killing you would do neither of us any favours, and handing you over to the commander..." Mateo paused. "It would be more merciful to kill you, I can assure you. You're fortunate that it was *me* who found you, others would be less inclined to negotiate." Daniel managed a curious look. He must've heard that wrong.

"...The hell do I have that you want to know?" Daniel sat up a little straighter.

"I know full well the 'cargo' that you've been transporting of late, the entire galaxy does. You consorted with numerous tainted, assisting in their escape from Gui-Lon. A concerned member of the public informed us of your present location, and so here I am. I presume that you have off-loaded your 'cargo' at some point since you somehow managed to cripple the *Gorgon*." Daniel's head was pounding again; he rubbed it with his right hand as the corporal continued, "You don't need to answer that. Captain Collette briefed the commander on the methods of those tainted, and I created an opportunity to 'peruse' the document. It told me everything, including your... special passenger."

There was only one person that Mateo could be talking about, and thinking about the monster made Daniel angry.

"...Get to the point," he muttered through gritted teeth.

"Very well, I shall be blunt. I want you to tell me everything you know about those tainted, including where you last saw them. I want to know what they're capable of, what makes them tick and how I can destroy them. Do this for me, and I'll see to it that your criminal record is erased in its entirety." That made Daniel start to pay full attention. "You were, of course, forced to work for them on pain of death, a captive that diligently assisted Z-Gen in their apprehension at the first opportunity. After all, they are dangerous agents of the Great Threat, while you are not. Their crimes were wrongly attributed to you, and so you will be pardoned and rewarded handsomely for your duties in protecting the galaxy. That is how it can be if you wish it. The galaxy will never hear of this meeting, or what really happened. All you need to do is talk. It's that simple."

It all sounded too good to be true, and that made him hesitate despite himself.

"...How can I trust you?" Daniel had to ask.

"It's fairer to ask how I can trust *you*, Daniel. You may not think it, but negotiating with you comes at considerable risk for me. Should your information be false, they might evade capture and continue their agenda, which no one in Z-Gen would like."

"And what's in it for you, a promotion? Two?" Daniel didn't expect him to openly admit his ambition before his crew.

"We can dispense with the pleasantries, and I can take you in for questioning if you would prefer that. As I said, the commander—"

"You think you can scare me with threats? Your commander can't do worse than they did to me." Daniel managed to stand shakily, resting one hand on the arm of his chair for support.

Questions had started to surface, and he didn't care less if he offended Mateo by asking them. "What do you lot know about the demons anyway?"

Mateo looked to his left to someone out of view, then back to Daniel.

"Does that matter to you, Daniel? I'm offering you a second chance: all you need do is accept it. You can start by telling me where you last saw them and what they intend to do." Mateo was being far more patient with him than he'd ever expected, and despite everything, that irked Daniel. He hated Callum and what had happened because of him, despised his former crewmates for forgiving him so quickly, but this... this didn't feel right.

"What will you do with them once you've got them?" Daniel did and didn't want to know, but he was too curious.

"We will follow standard procedures." That revealed nothing but set his mind whirring on the horrible possibilities.

"And what happens after they're captured? What will I need to do then?" Daniel asked. His eyes were only on the corporal, the empty gin bottle forgotten even if his aching head tried to remind him.

"Your silence on what you may have heard among the tainted is a given, after you have divulged it in full to us," Mateo answered.

"And then what?"

"Nothing." Daniel shook his head.

"I don't believe you, why should I? Everything here is loaded in your favour. I could tell you everything, and then you still lock me up or try and get more that I don't have." Daniel thought, and yet more questions surfaced with difficulty. "How did you find me so quickly, anyway? The galaxy is huge."

"We are Z-Gen, our reach is limitless," Mateo told him.

"Even in places you can't go? Even Otros, the Terran Empire?" Daniel moved back to his chair, the anger ebbing away and replaced with rekindled suspicion and something that nagged at him, a revelation unrealised and foggy, "Why would you need such reach?"

"We protect from threats without *and* within, Daniel, the better to ensure the galaxy is safe, and while you are asking these questions, the very threat that I'm seeking is getting further and further away from me. I'd like to think that you're just being thorough and not distracting me so that they can escape, because if you were" — Mateo looked directly to him — "if you were, it would not end well for you."

"Why the fuck would I do that? I hate them!" Daniel retorted.

"Do you? It doesn't sound like you hate them to me."

How dare he say that, dismiss his suffering and loss like it was nothing! They'd destroyed his life, he had every reason to hate them, and he did, didn't he? He had to, even though... He paused. He sought out the rage within him and couldn't find it anymore; instead, there was self-loathing and anger, not at Callum and the others but only Tyrus, the one who'd killed Monica. His crew hadn't turned on him like he'd convinced himself, brandishing no daggers behind their backs to off him.

They'd been making the best of a bad situation, one that had started back on Gui-Lon. He hadn't been there when it all went wrong, but one thing was clear to him now that hadn't been before: Callum and the others could have easily escaped by themselves, abandoning Siobhan and Monica to their fates if they'd wished it, but they hadn't. In their confrontation by the ship, the only one who'd been a threat was himself, ready to cast off even Monica to save his own skin.

He'd been about to do what Tyrus did so effortlessly, and he was doing it again right now, mere words away from selling them out for a handful of silver. How had Monica felt when he turned on her so quickly? He hadn't even asked, but they'd argued about it. If he hadn't taken the demon's offer, none of this would've happened; Monica would still be alive, he wouldn't be wanted by Z-Gen, and Callum... who cared what happened to him and his friends?

So, the demon said he was essential to defeating some horrible threat, most likely a lie, fabricated so he would serve them in their dark deeds. Z-Gen would be able to deal with whatever threat this 'Keiran' posed... or could they?

"If I'm going to do this, I want all my crew pardoned as well. They're still with them, but they're as innocent as I am." Was he innocent at all? Mateo sighed quietly.

"If we are able to apprehend the tainted without them being casualties, I will see what I can do. I can only guarantee your safety, of course, since you are apart from them."

The thought of Siobhan and Simon killed in a hail of laser fire stuck in his head and wouldn't shift. That would be their fate if he told Mateo what he wanted to know, he was sure of it. They were supportive of Callum and his goals, and even if Daniel thought it was ludicrous, he was the only one. What did that say about him, the only person who'd seen the call to action and turned his tail and fled? Monica wouldn't have fled: he knew that in his heart, even though she hated Tyrus as much as he did. "I am a patient man, Daniel, but even my patience has limits. Will you tell me what I need to know or not?"

Will eventually found Callum and Alexis a location to train their magic, a large empty room used to transport sensitive cargo. The walls were shielded and strengthened to protect the crew from any radiation or other effects certain materials had, but he assured Callum and Alexis that the place was safe and that nobody would disturb their training sessions.

The first they conducted together, practising their spells and, more importantly, how to dodge each other's attacks. Alexis was better at dodging his spells – harmless balls of energy that looked like fire and lightning, the better to not hurt one another – but she didn't have the reserves he possessed, needing to recuperate more often than him. Her daggers were no match for his sword – he never hit her weapons with his out of fear of breaking them – but still, they practised sparring as best they could. Callum also had shorter training sessions with Saresan, the guard agreeing to it 'to keep his wits about him', as he put it. His weapon looked a little different now, made of a shinier metal and with three buttons in the middle of the shaft.

"Simon came up with it, don't ask me where he found time to make it. My bet is he doesn't sleep." Saresan had pressed the first button and the weapon collapsed in on itself, folding neatly and quickly into the part he held until it was little more than a short rod. Callum had watched in amazement, his friend chuckling. "That was my reaction too." Pressing the button again reformed the weapon.

"That's really impressive. What else can it do?"

Callum had got a grin when he asked, watching as his friend pressed the second button. He'd expected something extraordinary, but nothing seemed to happen save the edge of the halberd's blade glowing a soft orange.

"He called it 'laser edging'. Long story short, this thing cuts through armour just like those beams do, but that's not all." Saresan had lowered the weapon till the point on top of the axe head was aimed horizontally. Pressing the third button caused Callum to almost jump when one of the red beams shot out of the tip and hit the opposite wall. "Don't think I'll be using that too much, I'm not good with it."

"You'll definitely catch people off guard with that," Callum told him. "Can it resist my blade?"

"Not a chance, so I'd appreciate it if you stuck to the sparring poles over there."

Callum didn't feel like he was improving in those training sessions, Saresan often overcoming his guard and easily resisting his own attacks, but apparently, he was far better than at the start, or so Saresan told him. He'd have a lot of time to practice, as Geladan was three weeks' travel from Otros.

It didn't take him long to locate the drinking establishment Jinar and Siobhan frequented along with the soldiers on board. Small and out of the way, it wasn't dark and full of loud, overpowering music like the place on Gui-Lon, despite it having similar beats which he didn't like.

The first time he'd found it, Siobhan and Jinar were the only occupants besides the bartender, the sorcerer's drink orange at the top and green on the bottom that he drunk from a straw. There was also ice and a tiny parasol, the purpose of which was lost on Callum. Siobhan's drink he recognised, spirits in a short glass. They'd been talking at his arrival, and though he couldn't deduce the topic, the two were comfortable and relaxed.

"Hey, stranger!" Siobhan shouted, motioning for him to approach. He did as Jinar eyed his new armour. "What you having?"

"Do they serve ale?" Callum asked as he sat down on the barstool next to her. The barkeep looked back to his selection and shook his head.

"Sorry. I've got some import beer if you like, Peruukian stuff. Got a hard edge to it," the man told him.

"That will do, thank you."

"Impressive workmanship, that hauberk. The smith did a fine job with that." Jinar was assessing the scales as Callum got comfortable.

"It was a gift from Telanthir. I'm surprised it's so in keeping with what I'm used to." The drink Callum received was in a tall, thin glass, black as night and bereft of a head.

"With your sword and our attire, it was likely not difficult to guess what we are used to." Jinar sipped on his drink, sighing with refreshment.

Callum tried his own and found that its taste was very bitter and with a lemon-like zest he didn't like at all. The barkeep noticed his involuntary grimace and offered to take the drink from him, which he gladly agreed to.

"Not my kind of thing either, but some of the crew like it. Can I get you anything else?" the barkeep offered.

"How clean is the water?" Callum got a funny look.

"Clean as any other on board, why?"

"I'll have some of that, please." It didn't take long before the glass was ready for him, crisp and cold.

"It is normally far busier than this, or so I am told," Jinar stated. "Sometimes Wilkinson is here, but I admit to not frequenting this establishment for long periods, unlike someone I know." Jinar gave Siobhan a knowing glance.

"And you don't come here for free drinks?" Siobhan scoffed, downing her glass with ease. "It's just coincidence that we're always here at the same time."

"That, or you enjoy our conversations enough to wait for me here." Jinar got a look which spoke otherwise. "I need not press the point when I know I am right."

"Has anyone told you you're delusional?" she asked him.

"Only moments before I prove them wrong with my staggering arcane power, why do you ask?"

The pilot rolled her eyes as Callum tried the water and found it just fine.

"Think I'm going to need a double this time," she told the barkeep, who nodded and reached for the bottle behind him. Jinar smiled at the spectacle.

"You might as well request the bottle for yourself. You could take it back to your vessel and partake while you make your... what did you call it? 'Twigging'?"

"Tweaking," she corrected, taking the refilled glass and drinking some more. "And no, you're not watching."

"Is it so bad to—"

"You touch the *Silverbolt* and you'll regret it," she warned.

"That sounds like a challenge."

"You don't want to call my bluff here, it ain't worth it." She finished her drink. Jinar simply smiled back, which provoked a frown. "You're weird."

"Says the lady with the peculiar hat," Jinar countered. Something about that made her stare with annoyance while straightening the topic of conversation.

"Nothing wrong with my hat." His smile persisted, and try as she might, Siobhan couldn't help but let a faint one slip on her lips as she looked away to her now empty drink.

Chapter Forty-Two

Gerasal shared far more in common with Gui-Lon than Otros, or so the images Callum found through his metal tablet had shown. Gloomy and lacking untouched beauty, tall buildings were prevalent in the sprawling settlements, which were in almost every image. The only thing more prevalent were the tell-tale signs of decay that most structures had, noticeable if you looked carefully; some buildings had been left abandoned, and the skies weren't as busy with vehicles as Otros had been. The streets were as crowded as Gui-Lon but lacked the suspended walkways, with everyone crammed in at ground level where the pathways were cracked and hole-ridden.

The numbers on the screen meant little to him as the tablet rattled them off, though the planet did sound heavily populated and only half the population were employed. He wondered how that was possible with all the wonders of the galaxy; surely, they needed people overseeing them for them to continue functioning. Perhaps the images were out of date, showing the aftermath of a conflict, before the great labour of repairing the damage began. With three weeks before their arrival, he had plenty of time to consider it as his routine of magical training and sparring continued.

Efforts to hone his skills with rifles proved ineffective, his accuracy and reaction times too bad when he had to fire in an instant. His magic didn't have such problems though, which Tyrus explained to be due to those energies being the implementation of his thoughts that were far more accurate and exact than any 'weapon wrought by humanity'. Alexis's magic was progressing well also, along with her teachings of words to him, Callum gaining more momentum as he used what words he'd already learned to help him work out more.

Word on the fate of Geladan was non-existent, the news channels instead focusing on far more mundane things, acting as if the world had disappeared off the face of the galaxy. Was that Z-Gen's work, or had no new news of importance surfaced?

Two weeks into their journey, Will introduced Callum to the pilot that was to take them to Geladan. Docked in the hangar, her ship was far smaller than Daniel's and entirely black in colour. The pilot was over half a foot shorter than him, with dark green eyes and messy hair, muddy blonde with streaks of black in it. The black couldn't have been natural, likely some kind of dye made from a wondrous substance.

She was older than him but still young, wearing a dark yellow padded jacket, sleeveless and with a metal fastening running down the front. Her arms bare, beneath the jacket was an unremarkable white shirt. Tucked into the collar of her shirt were silver reflective glasses, larger than the reading ones he'd seen some scholars wear. Her brown trousers had a large external pocket sewed into the right thigh, a pistol secured within. Her shoes were comfortable looking, designed to be slipped on effortlessly.

"Name's Luna." She offered a hand to shake along with a polite smile, which Callum took. "The sergeant filled me on what I need to know."

"Everything?" Callum double-checked.

"Enough for me to have her along." Luna motioned to her left, drawing Callum's attention to the figure some distance behind her.

The same height as Luna, her curly violet hair caught Callum's attention first, tied up in a ponytail at the back which ran to the base of her neck. Her body was athletic and barely concealed by her attire, a single dark grey suit that went from neck to foot. Heavy-duty boots and gloves of the same colour were the only other clothing she wore, examining a helmet that looked exactly like a Z-Gen one, only an even darker grey than her clothing. It also had a blue beam on the face of it rather than red. He spotted the rest of her armour not far away. It also looked like the equipment Z-Gen used, but there was no cloak. Because of her equipment, his initial feelings were ones of distrust, though he tried to shake them.

"Is she Z-Gen?" Callum asked carefully.

"Formerly Z-Gen. Drummed out two years ago, don't know why and I didn't ask," Will answered. The soldier ignored the conversation, checking a large pistol carefully. "When I mentioned the job would go to Geladan to the people I thought would be interested, she was the only one that stuck around to hear the offer."

"It didn't scare you off too?" Callum asked Luna.

"All I'm doing is getting you there, back and being paid a lot of money to do it. Xene's insurance just in case Z-Gen finds us, but they won't manage that in space." Luna looked back to her vessel. "The *Star's Shadow* hasn't been scanned by them yet, this time won't be any different."

"Have you been in trouble with them before?" Callum got a shrug from the pilot. Xene was now looking at Callum. She was unimpressed with what she saw.

"Does it matter?" came Luna's reply. "I don't ask too many questions, it's why I'm good at what I do. You just tell me when you want to go."

"We will," Will said to her. Luna turned to her ship and boarded it without another word. Will motioned for Callum to follow and he did, stepping away as Xene continued to watch them.

"I haven't told her about the demons or your enemies," Will explained quietly. Callum was surprised. "All it would've taken is one loose tongue to blow our cover before we even set off."

"Why not tell her now? She'll find out sooner or later, as Tyrus needs to come with us." Callum was worried, remembering his first encounter with the demons and how he'd panicked.

"The less she knows right now, Callum, the better. I don't like it any more than you do, but her ship's built for getting in and out of places without being spotted." The top of Will's right glove flashed a soft red, catching his attention. "We're needed on the bridge, Callum."

"We? What's happened?" Callum followed him as he quickly moved out of the hangar. Xene watched them depart without a word.

"A direct communication to the ship. Either someone we know wants to talk, or..." The sergeant didn't need to finish the sentence.

That the bridge was calm when Callum and Will arrived told him that the communication wasn't from Z-Gen. The room was far larger than Daniel's, and each station was manned by a crewmember, their attention entirely absorbed by the panels and displays in front of them. Despite the sheer volume of people, the room had a disciplined calm about it. There was no chair for the captain, but a large table in the middle of the room displayed what Callum guessed was the route they were taking and their location on it, a straight line without any deviation. Telanthir was stood in front of the table, looking ahead to the viewscreen.

"The communication is from Gerasal," Telanthir answered the question before Callum could ask it. "And a lot sooner than I'd expected."

"Do you think Z-Gen warned them of our arrival?" Callum walked up to the table, Will standing beside him.

"That remains to be seen. Let me do the talking for now." The king brushed off his shoulders before giving the nod to one of the bridge crew.

A second later the view of space was replaced with that of a harried elder man sat behind a metal desk. His short blonde hair was greying, and his clean-shaven face was lined with wrinkles, brown eyes focused not on them but on text projected in front of him. He wore clothing similar to Callum's attire for the banquet but dark blue, with a black shirt beneath it. On his head was a wreath of gold, a clear sign of status. The man didn't look up from his reading as he spoke.

"Telanthir, you've come earlier than I'd expected." His voice was a tired one.

"It's been too long, Fernisan," Telanthir greeted.

"Please, we've known each other long enough not be ensnared by diplomatic niceties." Fernisan finally dismissed the text and stood from his entirely metal chair. "What do you want, and be quick about it, I have a meeting in half an hour."

"I won't take up much of your time, my friend," Telanthir told him. "You have no doubt noticed that we are en route to your world."

"With the Great Threat an ever-existent problem, we've set up unmanned detection stations to alert us of any approaching vessel." Callum waited silently, hoping the news was good and immediately having that dashed. "This had better not be about what I think it is, Telanthir."

"Is the channel secure?" Telanthir checked with Will.

"As much as it'll ever be." Fernisan sighed and shook his head, making no effort to hide his frustration, followed quickly by disappointment.

"God, it's exactly that, isn't it?" Fernisan wasn't impressed. "When will you give up? It's been over sixty years, and what have you found in all that time? Nothing. Every time you come here, it ends the same way, and I've just about run out of patience."

"This time it's different," Telanthir told him firmly, prompting laughter.

"Oh, is it? How many times have I heard that from you? Five, ten? My father may have supported your crazy conspiracy, but he's twenty years dead and went to the grave without seeing a shred of your so-called 'evidence' amount to anything." Telanthir watched as the man shook his head again, his expression softening. "I sympathise with you, I really do. Losing your wife and daughter must have been hard."

"You have no idea how hard." Telanthir was doing a good job of keeping his anger at bay.

"It was just bad luck that pirates attacked your vessel, nothing more. There's no big secret Z-Gen are hiding, and the sooner you accept that, the sooner you can stop clinging to such self-destructive ideas and live the rest of your life in peace. How much have you spent forcefully extending your life in pursuit of this theory?" Fernisan said the last word with distaste.

"Pirates?" Will repeated. "Where did you get that information from?"

"It didn't take much research to find it. There's nothing to support your ludicrous ideas, but there *is* a swathe of hard, documented evidence for the pirate presence in that area and what happened to your ship."

"And you believe it?" The sergeant clearly didn't.

"A lot more than I would fanciful stories of red monsters emerging from the dark shadows and wiping out whole worlds. Just hearing it makes it sound as absurd as it is." That was enough to make Callum move from the table to present himself to the ruler, too fast for Will to stop him. Fernisan looked at Callum with disinterest. "And who are you?"

"My name is Callum Igannes, and I can tell you that Telanthir is telling the truth because I've seen them." He didn't expect Fernisan to believe him, so he continued, "My world was attacked by the same creatures." There was a pause, a nervous one for Callum.

"Is that so?" The man was doubtful. "What did you do, kill them with your sword?"

"And magic."

"Do you honestly expect me to believe you? Where's your proof, because if you don't have any, I've half a mind to inform Z-Gen—"

Fernisan's threat stopped dead in its tracks as Callum sensed the arrival of all the proof they'd ever need. One of the bridge crew noticed Tyrus in the doorway, drawing the attention of those next to him.

"Stand down, it's with us," Will ordered. "This conversation doesn't leave this room, have I made myself clear?" The sergeant's assurances did little to ease the fear among the bridge crew, but it wasn't them that Tyrus was focusing on. It stared directly at Fernisan, whose wide-eyed fright quickly faded into a deeply concerned nervousness.

"I... must admit, it's a very convincing projection you have there, Telanthir. You almost had me fooled." Tyrus didn't stop watching him as it walked slowly past Will and Callum to stand in front of all of them. Its stare unsettled the ruler as it did almost everyone else.

"It's real," Callum told him, holding his hand out for the staff the demon held. It gave it up without hesitation, the staff far heavier than any wood he'd come across. Fernisan's face went pale. "They killed everyone on Vedallan IV but me and my friends, who were saved by Tyrus here. We think the same thing happened to Geladan and want to find proof."

"...What *are* you?" Fernisan finally asked weakly, doubt washed away by fright.

"I am the only one of my kind that won't kill you," Tyrus told him simply, holding out its hand. A burning flame roared into existence, which startled the ruler further.

"It's on our side, from a small group not associated with the others," Callum clarified.

"Get it to stop," Fernisan requested urgently. "Please."

"Tyrus, that's enough." The demon ignored Callum's request, teleporting the staff back into its burning hand, the wood catching ablaze in an instant. Some of the bridge crew stood from their seats, terrified the fire would spread or worse, be directed at them. Fernisan was even more frightened now.

"You will meet our demands," the demon ordered with a snarl. Telanthir was looking to his friend, attempting to hide his own discomfort.

"O-or what?" The ruler stammered, eyes glued to the burning weapon.

"Or your world may suffer the same fate as Geladan. Not at our hands, but at those we seek to expose," Telanthir answered for the demon, stepping forward himself. Fernisan couldn't stop watching the staff ablaze with magic. "I do not ask that you help me directly or endanger your people, but we need to know that you will not betray the trust I'm placing in you."

Callum thought on Tyrus's earlier warning, of Telanthir endangering Otros by involving himself with them. Was Fernisan's world destined to be under the same threat? Was Tyrus prepared to kill him if he didn't agree? He'd try to stop the demon, but what could he do against such strength?

"...Alright," Fernisan spoke in a whisper, nodding just a little. "Just get that *thing* to stop, please." The fire died instantly, Tyrus's staff untouched. The man breathed a shaky sigh of relief, clutching his chair and slowly seating himself. The bridge crew were still wary of their inhuman passenger, neglecting their consoles to watch it.

"You'll delete all logs of this communication, I assume," Will checked. Fernisan shrugged vaguely, still trying to take in all that he'd learned in mere seconds. Callum sympathised with his confusion.

"I'm sorry," Telanthir apologised. "I was as surprised as you were."

"It's an alien." Fernisan was looking down at his table.

"It is."

"An alien. A real-life alien." Telanthir nodded to that. "...And if you're right – *if* you're right – they want to kill us all."

"That's what we're trying to find out." Telanthir gave a look to Will, who tapped on the table to change the image. It focused on six planets, one of them the end of the route their ship was taking and another highlighted in red. "Callum and his companions are going to investigate Geladan, and for that I need you to fabricate a reason for me to be on your world visiting you."

"Launching the mission from your world drastically cuts down the time of possible detection," Will explained further. A small red dot moved from Gerasal to Geladan quickly. "We have everything we need for the task on board and won't be asking for your assistance. Officially, our mission never happened, and we expect you to stick to that line." Fernisan couldn't stop glancing at Tyrus, the demon still staring at him.

"Z-Gen still have a task force in orbit of the planet. If they spot you—" Fernisan was still deeply concerned.

"We'll deal with that if it happens." Will didn't seem afraid.

"And if you don't? The odds aren't exactly stacked in your favour."

"That's not your risk to take, Fernisan. All we need from you is a pretence to dock at your spaceport, nothing more. We'll take care of the rest."

"If that's all you want from me... I'm sure I can find something." Fernisan sat up in his chair, looking to Telanthir with a grave expression. "If you're right about this, the ramifications... It'd change everything." The king nodded back.

"One step at a time, my friend. First, Callum will need to find that proof." The image before Will had changed into various different vessels, likely Z-Gen in ownership.

"Then I wish you all the luck in the world, Callum. You're going to need it." Fernisan was sincere enough, but it didn't make Callum feel any better. A flashing green glow began in the ruler's desk. "I'm sorry, but I need to take this. I'll see to it that you have clearance to dock when your ship reaches the system." He took one last look at the demon before the view reverted back to outer space.

Telanthir sighed slowly but with some measure of relief.

"What are the chances that Z-Gen were listening to that entire thing?" The king had to wait for his reply.

"We'd be hearing about it by now if they had, I think it's safe to assume we got away with it." Will turned off the images from the table. "That could've gone a lot worse."

"How many soldiers are in a task force?" Callum knew he wouldn't like the answer, but his curiosity got the better of him.

"Two thousand," Will's answer was quick. "Four cruisers, one crew carrier and a full squadron of fifty fighters. Vehicle complement depends on the commander in charge, but heavy weapons are a given. If they find us, we're unlikely to get off-world before their forces converge."

"Us?" Callum was surprised.

"I'm going with you, Callum, me and a group of my finest. You're going to need all the help you can get."

"How effective will your weapons be against the demons?" Callum couldn't help but be concerned.

"The soldiers on board are outfitted with state-of-the-art weaponry. If it can't take the demons, nothing can," Telanthir told them both.

Tyrus looked like it was about to speak but ended up refraining. Callum doubted it was because of their present company or the argument that would follow.

"We'll have a briefing before we arrive at Gerasal, sort out our plan. Leave the rest to us." Will looked back to the table, bringing up the image of their journey once more.

"Your men will die," Tyrus spoke with certainty. Will looked up from the image.

"They're the best Otros has, briefed with all the information we've got from Jinar and Saresan on the demons," the sergeant said back. "I appreciate the concern, but you need all the help you can get."

"The safety of your soldiers is irrelevant to me, as are you. Investigating the identity of the Great Threat and the protection of Callum are my priorities."

"I'll keep that in mind." Will was unfazed, returning his attention to the image before him.

"That your kind does not value individual lives troubles me, Tyrus." Telanthir didn't draw the demon's attention.

"The defeat of Keiran is the only thing that should trouble any of you," it replied as it uncharacteristically walked out the door. Callum exhaled.

"Tyrus is very focused on its duty." He couldn't explain it any better than that.

"I'll say," Will remarked. "That kind of attitude's going to get more people killed than any hostile force will, but it doesn't hurt to take its warning to heart. I'll have the quartermaster go over our equipment again, but truthfully, I've no idea if that'll be enough. No matter how much planning we do, we're going in blind."

"Is there anything I can do to help?" Callum offered.

"You let me worry about my soldiers, you focus on your training. That's how you can best help me." But worry Callum would, no matter what the sergeant told him.

Chapter Forty-Three

Warning: You are approaching the planet Geladan.

Geladan is a quarantined world. By order of Z-Gen, no vessel is to approach unless sanctioned to do so. Your navigation systems will now suggest an alternate route that bypasses the quarantine zone.

Those without authority who breach the quarantine zone will be removed by any and all means necessary. This will be your only warning.

—Automated message received upon approach to Geladan

Each day brought them closer to their mission to Geladan, and with it, Callum grew more distracted. Training became more difficult and his sleep restless, plagued with nightmares once more. They were all different but winded to the same conclusion, the deaths of his friends and Will's soldiers. Sometimes it was Z-Gen who caught them in an ambush, other times the demons overwhelmed them, ripped them asunder with tooth and claw. Once they didn't reach the planet at all, discovered by the strike force and killed in space.

Each time Tyrus saved him and him alone, leaving the others to their horrible fate without a moment's pause. No matter what he tried, he couldn't prevent it, waking each time with a start. The fatigue from his lack of rest did nothing to help his concentration, making him give up on training altogether after the fourth such night. Simon's arrival at his quarters that evening had been unexpected, the doctor handing him a clear bag of small white counters.

"Take one of these before you sleep," Simon ordered.

"What are they? Are they made of chalk?" Callum opened the bag and picked one of the counters up. "Why only one?"

"It'll kill you if you take two, that's why. Take them with a glass of water and not within an hour of eating."

"It'd kill me?" Callum put the counter back into the bag very carefully.

"Alexis told me that you looked like hell, and she's right. You'll be no good to anyone on Geladan like that. She's worried about you."

"I look that bad?" Callum moved to the mirror in the bathroom and was taken aback by the dark bags under his eyes. "I hadn't even noticed."

"Well, you can thank her for those pills. As a doctor, I'm obliged to tell you that you should take it easy for the next few days as well, but I don't think Tyrus would let you get away with that, so I settled for the next best thing. By the sounds of it, you lot have quite the task ahead of you."

"Are you going to be coming to Geladan with us?" Callum put the bag in his pocket.

"God, no. You're flying into a war zone: I'd just get in the way. If you need healing, you can use your magic till you get back." Simon looked beyond Callum to the kitchen. "Mind if I make a coffee?"

"Not at all." Simon moved over to that area, filling the kettle with water and pressing a button.

"I've been curious about something, Callum. How does your magic... work?" The doctor reached into his pocket for a tiny metal tablet, setting it down on the counter. It unfolded slowly into a normal-sized one as he found a cup in one of the cupboards. "I've been trying to get my head around it, but I don't know where to begin."

"I'm not the best person to ask. Jinar would be a better help." The doctor chuckled at the mention of his friend.

"He was my first choice, believe me. Where do you keep the coffee?" The doctor was looking about the counter.

"Where is it normally kept?" Simon grimaced at the jar he'd picked up.

"Never mind, I've found it. Otros has many things, but good coffee's not one of them," Simon remarked with a sigh. "Jinar knows a lot about how to use magic, but not the underlying science that makes it work. He can rattle off incantations and runic patterns until the cows come home, that doesn't help me understand how it all works."

"And Tyrus was no help?" Simon poured some of the pot's contents directly into the cup, observing the kettle impatiently.

"What do you think?" The kettle emitted a low hum. "Finally."

"I still don't understand why you came to me. I know less about magic than both of them; how can I give you the answers you want?"

"Everything has its place in the universe, and we have solid scientific theories to explain most of it. They tell us how it all works, and with them we can take educated guesses at things we don't quite know about, and there's a lot of that still to muddle through." Simon poured the boiling water into his cup, stirring the content gently with a small spoon. "In all my years I haven't seen a paper on magical theory or the things that fuel magic – we can blame Z-Gen for that – but it has to have a place where it fits, its niche."

"And if it doesn't?" Callum watched Simon try his drink, not quite happy with the results.

"Not bitter enough for my taste." The doctor set the cup down on the counter. "If it doesn't fit, then we'll need to figure out why not and adjust our theories to compensate. If we can't, we create new ones that make sense of it all. Science is many things, Callum, but most of all it's ever evolving. A hole drilled in the skull might not release evil spirits, but it can relieve pressure on the brain, and in rare instances, the recipient survives without immediate medical attention."

"It took a long time for us to figure out what was going on; centuries of trial and error, abandoned ideas and getting things right for the wrong reasons, not to mention when we got things wrong for the right reasons. The road to where we're at now was paved with failure, mistakes and more experiments than I care to think about, but we got here, and we'll get to wherever we're heading in time."

"That doesn't explain why you're asking me, though," Callum pointed out.

"As far as I've gathered, you and Alexis don't have a history with magic that runs deep enough for it to be second nature, so Jinar told me." Simon picked up the tablet, vaguely reading it. "The very idea of something like that being second nature to anyone is still mystifying, if I'm honest."

"It didn't feel natural at first, but the more I use magic, the easier I can call forth its power and the more there is." Simon began tapping on the tablet quickly.

"And how does it feel? Is the sensation painful? Where does it originate and how? Have you always had control of this power, and if not, what triggered your affinity with magic?" The doctor rattled the questions off without pause, and Callum barely had time to consider any of them before Simon smiled to himself. "Sorry, scientific curiosity. I may be a doctor by trade, but I've got a good foundation in many of science's other facets."

"That explains how you made Saresan's new weapon."

Simon reluctantly took another sip of his coffee.

"He wouldn't last five minutes against a Z-Gen squad with an ordinary halberd, it was the best compromise I could come up with," Simon remarked.

"I can't help you down there, but if I learn how magic functions, maybe I can help tip the scales in your favour a little in the future. I don't know how yet, but with a starting point, I can maybe come up with something." Callum thought on his magic and concentrated, bringing a globe of light into existence in front of him. Simon watched it with great curiosity.

"When I want to do something with my magic, I call for it... and it comes. I know what I want it to achieve, and if I have enough... of whatever it is that makes it work, it just works," Callum tried to explain as he made the orb hover closer to Simon. The doctor cautiously reached his hand out to the light, pulling it back when it got close. "It's not hot."

"How do you know?"

"Because that's how I made it." Simon furrowed his brow, then dared to reach out to the orb once more. He was surprised that his hand went right through it, then puzzled. "Is something wrong?"

"It's light without heat or an obvious source," Simon told him.

"I guess I'm the source, but that doesn't help you get any closer to the answers you want." Callum shrunk the light with a thought until it was like a jewel sparkling in the sun. "I can feel the presence of magic around when it's not hidden. You may not feel it there, but I can."

"What does it feel like?" Callum pondered that, trying to come up with a comparison that worked. Every time he fell short; he'd just accepted that he could sense it, being asked to explain the sensation had stumped him.

"...It just feels like magic. I'm sorry, that's the best I can give you."

"That's alright, it's more than what I started with." Simon's tablet collapsed back to its original size. "I've got a few experiments I might want to run later, once you're back from Geladan. Would you be willing to help me with them?" Simon had a lot of faith that they'd return, and he didn't want to ask why.

"Of course." Simon finished off the coffee in a few large gulps and returned the cup to the counter, heading to the door.

"If I don't see you before you set out, watch yourselves out there."

"We will, I promise." Simon nodded and left. The orb of light faded at the same time, Callum knowing his word alone couldn't make that be. He thought on Xiez and Alun, their demons and cultists, on Z-Gen and the devastating tools they wielded. Taking out the bag of medicine from his pocket, Callum poured a glass of water and took one, swallowing with difficulty. Settling into bed, he hoped it would gently lull him into a deep slumber. He hoped even more that it was without dreams, for the nightmare he couldn't wake up from was Geladan, and that was inching ever closer with each second. As he slumbered, he dreamed of someone – he couldn't see what they looked like – watching a news channel. The man speaking on the viewscreen talked about unimportant things, the words merging into one another, but between two woefully similar topics were two sentences, spoken off-hand and without care.

"Z-Gen forces stationed near Geladan apprehended collaborators of the Great Threat this morning. Z-Gen have refused to comment on the identity of the persons but have assured the public that they are following standard procedures concerning this incident."

"Good," coldly muttered the person whose eyes Callum saw through. The view faded into murky nothing moments later, plunging Callum into silent oblivion. Mercifully, it was the only dream that night.

Even though Simon wasn't going with them to Geladan, he was present with coffee in hand at the meeting Will organised to plan their mission to the doomed world.

The room that hosted the gathering was dominated by a huge table with far more chairs around it than people. Will stood opposite the door by a huge viewscreen that displayed information on Geladan, blocks of red words surrounding the view of the planet. Standing beside William was Davis and two other soldiers, the three wearing full combat attire and silently watching their superior.

Siobhan had her feet on the table, leaning back in her chair comfortably. Jinar was stood by the door out, stroking his beard as they waited for Tyrus to arrive. Callum was sat to the right of the door leading out, Alexis to his left and Saresan to his right. He was nervous at all the bad news they'd inevitably hear and concerned that even now, Will had decided not to invite Luna and Xene along with everyone else.

"Maybe Scaly won't show," Siobhan mentioned.

"Does it matter? It'd just object to everything anyway. It's probably listening in with magic." Saresan shrugged. "Might as well start."

"I will relay it again to Tyrus if needed." Will let the image on-screen zoom in to Geladan before continuing, "If our theory about the demons is correct, most of the main cities will be devoid of life. There was a planetside security force, but I doubt they lasted long. The cities also have extensive underground districts that, while not atypical, are larger than on most worlds."

"People might have survived down there. The demons are not especially bright, even mundane tricks to conceal a hidden entrance might work." Jinar got a nod from the sergeant.

"Naturally, we'll try and evacuate any civilians we come across, but we won't be able to take many of them." Will cast his eyes to Callum. "We won't be armed to fight a war, either with the demons or Z-Gen, but we'll do what we can."

"So where are we going to go if there's so many places?" Saresan got his answer when the image zoomed in on one location, a settlement by the sea.

"The capital, Hyval city."

"Named after its founder?" Alexis guessed.

"After its most recent ruler, actually. President Vandaal was killed en route to his home three years ago, and the commonly held opinion is that his son murdered him to take up the position."

"Doesn't sound out of place to me, happened all the time at home," Saresan muttered. "You couldn't go a year without word that some far off-duke had been offed by his son, stabbed or 'accidentally' killed while out hunting. Surprised anyone went hunting at all."

"There was never enough proof, and Hyval was much like his father, paranoid and reclusive. His home was deep in the city, but Telanthir visited him a year ago and discovered that that's little more than a front. His real home is *under* that building." The image zoomed in further, a red dot indicating to a walled-off area. "Heavily guarded and likely built to withstand orbital bombardment."

"Scared his son was going to poison him too?" The guard smiled as Siobhan asked that.

"Hyval never married or had children that we know of," Will told him.

"Is there a chance that he's still in that place, safe from Z-Gen?" Callum wasn't so sure but had to ask. "Wouldn't they have made sure to clear there?"

"That's what we're going to go and find out. If Z-Gen couldn't get in, the demons wouldn't have much luck either. My thoughts are that you could use your magic to get inside. If he's alive, perhaps we'll get the proof we need from him. His home is likely to have security systems that will have recorded the entire attack, at least in the vicinity of his complex."

Will left a pause for questions, of which there were none. "I don't expect him to hand it over willingly or be anything other than hostile if we can get in, but we'll cross that bridge when we come to it. We'll be recording everything through our helmets, so provided we can get them back on the ship intact, we only need see to the proof to document it. The *Star's Shadow* and the *Silverbolt* will land as close as they can to the complex, out of sight if possible. The *Star's Shadow* should be able to get past Z-Gen easily, it's your ship I'm more concerned about, Siobhan."

"I'll be fine. It's got some stealth tech in there, should be enough." Siobhan dismissed the worry with a shrug.

"Isn't that highly illegal? How long have you had that in there?" Simon asked.

"Does it matter at this point?" She didn't get a response, the doctor sipping his coffee.

"As soon as we've got the evidence we need, we withdraw to the ships and escape back to the *Janice*. Once we're back in Otros space, we'll consider our next move," Will finished explaining. "Any questions?"

"What if it goes wrong?" Callum knew that if he didn't ask, others would.

"If Z-Gen finds us before we land, we'll have to abort the mission and try to lose them, same if they find us on the ground before we reach the complex. We can't presume that they won't report our position even if we overcome the soldiers we come across. As for the demons..." Will looked to the sorcerers among them. "I'm not the expert on them, so I'll leave that judgement call to you. If we meet one of the talking demons though, I'll be pulling my men back; from what Jinar has told me, we're no match for them."

"Wise indeed, but if Xiez finds us, you will not escape by running." Jinar smiled confidently. "You need not fear, however: through my training I have grown far stronger than I ever was and shall be more than a match for it when next we meet."

"Bet you a crate of beer you're not," Siobhan chipped in.

"A pointless gamble, as if I am not, you will surely perish."

"Scared you'll lose?" She grinned up at him.

"And if I win this, what is in it for me?" He stroked his beard. "I shall have to ponder that on the journey." She raised an eyebrow, shaking her head.

"Beer's as good as mine." Her attention turned to someone nobody else had noticed in the right-hand corner. "Hey Scaly, glad you could join us. Clued up on the plan?" Everyone else then spotted the demon standing there, watching the proceedings in silence. How long had Tyrus been there, and why had she spotted it first?

"I will be unable to hide your presence from our enemies if you move too far from me," it warned. Davis was the only one of the other soldiers to continue watching it after his fellows had stopped. "Your pilot will be at risk of detection."

"Not to mention your armour's a dead giveaway as to where you're from," Siobhan muttered. Will shook his head.

"We're likely not on Z-Gen's databases due to our sole purpose of being Telanthir's guards. Besides, the alternative is going with less-than-optimal equipment against demons. I'll take Z-Gen figuring us out over those things clawing at us," the sergeant replied.

"We need to tell the pilot the danger she'll be in, her and Xene," Callum said to the others. "It's not fair not to."

"We cannot do this mission without her, Callum. The *Silverbolt* doesn't have enough room for everyone, even if I and my soldiers don't go with you."

"You sure she's not going to bolt if a demon attacks her ship?" Siobhan chipped in. "Money's no good to a corpse." Callum had heard that before, remembering Daniel's hatred as he'd stormed out. Will looked to his fellow soldiers, who said nothing, then back to Callum.

"I get the feeling that if I don't tell her, you will, am I right?" It seemed Callum didn't need to answer with words. "I'm right. She might get a whole lot more expensive though."

"Avarice has been the fuel for worse things," Jinar remarked quietly. The mood in the room had shifted since the beginning of the meeting, so subtly that Callum hadn't noticed until then. A gloom had set in, compounded by the magnitude of their task presented clearly and bluntly. They could've trained for a hundred years, and he still wouldn't have been ready for it, afraid the burning eyes of Xiez would stare him down as he died.

"We'll be arriving at Gerasal tomorrow evening, 2000 local time. Fernisan has assured me that at 2030 local time, there'll be a ten-minute window where the ship scanners and registry on the space station will be off while the program's upgraded. If you're not on the *Star's Shadow* when we set out, we're going without you." Will looked at them all in turn before nodding. "Dismissed."

Callum tried to focus on his training but couldn't, nor did rest come easily. Only with one of Simon's pills did he get to sleep, and it was plagued with his fears manifest. He felt no better when he woke, and a shower didn't help.

He wasn't hungry either but forced himself to eat, knowing he'd need all the strength he could muster when they arrived on the dead world. All the barren wastelands he could picture would be nothing like what was down there, the truth being far worse than any figment of thought. He resigned himself to a day of fretting, sat on his bed with the scale mail at his side. The door opened, and he didn't even notice someone walking in and sitting down next to him.

"Hello, Callum." It was Telanthir and he was smiling. "How are you?"

"As well as can be. Are your preparations for the meeting complete?" Callum asked, staring down at his feet.

"Fernisan had a few trade agreements that needed ratifying, he's going to use that as an excuse to meet with me." The room went silent as Callum thought on what to say. Telanthir found something first, though his smile had faded. "Thank you, for doing this."

"We haven't achieved anything yet," Callum reminded him.

"But you're willing to try. I can't pretend to understand the nature of the enemies you have, this 'Keiran' person." Telanthir looked ahead. "I asked Jinar about these foes, and he gave me far more detail than I ever could've asked for."

"He's good at that."

"Frighteningly so. He has a way with words, unlike any man I've ever met. Had he been born on Otros, I daresay he'd've made it into parliament with ease." Telanthir was the only one to chuckle and it died quickly. "No matter what happens, you're welcome to stay in Otros as long as you wish."

"I appreciate the thought, but if we did that, your world would be in grave danger."

"Jinar said that as well when he detailed the events leading to your world's... death." Telanthir watched him as he said that. Callum was too focused on what was to come to ponder what had been. The king looked concerned. "The galaxy must seem cold and cruel."

"The kingdom I grew up in was no paradise, Telanthir, I know that from experience. Most people were too focused on their own troubles to notice the misery of others. All it took was one poor harvest or a plague, and society would almost crumble around you." He had the king's full attention as he spoke quietly, "At least everyone gets a fair chance here, from what I've been told."

"People are still born with radically different opportunities dependent on a huge range of factors: you need look no further than me for that. I see your point though; so many things are taken for granted by so many. Education, healthcare, civil freedoms: all of them would've been great luxuries in your time – your world. Sorry, worlds like yours are associated with the far past."

"Would we have achieved the things you all have in time?" Callum asked. "Flying ships, weapons of red beams and everything else?"

"Not in the way you imagine. Some traders might've already made contact with people on your world, so there might've been some who knew of the galaxy beyond. It's unlikely your world would've gone ignored forever: an oxygen-rich Gaia-class planet would be a lucrative prospect for a multi-system mining corporation like HyGol. To buy mining rights to the world, they'd need to negotiate with each power centre on the planet individually; I can only imagine how much of a nightmare that'd've been if they got permission to do so."

"What would stop them? The armies of all the kingdoms wouldn't stand a chance against the soldiers on your ship."

"Laws that predate the collapse of the Terran Empire, for one. They protect the growth of pre-space societies from large-scale external influence. Some companies try to find loopholes to avoid them, but it rarely works." Telanthir looked over to the shining scale mail.

"But no amount of oversight and punishments could stop the tiny trickle of knowledge seeping into your society from small-scale meetings. Who knows what advances in science came about from such encounters with people from off-world, trading knowledge for precious metals, jewels or even land? And all it would've taken to throw your whole planet into chaos would be one person with enough riches to hire a mercenary force to assert their authority through superior technology."

"By the way you speak, that's not an uncommon thing."

"Z-Gen is good at quashing any would-be tyrants before they get a foothold when they find them, but there are near-forgotten parts of colonised space where they barely patrol for one reason or another. As your world was the only one inhabited in that system, Z-Gen didn't need to check there often." The king covered his mouth as he coughed. "Forgive me, I'm rambling. If you have something you need to do, don't let me stop you."

"I don't mind the conversation. I just wish I could concentrate on anything for long enough." Callum stood up and headed to the tap, getting a glass of water. "I feel like I'm the only one worrying about it, too. Everyone else was so calm at the meeting. The mood was sour, but... everyone was so calm."

"Believe me when I tell you that everyone there was worried in some fashion." Callum doubted the demon had been as the king also stood. "I'll be hoping for your success and safe return, all of you."

"Thank you, but I fear we'll need more than hope."

"Hope is the most powerful weapon you have, Callum. Without the hope of a better tomorrow, what are we? That's why we're doing this, for the dawn to be that little bit brighter." Telanthir headed to the door, turning back to him as it opened. "I'll see you when you return, Callum."

"You will. Take care, Telanthir." Callum hadn't touched his water.

"You as well." The king left, and though Callum felt a little better, he knew that optimism was unlikely to survive until the evening and their departure. Drinking deep from his glass, he clung to those faint embers of hope desperately. Telanthir spoke as if he were a hero, but that wasn't true, it couldn't be... could it?

Chapter Forty-Four

Everyone arrived early at the hangar, waiting for their departure. Callum wore his scale mail and had his sword drawn already, expecting the demons to somehow strike at them before they even boarded the *Star's Shadow*. Siobhan was making some final checks on her own ship, tapping at a tablet as she removed panels and glanced to flashing lights and metal wires. Callum noticed Saresan's armour was a suit of scale mail just like his, likely also a gift from Telanthir, who'd headed to the space station orbiting Gerasal earlier in a small shuttle Fernisan had sent to receive him.

The planet itself was half blue and green but with large blotches of grey infecting it, the scars of civilisation running deep across its skin. Tyrus made no attempt to hide its presence and Luna didn't seem too bothered by it, though she gave the creature the occasional look as she did some checks on her own vessel.

Xene looked the spitting image of a Z-Gen soldier at first glance, clad in her armour and holding a rifle larger than any other he'd seen before. The barrel at the front was as thick as the entire weapon, three or four inches wide. Her hefty pistol stuck to her left thigh through some unknown means. He was startled by two large spikes that retracted from the top of her gloves, thinking he heard the soldier chuckle softly at the hidden weapons.

Will's squad stood by her, the sergeant running through some final points with his soldiers. Davis was among them, looking to Tyrus as well as the other sorcerers every once in a while. His helmet hid his expression, and the stares would've made Callum feel uneasy were he not thinking on the mission ahead. His attempt to count the seconds to their departure had failed spectacularly, derailed by thoughts of what they'd encounter.

Alexis tried a smile, but it was fleeting and weak. Only Jinar was absolutely confident, floating a trio of prismatic orbs that crackled with lightning, fire and frost. Callum wanted to say something encouraging but nothing came to mind, so instead, he was silent. It was broken by a loud droning sound echoing through the cavernous room, and at that, Will nodded to Luna, who boarded her ship.

"It's time," the sergeant told them all, Davis and the other soldiers following him on board through the narrow airlock. Siobhan closed the panel she'd been looking at and stepped to her ship's entrance.

"Anyone coming with me?" Her offer caught Jinar's attention immediately, who stepped over with a smile. The others started to file into the *Star's Shadow* one at a time.

"Gladly. You may need my assistance if we come across trouble," the sorcerer replied.

"You touch *anything*, I'll shove you out the airlock," she warned.

"Does that exclude the floor? I can levitate if necessary."

"Just get in."

"With pleasure." He nodded, the pilot closing the door after him.

Callum and Tyrus were the only ones not to board, the demon giving him a look that asked why he was delaying. He didn't argue the point, stepping into the cramped space beyond. Tyrus followed behind, the ceiling just tall enough so that he didn't have to stoop. Their seating was a bar of metal that had been folded out from the walls, and it was a cramped fit even with Tyrus remaining standing. Callum squeezed in at the end closest to the entrance next to Davis, the private looking to him before turning to stare at anywhere else. The way out closed, and the door to the small but comfortable cockpit at the front of the craft did so a moment later. Luna's voice projected itself from the ceiling.

"ETA after we clear the airlock: twenty minutes," she told them.

"How can it be that fast?" Saresan asked, wedged in between two soldiers.

"Testing, testing. How's the line?" Siobhan's voice was next to be heard.

"Loud and clear. Ready to depart?" Luna asked.

"Ready as I'll ever be. Feel free to match my speed and course."

"Cute. You match *my* speed: this thing outruns blockades without trying," Luna corrected as Callum felt the ship take off.

"Sounds like a challenge." Callum could tell Siobhan was smiling.

"Is it wise to take on a second losing gamble?" He could tell Jinar was as well from his tone alone. The voices ended, plunging them all into silence as they departed the *Janice* and headed to Geladan.

Twenty minutes didn't seem like long, but the seconds ebbed by only slowly and with reluctance. Callum felt Tyrus's eyes watching him intently. Were the Council observing him too through the demon, judging his every action and word?

"This is going to be fun," Xene told herself while pressing some buttons on her weapon. Fun was the last thing on Callum's mind as time ebbed by, expecting everything to go horribly wrong at any point, for Z-Gen to notice their intrusion and attack.

"Crunch time. Silent running engaged," Luna's voice declared.

"Roger that, going quiet," Siobhan confirmed before the room went dark. This was banished moments later by Alexis conjuring forth an orb of light, which made Callum wonder what Luna's action had achieved.

"Turning off all systems makes the ship harder to detect," Will explained quietly.

"But how are we still moving?" Callum asked.

"Momentum. What are you, stupid?" Xene chided, much to Callum and Will's surprise.

"Our world was not at the same level of achievement as yours," Alexis answered with a frown.

"Mudders. Figures," the soldier remarked before returning her focus to the weapon she held. It was many minutes of absolute and tense silence before the lights turned back on and Luna's voice returned with them. Alexis dispelled her glowing orb at the same time.

"Good news, Z-Gen didn't detect us," she began, Callum relieved to hear that. "Thought they'd scanned us at one point, but we'd know about it if they had. Bad news—"

"What the heck happened to the city?" Siobhan interrupted, aghast. "It's blasted to hell!"

"That's the bad news," Luna finished.

"Orbital bombardment, most likely." Will shook his head. Callum was able to piece together what that meant in that instance, thankful he couldn't see outside just yet. "How are the radiation levels, Luna?"

"We'd all know by now if it was that," came her answer.

"Anywhere suitable for you to land?" Siobhan enquired.

"There's pockets of less damaged buildings. I'm setting a waypoint," Luna answered.

"Mine's better, less open ground to cover."

"Heading to your waypoint then," Luna confirmed. "You'll have ruins up to Hyval's complex. The north wall has been breached: I'd suggest you head there. It's nothing but scorched earth between the walls and what's left of the building in the centre though."

"Thanks." Will looked to his soldiers, then the others. "We all ready?"

"As much as can be, sir," one of the soldiers answered. She was nervous. "How will we know if the demons arrive?"

"We'll tell you as soon as we feel it," Alexis said. With a moment of shaking and a thud, the ship landed on Geladan. Callum stood with the others, taking a deep breath before the airlock opened for their departure.

"Secure the landing site," Will ordered his soldiers, disembarking first with a rifle in hand.

Xene followed behind with a shrug as Tyrus teleported away, likely to scout their surroundings also. Callum walked to the airlock cautiously and stopped at the exit as his eyes looked upon the desolation around them.

The quiet beyond the vessel was so unlike Gui-Lon that a coin falling to the ground would echo all around them. They'd landed in the twisted and broken husk of a building, the soldiers taking up positions ahead of them while looking to the other structures that were in no better condition. What did remain was blasted and badly melted. Further shattering his expectations was the complete lack of bodies scattered around, and though he was happy not to be presented with death, it troubled him; the demons cared not for the corpses of the fallen and Z-Gen surely wouldn't have cleaned them up, so what had happened to them? Slowly stepping out, he felt a chill wind brush across him that carried dust and silence with it.

"Geeze," Saresan mumbled as he too surveyed the land. The sky was dark and cloudy, the sun barely managing to shed a murky dusk. Xene had stationed herself by the entrance to the *Star's Shadow*, leaning on the wall nonchalantly.

"I wonder if this was the fate of our world," Alexis mused sadly.

"I damn hope not." Saresan had his halberd in hand ready.

"So, I don't see any demons around here, barring the one you brought with you." Xene was disappointed, again looking at her weapon and checking it.

"Demons don't leave bodies, they... turn into nothing after a bit," Saresan answered.

"Convenient." Xene then spotted movement to her left and raised her weapon, ready to fire in an instant. She paused when Jinar came into view, alone and observing their surroundings as he approached them.

"All clear where you were?" Saresan asked.

"It would be hard for it not to be. I fear that nothing lives here save us." Jinar was alone, thoughtfully gazing ahead as he closed the distance.

"It'll make spotting the enemy easier at least," Saresan muttered. Will approached them as the guard finished speaking.

"It's a half mile to the complex, and the sooner we move, the better. Any idea where your demon is?" he asked the pair.

"Hell if I know, but it'll be close," came Saresan's answer.

"Stick with us. If we get attacked, find cover."

Will made a hand gesture in the air and the soldiers silently obeyed his instruction, starting to carefully move down the blackened street. Callum and the others followed, watching the empty buildings around them for the slightest hint of movement within the withered husk of the city.

It was so quiet that Callum thought he could hear his heart beating, magic tingling in his arms as he tried to keep his fear in check. Will and his soldiers ignored the streets that turned off from the main one save for a cursory look down them, each as devastated and barren as the others. Nothing remained that could prove who started the battle which razed the city, though it was clear who hadn't won. Callum spotted Tyrus briefly ahead of them before it vanished once more, his mentor waiting for the threat that hadn't struck yet.

Despite the optimism that some had displayed, Callum knew it was only a matter of when things went wrong, not if, but as they continued unopposed, he found his thought grew bolder and more confident. Nobody let their guard slip for even a moment, and he was no exception, eyes scanning about even more as they moved further in.

Turning down a tight alleyway, Callum began to see traces of what the world had been like before the devastation; some discarded food packets, a section of a wall painted in vibrant colours, mundane things whose survival made them extraordinary. He stopped when his foot caught on something partially hidden beneath melted debris.

Kneeling down, Callum recovered a raggedy doll, its purple dress faded and one of the button eyes chipped. It stared blankly up at him and he couldn't look away, so many questions rushing to confront him. Who had owned it and where were they now? He knew the answer to the second one and couldn't help but be filled with sadness and anger in equal measure at the loss of such innocent life.

"You okay?" Saresan had stopped alongside him, noticing the doll. He had no words to say.

"If Z-Gen did this..." Callum wanted to clench his fists but couldn't bring himself to squeeze the doll, damage all that remained of the one who'd loved it so.

"Come on." Saresan patted his back as he continued walking.

He couldn't let it go, to be forgotten like Geladan would be one day. And so he held onto it, tucking the doll into his belt as he caught up with the others, the alley opening out into another destroyed avenue.

Only when they scaled the hill to reach the breach in the wall around Hyval's complex was the deliberate nature of its origin plain to see. All of the walls were burned but only that part had broken, blasted from the outside in by a tremendous force. The grass around and beyond the walls was torched, and what remained of the buildings was no better than what was all around them. The wrecks of what Callum guessed were large stationary weapons stood inert, and not a single thing moved within. Thunder boomed overhead, the herald of rain.

Alexis had noticed the doll, and her eyes spoke of her own sadness. Tyrus had rejoined them as they'd approached, not saying anything and keeping close to Callum. Will's soldiers had their guns trained on the inside of the compound while Will spoke into his gauntlet.

"We're at the breach. All things quiet on your end?" asked the sergeant.

"Dead quiet, no pun intended. No sign of Z-Gen or anyone else," Luna answered through the glove.

"We might lose contact with you once we go below ground. Relocate if you need to."

"Still surprised Z-Gen haven't swooped down on us yet." Siobhan opened a can of something as she spoke.

"It would make little sense to let us land, allow us to hide our vessels and explore." Jinar was surveying where they'd come from. "You are overthinking things."

"It's just *too* quiet, you know? There aren't even any fighter patrols scanning the cities."

"We delay," Tyrus declared, walking towards the remains of the main building.

"So much for caution," Saresan muttered, following with the other soldiers.

"Henry, cover our rear. Nika, Davis, you're with me," Will told his soldiers.

Henry nodded, backing up slowly as the rest of the group advanced. Callum spotted human remains at last and they were every bit as grim as he'd expected, skeletons charred black with fire, huddled around a heavy metal hatch in the centre of the ruin.

"Poor bastards," Nika exclaimed quietly, shaking her head. "Why weren't they let in?"

"Mad is the one who questions the madman," Jinar replied cryptically, examining the hatch with vague interest. "It would be a simple matter to open it with magic."

"And alert everyone inside that we're coming." Callum had approached the grisly spectacle. "There has to be another way to open it, a panel or a lock of some kind."

"Not likely, I'm afraid." Will's attention was on the way they came as Henry finally caught up with them.

"Teleportation?" Callum suggested next.

"Even with my skill, teleporting into an unknown area comes with considerable risk," Jinar explained. "I would need to be sure that a large room was beyond." The sorcerer knelt down and put his hand to the metal, humming.

"Does he... often do that?" Nika asked Saresan.

"Yep," answered the guard.

"I believe I can open it without significant noise if you wish it," Jinar declared then.

"It's our only way in, what choice do we have?" Saresan shrugged.

Jinar smiled and stood, stepping back as he began to mutter. The incantation took longer than most, giving those who'd experienced his magic before a chance to back up a few paces. Tyrus and the soldiers remained still, Henry and Nika watching the sorcerer as his magical energy focused into a thin, intense beam of heat that quickly melted a large hole in the metal.

"Whoa." Nika was stunned at the spectacle and stared even after Jinar had stopped, bowing like a performer after a show. Only Davis and Tyrus hadn't watched.

"If you are impressed with that, you have not seen anything yet," he assured her, looking through the hole. "It is quite a deep shaft, but they have been generous enough to provide us with a ladder."

"Henry, take point. We'll wait for the all-clear," Will ordered, getting a nod in return.

"Yes, sir." Henry approached the opening.

"The edges of the hole are no longer hot," Jinar informed him, the soldier holstering his weapon on his back before beginning the climb down. Callum stepped up to it and peered, surprised that the way was illuminated with dim lights and was entirely bereft of dirt and grime.

"They'd've already shot at us if they knew we were coming, surely," Callum said, continuing to watch Henry's descent.

"That's the hope." Will had his rifle ready to fire down the shaft, just in case. Eventually, Henry stopped after a minute of climbing down.

"Another hatch, sir, this one has a security code. Says it leads to the main security room. Want me to force entry?" Henry asked through Will's glove.

"How deep are you?" Jinar enquired.

"About a hundred fifty metres, why?" replied the soldier.

"Teleportation, good sir. I can assess the room beyond and open it from within. If there is a trap, they will not suspect my arrival and I will have the element of surprise."

"That's a big if," Saresan remarked.

"A few soldiers are no problem for myself." Jinar started muttering and then stopped mid-gesture, frowning quizzically. "Curious."

"Something wrong?" Alexis asked, looking around them in case he'd sensed the arrival of demons. Callum couldn't feel anything save Jinar's magic, which lingered within him before settling down again.

"I am... unsure," Jinar conceded, approaching the hole. "My magic is unable to reach beyond the level that Henry is at."

"Perhaps there's nothing down there but rock," Callum guessed.

"Magic is not so concerned with my well-being as to prevent me from doing something foolish, not that I would be so." Jinar was stroking his beard. "No, this is something unknown to me."

"There's a first for everything," Saresan joked.

"Sir?" Henry asked again, waiting for the go-ahead.

"Hold off for now," Will told him.

"I have never claimed to be omniscient, merely exceptionally skilled and highly knowledgeable," Jinar clarified. "I would like to examine that hatch myself and glean what secrets prevent my spell."

"Come back up, Henry, we need to check something out first." Will looked up at the sky as the thunder cracked louder than before. "It's going to be a big one. Should help hide us for a while."

"Perhaps Hyval has uncovered a way to block magical energies," Alexis suggested as Henry climbed.

"A possibility." Tyrus was focusing on the way they'd come, staring at the still nothing.

Callum couldn't see anything interesting, but his mentor's curiosity made him look more intently.

For a second Callum thought he felt something in the distance, but it was gone so fast that he had to wonder if he hadn't imagined it. Neither Alexis nor Jinar reacted to it, reinforcing that it was just his mind playing tricks on him.

Henry emerged shortly after, letting Jinar descend. He levitated down instead of using the ladder.

"Is there anything you can't do?" Henry was amazed, leaving his gun holstered as he continued to watch the sorcerer's descent. Davis turned away from them.

"It's best not to get him started on the answer to that," Alexis answered. She then paused. "What is the range of your concealing magic, Tyrus?"

"Insufficient to protect the location of the ships." Tyrus wasn't concerned at that fact.

"Everything still okay over there, Siobhan?" Will checked.

"Peachy. Not so much as a tumble weed since you left." Siobhan's chair squeaked as she spoke, relaxed. Callum imagined her feet propped up on one of the likely many consoles in the cockpit, staring at the ceiling. "Not that I'd even know if Z-Gen were after us, with the storm. Why you ask?"

"Just checking up on you three."

"Not me you should be worried about, buddy." Siobhan leaned further back in her chair.

"Xene's poking around the surrounding ruins, hoping to find something to scrap with. Not surprisingly, she's come up short so far. We'll keep you updated on if anything happens," Luna explained.

"Thank you—" The sound of Jinar's cry of fright cut Will off, the sergeant rushing to the hole at the same time Callum did to look down. "Jinar, are you alright?" Callum could see orange moving deep below them, a sure sign he was alive.

"I believe I have discovered something most peculiar," Jinar shouted up to them, trying his best to sound calm and collected. "I am currently unsure of the exact chain of events, but something is dampening my magic. My spell was disrupted, but I am quite unharmed."

"Explain," Tyrus demanded loud enough that Jinar was sure to hear.

"It is akin to a charged feeling in the air, not unlike lightning but also very much unlike it. It is most curious."

"He's talking about the force field," Henry stated, drawing all eyes to him immediately.

"You said nothing of a force field before," Alexis remarked.

"It's pretty standard for shelters like that to have them, they wouldn't withstand orbital bombardments otherwise. I thought everyone knew that." He paused, remembering his present company. "...Oh. Sorry, sir."

"Carelessness costs lives, soldier, remember that," Will bluntly remarked. Henry hung his head.

"Yes, sir."

"Be mindful of this," Tyrus told them all, Callum nodding. He had to tell Simon that when they got back to the *Janice*.

"I fear that my magic will be insufficient to teleport to the other side of this hatch," Jinar called up. "May I suggest more mundane methods of opening it?" Henry approached the hole and removed a small metal device from one of his belt pouches, dropping it down the hole.

"Catch!" Henry beckoned.

"And what is this?" Jinar enquired.

"Place it on the security panel with the red button facing you. Once it starts flashing, press it." A few seconds passed.

"It has been done. A most curious oddment," Jinar declared to Nika's disapproving tut. A few more seconds passed, and Callum heard a loud clunk echo up to them. "The hatch is open, and I can safely say that no one is awaiting our arrival, though the feeling from that force field is still present."

"Will you be alright down there, Tyrus?" Callum enquired, wondering if the demon could even fit down the shaft. It looked at the entrance.

"Yes," it replied, waiting for him to climb down.

He moved over to the hole and sheathed his sword before carefully beginning his descent, Alexis following directly after and Davis after her. Callum had expected the air to get worse as he got deeper, but it was the exact opposite; the temperature settled at a comfortable level, and the air was fresh and clean.

As he got halfway down, the force field made itself known; a soft presence at first, it grew more overpowering the deeper underground he got, suffocating his magical energies. Would it affect his sword as well?

Chapter Forty-Five

"I understand that those fortunate enough not to be caught in the Great Threat's attack on Geladan – those away on business or holiday – wish to return to their home. As someone who has spent most of their life battling the Great Threat, the idea of reclaiming that which was taken from us as a show of defiance is a powerful one, yet ultimately not viable.

"As with all such things, it comes down to economics. It's far cheaper to rehouse those left on neighbouring worlds – the cost of which Z-Gen will cover – than it is to construct a new settlement on a world that's been attacked. The Great Threat are monstrously efficient in their destruction, laying waste to the environment as well as settlements. It would take decades, even centuries to begin to repair the damage they cause, all with the danger that they'll return and destroy everything once again.

"Do not take what I say as conceding defeat, however. We WILL win against the Great Threat, end the danger they pose absolutely and utterly. Once they are gone forever, I promise you that we will reclaim every world they have attacked and return them to their former glory."

—*Statement from General Felix of Z-Gen*

Reaching the bottom of the ladder, Callum drew his sword quickly and took in the room. Nothing drew his eyes one way or the other, the room bereft of furniture or people. Every surface was an unblemished white, far too clean and sterile for Callum to be comfortable. A low hum emanated from the walls, likely the force fields that made the hairs on his arms tingle. The noise would've been lost to the background had there been any activity, but there wasn't. Jinar was to the left of the ladder, himself focusing on the only door that led further into the complex, a security panel to the right of it.

"This doesn't feel right," Callum spoke quietly without meaning to as Alexis finished climbing.

"I quite agree, our progress has been too swift." Jinar made room as Henry and the other soldiers arrived.

They'd also been expecting someone waiting for them and didn't let their guard down, guns trained on the only door. Jinar handed Henry back the small device, the soldier pocketing it with a nod of thanks. Tyrus didn't scale the ladder, teleporting into the room despite the presence of the force fields.

"I'm surprised you managed that," Alexis said to the demon, sounding concerned. By then everyone had scaled the ladder, Saresan watching the walls idly.

"Superior magic," Tyrus answered her. Henry went towards the door and started examining the panel when a loud voice spoke to them.

"Welcome. Please identify yourself with your unique sixteen-digit code on the panel provided. Oral recital is accepted as an alternative." It lacked any human elements, the words disjointed and monotone.

"Easy enough," Henry declared, retrieving the device once again and placing it on the panel.

"Hold off—" Will spoke too late.

As Henry pressed the button on his small contraption, a translucent red barrier emerged from the ceiling, trapping him in a small semicircle by the door. Alarmed, he tried to remove the device, only for the panel to also be shrouded in the same way. The barrier's arrival further dampened Callum's magic, causing him to be barely able to feel it as he grew fearful.

"What the hell?" Henry exclaimed in confusion.

"Unauthorised persons detected. Lockdown protocol engaged," a different voice declared. It was female and soft but, much like the room, had a sterile ring to it. The encased soldier reached for the pistol at his side.

"Nobody move!" Will ordered loudly. Everyone obeyed. "Until we know what this system is capable of, we don't want to do anything that might be perceived as a threat. And whatever you do, *don't* touch that force field, Henry."

"Will it hurt him?" Alexis warily watched the barrier as it shimmered with energy.

"I hope not."

"You hope not?!" Henry moved his back to the door.

"Don't. Move," Will repeated more sternly.

"And do what? Wait for it to kill me?" Henry's confidence had ebbed to nothing, and fright had taken its place.

"Is this one of the force fields you have spoken of, perchance?" Jinar didn't wait for confirmation. "Perhaps it obeys the same rules as our own magical barriers."

"We aren't in a situation to test that hypothesis, sadly." Alexis had drawn a dagger in her right hand.

"How did they even notice? There's nobody here," Saresan asked, looking at the walls and ceiling around them. "Is someone spying on us?"

"Surveillance was a given as soon as we entered," Will answered. "I'd expected a security detail on the way here, but Hyval must have thrown more money at this place than we could've ever imagined. I've heard that voice once before, a couple of years ago during a raid on an illegal smugglers ring, and if it's the same thing, we're dealing with a security-grade artificial intelligence, and a damn good one at that."

"A robot?" Callum looked back up in case someone was trying to ambush them. The ladder was clear, but his worry for Henry only grew. "What will it do?"

"That depends on how it was set up, if it's the one I think it is. Our best chance at the moment is to attempt to reason with it." Will took a careful step at that point and spoke firmly, "We seek the owner of this complex. We mean no harm."

"Assessing accuracy of statement," the voice responded, followed by a pause. "Damage sustained to outer hatch. Inner hatch security compromised. Attempt at compromising security of outer blast doors. Multiple persons possessing military grade weaponry and other armaments. Conclusion: statement dubious."

"We seek only information," Callum clarified.

"Statement dubious," the voice paused again. Callum felt like he was being watched from the very walls. "One unidentifiable person detected. Scanning database and comparing to known robot specifications." A thin red beam of light focused on Tyrus from the ceiling, slowly moving over the demon. While it didn't seem to be harmful, Callum knew its intentions weren't good.

"We need to get him out of there," Nika whispered worriedly, eyeing her trapped fellow, gun held tightly.

"I could use my sword to try to pierce the barrier, it might disrupt it," Callum suggested just as quietly, hoping the voice didn't hear him.

"It'll perceive that as a threat," Will muttered. All the while Jinar stroked his beard and observed studiously, eyes scanning for something.

"No matching specifications found," the voice concluded flatly. "Scanning database with discrepancy modifiers applied."

"It seems distracted by you, Tyrus. Perhaps you could further confuse it." Alexis was trying to muster her magic, but Callum felt only a spark of power within her, fighting to get out. She frowned, looking at her free hand.

"Needless risk," Tyrus remarked.

"We're knee deep in that already, too late to be sneaky." Saresan checked the way they'd come, "Your sword's his best bet, Callum." Callum didn't need to see Henry's eyes to know his feeling of powerlessness, but the very act of trying to free him could also condemn him.

"Unknown persons identified. Danger assessment completed. Hostile intrusion detected, deploying countermeasures."

At the voice's words, the shaft they'd climbed down was sealed shut with a hidden metal plate. Red lights flashed in the ceiling and a droning noise began to repeat.

"Damn it!" Will exclaimed.

The door behind Henry opened suddenly, revealing only darkness. He turned with his weapon ready and fired at something Callum couldn't see, screaming in horror right before a metal claw the size of his head punched through his chest.

"No!" Nika shouted in horror as what remained of her compatriot was discarded on the floor, twitching and gurgling.

Callum was horrified and he wasn't the only one, Saresan aghast and Alexis stunned. Tyrus watched with absolute indifference as the force field died and something emerged. Lumbering forth from the black was a huge, bulky robot that was even larger than Tyrus. It had four legs that it walked on like an oversized dog and an equal number of arms. The top two were bulky and ended in claws, while the bottom two were large rifles. It didn't look human at all, more akin to a monstrous wolf, sparkling white and pristine save the blood that soaked one of its claws.

Davis and Nika didn't hesitate to open fire, but their shots were ineffective, bouncing off the robot's body and scorching the walls. Callum charged forward, fuelled by his anger without thinking of the danger. Fortunately, the robot didn't perceive him as the primary threat, opening fire on the rifle-armed soldiers. Alexis and Jinar were barely able to save them with their combined spell casting, conjuring a weak and brittle barrier that quickly failed under continuous fire. It gave them the seconds Callum needed to get close and swing at the upper arms.

His sword cut through the metal with ease, but their foe noticed its appendages clatter to the ground, trying to grab him with both claws. His magic fought violently to be heard, pushing past the suppression of the force fields to answer his gut instinct to make some distance. It shunted him forcefully back, leaving him safe but disorientated. The robot closed the distance immediately and he swung again, managing to take off one of the claws that had so coldly killed Henry. No, there was still a chance to save him, he had to try! Tyrus moved forward, grabbing the final dangerous limb and holding it still so Callum could slice that off also.

Even as the stumps sparked with the lifeblood of the robot, it continued to struggle, trying to bludgeon Tyrus and Callum with what remained. Tyrus took a blow to the chest, and though it recoiled, the demon did not yield. Callum ducked a swing aimed at him, the robot's stump smashing into the wall and leaving a hefty dent.

Callum wasted no time in driving his blade through the body of the thing, slicing it in half, whereupon it finally fell inert. Callum didn't revel in his victory however, rushing to Henry's side, only to see that he was deathly still, lying in a pool of his own blood and innards. He'd had the power to save him all along but instead let him die.

"Siobhan, Luna, come in," Will spoke into his gauntlet and got back only silence. "We need to go," Will told them then, his remaining soldiers regrouped around him.

"The way out's blocked," Saresan reminded him.

"Not out, in," Will corrected.

"In? They know we're coming!" Nika protested, voice strained with loss.

"You want to stay here and wait for more of them?" Will didn't wait for an answer, heading to the door the robot had emerged from.

"Irrelevant. The information on the Great Threat must be obtained," Tyrus told them, looking Callum over once. "Move."

"But—" Callum barely got that word in before a large panel in the ceiling opened and another of the robots fell down from above.

"Move!"

He obeyed even as it hurt to abandon Henry, though he wasn't alive to care. He couldn't help looking back as they rushed down the corridor to the blaring sound of the alarm and the sight of the robot thundering after them, firing as it did. Only through Tyrus creating well-timed barriers did they survive its barrage, losing sight of it when they rounded a corner.

Siobhan had stepped out of the *Silverbolt*, even though outside offered nothing more to stave off boredom than within, giving the systems a once-over as she often did. They'd heard not a peep from Will or the others since they'd reached the compound, but she didn't worry; with all their magic, they were more than capable of taking care of themselves, or so Jinar would've told her. She rolled her eyes at the thought of the quietly smug sorcerer declaring his 'endless affinity with the arcane' or whatever rubbish he'd pulled out of his ass at that moment. He was so insufferably self-assured, but his power was undeniable.

She'd imagined sorcerers letting the power go to their heads, but Alexis and Callum had been far from that; Jinar too, for all his posturing. He'd even managed a few genuinely funny remarks in their frequent meetings at the bar, though she'd denied it at the time. She'd thought of suggesting that one of the sorcerers remain with them to guard the ships, but Jinar would've volunteered, and his presence lingering over her shoulder as she worked was the last thing she'd wanted. Luna hadn't disembarked from the *Star's Shadow*, but her guard was watching the horizon impatiently, pacing with her cannon ready for a fight that she was itching for.

"Come on, come on, where are you?" the soldier muttered to herself.

"You really want a fight, don't you?" Siobhan asked as she worked.

"You hired me to shoot people, that's what I do." Xene pressed a button on the side of her cannon which flashed blue. "Pirates, criminals, Z-Gen. Don't care who."

"So, why'd you leave Z-Gen then? All the fighting you could ever want right there."

"We don't fight crap. We 'patrol' and 'guard', putting on a pretty show for the civvies who lap it all up." Xene had stopped, holding her cannon in her left hand so she could quickly draw her pistol with the right. "But boy, when there was a real fight, it was great."

"Doesn't explain why you left," Siobhan stated idly, checking the power cycling on the ship's cannons.

"Kicked me out. Their loss. Better off without them anyway."

"And your equipment? Isn't that illegal now you're out?" Siobhan turned quickly at the sound of a shot, only to see that Xene had fired at a lone beam of metal in the distance. "Hey! If there's anyone out there, they might've seen that!"

"Good." Xene holstered the pistol as quickly as she'd drawn it. "Then maybe things will get more interesting around here."

"I'm quite happy with it remaining dull, thank you very much." Siobhan looked back to the readout, seeing that it was all within acceptable parameters.

"That's what the others said; they were too soft. They just let people get away, 'to avoid collateral damage'."

"Collateral damage?" Siobhan repeated, attention once again caught. "What the hell were you shooting with?"

"This." Xene pressed the blue button on her gun again, vents opening on the sides. "If the civvies don't know better than to get out of the way, then they deserve to get caught in the crossfire." That was all Siobhan needed to hear to know why Xene had been drummed out of Z-Gen, but the conversation had brought her thoughts to the feral demons that everyone had spoken so much about. The prospect of facing off against them wasn't something Siobhan relished, but they seemed long gone, along with everyone else. If they'd caused this devastation, she pondered how the rest of the galaxy would fare against them.

Were the sorcerers among them so powerful that whole worlds fell to their power? What chance did she stand, even with the *Silverbolt*, against one of them? Having grown up in a bustling metropolis of one and a half billion, the quiet of the ruins had crept under her skin more than she'd thought it would. Keeping herself busy helped somewhat to take the focus off it, but the chilling wind couldn't be ignored.

"And there they are." Xene's words caught her attention. Siobhan looked about in time to spot a huge vessel briefly piercing the clouds in the distance before rising above them.

"Shit." Closing the panel on the *Silverbolt* quickly, she rushed into the cockpit of the fighter and began powering up the systems. "You see that?"

"A Z-Gen cruiser with a squadron of fighters, I saw it," Luna answered over the speakers. "And you know where they're headed."

"You sure?" It didn't take long for her ship to estimate their destination. "Damn it, how did they know? We've got to warn them."

"Already tried, no signal. Maybe they spotted us on the approach after all, I don't know." Luna was trying to work it out. "But they'd've fired on us there and then."

"Unless they wanted to know why we came here." Siobhan was sitting up in her chair, watching the ships get further and further away on the scanner with each moment.

"They could've captured us before we reached the surface, no sense in letting us get away." Both of them were silent as Z-Gen got further away still.

"Nothing for it then." Siobhan primed the laser cannons, taking a breath. "We've got to buy them some time."

"Very funny. They'd swat you out of the sky."

"You hear me laughing?" Siobhan readied to take off, already working on how she'd divert the fighters through the ruins if she had to. "I can use the storm as cover and pick the fighters off one at a time, that'll get the attention of the cruiser for sure."

"And they'll shred you with a single barrage."

"If they can hit me," Siobhan countered back, priming the engines for immediate take-off.

"*When* they hit you! You're one fighter craft, what can you do?"

"Less the longer I sit here arguing with you."

"We're to wait for them to return or bail out if we're compromised, we're no good to them dead," Luna told her. Her ship wasn't readying up. "They haven't detected us, so we stick to the plan." For a second, Siobhan paused to consider the odds. She was outgunned and outnumbered, but that was nothing compared to what Callum and the others would suffer when they landed the cruiser's soldiers.

"Damn it," she muttered, knowing exactly how dumb it was but also that she had no real choice. "You stick to your plan, Luna, I say the plan's gone to crap already. There's no way in hell I'm abandoning them, so it's time to make a new plan!"

"Siobhan!"

Luna's shout was ignored, the *Silverbolt* taking off with a thunderous roar. If that somehow got the cruiser's attention, then that was just as good as her initial plan, her craft shooting off with speed in pursuit of the imposing vessel. It was crazy, but so was getting comfy with front row seats for the deaths of her friends.

"You got this," she told herself, hoping it'd be convincing enough to push back the gnawing concern that she was, in fact, flying headlong into death. But that was the fear which kept her sharp, fed her piloting instincts. She'd gone toe-to-toe with Z-Gen fighters before, and this time she'd be getting the first strike. It would be a piece of cake.

The *Silverbolt* pierced the clouds for a second, her viewscreen adjusting instantly for the bright sun, highlighting the squadron of fighters and the cruiser they swarmed around. It was even larger than she'd guessed from a distance, but she'd dance circles around it, or at least that was the plan.

Quickly identifying the two laser cannon batteries and presuming it had point defence, she submerged once more into the clouds, waiting for a few seconds as thunder boomed around the *Silverbolt*. As it rose up once more, the targeting systems focused on the closest fighter and she fired without hesitation, hitting the engine of her quarry with two shots. It exploded as she once again submerged, hoping that they hadn't pinned down her location in the panic.

She waited a little longer before surfacing again to see that all the fighters had disappeared, likely scouring beneath the clouds for her. The cruiser hadn't slowed, however, its intent still clear, and as much as she was tempted, Siobhan knew that picking a fight with that was suicide. Her best hope of distracting it was to take out its escorts, give them a reason to pause. So, she dived back beneath the protective clouds to see the squadron was still unified. Worse, the thirteen craft immediately changed course to intercept her.

"Damn it," she cursed, taking a few potshots before diving further to take the fight to the city ruins.

"This is Z-Gen. You are in violation of planetary quarantine. Power down your weapons and surrender into our custody," an automated communication informed her before repeating.

"Yeah, no."

She blocked it quickly, lasers flying past her view as she reached the scorched shell of civilisation. Heart pounding in her chest, Siobhan took deep breaths to calm it down as she navigated the controls on memory alone, her eyes glued to the screen.

There wasn't much to make pursuing her difficult, but she'd take any terrain over nothing. Siobhan reached for a button she'd never pressed before. There was a loud thunk from outside, and a small screen overlaid on top of her view in the bottom left, showing what was behind her vessel. The Z-Gen fighters were lagging a little behind, her ship faster than theirs when not boosting.

"Reverse fire activated," a young female voice informed her dully.

"Time to see if you were worth getting over the G-8. Don't fail me now."

She focused on dodging and weaving around the ruins, firing when a target was roughly lined up in the small window. It gave her pursuers pause, and they broke off into three smaller groups, two flying up while the smaller one continued to give chase. A lucky hit took out the cockpit of one of them, it crashing into the carcass of a building with a hefty explosion. With a grin, she opened up communications again.

"Had enough yet?" she taunted.

"We've got you outnumbered, give yourself up!" a stressed-sounding man responded. One ship barely avoided getting hit by another of her shots. "Damn, that was close! She's good!"

"Channel's still open, hotshot. You guys seriously the best Z-Gen has?" Her grin lingered as the channel went silent. "Why don't you call down your little cruiser since you can't hit one tiny fighter—" The ship rocked suddenly, the controls to her left sparking and the lights flickering.

"Hit sustained to left hull. Targeting matrix offline," the voice helpfully informed her.

"Damn it," she muttered under her breath, rushing to patch in the backup targeting matrix as she dodged more intently.

"Oh, I'm sorry, did I wound your pride and joy?" the Z-Gen pilot asked mockingly. That hit a nerve, her cockiness vanishing instantly.

"Backup targeting matrix online," the voice informed her, in time to notice the bulk of the squadron which had boosted ahead of her, hoping to cut her off.

"Now, are you going to back down, or do I have to rip your little relic apart?" the pilot asked smugly.

"This 'little relic' is done playing with you now." All thoughts of taunting the Z-Gen pilots vanished as she turned the ship around sharply, returning her cannons to their original facing just as fast. "Because you're screwed."

Boosting towards the oncoming fighter, she aimed for the man who'd dared to insult the *Silverbolt* and fired.

Chapter Forty-Six

The corridors Callum ran through were all alike and devoid of anyone, and try as they might, the hostile robot was in hot pursuit. Will reached for a small cylinder at his belt and pressed the top before throwing it behind them. Seconds later, the robot passed where it landed and the cylinder exploded, knocking the foe off its footing long enough for them to gain a tiny bit more distance.

Callum was winded, however, his legs aching in exertion and frustration as he carried on anyway. Jinar turned to fire upon it with his magic, managing to send a thin, wavering bolt of lightning at the metal beast. It seemed unaffected by it, continuing its pursuit as Will darted to the right into an open door.

Callum and the others followed, and once they were all in, the sergeant pulled a hefty switch which shut the door and encased it in an even thicker door. Callum then took in their surroundings and barely contained his revulsion at the butchering before him. Scattered around the barracks – it was his best guess with the many bunk beds present – were what remained of the garrison in various states of dismemberment. It was unclear what had killed them, but it was unlike even the attack on Callum's world. The room had a putrid smell of rot and death, but no flies were swarming the cadavers or rats gnawing at the spoiled flesh.

"Good gods!" Alexis exclaimed, turning away quickly. Saresan didn't avert his gaze, looking instead for a way out of the room.

"What the hell happened here?" Nika stayed exactly where she was even as Davis strode out to examine the dead.

"A massacre." Will's answer was punctuated by a dull thud on the other side of the door, then another. "I don't think it will hold forever."

It couldn't have been the demons that did this, Callum thought to himself; the rest of the complex wasn't littered with corpses that the monsters would've left in their wake. He was starting to wonder if the demons were a worse threat than humanity was to itself.

"It'd better, there doesn't look to be a way out." Saresan was checking the ceiling for anything they could lift away, but there was nothing.

"No claw marks," Davis remarked, looking at one of the more intact bodies.

"Could the feral demons get into this place with the force fields? It would explain how the AI was able to identify Tyrus." Alexis was trying to ignore the continued thumping from the robot beyond. She looked at the demon. "Can you get us out if this gets worse?"

"Myself and one other, possibly." The demon stayed next to Callum, leaving nothing to chance with the meaning of its statement.

"I'm not abandoning anyone here." Callum felt he had to repeat that. "And we don't have time to argue, before you start. Either we all get out of here alive or none of us do."

"The force fields seem somewhat similar to the countermeasures Kole had set in place, though they are likely more fallible," Jinar mused out loud. "Perhaps that is why this place escaped the wrath of the demons relatively unscathed, as they could not sense the presence of the occupants through the energy. This, of course, does not help us in our current predicament, but disabling the force fields would be desirable. With our magic uninhibited, the robots would be no problem for me to dispatch."

Another dull thud on the door.

"Finding Hyval is our first priority," Will told him, turning his guns to the door as a dent began to appear. "Nika, Davis, to me. We'll hold it off as long as we can, you lot find an exit. We'll need your sword too, Callum."

"Of course." Callum held it ready to strike at a moment's notice, Tyrus readying the familiar teleportation magic that he'd fight against if needed. The two exchanged a look that carried the debate between them without words.

"Found something!" Saresan had pulled a metal wardrobe from the wall, and behind it was a sturdy grille and a passage beyond it, large enough for them to crawl through. If Tyrus would fit was another matter. The guard was about to swing his weapon at the grate before Davis stopped him, pressing the button beside it which made it fold into the wall. "Thanks."

A hole was blasted through the door then by the robot's cannon, the shot barely missing Callum and melting some of the ceiling. It said nothing, which made him wonder if there was any empathy in its metal chassis at all. Had it cared for Henry's death at all, or were they just intruders to be dispatched and discarded? Callum struck at the claw which tried to grab the hole, severing most of it with ease as Will prepared to throw another grenade.

"Go," Tyrus ordered suddenly, stepping in front of them and preparing its sizeable magic. Even with the force fields, it could still muster so much. Will and Nika didn't need to be told again, falling back to the open grate that Saresan and Davis had already crawled into.

"I can't leave you here," Callum insisted as another hole was shot through the door. He surprised himself with those words.

"I cannot fit through," Tyrus told him flatly, summoning forth a barrier to cover the door entirely. It blocked two shots, and through one of the new holes, Callum could see a second robot that had arrived.

"If you stay—"

"Why do you linger?" it snapped angrily.

"Because I'm not leaving you here to die! You can teleport after us like you did before." Callum wasn't going to give up so easily on his mentor, despite their disagreements. Only Will waited by the grille for Callum.

"The force fields are too strong in that direction." Another hole was shot through the door; it wouldn't hold much longer. "Disable the force fields and I will follow. Until then, I will provide them something to fight."

"Callum, we have to go." Callum ignored Will, refusing to move.

"My utmost priority is to protect you. All else is irrelevant," Tyrus spoke with finality, facing its potential death as it was.

"What about the magic concealing us from Keiran?" Callum was grasping at straws as the door finally gave, crumpling into broken fragments of metal.

Three robots struggled against the barrier Tyrus stubbornly continued to maintain, drawing upon more power than Callum knew was within the demon. He used what little of his own magic he could to strengthen the barrier, but it was negligible.

"We need you!" Callum told him honestly.

Despite all the pain it had caused and despite himself, he found that he was worried for its safety. He'd never thought at their first meeting it would happen, but there he was, pleading with the thing he still thought of as a monster. It didn't react, perhaps it couldn't.

"Incorrect. I am replaceable, you are not. Go." Tyrus had run out of patience, shoving him with exceptionally powerful magic to the corner where Will still waited. Callum couldn't fight against the force that the demon was exerting on him, overwhelmed by the sudden surge in power. "Guard him with your life," the demon ordered Will.

"Of course," the sergeant answered with a nod. Callum was shaking his head. "Come on."

"But—"

"It's doing this for you, don't make it be in vain."

But Callum didn't want it or anyone to do that, not for him. Then the barrier Tyrus had been using to stall the robots vanished and it fought toe-to-toe with them, blasting one of them with a ball of fire as it blocked another's claw with its staff, the wooden weapon managing to buckle the metal. Despite its calm, there was a pent-up ferocity it also battled with, the inner rage they sought to control which it was tapping into.

Anguished, Callum felt Will's stare and knew that, like Tyrus, he wouldn't back down from his orders either. With great reluctance he sheathed his sword and followed the others into the opening, crawling into the dark. Will blocked almost all the light from the room with his presence behind him, and with a press of the button in the crawl space, they were plunged into blackness.

"Not bad for a relic, don't you think?" Siobhan taunted as the penultimate fighter craft detonated in a fiery explosion, focusing her sights on the now sole foe that had managed to elude her. "You know I'm faster than you. I'll get you eventually."

"This is Alpha Squad leader calling on all channels. We're under heavy fire, requesting reinforcements." Only the one who'd mocked her ship remained, a far more skilled pilot than the ones he'd commanded. He'd been ignoring her, broadcasting the same message for a minute without reply. The storm above, however, continued to do an excellent job of blocking short-range communications, stranding the sole survivor.

Of the cruiser she'd seen no sign since leaving the clouds. She wanted to break off and seek it out but knew the straggler would take his shots in the open air above the city. She was planning to do exactly the same if he tried to retreat, so the game of cat and mouse continued.

"*You're* under heavy fire, get it right," she corrected with a smile. She fired on her foe once more, who deftly weaved between two large buildings. The *Silverbolt* had taken a few hits – most of them from him – but the Z-Gen fighters simply didn't have the grunt to punch through her hull properly. The leader's craft was a little bit better, perhaps a newer model, but it was nothing compared to her own.

"Got to hand it to you though, you're not bad for Z-Gen. What's your name, anyway?"

"This is Alpha Squad leader calling on all channels—" the man started from the top, swerving right and low, skimming street level.

"Oh, knock it off, you know they're not coming. You're the meat shield." She followed, trying and failing to hit him once again. The targeting matrix was just a little too slow to keep him in her sights, she'd have to look into that after they left Geladan.

"And you're not?" the man countered, engaging his reverse thrusters suddenly to get behind her. She boosted forward to counter, but not before he managed to land another laser.

"Damage to reserve thrusters. Maximum speed reduced by seven percent," the voice informed her as she heard sparking from the back of the cockpit. She kept her anger internal, not wanting to give him any clues of how annoying his lucky hit had been.

"You even know what *really* happened here?" Siobhan turned only to not see her quarry, which confused her. She checked the scanner, and though it showed nothing, she knew better; fighter craft didn't simply vanish into thin air. "It wasn't the Great Threat that blasted this place to kingdom come, surely."

She didn't get a reply, the silence playing on her nerves. He was playing mind games with her, seeking to provoke a wrong move, but she refused to go along with it, taking a deep breath to try to clear her head and moving to minimise the angles the man could shoot her from.

"Do you even care about the people who died here, or are they just another statistic?"

At the quiet, her eyes flitted between the view ahead and the scanner nervously. Where was he? A part of her thrilled at the challenge the man was giving, but it was tempered by her survival instincts. She couldn't contact Luna, no matter how tempting it was; the risk of giving away her position wasn't worth it. Suddenly, a torrent of beams from high above startled her, blasting through the building to her left. The ship's emergency dodge protocols kicked in, thrusters shoving her right with all the grace of paper caught in the wind.

"What the hell was that?!" The scanner showed a large concentration of dots rapidly approaching her position. "Oh, damn it."

"My reinforcements," the man spoke at last. A corner of the viewscreen showed the squadron and, more worryingly, another large craft in the distance. It appeared smaller than the cruiser but was no less intimidating, capable of startling accuracy even at that distance. "This is Sergeant Siegfried of Alpha squad, reporting in." All the while she still couldn't spot him on the scanners. Then she figured it out and kicked herself.

"You landed and powered down," Siobhan stated out loud. "Sneaky bastard."

"Sergeant Gabriela, Delta leader. We have the target in our sights. Where's the rest of your squad?" a stern female voice asked.

Why were they still publicly broadcasting? Perhaps they sought to demoralise her with more than overwhelming numbers. Siobhan tried to get more distance between her and them, but it would only delay the inevitable conflict.

"Dead. Don't underestimate her, she's good." There were at least twenty of them roughly a minute away from her, and more than one was the larger model of fighter craft. Her database didn't recognise those, which concerned her even more.

"Roger that. Fall back, we'll take care of this," Gabriela informed him.

"Negative. You'll need all the help you can get," Siegfried answered back.

"Report back to your cruiser. I speak with the authority of General Cadmus," came her order.

"...Roger that. Falling back." Siegfried's dot reappeared on the scanner remarkably close to her, but pursuing would bring her closer to Delta squad and the mess that entailed.

"I'd ask you to surrender, but I don't think you're the type," Gabriela told her, rushing ever closer by the second.

"Damn straight," Siobhan answered back, allocating reserve energy to the cannons.

"All the more fun for me," Gabriela replied darkly. "Kill her."

A direct communication came in then, which she couldn't block.

"You should've surrendered, it would've been easier." It was Siegfried. Gone was the arrogance he'd started the fight with.

"For you lot, maybe. Once they're gone, I'm coming after you," Siobhan promised angrily, double-checking that her weapons were primed.

"I look forward to it, if you live." Siegfried's ship boosted off and away, continuing to use the buildings as cover even with the overwhelming suppression fire he'd have gotten with the more direct route.

With her original quarry gone, Siobhan considered her situation and quickly decided not to dwell on it too much; it didn't matter how badly the odds were stacked against her, just that she overcame them. Besides, how was she going to win her bet with Jinar if Z-Gen killed her?

"You're not getting out of it this easy, you smug git," she muttered to herself with a smile, turning to face the oncoming squad and already starting to devise a plan. How hard could it be?

The group felt incomplete without Tyrus silently judging their every action. Even now Callum wanted to go back and help, but Will wouldn't have let him.

All the way along the linear path the interference from the force fields grew, until his magic was all but silenced by it. The quiet hum had grown louder, to the point that it made concentrating difficult. The crawl space ended abruptly with another grate, which opened into a small room that didn't have the alarm sounding.

The hum was also far quieter in there, but space was at a premium, the group barely managing to fit. Stacked all about them were sealed crates, each labelled with complicated lists of their contents. Nika and Davis were covering the only door leading out, guns ready for anyone unfortunate enough to open it. Jinar's smile to Callum was weak, understanding the predicament they were in now they were without Tyrus. Saresan had been none the wiser, however.

"Where's Tyrus?" the guard asked.

"It stayed behind to buy us time," the sergeant answered with finality, closing the grille behind them.

"Don't we need it for the concealment magic?"

"We do," Callum answered back grimly.

"Well, the situation just got a whole lot worse."

"And we cannot teleport away until we weaken the force fields protecting the complex, which will make it susceptible to demon attack." Jinar stroked his chin thoughtfully. "Quite a conundrum."

"We can't go back even if we wanted to, so that's out of the question. The alarm isn't active here, but we can't presume we won't be noticed immediately when we emerge," Will warned.

"They'll pay for what they did to Henry," Nika promised.

"Don't let your anger get the better of you," Alexis warned the soldier moving up to the door. Listening to it, Nika paused.

"I think someone is in the next room," she whispered to them.

"Another robot?" Callum inquired, blade ready.

"No, someone." She stepped back. "It's faint and he's some distance in, but it's a person."

"We open it on three," Will declared. Nika and Davis nodded, the latter closest to the door panel. "One—"

"Why wait until then?" A voice echoed around them, surprising everyone but Davis, who stood unwavering with his rifle ready. Callum found something strange about the way it spoke, unsure if the man's tone was laced with sarcasm or self-importance. "I know you are there, little rats. Make yourselves known to me and I will delay your extermination."

The door opened without their input into an immaculate space. All the furniture Callum could see was white as snow, a single seat sofa and a compact kitchen area making him guess it was a living area of sorts. The air within was colder than elsewhere in the complex, and there wasn't a single robot in sight. Nika quickly regained her composure, seeking the threat that wasn't yet there.

"Come on, come on. You don't have all day."

"I presume that you can hear us?" Alexis asked, looking around the room for the method of his divining.

"You presume correct, my dear." The voice took on an entirely different tone with her, softer and quieter. It unsettled Callum. "You have scurried through the maze like obedient little vermin and have found your prize."

"You wanted us to come here?" Alexis inquired. She didn't react to his change in tone, though her daggers were held firmly.

"I wanted you dead, but we can't always get what we want, can we?"

"Are you Hyval?" Callum then asked cautiously. A nervous chuckle bounced around the room.

"I refuse to continue this conversation without you partaking in the amenities I so graciously provide." The tone shifted again, more forceful and threatening. "Now show yourselves!"

Saresan glanced at the others and shrugged.

"Can't say we have much choice."

With that, he walked out into the room. One by one, the others followed suit into the spartan yet luxurious space beyond.

The whole place now visible, Callum spied an impressive throne of white metal, and sat upon it was a middle-aged man, dressed in an immaculate suit that was somehow even whiter than everything else around them.

His attire was a stark contrast to his dishevelled brown beard and the heavy bags under his eyes, his left hand gripping the arm of the chair tightly as they presented themselves to him. His stare was sharp and piercing but never lingered in any place for long, save the impressive knife in his hand that he was fiddling with constantly, almost fascinated by the glints of reflected light. He was nothing like Callum had imagined, far from the regal ruler surrounded by loyal subjects, yet he sat without fear before them, which told Callum there was something else at work here that they hadn't realised. Nika and Davis kept their guns trained on him, but the figure didn't care.

"Are you Hyval?" Callum asked again, watching him and their surroundings for the inevitable trap.

"Not yet, not yet..." The man appeared to be whispering to the knife like it were a baby. "We have guests." A shiver ran down Callum's spine.

"Mad as they come," Saresan muttered, not quiet enough to stop the man from hearing it.

"And who are you to speak?" The seated man stood quickly, glaring at the guard with his blade gripped tight. "You who have broken into my home, an interloper seeking my life like all the rest?"

"*Are* you Hyval?" Jinar enquired casually, not in the least concerned with the man's threatening tone. After a pause, the stranger slumped back in his chair weakly, glancing about the room.

"What is a name when you have seen oblivion?" Once more had the tone shifted, this time to defeat.

Callum couldn't see an obvious exit to the room, but there had to be one; he couldn't believe the man had sealed himself away in a gilded cage with no hope of retreat.

"I shall take that as a yes," Jinar finally said. "We seek information that your complex likely has collected, with which we can better prepare the galaxy—" Hyval laughed quietly, shaking his head.

"I was as prepared as anyone, but their assassins reached me anyway. That is what you are, is it not? Assassins sent to finish what you have started." Hyval leaned forward in his chair, watching Jinar intently.

"You are mistaken. Would we not have tried to kill you already?" the sorcerer countered.

"Information is difficult to extract from a corpse, though not impossible. Not that you could kill me in your present situation."

"You hid away from the attack on this world here, but what were you hiding from?" Callum stepped forward, wary of the idle threats that may very well have had merit. "Was it the demons?" At the mention of the creatures, Hyval shot Callum a glare, gritting his teeth.

"Whisper they did to me, as they do you," he murmured, looking frantically around the room. Saresan sighed. Callum tried to see what the man was looking for. "They are everyone's master in the end."

"This is going nowhere." Saresan approached with weapon in hand.

"Saresan—" Alexis warned him too late, the guard colliding with a force field that only made itself visible with his impact, sending him recoiling back in pain. It shimmered a brief blue before fading into nothingness once more. Hyval laughed again as Jinar went to check on Saresan, but the guard waved him away.

"I'm fine, I think." Slowly he stood, dusting himself off despite the lack of dust.

"You thought me a fool, yet you are the fool." Hyval pressed a button on his throne and from the ceiling emerged weaponry on extending arms, all aiming at them all. Davis and Nika moved to watch them instead. "No others have made it this far, so I commend you for that, but you shall not take me down! We had a deal and you're breaking it!"

"A deal?" Alexis repeated, concerned and surprised. "Did you... negotiate with the demons? Why?"

"Silence, else your words will be your last!" threatened Hyval.

"We *aren't* here to kill you. We really aren't working with the demons: we just want information. I know we have a demon with us, but—"

"But what, little rat?" Hyval again watched Alexis intently. "But what?"

Callum thought on how best to explain, but what would reason with a man beyond reason? Alexis cautiously looked at him, mirroring how the others likely felt. In the end, it was Callum happening to glance at the doll on his belt that gave him the inspiration he needed, the most simple and obvious of things to pierce the veil of madness Hyval was shrouded in. So armed with truth and a deep breath to steady himself, Callum began to explain plainly and directly.

"The demon with us does not work for the same master as the others you obviously know of." Hyval watched and listened. That itself was progress, so Callum continued, "It is one of a small cabal hidden away that seek to defeat the leader of the other demons. We really haven't come here to kill you, no matter what you think: all we want is evidence of who did this to your world. If you give us that, we'll leave and tell no one that you're here. That I promise on my honour."

Chapter Forty-Seven

*It takes only ONE agent of the Great
Threat to doom your world.*

Don't leave it for 'someone else' to deal with. See it, report it.

Z-Gen: Protecting Tomorrow

—*Z-Gen advisory poster*

There was quiet after Callum had finished. Everyone waited as the king glared at him. Slowly the ferocity in Hyval's look faded, eroded by his words into tiredness and tentative clarity. Once more the man slumped on his throne, and the knife he wielded fell from his fingers, clattering to the ground.

"They were absolute and brutal, unflinching in their task," Hyval spoke in a pained tone, eyes downcast. "They slaughtered and destroyed that which my forebears had taken centuries to build. A life was nothing, a million even less, little more than a block of time chiselled out for their deaths."

"The demons?" Alexis guessed. Hyval shook his head.

"...Z-Gen." Callum had half-expected the answer, but that made it no easier to hear.

"Telanthir was right," Alexis said to herself.

"So, *he* sent you," Hyval spoke with disdain. "He should know better."

"He wants to show the people of the galaxy what Z-Gen have been hiding, who did this."

"He doesn't know what he's stepping into, and neither do you," Hyval warned harshly. "The monsters were savage, but they had come only to destroy. The people looked to Z-Gen as their saviours, but the olive branch was barbed with poison."

Hyval pressed another button on the throne, and for a second it seemed like they'd have to fight after all, but the guns returned to the ceiling and the wall behind the ruler began displaying static images unlike any horror Callum had ever seen. The first few were from above the conflict and showed demons washing over the streets, tearing every living thing they found to pieces. Nothing was spared nor could resist the tide of blood and terror, but the buildings remained intact. Callum thought back to his own world and wondered if that was how it had ended.

"Oh god," Nika exclaimed, eyes glued to the spectacle like everyone else. "You getting this?"

Will nodded subtly. Unbelievably, the images got worse, a brief picture displaying the bloody carnage left in the demons' wake. Hyval shivered even though he couldn't see it, eyes closed.

Then the view changed, and it was not demons but a rain of death that obliterated everything it hit. Explosions in the distance were captured destroying whole streets in that single moment, and huge beams not unlike the ones from rifles pierced the structures of the city, melting everything they touched. Demons and humans alike were caught in the crossfire, though few people remained at that point. A snapshot of time caught the devastation crystal clear, it leaving no doubt as to the events leading up to the city's present condition, a silent ruin.

"Perhaps some people yet live, hidden away in tiny pockets untouched by the onslaught," Jinar hypothesized.

"And you think Z-Gen will have left them alive?" Will asked back. "That must be why the Z-Gen ships are still in orbit. Any communication tries to get off-world, they block it and track down whoever sent it. There might be some in the underground sections of the city—"

"Dead," Hyval cut him off. "The incinerator missiles took care of that."

"But they're illegal!" Nika objected. "Banned under every law governing war!" Hyval laughed at her.

"Poor child, to think war plays by the rules set out for it."

Callum didn't need any detail on what an incinerator missile might do, knowing how flames spread through enclosed areas. Before Hyval could speak again, the room was bathed in the flashing red light and the blare of an alarm.

"Intruders detected. Activating countermeasures," the AI declared as the image behind Hyval shifted to showing the entrance room. The new arrivals were immediately identifiable.

"Z-Gen," Callum murmured. A constant stream of soldiers was climbing down the ladder, with one standing by it giving orders. "How did they find us?"

"Perhaps we were not so subtle in our arrival as we first thought," Jinar answered back. Hyval's expression shifted dramatically to one of suspicion and hate.

"...You led them to me, deceived me after all!" accused the ruler as he reached for the discarded knife. "Made me confess so they can execute me!"

Will was already looking around for an exit to the room even as the weapons emerged once more from the ceiling.

"It isn't like that. We came by ourselves—" Callum began to protest.

"Yes, my dear, now it's time to dispose of them." Hyval wasn't speaking to them, gazing upon the knife that rested on the floor as he pressed another button. "Scurry, little rats, so that your final moments may amuse me!"

But the weapons did not fire on them. Instead, the room was plunged into darkness and the siren died, along with a yelp of surprise from the ruler moments before two loud clunks from his direction. With the dying of the background hum, Callum's fear was overwhelmed by the feeling of his magic flooding through him, and he couldn't have been happier. That he couldn't sense Tyrus's familiar presence stifled his joy, hoping it was merely hidden to protect them from any demonic onslaught. The flashing red lights in the ceiling were the only ones to return, bereft of the siren. Of Hyval there was no sign.

"Main generator failure. Internal force fields deactivated. Countermeasures disabled. Emergency protocols engaged. Opening doors and unsealing bulkheads. Redirecting power to emergency life support and external force fields. Blocking main entrance with external force field." The AI was quieter than before. Will and the soldiers activated beams of light that shone from the bottom of their rifles, quickly highlighting a new opening in the left wall.

"Can you teleport us out?" Will asked. Davis turned to his superior at the question.

"Sir—"

"Can you?" Jinar shook his head. "Why not?"

"For the same reason you cannot communicate with Siobhan or Luna. The external force fields would likely prevent such an escape, and I do not wish the spell to go awry were I to try. We *could* relocate to the entrance that way, but I fear such a move would be unwise. More concerning is that I cannot feel the presence of Tyrus nearby," the sorcerer answered.

"Then we're as dead as it is as soon as we leave the complex." Saresan was watching the illuminated exit.

"I did not say it was dead, merely that I could not detect it. It may be beyond the complex."

"It wouldn't abandon Callum in here, not even for its own survival," Alexis pointed out. All the while Callum wanted to move, make away before things got worse. "We'll have to take our chances outside unless you want to be in Z-Gen's hands. You got what Hyval showed on the wall, right, Will?"

"From start to finish. Stick together, everyone, and keep your eyes open. Let's go."

Will was the first to head into the corridor beyond, flanked by his remaining soldiers. Callum couldn't believe that Tyrus had been taken down so easily by the robots, not after all he'd seen of its power. Despite that, there was a gnawing voice in his head that said exactly that, trying to weigh him down with worries he could do nothing about. He shoved it away when he moved with the others, knowing that now wasn't the time to dwell.

The corridor they moved through was narrower than the ones before and lacked doors leading off it, making him hope it was a secret escape tunnel Hyval had used to flee the complex. That dream quickly died as they heard the distant noise of people running ahead of them and around a corner. There was nowhere to take cover or hide, and heading back wasn't an option, so Will and his soldiers kept going.

Stopping at the corner, Davis peeked past it for a second and held up four fingers with his left hand. There had to be more than that, though Callum wondered how they'd got there so quickly or how they'd known of their destination at all. Each possible answer was worse than the last, so instead he focused on his magic, readying it to defend himself and the others if it was needed. Davis checked around the corner again and held up more fingers. There were eight now.

"I saw something, sir, could be survivors," a distant female voice stated.

"Or our targets. Proceed with caution, you've been briefed on their capabilities," a male voice answered.

"Subtlety does not serve us here," Jinar declared before stepping beyond the corner with a confident smile. He illuminated himself with a soft white glow that was sure to get Z-Gen's attention, and it did.

"Over there!" the first voice shouted.

"How observant," Jinar called back while launching a corridor-spanning wall of flame ahead of him at great speed.

"The hell—" The shout was cut off by a horrifying scream, then silence. Callum winced at the deaths Jinar had wrought, even though they sought to mete out the same to them.

"I believe our path is clear now. Let us—" Jinar blocked a shot aimed at him with a barrier, sighing in mild annoyance. "My apologies, I appear to have missed one of them." A mutter later, and a bolt of flame shot from his pointing finger. After another second, a cry rang out that died quickly.

"Have you finished showing off?" Alexis asked, annoyed.

"I am flattered that you are impressed with my display of arcane prowess."

She didn't respond, Davis looking around the corner again before giving a thumbs up to them, whereupon they moved quickly forward and closer to freedom. Callum tried not to look at the bodies of the dead but couldn't help it, their armour scorched and melted. He was only glad that their eyes were obscured by what remained of the helmets and that their suffering was likely brief.

They didn't get far before more Z-Gen soldiers blocked their path forward. Callum had dared to look around the corner they'd stopped at and was surprised to not be shot. Then he saw the fortified position the soldiers held in front of stairs leading up. If Hyval had gone that way, he'd have met them on the stairs, likely sealing his fate. Fifteen Z-Gen soldiers were protected by a dome-shaped force field, and a bulky device sat in the middle of the group.

"Portable force field generators are cutting edge military tech," Will explained quickly. "Heard Z-Gen wants to incorporate them into their ground vehicles at some point. I wonder if they know that the force fields protect them against your magic."

"I don't think they'd tell us either way. Teleportation is out of the question until we turn it off," Callum remarked.

He thought about using his sword to attack the barrier directly, but if they had a way to fire back through it, he'd be too vulnerable. His experience with them told him they couldn't, but he was the first to admit he knew little of anything concerning the current weapons of war. He tried his own magic against it from a distance regardless, flinging a concentrated ball of lightning at the barrier, which made it waver for a moment.

"Strengthen the field!" one of the soldiers shouted, and the barrier grew less translucent. "There's no way out, servants of the Great Threat! Surrender and we shall take you into custody!"

"And get killed? What do you take us for?" Saresan shouted back. He knew better than to take a shot with his halberd while the barrier was still up.

"Last chance, though you do not deserve that leniency," the soldier called to them.

"Then why even offer it?"

"Do you surrender?" they were asked again.

"You *do* realise that we are powerful sorcerers, yes?" Jinar checked. "We could end your lives with a thought, and you dare to provoke us to do so?"

"Then do it, I'm not afraid of you. I've killed tainted in my time, and they were just like you, stuck up and dead." The soldier spoke with vitriol, though Alexis couldn't help but smile a little at the remarks holding some truth in Jinar's case. "More soldiers are on the way: you can't kill us all." Callum looked to the others, not to check their opinion on the question but for options.

"A combined spell may weaken it enough for us to attack," Alexis suggested quietly. "But we'd have to time it well."

"I can't think of anything better." Callum got no objection from Jinar. "On your mark, Jinar." Callum prepared most of his magic, hoping it would be enough. Jinar gave a nod, and together the three stepped out and launched their spells. Jinar used a bolt of lightning while Alexis sent forth an instant beam of white energy, lacking any distinct element. Callum settled on the spell he was best at, a large fireball that hit the barrier last. It wavered from the first two impacts and fizzled with a satisfying crackle at the third, leaving the soldiers exposed.

"How..." the commanding soldier shouted before pointing to the trio of casters. "Open fire and get that thing back online!"

The barrage was immediate and intense, with only Jinar acting fast enough to protect the three of them. Will gave a silent order to his soldiers, and they started firing from the corner at the Z-Gen fortification, taking out a few quickly. Alexis aimed for the one shouting orders and fired another beam, but it was blocked by a soldier interposing himself in front of his commander. His sacrifice worked, and a moment later the force field turned back on. Now that they knew their foes couldn't fire on them, Callum didn't move back to cover. His former mentor smiled to himself, also remaining in place.

"That was but a taste of what we can do, soldiers of Z-Gen," Jinar proudly declared. "You cannot overcome us, but if you surrender, we will be lenient and spare your lives."

"If that is how it must be," the commanding officer said back as the force field deactivated in time for the reinforcements on the stairs to shoot at them.

An even more torrential hail of fire suddenly bombarded them. Only through their combined magic were they able to make it back around the corner safely, though it had cost Callum nearly all his reserves.

"Cover your eyes!" Will suddenly shouted.

Callum didn't notice the small metal cylinders that clattered against the wall by them until they detonated.

An intense flash of light blinded him and the accompanying bang messed with his hearing, panicking him; he should've felt pain, but there was none. Powerless to do anything, Callum could vaguely hear shouts and people rushing towards him. Staggering and finding the wall, Callum felt a padded hand grab his arm and he reflexively swung his sword out.

His vision sluggishly returned in time to see his handiwork, the Z-Gen soldier before him clutching the stump where his arm used to be in howling agony. He'd been armed with a humming baton, Callum glad he hadn't discovered first-hand what they did. He quickly looked away to see that the enemy was among them and numerous, having taken advantage of the brilliant white flash to break the stalemate.

Will and Davis were taking precise shots at approaching soldiers, with Alexis protecting them as best she could with her magic, but there were just too many of them. Saresan was locked in melee combat with two soldiers but had the advantage of range, felling one with a hefty swing and the second with a beam from the spike.

"That all you got?" Saresan taunted, drawing another baton-armed soldier's attention.

Then Callum noticed Nika slumped on the wall ahead of him, clutching her stomach as blood seeped through a hole in her armour. Jinar was trying his best to keep the soldiers from her with all the fire and lightning he could muster, but his magic wasn't enough, and lacking a weapon of his own, he was quickly overwhelmed by three soldiers who tackled him to the ground.

In the dark moments of despair, Callum found not hopelessness but determination; no one was going to die if he could help it. Rushing over to help Jinar, Callum forced his magic into the blade itself, which was wreathed in flame. He cleaved one soldier down just as he looked up, and the second lost his head a second later. The third let go of Jinar and scrambled back desperately, drawing Callum's eyes to a pair of robots that he recognised as the same type from the *Gorgon*.

Quickly, Callum rushed them before they could begin firing, lopping off the arm of the one on the right. They refocused their attention from Jinar and Nika to attack him, and that was when Callum learned that only one of their arms had the rapid-firing beam weapon. The other struck Callum in the chest, and a surging pain shot through him, setting every nerve in him alive with torment.

"Callum!" Will shouted from the corner, readying another cylinder to throw.

The robot noticed too and fired back, hitting Will in the helmet with a beam. He collapsed with a cry as soldiers rushed past the robots. Callum tried to fight the pain but couldn't, sword dropping from his limp hand as he finally blacked out.

Chapter Forty-Eight

When Callum awoke, he wasn't shocked that he didn't feel the sword at his side, though the doll remained looped in his belt. His body ached all over, and not just from the uncomfortable position he'd been slumped in. He rose to his feet to discover that his hands were manacled together and that he was contained within a circular force field prison.

They appeared to still be in Hyval's complex but not a part he'd seen before, a large room where Z-Gen soldiers worked at consoles that spanned two of the walls. In a corner he spotted two people depositing what looked like Will and Nika's rifles into a small metal box, closing it and pressing on a panel that fastened sturdy locking latches on the outside.

Already he was thinking of escape, but what hope did he have, contained, magic-inhibited and unarmed? Looking around more, he saw that beside him were other force field prisons and in them were his friends. To his great relief, they were all alive, but some were worse for wear and all were unarmed; Will's helmet was gone, and the right side of his face had been bandaged up, including the eye.

"Will, are you alright?" Callum asked, hoping that his friend could hear him.

"I've been better." The sergeant sounded like he was in great pain. One of the Z-Gen soldiers nearby was watching them intently.

"How long have we been here?"

"An hour, maybe a little more. The others woke a while ago, though considering what you went through, I'm surprised you're still alive." Nika and Davis were also without helmets.

They were hooked up to a device that was being observed by a Z-Gen soldier with an orange cloak. Nika's wound wasn't bleeding at least, though the brown-haired soldier was downcast in her confinement. Saresan definitely looked worse than the others, sporting many bruises on his arms and face as well as multiple holes in his scale mail. He noticed Callum being awake, getting Jinar's attention with a hand gesture. Jinar had a bruise on his forehead but was otherwise unharmed, thoughtfully observing the soldiers and the force field that contained him and likely trying to figure out a way to escape.

Callum couldn't even feel his magic, so intense was the barrier around him. Alexis was unharmed and relieved to see that he was alright, and likewise he felt the same for her. Tyrus wasn't among them. Callum didn't give up even then, frantically looking around the room for anything that could help them, no matter how slight. The soldier that had been observing them looked over to one clad in a green cloak.

"Sir, he's awake," he informed his likely superior.

Roughly Callum's height, the green-cloaked man stepped away from the one talking to him and stopped by his prisoners. Only then did Callum realise that, along with the rifle slung over his back and the pistol at his side, there was the sword in his hands. Callum couldn't keep his eyes from the weapon, afraid of what the man would do with it. Callum still hadn't gotten used to not seeing their eyes but could tell the green-cloaked man was looking at him.

"My name is corporal Arad," he introduced himself with a commanding voice that was gentler than he'd thought it would be. "And you are Callum Igannes."

"How did you find us?" Callum asked the question that burned most on his mind.

Lying about who they were would achieve nothing, as they could check their chips for the information. How much did this man know about what happened to the world? Had he been there, ordering the deaths of billions?

"I'm not here to tell you how we located you, only to bring you in for interrogation and imprisonment." A soldier passed Arad a tablet, which he glanced at. "If you wish to better your situation, you can start by telling me where the Great Threat plan to strike next and of this blade you possess."

"Be careful with it, it's wickedly sharp," Callum warned.

"We learned that firsthand when our technicians examined it. The metal it's made of doesn't match any known material. How did you come across it?" Arad awaited an answer Callum wasn't willing to give. Everyone else mirrored his reluctance. "I'm trying to make this easier for you, but if you insist on silence, I'll move on. What do you know of the Great Threat's plans?"

"We're not with the Great Threat," Callum told him honestly as Arad passed the sword to a soldier who carefully placed it within the same box the other weapons had gone into. "We're here to try and stop them, not that I expect you to believe us."

"I'm certainly sceptical, but while we're sending the databanks in this complex for analysis, I have nothing but time." Arad handed the tablet back, the soldier walking off to continue his work. "Suppose, however, that I believe you. If you aren't working with them, what is the thing that we found on the upper levels?" A spark of hope fired up in Callum's stomach.

"Tyrus is alive?" Alexis was surprised.

"So, it has a name. We were unable to glean any information from it. It killed twenty of my soldiers before we could contain... whatever it is." The fragile hope of Callum wavered.

"An impressive feat for a non-sorcerer. How were you able to achieve it?" Jinar enquired casually.

"I'm the one asking the questions," Arad reminded him. "What is that thing?"

"A demon," the sorcerer answered frankly.

That grabbed the attention of a few nearby soldiers, who stopped what they were doing to listen.

"...A demon," Arad repeated slowly.

"That is what they refer to themselves as, yes. It could explain better than we can, naturally." Arad turned to the soldiers who'd stopped working after a pause, his stare all that was needed to get them busy once more. "What do you intend to do with us, if I may ask?"

"That is beyond my remit. My duty is only to capture you and send you on. If I were to guess, your... demon will be examined in one of our laboratories. You will be shipped to a secure detention facility for interrogation and incarceration." Arad walked over to Jinar. "I will also be passing on to my superiors our findings on how force fields affect your talents." Callum had hoped they'd not make the connection, but there were more pressing issues he had to warn Arad about.

"You need to let us go," Callum told him. "You're all in great danger while we're here."

"I have no intention of releasing an agent of the Great Threat, especially not because you asked nicely," Arad answered back.

"We're not with them, damn it!" Saresan was frustrated. "How many times do we have to tell you that?"

"Only once if you can prove it, which so far you haven't. All the evidence points towards you being dangerous criminals who are a risk to the public. Your presence on a world recently attacked by the Great Threat does little to help your case. I've also received reports of a single fighter craft that took down our escort fighters during the approach to this complex."

"She is good at what she does, or so she has told me," Jinar explained simply.

"Sir, Hyval has been received on board the commander's vessel," a soldier informed Arad calmly. "All sensitive information has been sent forward for analysis, and the AI has been deactivated."

"And the recordings from the helmets?" Arad enquired.

"Sent on as well, sir."

"Good. Purge the originals." The soldier nodded at the order and went to work.

"Fuck," Nika muttered angrily as all the evidence Henry had died for was lost forever. Will sighed.

"We're ready to escort the prisoners to the extraction point on your order, sir, as soon as we deactivate the external force fields," another soldier informed Arad.

"You mustn't!" Callum exclaimed, alarm bells ringing in his head.

"And why not? What do you know?" Arad asked him. Before Callum could answer, a third soldier called for Arad's attention.

"Sir, we have a communication coming through, priority one," a woman working at a large machine told him. "They're asking for you by name." The corporal stepped away.

"We'll continue this later. Take the time to consider how you will answer my questions." Arad stepped away towards the machine, pressing a button that brought up the view of a bridge manned by Z-Gen personnel, projected onto the opposite wall. In the centre of the image was a man in full military attire with the same colour cloak as Arad.

"This is corporal Mateo of the *Alexandria*. What is the current situation?" the man asked, stern and to the point. Arad walked to a more central position, looking to his equal. Callum listened, hoping to glean something that would help them. All the while he worried about Tyrus and the imminent peril they'd all be in when the force fields were shut off.

"This is corporal Arad. The situation is under control. My soldiers are checking the final unexplored areas of the facility. We've apprehended a group within, wanted for numerous crimes," Arad answered.

"I wonder how many of them speak of chairs," Jinar joked idly to Saresan's weary glare.

"I was unaware that the *Alexandria* would be in this area. We were assigned the task of watching over Geladan alone," Arad remarked.

"We'll be landing a squad to take your captives into my custody," Mateo informed him. "I trust we'll have no difficulties extracting them out of the facility?" There was a pause.

"The prisoners are in *my* custody, corporal. We're quite capable of transporting them off-world ourselves. Your offer of assistance is appreciated, but we do not require it," Arad answered calmly, though there was a hint of suspicion in his tone. "You haven't answered the question of why you are here."

"I'm following up on intel provided by a helpful citizen, which led me here. Cadmus has ordered that I see to the disposal of the prisoners in your custody," Mateo answered plainly.

"My orders come from general Olahnir," Arad countered. "Under no circumstances am I to release or relinquish the prisoners once captured. I'm sorry that your journey has been in vain."

"This isn't going to end well," Saresan warned quietly. All Callum could think about was the order to take them to the surface, the ticking time bomb under all of their feet.

"Ah yes, Olahnir," Mateo spoke without reverence. "A man yet to whet his teeth in the conflict against the Great Threat. How you must miss Kalton's steady guidance."

"His death was a tragic accident, but I'm confident that Olahnir will be capable in his new position." Callum recognised neither of the names. "As I said, I'll be taking the prisoners from here. Your presence isn't required."

"And I'm afraid I *must* insist that you hand them over. They are dangerous criminals that must not be allowed the opportunity to escape captivity." Mateo looked past Arad to Callum and the others. "If you're concerned about your orders, Arad, I'm sure it can be explained reasonably enough. Suppose they broke free from their confines, and you were forced to kill them to protect your own soldiers. No one would be any the wiser but those here, and you can guarantee their silence."

The soldiers in the room were now listening to the conversation themselves, distracted from their work by the casual discussion of execution. Callum grew even more concerned with every statement Mateo made, but Arad remained resolute.

"I'd know," the corporal replied, shaking his head. "My orders are to keep them in my custody and I'm not going to deviate from them."

Mateo glanced to his left and gave a nod to someone out of view.

"Are you sure that your judgement has not been clouded by the very prisoners you seek to protect from due punishment?" Mateo asked thoughtfully. "It wouldn't be the first time that a Z-Gen officer has been swayed in such a way."

"I hope you're not implying that I'm in league with the Great Threat. That's a serious allegation." Arad folded his arms slowly.

"And you've given me reason enough to suspect that this may be the case. I'm merely following protocol," Mateo replied bluntly. "I'm sending a task force to examine this possibility. I hope that you will do nothing to impede their investigation." Callum didn't like the sound of that at all and neither did Arad's soldiers, but their commanding officer nodded slowly.

"We have nothing to hide, Mateo, but if you attempt to take matters into your own hands, we are well within our rights to stop you."

"Of course." The communication ended abruptly.

"Sir, do you suspect—" one of the soldiers began to ask.

"I don't need to suspect. I know," came Arad's ominous answer. "Can we get a communication to Olahnir?"

"No, sir; the external force field is interfering with our signal. We'd have to relay through another ship, and the only one in range is the *Alexandria*." Arad considered their options, looking to Callum and the others before turning to his soldiers.

"Fortify the perimeter. We may have some unwelcome company soon." Arad turned his attention to his captives once more as the soldiers about him changed focus instantly; orders were being issued, people redirected to other places within the complex. Arad muttered something under his breath before addressing Callum.

"You've made a powerful enemy, Callum. It seems General Cadmus wants you dead, no matter the cost," the corporal announced to them.

"So, you're going to fight to keep us alive just long enough to dispose of us yourself?" Saresan was bemused. "Aren't you both on the same side?"

"We are, but the six generals have diverging views on certain things. Cadmus is a man of action and has fought the Great Threat for most of his career. His record is full of exemplary military actions against our foe," Arad explained, going directly against what he'd said earlier about not revealing anything to them.

"Doesn't sound like you agree with his methods much, but is that worth risking your men?" the guard inquired.

"There are many who don't agree with Cadmus's methods, but he has the full support of the High Marshal. His position is assured as long as that's the case and so are his methods, but this is the first I've heard of Z-Gen forces willing to fight their own."

"Is it that difficult to contain a sorcerer in prison?" Jinar enquired casually.

"You're one, you tell me." The corporal didn't wait for an answer. "My men are prepared to lay down their lives in the line of duty. You are right, I'd rather none of them needed to. I cannot let that blind me to my purpose here." Arad clasped his hands behind his back. "Why are you so afraid of me bringing you to the surface?"

Callum wanted to answer immediately but found himself hesitating; would they even believe the truth, and if Arad did, would he kill them to save his men?

"Aren't you kind of proving that guy's point by asking us that?" Saresan asked.

"It's prudent to gather as much information as you can on your enemy, even if its source is of dubious credibility." Arad unclasped his hands as a trio of soldiers passed behind him, rifles out, ready for combat. "The only reason you'd have to want to stay here that I can think of is that you're expecting someone to save you, but I doubt they'd be able to get past the *Alexandria*."

"We don't gain anything by telling you what we know." Will caught the corporal's attention with his words. "You're not going to let us go if our information saves your lives."

"That's correct. It will likely save your lives as well, however, as you're in no situation to defend yourselves." Alexis and Callum shared a look, and he could see in her eyes that they'd both reached the same conclusion.

"There are more creatures like the one you have imprisoned, a lot more of them," Alexis began. Callum continued for her.

"They're savage, monstrous and focused only on killing." His words caught the attention of some of the soldiers, who muttered amongst themselves, though most quickly dismissed it. Arad didn't interrupt, waiting to hear more. "Once they've killed us, they'll have no qualms about killing you too."

"The force field surrounding this place is the only thing preventing them from noticing that we're here, and once they do notice, they'll attack," Alexis added.

"The *Alexandria* and the task force in orbit would stop them." Arad's point was immediately dismissed by Jinar.

"Not so. You are quite unprepared for what they are capable of, but they are only after us. Were you to let us and Tyrus go free—"

"I cannot do that," Arad interrupted him. "Not even to save ourselves."

"We're trying to help you avoid needless death," Alexis told him. "We're criminals only because you decree that sorcery is that. Had you not tried to arrest us on Gui-Lon, we'd've never been the danger you perceive us to be. We tried our best to avoid killing people in our escape." Alexis was trying to reason with him, something Callum hoped would work. "You seem like a sensible man, Arad, please heed what we've told you. If our enemies find out we're here, you'll all die, and we don't want that."

Arad thought on her words, and though Callum couldn't see his face, the corporal's posture spoke of conflict.

"Sir, we cannot trust the tainted. They speak with forked tongues," a soldier reminded her superior.

"Not the first time we've heard that," Saresan muttered to a warning stare from Alexis.

"They even admit to it, sir! We have to disable the force field so we can communicate Mateo's actions to the general." The soldier didn't get a reply, which puzzled her. "...Sir? We don't have much time."

"And we may have far less if we don't heed their warning," Arad stated to the shock of his fellow.

"Sir, you can't be serious!" she exclaimed.

"I want you to take a squad with a communication relay to look for an alternate exit, there's bound to be one somewhere. Broadcast to the general once you're out and then signal for the ship to prepare for a hot extraction of the prisoners. Under no circumstances will you mention *anything* that they've said, do I make myself clear?" The soldier hesitated. "Do I make myself clear, sergeant?"

"...Yes, sir. Right away, sir." She motioned to three other soldiers, one of them grabbing a carrying case by the handle before they departed through a door on the right. Arad sighed.

"I want the force fields on our perimeter at maximum power and heavy weapon platforms set up behind them. Deploy what remaining combat robots we have." Arad's order was obeyed instantly, the soldiers' focus again shifting. He spoke then to his captives, "We would have more, but your creature destroyed most of them."

"Sir, I'm getting reports of heavy fire directed at the complex, ship-grade laser cannons," a soldier declared abruptly.

"Mateo's trying to take out the force fields," Will guessed. That filled Callum with imminent dread.

"Please, you have to free Tyrus," Callum implored his captor desperately, but to no avail.

"How long till they breach it?" Arad asked his soldiers just as the lights died. There was a moment of silence, but for Callum it was anything but that; even through the force field, Callum sensed the arrival of a large concentration of magical energy not too far from them. They were too late; the demons had arrived.

Chapter Forty-Nine

"But how do they do it? How do six generals oversee the entirety of colonised space?"

"I thought it was obvious: delegation."

"Delegation?"

"The High Marshal delegates a sixth of the galaxy to each of the generals. They, in turn, delegate sections of that to their commanders, who in turn delegate to the captains, and so on and so on."

"But how can the generals keep on top of everything going on if they're not actively watching it?"

"They don't. Their aides filter through the reports sent their way and only pass on important stuff, allowing them to focus on what matters."

"Like what?"

"...What?"

"What do they actually do that matters?"

"Important stuff!"

"Like?"

"..."

—Exchange between patrons of the Five Lasers Bar on Kavadran

The lights returned quickly enough, and Callum knew that Alexis and Jinar had also felt what he had. They looked to one another and Saresan recognised that expression.

"Damn it," the guard voiced Callum's sentiments nicely, just as the soldier who'd broached the bad news from moments before spoke again.

"We've lost the outermost fortification, sir."

"What?" Arad walked over to the soldier's console. "How did Mateo's forces mobilise so quickly? Did they say how many attacked?"

"No, sir; the monitoring station feed was cut before that. The next one in is under attack now, they're reporting..." The soldier gave a puzzled pause. "...This can't be right, they're reporting—"

"Display the feed, now!" Arad ordered sternly, taking immediate charge of the situation.

Callum knew what they'd see and was too slow to warm them as the grisly and macabre scene was laid before them. The soldiers were being overwhelmed by a large group of demons, ripped apart and cut down by their brutal savagery. They spared no one, ignoring pleas of mercy and butchering those who tried to run. Nika couldn't look away, terrified beyond measure.

"The hell?!" one soldier shouted, as stunned and horrified as all the others. It was like his world all over again, Callum thought, helplessly watching as people died because of him.

"Inner defences are failing, sir. ETA to… their arrival, one minute, maybe less," came the grim proclamation. Arad turned to one of the sergeants there quickly.

"We can help!" Callum suggested then. "We've fought them before."

"I can't take the chance that you're in league with them," Arad told them.

"We're going to die," Nika murmured to herself hopelessly.

"Stay focused," Will ordered her to no avail.

"Why? They're going to rip us to pieces! I should never have volunteered for this suicide mission!" She sunk down to her knees, breathing light and erratic.

"Why would we warn you about them if they were on *our* side?" Saresan had had enough, glaring in frustration at their captor. "You may not trust us and I sure as hell don't trust you, but none of that matters if we're dead! Stop being a stubborn ass and let us help you!"

The door to the left opened, and in staggered a wounded soldier clutching his chest, armour clawed open. From down the corridor, there was the sound of horrified screams of pain and a presence of magic all too familiar to Callum, setting his heart racing.

"…Help me," the injured man gasped before he collapsed. Two soldiers rushed to his aid while Arad stood in the middle of the growing panic, torn between his duty and his life.

"Sir?" he was asked fearfully by one of the privates who clutched her rifle tightly. Those present were readying their weapons on the door the demons would eventually reach, prepared to give their lives needlessly.

"Give the order to all remaining fortifications to fall back to this point!" Arad ordered.

"…There's no one else left." The reply was barely whispered, full of silent dread. Callum wanted to plead with them more, but Arad wouldn't listen.

"Then we have to hold out for as long as we can. Mateo wants the

prisoners, so he'll have to fight his way through those things to reach them."
Arad drew his pistol, pressing a button on the side which made it emit a quiet
hum. "What they are is irrelevant, that they must not reach the prisoners is
all that matters. You are soldiers of Z-Gen, the best there is. Give them no
quarter and let them pay for every inch of ground they gain with their blood!"

"They bleed a black ichor-like substance, very unlike blood," Jinar
corrected politely, hand gestures hinting that he was trying to find a way to
escape confinement from within. "And they will give far less quarter than
you can ever rescind from them, we can assure you."

"Please, let us help you," Alexis implored one final time.

"You're wasting your breath." Will was looking around at unattended
weapons, planning for the inevitability that the force fields containing them
failed.

Callum knew what Tyrus would do if it still lived once that happened;
he'd be teleported out of the complex within moments, leaving the Z-Gen
soldiers to their inevitable fates, but perhaps that would spare them the
brunt of the demons' ire. Callum had his eyes not on the box with their
weapons but the door the demons would burst forth from, the presence of
magic growing closer and far more powerful than he thought it should've
been. The door started to turn a searing red which intensified until the
metal melted into a pool of slag, the work of strong magic which allowed
the demons to rush into the room.

"Fire!" Arad ordered and his soldiers obeyed, unleashing volley upon
volley, which was surprisingly effective against the demons.

They aimed for the head with great accuracy, felling the first clump in
little order. There was no time to reflect on their minor victory, however,
as more surged in to replace their fallen brethren, rushing over the dead
with no regard for their existence, and all Callum could do was watch. One
demon got within clawing distance of a soldier, but Arad shot it with his
pistol without a moment's hesitation, blasting a huge hole through it which
it couldn't recover from. As soon as the attack had begun it was over, or so
it seemed; but the strong magical presence remained, one that Callum now
recognised for some reason.

"Sir, what... did we just shoot?" one of the soldiers asked as the bodies
evaporated before them into nothing.

"The enemy," Arad answered simply.

Something caught their attention and they fired on a target out of sight but quickly stopped, one looking to their rifle.

"Keep firing!" the corporal ordered, shooting at their foe himself, only to stop when a narrow and momentary beam of light hit one of the assembled troops, boring its way through his body and into the wall on the other side of the room. Nika flinched as the unfortunate victim fell backwards, a perfectly circular hole of nothing in his chest, very dead. The ones on either side of the corpse couldn't look away from it.

"Quaint, but futile," came a reply that brimmed with self-certainty. "I would suggest not firing if you value your lives."

The voice left nothing to the imagination of Callum as a figure emerged through what remained of the doorway. Wearing ever-familiar purple robes, Alun stepped into the light with a quietly confident smile. The soldiers behind Arad readied to fire, but the corporal held up his hand.

"Hold your fire," the corporal ordered.

"B-but sir—"

"Hold." The order was obeyed.

Callum had expected Xiez, but the arrival of the leader of the Silent Hand was little consolation, though he was alone. Alexis scanned the area behind the new arrival, hoping to see Johnathan hidden in the shadows. One of the soldiers manning a console reached for a pistol despite Arad's warning, only to stop when Alun waggled a finger at him admonishingly.

"What did I just say? Weapon down." Slowly the soldier did just that, provoking a wider smile from the sorcerer. "Good man."

Fear rose up in Callum's stomach that he couldn't suppress. The sorcerer was wearing something under his robes, a bulky piece of attire that Callum guessed was armour of some kind. The man had no other weapons, armed only with his sinister charisma and overpowering magic.

"Who do you serve, the Great Threat?" Arad asked. His pistol wasn't aimed at the sorcerer.

"I would answer, but for you it doesn't really matter." Alun hadn't raised his voice, and unlike before, the words were not laced with honey. Instead, they reeked of absolute confidence.

Alexis and Callum glanced at one another again, both knowing the man's fearsome power. Will read the expression well, though none of them could do anything about it.

"I will dispense with the initial formalities and begin by stating that I have the advantage here, soldier."

"I don't think so," Arad spoke as the door on the opposite side of the room opened, not to more demons but soldiers who, after a moment to take in the situation and their foe, levelled their weapons on the purple-clad man. "If you had the advantage, you'd've already attacked, but instead you negotiate."

"Do not underestimate him," Alexis warned Arad. Jinar was still muttering to himself, the gestures getting more complex, but nothing changed.

"Unlike others who might have come here in my stead, I am... far more reasonable to deal with," Alun informed Arad. "You would not wish to meet the diplomatic face of my fellows, nor ignore the offer that I have for you."

"Don't listen to him," Callum warned, wanting to prevent a repeat of what happened to Johnathan.

"No offer you give me will change my orders," Arad defiantly stated. Will shook his head at the stubborn bravery. "Know this before you speak again."

"It is duly noted." Alun paused and laughed softly. "You know, I do not know your name. I believe introductions are in order. I am Alun, High Sorcerer of the Silent Hand, though that name should not mean much to you."

"Arad," the corporal responded. One soldier by a console started quickly tapping on a screen.

"A curious name. No more than the ones I have encountered in other places, but also exactly like them: insignificant," Alun said with finality. Callum knew where that line of conversation was heading. "I must commend you though for the fine work that you've done here, soldier, though it is somewhat brutish. How long did it take you to finish what the demons started?"

"What are you talking about?"

Arad didn't know. How could he answer like that if he'd known? Did any of the soldiers know? How could they not, working for the very group which committed the atrocity?

"Oh, come now, I thought it was worst kept secret in all of Z-Gen." Alun moved forward a step. Nobody fired. "We only need to light the fire; it is *you* that fan the flames and lets the worlds burn."

Alexis stared angrily at being reminded of what they'd seen. The soldiers looked at each other, and though Callum couldn't see their faces, he guessed puzzlement and worry adorned them in equal measure.

"Z-Gen has stood firm against the Great Threat for a century, defending worlds from the desolation Geladan has suffered," Arad answered. "We would do nothing to endanger the lives of those here. It is our duty to protect them and the galaxy from the Great Threat and all other harm." That only reinforced that Arad didn't know. He then addressed the soldiers present, "Do not be swayed by his words. He seeks to break your resolve, but we will not yield to falsehood. We are the defenders of humanity, and whatever minor victories the Great Threat may have, they'll pale in comparison to the day Z-Gen are victorious."

"Oh geeze." Saresan shook his head. Alun's face moved to a pitying frown, masterfully crafted.

"Then I am so sorry to break the bad news to you and your soldiers. Your superiors are lying to you, Arad, to all of you. Z-Gen didn't come to save anyone, merely to... tidy up the mess. You did the rest of their dirty work when you blindly erased the records in this complex of what has happened here, but now we all know the truth."

Alun's words didn't affect Arad, but more of his men hesitated, unsure and conflicted.

"How do you know about our activities here in this complex?" Arad enquired cautiously.

"With remarkable ease. Your communications are shockingly easy to pry upon, and I have been doing so since the capture of those I seek."

Callum was amazed the situation hadn't already ended in violence, but he was unsure if it was a testament to Alun's patience or truly a sign that neither side had the advantage. The sorcerer before them spoke once more, ensnaring the attention of all who'd wavered.

"My terms are simple and shall be said only once. Hand over him and his blade, and I shall not kill you."

"Only for you to go against your word as soon as we do that?" Arad wasn't at all convinced.

"The alternative is death, which I am willing to provide if you are not willing to comply." Alun's offer was given flatly and simply. "You have seen what your captives are capable of, I assume? Know that their power is nothing compared to my own, and if you do not comply, I will not hesitate to break each and every one of you until nothing remains of your shattered minds."

Callum took a shaky breath, considering that those moments might've been their last, but still he pondered on why Alun didn't act; he was so sure of himself back in his enclave and in the burning ruins of the town where he'd stalled, why would he—

Callum stopped and remembered why the man had dallied before, his scheme to absolutely overpower them with Xiez who arrived later. Surely he wasn't doing that now, was he? Jinar still muttered, as did Nika, but her words were those of despondency and hopelessness. He wanted to plead with Arad, as futile as the effort would be without his sword, but the corporal didn't need time to consider options, levelling his pistol up towards the purple-clad invader.

"No. I won't hand them over to you or anyone else. Callum and his companions are my prisoners, and if you want them, you'll have to get through me, my soldiers and Mateo." Some of his men were faltering, but one look from their commander kept them in place, barely.

"Don't do this, let us help you," Callum urged, begged as the soldiers again aimed at Alun. Their hands were shaking.

"It's their funeral," Saresan murmured grimly. "And ours."

Alun smiled pleasantly as he dusted off his hands, a look that was entirely natural and yet not.

"Alas, at times one does not get what one wishes, even when asking nicely," Alun remarked to himself. As his gaze returned to Arad, the eyes of the sorcerer were glowing a fiery white, the man radiating power. "So be it. If it is death you seek, I shall gladly provide it for you, Arad."

In an instant, the magic within Alun was unleashed upon the unsuspecting soldiers in front of their commander, a wave of all-consuming raw energy fanning away in an outward arc from the man's hand. It was so intense and dizzying that it nearly scalded Callum even through the force field, warping the metal floor.

The soldiers barely had time to consider their fate, one moment there, the next gone. Arad had been spared only because he'd been a few steps away, and in the seconds of continued laser fire that followed, Callum saw the soldiers' futile resistance. They gave their all, firing everything they had at Alun, but he didn't even react, each shot dissipating harmlessly on a barrier that was entirely invisible save for the brief ripple of blue.

One after another, Alun killed the soldiers, each with a focused beam of magic which left nothing of the poor souls but a few minor pieces of equipment. Determination quickly faded into panic at the overwhelming and unstoppable might of the sorcerer. Callum wondered if Alun was so confident of victory that he sought to demoralise him and his companions before slaying them, trapped as they were. If that was the case, it was working for the soldiers, but perhaps instead it was the first sign of weakness that their foe had displayed.

Arad's orders to hold their ground were ignored by some, who scrambled to flee certain death, only to run into the claws of demons that now blocked the way they sought to escape to. Surrounded on both sides with no way out, one of the people manning a console pressed a button just before being reduced to nothing by Alun, and with a dying hum, the walls of Callum's prison vanished.

In that second, three things happened in quick succession; first, Alun turned his attention from the soldiers to Callum. This occurred exactly as Jinar pulled the chest containing their weapons to them with a burst of magic, it crashing into a Z-Gen soldier as it hurtled across the room. Finally, a demon appeared without fanfare right in the middle of the room, ripping Alun's attention from Callum once more, long enough for it to strike with the staff it conjured from nothing.

The enemy had not expected this and was struck, reeling from the sheer force of the attack as the weapon snapped in half and was discarded by the new and welcome arrival. Its scales were scorched in multiple places, cloak shot to tatters, but who it was was unmistakable.

"Tyrus!" Callum exclaimed in surprise and happiness.

It didn't share his relief, snarling with barely contained anger as it teleported his companions away in quick succession, starting with Alexis. That the demon even considered her as the first choice was startling. Had it finally conceded his point, or was that purely out of pragmatism for the moments it would take to get to where Callum was by foot? Saresan had quickly assembled Will and his soldiers so they could teleport together, while Arad stared at the situation for a moment, Callum worried he'd still try and stop them escaping.

"Fall back!" the corporal ordered with a shout, taking the opportunity to move past Alun while he was sprawled on the floor, with what few of his soldiers had survived and weren't routing. Even as they retreated into the corridor, they were shooting at more demons.

"Catch, Callum!" Jinar called out before throwing the sword towards him.

Fortunate to be looking that way, he managed to grab the handle and once again felt complete as Tyrus appeared next to him. Distracted as Callum was, he didn't fight the spell and in an instant was somewhere else entirely.

Chapter Fifty

Callum quickly looked around him as his senses returned, finding that they were a small distance away from the now demon-infested complex. Looming above it was a colossal spaceship, as well as a smaller one that had just landed outside the breach in the complex wall, unloading Z-Gen soldiers who were heading for the underground facility.

That they didn't spot Callum and Alexis was a relief, and yet he wanted to warn them of the horrible death they were hurtling towards, but they probably had only seconds before Alun caught up. Tyrus had already vanished, hopefully to rescue the others as Alexis took in their situation.

Callum's heart was thumping furiously, him only now able to fully comprehend how terribly wrong things had gone and how close he'd been to dying once more. Tyrus appeared with Saresan and the others he'd assembled, while Jinar did so a moment later with Davis, who held the box of weapons they'd rescued. Saresan didn't take long to recover, but Will nearly lost his footing. Davis didn't fare as badly, quickly turning to Jinar and staring at him.

"You will not do that again," Davis told him sternly, almost threateningly. The sorcerer stepped back a pace, looking up at the imposing figure.

"You are most welcome," Jinar answered sarcastically. "Next time I will not save your life."

"Davis, not now," Will ordered weakly, getting a look from the private. "Not now!" Davis stepped back but didn't apologise, looking to the box where his weapons were stored.

"Alun cannot detect us at present, but he will in time. We must move," Tyrus informed them with a quiet snarl.

The demon was struggling with the pain it had endured, and now that they had a moment of quiet, Callum could see the full extent of its injuries. There were more burn marks than Callum had originally thought, and ichor had seeped from several places. He stepped up to Tyrus to try and heal it, but his mentor objected, stepping back.

"Your magic is better saved for something important."

"You're important," Callum objected, channelling restorative energies into the demon's body as the others re-equipped themselves. The demon stepped away again after a second, though it stopped snarling and some of the scorched areas looked a little better.

"We must move." It was more agitated now. Jinar started to muster people together for more teleportation. "No. It will be detected immediately."

"A fair point," Jinar conceded, looking back to the complex they'd been trapped in only minutes before. "As you said, however, they will find us in time."

Nika was looking back too, shaking her head, with memories of the horrors she'd seen playing on her face. With their weapons retrieved, the group began to retrace their steps quickly. Will spoke into his gauntlet as they began.

"Siobhan, do you copy?" were his hopeful words.

They were answered immediately.

"There you are, what kept you? How did it go?" Siobhan asked cheerily.

"Z-Gen kept us," Will answered.

"And you got what we came for?" Silence answered. "No?"

"Things got messy, Henry's dead. What's your present location?" he asked.

"Well away from that cruiser, running a systems diagnostic for any lasting damage. Already had enough problems with the fighters they sent after me, but it's nothing I couldn't handle. Where are you? I'll get Luna to pick you up." Callum didn't trust the silence around them, searching for the tiniest hints of movement, of demons pursuing them, but there was nothing.

"Next to 'that cruiser'," Jinar answered politely.

"Should've guessed you wouldn't make it easy." Siobhan didn't seem disheartened. "Give us a location and we'll pick you up."

"The LZ will be hot no matter where we are," Will warned her. "We'll return to Luna's position. Avoid confrontation wherever possible."

"You're the boss. If you get into bother, give me a call."

The communication ceased, and the overbearing nothingness around them once more took hold. Callum again glanced back to the complex. He wanted to warn the Z-Gen soldiers, but they wouldn't listen, answering only with hostility.

"We did all we could," Alexis tried to reassure him, though she seemed to question her own words.

"Nothing makes up for Henry," Callum told her. He looked to the doll looped into his belt, which had somehow survived their battles unscathed. "Or the people of this world."

"But now we know that Telanthir was being truthful, we can work to expose what Z-Gen do."

Alexis stopped suddenly, looking to her left at something Callum hadn't seen.

He acted before turning, readying his magic defensively to prevent a shot aimed at his head even as Davis shot back at the Z-Gen soldier who was far too close for him to be alone. Callum's eyes scanned their surroundings, and sure enough, there were more lying in wait, concealed within the twisted remnants of the buildings that once made up a likely bustling avenue. Were they Arad's men or soldiers of Mateo? Either way, it was bad news.

The other soldiers began firing as well, but the failed ambush had spent the element of surprise and now Callum was ready. Will didn't try to shoot them, instead moving to Jinar, who protected him while also dispatching soldiers effortlessly with his magic. He risked alerting Alun to their presence, but when death was the alternative, there was really no choice.

Alexis noticed one in the building next to her and threw not a dagger but magic in the shape of the blade, it searing through the soldier's armour and killing him. Saresan's armour held against the lasers, but it wouldn't for much longer, each shot weakening the glistening scales and one managing to melt a tiny hole through it. The guard gritted his teeth and groaned at the burn on his chest, responding with a spread of shots from the tip of his halberd which forced the shooter behind cover.

What ones they hadn't killed didn't re-emerge, but they didn't know how many there were or if they were calling for reinforcements, and neither did Tyrus, who started to move ahead of the group. A chuckle came from the building to their left, which made Tyrus pause, though it was distorted and tinny. A soldier emerged, not from behind a wall but through it, translucent and blurry, an orb hovering above the wall to facilitate the fantastical feat. Callum recognised it as a hologram that was being projected by the orb, though he hadn't imagined such a thing was possible from something so small. Callum guessed who the hologram was by the colour of his cloak as well as what he had to say.

"Callum Igannes," Mateo said as he turned to face them. "My presumption that you would escape Arad's clutches was correct. I'd ask if he's alright, but even if he lived, he won't for much longer. My soldiers will make sure of that."

Tyrus continued moving, ignoring the projected threats, and Callum did too along with the others; they didn't have time to waste on words when a far more dangerous threat could strike at any time.

"You can try to run if you like, but my soldiers are convening on your location, and when they find you—"

"Oh, shut up!" Saresan tried to shoot it, but the orb dodged out of the way deftly, the beam skimming just past the floating device. Callum continued to move, hoping that audacity alone would whisk them to their escape, but the orb followed.

"Stubborn to the end, I see. Many of your kind are like that, so certain their taint will save them."

Mateo's projection didn't need to step in time with them, the orb managing to keep pace. One of the soldiers that had survived the initial skirmish emerged from behind them to try her luck, but Davis had been expecting it, killing her with a single shot.

"Impressive, for an... Otros soldier? It certainly has similarities to their garb." Tyrus continued to ignore the orb, something Callum couldn't manage.

"Don't say a word," Will ordered Davis even as it floated next to the sergeant. Jinar was pondering something.

"I shall have to pay Otros a visit once my soldiers are done with you, escorted, of course, by a fleet or two, to deal with their breach of the treaty." Will didn't speak, and that was when Mateo noticed Callum staring at him. "Some may call your taint wondrous, but they are fools. It is you and your kind who bring about the devastation around you, and in killing you, I will take one small step in righting the wrongs you commit."

"Magic is, as a tool, bereft of evil or good. It is no more corrupt than the weapons any of your soldiers have pointed at us," Jinar announced then. "And for all your words, you have yet to give the order to kill us. I wonder if you question their capability to do it."

"Don't taunt him," Saresan muttered.

"Why not? It is all he himself is doing." The guard shook his head in frustration but couldn't stop Jinar from continuing, "Now, if you are quite done, we shall—"

Callum noticed another soldier ahead of them emerging from the ruins. This time they weren't being subtle, and when another thirty or so revealed themselves, he knew why. Some were armed with large weapons, but none of them fired immediately, nor did they react in surprise at Tyrus being there. What were they waiting for?

"—Die? Quite correct," Mateo finished the sorcerer's sentence for him, and Callum knew that he was smiling under that helmet. "And when you die, I will be commended. My transgression will be naturally forgiven when I present your deaths to General Cadmus."

"Is that all you're doing this for?" Callum was shocked and appalled. "You've no idea what danger your soldiers are in, being near us. If Alun finds us—"

"They are the best at what they do. They have nothing to fear from you or your little pet."

"If you know of Tyrus, then you must know of the demons. They'll kill everyone here, your soldiers included." Alexis's words were all-but-ignored by the corporal, who looked to his soldiers.

Callum was ready to defend himself, and he knew Tyrus was preparing to spirit him away, but then they'd just be facing Alun alone. No, no matter the odds, they had to hold out here, together.

"You may—"

Mateo didn't get to finish his words before chaos broke free, bringing havoc in tow.

No one had time to speak or consider how they'd escape as Alun appeared, much like Tyrus had, next to Nika and the other soldiers. Davis and Will threw themselves away to the ground while Saresan darted back, but Nika didn't; unable to see what they'd moved to avoid, she turned to face the sorcerer, looking up to him and gasping in fright.

As she raised her weapon to shoot, Alun's expression was one of disappointment. If Nika fired Callum didn't know, for a bright flash of white dazzled him. The sound of her shattering, melting and boiling was broken only by a brief and abruptly silenced wail. When Callum's vision returned, Nika was no more. Pain and sadness flared up in him all at once, for another life that the man had taken right before him. Mateo's gaze was fixed on the new arrival, the hologram stepping back even though it didn't move.

"Fire!" one of the soldiers ordered with a shout, shooting at everyone, including Alun.

Jinar and Alexis conjured up defences, enough to shield them from the initial barrage, but already the barriers were failing, their magic running low. Alun didn't take kindly to being shot at, even if none of the beams harmed him, and in an instant he was off the ground.

He floated up into the air gracefully before firing a single intense bolt of lightning at the closest Z-Gen soldier from the same finger that had eradicated Nika. The target cried in agony and collapsed dead, his comrades barely having time to react before the spell bounced from the corpse to the others, one at a time.

The volleys of fire ceased on Callum and his friends immediately as cohesion in the squad broke down; some tried to run, while others sought to hide, in the hope a physical wall would stop the arcing energy of death. Much like Davis's shots on the sorcerer, Z-Gen's efforts were entirely ineffective.

Mateo watched as his squad died horribly, including those that had tried to retreat, the lightning dancing off the twisted metal remnants that jutted out of the buildings to catch up to them. The energy didn't strike at the orb, however, letting Mateo continue to witness what Callum knew Alun had planned.

In desperation, Callum let loose a ball of flames directed at the one who'd caused it all, hoping his fury alone would melt the man away to nothing. Alexis and Jinar joined in with spells of their own, the former firing orbs of white energy and the latter lightning, that crackled with the final reserves of their power. Alun's barrier held for a few seconds before he floated back a little, smiling calmly.

Davis and Will had risen to their feet, the latter's weapon now recovered. Will only glanced momentarily at where Nika had been before taking aim at their foe along with Davis.

"All of that, and yet you delay once more?" Jinar was taunting again, a ball of fire dancing between his palms. "Perhaps you should have slain us while the Z-Gen soldiers had distracted our attention, but that is your folly."

"Jinar," Alexis warned silently, ignored.

Every moment gave Callum time to recover, as best as he could with his heart going into overdrive.

"We have grown far stronger since you last met us, Alun," Jinar boasted. "It would be wise of you to leave before I unleash my full power against you and unmake you entirely."

Callum was considering their options. Teleporting to the ship would be folly, Alun would destroy it with ease. Running was even more futile. No, they had to take care of the man now. He wanted to charge forward, avenge Nika, but he managed to hold back; he'd achieve nothing with such recklessness.

Tyrus stood beside him, wounded but as ready to fight as ever – until the opportunity to flee appeared, of course – with its staff reformed and in hand. Davis and Will had their weapons ready but neither fired. All the while Mateo's hologram watched Alun silently, Callum having to remind himself that he wasn't really there, so he didn't waste magic trying to protect a projection.

"This world was destroyed by my hand. More will follow after you are gone, Callum," the leader of the Silent Hand proclaimed simply.

"*You* did this? Killed all these people?" Callum's anger was only further stoked by the sorcerer's proclamation. It took all his willpower not to act on it. "Why? Why do this? What do you gain from this? You're not a demon, what can you possibly hope to achieve by siding with them?" Alun looked at the clouds above and took a deep breath.

"I have seen what is to be, Callum, the one who seeks the end of humanity," he answered.

"Keiran." Callum didn't need confirmation.

"There is to be no victory for humanity as a species," Alun spoke as if he were certain. Jinar shot a bolt of lightning at the man, but he effortlessly deflected the attack into a nearby building. "If *that* is the full extent of your power, then you have no grasp of what power truly is."

Callum refused to believe it, but Johnathan had with ease, seeing something that he had not. There was no truth in the lies the man had weaved, surely? The worlds of humanity could not all fall, could they? Could they?

"And yet for all the power that this one person has, he cannot appear and defeat us himself." Jinar got another look, this time from Saresan. "It is a perfectly valid point." Callum looked back to the image of Mateo, wondering just how much of what he was hearing was new information.

"You are little different from the rest of these criminals," Mateo declared, though his tone wavered. "They'll fall before the might of Z-Gen as you will, as will the Great Threat." Alun stared into the eyes of the projection with his own burning ones. Mateo couldn't maintain the gaze long.

"The might of Z-Gen is a hollow falsehood."

Behind Alun, the recently disembarked soldiers were suddenly ambushed by demons that swarmed out of every shadowy nook and cranny of their surroundings, overwhelming them instantly. Mateo saw that and a trio of fighters flying towards their location, which Alun half turned to. One by one, the vessels were hit by bolts of magic fired from the buildings around them, exploding violently in sudden and potent bursts of might. The final one crashed unceremoniously into the ground with an even larger explosion.

"A falsehood you will witness die."

"Damn," Saresan exclaimed quietly.

Callum now noticed the Silent Hand sorcerers hidden amongst the ruins that had destroyed the fighters, that had waited for their time to strike. There were no demons yet, but it was only a matter of time before they closed the distance.

As his friends noticed their predicament, Saresan prepared his halberd for their inevitable attack while Alexis reached for her second dagger. Callum also spotted a shadowy figure looking from a barely intact window to their left. He saw the glint of an axe head and knew it was Johnathan, the shackled puppet of Alun who watched the spectacle. Upon catching his eyes, the man vanished, appearing beneath his liege. Alexis was both relieved and frightened all at once, defeating her urge to rush to him and instead staying where she was.

"Divert all remaining forces to the target's location!" Mateo ordered someone beyond the projection. There was a pause. "*All* of them are under attack? Impossible! They were ready for this, how can they—"

Mateo looked back slowly to Alun, who merely continued to watch as the corporal slowly realised how doomed his soldiers were. The fear which had overcome Callum before was slowly fading, however; instead, determination once again emerged in a way that he never thought was possible when Tyrus first presented its impossible task before him. Words came to him, and he spoke them without hesitation.

"Every time we've met, you've thought yourself above me, elevated by your knowledge and learning," Callum declared. "Now I see the truth, that you're no better than the monsters you stand beside. In fact, you're worse than them!"

Callum's conviction attracted Alun's attention.

"Do not be so quick to condemn me, Callum. Were you in my situation, you would have done the same. To seek to survive is only human."

Johnathan looked again to Alexis, his eyes pleading. Will and Davis kept their weapons trained on Alun, ready for a time to shoot.

"At what price? One world? Two? A hundred?" Alexis asked him. Alun did not answer her. "Is the entire of humanity worth your life?"

"You presume that my opposition of Keiran would have done something to save others. It would have only hastened my doom and that of our world. You would have died a decade ago, not knowing it was because of the stubborn and futile defiance of one man you never knew. You owe me your life, but I do not expect any gratitude for that."

"I owe you nothing but the death you deserve for the ones you've killed," Callum told him firmly. Alun smiled as a parent would to an ignorant child.

"You are a loose end left after the destruction of our world, you and your friends, one whose patience with me has worn thin. If others cannot do what must be done, then it falls to me to finish what I started." Callum would've wavered just months ago, but not now. He wanted to question where his bravery had come from but decided against it, hoping that not pondering it would prevent it from ebbing away as he readied for combat.

"He is too strong," Tyrus warned. All the while Alun watched. Johnathan's eyes were on his sister alone, who tried not to look at him. Would he fight against her if Alun ordered it? Would a fight happen at all? Callum was shocked it hadn't yet.

"We have no choice. I have to do something!" he answered back to the demon with finality.

The others knew it as much as his mentor, but only it refused to listen. If it was a hopeless fight, then it would at least be for the right reasons. Callum gripped his sword so tightly that it hurt. What magic had returned to him begged to be unleashed on the one who'd wiped life clean off Geladan, and all the while Alun still watched, believing himself in absolute control of their fates.

"You will do something, yes," Alun promised as he teleported a distance away from them to the ground.

Mateo's image flickered out of existence then, the orb trying to withdraw away from the inevitable conflict. It was detonated, just as the fighters had, by Alun's hand, leaving nothing but dust.

"You will die and no one will care. It is the way of things."

Chapter Fifty-One

"Hope is the shield of the righteous, for even in death it shines eternal."

—*Vedallan IV knightly proverb*

From around them, a small hail of magical attacks signalled the start of the Silent Hand's assault. Tyrus protected Callum with its magic while Jinar and Alexis did what they could to shield the others, but that left only a few free to fight back.

Though Will's shooting wasn't as accurate with one of his eyes bandaged up, his shots still forced a sorcerer to take cover. Davis wasn't so hindered, focusing on one of their foes and downing him with a single blast of his rifle. The man screamed as he slumped and fell out of the broken window, landing with a sickening thud.

"Good riddance," the soldier muttered quietly before taking aim at another.

Alun could've struck at any moment but did not, he and Johnathan watching as the group struggled to defend themselves. Callum expected Xiez to appear much as it had before on their world, all of this an elaborate stalling tactic so Alun didn't have to do the dirty work of fighting them himself. If that was the plan, it hadn't happened yet, and Xiez hadn't been much too pleased the first time around.

Callum looked about in time to see that a pair of demons had tried to close in already, feral savagery in their burning eyes, no doubt drawn to them by the bursts of magic. Callum struck out with his blade and saw for the first time the difference his training had made, felling the first in a single strike.

The second got within clawing distance but was dispatched by Tyrus, engulfed by an all-consuming blanket of flame. Callum hadn't expected another foe right after that, so he was shocked by the figure who ran through the fire to attack him.

It was Johnathan, and his eyes were full of hate as he swung with his axe, a blow Callum just managed to parry with magic. Tyrus's attention was torn away from its charge to the demons that were emerging from all around, a trickle that was sure to become a tide.

Callum noticed that it made efforts to draw as much attention to itself as possible, luring the majority of the demons into a battle with it alone. This left Callum and Johnathan to square off against each other, each assessing the other for any weaknesses. Callum saw none in his former friend save the gem strapped to his forehead, something Johnathan noticed. Still within Callum gnawed reluctance, seeing past the purple robes he wore to the man he once knew.

"You don't have to do this," he implored, hoping beyond hope that Johnathan could see the madness in what he had planned.

"Alun is right. There is no hope for us," Johnathan countered grimly as Saresan moved to stand beside Callum, firing a beam from his halberd as he did. It burned through his robes and hit his chest, but the sorcerer didn't so much as flinch.

"What the hell happened to you?" Saresan asked in horror. Alexis saw the imminent confrontation but could do nothing to get involved, fighting demons in hand-to-hand combat, her daggers infused with white magical energy. It was only a matter of time before they were overwhelmed by sheer numbers, but they couldn't hope to escape until Alun was dealt with and their enemy knew that.

"You did." Johnathan looked to Callum, speaking with disdain as he held out his palm.

A continuous torrent of fire shot forth from it that Callum tried to deflect, but it was just too strong. His barrier held for only a second before he dived to the side, Saresan darting in the other direction. From the ground he could see Alun floating above the melee, watching his struggle with a serene expression.

The view was quickly blocked by Johnathan, who swung down at him once more, Callum again managing to dodge. Saresan had sprung to his feet and struck at the man, only to have his attack blocked. Before either could land another blow, there was a whooshing sound overhead, along with a withering rain of red beams that cascaded from the heavens, slaying demons left and right.

"Someone call the cavalry?" Siobhan asked through Will's gauntlet as the *Silverbolt* finished its strafing run.

"Damn, am I glad to see you!" Will exclaimed even as Davis took out another Silent Hand sorcerer with three successive shots that wore through her protective spells.

"Can't have Jinar get out of his bet by dying, can we?" she remarked as she flew past Alun.

"I never intended on dying, though your concern is touching," Jinar remarked as he incinerated an approaching demon with the click of his fingers and a smile.

Callum and Johnathan both looked to the ship while Alun shook his head dismissively. Not even he could've expected the guns on her vessel to revolve back to face him, firing with unerring accuracy. Alun blocked most of the shots but, after a few seconds, had to teleport out of the line of fire, allowing Siobhan to do another flyby on the demons that were already starting to replenish their numbers. Callum tried to get to his feet, but Johnathan stopped him, striking again with his axe and keeping him stuck on the ground.

"Johnathan, stop! You don't need to do this!"

His words fell upon deaf ears, the axe now ablaze with flame. Saresan's attention had been wrenched from helping by a demon that was gotten too close, the guard fighting it instead with all the lessons of his employed years serving him in good stead.

"With you, she will die. I cannot let that happen, I will not!" Johnathan declared with anger, once again drawing Alexis's attention.

Again, she was unable to act on it, almost caught off guard by a pair of demons due to her focus shifting from her surroundings. How could Callum make the man understand? Alone with his foe, Callum's fear swelled along with the anger for all the death on this world, culminating in a powerful blast of magic that erupted from his free hand at Johnathan, knocking him back but dazing himself in the process. With no current opponent, Jinar turned his attention to Alun and prepared his magic. Alexis noticed where his gaze was.

"It is time to teach you what the definition of power is, Alun, for it is not what you think," declared the sorcerer as he prepared a spell.

"Jinar, that's not—" Alexis began.

He didn't let her finish, teleporting up into the air right next to Alun. The cabal leader had anticipated it, however, and was ready with a spell of his own that went off first. A bolt of lightning shot straight through Jinar. Callum's heart sank and Alexis gasped as he fell like a discarded doll.

Thinking quickly, she used her magic to try and cushion his fall, conjuring an elastic net of magic for him to land upon.

"Oh, you did *not* just do that!" Siobhan's voice was coming from the exterior of the fighter, shocked and angry.

The *Silverbolt* swerved back towards the fray sharply, firing exclusively at Alun, who retaliated with the same spell. It did little more than leave a scorch mark, allowing her to continue her assault. Again, Alun had to re-locate away, just as a trio of Z-Gen fighters swooped down from the clouds towards her. "Aw, damn it, not now! I've gotta bail, can't have them finding you! I'll be back once I shake them, promise!"

The *Silverbolt* took off into the distance quickly and the chasing fighters pursued, leaving them without her vital support once more and Callum still in a daze. Jinar was shifting but only just, Davis and Will having moved to protect him as they all fought on. Exhaustion was starting to catch up with Callum, and even as he shakily stood, he could feel that his magic was all but spent. Yet more demons were arriving, more of the endless stream of monsters which had claimed his world, claimed Geladan and might soon take them as well. His courage still burned brightly, but it was being chipped at piece by piece. Before Johnathan could move to re-engage, Alun teleported to ground level once more, a headache-inducing amount of magic building up in his hands. His expression was one of mild annoyance.

"Enough," he declared as his spell was unleashed.

The bolt of lightning first jumped to Callum. Guessing that he'd be the only target of the spell, he used what little magic he had left to try and block it. It proved woefully ineffective, his body overwhelmed by terrible pain and losing consciousness a moment later.

Callum was surprised when he awoke, though not why he did. Tyrus had healed him, but the demon looked in a terrible way. Its scales were scorched in many more places and ichor seeped from many more wounds, it snarling in pain it tried to suppress. Callum looked about and realised then that Alun's spell hadn't just been for him but everyone, spying Jinar's collapsed form alongside Will and Davis. He felt the familiar sensation of teleportation magic and cast his mentor a glare.

"Don't you dare," he warned quietly. To his surprise, the magic faded, though Tyrus was baring its teeth at his words.

"Will, you there?" Siobhan's voice came from the direction his friends had been fighting. Will was down just like the others. "I damn hope so. I'll be on my way back soon!"

It would be too late by then, but hearing it made his worries focus outward again. His eyes turned not to the enemy but all around, checking if anyone had managed to withstand Alun's might. One of them was still standing, though she was even more shocked about it than he was.

Alexis stood alone, the only one untouched by the lightning. Her saviour stood in front of her, robes scorched as he stared with confusion and fury at the one who'd tried to kill her. All at once, Callum understood.

"You said she would not need to die!" Johnathan protested to his master even as a smattering of demons closed in upon the fallen.

Alexis wanted to cry and smile all at once but did neither, turning her head to see the monsters that had eyes only for her as they approached. Alun took a single step forward as a chill wind blew, catching his robes softly while he closed the distance. Magic was building within him, powerful magic that wasn't aimed at Callum. Why was he not finishing the job?

"She has chosen her side, Johnathan. You could not persuade her then, nor will you now," Alun told him bluntly.

Callum noticed that Davis was stirring ever-so-slightly; perhaps some of the others were alive also. While Alun's focus was off them, they could yet be saved. Tyrus saw that also and gave Callum a look, one he'd seen before, but not for the same reason.

"Not until he is more distracted." Tyrus whispered the words so quietly that Callum barely heard them. It sounded sinister and unnatural, sending a chill shiver down his back. If they had to have Alun more distracted, then that meant that their only hope laid with...

"...Johnathan?" Alexis spoke fearfully.

Only one of her daggers was infused with magic now, stabbing at the first demon that reached her in the head. It fell, only to be replaced by a second. Fright rushed through Callum and Johnathan at the same time, the latter turning around and decapitating the threat to his sister with a single blow. She hadn't expected that, and as Alun stopped walking, it was clear that he hadn't either.

"You would've killed her with that spell!" Johnathan shouted. "You promised you would let her live!"

Johnathan dispatched another demon with his axe, followed by a third who was incinerated with fire. Callum struggled to his knee, wanting to go to Alexis but just not able to. Tyrus placed its hand firmly on his shoulder to stop that, watching Alun intently.

"The circumstances have changed, Johnathan, or have you remained blind to that which is before you?" Alun's tone had shifted; the serenity was gone, replaced with the gilded tongue he'd used so well to capture Johnathan's heart and mind before.

The demons had stopped advancing, perhaps confused at their deaths at the hands of someone meant to be on their side. If they could even tell that was another matter. Perhaps Alun had ordered them to hold instead – and their numbers were far less. Had all the ones outside the complex been dealt with?

"Look to your sister, Johnathan, and see that she is not the woman you once knew."

Alexis turned to her brother, and the two stared into each other's eyes. Slowly and cautiously, he reached his free hand out to her face, but she shirked away. He saw the daggers she had ready to defend herself, could no doubt feel the magic that was building up within her to do the same thing. Johnathan looked at the hand that had been rejected, blinking.

"All you've seen, all you've done... All those you've killed to save me," Alexis told him with so much emotion she was fighting to contain, though she could not stop the tears. "Did you kill the people here on Geladan? Did you kill them alongside the demons?"

Johnathan looked back to her and was about to speak but did not. Alun smiled slowly, taking another step.

"Tell her, Johnathan. Tell her of how you slaughtered those that ran from you, that your axe bathed in the blood of those who died terrified of you." Alun watched as Alexis's eyes widened. Callum knew what he was up to, but this time he wasn't sure if it was a lie. "Tell her of the children, Johnathan. Tell her what you did when you found them, hidden away in a dark basement that the demons had overlooked, huddled and crying. Tell her *everything* that you have done, for her."

Alexis shook her head over and over, unwilling to believe it. Johnathan took a slow, shaky breath that was very unlike him, and yet so very human that it filled Callum with a small ounce of hope as his magic returned ever so gradually.

"...One fireball was all it took." Johnathan's words were quiet. "They did not suffer long."

Callum could imagine just how long an eternity of pain that moment would've been and so could Alexis, her breath stilled as she stepped back from him once more, horrified and heartbroken. Johnathan didn't follow.

"Alexis—"

"Don't." Her harsh tone was unexpected by him.

"Callum brought the demons to our world, brought all that death. If he hadn't—"

"And you betrayed him!" she shouted back, which succeeded only in angering her brother. Alun chuckled to himself quietly.

"Oh yes, I betrayed *him*! That's all that matters, isn't it, that he felt hurt that I did what I had to—"

"You betrayed *me*." Johnathan's words died in his throat. Alun stopped again, mere steps from Callum. It was so tempting for Callum to take a chance and strike, but he knew he'd never make it to him, reduced to ash with a thought. "What would our parents think if they saw what you've done, Johnathan? They'd die all over again in grief to see how the good in you has gone."

"...I... I did it for you..." He was confused, hurt.

Both of those were emotions Callum had never seen in the warrior before, and Alun's expression had shifted to a frown. Alexis's gaze wasn't on her brother's face but the gem on the headband. Her eyes were on the prize, even if her heart was clinging to the memory of what her brother was.

"No, you did it for yourself. You did it in fear, without thinking, and have been unable to step back from your mistake. You thought it was to protect me, but I was always safest away from them, you knew this." She spoke with such pained affection, the kind that only siblings could have. "You've always been the big brother trying to protect me, but you never sought to protect yourself. Let us protect you, let us undo what Alun has done... please."

Johnathan took another breath, swallowing slowly. Alun prepared his magic, though he wasn't distracted enough by Tyrus's reckoning for its plan to be enacted.

"The proof is there before you, Johnathan. She sees the fate of humanity, and still she refuses salvation." Alun turned his eyes to Callum and Tyrus. "It's time to cut the loose ends. Finish what you sought to do back then."

Johnathan's expression hardened, and for a split second, Callum thought all of Alexis's words had been for nothing. But the warrior turned to look at Alun instead of raising his weapon, exposing the back of his headband to his sister without knowing it.

"...Even if she is not who I knew, she is still my sister." For the first time since his death, Callum saw on the man's face the familiar expression of stoicism. "And you tried to kill her."

"And I gave you an order, acolyte," Alun sternly reminded the man.

"Who cares?" Johnathan's weapon was bathed in flame once again as Alexis carefully began to reach for his headband. "You may have wrenched me from the beyond of death somehow, but you don't own me. You want to kill her? You're going to have to go through me first!"

Alun blinked and shrugged softly, though Callum could see a wave of simmering anger that he was holding back. The magic within Alun built up further, making Callum's skin tingle.

"You are wrong, Johnathan. I *do* own you."

Alun's spell was unleashed upon Johnathan exclusively, wrenching the glowing gem from his headband just as Alexis managed to undo it. It rushed to the sorcerer's palm, and in an instant, Johnathan stumbled forward in great pain, clutching his gut. Alexis was startled.

"Johnathan?" Her brother shrugged dismissively.

"...I'm fine," he said to her before charging forward, launching a spell at his master.

The trio of fire beams was deflected away with little more than a flick of Alun's free hand, which then called forth the white entrapping spell that Callum had once been a victim of. This time, however, it wasn't just keeping the man in place but crushing him, constricting and breaking him as he exclaimed in pain.

Alexis cried out in fright and tried to stop the spell, but Alun didn't even notice her efforts. Callum had to do something now, but again Tyrus held him back with an even more powerful grip just as he panicked for Alexis and Johnathan both. If then wasn't the time, when was?

"I am the one who ensnared your soul, Johnathan, kept it here when you should have passed on," Alun's voice boomed. "You became my little test subject to see just how useful this spell would be, to live beyond a natural life. Your arrival was perfect for it, and your mind so easy to break, so simple to sway."

Alun held forth the gem, which shone brighter. The normally calm man was agitated, and Callum didn't like that at all.

"That body of yours is a puppet that you control from here only because

I wish it. Your freedom to be yourself was only so long as you were loyal to *me*. The Silent Hand has no space for doubt, for traitors like you or Jinar's mentor. You are ordered and you do! And this is the price of your ignorance!"

The interior of the white prison flashed brightly as a pulse of powerful magic detonated within, and with a final cry of pain, Johnathan was gone once more.

Alexis dropped the headband she'd saved as she once again witnessed her brother die, tears trickling down her face. The imprisoning magic winked out at that moment, leaving nothing but white ash which blew away in the wind. Alun took a deep breath and his anger subsided, but for Alexis, it had only just begun.

"...You monster," she said through grief and fury, readying her daggers once again to fight. "I will kill you myself, Alun, even if I have to follow you to the ends of the galaxy!"

But Alun wasn't done, clenching his fists around Johnathan's prison as he approached her.

"In a way, I should be thanking you for pointing out the faults in my spell's design. Had I have used it on someone of actual worth, I would not have expected the prospect of betrayal." Alun's eyes scanned the orb and he smiled darkly. "Now I will have the chance to right what I did wrong, shape him into the tool of your destruction. A mind is easy to mould when it is at your whim, and a soul is little different, Alexis. I will take every part of the man you loved as a brother and kill it, till what remains is only hate and unswerving loyalty to the one who gave him life."

Alexis tried not to let it show that his words cut deep but couldn't help it.

"He will be the first but not the last, though yours will be the last life he takes, and when he does, I will return to him all that I had taken, piece by piece. He will watch you die by his own hand. Only when you are gone will I kill him, a fitting punishment for a traitor."

"The only traitor here is *you*, Alun, a traitor to your own kind! If we're making promises, let me reiterate mine for you: the last person you will see is me, ending your sorry, miserable existence as we triumph over the demons, over Keiran!" Alexis got a laugh from the leader of the Silent Hand, and it was then that Tyrus prepared its magic subtly, slowly, trying to conceal the build-up. Callum got ready himself, though he had little power to spare.

"How little you all understand of what's truly going on here, Alexis.

If only you knew, we would've been on the same side after all, and your brother would still be alive."

She teleported suddenly in front of Alun and slashed at both his face and the arm which held Johnathan's gem. Even though her footing was shaky, the blade to his face found its mark, for he focused his efforts on keeping the gem from her even in the moment of surprise.

"Never," she told him, voice full of hate.

The man stepped back as blood splashed across his robes, and that was when Tyrus acted, calling forth an intense cloud of green healing energy that encompassed all those that were downed. It lasted only a second, but the effect was instantly noticeable, Jinar getting to his feet quickly along with Davis, who recovered his gun.

Alun wiped the blood away from his face and healed the wound at the same time, though a tiny mark remained just above his eyebrows. He looked about to see that all his work had been undone. Will had joined Davis in finishing off the remaining demons before training their rifles on the cabal leader, and Jinar was beside them with a pulsing blue orb dancing between his hands. Saresan had moved back to stand beside Callum and Tyrus, giving his friend a look.

"You okay?" he asked. "Thought we were goners there."

"There's fight in you yet, Saresan, in us all," Callum said.

Alexis stepped back slowly from the sorcerer she'd struck, amazed she'd succeeded. Her breaths were light, arms shaking in anger and fear as the magnitude of what she'd risked dawned on her.

"Siobhan? Get our ride ready to flyby ASAP. We'll board in transit," Will spoke quietly, hoping Alun wouldn't hear.

"Gotcha," Siobhan replied. Callum stepped up to Alun then, blade ready to defend himself or any of the others if the need arose. The man's attention was his.

"We know the truth, Alun. We know what the Great Threat is and we're going to tell the galaxy," he said defiantly. Alun didn't attack any of them, nor did he retreat. Instead, he simply smiled once more.

"There are those here who would not wish it." Alun's head subtly shifted, and Callum's eyes glanced to behind the sorcerer.

There, he spotted three figures in the distance that were but silhouettes, and yet he knew exactly what they were. They were stood atop a small pile of collapsed material, and each was a demon, but they were very unlike the feral monsters they'd fought before. On the left was one that held a polearm in its right hand and wore a cloak that billowed softly. To the right was one that hefted a two-handed weapon and had something adorning its head, and between them both was Xiez, the robed demon being the only one that had any kind of magical presence he could sense.

Was that to draw his attention to it or to provoke fear? Xiez vanished just as the whooshing sound of the *Silverbolt* heralded the craft's arrival along with a hail of fire. Together with it, the *Star's Shadow* flew with Xene firing at some approaching demons through the open airlock. Suddenly, Xiez was among them, the fearsome demon standing between Callum and Alun with a spell ready for both him and his friends.

Even as Tyrus sought to teleport him away, Callum knew he had to act first, else the demon would be rescuing a corpse. How he wished the golden warrior would appear from nowhere and save them, but no, it was just them against it all.

And so he stepped away from the salvation his mentor offered even as it tried to grab what remained of his hauberk, and did exactly what Xiez didn't expect of him: attack head-on. Its smouldering eyes widened at the realisation, and it moved all its attention to him alone. Taking a leaf from Alexis just a minute before, he focused all his magic and more into his blade, and it erupted into white-hot flame, striking just as the demon's power was unleashed upon him. He blacked out once again even as he felt the rushing adrenaline of the teleportation spell take hold, though it was mixed with a nearly unbearable amount of pain and the briefest moment of a demon growling.

Callum slipped in and out of consciousness for fractions of time. He was lying and in agony, and all around was a chorus of different voices and words. Some were arguing. He also caught moments of Siobhan and Jinar in discussion. He felt magic being used on him and thought he could pick out a few words in particular: he made out 'not a lot', 'hold' once, 'please' several times and 'irrelevant' a lot. He also caught the word 'Alexandria' and presumed it was about the ship. Only when he heard a deafening explosion did he black out again from sheer suffering.

Epilogue

Mateo was lucky to be alive and he knew it.

Already close to the hangar when catastrophic damage was sustained, he and a handful of soldiers boarded his personal runabout frantically, throwing all safety procedures out of the window in what he could only describe as a miraculous take-off. He'd told the few who'd escaped with him that it was pure chance he'd been there, but that was a lie; having seen the proficiency with which Alun had wielded his tainted power, he'd guessed that something bad might happen, but never to that extent.

He'd presumed they might make an attempt to damage the *Alexandria*, but to obliterate the engineering decks and the entire engine system with a single spell? It hadn't even been aimed at them but the fleeing criminals, the ones they'd been trying to take out with their laser batteries when the incident happened.

Surely they too had been destroyed, they had to have been; no ship could survive being hit by something with a power ten times that of any orbital cannon. He hadn't looked back at the colossal explosion the vessel made nor spoken beyond a few words to his crew, leaning back in his chair and considering his next step despite all the questions that rang in his mind.

He had to be ready for the cross-examination, and more importantly, he had to get his story straight. That a Z-Gen cruiser had been destroyed with that hideous power was unheard of, but at least he didn't have to worry about the criminals; that they'd been reduced to nothing cleaned up the loose ends quite nicely.

His report would naturally omit the truth of what happened in favour of his own version of events, ones that painted Z-Gen and himself in a far better light. With Arad almost certainly dead – there was no way he'd have been able to escape that facility with the monsters in it – and only a few soldiers around him to sway, he couldn't help but smile to himself just a little. It was almost too easy to make this work out for him.

"Any other ships make it?" Mateo asked half-heartedly.

"A fighter or two might've escaped the blast radius, but if they did, they're not in scanning range. It's just us here," a private responded. "I've activated the distress beacon; the task force should be picking it up any minute now."

"Put the communication through when it arrives, let me do the talking."

"Sir." The private tapped on the screen ahead of him and focused on his work, at least for a few seconds. Then he spoke, "Sir, what was that thing?"

"What thing?" Mateo was only half listening as he began to draft the beginnings of the report on his tablet.

"...The *thing*, sir. Was it an alien, a figment of magic?"

"All that matters is that the criminals are dead. Cadmus will be pleased with that outcome."

"Sir?" the man asked quizzically.

"We have accomplished our mission. You need think no more on it." Mateo was firm enough that he hoped there'd be no more objections. The others in the cramped bridge looked to the corporal before returning to their duties.

"But the cruiser is—" the private continued.

"They'll build a new one." Mateo smiled more. "A bigger one befitting my new rank."

The viewscreen switched from a view of the stars to the Z-Gen logo, the sign of a communication request. A moment later the image changed again to show the commander that had been with Cadmus. Her helmet was on, and oddly, she was alone, looking only to him. Commanders were often accompanied by an aide or two, but there weren't even guards at the door of the absolutely featureless room she was in, the walls unpainted metal.

"Corporal Mateo." She didn't sound pleased, but then she never did.

"Greetings, commander, I hadn't expected to hear from you—"

"Explain," the commander cut him off abruptly and without giving any clues about what she wanted from him. Still, he sat comfortably, confident she'd end the communication thanking him for his tireless work.

"I'm happy to report that I located the troublesome criminals that crippled the *Gorgon*. They have been dealt with as per Z-Gen protocol, though the toll has been heavy. You'll have my report within the hour," Mateo informed her.

He expected that to be the end of it, but she didn't even react to his words, still staring at him. The bridge crew grew uneasy, but Mateo took it in his stride.

"Are you with the general now? I can relay my report directly to him if you'd prefer."

The silence continued, and now he too was feeling unsettled, shifting a little in his chair.

"I know what you did, corporal," the commander told him. The penny dropped, but he tried to play it off.

"I was only following the general's orders—"

"Theft of confidential documents is beyond your remit, soldier." Her tone didn't shift, but she was annoyed. He shuffled again in his chair as the crew around him looked to their superior.

"You did what?" one of them asked, aghast.

"I needed that information to fulfil my mission. Would you send your soldiers out unprepared for the enemy we would face?" Mateo asked back, standing up so he didn't look uncomfortable. His heart was beating faster. "You and I both know that the High Marshal doesn't care *how* things are done, only that they get done, and I got it done. The criminals are dead."

"I see no evidence," she replied. Her gaze hadn't left him since the communication began, as if she could see through the helmet at his now growing concern.

"My report will detail everything at length, of that I assure you."

"That is not evidence, nor justification for your acts." The commander finally moved, clasping her hands behind her back as she looked to the other crew. "You say they are *all* dead, corporal?"

"Down to the last," he said firmly, lying through his teeth as best he could. She seemed to consider the answer, then nodded. The worry faded from him slowly; they were in the clear at last. "The task force will be here to pick me up soon, I'll send my report then. When will I next hear from you?"

"I won't need your report, corporal. I've heard all I needed to." She nodded to someone off-screen, and with that, Mateo was plunged into darkness as all the systems barring the communication died. The emergency lights activated, as well as a single panel ahead of them, small and flashing red.

"Sir, I've lost all control! Trying to activate manual overrides!"

Worry blossomed in Mateo's stomach, then engulfed his feet as if it were concrete, ready to throw him into the bottomless depths. The other soldiers frantically tried the controls in vain as Mateo approached the single flashing panel. It confirmed exactly what he feared.

"...Why?" he asked loudly, tearing his eyes from the countdown to look pleadingly to his commander. "I did what you asked. I did what you asked!"

"Protocol is clear, corporal," the commander told him coldly. "Those of insufficient rank to know what you know are to be promoted to sufficient rank or discharged from service, at the superior officer's discretion."

"Fuck protocol, turn this off!" She didn't answer his order. "TURN IT OFF!"

"Congratulations on your successful mission, corporal. I will give Cadmus your regards." She was to the point and formal, like this was no different to anything else in her day, before she turned from him.

"Commander!"

The communication ended, the viewscreen pitch black as panic descended upon the bridge and his crew. One tried to rush to the escape pods, but the door out wouldn't open, not even when the manual switch was pulled.

Mateo slumped back in his chair slowly, attention fixed on the screen that counted down to the end of everything, knowing that struggling was useless. Many emotions flashed through him in those few seconds: anger, despair, but ultimately fear. Try as he might, sheer force of will couldn't stop the numbers, and when they reached zero, he felt a flicker of pain as everything went white, then nothing.

Callum awoke with so many questions fighting to be asked that none of them got out. He'd expected to still be on Geladan, surrounded by his friends fighting for his life, but he was not. Instead, he was in the comfort of his room on board the *Janice*, lying on the bed and above the covers.

He checked for his sword first and saw it next to him, sheathed in its scabbard. This made him notice that he was shirtless save a bloody bandage that covered where Xiez's spell had likely impacted, as well as a very thin tube in his left arm that connected to a small machine. A rhythmic beep emanated from it, and beside it was Simon, alleviating some of his confusion. The doctor looked as tired as ever, checking a syringe full of clear liquid, his cup of coffee next to the sword.

"Try not to move, your chest is still on the mend," the doctor told him. Even as Callum stayed still, pain jolted through him, making him try to reach for the bandages. "This should help."

Simon injected the liquid into his left arm and a numbing sensation washed over him, hushing the pain quickly.

"...What happened, Simon?" Callum asked finally. "Is everyone alright?"

The doctor paused before replying.

"They're alive, but alright isn't the word I'd use to describe them," came the answer as Simon walked over to retrieve his cup. "Jinar filled me in on your mission in excruciating detail. We're on our way back to Otros."

"But how are they?" Callum wanted to sit up but refrained.

"Will's eye is a lost cause. Most of them sustained non-life-threatening injuries, barring you and the demon; at least that's how it was when they got to me. Who knows what they were like before your magic patched them up. It didn't let me tend to its own injuries, and I wouldn't even know where to begin." He indicated to the bloody bandages as he returned to the machine by the bed. "It's going to leave a nasty scar, but I've managed to set right most of it. Three quarters of your ribs were broken where you were hit by... whatever hit you. Had they punctured something..."

"It was a spell, a powerful one," Callum told him.

Simon nodded, though that told him little.

"The skin I had to grow on short notice, it's going to take a day or two for you to recover more fully."

"A day or two? Growing skin? How is that all possible?" Of all the questions, that one was the loudest in his head.

"The skin wasn't the hardest part. You had to have a blood transfusion pretty quickly to stabilise your condition, after that it was all routine. I reset and reconnected the broken ribs, checked for any internal organ damage and ran a few tests. That's not even mentioning the cocktail of drugs in your system knitting everything back together till you're good as new; well, almost." Simon was referring to the soon-to-be scar. "That reminds me, until I say so you can't take the pills that help you sleep."

"Because it'll kill me?" Callum guessed, getting a nod.

"And no using your magic to heal yourself either. I'm not saying it won't help, but I don't know exactly what it'll do, and with the drugs in your system I don't want to take any chances." Simon indicated to a stack of very thin parchment by the machine Callum hadn't noticed before. "I also performed a few general tests, checking your health and such. Did that with everyone, you're the last."

"I never cease to be amazed by everything I see," Callum remarked, though the events he wasn't awake to witness still worried him. "Can you restore Will's eye?"

"That's a little more complicated. The eye's one of the most advanced natural cameras ever created. It's possible but beyond my means, even on this ship. I'll sort out a stopgap measure in the meantime." Simon was staring at the bloodied bandages, frowning. "That wound should've killed you, you know. Internal bleeding alone would've got you in minutes. If I had a machine that could do what the magic that saved you did, I think all doctors would be out of a job."

"They might've defeated Xiez if they hadn't had to save me." Callum sighed. The doctor shook his head then, sipping his coffee.

"Jinar said that without the blow you landed when it appeared, they wouldn't have been able to escape in the first place." Simon put the cup down on top of the machine. "Don't be too hard on yourself."

"Did he say anything else?"

"I couldn't get much between Siobhan and him debating over who won their stupid bet." Simon sighed. "I expect that one to rattle on for some time."

"And what did Tyrus say? I'm surprised it's not here now, judging me." Callum expected the demon to appear, but it didn't.

"Nothing. Didn't expect anything less. Alexis asked after you after I got you stable. I can let her know you're awake if you'd like."

"Please." Callum was pondering the mission, everything that went wrong. "I'm surprised it didn't chide me for not being strong enough or doing something so reckless."

"I can't speak for it, heck, I don't think anyone can here. You'd have to ask it yourself when you're better."

"Henry and Nika are dead." Simon nodded at that.

"They knew the risks of going down there, you all did."

"Did they? They'd never met the demons before, how could they know what was coming?" Callum shifted just a little, the pain far less than before but enough to make him stop. "We didn't even get what we wanted."

"Telanthir has already informed their next of kin." Simon picked up his cup again. "We know at least that he was right, that Z-Gen is covering up the demon attacks. That's a victory all on its own."

"But we can't hold Z-Gen to account for it. It's our word against theirs, and everyone thinks we're criminals." Simon sighed.

"Look, I'm terrible at this sort of thing, so I'll be blunt. Nothing I can say will make you feel better about this. It went as it went, it's up to you to make your peace with what happened."

"I wanted no one else to die for me, but I couldn't stop it," he said to no one, closing his eyes. He could see Henry and Nika, their final moments of life, the fright they felt as it ended. Monica and Azure's deaths mingled with them, a cacophony of loss.

"Could you have when it all began, back on your world?" the doctor asked. "You're still growing into what you'll become, Callum. I don't know what that's going to be, but you're not the scared and confused man I met after we saved you."

"I'm still scared, Simon."

"Attacking the demon like you did wasn't the act of a coward," the doctor countered.

"It was one of desperation." Callum opened his eyes slowly. "It was the only way I could try and save everyone else."

"That sounds like bravery to me. I know you don't want to hear it, least of all from me, but on the road we're treading there's going to be a lot more death before it's all done." Simon stepped away from the machine. "Now, I don't want you out of that bed unless you have to. The machine is on wheels, use it for support as you walk."

"And if I don't listen?" Callum asked when the doctor was near the door.

"Then I'll strap you down." He wasn't sure if that was a joke or not, nor did he ask as the doctor left.

It wasn't long before Alexis came in, immediately looking at him with concern. Her injuries were all healed and clothes repaired, as if the fight had never happened. Her worry didn't leave when she saw the machine he was strapped to, heading to the bedside and scanning him with her eyes as she did. They lingered on the bloody bandage, then drifted to his face. He was just glad to see that she was alright.

"Hey," he greeted, unsure if either of them would ever speak otherwise.

He wanted to tell her how he appreciated her risking her life back on Geladan, but he couldn't find the words, nor did he think she'd want to hear them. She was managing to hide the pain from her encounter with Johnathan well, but it was there, he knew it.

"You look well."

"You look a lot better," she said in return, managing a fleeting smile. "When I saw what Xiez did to you, I was worried."

"Simon said I'm lucky to be alive." Her eyes looked away for a second.

"We all are," she answered. Wanting to make room for her, Callum attempted to sit up but felt a jolt of pain which stopped him. Noticing his discomfort, Alexis placed a hand on his shoulder. "You need to rest."

"I'm not good at being idle, but you know that. Can you help me sit up?"

Nodding, Alexis placed her other hand on his back as he tried to move more upright. He gritted his teeth at the stinging in his chest but tried to conceal it, though he doubted that worked. With some effort he was sat up, Alexis moving the pillows to support him as best they could.

"Thank you. You can sit down if you'd prefer."

"I'll stand. Thank you though."

"I'm sorry I worried you." At those words, a smile crept onto her lips. "What?"

"Even now you find something to be sorry about, though you'd worry too if the situation was reversed." He nodded, leaning back more into the pillows. "Telanthir wants to discuss with us our next course of action once we reach Otros, provided that you have recovered."

"What can we do next? Geladan was the best chance we had to get the evidence against Z-Gen, and we failed. The demons could attack anywhere next. How would we get there in time?" Callum asked.

"He told Fernisan of what we saw. Without the proof, I don't know how that went, but it can't have gone that badly if they didn't order us to leave." Alexis looked again to his bandaged wound. "I can help with that if you like."

"Simon told me not to have magic used on it, just in case it interferes with his treatment. He said it'd scar, but I expected much worse." She wasn't happy with that answer but respected the doctor's wishes. Callum reached for the sword carefully, freeing it from its scabbard and looking to the weapon that started him on the path he now travelled. "I don't feel like much of a champion right now."

"Me neither, but we did the best we could, though I wish I could've done so much more." She carefully sat on the edge of the bed then, turning to face him.

"Did we defeat Alun?" She shook her head in reply.

"We could barely get out of there as it was. He just... watched us go. There's a part of me that thinks he *wanted* us to get away." She went silent, eyes drifting from his face and back to sadness. "I never thought when we met that I'd be here, doing all this. Talking about defeating spellcasters, fighting monsters, working to save other worlds... or other worlds in general. I sometimes forget that not long ago, my world didn't extend beyond the kingdom we grew up in."

"I'm—"

"Don't," she interrupted him. He stopped speaking and she did too, as if she hadn't worked out the words to continue. "I have... few regrets, Callum.

I can't say I don't want some things to be better, but wishing for the impossible will only bring me more pain. No matter how hard I tried, I couldn't save my brother. He's lost to us now, just after I finally persuaded him."

"Tyrus told me to wait."

"It was right to, you'd've only been killed." Alexis sighed shakily, blinking away a tear. "All I can do now is look forward and work to right what's wrong. We'll get another chance, Alun promised me that much."

"That's easier said than done."

"It is, but we'll do it one day at a time." Her hand returned to his shoulder. "Together."

Her hand was comforting, rousing a smile without him knowing it. The way she looked at him was just as soothing, a warmth that was so familiar and yet not all at once.

The presence that appeared in the room behind her wasn't familiar, but how it arrived was. She turned to see not Tyrus but Baylon. Alexis quickly removed her hand from his shoulder, surprised that it wasn't their mentor looking down upon them.

"Callum," Baylon spoke first, its greeting very unnatural.

"What are you doing here?" Alexis asked the question on Callum's mind also.

"Tyrus was summoned by the Council. I am overseeing its duties during its absence," Baylon quickly responded.

"Summoned? What for?" Callum inquired, concerned already.

"To report on your recent actions and your progress."

"And if they aren't satisfied? Will they stop protecting us?" Callum knew the answer but asked just in case.

"I cannot speak for the Council. The Seven's minds are theirs alone to know." The demon paused. "They balance the risks of continued support with what you have achieved. Tyrus spoke in brief of your achievements."

"What did it say?" Alexis asked the demon.

"That you have far to go."

"They can't expect the impossible from us," she objected, standing from the bed, annoyed. Baylon matched her stare.

"Their minds are theirs alone," it repeated. "Tyrus will give its report and a decision will be made."

"Without our input?" she asked.

Baylon's silence was all the confirmation either of them needed.

"Your input is irrelevant," it told her bluntly. "It is the way of the Council. They seek external viewpoints minimally."

"Then how can they make a proper decision?" Callum asked. "It sounds like they've already made up their mind."

Baylon paused once more.

"I cannot speak for the Council." Alexis was about to object, but the demon spoke first, "But I *can* speak for myself and what Tyrus spoke of you."

"And what do you think?" Alexis carefully asked. Callum held his breath.

"Tyrus said you have far to go... but conceded that you have made progress. That progress is immediately tangible within your presence. The information on the Great Threat that Tyrus will bring to the Council is significant, if minor in the scope of your task." Baylon paused again. It only made Callum more nervous. "Tyrus questions your drive, your methods and the value you place on those around you. I do not."

Callum blinked.

"You don't?"

"It is... difficult for my kind to understand what motivates humans to act, more so for the Council, who have never seen the galaxy at large beyond fleeting moments."

"And you have?" Alexis's question provoked a longer pause.

"To expect immediate results is folly. That is what Tyrus will tell the Council. It is up to them to decide what to do with you and your blade." Baylon glanced at the weapon momentarily. "You would not relinquish it if asked."

"Keeping it has cost us too much as it is," Callum told it honestly, gripping the handle tighter than normal without realising it. "To give it up now would make it all for nothing."

Baylon didn't react to his words aside from heading to the door.

"That is why they will not discard you," it assured him as it reached the door. It felt unusual to hear that from a demon, but it soothed his nerves somewhat. "I will inform the security detail on board of my presence. If you need me, I will find you." With that, Baylon left.

"I hope it's right," Alexis said before looking to the door herself. "Do you want me to leave you to rest?" Callum thought about it, then nodded.

"Only for a while. Would you be able to teach me again later?" She nodded.

"Of course. Sleep well, Callum." She went to the door as well but stopped partway there. "If I catch you out of bed, I'm not going to be happy."

"You sound just like Simon," Callum remarked with a laugh that caught him off guard. His laughter made her smile again.

"I'll take that as a compliment."

It didn't take long after she exited for Callum to drift to sleep, even though the lights were on. Try as he might, his dreams were dark and troubling, and though they lingered a little less on what had already been, that which was to come worried him more.

Tyrus was right; they did have far to go, and the road ahead was shrouded in a terrifying unknown. He thought he spotted a brief shimmer of light piercing the gloom, and even as it was swallowed by the dark it shone again, a little stronger than before. He didn't let go of the sword, his silent and stalwart companion even in his dreams, taking comfort in its presence and emboldened by the sight of the light at the end of the darkness. He took a shaky but determined breath, and together, they stepped forward.

Dramatis Personae
(In order of introduction)

Callum	*Village Labourer*
Terrance	*Aged friend of Callum*
Cuthbert	*Pompous Noble*
Saresan	*Guard*
Azure	*Knight of King Franci*
Alexis	*Merchant's Daughter*
Johnathan	*Merchant's Son and Warrior*
Grimsal	*Vicious thug*
Jinar Yelandan Fakkal Genai Lae	*Self-proclaimed master of the arcane*
Alun	*Master of the Silent Hand*
Xiez	*Demon lieutenant of the feral demons*
Daniel	*Former soldier and owner of the* Winter's Mourning
Simon	*Doctor and engineer of the* Winter's Mourning
Tyrus	*Demon mentor of Callum*
Siobhan	*Gunslinger and Ace Fighter Pilot of the* Silverbolt
Monica	*Copilot of the* Winter's Mourning
Keiran	*Enigmatic leader of the feral demons*
Baylon	*Demon warrior of the Enclave*
The First	*Leader of the Demon Council*
The Second	*Member of the Demon Council*
The Third	*Member of the Demon Council*
The Fourth	*Member of the Demon Council*
The Fifth	*Member of the Demon Council*
The Sixth	*Member of the Demon Council*
The Last	*Member of the Demon Council*
Colette	*Captain of Z-Gen in command of the* Gorgon
Telanthir	*Venerable king of Otros*
Davis	*Private in Telanthir's Guard*
Mateo	*Corporal of Z-Gen in command of the* Alexandria
Cadmus	*General of Z-Gen in command of the* Viridian Eclipse
Will	*Sergeant in Telanthir's Guard*

Fernisan	*President of Gerasal*
Luna	*Smuggler for hire in command of the* Star's Shadow
Xene	*Z-Gen First Class Private and mercenary*
Henry	*Private in Telanthir's Guard*
Nika	*Private in Telanthir's Guard*
Siegfried	*Sergeant of Z-Gen and fighter pilot of Alpha Squad*
Gabriela	*Sergeant of Z-Gen and fighter pilot of Delta Squad*
Hyval	*Mad king of Geladan*
Arad	*Corporal of Z-Gen*

About the Author

Damien Jennison grew up in South Yorkshire, England, and while he's better known as the online personality and content creator Kikoskia, his first and true love has always been writing.

Ever since he was first introduced to writing fiction at school, his mind has been awash with worlds that have cried out to escape from its confines. Pulling inspiration from the science fiction and fantasy media of his youth and the lessons learned throughout his life about overcoming adversity – self inflicted or otherwise – he has finally done what most people said he wouldn't and published the first book of the *Sword Saga: Errant Hope.*

You can learn more about Damien and his work at his website: https://kikoskia.com/

Printed in Poland
by Amazon Fulfillment
Poland Sp. z o.o., Wrocław
03 August 2022

70431e62-5b9b-4f7e-a106-88e2048d5bddR01